SelectEditions

SELECTED AND EDITED

SelectEditions

BY READER'S DIGEST

VOLUME 4 2001
THE READER'S DIGEST ASSOCIATION, INC.
PLEASANTVILLE, NEW YORK

SelectEditions

Editor-in-Chief, Global Select Editions: Tanis H. Erdmann
Editor, U.S. Select Editions: Laura E. Kelly

Volume Editor: Paula Marchese

Editors: Dana Adkins, Maxine Bartow, Karen Bruno, Barbara K. Clark,
Thomas S. Clemmons, Tatiana Ivanow, Eva C. Jaunzems,
Marilyn J. Knowlton, Joseph P. McGrath, James J. Menick,
Angela Plowden-Wardlaw, Mark Poirier, Amy M. Reilly

Art Director: Robin Arzt
Art Associate: Janine L. Megna

RIGHTS AND PERMISSIONS
Director: Alfredo G. Santana
Associate Director: Lisa Garrett-Smith
Manager: Carol Weiss Staudter

INTERNATIONAL EDITIONS
Executive Editor: Gary Q. Arpin
Senior Editor: Bonnie Grande

CONTENTS

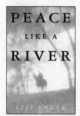

PEACE LIKE A RIVER

LEIF ENGER

In the Old West, outlaws traveled
the Badlands of North Dakota
in search of peace and freedom.
My father took my sister and me on such
a journey one cold and desperate winter.
What we found was a peace greater
than any we could imagine.

clay

FROM my first breath in this world, all I wanted was a good set of lungs and the air to fill them with—given circumstances, you might presume, for an American baby of the twentieth century. Think about your own first gasp: a shocking wind roweling so easily down your throat, and you still slipping around in the doctor's hands! How you yowled! Not a thing on your mind but breakfast, and that was on the way.

When I was born to Helen and Jeremiah Land, in 1951, my lungs refused to kick in.

My father wasn't in the delivery room, nor even in the building. The halls of Wilson Hospital were close and short, and Dad had gone out to pace in the damp September wind. He was praying, rounding the block for the fifth time, when the air quickened. He opened his eyes and discovered he was running—sprinting across the grass toward the door.

"How'd you know?" I adored this story, made him tell it all the time.

"God told me you were in trouble."

"Out loud? Did you hear Him?"

"Nope, not out loud. But He made me run, Reuben. I guess I figured it out on the way."

I had, in fact, been delivered some minutes before. My mother was dazed, propped against soggy pillows, unable to comprehend what Dr. Animas Nokes was telling her.

"He still isn't breathing, Mrs. Land."

"Give him to me!"

Dr. Nokes did not hand me over. He rubbed me hard with a towel, pounded my back, and massaged my chest. He breathed air into my mouth and nose. My chest rose, fell with a raspy whine, stayed fallen. Years later Dr. Nokes would tell my brother, Davy, that he'd never seen a child with such swampy lungs.

When Dad skidded into the room, Dr. Nokes was sitting on the side of the bed holding my mother's hand. She was wailing—I picture her as an old woman here, which is funny, since I was never to see her as one—and old Nokes was attempting to ease her grief.

I was lying uncovered on a metal table across the room.

Dad lifted me gently. I was very clean from all that rubbing, and I was gray and beginning to cool. A little clay boy. "Breathe," Dad said.

I lay in his arms.

Dr. Nokes said, "Jeremiah, it has been twelve minutes."

"Breathe!" The picture I see is of Dad, brown hair short and wild, giving this order as if he expected nothing but obedience.

Dr. Nokes approached him. "Jeremiah. There would be brain damage now. His lungs can't fill."

Dad leaned down, laid me back on the table, took off his black canvas jacket, and wrapped me in it. He left my face uncovered.

"Sometimes," said Dr. Nokes, "lungs can't expand to take in air. In these cases we must trust in the Almighty to do what is best."

At which Dad smote Dr. Nokes with a right hand, so that the doctor went down and lay on his side with his pupils unfocused. As Mother cried out, Dad turned back to me, a clay child wrapped in a canvas coat, and said in a normal voice, "Reuben Land, in the name of the living God, I am telling you to breathe."

THE truth is, I didn't think much on this until a dozen years later—beyond, of course, savoring the fact that I'd begun life in a dangerous and thus romantic manner. When you are seven years old, there's nothing as lovely and tragic as telling your friends you were just about dead, once. It made Dad my hero, as you might expect, won him my forgiveness for anything that he might do forever, but until later events it didn't occur to me to wonder just why I was allowed, after all, to breathe and keep breathing.

The answer, it seems to me now, lies in the miracles.

Let me say something about that word, miracle. For too long it's been used to characterize things or events that, though pleasant, are entirely normal. Peeping chicks at Easter time, spring generally, a clear sunrise after an overcast week—a miracle, people say, as if they'd been educated from greeting cards. I'm sorry, but nope. To call such things miracles evaporates the strength of the word.

Real miracles bother people. It's true. They rebut every rule all us good citizens take comfort in. Lazarus climbing up out of the grave—now, there's a miracle, and you can bet it upset a lot of folks at the time. A miracle contradicts the will of earth.

My sister, Swede, who often sees to the nub, offered this: People fear miracles because they fear being changed—though ignoring them will change you also. Swede said another thing too, and it rang in me like a bell: No miracle happens without a witness. Someone to declare, Here's what I saw. Here's how it went. Make of it what you will.

The fact is, the miracles that sometimes flowed from my father's fingertips had few witnesses but me. Yes, enough people saw enough strange things that Dad became the subject of a kind of misspoken folklore in our town, but most ignored the miracles as they ignored Dad himself.

I believe I was preserved, through those twelve airless minutes, in order to be a witness, and as a witness of many, let me say that a miracle is no cute thing but more like the swing of a sword.

If he were here to begin the account, I believe Dad would say what he said to Swede and me on the worst night of all our lives.

We and the world, my children, will always be at war.
Retreat is impossible. Arm yourselves.

his separate shadow

I NOW think of my survival as my father's first miracle. Dr. Nokes himself named the event miraculous once he woke up and washed his face and remembered who he was.

The second, I suppose, is that the doctor turned out to be wrong about the brain damage. I'm happy to say none surfaced until I entered tenth grade and signed up for plane geometry, but since I can still feed myself and grind out a sentence in English, you won't hear me complain.

Dad's third miracle—and one of the most startling, if not consequential—happened in the middle of the night, in the middle of North Dakota, just after I turned eleven.

It was the trip when I shot my first goose, a medium-sized snow. We were staying at August Shultz's place, four hours west onto the Great Plains, hunting near the homestead Dad grew up on and still quietly longed for. The goose was a joyous occasion, and for a while we could all speak to each other again. That is, Dad and Davy could speak again. Swede and I rarely quarreled, for I never held opinions in those days, and hers were never wrong.

The tension in the car, going out, was so potent I fell asleep as soon as I was able. Davy was sixteen then, a man as far as I was concerned, with a driver's license, a knockout four-inch scar down his right forearm, and Dad's own iron in his spine. That night they sat in the front seat of the Plymouth not speaking at all.

We were late getting started, as happened often, because Dad had to lock up the school after the football game. Swede and I yawned in the back seat, boxes of shotgun shells stacked at our feet. That Plymouth had a worthless heater. We rode cocooned in gray army blankets and stocking caps. Twenty miles into the trip, Swede slipped off her rubber boots, and I felt her toes creep up against my hip. Oh, but they were cold. I pulled them into my lap and rubbed them while up front Davy opened a thermos, poured coffee into the lid, and, without looking at Dad, handed it over.

In a few minutes Swede's toes felt warm, and she was breathing evenly through her nose. The road bent backward under us. I laid my head against the seat and slipped away as well.

Before dawn we were settled among decoys in one of August Shultz's barley fields. Dad and Swede lay on their elbows side by side under a swath. Davy and I took the opposite flank, he with his clawed-up Winchester goose gun. I was too young to shoot, of course, and so was Swede. We were there purely, as she said, "for seasoning." In all the years since, I don't remember a colder morning afield. Rain can outfreeze snow. We lay between soaked ground and soaked swaths with a cold wind coming over our backs. As the sky lightened, the rag decoys puffed and fluttered. I yawned once.

Davy said, "Don't go to sleep on me now, buddy."

He could say it. He wasn't cold. Though his gloves were cotton, he could handle an icy shotgun in evident comfort. When he said softly, "Old Rube, I could live out here, couldn't you?" I was too frozen to tell him yes.

Minutes later I woke. Davy was poking me in the side. Finger to his lips, he nodded east. A lone snow goose was approaching, fighting the wind, making low, questioning honks at our flock of rags.

Davy jammed the Winchester into my hands. "Take him, Rube."

The goose was straight overhead. Not twenty feet high! I flung off a mitten, tried to aim, and yanked the trigger. Nothing happened. Davy's hand zipped out and clicked the safety off. The goose was just beyond us but still so close. I yanked again, shot wild, and the recoil slammed my shoulder into the mud. The goose tilted off left while I pumped another shell into the chamber. Blind with despair, I fired again. The goose had to be out of range, yet somehow it shuddered, went graceless, and made a controlled fall to the ground some eighty yards away. "You did it," Davy said. "Good shot. You took him the hard way, buddy. Better go finish him."

But Swede streaked past in her corduroy coat, yelling, "I'll get 'im, I'll get 'im," her yellow hair bouncing behind her stocking cap.

Downfield, though, the goose seemed to have recovered its wits. It stood upright, taking stock, its head high and perky. When it saw Swede coming, it turned and sprinted away.

I'm telling you that goose could run.

Swede lowered her head and went full steam, mud and chaff raining off her boot soles. Dad started laughing, whipping off his cap and whacking it on his leg while the goose stretched out its neck and bolted across the barley. Reaching the end of the field, it encountered a barbed wire fence. It stopped as Swede closed in.

Did you ever see an angry goose up close? Swede got within a yard and stopped cold. Later she told me she saw a decision being reached. "It decided to kill me," she said.

From where we stood, though, all we saw was the goose raise its wings and poke its beak at Swede. She spun, then was shutting the distance between us, that goose coming after her just as hard as it could. Dad was laughing so hard he had to sit down, wiping his eyes. Swede led the bird straight toward us, and when she pounded past, Davy leaned over and snagged it just behind the head. A quick twist, and he handed it to me, wings quivering. He grinned. "All yours, Natty"—after Natty Bumppo, James Fenimore Cooper's matchless hunter. I held my goose with one hand and Davy's Winchester in the other, smelling gunpowder and warm bird, feeling something brand-new and liking it quite a bit. Swede, though, was crying, her face in Dad's belly even while he laughed helplessly on.

SWEDE felt bad about that goose for a long time. For an eight-year-old girl she put enormous stock in courage. To be routed across a barley field by an incensed goose gave her doubts about her character.

"He's really a big one. Look at him," I said once we were back at August's farm. Behind the barn was a hand pump and an old door set up as a cleaning table. Maybe it was just the thought of cleaning that goose by myself, but I had, of all things, a lump in my throat.

Luckily, Swede was standing at my elbow and said, "First thing, you have to cut his head off."

"Well, I know that."

Swede stepped over to the ruins of a grain truck that had been parked behind the barn to rot. She shinnied up the big rumplike fender and sat. I picked up Davy's knife and beheaded the snow.

Watching, Swede said, "Forgive me running, Rube?"

"From the goose? Swede, it wasn't any big deal." I tossed the head into a cardboard box, then went to work on the wings.

"Forgive me out loud," she insisted.

"Swede, I forgive you. Is it all right now?"

She hugged her elbows. "Thanks, Reuben."

My hands were freezing, and I dreaded the next part. Aiming at a spot under the breastbone, I plunged in.

"Swede," I said—just talking so she'd stay with me—"I don't get what's wrong with Davy."

She didn't answer at first. Finally she said, "He's mad about Dolly."

"Oh." Davy's girlfriend. "How come?"

"You heard. Last night, driving over."

"I was sleeping."

"You were faking, I could tell. Just like me."

We heard the screen door open, up at the house. "Pancakes in five minutes," Dad hollered. The screen slapped shut.

"Really, I was asleep—I swear it, Swede."

"Israel Finch and Tommy Basca had Dolly in the girls' locker room."

"What? How come?" Two boys had gone into the girls' locker room?

"They beat her up, Reuben. During the football game. Dad caught 'em."

It was only then that the names sunk in. Israel Finch. Tommy Basca. I shrunk up inside my coat. "How bad, Swede?"

"She's okay, I guess. I heard Dad say he got there in time."

"Then why's Davy mad? Wasn't he happy Dad caught those guys?" I didn't even want to say their names aloud.

"I don't know. Ask Davy if you want."

I wasn't sure I could do that. Though there were only five years between Davy and me, lately they'd seemed a weighty five. At times it felt like he was Dad's brother instead of mine.

DAVY missed the pancakes Dad had served up merrily to Swede and me, not commenting on Davy's absence. Then Dad stoked the woodstove, and the three of us went to our rooms to snooze. That's how goose hunting is. You rise early and do the cold, thrilling work, then come in and eat; then fatigue sneaks up and knocks you flat. I pulled up the quilt and slept like a desperado.

I woke to Davy sitting on the bed across from me, wiping down his shotgun with an oiled rag. "Hey, Natty," he said, seeing me stir.

"Hey, Davy. We going back out?"

"A little bunch went down on the west quarter. Canadas." He hiked his eyebrows at me. "We're gonna crawl up."

"Okay!" I threw the covers back and tried to shake out the murky dream I'd been having.

Davy leaned forward. A warm tobacco smell clung to him. "Listen, Rube, you heard us talking about Dolly last night, didn't you?"

"I was asleep. Swede heard, though."

"Well, she didn't hear everything. Dad kept shut, to keep from scaring you guys, but you should know this. Finch and Basca made some pretty vicious threats. To Dad, I mean." Getting me by the eyes, Davy said, "They talked about hurting his family."

It took me a second to realize he meant us. Dread landed flopping in my stomach. I watched my brother closely.

"They're basically loudmouths," he said. "Cowards, windbags. They won't do anything. Just keep an eye out, that's all. And let's not mention it to Swede, Natty. All right?"

"Nope. We don't need to scare her, I guess."

"Good." He reached down and picked up my boots and set them in my lap. "Now let's crawl up on those Canadas."

A crawl-up, if you're not familiar, is a different kind of hunt from waiting among decoys. I stuck with Davy again, Swede with Dad, and we squirmed on our bellies up a shallow rise beyond which a few dozen honkers were feeding on stubbled wheat. The light was almost gone, and though we supposed the geese were close, we couldn't hear them and had to crawl on faith that they were there at all.

At the crest of the rise lay a small rock pile. We wiggled up to it, and Dad peered over. "They're pretty far," he whispered. When Davy had a look, he said, "They're walking away from us. Look at 'em waddle."

There wasn't a thing we could do; the geese were out of range. Then came a great racket of honks, and the Canadas rose up in a panicked layer and beat westward. Their voices faded to a dim, disorganized music, and we rested against the rocks.

"Well," Dad said.

He was just getting up when Davy said, "Wait." He watched the dirty western sky. "One of 'em's broke off from the group." He pointed at something none of the rest of us could see.

Half a minute later we saw the goose coming toward us. My, it was high. Dad relaxed. A bird that far up is all but beyond the reach of lead shot. Swede soughed in defeat.

"Stay down," Davy said.

The goose now commenced a wide swing round the field, while Davy melted into that rock pile as if to join it forever. I remember his shadowed, patient eyes. The odd thought came to me that Davy was hunting alone—that Dad and Swede and I weren't even there really, that we existed with him as memories or fond ghosts watching his progress.

The goose circled the field once and gained altitude; it might've been considering Mexico, it was that high. It flew over the rock pile, and when it did, Davy rose to one knee and shot it out of the sky.

THAT night Swede and I lay somewhat breathless under a hill of quilts. For drafts there was no place like August's farmhouse.

"What do you think Davy'll do—about those guys?" Swede whispered, eyes alight. Though I'd promised not to scare her with any Finch and Basca talk, she kept coming back to them.

"What do you mean, do? They're just cowards, windbags." An unsatisfactory answer to a warrior like Swede. She jounced a little under the quilts, and we listened to talk from the kitchen—August and his wife, Birdie, larking through the old stories with Dad. Davy was there, drinking coffee with the grown-ups, keeping his silence.

"You think he'll fight 'em?" Swede asked.

"Why would he? Dad took care of those guys, didn't he?"

Swede said, "Davy thinks they got off easy, can't you tell? Boy, I'd hate to be those guys when Davy gets hold of 'em."

I thought that was awfully bold of Swede on Davy's behalf. These two fellows were as serious a kind of trouble as you could purchase in Roofing, Minnesota, back then. To call Finch and Basca the town bullies doesn't touch it, as you will see.

"Maybe," I said, "we just ought to wait. All right?"

We settled, yawned, and listened to August Shultz talk about days of yore. As kids, Dad and August had been neighbors. August would ride his horse over in the mornings and pick up Dad, who'd be saddling his paint in front of the barn, and they'd race the last half mile to school. Dad was by nature a flat-out rider, whereas August had the cautious temperament of his German forebears. Though this cost him transient glory, it probably saved his farm any number of times. It probably accounted for his now owning three farms, including the one he loaned us to hunt on every fall. Dad's family, the Lands, had not only lost their farm toward the end of the Dust Bowl years, they'd never owned anything again. We'd become renters—which was, in our case, about all that the family of a small-town school janitor could expect.

Swede murmured, "I'm sleeping, Reuben."

"Back to your room, then." She'd slipped in with me because the room I shared with Davy was nearer the kitchen, the better to rubberneck on the grown-ups.

She got up and stood in her cowboy-print pajamas. "Rube, you're almost like Davy now. I mean, you shot a goose this morning."

She meant to compliment me, but the fact was, I'd been thinking this over. By the time we left to steal up on that little bunch of

Canadas, I'd almost begun to believe I'd taken that goose on account of my own skill. But Davy's work on the lone Canada had slapped me awake. I had in my mind, that night, the image of him I'll carry always. It's Davy at the very top of his motion—risen to one knee, Winchester at his shoulder. His hat's fallen to the rocks, his short blond hair stands stiff as a wolf's, and on his face is nothing at all but the knowledge that the goose is his.

I squeezed Swede's arm. "Sure I am," I said. "Good night."

Waking past midnight, I departed this dream: I was crossing a shallow river that smelled of dying plants, the far shore concealed by fog. Then the mist corkscrewed away, and a dead horse lay swollen there, tail in the river. I woke gasping to the windowful of moonlight and Davy in his bed snoring, arm thrown across his eyes.

I was scared to go back to sleep. There'd been something worse on that riverbank than just a dead horse, I was sure of it. Sitting up, I realized with some relief that I had to go to the outhouse. Normally I'd have dreaded this, for the usual dark and scary reasons, but this time the idea seemed a chance to walk that vision off. I slipped from bed and pulled on my pants and carried my boots into the kitchen. A kerosene lantern was lit on the table. I took my coat from its hook and went out.

The privy stood next to a corncrib downhill from the barn. I hunched my shoulders and headed for it, the moon bouncing my shadow off the grass. Then I heard footsteps.

Nothing stealthy about them—just shoe leather on wood. Still, the noise raised my short hairs, until I figured it must be Dad pacing the flatbed of the old grain truck behind the barn.

But it was the dead of night. The smell of the dream hung around me. So I crept up quiet next to the barn until I could peek round the corner. Dad, sure enough, was pacing the flatbed. He was praying—nothing unusual. Dad liked to walk as he prayed.

Dad's hands were clenched to his eyes; his lips were moving. Though he often comforted Swede and me by quoting from the Gospel of John, *Let not your hearts be troubled,* it was plain Dad himself was suffering the labors of a troubled heart—over the business of Finch and Basca, I figured, or over Davy, who clearly saw the matter as unfinished.

And then, as I stood watching, Dad walked right off the truck.

I saw it coming—his knuckles jammed to his face, his steps not slowing. I stood there with my knees locked and my heart gone to water, while Dad paced over the edge.

And did not fall.

He went on pacing—God my witness—walking on air, praying relentlessly. As he went, the moon threw his strangely separate shadow to the earth. Dad's boots touched the tops of a thatch of tall grama, and they waved as if stroked by wind. I will forget none of this. Nor the comfortable, fluttery feeling it gave me, as though someone had blown warm smoke through a hole in my center. Dad went perhaps thirty feet, paused, and started back. Then his boot soles struck the flatbed again.

In growing discomfort I looked at the outhouse. Getting there meant lurching straight past Dad—and him walking on the hand of God! I knew what heretic meant, for Swede had read me more than a few bits of gruesome history. There was a willow thicket across the yard, and I took myself there in a hurry.

WE ARRIVED back in Roofing to find our front door tarred black, top to bottom. It was late, a cloudy night, and none of us saw anything amiss at first. For my part, I was too preoccupied with the task of breathing. All the long drive I'd felt the air changing, turning warmer, thicker, filling with invisible mites that colluded against my lungs. By the time we got home, it was all I could do to totter up the steps with the two news-wrapped geese in a sack. Dad was right behind me, his arms full of unconscious Swede. Then Davy, who had the house key, said, "What's this junk all over the door?"

What it was, was most of the contents of a one-gallon can of Gamble's roofing tar spread thick over our sturdy portal by means of a putty knife. Next morning we were to find both can and knife tossed among the junipers flanking the house. For the present, Davy simply turned silent and Dad businesslike. He carried Swede across the violated threshold and put her, still dressed, into bed. Then, noticing my shallow gasps, he ordered me to sit in his own stuffed chair and not move until he could attend to me.

A word here about this business of taking a breath. If you're someone who's never had to think about it—never had to exert muscular effort to do it, never lay awake through endless dark hours knowing you'd stop doing it forever if you happened to fall asleep—then indulge me. Think of a bellows, such as you use to rouse a fire. Really moves the air, doesn't it? Now imagine a tiny, malignant, wind-carried seed entering that bellows on the inhale and sticking inside. Slowly—slowly!—a sponge begins to grow. As time passes, you see that the bellows won't close all the way. It's taking shallower gulps. And down inside, the sponge keeps growing. You shut your eyes and concentrate. Air in. Air out. Your breaths are sips, couldn't blow out the candle on a baby's cake. The air gets close and sticky, and you understand, in a frozen sweat, that morning is miles and miles away, and the house is quiet with the smooth respirations of your family, and if you fall asleep from pure exhaustion, the sponge will win and you will be singing hymns by sunrise, at the feet of the Lord, in a body glorified.

I sat on Dad's chair with my bellows full of sponge while he lit the kitchen stove and laid a pan of water over the flame. He shook some salt into the water, then soda, then disappeared downstairs and returned with a quart canning jar.

"Kerosene," he explained. "Let's see if it strips the tar." He winked at me in such easy form I recalled the sheltered feeling I'd had witnessing his walk off the grain truck. It was comforting, but I'll have to say it didn't make breathing any easier. For the first time the thought ingressed that if this man, my father, beloved by God, could work miracles—if he could walk on air—then fixing my defective lungs ought to be a picnic. A day at the old beach.

When the water boiled, Dad set the pan on a cutting board and that on my lap in the chair. He draped a blanket over my head for a steam tent. "All right?" he asked.

I nodded under the blanket. He opened the door, and cold

poured in. I could hear him unscrewing the jar of kerosene, tearing up rags, working at the tar. The door had been a lovely dark green—hunter green, Dad called it—the single adornment to a clapboard house as white and midwestern as any you've seen. Come December that green door gave the place a Christmassy look that atoned for our want of pretty lights. I felt awful for Swede, by now the chief deliverer of Christmas spirit in the family.

Dad said, "I think I better tell you how this came about."

But I didn't want to hear any more about Israel Finch and Tommy Basca. It's true I'd been curious enough earlier, but then we'd been four hours' drive distant, which made the problem abstract.

"I know about Dolly and those guys," I told Dad.

He took his time with this information. He'd not wanted Swede and me to know. Finally I heard a low chuckle. "Well then, here is your chance to learn about the principle of escalation."

I'd heard the word before. "Like in wars?"

"Yes, exactly like in wars. How's the steam? Working good?"

I nodded.

"Fine. Now. Let's say a war begins. One nation wants what another has. Property, gold mines—"

"Helen of Troy," I contributed. Swede had told me all about her.

"Sure. Now. This nation has no intention of giving over its bounty, so the aggressor decides to take it by force. However, after the first engagement the defender's allies step in—"

Well, so it went. At one in the morning, smelling of tar and petroleum, Dad framed his locker-room skirmish as a composition on wartime ethics.

Here is what I learned later from Davy. Dolly, a bouncy clarinetist, had been playing in the pep band during the football game. After halftime she and a few others ran up to the band room to put away their instruments. Dolly meant to accompany friends to the bowling alley, but she remembered a pair of shoes she'd left down in her athletic locker. She told the others she'd catch up.

About this time, Dad was in the boys' locker room, pushing his wide broom, when he heard a rowdy laugh just beyond the cinder-block wall—in the girls' locker room. He listened just long enough to hear a second laugh, this alongside a scared yelp. Then he took his long broom and unscrewed the hardwood handle.

Dolly told Davy she was kneeling at her locker when she heard the wheeze of the locker-room door. Then the lights went out, and nobody answered her nervous call, and Dolly saw the jumpy beam of a flashlight. No screamer by nature, she clutched the hardest thing she could get her hands on in the dark—the Master padlock hanging from its hasp.

Simple! Nothing to it, those boys must've thought, seeing Dolly crouched with her sweet chin set hard. Imagine the crazed gladness in their hearts! Israel laughed once. Then Dolly up and fired that padlock at the flashlight, God bless her all her life, and it struck Israel Finch to the left of his Adam's apple, so that he dropped the light and seized his neck. "I'm all bloody," Israel yelled—but unhappily, the padlock had missed the all-important jugular. Slipping past him, Dolly bumped straight into Tommy Basca, who clutched onto her with a snort.

Then Israel Finch got to his feet and pointed the light at Dolly. He told Tommy to hold her arms, and Tommy roared as if these were the funniest words in his reduced language. Israel slapped her across the mouth; told her she was in for deep regret now, boy; and reaching forth his strong, smelly hand, rent open the front of her sweater. That is when Dolly saw Dad coming. Keep in mind he ought not've been visible at all. There were no lights on but the flashlight. She said Dad's face coming toward them was luminous of itself, glowing and serene, the way you'd suppose an angel's would be—that it rose up behind Israel Finch like a sudden moon, and when Tommy Basca saw it, he dropped her. She said Dad was silent; he made no sound except a strange whistling that turned out, of course, to be the broom handle en route to any number of painful destinations. Tommy went screeching to his knees, and Israel prostrated himself and moaned as though the devil had hold of his liver. The two of them just lost their minds, Dolly said, while she suddenly could not stop laughing. Here was Dad, smiling

(Dolly said) though his eyes looked terribly melancholy, whacking Finch and Basca every second or two while the pair of them shrieked in no English you'd recognize.

So Dad gave Dolly a ride home, talked briefly with her father, and returned to the school to lock up. The football game was over, and when Dad stepped outside in his overcoat, there stood Israel, his face swollen and discolored. He said, "Something you should know, janitor. Tommy and me are watching your family. All of 'em. You understand?"

"Escalation," Dad said to me now.

The water had cooled under the steam tent. "Well," I wondered, "what should we do back?" It was our turn, after all, though I couldn't picture Dad carrying the battle back over a wrecked door.

But Dad chuckled and swept the blanket off my head. "Nothing. Of course, nothing! What those fellows don't realize is, we've already won. The victory is ours."

I blinked up at him. He said gently, "You don't understand." And he swung me up and carried me off and tossed me on my bunk just as if I hadn't done a whole lot of growing up in the past few days alone.

I SUCCEEDED in worrying about this escalation business for a good day and a half before worry died, as usual, at the hands of routine. Swede and I rose muddy-eyed each morning at six—Davy being already up and out, running his line of muskrat traps. Dad would be sitting at the kitchen table, his King James open before him, coffee on the stove. We fixed oatmeal with bowls of condiments set alongside—white sugar, currants, flaked coconut. As the oatmeal puffed and steamed, Dad would lean back, shut his eyes and his Bible simultaneously, then pop up, declaring what gifted chefs we were, dipping a spoon into the pot as if it contained something exorbitant and full of clams.

And then to school, where I swam upstream through geography and grammar, and where Swede, who disliked long division, tried to win her teacher's favor by composing heroic verse. What was Miss

Nelson supposed to think when Swede, dimpled and blond, coming up on nine years old, handed in a poem like "Sunny Sundown Delivers the Payroll"?

The men who worked the Redtail Mine were fed up with the boss.
They swarmed around his office door like blackflies round a hoss.
"No wages these three months!" one cried. "Let's hang the lousy rat!
He'll starve our very children, boys, while he himself gets fat!"
And true enough, behind the door, a fat man shook and wept;
The wobbling bags beneath his eyes said this man hadn't slept.
A messenger had brought him word that made him feel his age:
Valdez, last night—the third straight month!—had robbed the payroll
*   stage.*

Swede had lost her heart to the West early on, something that gave Dad no end of delight. He supplied her with frayed Zane Grey paperbacks thrown out by the school library. Swede popped them down like Raisinets. You have to admit she learned the language.

And now the mob broke down the door, and now they found a rope,
And now the boss was on his knees, a prayer was his last hope.
"Oh, God, I'm not an evil man, though everybody says
It's all my fault that we ain't caught the devil called Valdez."

There's nothing like good strong meter to make a poem mind its manners. Show me free verse that nails a moment like this does:

Then each man felt the air go still, each felt a stab of dread;
Each heard the sound of danger in a dancing mustang's tread.
They watched the horse come down the street, they watched the rider
*   halt;*
They watched him size them man by man, as if he knew each fault.
He said, "You want to hang this man, I'll give you each the same.
I don't much like a mob," said he, "and Sundown is my name."

And it goes on: Sundown takes the payroll job, as you might expect, and gets bushwhacked by Valdez, and the ensuing chase leads into country where the sun is hot as madness.

YES, YES SIR—ROUTINE IS worry's sly assassin. It only took us till Wednesday night to get a little careless.

It was church night, of course. We went to a Methodist church. Though not yet members, we'd switched from Roofing Lutheran the previous year, a move I didn't wholly understand. The new minister, Pastor Reach, wasn't half the exciting preacher the old one was. Our former pastor could exhort like everything, and he owned what Dad said must be a special edition of the Holy Bible, for it contained things omitted from our own—references to card playing, for example, and rock and roll, and the Russian people. Pastor Reach had a plain Bible, like ours, and preached right out of it. He was a great advocate of forgiveness. Thrilling he was not.

Yet this Wednesday night I was especially keen to be at church, for two reasons. A revival crusade was setting up in Montrose, and Pastor Reach had prevailed on the esteemed Reverend Johnny Latt to come over and preach. Also I suspected the black-haired and winsome Bethany Orchard would be at the service.

In the car Dad said, "I suppose you've heard things about the Reverend Johnny."

"Jeff Swanson called him a Bible-thumper," I ventured.

Dad considered this. "Everybody thumps something, Reuben."

"Do things happen when he preaches?" Other things I'd heard: how at a word from Johnny, people fainted down to the floor to twitch, while prophecies flew through the air like bats.

"I hope so, Rube," Dad said. We pulled up to the church, which appeared crowded already. "Reuben, do you know why Swede stayed home with Davy?"

"No sir."

"Because I'm not sure Swede is ready for this. In fact I'm not sure you are."

"I am," I said a little abruptly. Bethany Orchard had just traipsed into the church, and a moment before the door closed behind her, she had poked her head out and smiled at me.

Dad said, "Goodness, what a cutie," and my ears heated up, and in we went.

Did you ever go to church and see the minister rise with a trumpet in his hand? That's what the Reverend Johnny did. The reverend played like Gabriel, by which I mean loud and with the authority that comes of a good ear and large lungs. He had with him a saxophonist younger brother, an organist wife, and a heavy, weak-looking son who played the flute. The music alone lasted as long as our normal service—fine music, I believe to this day, but all the same, my head throbbed after half an hour. For relief I looked sideways, where Bethany looked cool as a May morning. On we bore through "He Leadeth Me," on through a trumpeted rendition of "Shall We Gather at the River?" at once so beautiful and calamitously loud I could've wept for either reason. Peeking sideways, Bethany glimpsed my eye on her. "Onward Christian Soldiers."

Near the hour mark I closed my eyes and saw a picture of myself from the side, a runnel of blood sliding out of my ear. This, followed by a glance to find Bethany gone, and I rose from my seat and slouched from the sanctuary. Feeling Dad's gaze, I turned and sought his approval. Dad winked at me to go ahead, take a break, understanding that the trumpet in its glorious proximity was hero enough for any mortal ears.

I found Bethany downstairs in the kitchen, peeling an orange from the Westinghouse drawer. When I put my head in at the door, she said, "Reuben, are you hungry?"

"Sure."

"Come on, I'll share it with you."

Bethany Orchard was twelve—only a year ahead of me at school, but in the universal race children run toward the doubtful prize of maturity, she was leagues out front, a realization that arrived as I stood with her in the basement of Roofing Methodist and she fed me orange slices with her fingers. As she peeled the sections away one by one, a locustlike buzz entered the back of my brain. Her fingers were long, capable, conversant: a woman's fingers, slightly reddened from some recent scrubbing. Her fingers were the oldest part of her. I couldn't think of a thing to do with this information. I couldn't think of anything at all. The locusts neared. The bits of orange her fingers placed in my mouth were so ripe I barely chewed.

What brought us up at last was a hard thump from overhead. A light fixture wobbled. We froze and heard the reverend's voice. A second thump rattled the fixture. Somebody shouted, "Amen," and then it was as if Armageddon opened out above us, such salvos of thumps and whacks shook the church.

Did we zip! At the sanctuary door, I heard an urgent voice say, approximately, *"Bahm, toballah, sacoomba-raffay."* Straight off, a different voice raised up to translate. "I am among you tonight, my children," it said amid blooming amens. Cracking the door, we saw the Reverend Johnny Latt reach out to touch a man on the forehead. It was Mr. Layton, who'd stood behind his dime-store counter these endless years, an egregious miser and congenital grouch. He fell backward without utterance, slipping between the ineffectual arms of the younger Latt brother—who'd crept up behind to make the catch—to lie at peace in a room littered with supine Methodists.

There was a pressure on my arm, which I recognized as Bethany's hand. She asked in a whisper if they were all right, these folks lying about. It's true the place raised neck hairs. "They're fine," I said, looking for Dad, who'd know.

"Therianus-dequayas-remorey-gungunnas," a man called out, plus a paragraph or so more. The language was complicated and musical, outside human usefulness. The Reverend Johnny surveyed the room. Bethany's hold whitened on my arm. "Oh, Reuben," she said, "your dad's down!"

He was stretched on his back right up by the pulpit, as if he'd been first to go. I had a fleeting sense of forsakenness. The sight of Dad out cold on the floor momentarily tipped bedrock. I went and knelt at his side.

But how do you wake a man knocked cold by love? Because as he told me later, that's what it was: the electric, unearned love of the great Creator, traveling like light down the nerves of the Reverend Johnny's arm, crackling out the tips of his fingers. Then a jolt hit my shoulder. Lights snapped in my eyes, my ears plugged and opened, and there was a sudden easing in my lungs that showed me how hard I'd been working to breathe. Charged with fear and oxygen, I turned to see who had hold of me. No one did. No one in fact was near me except the Reverend Johnny. He wasn't even looking at me.

But his hand, his right hand, was brushing my shoulder.

I can feel it still—that sizzling jump inside my organs. It didn't feel good, not as I would've suspected the touch of the Lord might feel. It only felt powerful, like truth unhusked.

Had I Swede's gift for getting to the core, I'd be tempted to chew on this awhile. But a witness must obey his strengths; and mine, forgive me, lie in keeping the story moving. So here is where my father wakes. He sits upright, and his eyes are troubled. "Son," he says, "we have to leave." He knows we've stayed too long.

Because he knows, somehow.

At home, the hard and escalating war has paid a visit. And it's Swede, my darling sister, who has met it at the door.

A canyon dim and deep and cool was where he'd made his lair,
A labyrinthine cavern strewn with bits of bone and hair.
It smelled within of smoke and sin and blasphemy and dread,
And none would choose to walk that way who were not walking dead.
Yet down the quiet canyon wall a weary rider came—
A rider bent with grief yet bent on justice all the same.
And while the storm clouds rise on high, and ruin moans and grates,
The rider Sundown draws his Colt, and Valdez grins and waits.

Swede was alone in the house. Dad and I were at church, of course, and Davy was in the garage loft working on a secret, Swede's ninth birthday being two days off. Who could imagine someone would come to the door, in plain sight, such a lovely October evening, with evil in his heart?

But Dad had spoken correctly: They did not know they'd already lost. Israel Finch didn't know it as he heard Swede running to answer the door. Davy didn't know it as he worked in the garage. Swede certainly didn't know it as she lurched across the yard toward a smoking Chevy with Tommy Basca at the wheel and

Israel's hand against her mouth. Seconds ago she'd been writing down rhymes to describe the bandit king Valdez, *daring, eagle-hearted thief,* and growing a soft spot for the bad guy, like every other writer since Milton. Well, no more. The bitter taste of Israel Finch's palm, his unwashed smell, took the sheen off villainy.

Israel made her sit on his lap in the Chevy. Tommy pulled away from the house, dumb as any good chauffeur.

I won't give a detailed account of the ensuing twenty minutes. Later Swede would characterize the interlude as "a small and dirty time," and to think of it still hurts me physically.

A nine-year-old shouldn't be dragged from her house by someone who hates her. Nor be forced to hear the language of the unloved. Nor be jiggled in the laps of perverts. A nine-year-old shouldn't be told, "We'll take you home now, but we'll be back."

The first Davy knew of Swede's capture was her return. Finishing his work in the garage, he came into the house to make coffee, entering at the back door just as Swede slammed in the front. Her shoulders were bent forward, but she was not crying. Her face was white. Davy saw her looking thus and swept her up and smelled the oil-smoke rush of the departing Chevrolet.

That night I eavesdropped on Dad and Davy and Ted Pullet, the town cop, in the kitchen. Swede was asleep for real, which somehow made me fearful—that and Pullet's manner.

"I'll talk to those boys in the morning, Jeremiah," Pullet said.

Dad said, "You can do better than talk, Ted. You know Finch."

Davy hadn't wanted to call Ted Pullet at all. This was Finch and Basca's third offense, and as far as Davy was concerned, their woeful moon had risen. He had his jacket on and car keys in hand when Dad pulled rank and called the law.

Waiting, Davy asked, "How many times does a dog have to bite before you put him down?"

And now here came Pullet with his timid logic. "You gave them a pretty bad scare that night in the locker room, Jeremiah. They're just kicking back a little." He smiled.

Davy got up from the table at this and left the house.

"They pulled her out of the house, Ted," my father was saying. "Her own home. Threatened her, put their hands on her." A pause, then, again, "You know Finch."

This referred to Israel Finch's departure from school the previous year. One day he'd got up to leave in the middle of remedial math. The teacher, young and uncertain, moved cautiously to block the door. Israel seized the teacher by the hair, bent him toward the floor, and delivered a kick that ruptured something inside. Israel went briefly to a reformatory, which failed to prove up to the name. By the time he returned, Tommy Basca had quit school also, his options there seeming limited.

"I'll talk to them in the morning," Ted Pullet said. But by now I recognized the fear inside his voice.

He was no good to us.

This he would verify the very next day, returning after visits with Finch and Basca to tell Dad that those boys were just playing—had meant no harm. I remember the clear contempt in Davy's eyes and the set of his mouth as he listened to this folly.

Swede for her part said nothing to me about Finch and Basca. The day after it happened, we went to school as always, and getting home, she pulled out her little hardheaded doll, a toy that hadn't seen daylight in months. She changed its clothes impatiently, ran a brush over its stiff hair. Once, as Swede was rocking it, her blouse rode up, and I saw two black thumblike marks low on her side. That night she worked fiercely at her tablet.

"Just writing," Swede told me, but she was doing more than that. She was killing off Valdez.

And in the morning she turned nine years old. In reckless celebration we sneaked to her bedroom, where she lay awake pretending otherwise, according to tradition. Then Dad softly sang "Happy Birthday," and she sat up, rubbing her eyes like some storybook child. I can't tell you how relieved I was to see her so glad.

She wanted my present first, probably because it was smallest— a secondhand paperback western by one Frank O'Rourke.

"I'm sorry it's not a Zane Grey," I said.

"It's all right," said Swede, smoothing the cover. The book was called *The Big Fifty*.

"It's about a buffalo hunter."

"It looks swell," she said, then, "Daddy!" because he'd laid on her bed an awkwardly wrapped package that came untaped with no help at all and revealed a great solemn typewriter, black as a Franklin stove, its round keys agleam.

"Daddy," Swede said again in disbelief.

Grinning, he handed her another package—a ribboned ream of twenty-pound bond. "Now put those cowpokes of yours in print."

She touched the keys, pinched the curling ribbon, and waved inked fingers. I never saw Swede look happier than she did with that machine sinking in her bedclothes, as if her world were nothing but huge blue-skied future. But the smudges on her fingers made me think of the bruises, and I wondered how much they hurt.

"Thanks so much," she said, and may we all be paid one day with looks such as she gave Dad.

Then Davy, who'd smiled silently through everything so far, knocked us all flat by stepping out of the room and back in with a Texas stock saddle on his shoulder. He said, "Someday you're going to need this," and laid it on the floor beside her bed.

Swede opened her mouth and couldn't find a word in it. There's magic in tack, as anyone knows who has been to horse sales, and a rubbed saddle owns an allure only dolts resist. Swede's was double rigged with red mohair cinches, tooled Mexican patterns, and a hemp-warn pommel. It was well used, which I believe gave all our imaginations a pleasing slap. Davy had brought the thing back to near perfection; the smell of soaped leather, which is like that of good health, rose around us. It was flawed only in the cantle, where the leather had split and pulled apart and he was unable to mend it. "But it doesn't matter for riding," Davy said.

"That's true," Swede said practically, just as if there were a pony out waiting in the yard.

Well, the day defined extravagance. Swede seemed joyously forgetful of recent evils, and we kept the momentum as long as we could: waffles for breakfast, sugar lumps dipped in saucers of coffee. I remember it as October days are always remembered— cloudless, maple-flavored, the air gold and so clean it quivers. After lunch Dad opened the coat closet and with great care unfolded something scarlet, crinkled, shroudlike. A balloon of tissue paper ten feet high, it had an open bottom weighted with a circle of wire.

In the backyard, Dad lit a coffee-can mixture of gas and fuel oil, and in minutes the balloon commenced to tug. When it was pulling hard enough to lift a good-sized cat, we let it go. It went up quickly. A light wind slipped in from the east, and the balloon caught it. "Ah, Swede," Dad said, "nine years."

A car horn sounded out front. Davy trotted round and came back looking like he'd burped sour. He said, "Dad, it's Lurvy."

Swede looked aggrieved but said nothing aloud, to her credit.

"All right," Dad said. His carriage drooped an inch or so, but you couldn't have guessed a thing from his face. The horn honked again, and Dad went and told Tin Lurvy to come in for coffee.

Picture a fat man, suit full of sweatspots. Imagine the voice of a much picked-on yet somehow hopeful child. If John Calvin was right, destiny had a serious grudge against Tin Lurvy, a purple-faced, futile, tragically sociable traveling salesman. Had he only been pushy, he wouldn't have been a problem. Dad never minded hurrying Fuller Brush men along. But Lurvy never mentioned what he was selling unless you asked. I suspect few people did. Along American turnpikes Lurvy had failed to peddle vacuum cleaners, patent medicines, cuff links, hairpieces. Though he probably came through Roofing but once or twice yearly, it was more than enough.

The arrival of Tin always turned your day in unexpected directions. Here we'd been trying to give Swede a birthday to make her troubles flee; now we wanted to flee as well. It had to be done quickly if at all. Otherwise, protocol took hold, like the death rigor, requiring a person to respect company and sit and listen, in the case of Lurvy, to pointless recitations about people you didn't know, most of them Democrats. Illinois Democrats, Delaware Democrats, Ohio Democrats. "The Democratic Party is the best family I got," Lurvy liked to declare, a truer statement than any of us knew.

So Swede gathered Davy and me behind the house. "It's my birthday," she said. "I didn't invite Mr. Lurvy!"

She never would've pouted so in Dad's presence. It was unacceptable form, and anyhow there was something about the salesman that brought out the Samaritan in Dad. We all recognized this, including Lurvy. The advantage was all his.

"Maybe if Dad bought something, he'd go away," I suggested.

Swede was suspicious. "What's he selling?"

"Encyclopedias, cost a couple hundred dollars," Davy said.

From inside we could hear Dad setting out cups and opening cupboards, and also the cheerful insensibility of Lurvy's monologue.

Swede said, "I'll just go help Dad find the cookies."

"No. Let's go to the timber," Davy said. "Let him find them, Swede. He knows where they are." The timber was a hundred-acre woodlot at the edge of Roofing, wherein lay solace for the hard hit.

"No, he doesn't," Swede said bitterly. "He doesn't."

"They don't need cookies anyway," Davy said. "Let 'em eat cake."

There was a joke here I didn't get. Swede giggled and replied sagely, "The cake's what I am trying to save." It was her birthday, after all. I suppose she'd baked that cake herself. "If I'm not back in two minutes, you guys go on without me."

And do you know, she wasn't back—not in two minutes nor five nor ten. Then Davy said, "Let's pull out, Rube," and peeking through the kitchen window, I saw poor Swede installed at the kitchen table. I could hear Lurvy talking through the glass: "I tell you I ordered me an Airstream trailer? Twenty foot."

It grieved us, leaving Swede that way, but off we tramped down county blacktop. The afternoon was still bright and smelled of wheat stubble. Sometimes we stepped down into the high killed grass to spook hares out of the ditch—Davy had snagged his little carbine out of the garage, but we weren't really hunting, and he just sighted down the barrel at them zigzagging away.

The timber, I should tell you, was one of the best places God ever made. The trees were mostly bur oaks—wide, knuckly giants whose leaves in autumn turned deep brown and beetle-back shiny. A fellow named Draper owned the land then, a happy old crank, and he ran a few independent Jersey cows on it to keep the grass down. In the timber we'd seen badgers, mink, fox.

Abruptly Davy asked, "Did you see Swede's bruises?"

I nodded. "She didn't say anything. I just saw by accident."

"You think Dad knows?"

I didn't, really. "Maybe." My lungs were getting a little stiff on the intake, and Davy was keeping a quick, frustrated pace.

"You think," he said, "that Dad is afraid?"

I stopped—had to—crouched for breath. "Afraid of what?"

"Finch and Basca. Are you okay, Rube?"

I nodded, shut my eyes, took in as much air as I could, and let it out slow. I said, "He beat 'em up in the locker room that night."

Davy said nothing. Maybe that was what had him so irritable: He thought Dad was scared. Maybe it scared him in turn, or maybe he thought it was weakness. Finally he said, "Are you scared, Rube?"

"Naw."

He watched me breathe awhile. "You think God looks out for us? You want Him to?"

"Well, yeah," I said.

We had a strange encounter in the timber that day. We came across a tramp curled up houndlike in a tiny clearing beside a ruined fire. We heard him snoring, sawing away like Sunday afternoon.

We backed away and didn't speak and moved a bit more quietly going home. I'm not sure why I mention him here. He'd make a good harbinger, beside his sorry coals, but I doubt he was.

Still, when we stepped out from the trees—stepped out into a peevish wind, the evening-colored sky telling of winter—shouldn't I have felt something then? As we walked home toward lighted windows, shouldn't I have sensed the Lands adrift, pushed off course?

Supper that night was Swede's favorite, a red-potato chowder Dad mixed up with hunks of northern pike. Seasoned with vinegar and pepper, this was our king of soups. My heart sank when I entered the kitchen and saw Dad stirring while Lurvy talked on.

Lurvy was expounding on his most cherished road meal of all time, a bowl of fisherman's stew he'd ordered in Seattle, when Davy said with mild impertinence, "Where's your next stop, Mr. Lurvy?"

But Lurvy only smiled. "No scheduled stops, son. It's thoughtful of you to ask. Interested in traveling, are you? Let me tell you about a little seafood place I found up in the Cascades—"

Meantime I peeked into the pan and became alarmed. Why, Dad had made a regular batch. He ought to've tripled it—even I knew that. Lurvy could eat this much all by himself!

"Something wrong, Reuben?" Dad said.

"Is this all the soup?"

Dad grinned, saying, "Well, of course."

Lurvy said, "Better wash your hands, kids. No dirty fingers at this table." Then, without rising to wash his own, he reached for two napkins and tucked them into the top of his shirt.

The soup, I must tell you, was peerless. Lurvy ate a bowl in owlish silence, confounded I guess by excellence, and seeing this, we kids all ate the faster. He said nothing of Seattle.

"More, Tin?" Dad offered, and Lurvy held up his bowl.

With that second helping, the silence broke. Lurvy had found joy at our table. Spooning up soup, he looked benevolently at us. He said, "I had my appendix out last month; they showed it to me when I come to. It was yellow as paint and six inches long. Your normal appendix goes about three. Did you know that?"

Well, none of us had known it until that moment. There commenced an education on appendixes and their ailments, Lurvy's in particular, that—speaking for myself—I'd rather have heard after supper. During this discourse Lurvy ate at least five bowls of soup, I had one bowl, and Swede ate three, probably out of principle, it being her birthday. Later, after cake, when Lurvy had gone, Dad admitted he'd had two bowls of soup despite the morbid narrative.

All this from a pot of soup meant to feed the four of us and no more. A small pot of soup. Cleaning up the dishes after supper, I beheld a pot still more than half full of our king of soups.

Make of it what you will.

But onward. I remember a cold rain dripping off the eaves as Lurvy's taillights eased away. I remember Swede's head against my shoulder and her saying, "You think it'll turn to snow, Reuben? Oh, I hope so!" I remember Dad moving slowly in the house, a terrible headache having taken him almost the moment Lurvy departed. Walking stooped, reaching to turn off lights that hurt his eyes, Dad tripped over Swede's saddle, which she'd dragged into the living room. When she ran to him, he said, "Don't worry—don't worry," and picked up the saddle and carried it to her bedside.

Swede and I went to bed early. Davy slung on a coat and left the darkened house. I lay wakeful, conscious of breathing, discomforted at Dad's stumble, at the pain that blinded him. Rising, I looked out the window: Davy's lit tobacco was an orange dot in the rain. I crossed the hall, whispering, "Swede, are you awake?" But she was already far gone into night, mouth open, her breathing faintly snotty. Beneath the rainshot window the saddle camped in a pearly glow. I knelt and touched the leather. I ran my hand down the slope of the horn, down the slick sitting place, and up the swept cantle, and that's when I noticed that the flaw—the pulled-apart leather—was gone. The wound had simply healed up. I remembered how Dad had picked it up in his patient hands. I touched the cantle: just smooth leather, not even a seam.

Make of that what you will.

Sometime past midnight the rain turned to snow. I could tell by the difference in the sound against the window—a less sharp, wetter sound. At first I thought it was what had wakened me.

Then the door handle turned—the back door, off the kitchen. I knew that little squeal. How I wanted it to be Davy coming in, smoky and quiet and shaking off water, but Davy was sleeping not five feet from me. Nor was it Dad, for I could hear him rolling to and fro in sleep, wrestling his headache.

I heard the dry complaint of the kitchen floor, of the place beside the broom closet where joists groaned underfoot, and if I'd had any doubt that someone had got inside the house, it vanished.

Davy smacked, swallowed. My lungs shrank with expectation; my whole surface hurt. I ached to creep across and wake him but felt benumbed, crippled. Footsteps crossed the living room. A shoulder bumped the mantelpiece. The steps came forward. They stopped at my door. I felt, more than heard, someone's hand upon the knob.

Then Davy spoke from beside me—"Switch on the light"—his voice so soft he might've been talking in his sleep. But he wasn't. He was talking to whomever stood incorporeal in the doorway. "Switch it on," he commanded, and next thing we were all of us brightsoaked and blinking—me beneath my quilt, and Israel Finch standing in the door with a baseball bat, and poor stupid Tommy Basca all asquint behind Israel's shoulder. Davy was sitting up in bed in his T-shirt, hair askew, somehow holding his little Winchester. And holding it comfortably: elbows at rest on his knees, his cheek against the stock as if to plink tin cans off fence posts.

It is fair to say that Israel Finch had no chance. He lifted the bat, the knothead, and Davy fired. Israel went backward into Tommy Basca, and Davy levered up a second round and fired again.

Did you ever hear a rifle shot inside a house? Inside a plastered room? You may imagine how the place came alive even while the opposite was happening for Israel Finch. The round made a bright black raindrop above and between his two eyebrows. He was on his back in the hallway when Swede came flying from her room. She saw, besides Finch, Tommy Basca on his stomach and Davy stepping up behind him. And she saw me, I suppose: me watching the end of all our lives as we had lived them heretofore. I remember the sound of Swede's exhaled huff as Dad yanked her into the bathroom and slapped the door shut. I looked at Tommy Basca, who was shot too, though not cleanly as was Finch. Tommy clawed the floor, bawling incomprehensibly.

Davy levered up a third cartridge. He lowered the barrel to the base of Tommy Basca's skull and fired. Tommy relaxed. The house went quiet except for Swede, sobbing behind the bathroom door. Davy straightened, not looking at me or at Dad, who emerged with arms scratched red from restraining Swede. Davy wiped his face, said, "Well," then stepped over Tommy and out the door.

peeking at eternity

NO ONE would be more annoyed than Davy if I tried to recast the predicament under some redemptive glow. Two boys were dead in our house, and there was no bright side to the matter. I recall Davy sitting on the basement stairs under a yellow bulb, his face oily with rain. He wouldn't speak, and his eyes showed a narcosis that was fearful to me. We waited together for Ted Pullet to arrive. Dad, far gone in prayer, held Swede in one arm and gripped Davy's shoulder with the other. I babbled to Davy that it would be all right, that he had not meant to do it.

Which woke him from wherever he'd been, for he turned and snared my wrist. "Don't say it's all right, Rube. I meant to do it. I meant to. You hear me?"

I could only nod frantically. Cars had driven up while he spoke, and we heard voices and doors thumping.

Davy said, "Here we go, then." He was always impatient with our family's general insistence that things turn out for the best.

TRUE story: In the spring of Dad's twenty-eighth year he was raised up by a tornado, along with most of the roof above him and a few loose boards he was setting into the floor.

This was when he was married to my mother, attending a little school in Iowa under the GI Bill. One of those honorably ambitious self-educated men, his scholarly quest kept him happily consumed. Possessed of unusual compassion, he leaned naturally toward medicine, and I imagine my mother falling easily for this generous, handsome, and obviously rising young doctor-to-be.

From what I heard, those were fine times. Davy was a year old and tottered roguishly around the glad-hearted poverty of married-student housing. Mother fed him and wore thin from the chase and

read him to sleep from Robert Louis Stevenson. When not studying, Dad worked, sweeping and painting in the athletic building
twenty hours a week. It was the athletic building, Dewey Hall, that
the tornado struck, just past eleven one heat-soaked night in
September. This, by the way, is the only story Dad ever told us in
whispers: how the tornado came cruising up out of the south, birthed
from a yellow cloud; how it touched earth at the fringe of town, a
pale umbilical rope, to corkscrew almost shyly up College Drive.

Dad was working late, installing a few new floorboards on the
basketball court. Dewey Hall was the only building on campus not
made of brick, and the tornado came for it in absolute maturity—
jumping Old Main and the library and lighting on Dewey, where
Dad toiled alone. He said it didn't sound like a train, as the wisdom
goes, but like a whole mountain skidding sideways. He heard the
great slab of ceiling tear loose, and he felt himself move upward,
ascending in bodily confusion out of the range of gravity and earth
and earthly help.

Meantime my mother, awakened in their third-floor garret by the
hissing wind, leapt up in time to see the rotating head of the funnel
coast overhead.

Gusts of sand raked the panes. No accumulation of hard feelings
can diminish my admiration for what she did then, which was to fly
nightgowned into Davy's tiny room, seize a folded quilt, and brace
it against his window. Thus she stood as all lights failed and glass
burst elsewhere in the building and the noise became everything a
mind could hold.

As Dad told the story, this was always the moment of triumph,
the turn of the war toward winning: Mother is leaning against the
window, standing between the gale and little Davy, and at the
storm's very crest, when it is like a war come seeking what it might
devour, she feels the slightest easing in the glass. At the same time,
Davy stirs and smacks, he rolls to his stomach, the glass goes still
beneath her hands, and by the time Davy's settled back into sleep,
the war's moved on, to the north.

(But do you think the worst is over? Remember, Dad is only now on the ascent. Hammer in hand, he's peeking at eternity. Mom's tears of relief are just standing at the corners of her eyes. Nope, the worst, for Mom at least, is still to come.)

First thing she did, Dad told us, was to run for the hall telephone they shared with the third floor. To ring up Dewey, check on Dad. The line was dead, no surprise, but a strange thing: The handset was hot, voltage-goosed.

Within the hour, someone knocked. In the dark Mother opened the door to a small committee of men, their lantern-lit faces the color of burning paper. One man said, "Mrs. Land, Dewey Hall is down."

As to my mother's state of mind in those next hours, I can only guess. Once in my life I knew a grief so hard I could actually hear it inside, scraping at the lining of my stomach, dredging with hooks as rivers are dredged when someone's been missing too long. I have to think my mother felt something like that.

All I know for sure, from Dad's telling, is this: She was at the kitchen table late the next morning, feeding Davy, when the hall phone, restored to service, began to ring. She waited a long while, wanting someone else to get it, but the whole floor had emptied, gone to class and to work and to walk blinking round the former Dewey Hall. At last she answered. A woman asked for Mrs. Jeremiah Land.

"Speaking," said my mother.

"Mrs. Land," a woman said, "I'm Marianne Evans. Our farm is four miles north of town. I got a man here drinking coffee on my porch. He says he's your husband."

Dad would say he was baptized by that tornado into a life of new ambitions—interpreted by many, including my mother, as a life of no ambitions. Finishing out that semester, he found work as a plumber's assistant. Having been whisked through four miles of debris-cluttered sky—having been swallowed by the wrath of God and kept unbruised inside it—Dad's response was to plunge his hands joyfully into the sewer. An explanation is beyond me other than to repeat what he would often say, the story ended, his hands tucking up the blankets: "I was treated so gently up there, kids."

But the whole thing bothered Davy, and with Dad out of earshot he'd say so. You couldn't get blown around in a tornado, he said, and not get banged up. It didn't make sense. It wasn't right.

Swede challenged him. "Are you calling Dad a liar?"

"Of course not. I know it happened. It just shouldn't have."

I saw what he meant. Davy wanted life to be something you did on your own. The whole idea of a protective, fatherly God annoyed him. But I was weak, and the weak must bank on mercy—without which, after all, I wouldn't have lasted fifteen minutes. Davy's hands were hard as any man's, and quick. They moved always as with a purpose long known. History was built into Davy so thoroughly he could never see how it owned him.

And Mom? How she must have rejoiced after that phone call, how frantically she must've driven to the Evans farm. That reunion must've been a thing Marianne Evans would tell her neighbors about. Happily for Marianne, she would not see my mother's puzzlement as Dad surrendered his prosperous future, nor my mother's attempts to make the best of it. These attempts lasted quite a while, really—long enough to bear Swede and me—but she must've felt Dad had violated some part of the covenant between them. She departed without explanation. We heard later that she married a doctor in Chicago; we heard they patronized the symphony, the theater. But none of this did we hear from Mother, for no letter or call did we once receive; nor did we ever meet the gentleman on whose behalf we'd been erased.

THEY put Davy in cuffs and drove him to the Montrose jail and the rest of us to a motel for the night. Easing away through the dampness, we saw an ambulance backed onto our lawn and the freeze and fade of windows struck with camera flash.

The whole thing was no less a tornado than the other.

Next day when we went to see Davy, Swede tried to kick him. She was crying and incensed, and he reached to comfort her, and she gave it a stout try between the bars, only to clank her shin.

"Good grief, it's lucky I'm in here," Davy remarked as Swede hopped about, biting her lip. Grim as it was, I could see Dad was glad for the joke. Davy'd shaken off the concussed glaze of the night before. He was in a cell with tan lighting and squashed flies on the wall, but he'd not become a creature changed beyond knowing. When Swede had got the mad out and hugged Davy through the bars, Dad told us to say good-bye and wait in the hall.

He was quiet when he joined us. We walked out to the car, the wind flapping staleness off our clothes.

"He seems all right, doesn't he?" I said.

"Sure he does," Dad replied.

We got home, and Swede and I looked around in the cupboards. Normally Dad would've taken over, but instead he just sat in a kitchen chair and leaned back shut-eyed.

Thinking of supper, I asked, "You want us to do anything, Dad?"

"Persevere," he said. It was a better answer than we wanted. What else to do when the landscape changes? When all the mirrors tilt? That first week Swede rose as usual and demanded that I help her cook Dad's oatmeal, but he could no more eat it than he could wave and run for Congress.

Suddenly lots of people we didn't know were calling and dropping by. Reporters, yes, and two different radiomen, and the first TV correspondent ever sighted locally. Meantime a lot of people we did know, whose cheerful encouragement I'll bet Dad could've used, were staying away. I don't know. Maybe they figured they'd wish for no one to say a word if their son shot down two boys. Or maybe—could this be?—they just reasoned Dad was due some grief. That a man like him couldn't be exactly what he seemed.

Two men I remember who did not desert—no, three. They were the Methodist preacher, James Reach, and Dr. Animas Nokes, and also Mr. Layton, first name of Gerard, the dime-store man who'd been struck of the spirit at the hand of the Reverend Johnny Latt.

Strangely, it was Dad who seemed to suffer most and Dad who these few rallied round, while Davy seemed on the whole the same boy who'd always been my favored brother. I remember a moment when he rose from his seat against the cinder block and put his arms around me through the bars, and I put mine around his narrow waist. He grinned and wouldn't let me cry. "Say, Natty, don't you eat those geese yet. You keep those in the deep freeze till I get out. Just a little while." At this I recall a stirring of the jailer who stood close by, a fleeting chuckle of his keys as if at Davy's words, "till I get out . . . a little while." But I held my eyes on Davy's, and I knew in whom I could believe.

If Davy didn't get much reassurance in person, he surely did get it through the mail. Especially those first days, when the newspapers leaned graciously in his direction. Not the Montrose *Observer,* which had the Finch and Basca families to live beside, but the Minneapolis daily's first headlines were the stuff of scrapbooks. Teenage Son Defends Home and Family: held without bail at sixteen for shooting assailants.

So many letters came those first two weeks that one of the deputies, Walt Stockard, brought in a shoe box to hold them all. In slow hours Stockard would pull up a chair and prop his boots on the bars, dipping into the mail and reading aloud. "Here's one from a Maggie in St. Paul:

" 'Dear Davy, I am in the ninth grade, we have just begun to read William Shakespeare, our teacher Mr. Willis demands we read Julius Caesar even though he knows it is Romeo and Juliet we all desire. I hope you will write back, I would like to have a pen pal, maybe we could tell each other our thoughts.'

"And say, Davy," the prison guard added, "it's got perfume on it."

None of this was comforting to Dad. There arrived a day when we were informed that Davy would be charged with two counts of manslaughter—that charge instead of murder because of Davy's age and because the victims had entered the house bent on mischief.

We were now beset with a whole lexicon of legal applesauce. Swede and I eavesdropped on a man in a beard and a tan, baggy suit who sat at the table drinking the coffee Dad so tiredly poured, the two of them talking in quiet voices about jury selection and presumption of innocence and judicial prejudices against violent youth.

The bearded man, Dad told us next day, was Thomas DeCuellar. He was Davy's defense attorney, appointed by the state. We knew he was a good man, because he was on our side and had twenty years' experience in various courts of law and because he'd brought with him, from his wife, a quart jar of dill pickles she had put up herself, with cloves of bluish garlic and, DeCuellar said, somewhere in there, a jalapeño pepper.

Days came, went. Davy sat; reporters left town in search of new misfortunes; the mail dropped off. One morning Swede didn't come out of her room and foiled my snoopish concern by propping a chair beneath her doorknob. "I'm working," she declared. "Don't bother me."

She was writing, of course. I could hear the whir of the typewriter carriage as she rolled in a sheet. The fact made me nervous in some abstruse way. "Is it Sunny Sundown?" I asked—sounding, I know, like some dumb, jealous boyfriend.

She didn't answer, so I moped away to the kitchen to eat corn-flakes in solitude. Dad was back at work by now, having taken leave after the shootings, and by rights we ought to've been back in school, but Dad, though a believer in education, had never respected the glowing objective of perfect attendance (a goal set for kids, he said, "by adults with ruined imaginations"). He'd sat and asked Swede and me if we felt ready to undertake classes again or whether we'd like another week at home.

What do you think we were, idiots?

Besides, I suspect Dad didn't want us back in school yet. He was weathering quite the gale there himself, though we didn't know it. Superintendent Chester Holden, a man whose face was a minefield of red boils, had decided to "scour that janitor's teeth."

I will give you an example of such scouring. Remember the rain the night Finch and Basca broke in? Well, the rain came cold and steady for days, so that the gutters of Roofing ran with brown water. Had the city been more carefully engineered, this would've been harmless enough. And yet on Saturday afternoon, two days before Dad returned to work, the Roofing sewer system came full.

It was stuffed! When Dad got to school Monday morning, he encountered a basement shin-deep in soft terrors, a furnace choked and dead, a smell to poise your wits for flight.

Superintendent Holden called off school, of course.

But do you think he called a plumber?

The first two days, Dad didn't even come home. He telephoned to ask that I bring him a sandwich and a clean shirt; his voice betrayed the headache that had been riding him all week. Of note, I think, is that Roofing Elementary actually had a contract with a pipe-and-furnace man to deal with just such catastrophes. The school had no compunction about calling on him until Superintendent Holden decided Dad's teeth needed scouring.

But Dad just bent to work, firing up a widemouthed pump. He dismantled the furnace, cleaned it piece by piece; he mopped and disinfected, his fingers and lungs corroding from Borax. His lack of complaint must have provoked Superintendent Holden, who came to our house after Dad finished up. It was eight in the evening.

I opened the door and stood in it.

He said, "Your dad here?"

"He's taking a bath." I stayed put.

"Well, tell him something for me." Holden was angry. "I bet he's forgot the parent-teacher meetings tomorrow night. He spent so much time cleaning up his basement mess, he never swept the classrooms. Tell him I said to come in early." There was nothing in his eyes but spite.

So home we stayed, Swede and I, for one more week. The lawyer, Thomas DeCuellar, came by several times. He said little to us about his hours spent with Davy, though he later remarked that he had never represented anyone so unconcerned with his own defense. Mr. DeCuellar saw the shootings as a clear and winnable self-defense in which Davy's hand was forced to violence, a rhetoric that displeased my brother. He was not forced, he told Mr. DeCuellar. If he hadn't wanted to shoot those fellows, he wouldn't have done it. Though he allowed he felt bad, about Tommy especially, Davy couldn't see what this had to do with his defense. Poor Mr.

DeCuellar! Even his petition to have Davy tried as a juvenile was slapped down.

SWEDE meantime sat in her room, whacking at the typewriter. One afternoon I went out to the garage and was startled to see Dr. Animas Nokes standing outside her bedroom window. He was carrying a sack, and seeing me, he motioned for quiet. Swede's window shade was pulled, and strange noises issued from behind it: typewriter keys, yes, but also a sort of desperate chant, Swede's own voice rendered distant and tribal, searching for meter. Dr. Nokes looked a question at me.

"Doggone poem is giving her trouble," I said.

"Ah," said Dr. Nokes, as if a great mist had parted; then, "Reuben, you look like a boy who understands how to treat a pecan pie."

That same night, Swede showed up in my room dragging her sleeping bag. It was one of those cheapies with a vinyl shell, and I heard it crinkling all the way from the hall closet. She spread it on Davy's bed and snaked down into it and thumped Davy's pillow until it was comfortable and she was sure I was awake. I whispered, "Hi, Swede!" not caring a bit that I sounded overjoyed to see her.

"Reuben, can I sleep in here from now on?" she said.

"Sure," I said. "Till Davy gets back."

"Reuben, you really think he'll come back at all?"

Out of nowhere my throat lumped; I kept still.

"Reuben?"

But I couldn't talk about Davy right then, and it made me cross how close I was to crying. "How come you been in your room so much anyhow? Don't you know others of us live here?"

She was quiet a moment, during which I regretted being harsh. "Well, I'll tell you about it if you want—you grump."

I sure had missed my sister.

What happened to Swede was that she couldn't kill Valdez. That is, Sunny Sundown couldn't kill him. Bear with me. After Finch and Basca grabbed Swede that day, old Sunny's adventures had turned a little grim. He kept trailing after Valdez, finding worse and worse.

One day an upturned stagecoach and its driver's ghastly hue,
The next a blackened farmhouse with its family blackened too.

I began to understand how truly scared Swede had been. I'd been picturing Valdez as one of those banditos in *Zorro:* sitting a scrawny horse, sneaky grin, the kind of villain who'd dig for ear-wax to groom his mustache. Now, overnight, Valdez had come unbound. He was a monster.

I said to Swede, "What do you mean you can't kill him? Can't you think of a word to rhyme with dead—"

"Reuben, that's not what I mean." How quietly she interrupted. "It's not that I can't write it. I've already written it ten ways."

If she could write it, then what was the problem? I sat confounded. Mistaking my silence for doubt, Swede recited:

"And as the gunshots echo back against the canyon walls,
Valdez begins to totter—now he staggers—now he falls."

"Yeah," I said. "Yeah!"

"And later, Sundown finds a match, and lights it with a stroke;
'Cause graves in sunbaked ground come hard—a man can use a smoke."

"Swede, that's great! He buries him and everything— *Now* what's the matter?"

She'd flopped back on the pillow. "Just because I write it, doesn't mean it's what really happened."

I had to hold that in my head awhile. I knew she knew what she meant. She said, "It doesn't matter if it sounds good. I can't write it so he's really dead. It doesn't work."

Swede was talking some language to which I knew the words but not the meanings. It scratched my pride. I tried making my voice gruff, like Davy's. "Listen, Swede, who's running this story anyway?"

She didn't answer. She was right not to. It was a dumb question.

TEN days before the start of Davy's trial this article appeared in the Minneapolis *Star:*

A Victim's Story

His aunt called him Bubby, because as a child, nothing made him happier than sitting on her back step blowing soap bubbles that rose and drifted across the yards of this small middle-American town. "I was a second mother to him," Margery Basca said. "Bubby lived with me when his parents had difficulties. Oh, he was sweet." Last month Bubby—Thomas Basca, age seventeen—was shot dead in a house across town. His parents have been unwilling to talk with the press about the loss of their only child. Now that child's favorite aunt has agreed to tell her story to the *Star*.

I won't belabor you with the rest. Yet for all its mawkishness, the story had sway; it can't be denied. Looking back at how the Finch and Basca families shunned the papers at first, the timing of their turnaround seems predestined, as all history does when you think about it. By the time Margery Basca decided to talk, the reporters had pretty well run the string out on Davy Land's heroics, and they seemed cheerful at the prospect of laying him low. Tommy's bereaved folks, Stan and Karen, patched things up long enough to pose for an AP photographer. You never saw people of more threadbare hopes.

This troubled Thomas DeCuellar. The trial would start Wednesday at the courthouse in Montrose; on Sunday night he sat down tiredly at our kitchen table and told us how it was.

"People are placing their sympathies with the dead boys," he said. There was bread and cheese on the table, and he built a sandwich. "Jeremiah, have you been reading the papers this week?"

Mr. DeCuellar chewed his bread and cheese. Swede and I sat quietly. "I've read them," Dad said.

"You have to assume the jury has also. Of course they'll be sequestered once the trial starts. Until then they're quite free." Mr. DeCuellar turned unexpectedly to us. "You know, compadres"—using that word because Swede liked it—"the situation could be worse. Do you know how they conducted trials in Saxon England?"

Swede shook her head. She liked most everything about Mr. DeCuellar: his black-coffee eyes; his pipe, a small, neat meerschaum; and his way of speaking to us, which, Dad said, was in the manner of men who had wanted children for decades and never had them.

"Do you remember the Battle of Hastings?" he inquired.

"Ten sixty-six," Swede replied.

"Exactly." Mr. DeCuellar beamed. "Well, before that, England was in Saxon hands. The Saxons invented jury trials, but they also tested for guilt *by ordeal.* A man might point to his poor neighbor and say, before the judge, 'He stole my grain.' Henceforth the accused would have a red-hot iron laid across his palm! *Tsssssssssss!*"

"But if he was innocent!" Swede protested.

"If innocent, he would pass the test. His flesh would be unharmed," he said pleasantly. "So people believed."

"Then no one ever passed," Swede observed darkly.

The lawyer looked at Dad. "Probably not many, hm, Jeremiah?"

Dad said, "Maybe, Tom, you ought to tell us what we can expect of the trial—how it all works."

"Yes, of course. It's quite simple." And Mr. DeCuellar spoke a brief, clear paragraph about the properties of justice, about the efforts the prosecution would surely make to discredit our brother and portray him as a brutish reprobate, and, finally, about Davy's brave defense of us, his family. When Mr. DeCuellar stood to go, Swede hugged him hard. Then he offered Dad two counts of advice. First, maintain a happy composure at work; second, answer no questions, especially from reporters. We were to stay out of the newspapers, which, he said, had never really seen the problem with Saxon justice.

GOOD advice is a wise man's friend, of course, but sometimes it just flies on past, and all you can do is wave. Because the next day, speaking of ordeals, Dad went and got fired by his boss, the boil-faced Mr. Holden, with half the school looking.

It transpired in the cafeteria. Several classes, mine included, were assembled for the morning milk break. Because of impending Thanksgiving we all had on Pilgrim hats cut from stiff black paper, and Mrs. Bushka at the bakery had sent over some gingerbread turkeys bedecked with orange and yellow frosting. Even as we sat prying lids off milk bottles, we could hear the persecuted cooks banging around back in the kitchen, grandmas barking at each other, preparing the daily grotesque. I remember Peter Emerson, looking uncharacteristically solemn because of his Pilgrim hat, predicting meat loaf: "The butcher's truck goes to the dump every Thursday. This smells like the dump Fridays."

It was, nonetheless, a glad-hearted gathering, at least until Mr. Holden came down to make some brooding remarks about Thanksgiving, probably having to do with privation and death. He'd certainly picked the right career, had Mr. Holden. His every feature spoke of annoyance and, to people under five feet tall, of physical danger. His poor face looked always festering with some imminent parasitical hatch. Nothing could quiet a happy crowd of kids like Mr. Holden's appearance. He loved superintending; he was made for it. So when he marched in with a determined grin on his face, we froze. Boys and girls recognize sinister as handily as dogs do. Here it was. But when he produced a paper Pilgrim's hat from behind his back and put it on his own head, I think we all nearly bolted.

Then Mr. Holden said his few words. I've forgotten them—doesn't matter. No doubt he thought we were all spellbound. What had my attention, though, was something I hadn't noticed before. The neatly scripted letters near the squared-off top of his hat. Very small capitals in white chalk, easy to miss but really quite readable: SHOOT ME! they said.

Well, I saw that and wanted to laugh. Not just wanted to. I tell you, that laugh was down in my stomach, like bad beef. It meant to come out. A giggle crept up the old esophagus; my eyeballs watered. The worst of it was, I seemed to be the only kid who'd noticed. Either that or everyone else had iron control—a terrible thought. Mr. Holden talked on. Then Peter Emerson leaned over to my ear. "Bang," he whispered. The laugh ripped forth—*hoo hoo ha ha wha wha wha.* I laughed so hard my sight went dark. I laid my forehead down on the table to sob. Did anyone laugh with me?

Who knows? I do remember looking up through tears to see the glaring superintendent, death in a hat, SHOOT ME! still writ upon his mighty crown, and I remember wishing *I* could arrange to be shot at that moment and have it done with.

Well. He didn't kill me, though I don't doubt his intention; he started for me but was so anxious about it he clipped his thigh rounding the table. Do you remember how tippy those school milk bottles were? Mr. Holden took that corner, and half a dozen of the little soldiers leapt from the tabletop and burst wondrously at our feet. The cafeteria was silent except for the contents of one tipped bottle streaming off the table. Beside me Peter Emerson moved his elbow furtively. The bottle tipped, sailed out, exploded.

And then, as would happen, Dad appeared. Instinctively I feared for him, for a curse seemed hovering in that room.

But Dad was in his usual fine humor, diagnosing the breakage, catching my eye and Peter's as we watched from our benches, and sending us a wink. His face betrayed delight, for he'd entered at the moment of Chester Holden's fabulous lurch. It took him perhaps twenty seconds to unlock a supply closet and set to work with a rag mop and bucket, and in that time Mr. Holden saw before him an opportunity to set an example. To superintend. To *scour.* As Dad knelt for broken glass, Holden stepped up next to him, so that Dad was working around his knees. Dad looked slavelike down there.

Mr. Holden said, "Land, we have to talk."

Dad looked at his boss, surprised by some alteration in his voice.

"There've been complaints," the superintendent said.

Miss Karlen, our teacher, said, "Children, we must go now."

Holden held up one hand. He wanted everyone there.

"All right," Dad said.

"Last week when you were cleaning the basement, two people reported you stumbling around down there. Talking to yourself."

Dad said nothing. I didn't know what Holden was getting at, saying next, "This isn't the first time. I've seen it myself." He spoke with quiet reason, as if Dad were some disturbed child. "Jeremiah," he said, "I'm aware you passed clean out a couple of weeks ago—

in *church*. Don't you think your problem is getting out of hand?"

I entered here into some sort of shock, for I understood two things at once: first, that Superintendent Holden was accusing my father of drunkenness, a charge so preposterous that God would surely flatten him before our waiting eyes. I also understood that Dad would not defend himself within our hearing. I do not doubt that Holden understood this also.

Miss Karlen began quietly rallying the children to leave. As we clattered up our trays, I heard Holden demand Dad's explanation. I saw Dad voice a soft reply. At this the superintendent made the most fitful transformation. His neck compressed into his shoulders; his hands clawed upward into his sleeves. He was Mr. Hyde! He roared a few words, and Dad became a former janitor.

Most boys, I am guessing, have never watched outright as their father was stripped of his livelihood, and I don't want to pound it too hard, but the cruelty of that moment still impresses me. I left my classmates and headed for Dad, who stood in rapt surprise facing Holden. I hadn't in mind to say anything, and indeed I didn't, for as I approached, Dad lifted his hand, sudden as a wind shift, touched Holden's face, and pulled away. It was the oddest little slap you ever saw. Dad turned and walked off, and the superintendent stood with his fingers strangely awonder over his cheeks and forehead. Then I saw that his bedeviled complexion—that face set always at a rolling boil—had changed. A hale blush spread over cheekbones that suddenly held definition. Above his eyes the shine of constant seepage had vanished, and light lay at rest upon his brow.

Listen: There are easier things than witnessing a miracle of God. For his part Mr. Holden didn't know what to make of it. He looked horrified. He covered his face and slunk from the cafeteria.

I knew what had happened, though. I knew exactly what to make of it, and it made me mad enough to spit.

What business had Dad in healing that man? What right had Holden to cross paths with the Great God Almighty?

The injustice took my breath away. Truly it did. I felt a great hand close against my lungs, and Miss Karlen escorted me gasping to the nurse's office, where Mrs. Buelah plugged in her teapot and made a steam tent from a bolt of tan canvas.

When Dad came—having boxed up the contents of his single drawer in the boiler room—he lifted a corner of the canvas. "I'm sorry you saw that," he said. His getting fired, he meant, not the other thing. "How about we go home?"

But I shook my head. I just couldn't go with him. Nor could I tell him it wasn't his public mistreatment that stole my breath; it was something too mean to explain. It was the fact that Chester Holden, the worst man I'd ever seen, got a whole new face to look out of and didn't even know to be grateful, while I, my father's son, had to be still and resolute and breathe steam to stay alive.

late in the night
when the fires are out

EARLY Wednesday, under red skies, we drove to Montrose. We'd been told to be at the courthouse at nine a.m., but the DeCuellars insisted we breakfast at their house. There's no way a person can really prepare for someone like Mrs. DeCuellar. Buxom and businesslike on her doorstep, once she had you inside, she became the woman you wish had lived next door all your childhood days.

And breakfast? What would you say to butter-crumbed eggs that trembled at the touch of your fork? To buttermilk biscuits? To peach pie baked that very morning? And through everything Mrs. DeCuellar, like a small sun, beamed down on Swede and me.

Thus braced against the evil of the day, we came to the courthouse. We'd thought to visit Davy before it all started, but we were informed this was impossible and advised to wait on benches in the hall until the jury was seated and given instructions.

Trials are mostly a succession of waits. We waited all morning. The prosecuting attorney, whom I remember only by his first name, Elvis, had detected an attitude problem in one of the jurors.

"Will it be a long time?" Swede asked.

Mr. DeCuellar brought out his meerschaum. Lighting the pipe, he said, "Swede, who in your family is champion in war at sea?"

Swede blinked, and Mr. DeCuellar slipped a notebook from his pocket. "You've grown up so big not knowing how to play war at sea? I don't believe it. Here." It is thus I most often remember that good lawyer: he sitting slouched on a folding chair, notebook on his knee, Swede leaning into him as he pointed and strategized.

We played war at sea right up through noon, Swede and I, and then the door opened. The trial was about to commence.

You've seen courtrooms. This one had a raised jury box fenced by a brass rail, and after we'd all stood up and sat again, it had a judge by the name of Raster sitting behind his high desk. The judge had the kind of wavy white hair I associated with benevolence, the hair of soft-touch aunts who keep mints in candy dishes, though his eyes evoked no such hopeful impressions.

Davy was in the front pew beside Mr. DeCuellar. I was surprised what a short and unrakish figure he cut. Nobody seemed to be looking at him. I wanted to run forward and make him look into my eyes.

After certain formalities Elvis, the prosecutor, rose to get things started. He cleared his throat and preached an eloquent and transparent sermon on violence, a five-minute redaction in which Davy ceased being any human's brother and became an icy double murderer. Israel Finch grew into a lost boy of great promise, who despite his broken home and juvenile record, showed natural talent in auto mechanics. And Tommy Basca was just some forlorn kitten out mewing in the dark and rain. Through all this I gaped occasionally at Swede, who appeared snakebit and vengeful.

Then up stood Mr. DeCuellar to respond. I don't remember his words, but in general feeling—well, remember how the great Daniel Webster argued against the Devil for the soul of Jabez Stone? The Devil had him beat, you recall, as long as Webster stood on logic. You can't argue with a signed contract, and Jabez, the dolt, had signed. But Webster calmed himself and began to speak instead about what makes a man a man and the nature of the soul and its very Creator, whence comes all freedom. And the Devil himself did wither in the face of this bigger logic, and so, it seemed to me, must Elvis wither, and judge and jury also.

They didn't seem impressed, though.

In fact there came some fairly bad moments after that. One came when Elvis called Stanley Basca to testify. Till now I'd thought I had the facts by the tail, but Stanley had a zinger to impart to the court.

"Davy came around to Finch's place that night. Rotten night out. Nine o'clock or thereabouts," Stanley said.

ELVIS: "Did you see him yourself?"

STANLEY: "Yes sir. I was over to the Finches', looking for Tommy."

ELVIS: "And what did you see Davy do?"

STANLEY: "Well, he had something in his hand. A tire iron I guess, or pry bar. He whacked every window out of the Finch boy's car."

Those gathered stirred audibly—a surprise revelation! For me, of course, the surprise quickly deadened into a recognition that it was perfectly true. Swede and I had gone to bed early; so had Dad. Davy'd gone out into that freezing rain. And later, when the footsteps entered our house? Wasn't I amazed when the lights came on and there was Davy holding his Winchester?

He'd issued them an invitation. I saw it now.

I looked at Davy's face, couldn't read it, and looked at Dad's, seeing not shock but sorrow and austerity. I checked Mr. DeCuellar. He knew it too. At that moment a wall inside me shifted, and I knew my brother had no chance inside that courtroom. Piece by piece our defensive architecture failed. Margery Basca testified, the tears standing in her eyes, how poor Bubby had gone to the store for her twice a week, getting the bread and milk, doing his uncomplaining best. Yellow-eyed old Mr. Finch, Israel's grandfather, told in quiet, convulsive tones how Israel was without doubt the most maligned young man in Roofing—"He didn't make friends that well." Davy's erstwhile girl Dolly was sworn in, throwing tragic looks at him, and recounted her experience in the locker room, establishing for the jury the extant hate between Israel Finch and Davy.

All this time I was fighting a magnificent swarm of butterflies. Mr.

DeCuellar had told me I'd have to testify, as the single eyewitness of the shootings. In craven dread I sought Swede's help in rewriting events, but Mr. DeCuellar reassured me, saying to be forthright though frugal in detail.

"WE'RE going to lose, Reuben," Swede told me that night.

We were socked into sleeping bags on the floor of Mr. DeCuellar's study, and I agreed with Swede, though not aloud.

She then said, "We've got to break him out."

I should've known it was coming. "Oh, Swede, don't now."

She sat up in her sleeping bag. "We could do it—bust him out of there. Tonight!" She had hold of my shoulder. "They're gonna convict him, Reuben. You want Davy in prison?"

"We can't even drive, Swede," I said, but it carried no water.

"We'll wait till they're asleep—take some of Mrs. DeCuellar's cookies—offer 'em to the guard. When he turns to me, you grab his gun," and so on. It was one of those rare moments when I actually felt older than Swede. Seizing it, I told her to grow up. She went silent and fell to studying bookcases. Mr. DeCuellar had left a reading lamp on in a corner as a night-light—had he children of his own, he'd have known better. She returned to bed at last with a book of poems by Robert Louis Stevenson.

I said, "Read me one, Swede." Few writers can match Stevenson. Both danger and peace inhabit his verse; it throws a very wide net. So Swede lay beside me reading.

"Whenever the moon and stars are set,
Whenever the wind is high,
All night long in the dark and wet,
A man goes riding by."

Gooseflesh rose. Outside, the wind thumped around; the reading lamp flickered but stayed on. She whispered,

"Late in the night when the fires are out,
Why does he gallop and gallop about?"

I said, "Let's sleep, Swede," though I couldn't have—not anymore. There was a prescient chill in those lines, in her voice.

"Whenever the trees are crying aloud,
And ships are tossed at sea,
By, on the highway, low and loud,
By at the gallop goes he.
By at the gallop he goes, and then
By he comes back at the gallop again."

"What does it mean?" I asked.

"I don't know." She shut the book and turned out the light. After a while she said, "I think it means we ought to break him out."

NEXT afternoon they put me on the stand. I felt like a parakeet up there: new chinos, a green wool sweater that itched at the neck, my hair slicked to pudding. I looked at Dad, who smiled back; at Dr. Nokes, who winked. I laid my hand on the Bible and, when finished, looked at Davy. He was making faces, trying to bust me up, just like back in church.

Elvis came up in his bow tie. He asked some chatty questions about friends, bullies, stuff I liked to do—getting me comfortable, warming the clay. I gave him nothing at first, I promise you.

But gradually—oh, it hurts!—something began to work on me. I began to have, of all things, self-confidence. It crept up like an oily friend. I sirred Elvis to death; I sirred him with a disrespect he had to comprehend. And hearing these things from my own mouth, I thought, Not bad. Pride is the rope God allows us all. At some point I looked at Mr. DeCuellar and saw alarm in his eyes. I actually wondered what was wrong, which tells you how far gone I was.

Then Elvis said, "Reuben, the night the boys came by and took your sister for a ride—was Davy angry that night?"

He thought I hesitated out of fear to answer the question. I confess I was only looking for the right voice.

Elvis prompted, "Something like that happening to his little sister—say, I would've been upset, a thing like that."

Reaching down for a good low register, I replied, "No sir. Davy was as easygoing as anything."

"He didn't have a thing to say after Tommy and Israel brought her home? Scared as she was by those boys?"

Posed like that, it did seem unlikely. I thought it over, sensing the court waiting. Davy *had* said something, hadn't he? Just before Ted Pullet drove in? I looked at my brother and tried to recall.

And do you know, when Davy looked back, something was different. Something in the look itself—it was untethered somehow. He smiled at me from some planetary distance. And I thought of his way in the kitchen that night, how he'd yielded the car keys to Dad wordlessly after a long and inner weighing.

"Why, yes sir. He asked Dad a question. He said, 'How many times do you let a dog bite you before you put him down?'"

And the court did not erupt, nor the jury gasp in wonder at this revelation. Only Elvis's eyebrows rose slightly. "Reuben," he said with approval, "you have been holding out on us."

Why, you're wondering, did I toss Elvis that line of Davy's? Well, I suppose I had to, once I'd remembered it. I was tied to honesty by oath. What I regret is how I said it: I said it with belligerence, a trait ever cultivated by fools. And predictably, chaos accompanied belligerence into office. For that putting-down-the-dog remark led Elvis to seek and pull from me other facts pointing to ill intent: that Davy already had his coat on to deliver vengeance, when Dad stopped him; that Davy, waiting on the stairs for his arrest, had grabbed my wrist and spoken the words, "I meant to." With despair I heard myself answer. Oh, I was meek enough now, but it didn't matter. Elvis drew these facts from me and unfolded them to view and laid them before the court like a series of bloody hankies.

THAT night I agreed to break Davy out of jail. Swede and I went to bed jittery, faking weariness, even as Dad prayed over us for forgiveness and joy and a night of peace. We shut our eyes, slurred our good-nights. The moment Dad left the room, Swede bounded up and pulled jeans over her pajamas. I buttoned up a flannel shirt.

We'd have sneaked out then, except Dad and the DeCuellars decided to have their coffee in the living room. The front door was in the living room, and we weren't likely to just waltz out through it.

"We'll go out the window," said Swede. But Mr. DeCuellar, in his efficiency, had put his storms up right on schedule.

"I guess we'll have to wait," I said. It was fine with me. Outside, the trees were leaning in the wind; the pane was so cold it felt wet.

But Swede was intent. "After they're asleep, then."

After a while we lay down on top of our sleeping bags, just to soften the wait; a fine freezing rain began against the window.

Next thing I recall is Dad kneeling between my bag and Swede's, waking us before sunup. There was an agitation in his voice that made me think, just for a moment, that we were on our way west, the car packed and pointed toward the faint cries of geese.

Then I heard Dad say, his voice part of sleep, "The sheriff was here an hour ago—wake up, kids—the sheriff has been here. Kids, are you listening? Davy's broke out."

ALL we knew that first morning was that Davy'd got out—that he'd taken with him a police-issue revolver and that a posse had been formed. Twelve men in six cars were out parsing the county.

It was Swede's contention, as the morning stretched on, that a posse of twelve *hundred* couldn't catch Davy. Let 'em try.

Dad said, "Swede, if you can't talk sense, don't talk at all."

They were the harshest words I'd ever heard him speak. I watched him sipping his coffee, his face foreign with misgiving. How I wanted to understand him! But I was eleven, and my brother had escaped from the pit where my vanity had placed him. Who in this world could ask for more?

The following days must've been excruciating for Dad—dreading Davy's recapture yet fearing worse. The state police were advised, and locally the posse grew exponentially. After early radio reports, fifty men appeared at the courthouse, every one of them armed. Though the word posse sounds archaic, it made all sorts of sense at the time. For one thing, Davy was believed to be on foot. Since no one in Montrose County had reported a stolen vehicle, it was assumed he was still nearby, shivering in some hidey-hole.

"Unless he got out to the highway and hitched a ride," Dad suggested. He was trying to sell Deputy Walt Stockard on calling off the posse, something Walt hadn't the authority to do anyway. It was Davy's second day out. Walt had come by the DeCuellars' for coffee. No doubt the sheriff thought it wise to keep an eye on Davy's family. "He could be in Kansas City by now," Dad said.

"Possibility," Walt admitted. "Though it was raining buckets. Besides, he's got the best-known mug in the state right now."

What actually happened—and we got this from Walt, whose colleague Stube Range was on shift—was this: Shortly before eleven Stube was sitting at the night desk reading a Mickey Spillane paperback mystery. Suddenly he was distracted by a polite call from Davy. The toilet in his cell wouldn't flush, he said.

"Don't flush it, then," Stube answered.

"There's a need to," Davy replied. "Sorry about that, but there's a need." Davy jiggled the lever audibly. No flush.

There was apparently some back-and-forth between them, but finally Stube Range put down his book, let himself into Davy's cell, locked it behind him, and peeked into the toilet.

No suspense here. Stube awoke propped against the wall of Davy's cell. His head was sore. The toilet, incidentally, worked fine. He had to use it before his replacement released him from the cell.

Swede would point out, rightly enough, that he ought to have known better, but Stube Range, as they say, had a good heart. At this crossroads in his life he would in fact leave law enforcement to begin a new career as a school janitor over in Roofing. The district was hiring, you see.

WE STAYED at the DeCuellars' three days after Davy's escape. Walt Stockard visited every morning, bringing us news of the county's frustration. Crisscrossing the area, talking to farmers and rural-delivery men and others who might've noticed a bedraggled boy slouching hastily elsewhere, the posse had come up dry. By the time a bloodhound could be borrowed from a neighboring county, the great rains had blotted out Davy's scent.

That afternoon a farmer name of Nelson Svedvig came into Montrose and filed a complaint about a stolen horse. An Arabian mare taken from his south pasture. "Taken when?" Sheriff Pym asked. Walt was standing right there listening, is how I know.

"Not sure," Nelson Svedvig admitted. "Those ponies kind of look after themselves this time of year."

That night the sheriff paid off what remained of the dispirited posse, and we took our leave of the DeCuellars. Oh, it was good to get home.

OUR first night back, Swede propped herself in bed, typewriter before her, and whacked away steadily. Here's what I found in the morning, laid on the floor beside my bed:

The moon was black as a miner's lung,
The sky was black as a shroud,
And deep in a cell that was black as a well
Two men lay moaning aloud.
And one was Rennie, who'd robbed a man,
And one was Bert who had killed,
And the gallows outside hadn't ever been tried
But its mission would soon be fulfilled, lads,
Its mission would soon be fulfilled.
Three nooses swayed loose in a breeze like a sigh—
But who was the third who was waiting to die?

Swede came in while I was reading and perched on my bed like a satisfied cat. I said, "Is it Sunny?" But she only shrugged.

He'd been awake in his room one night,
With his darling asleep by his side,
When the bold Reddick boys, hardly making a noise,
Pushed the front door open wide.
His bride they had threatened not once but three times,

When his travels had fetched him away.
They had followed her round as she walked through the town,
Calling names I would rather not say—no,
The names I would rather not say.
And what do you think any good man would do,
No matter what judges or laws told him to?

"Swede," I told her, "this is awful good!"
"Aw, don't," she said.

They opened the door and they crossed the broad floor
With their minds full of evil intent.
For in town they had heard the fortuitous word
That Sundown on business was sent.
And as they approached Sunny rose to his feet,
Like a spirit he made not a sound,
And his blood rose inside as they came near his bride
And he shot the bold Reddick boys down, lads,
He shot the bold Reddick boys down.
So may a good man who has spared his wife hurt
Face death with the likes of poor Rennie and Burt.

"That's it?" I couldn't believe it; there wasn't any more! "He shoots them? Then they hang him with those two guys?"

"Reuben, how fast do you think I can write this stuff?"

"Oh—it's not done?"

"Reuben!"

"Well, I'm sorry!" The truth was, old Sundown really tugged at me. Cautiously I asked, "What about Valdez?"

She didn't look at me. She had tears in her eyes, just that quick! "Sunny couldn't beat him, Reuben."

"So he got away?"

Her silence placed a nub of fear in me that Valdez was no invention. That he was real and coming toward us on solid earth. A preposterous idea, yet it blazed up, so scary in its brightness that I made a wall against it in my heart, in the deepest place I owned.

THE WEEKS WHEELED ALONG unbalanced. One day Walt Stockard reported to us that the Svedvig mare had come trotting home, whickering for oats. There was speculation that Davy'd ridden a dozen miles across country to the highway. Swede also took satisfaction in the newspapers' latest reversal of attitude, so complete that a stranger now reading his first Davy Land article would've finished it believing the world was improved without these Finch and Basca characters anyway.

There was no comfort in it for Dad, though. He seemed to believe he had lost his son forever. He stopped answering the telephone; he became restive and joyless. Many a night I woke to the murmur of paper and knew he was up, sitting in the kitchen with King James. He held to that book like a rope ladder.

I remember creeping out once when my breathing was poor, and there he was, bent to it. I told him my lungs were tight.

"All right." He sat still, not rising to put water on the stove.

"What you reading?"

"Ninety-first Psalm."

"Does it help?"

He went to the sink and held a pan under the tap. He didn't answer, and I thought he wasn't hearing me. I repeated the question.

Dad lit a burner. When the water boiled, he threw in baking soda. I said, "You could read me a psalm if you want to, Dad."

But he said, "Not tonight, Reuben. My head hurts so."

WE DIDN'T go back to school. Dad hadn't the will to send us if we truly didn't want to go, and we knew it. Preying on his depression, we made ourselves useful. We washed clothes, scrubbed floors, swept cobwebs, cooked soup. When he approached us one day with the reluctant suggestion that we return after the Christmas break, Swede took him into her room and displayed a stack of geography and arithmetic books. "From the library," she said. "I certainly don't want to lag behind my classmates."

"Ah," Dad said, looking at me over Swede's head. He was onto her and wanted me to know it. He didn't send us back, though. It wasn't as if we didn't read; while at the library, Swede had checked out every Frank O'Rourke on the shelves, having finished *The Big Fifty* long ago. O'Rourke, she confided, wrote much better westerns than Zane Grey.

"It's his women. They don't talk all the time, and when they ride, they ride like men. In Zane Grey the hero always starts off with the wrong girl, and she has eyes that are too close together, and she has a bad attitude, like a stubborn roan."

"Swede," I said, "Sunny's wife—she was the right kind of girl, wasn't she? Like one of O'Rourke's you were talking about."

The question made her indignant. Sunny Sundown was no dummy, she said; he'd ridden some miles in his time; he would never have married a roan. I was glad to hear her say it. Last I'd read of Sunny, he had his hands full enough:

Till late in the night he had fought the good fight
With his fear, and had kept it at bay;
And he dreamed of his wife, and their satisfied life,
And he woke to a wicked new day.
Then he rose in his shirt and he nodded to Burt,
Who was empty and mute as a hole,
But down on his knees Rennie wept aloud, "Please,
Have charity on a thief's soul, Lord,
Forgive my poor dry-rotted soul."
Three nooses swung loose as a clergyman prayed.
Three men were marched forward—and two were afraid.

Swede meant this to be suspenseful, of course, but even at eleven I recognized what had to happen next: Somehow a woman had to come on the scene. And she had to be young and black-eyed and lovely, and touched by the bravery of the condemned hero.

Then up the tight street came a rider so sweet,
She was light as the dawn, and as free—
And her hair was as black as her stallion's back,
And she parted the crowd like a sea.

"Is it Sunny's wife?" I asked.

"Nope—just a woman." She deliberated. "You know, that's not an awful idea. But it's a different woman." It was a problem.

"Why don't you change it?" I suggested. "Make this girl his wife, see—they ride away together."

"She wasn't his wife," Swede flared. Past tense, you notice—history, even the fictive kind, being beyond our influence.

The problem got worse when the girl actually pulled off the rescue, for then Sunny, though rushed in the moment,

leaned down from the black and pushed her hair back
and kissed his deliverer twice, my lads
He kissed his deliverer twice.

The last thing I wanted was to fight Swede, but this was terrible. "Now he's kissing her," I complained.

"Reuben," Swede said, holding herself back, "say you're about to be hanged. The rope's on your neck already! Then out of noplace this beautiful girl comes riding up and saves you. Are you telling me you're not going to kiss that girl? Look, Reuben. Let's say Sunny just thinks of her as a really great sister. Like me."

I nodded, but in truth this picked at me for some little while.

by the grace of lurvy

CHRISTMAS looked a little meager going in. You understand: Kids of my generation grew up with stories of their parents' deprivations—tales of treeless Christmases, scrawny old stockings containing naught but a polished apple. In 1962 the Great Depression was a reach back of less than thirty years—surely a millennial distance for residents of Minneapolis, but not so far if you lived in Roofing, on the edge of the plains.

Dad had found but irregular work. He repaired a furnace for the

Lutheran church, mended furniture in the basement, and, capitalizing on a rash of chimney fires in town, borrowed a brush and swept chimneys until he caught cold. "I'll work through it," he told Swede, sniffing the hot lemonade she handed him, but another day on the rooftops drove the cold lungward until he wheezed as badly as I did. I suspect he was almost grateful. I know we were. That chimney business was nasty work, the wind snapping his coat around, him up there in his janitor's boots traipsing on icy shingles.

Still, an unemployed father meant the sort of Christmas Swede and I had always heard of. We wondered how well we'd do in front of Dad—how grateful we could appear for a gift of, say, a navel orange. What Swede really wanted that year was something extravagant. "A trip," she said, "out west. I want to ride west on a horse and find Davy." She was sure he was out there, sitting on a blanket eating buffalo meat. How great it would be!

A navel orange just seemed a little weak in comparison.

Then, ten days before Christmas, Dr. Nokes stopped by. Drinking tea—our coffee was long gone—he grew alarmed at Dad's deepening cough. He set his cup down and retrieved a stethoscope from his car. "Jeremiah," he said warily, "how long have you been croaking this way?"

"I actually think it's getting better," Dad said.

"How much do you bring up?" asked Dr. Nokes.

Dad said he hadn't been measuring. Then, "Swede, Reuben, is your homework done?" We hadn't any homework, of course, but we went to my room anyway.

On our way out we heard Dr. Nokes ask, not fooling around, "What color?"

HE'S told me since—Dr. Nokes has—that his main worry was not Dad's pneumonia. He was confident antibiotics and Dad's own constitution could handle that. What worried the doctor was that I might come down with it. A set of lungs like mine could turn to peat moss with very little prompting. Before leaving that night, Dr. Nokes stepped me aside and spoke in confidence.

"Reuben," he said, "I've a hunch about your sister—that she has the makings of a doctor when she's grown. So listen: Let her take care of your dad. You stay out of her way. What do you say?"

I should've been far too old to fall for this sort of ruse.

"I'll drop some medicine by," he added. "Swede should take him his meals too. It's where she needs practice. Her bedside manner is a little rough."

"Well, what can *I* do?" Two weeks Dad was to stay in bed.

Dr. Nokes said, "You know, I was talking to Mr. Layton today. He's got a bad spine, did you know that? You're familiar with that old eyesore of a corncrib back of his house. Mr. Layton would probably hire a boy to tear it down—if the boy had a strong back."

A strong back? I had never imagined myself with a strong anything. Even had I guessed that the doctor only wanted to remove me from the house, put my lungs outside in healthy air, I wouldn't have cared. No words he spoke could've pleased me more.

GERARD Layton's corncrib was indeed an artifact. Tall as a boxcar, nailed up of laths spaced on oak posts, it leaned back in time. I stood in front of it holding a crowbar, not knowing how to begin.

It was December 16, and already we'd logged three or four notable snowstorms. Winter was a train crawling north. I walked all round Mr. Layton's corncrib, up to my hips in snow every step. I remember thinking the corncrib looked about ten minutes from falling over on itself, but when I poked the crowbar through its ribs and leaned down, nothing happened. I heaved to and fro. At last, after extravagant effort, a nail squealed and dropped me into a drift.

Swede fretted over me appreciatively when I came in at noon. "Oh, you're frozen! Come *on*, Reuben, I've got soup ready!" She squared me up at the table and set down a bowl of something white. "It's villing!" she announced.

I knew what it was. It was hot milk with dumplings, and a little sugar stirred in, also some butter and a shake of cinnamon.

I'd been out all morning doing a man's work. Villing was *sick* food. "Do we have any cheese?" I asked.

Swede shook her head. Off in his bedroom, Dad hawked something up, a dispiriting sound.

"Dad's worse," Swede said abruptly. "He's in there pounding his chest—hear him thumping? He's been doing it all morning."

"Be right back," I told her. It was strange—my fingers started to tremble.

"Wait, Reuben, you aren't to go in," Swede said, but I was compelled. Who knew constriction better than I?

Dad stopped pounding when I opened the door. Sitting up in a flannel shirt, blankets over his lap and on them an aluminum pan, his face filled with chagrin. "I sound like a threshing crew. Ack."

"Is it hard to breathe?"

"Reuben," he said, "is this what you feel like in the night?"

His breathing was like ripples on a sand beach.

"Yes sir."

He nodded—exhausted but watching me, it seemed, more closely than usual. "Say, Reuben, what did you think of Swede's villing? Good, wasn't it?"

"I haven't eaten."

"Mm." Shallow breath. "Well, you're going to like it."

And it's funny, but I did.

BACK at the corncrib, I was distressed to realize all my efforts of the morning had brought down only six lengths of lath. Elementary math revealed I'd be working till Easter unless I got the hang of this. I chose a junction of oak and lath and wedged the bar in.

A kid somewhere said, "Hey!"

He was in the corncrib, crouched and peeking through laths. I had a slatted view of a boy in a corduroy coat, a fat, grinning boy with plugged nostrils. You could see what was plugging them too.

"Who're you?" I asked.

"Raymond." He said it *Raymod,* the *n* getting detained up in nostril country.

"I'm Rube. Why don't you come out of there?"

"Whatcha doig?"

"Ripping this old thing down," I told him. "Mr. Layton hired me. Come on out of there."

Outside the corncrib he was more of himself. The coat was unbuttoned and showed layers of shirt. His cheeks were rubbed scabby and looked like sallow Texas grapefruits.

"How old are you, Raymond?"

"Six." He waved at a house across the alley. "That's Gramma's. We live with her, Mob an' Dad an' me. Can I watch?"

Raymond was a good watcher. "We jus' moved here las' summer. Gramma's house idn't built good. My dad's a buskrat trapper, got two hunderd buskrats last year."

A lath sprang free from the crib. I managed to stay on my feet. About this time I discovered a principle of physics. Mr. Layton's crowbar had been broken off and resharpened and so lacked a slight angle. In my ignorance I worked without fulcrum, until finally a loose lath fell down, wedging itself between bar and post. I shoved, and the lath I'd been worrying squealed loose instantly. Thereafter things accelerated.

Raymond sat in the snow, talking away. "How strog are you?" he inquired bluntly.

I tore down a lath and flung it on the pile. "I'm tearing down a building, aren't I?" Boy, it felt good saying that.

"You're pretty strog." Of course, he could've outpulled me in any contest you might name, but at six he was too kind to know it.

I said, "Well, I'm older than you."

"Rube, is your brother a burderer?"

I regarded Raymond for malice. "Where'd you hear that?"

"My dad said he was." Then, "My dad's really strog—he could tear that shed down with his bare hads. Could your dad do that?"

"Sure. Not right now, though. He's got pneumonia."

"Oh," Raymond said. "I had a uncle with pneumonia. He died and had a funeral, but we didn't go."

THAT corncrib represented the hardest work I'd ever done. Still, I suspect Swede had the tougher job back home. When I arrived from Layton's those late afternoons, brimming with my own success and breathing deep as I ever had, she seemed frighteningly burdened. Of course with Swede you got used to periods of deep thought, but this was different, for she was Dad's nurse, and anyone knows a downhearted nurse signifies a sinking patient. This didn't register with me until I crept in one evening hoping to find him awake. I stood beside him, a boy just wanting his dad's attention, and then, standing there, I had the dreamlike thought that he'd become me—his breathing something you had to listen hard to hear at all. I grabbed Dad's shoulder and brought him awake.

"Reuben." He was startled. "Is everything all right?"

"You want me to boil some water and soda? Loosen you up?"

He sat upright and breathed as deeply as he could. Oh, but he was bound tight. "Look, Reuben, I don't think steam's the thing. Maybe you'd pound my back a little."

So I sat on his bed and whacked him between the shoulder blades as hard as I dared, never having touched my father in this strange way before. He couldn't shore up against even my feeble thumping for more than a minute, but when he sagged back onto his pillow, his breathing was discernibly easier. He smiled.

"That corncrib work is helping you, boy."

I FINISHED December 20, a huge day for me. The crib had a roof of sheet tin held tight by a thousand galvanized nails, and I had to haul the ladder in and hammer upward to loosen it. When finally the tin whuffed to earth, I tilted into a snowbank to rest. I wished Raymond would show up. I missed his six-year-old admiration. Nothing remained of the crib but its black upright timbers, which I shoveled to bare earth and sheared flush with a crosscut saw. It took all afternoon. When the last post toppled, stars were appearing, Venus in the east.

When I got home, Swede was chafed beyond reason. She clattered out the bowls for supper, poured the cornflakes, made Dad's hot water with a spoonful of lemon juice, and slapped it all on a metal tray. I said, "Are you mad about something, Swede?"

She stayed clammed, entered Dad's room to lay supper across his lap, and returned somewhat mellowed with his praiseful thanks. Still, she didn't speak to me. I was certain I'd done something thoughtless, until she sat down and began to blink. "Look at 'em all," she said, pointing at the hallway door.

She was talking about the Christmas cards she'd taped up, ten or twelve of them, a bumper crop. Because we hadn't much family, we'd never received more than six or seven a year. This time there were new ones—from the DeCuellars, the Stockards, a few others.

"What's the matter?" I asked.

"We haven't got nothing from Davy," she said.

It hadn't occured to me that Davy might send us a Christmas card, him being a fugitive from justice and everything. Was there even precedent for such a thing? Mentally I ran down a few examples. Cole Younger? Butch Cassidy? John Wesley Hardin? Maybe these fellows were just flush with Christmas spirit, but I'd never heard about it. I mentioned these doubts to my sister.

"Wesley was illiterate," Swede said, using the middle name as if on personal terms with the outlaw. "Also, he was a skunk. He wouldn't have sent cards to anybody, and he never got any either."

"Well, what about those others?"

"Cassidy was romantic—you know that." In fact I did know it. Swede had read all about the heroic Butch, how he had a fondness for the afternoon siesta, also for the words pardon, senorita, and other poetical phrases. It was easy to believe Cassidy would've sent off his Christmas cards, and on time too.

I was going to ask about Cole Younger, but someone stepped up on the porch and knocked. It was Mr. Layton. He stood out there like a big hunched beetle and wouldn't come in.

"Boy," he said, "you finished. Come out here and settle up." This was the first I'd seen of him since he'd handed me the crowbar. "You done a good job," he said.

"Thank you, sir."

Mr. Layton reached for his billfold. He pulled out two ten-dollar bills and a five, then patted another pocket and came out with two chocolate bars. Mr. Goodbars—you know that yellow wrapper. "One for you and one for your sister," he said.

TWO whole days I dreamed with Swede about the things twenty-five dollars could buy. The bills were straight voltage, juicing all sorts of hallucinations. Could you buy a Hiawatha bicycle for twenty-five clams? Swede thought you could, and she figured there was room for her on the handlebars. I was also tempted by the thought of water. "I think a canoe," I told Swede, thinking secondhand.

"Telescope," she replied.

Then again, it was almost Christmas. What about presents? Shamefully, the first person who came to mind was Bethany Orchard, whom I hadn't seen in weeks. What did Bethany want for Christmas? I would've given half the money just to know.

The next day—December 23—Dad got out of bed. I woke from dreams of a gravel road along which I walked shoeless, picking up nuggets of gold the size of baby turtles. We had in our bathroom a hot-water tap that squeaked persistently when turned. On and off it squeaked, and then I was awake and knew Dad was up and shaving. Bounding up, I rapped at the door and was admitted to the sight of him standing at the mirror, grinning, soap on half his face.

"Morning, Reuben." His voice was quiet, tired, but free of the congestion. "You look starved. Go start some oatmeal."

So off I went, rejoicing, banging around the kitchen until Swede awoke and came in to issue instructions. Stirring the pot, she told me it was a big day and to get the maple syrup out of the back cupboard. I looked. The syrup was gone.

"Brown sugar, then," she said. "Above the toaster."

I shook my head. "We used it up."

"White sugar." But that bowl too was nearly empty, and when I got out the ten-pound canister, the scoop rattled sorrowfully inside.

Swede was disgusted. "Well, get out some apples."

We had a bag of old apples in the refrigerator. I peeled them down and chopped them small, and Swede found some Karo syrup and poured it into the oatmeal and told me to round up Dad.

He'd finished shaving and was in his bedroom. I knocked and, getting no response, went in. As I did, he stepped from the closet, where he'd been rummaging. A scream formed in my gut and emerged as a whimper. When shaving, he'd worn a big T-shirt that fell below the waist of his pants, disguising his exsiccated frame. Now he came out of the closet bare-chested. His torso was not his but someone else's—a drawn maroon's from some sea story. How had this escaped me? He looked at me with a mercy and pain that confused me.

He nodded slightly, I suppose wondering what to say. "You and Swede get that oatmeal ready?"

"Yes sir." I couldn't stop looking at him, at the way his khakis were belted across his hipbones.

He said, "I'm a little surprised myself, you know."

IN RETROSPECT it's hard to believe I didn't see instantly what to do with that money. But when it's the first you've earned by sweat, you see it as special and, by golly, not to be spent on less than the desire of your grasping heart.

"We're out of food, Reuben," Swede said.

"Well, let's go get some, then." The truth is, I'd been wondering when she would take the initiative and suggest we go up to the Red Owl for groceries.

"We can't. If we spend any more money, we shall be broke."

Her emphasis on *shall* put me in mind, as it was certainly meant to, of Pastor Reach, whose inflections left you in no doubt of his good sense. I was smitten into silence while Swede stacked dishes in the sink and waited for me to make myself gallant.

But I was annoyed that we were out of money and Christmas almost here. I was annoyed that I'd worked hard to earn twenty-five dollars and now would have to give it to Otto Schock, the Red Owl man. There was a lot to be annoyed about, and I could afford to grouse because Dad had eaten his small breakfast and thanked us and gone back to his bed of exhaustion. I stood festering in the kitchen.

"You don't want a canoe, then?"

I stood glaring at the back of Swede's little blond head, which was tilted in thoughtful mien. Sensing she was going to say something sagacious, I started to leave the kitchen but was too late.

"In *Little Women*," she said—see?—"when Jo cut off her hair and sold it to pay for Marmee's train fare—you remember?"

Well, of course I remembered.

"If Marmee had begged Jo to go cut off her hair," Swede hypothesized, "I wonder how heroic a thing it would have been."

I didn't say anything. But I thought, Aw, crumb.

HERE are some of the things we bought, Swede and I, having propped Dad in bed with a cup of beef tea: Aunt Jemima syrup in a brown bottle, twenty pounds of white Robin Hood flour, a sack of raisins and another of currants, two gallons of whole milk, a box of chocolates, a three-pound can of Hills Brothers coffee, and a Christmas turkey. Strangely, it was the coffee Dad seemed most happy to see and which, brewed, caused our home to feel again like a place where we might live right side up. Dad hummed "God Rest Ye Merry, Gentlemen" as he measured grounds into the basket and lit the gas. The pot ticked as it heated; and as it perked, a smell came forth like the sunlit hillsides of Mexico, a smell like morning camps described by Theodore Roosevelt in his days as a rancher in North Dakota. Dad sat at the kitchen table with a white ceramic cup all asteam, and seeing me, he reached out to seize me at the muscle.

"That's a hero's arm," he declared. "Thank you, Rube, for stepping in. I'll get strong now—look here," and he shadowboxed a moment where he sat, his hands quick again like Davy's.

Then somebody knocked, and when I poked my head out the kitchen, Swede was admitting a man in a gray pinstripe suit. His hair was brown and flattened round his temples, as if he'd just removed a fedora. He held a slick ID card. "Is that coffee fresh?" he asked.

It has been a defining trait of our family: The moment some simple but meaningful treat is prepared, a good soup or the first pot of coffee in weeks, up trots some uninvited person with an appetite.

The man in the suit was named Andreeson. He was a federal investigator and had the boldness to state that he expected to *nab* Davy before the turn of the year. He used that word, nab, and I thought Swede might kick him or lurch suddenly with the coffee, for she was serving him a cup. Andreeson sipped it without acknowledging the hospitality and said, "He's just a kid still, Mr. Land. Gonna get pretty lonesome this time of year. He's going to make contact. You want to do the right thing when he does."

"Which is?" Dad didn't care much for Andreeson either.

Andreeson could tell it, and he eased his tone a little. "I know you don't want your son hurt." He slipped a card from the vest pocket of his suit. "You can reach me here."

"I didn't know you fellows were interested," Dad said. It was the truth. Andreeson was our first fed. Naturally, I disliked him.

"We suspect he's crossed state lines. That makes him our job."

Dad stood. He said, "Well, thanks for coming by."

"When he gets in touch, Mr. Land, you've got my number."

Dad smiled at the floor a moment—he was so thin you could see his strength was not his own—then looked up and replied, "Mr. Andreeson, you and I will not speak again."

THE good thing about our reduced circumstances, going into Christmas, was that our expectations changed. They lowered themselves to a worthy place. Of course we missed the suspense associated with lumpy stockings; we missed the call of the parcels; we missed the Christmas spruce. Swede especially wanted a tree and at the last minute hung a few pathetic bulbs in a hackberry tree visible from our kitchen window.

Swede rose early on Christmas Eve day and set about preparing more Christmas dinner than we could ever consume. We'd got that turkey I mentioned. He went more than fifteen pounds. We had sweet potatoes and a heavy glass bowl of cranberries Dr. Nokes had brought over, along with a pie from Mrs. Nokes called a Bob-Andy pie, a creamy thing I have looked for since without success. Swede simply could not wait for the twenty-fifth. "I need Christmas *now*," she said.

And so during the day our appetites rose. Food appeared raw on counters and was pounded and rubbed, seasoned, and put to cook. Dad slept the morning through and woke agitated under the weight of smells. When he walked past me, I heard his stomach growl. No, it snorted, like a buck in rut, the healthiest sound he'd produced in weeks. All that long afternoon Swede fussed and the smells rose up and the sun sank down, and when finally the plates were arranged and the cider poured and Swede lit a candle and pronounced a call for Christmas dinner, two things happened.

Dad laughed aloud for pure delight.

And someone climbed up on our porch and knocked.

Did you see that coming? You ought've by now. And yet so glad were we to simply have our dad upright and able to laugh, not even uninvited guests could quench us. And Dad himself went to the door, and when he opened it, in stepped our good friend Mr. DeCuellar with his wife, shouting, "Merry Christmas, Merry Christmas!" To me they handed a long box that turned out to hold a reflecting telescope of astonishing power, and to Swede they gave a pair of boots and a lariat, and into Dad's hand they pressed a key and told him to look, look out at the street. Four weeks ago the traveling salesman Tin Lurvy had taken ill in a hotel room in Idaho, and though he had driven himself to a hospital in the wee hours, his poor heart burst before he turned off the ignition, so that he sat behind the wheel until dawn. And in his will Tin Lurvy had left Jeremiah Land his brand-new 1963 Airstream trailer. And the reason we didn't know this earlier was that our telephone service had been cut off. I'd wondered, once or twice, why nobody called.

I don't have the gift to aptly describe the rest of that evening, except to say it was a Christmas Eve beyond all gasping wishes and that even the absence of Davy seemed somehow more temporal and bearable because of the DeCuellars' appearance and Tin Lurvy's marvelous benediction. And later, when the conversation was low and I had set up the telescope and was taking turns with Dad and

Mr. DeCuellar looking at the moon, I asked Dad why he kept laughing. What a sound that was, his laugh, low and confident again, like your best friend's laugh in the darkness when you've believed he was gone forever.

And Dad said, "Because I was praying this morning, and I prayed, 'Lord, send Davy home to us, or if not, Lord, do this: Send us to Davy.' "

REMEMBER August Shultz, in whose barley I made the most panicked job a boy ever did of shooting a wild goose? At the bottom of a January cold snap we received a three-cent postcard:

Hello All
    Old friend Speedy came by. Weaselly skinny but strong, sends regards, Birdie had kielbasa, it went fast!
                                                            Aug & Birdie
P.S. Best to your friend Andreeson

Do you think that put Dad in an excellent humor? Swede came from the post office in high color, flag-waving that card, which confirmed that Davy was all right, that he was gone west, that he remained the big brother who loved us all, Christmas card or no.

Well, Swede was ready right then to step into the Airstream and ride to the western sun. Dad himself had begun preparing to leave the day after Christmas. Keep in mind that this was before we'd heard from August Shultz, yet Dad began to stock up. Cash was a difficulty, so he commenced to lay hold of unattached items around the house and sell them, doing so with an impish glee. His bedroom mirror went first, and it brought three dollars. Fifteen cans of pork and beans from the Red Owl went into the deep, mesmerizing pantry of the Airstream. Dad next sold two pine dressers for five dollars each. He bought a case of Dinty Moore, two canned hams, some hash. Each day familiar things went away from us; each day Dad tallied up the take.

"Where do you think you're going?" Dr. Nokes demanded. I think he feared the sickness had touched the part of Dad's brain in charge of good sense. "What do you have for directions?" he asked.

And Dad, eyebrows raised in delight with his forthcoming answer, said, "I have the substance of things hoped for. I have the anticipation of things unseen."

Dr. Nokes told him point-blank he was out of his mind. Dad laughed aloud. How could we not believe the Lord would guide us? How could we not have faith? For the foundation had been laid in prayer and sorrow. Since that fearful night, Dad had responded with the almost impossible work of belief. He had burned with repentance as though his own hand had fired the gun. He had laid up prayer as if with a trowel. You know this is true, and if you don't, it is I the witness who am to blame.

WE PULLED out after a frostbit sunrise, the twenty-second of January. For two weeks the average night had reached thirty below. Very dismaying to Swede and me, since we'd intended to ride in the plenteousness of the Airstream. Yes, the trailer had a gas heater, but Dad couldn't be persuaded to travel "lit." Of course the Plymouth's own heater was a foreseeable disaster—we probably weren't much warmer in our back-seat army blankets than we would've been in the trailer, or outside in the blistering wind, for that matter.

From Roofing it is some eighty miles to North Dakota. We drove without talking. After weeks of anticipation I'll confess to feeling let down. It was so cold my limbs seemed heavy. Dad drank coffee, looking at the frozen farmsteads we passed, clumped at the end of their long driveways. The Plymouth itself moaned as we drove, sounding perhaps not up to this long and heavy haul. We crossed the state border late in the morning and reached August's late afternoon. Having retreated to sleep, I snapped from a dream in which Swede's badman Valdez had got into the Airstream and crawled into my bunk. I knew he was there but couldn't tell anyone.

"Wake up, Rube," Dad said as we bounced into August's yard.

I stumbled up to the house with the dream still attached. Unbundling us in her hot kitchen, Birdie teased, "Somebody's sleepy."

But that was only part of it. In truth I was a little scared, and preoccupied about where we'd go from here. For I had asked this of Dad straight out the previous night. He didn't know. We'd simply go forth, he said, like the children of Israel when they cameled out of Egypt. He meant to encourage me, yet the trip thus far had reminded me what a hard time the chosen people actually had of it. Once traveling, it's remarkable how quickly faith erodes. It starts to look like something else—ignorance, for example. Sure it's weak, but sometimes you'd rather just have a map.

OF COURSE fear and doubt must flee when such gentle hosts as August and Birdie take charge of you, and a supper of creamed chicken and beans and sliced nut bread can go a long way toward the devil's discredit. Yet for all the Shultzes' home-cooked benefi-cence, their most nourishing offerings were details.

"He walked into the yard just before midnight," August said. "Ricky"—their Walker hound—"barking his dumb head off. I turn on the porch light, and there's Davy sitting on the steps."

"Tell how he looked," Dad said.

"Why, same as always," August said, "just more grown up."

"He was dressed warm?" Dad asked.

"Why, I guess so," August said, at which Birdie rolled her eyes.

"He was underdressed," she said, "wearing an old barn coat. I sewed on some buttons. And Jeremiah, he was awfully thin."

"Does he miss us?" Swede asked. "Did he say he missed us?"

"Well now—" August said.

"Like sunshine," Birdie put in. "He said it's like having no sun in the sky, Swede—he misses you that much."

I remember thinking that was a funny thing for Davy to say, him not being generally lyrical, yet Birdie looked so sternly at August I knew she must be remembering correctly. Swede teared up and put a hand over her mouth.

"August," Birdie suggested after a beat, "tell about that fellow who gave Davy the ride."

What a tasty particular! Thumbing west, Davy'd been picked up by a man in an Oldsmobile full of musical instruments. They lay in the back seat—a button accordion, saxophone, tin whistle, and trumpet. The man told Davy he was heading for Los Angeles, where he would certainly get on television. He asked Davy for money and offered to stop right there on the highway and play for him.

One more gratifying detail? Sure: Davy, retiring upstairs, had twice laughed in his sleep—a strange thing to hear, said Birdie, who lay wakeful—a boyish laugh drifting down those stairs again.

I can't describe the peace this conversation gave me. Davy was practically in the room with us. Every creak of the old house was like his footstep. Dad said, "I'm grateful to you for helping him."

Birdie said, "Jeremiah, he doesn't know the trouble he's in. We talked to him the best we could. He seemed careless about it. He said he hadn't read the papers or heard the radio."

"Jeremiah," August said, "was it like the newspaper said?"

"Pretty much," Dad said. "Yes. He shot them down. That jury would've had to convict him."

Birdie said that she had pressed Davy to return home and offer himself up for justice. In such public repentance, she told him, lay his best chance for what might yet become a fruitful life. And this, Birdie said, brought a great smile to Davy's face, and in that smile the Shultzes saw the truth—that turning himself in would be the very last thing Davy would do in his life, however long it lasted.

I WOKE next morning smelling change. No metaphors here— something was different to my actual nose. The air felt heavy, the quilts too, as blankets feel on camp-out mornings. Rising, I dressed and went down to the kitchen. I've always liked being the first one awake in the morning; it makes you daring somehow.

I poked around carefully—didn't turn on any lights for fear of rousting August or Dad. Lifting the coffeepot off the stove, I found it half full. I lit the gas, which made a lovely blue light in the dark kitchen, and in no time the pot was ticking away. I felt self-sufficient and borderline sneaky. Then August scuffed into the kitchen in his nightshirt, an electric candle in his hand.

"Feeling better, Rube? You coughed some in your sleep."

"Yes sir. I didn't mean to wake you."

"Making coffee?"

"Just heating it. Is that all right?"

He opened a cupboard and reached down a box of sugar lumps. I opened another and set out two cups.

He moved to the table, a strangely discordant sight in that nightshirt of his. He said, "You smell that this morning?"

He meant the change I mentioned earlier. "I don't know what it is." It smelled to me like a shovelful of earth. A wet day in spring.

"It's fog," August said.

He put out the electric candle, and we sat there smelling the air.

"Doesn't matter when it comes," August continued, "it smells like April. Birdie was born April twenty-second. Every time it fogs like this, I tell her, 'Happy birthday, love.' "

On receipt of this intimate remark I suddenly understood what had been given me. Never before had I been with Dad's best and oldest friend, the beloved August Shultz, without Dad present. Nor had I been old enough to appreciate it. Now here we sat together in his dark kitchen, the house asleep.

"Coffee hot?"

It was. August lifted the candle so I could see to pour.

"Would you guess your dad is on the mend?" he asked.

"Oh, he's fine. He's well," I replied.

"I never saw him so skinny before."

I nodded. August's concern bothered me. Dad hadn't coughed in a week. Anyone could see he was all right.

"Did he go to a doctor?"

"Dr. Nokes is a real good doctor. He's the one who delivered me," I added, which credentialed Nokes as far as I was concerned.

August sat considering this. "Yup," he said. "Yup."

About that time the others began drifting down, and Birdie set out breakfast. During it I got distracted watching Dad. August had this much right: Dad was skinny. He'd lost all superfluous flesh, and I saw now it had stayed lost. Skinny didn't say it. His very bones seemed loose-joined. And I'd simply gone and adjusted to it.

at war with this whole world

WHEN we drove out of August and Birdie's that morning, Swede rode ensaddled on a swaying sawhorse in the Airstream kitchen, her typewriter before her on a fold-down table. When we'd first packed the Airstream, she had begged not to leave the saddle behind, and Dad at last had said, "Well, why not?" Then she asked to bring one of the sawhorses from the garage, and her design began to emerge. Now she had her coat on, though Dad had lit the heater briefly and goosed the temp to around sixty, and she had paper rolled in:

> And so we forsake the encouraging company of the last friendly outpost, riding alone into a wide cold land in pursuit of our brother. What a speck we are on this vast prospect!

Plainly this excerpt represents Swede at her happiest, though it made me feel bleak at the time. That part about the last friendly outpost. Once we'd boarded the trailer, August came coatless around the Plymouth and put a bear hug on Dad, a man so thin he oughtn't have survived. Then Dad sank behind the wheel, and off we rolled, a great drop of tin glinting on the snowy plains.

> We are headed for the Badlands. August called it a big busted-up place and believes our Davy has gone there. Practically every wanted man goes to the Badlands sometime. Butch Cassidy, Mr. Younger, Sam Bass. The Badlands are as good a place as any.

Swede was to write dozens of pages before we returned to Roofing, which is plenty of typing for someone using only index fingers plus thumbs for the space bar. Reading through them, you will find many an allusion to distinguished outlaws of eras past and not one to the fact of motorized travel. Always it is a "long ride west"; Davy is surmised to be out front of us by "six days' trail." Though I'll

defend her narrative to the last, Swede's journalistic technique pre-
cluded the attendance of one or two facts. For example, Davy was
driving a Studebaker, its floorboards rotted to mere embroidery.
August for years had kept the old boat for a field car, and seeing
Davy's unwillingness to return home with his hands in the air, he
decided it needed a change of mission, also of oil. So that freezing
sunup found August beneath the chassis, heart flailing with the loyal
and grossly unlawful business at hand. Before Davy finished breakfast, August had affixed old license plates and placed bread and a
sack of canned goods in the trunk.

> *And will we find our Davy safe,*
> *Along this stealthy track?*
> *And might all our implorings steal*
> *Our outlaw brother back?*

The question niggled. I tried to remember a time when I had persuaded my brother to change his mind—not just to humor me,
which he did often. It had never happened.

I said, "Swede, do you think we can talk him into coming back?"
She unstirruped her right foot to face me sidesaddle. "Do you?"
"I don't know."
Swede said, "What would you give to get Davy home?"
"Well, most things. I guess anything."
"And what if they stick him in jail? You still want him to come
home?"
I couldn't answer. If I said what I sensed was the noble thing—
better not to see him at all than pale and dumb during visiting
hours—might that not bring despair on this whole crusade of ours?

WE STOPPED at noon. Dad pulled over in a municipal park in
Linton, this being midfield North Dakota, and stepped up into the
trailer. "Well, amigos? Shall we cook beans?"
We did, Swede ending up with the coveted knob of fat from the
can. Then Dad cranked the heater again, professing intent to nap.
Lulled by warmth, I did likewise, going sound asleep to Swede's

typing. She woke me minutes later. That stinker Andreeson was sitting in his car across the park.

"No, Swede, it can't be him. Go look again."

"It is him. He waved at me, Reuben!"

That sat me up. "Is he coming over here?"

"Wait." Swede ran to a window, peeked edgewise. "Nope. He's just sitting there. His car's running."

I slipped to the window. Sure enough, there sat our self-satisfied fed in a clean beige Mercury across the narrow little park. There weren't fifty yards between us. He had a plate of something in his lap and a cup of coffee in his right hand.

"Look at him," Swede said, "chewing his french fries. He wouldn't even eat them in the café—afraid we'll pull out and he'll lose us." This appeared to be true, for Andreeson kept looking our way between bites. "How come he doesn't just talk to us?"

"Maybe he just wants us to see him. To make us nervous."

"We haven't done anything," Swede said defiantly. "All we did was go on vacation. People do it all the time."

"Maybe we better wake Dad. Wait a second. He's done."

"Is he coming?"

"Nope—going." For Andreeson had balled up his paper plate and crept the Mercury forward to a public trash can. He made his deposit, caught me watching, saluted, and tooled away.

"Chicken!" Swede said. "Shyster! Putrid fed! He's desperate—following us because he can't think of anything else to do."

I admired Swede's certainty but didn't share it. Desperate guys don't salute. Andreeson had looked canny, or borderline humorous. "So where do you think he went?"

"Probably to the public toilet. Let's wake up Dad and get out of town."

"You think we should? Won't we get in trouble?"

"Did we do anything wrong?"

"No." But it felt like we had—or were about to.

In the end, all our stratagems came to naught. Dad woke with a record headache to suggest, in a distressed whisper, that we stay till morning. Instantly I recollected August's apprehensions about Dad's health, but he swallowed two aspirin and promised to be better by supper, provided it was chicken and dumplings.

WE MADE the dumplings with a Swanson chicken, and Dad emerged to eat. He didn't look much better, but it was hard to see him. Rather than use the Airstream's lamps, Dad claimed to prefer the ambient dimness of Linton's streetlights. It was more romantic, he said—obviously cover for his light-pained eyes—but we went right along. Someone banged on the door. "Yes?" Dad called.

"Mr. Land, it's Martin Andreeson."

Dad was silent a moment. He struck a match, lit a mantle in the kitchen. "Come in."

Andreeson was hatless and smiling in a fresh haircut and tan knee-length topcoat. He said, "Lovely weather. I enjoy the Dakotas. Don't get out here as often as I'd like."

Dad stood with his hands on the back of a kitchen chair, his face all pouched with headache. I couldn't help but remember that he'd said, "You and I will not talk again." How prophetic and incontestable he had sounded! Dad seemed to be thinking similarly, for he gave me a wry, so-much-for-pronouncements look and said, "Do you have news for us, Mr. Andreeson?"

"Why, no, I don't."

"Then your purpose here is abstruse," Dad said politely.

"I'm glad to explain. You departed suddenly in the middle of January. Your rent is paid through April, though you no longer draw a salary and you have no savings. Half of Roofing thinks your mind soured. They think you're out here eating locusts."

Dad chuckled. "How about the other half?"

"They believe you heard from your boy."

"Which theory appeals to you?"

"I'm trying to think what else brings you here—now." He meant to the Great Plains in midwinter. It wasn't a bad question.

"We're looking for him," Dad said.

Andreeson waited, finally prompting, "Did he contact you?"

"No."

"Did he contact August and Birdie?"

"Yes, he did," Dad said.

"August told me differently," Andreeson said. "Very loyal, though it does leave him open to accessory charges. What directions did your boy leave him?"

"None."

"Mr. Land, it's my responsibility to find your son. At the moment it's my only responsibility. I believe we are close to him right now. If you know more than you're saying, you could save his life."

"I've been honest with you, Mr. Andreeson."

"You could also save August and Birdie some grief down the line. It's a shame they lied to me."

Dad said, "You yourself have lied twice since stepping in here."

That set Andreeson back a step. I was still wondering which two statements were false when he nodded, set his hand on the door, and said, "Mr. Land, you and I don't have to be enemies."

"Mr. Andreeson," Dad replied, "it appears that we do."

So departed our putrid fed, and a few moments later in popped Swede in her overcoat. We hadn't even noticed she was gone.

"I had to run to the gas station," she said breathlessly. There was a Phillips 66 we were using. Hanging her coat neatly in the closet, she slipped into the saddle, where she dashed off the following:

The blizzard shipped in from the west like a grin
On a darkened, malevolent face,
And the posse that sought Mr. Sundown was caught
In an awfully dangerous place.
For their horses were sore and their chances were poor
Of locating warmth or repose,
When the sweet sudden sight of miraculous light
Shone dim in the dark and the snows, my lads,
A light through the dark and the snows.
And the lady who answered their knock at the door
Had answered another, an hour before.

So fully did Swede own these lines, so resonant were her strokes upon the keys, that Dad said, "My goodness, Swede—don't you know *Moby-Dick* has already been written?" But no response. I guess she was just too elevated to hear him.

> *She bid them to stay, in her courteous way,*
> *And insisted they sit by the fire,*
> *And she poured them all brandy and sang them a song*
> *And they slept as though lulled by a choir.*
> *The sheriff next morning was first to awake*
> *And he called all his men to the chase,*
> *For a dream had suggested their quarry sought rest*
> *In the hay in the barn on the place, lads—*
> *He'd slept in the barn on the place.*
> *But when they crept into the building to spy*
> *Gone horses, gone lady, gone outlaw, good-bye!*

DAD'S headache was gone in the morning. In fact he suggested pancakes after Swede routed us from bed. The routing itself should've alerted me to something; Swede was rarely awake before Dad. "Can't we get going?" Swede begged. It was close to wheedling. "Let's just have cornflakes."

Dad felt none of her urgency. No mistake, Andreeson had tossed a wet washcloth on the trip. In fact Dad was inclined to laze around Linton awhile and wait on the Lord.

"But Davy—" Swede began.

"Davy's in the palm of God's hand, like all of us are. A few days' wait may be best for everybody. Now, what about pancakes?"

"I don't feel very good," Swede said.

Dad leaned at her. "Why, you are pale. It's early yet. Why don't you go back to bed?"

Swede climbed back in her bunk. Dad turned the gas low so the trailer was dim and warm and restful. I dozed myself, hearing only the occasional turn of a page as Dad read King James.

Then Swede said quietly, "Dad?"

"Mm."

"I have been praying, and I believe it is the will of God that we get going."

Dad sat back and stretched. "Well, Reuben," he said, "get out the cornflakes. At the very least it's the will of Swede. Let's go."

IT WAS on this day that we began to imagine ourselves truly far from home. By sunup we'd bumped into the great Missouri River and struck north along its banks. Dad had informed us that when we crossed the Missouri at Mandan, we would enter mountain time, a concept he ought've cleared up, as it put all sorts of snowcapped expectations in our heads. Meantime it was a good drive yet to Mandan, and the trailer was freezing.

Remember the fuel economy of the 1955 Plymouth wagon? Thirsty power under the best conditions, when pulling great weight, our car became a carping slave demanding refreshment. Yes, gas was cheap, as I am constantly reminded, and yes, the Plymouth had an ample tank. Still, service stations were not the frequent, well-lit, prosperous concerns they are today, and Dad had filled two red five-gallon cans to extend our range another hundred miles— generally enough to reach a gas pump even on the Great Plains.

Sometime in the middle of the morning, just as I was bequeathing Swede all my stuff should I freeze to death, Dad pulled into a Sinclair station, and Swede and I hopped numbly down.

"Nobody here," Dad said. It was a little white gas station with a green stripe. Emptiest spot you ever saw. All morning the wind had risen, and the Sinclair sign with its green brontosaurus rocked and groaned on high. "I guess we can get to Mandan. We can easily get that far. Besides, we have the reserves."

But we didn't gas up in Mandan. We crossed the Missouri ("The mountains must be a few miles away," Swede remarked), but at the first service station we came to, Dad slowed way down, then slid by.

"Why didn't we stop?" I asked.

"Nineteen nine a gallon," Dad replied, his eyes on the rearview. "We can do better." An explanation I bought—why wouldn't I?—

though Swede whispered there'd been a state car at that very station, a trooper in sunglasses inside it, watching traffic.

We cruised along into Mandan, a good-sized town. Dad passed another gas station. "There was one," I told him.

"Mm, yes, there it was," he said.

"Can we get something to eat when we stop?" I inquired.

He didn't answer and, moreover, didn't slow when we approached yet another station. I opened my mouth, only to have Swede grip my coat sleeve. As we went by, I saw a trooper in his parka and ranger hat, leaning against his car in the wind.

I'll admit the sight thrilled me. Not that I believed the trooper was looking for us, but Swede plainly believed he was, and Dad—well, Dad wasn't stopping.

Swede signed me to keep my mouth shut.

We were all so quiet, in fact, that Mandan in my memory is a silent movie: people on the sidewalk shrugging in the hard white useless sun, and every thing and person getting knocked around by the bossy wind—except the troopers, who on that day were sitting in their state cars at every gas station in Mandan, North Dakota. And so still were these men, and so flat-out many were they, that I knew they were indeed looking for us, and for Davy through us. I took a fierce chill. A sob rippled up, and I couldn't do a thing about it. It is one thing to say you're at war with this whole world and stick your chest out believing it, but when the world shows up with its crushing numbers and its predatory knowledge, it is another thing completely. I shut my eyes and rocked.

Later the putrid fed himself would confirm it. He'd twisted the arm of the weak-willed chief of the North Dakota State Patrol, who'd ordered a disproportionate measure of his force to Mandan, plus a few more spots along the route Andreeson had guessed, correctly, we would choose. An easy assignment, wouldn't you think? Stopping a Plymouth wagon pulling a twenty-foot Airstream trailer?

They didn't get us. Not one of them even saw us, though we saw *them,* as I've described. We tiptoed through that town like a fat boy through a wolf pack. Make of it what you will.

One thing bothered me: that Andreeson had gone to such exertions. What cause had the putrid fed for hounding us?

"I was actually expecting it," Swede said.

"Well, bully for you." Sure, I was a little sour. "You know he's still looking for us. Now everyone else is too."

"Andreeson's back in Linton," Swede declared. "I crept over and spoiled his car. It was an act of sabotage. Don't tell Dad!"

This was so far outside what I expected, it rendered me stupid.

"Maple syrup down his gas tank," she explained. Oh, how scared and proud she looked. "I used the whole bottle, to make sure."

Well. No wonder she'd been against having pancakes.

MEANTIME we still hadn't got gas. We'd stopped ten miles out of Mandan, poured in our spare ten gallons, and driven west until Dad said he had to lie down. He had a headache: another monster, or maybe the same one never truly gone away. His face was lined like a Renaissance painting. He pulled off the road beside a great empty misplaced-looking barn, no house in any direction, and said he believed we had propane enough to keep the Airstream tolerable until morning. Swede asked in alarm whether we shouldn't get farther along, and he replied in a tone of declining patience that if he didn't lie down, his head would fall off and land in his lap.

"It's Saturday night," Swede informed him. "Gas stations'll be shut tomorrow."

Dad nodded. He'd lit the heat and tucked us in—both of us in Swede's bunk. We all knew it was going to get cold. He said, "Swede, are you going to pray tonight?"

She nodded.

"I'm going to as well. One thing I mean to ask Him is to save us some gas. Will you do the same?"

"Okay."

"Okay," Dad said. He didn't kiss us good night but bent near us, then pulled away, as though you could catch a headache.

"Are you tired?" Swede said when Dad had slid his door shut.

"Nope."

"I bet it's not eight o'clock."

"I'm awake," I said.

"I bet it's not even seven!"

Dad's door slid open. In the amber gloom he looked scary and sunk-eyed. A man looks like that in the daytime, and you'd glance around for a phone. "Pretend it's midnight," he said. "Whisper."

The door slid shut. "Wow," Swede said, whispering.

We had the lamp on and quilts piled up. My nose was running, and my cheeks felt like little blocks of pine. Outside, the wind had picked up. It was bumping the trailer around gently.

"Look, I can smoke." Swede feigned a cigarette in the V of two fingers, raised one brow, and blew out a long strap of steam. She said, "I am zoooo cold, dahlink," which gave me the giggles, which made my nose run faster, which led to my desperate use of a corner of the uppermost quilt—a horror that goosed our giggles into full-tilt hysterics. Know what we did? We laughed ourselves warm.

"Reuben," Swede said, whispering, later when we'd turned the light out and gone quiet in a sudden spell of conscience. "How come we even have to worry about buying gas?"

"Because we used the ten gallons already."

"What I mean is, we had that thing today. With the police. Do you think Dad prayed for that to happen?"

"I don't know if he prayed, Swede. Maybe it just happened. I don't know if he ever prays for them or if they just come."

A brief cold moment, and then she said, "What do you mean, if they come? What other ones are you talking about?"

"Well, like when I was born. You don't call that a miracle?"

"Oh. Yeah," she said. "I thought you meant other times."

Of course I'd meant other times, and it now seemed like some wretched betrayal not to say so. "He walked one time on nothing but air," I told her. It was probably the wrong place to start.

Strange, isn't it, that we'd never had such a conversation before? Strange that I could see my father step out supported on the void and not go tell my sister? Or watch a pot of soup multiplied and keep all my wonderment to myself?

"Why didn't you tell me?" Swede said when we'd finished.

I didn't know. Why does any witness keep shut about something? "You could've noticed some of this yourself, don't you think? Like the saddle. I can't believe you didn't notice that."

The saddle was a clincher of sorts for Swede. She climbed over me out of the bunk and crossed the trailer in the dark, until she found it there aspraddle the sawhorse. There was silence. Then there came a hazy sigh. She whispered, "I've been sitting on it just like normal." Cold as it was, she stood by that saddle a long while.

In the morning it was a brisk nineteen degrees according to the Roofing Co-op thermometer Dad had rubberbanded to the bedrail. In case you were starting to think miracles were a convenience of mathematical dependability, we'd run out of propane during the wee hours, which also meant a cold breakfast of dry cereal and bread. The milk was a frozen cardboard cube. The wind still pushed and grieved round the trailer, and we stumbled about inside, snugging it down with an urgent quiet in our hearts, a fear strangled by cold and hurry. Dad's head still ached, but he'd regained himself enough to stretch and shadowbox and chide us toward warmth. Kneeling atop the stove, putting the coffeepot away in its high cupboard, my numb fingers hit a stack of cups, and down they all came to explode around my knees. At this Swede began inexplicably to weep. I remember the clamor of breakage, the noise delaminating into crying and bursting ice. A few moments more and I'd have cried too from pure confusion, except then Dad began to sing lightly, almost offhandedly: *"Mine eyes have seen the glory of the coming of the Lord. . . ."*

This lovely, warlike anthem Dad sang with increasing good humor straight to its end, steadying me with his hands, picking up wicked white shards—*"I have seen Him in the watch-fires of a hundred circling camps"*—dropping the shards in a paper sack—*"They have builded Him an altar in the evening dews and damps"*—sweeping up the glistening dust, my mind brightening the while and Swede's grief fading to a series of exclamatory sniffs. *"His truth is marching on!"* Certainly it was our battle hymn as much as the Republic's.

ALL THAT MORNING WE drove cold through wind-sacked, immo-
bile towns with Presbyterians and Lutherans and secure Methodists
standing around their church doors with no need for fuel, while we
moved slowly past, wondering when the last spoonful of gas would
drain from the tank. In no place did we see a state trooper, in no
place a gas station lit from within. We drove for hours. That we
didn't run dry may indeed have been the miracle Swede wanted.
Nearing midday, we began seeing what looked like mountains shorn
off at the roots. Swede pointed them out as buttes or mesas and said
it meant we were in the West for certain, a fact also evident in the
presence of beef cattle and oil derricks, often in the same matted
grasslands. We saw fences rarely. North Dakota was a big state.

Sometime after noon the Plymouth began to miss. Not like your
small cars, bless their dainty hiccups—the whole car seized backward, cousin to a bucking horse. You had to hold your head against
whiplash. Dad pulled over, and Swede laid the atlas across her
knees and judged us close to a town called Grassy Butte.

"We'll stay there," Dad said. "Grassy Butte. I wonder if there's a
garage. Say, you two, let's get something warm there!" And in that
moment I loved the old Plymouth, for something warm was just
ahead and we were heading for it. Already I could imagine a café,
that rare pleasure, with cocoa in a thick white cup. We'd all take
our coats off—honestly, Swede and I were so pleased we got giddy,
poking each other as the wagon bucked along.

Before reaching Grassy Butte, though, Dad spied a farmhouse
with two pumps in the drive and a red-and-white sign out front saying DALE'S OIL COMPANY. Another sign said CLOSED, but a light
was on in the house, and Dad pulled in.

When he went to the door, no one answered his knock. He
knocked again, and this time the door opened and a woman was
standing there with a baby goat in her arms—just a little goat suck-
ling at a bottle she held.

"It's Sunday," she said. "We're shut."

"Is Dale here?" Dad inquired.

"Sir," the woman said, "Dale has not been here since November."

It's hard to look back and describe Roxanna to you as she was when we first saw her. Big-boned, yes, but not in the cushiony sense people often mean. Tall, dirt-road blond hair in a back-swung braid, windburned in the face. She looked like some woman from a polar dogsled expedition recounted in the *Geographic*.

"My sympathies," Dad said.

"Appreciated, but gratuitous," the woman replied, and Swede would have loved her forever for that phrase alone. "Dale left November twenty-fifth. Every day since has been Thanksgiving."

Well, what does a person say to that? I watched Dad look down at his feet, smiling, one hand rubbing the back of his neck. The woman stood there holding her goat, which was yanking at the bottle single-mindedly.

Dad looked up. "Ma'am, I sure hope you'll sell us some gas. I know you'd rather not on a Sunday."

At this moment a better observer than I would've seen some acquiescence in the woman's eyes, some raising of the gate. I saw nothing of the kind, but Dad must have, for when she abruptly shut the door, he stayed right where he was. The wind snapped our coats, and now it carried a few gnats of ice. Then the door opened again, and the woman came out in a parka with the fur up round her ears and walked fast ahead of us to the pumps.

"Check your oil?" she said while the tank filled.

"It's fine," Dad said. Swede and I had climbed back into the Plymouth, under our blankets.

"You mind if I don't do your windshield?" the woman said.

"What's your name, if I may ask?"

"Roxanna." The pump clicked off, and she finessed it a little.

"You should change the sign to Roxanna's Oil," Dad said. "It's a more attractive name, if I may say it."

"Five fifty," Roxanna said, her furry hood studded with ice bits.

Dad said, "I don't guess you'd have any propane."

Roxanna Cawley did have propane, in a bulk tank behind the house. We waited inside while she filled our cylinder. There was a glass counter with boxes of Butterfinger and Three Musketeers alongside some Dutch Masters cigars and a clip display of Dr. Grabow's pipes. There was a gumball machine, and there were two goats, kid and nanny, stabled in a bathroom behind the counter. Seeing us gawk, Roxanna opened the door to show the satisfied mother standing on a hummock of straw, the kid curled asleep by a claw-foot tub. It wasn't as dirty as you'd expect. The billy lived in the barn out back. Roxanna said he'd be rejoined by his family as soon as the kid, Beth, got stronger.

"What's wrong with Beth?" Swede asked.

"Born blind. The billy kept pushing her away from Momma. He wouldn't let her eat. So I moved them in here."

"Ruffian," Swede said. "Thug. Miscreant."

Roxanna smiled. "Knave," she said.

"Scapegrace," my sister sang out. "Brigand."

At which Dad herded us out the door, saying something about finding a place for the night. Turning back to Roxanna, he asked whether Grassy Butte had a garage or a motel.

"Garage is closed. The Hi-Way Motel is by the water tower."

Dad held up a hand in thanks and shut the door.

We hadn't made it back to the car when we heard the door open again. Roxanna Cawley was standing there looking thistly.

"Or if you'd like," she said, "I have a couple of rooms."

the skin bag

IT MAY surprise you, after the goats in the bathroom, that Roxanna Cawley set a pleasant and even cultivated table. Against the grassy barrens she managed to coax forth string beans and acorn squash and to put them up in quantities reaching to late January. She also had sweet corn, which froze well right on the cob. Did you ever sit down to white cobbed corn, freshened with butter and salt, snow meantime beating the windows on the coldest evening of a cold new year? We ate roasted chicken, pickled beets, tender potatoes, and gravy stirred up from the cracklings. Roxanna went to a lot of trouble for us, who were after all just one small family paying a few dollars for a night's room and board. Swede looked often at the windows, and I knew she was growing the storm in her mind, abetting it until the world should be slowed and the roads stopped and us buried at some happy length in the contentment of this house.

And what things we learned around that table, what lessons in the ways of independence! For Roxanna Cawley had grown up motherless, just as we were doing, and had learned from her father the principles of business. Having failed at ranching in the Dust Bowl years, Mr. Cawley had borrowed from an uncle to purchase a long-closed theater on the main street of Lawrence, Montana. Roxanna remembered the care her father practiced in choosing films: selections like *Tarzan the Fearless* and *Tarzan Escapes*. Johnny Weissmuller, Mr. Cawley informed young Roxanna, could be counted on.

To this bit of talk Dad added nothing, but leaned back in a ticking-covered chair, smiling, with his hands clasped behind his neck and his legs crossed as though at home. Roxanna Cawley was talking to us in a warm fashion we couldn't have guessed at when we pulled in for gas. I'm ashamed to recall thinking it was too bad she was not lovely. I recall believing if she were only beautiful, she would somehow come to spend the balance of her life entertaining us in just this way. Wrapping us in just this sort of comfort. My selfishness should no longer surprise you. Rather, the surprise might be that I thought of Dad at all, for it came to me that he was regularly alone after Swede and I went to bed at night. That he would one day be alone when we'd gone away. I watched him lean back in his chair, looking tired and pleased. We were warm finally, and I rose to the window, where hard snow was spatting against the glass.

"Reuben," Dad said, "how's the breathing?"

Boy, I wished he hadn't mentioned it in front of Roxanna.

"Sounds a little ropy," he said.

"It's okay. I'm tired. Can I go to bed now?" I asked.

"Of course. I'll be up soon too. Go on, you two."

I DREAMED A DEVILISH LITTLE man came and stole my breath. He stepped through the door with a skin bag strung over his shoulder and with dispassionate efficiency crouched back and slugged me in the stomach. Such an incredulous exhale! Not a wisp of air remained. In that agonized vacuum I rolled my eyes upward and beheld the stranger tying up the bag with a leather thong. He had the opening squeezed shut and was throwing half hitches around the bag and yanking them tight. The bag was barrel-size and taut as a blimp. Inside it was all my breath. The little man crouched again and looked at me closely. He was a pale one, a horror. When he went out the door with the bag on his shoulder, I thrashed and lurched and arched my back. On waking, I saw Dad kneeling bedside, holding my upper arms; I heard Swede crying distantly; someone I couldn't see was thumping my back. I'd never felt such thumps. They were like car wrecks. But I got a little breath back with each painful thump. Confused, I managed to turn enough to glimpse Roxanna Cawley in a flannel nightgown hammering my corporeal self with the strictest resolve. She was panting hard when she stopped. She sat beside me on the bed while Dad asked the usual questions. Yes I was better. Yes I was still wheezy. Yes I thought steam might help. Roxanna asked if she should go heat some water, and before leaving, she bent and put her cheek to mine. Her hair was in a single thick braid, and moist coils of it had come free. They clung to my face as she pulled away.

NEXT morning all geography lay snowbound. Maybe two feet of snow had fallen, or maybe six—you couldn't say. The wind had whipped it into dunes and cliffs. It was a badlands of snow.

Swede's bed was empty. The whole house sounded empty. Crossing the hall into Dad's room, I heard muffled scrapings and ran to the window. Sure enough, all three of them were out back. The sun was out so hard on the snow I could barely look. Dad and Roxanna were clearing a wide path to the barn.

"Wait!" I yelled. I ran to my room, hooked my pants and shirt, ran back to the window. "Wait for me!" I banged on the glass, but they couldn't hear. I shouted again, "Wait up!" What were they doing there out in the new snow without me? Then, surprise, I had to lean quick on the windowsill. All that yelling had used up my air. I had to sit down. I was sweatier than I'd ever got taking down Mr. Layton's corncrib, and here I hadn't even got my pants on. I heard the barn door screel open, and Swede's outcry of wonder and pleasure, and Roxanna laughing. I tell you no one ever felt sorrier for their sorry lot. I crawled back into bed, and I thought dangerous things to myself. Back to mind came every hurt I'd endured for my defect, every awaited thing I'd missed. It seemed to me that I'd been left alone here by the callousness of my family; that should the man with the skin bag return, I might not fight so hard next time; that this house was so empty even God was not inside it. He was out there with the others, having fun.

LATE in the morning Swede came in red-cheeked with the news that we would stay at Roxanna's another night.

"Dad walked out on the road. There's drifts up to his chest! Roxanna says she never saw this much snow! She says it snowed a foot one year, and it took the county two days to plow the roads. For one foot, Reuben—and we got four or five!"

It was plain nothing could've pleased her more. Nor me under other conditions. But I'd lain the morning in a sump of self-pity.

"We're not gonna find Davy sitting around here," I told her.

"Well, we don't have a choice. We couldn't get out if we tried." Swede was wearing a fur hat of Roxanna's. Snow was stuck to it and turning to water. "Reuben, you've got to see that barn! There's the billy goat and six sheep and a bunch of roosting chickens. We picked eggs, and there's a rope in the hayloft!"

I said, "You tell me what good it does, staying here. Tell me one way it helps Davy."

She glared. "You don't care about Davy. You're mad on account I went out to the barn!"

So dead center was this that I leapt up and tackled her at the waist and landed half on top of her on the hardwood floor, a strategic mistake. We scuffed around a little, she getting me twice on the jaw before the energy leaked out of my muscles. She wiggled away and stood over me, and I was a gasping ruin.

"I win," she hollered. "Ha—look here!" She took a gigantic, wrathful, chest-filling breath. "Look what I can do!" She blew out the breath and snatched another. She did frantic jumping jacks. "See? I could do this all day! I could do it all year!"

I couldn't speak. I rolled my eyes up at her like the betrayed steer at slaughter. I could hear my heart, boy, blacksmithing away.

"I win!" Swede shouted. "Come on, Rube, say uncle."

I shut my eyes.

It is one thing to be sick of your own infirmities and another to understand that the people you love most are sick of them also. You are near then to being friendless in this world. "Please," I whispered.

Swede said, "Reuben? What's the matter, Reuben?"

I gathered enough air for a sentence: "You went outside without me." Which set her off sobbing. She wilted down on the floor next to me. It was hard to fathom after such a fight. She put her arms around my neck, but when it is like breaking cement with a hammer just to breathe, a tight hug isn't helpful, so I had to shrug her off. We lay there quite some time, a very woebegone set of penitents. Swede took my hand and held it while confessing all sorts of things, cheifly related to piggishness, but also the surprising fact that she actually had forgotten about Davy—just for a little while.

At last I had achieved basic respiration. "I like being here," she said, "with Roxanna. Don't you like her, Reuben? Do you really want to leave?"

"I like her a lot."

"We parked the trailer in the barn. Roxanna thought of it. It's just a huge barn, Reuben. You have to see."

I didn't see it right away, but this was certainly the work of the Lord. It was a cup running over.

ROXANNA was correct about the county snowplows. They weren't up to the job. Days opened and filled with work and talk and closed early. My lungs relaxed. I was allowed in the barn and taught to candle eggs. Swede climbed to the loft and pitched down hay for the sheep. Following these modest chores, we cinched on scarves and went walking atop snowdrifts so hard they stayed track-less. We were good and stuck, and dangerously happy. Late in the fifth day we saw jets of smoke in the east. We expected chuffs and growls, but the plow trucks were still too far for sound.

Next morning Roxanna and Swede cleaned out the goat pen—in the bathroom, back of the cash register—while I investigated the pictures on the office walls. "What's this one of the town?"

Roxanna poked her head out the bathroom. "Main street of Lawrence. That's Dad's theater on the right."

"How come you've got this of the Wild Bunch here?" It was Butch Cassidy and the rest posing in new suits. You've seen it—the one with the bullet holes.

"My great-uncle spent time with Cassidy," Roxanna called.

Whatever Swede had in hand dropped to the floor. "Your uncle knew Butch Cassidy?"

"Great-uncle. They were friends," Roxanna said.

A revelation of this nature might've rendered Swede paralytic until the whole story was told, but Roxanna said, "No. You said you'd help; let's keep at it," so Swede scraped and moiled. Roxanna's great-uncle had been a gunsmith and doctor in Casper, Wyoming, at the end of the nineteenth century. Taken to visit him by her father, Roxanna remembered a kitchen table spread with trigger assemblies, firing pins, bolts grooved silver for want of oil. He had a workshop in the basement but preferred the kitchen. A lifelong bachelor, he baked himself cinnamon rolls almost every morning.

Swede asked, a trace impatiently, how the great-uncle knew Mr. Cassidy. The answer was, same way he knew all sorts of other peo-ple. You couldn't ever visit Uncle Howard without shooing away salesmen from the Remington and Winchester and Savage compa-nies or medical men come inquiring after his particular advice in the treatment of gunshot wounds.

This is how Uncle Howard had met Mr. Cassidy: Arriving home

from church on a lovely June Sunday, Howard had been surprised to find a boy propped spraddle-legged on his front step. That's how the great-uncle described him—as a boy. The boy had a parcel in his jacket and wondered if Howard might have a look. He was so engaging that Howard allowed him into the kitchen, where he unstrung his oilcloth parcel. With great sadness he lifted forth a smashed revolver. He said a train had struck it. Howard said he couldn't fix it. All the king's horses and all the king's men . . . The young man sat at Great-uncle Howard's table looking down at his knees. It made Howard ache.

The cinnamon rolls were just browning up, and he offered one to the youngster. Roxanna remembered her great-uncle's rolls. His especial pride was the frosting. He ordered back east for confectioners' sugar, fifty pounds at a time. After several rolls the young man's spirits lifted. He told Howard to call him Butch. He said the revolver meant a lot to him. He'd ordered it for its long barrel because he was a poor shot. Moved by Butch's earnestness, Great-uncle Howard offered to sell him a refitted 1860 Army which similarly had that ungainly length. Butch was interested but strapped. He waged negotiations upon which he was allowed to leave Howard's kitchen with the gun at half its value, the rest to be delivered upon arrival of Butch's next pay, which Butch affirmed was coming along soon.

By the time Dad stamped in—bathed in dirty oil and bits of straw—we'd learned that Butch Cassidy had indeed paid off the revolver, that Great-uncle Howard had liked the young man's company enough to close shop occasionally and dabble in outlawry, and that he'd once had the strange experience of shooting an unruly trainman in the thigh, then removing the bullet four hours later at his town practice, having not even changed his clothes.

Dad said, "Can you hear the plows? They'll have us clear by dark."

"Now that's auspicious," called Roxanna. "I'm out of milk."

"Also the Plymouth is running better. Plugs were a mess."

Swabbing noises from the bathroom.

"So we'll be able to settle up, Roxanna. Get out of your hair."

I can hear him yet: *Settle up. Get out of your hair.* In that dread moment I realized some huge, imprecise, and desperate expectation had begun to form inside me. And so swiftly—I'd had no idea!

Then he said, "Swede, Reuben, go get your things together."

Dad seemed so determined, I supposed he'd received orders from the Lord at last. Upstairs, I offered this idea to Swede. I only meant it as comfort.

She was crying mad, firing balled-up socks into her suitcase. "If God told him what to do, how come he didn't tell us?"

"Who—Dad or God?"

"Who cares? One of them ought to've mentioned it." Swede slitted her eyes and peeked into my heart of doubt. "Okay, Reuben, is it your true opinion God told Dad the whereabouts of Davy and we are going there in the morning?"

"No," I had to confess.

"Then shut up about it," she said.

Suitcases packed and clothes set out for morning, we went downstairs to help with supper. It was our routine now, and a busy one, Roxanna being a thorough cook. Generally I was sent to retrieve wax beans or yams from the webby cellar while Swede sliced bread or laid out plates and glasses. We did with conviction—devotion—all the things we'd done so gracelessly at home.

Roxanna was standing at the counter with her back to us. Standing in a dark wool dress pulling tight across her shoulders.

"Children," she said, turning to us. Though her eyes glittered, she was not crying. In fact she pulled a smile from somewhere. Her hair was roped back in a French braid from which it was very winningly coming loose, and she held before her a picnic basket with a clasped lid. Does all this make her sound beautiful to you? Because she was—oh yes. Though she hadn't seemed so to me a week before, now when she turned and faced us, I was confused at her beauty. Later Swede would render into verse Roxanna's moment of transfiguration, but truly I suppose that moment had been gaining on us secretly, like a new piece of music played while you sleep. One day you hear it—a strange song yet one you know by heart.

YOU'RE MAYBE WONDERING about the picnic basket. Though North Dakota is a fine place to picnic, for most this holds only in summer. But Roxanna Cawley was exempt from assumption. She knew there are times you need a picnic most, and the fact is, if you were lucky enough to live in the North Dakota Badlands in 1963, you could load up and have one at will.

We didn't know where she was taking us. Dad, driving, just followed her directions. We were a quiet troop. Swede was curled away from me, and my throat ached with coming departure and with the beauty I had perceived in Roxanna.

We went round a bend, and Roxanna suggested we park, a difficult trick because the road was so skinny. Dad scraped the hard snow wall to the right, and we piled out left. The moon showed us a white hillside up which Roxanna led us, her wool dress whipping. Climbing at last to the top, we looked down at what seemed a garden of fire.

Fire and rising steam and specks of light—the specks pooling and runneling, then blinking out. The fire came from a split in the earth that zigzagged away, branching outward. Smoke and heat and sporadic low flames. It was a fearful sight—I know *I* was nervous— but down we went, descending the hillside lit by orange snow, down into the lee of the hill where the wind couldn't reach. And the snow got softer and wetter, and now we could see that the specks of moving light were streams of snowmelt, and the streams grading down into the crack were what created the steam and made the air so warm and sociable the lower down we went. Roxanna told us how generations ago lightning had sliced into an aged cottonwood whose roots ran across a vein of lignite. The fire settled into the coal and spread inchwise until here, a hundred years later, it lay before us, a snaky, glowing web reaching away into the evening.

"Mr. Land, right here," Roxanna said. Dad took a blanket off his shoulder and flung it across a flat rock by the flames, and for radiant warmth it was like sitting on a rooftop. Before us the crack was more than a yard across, and the fire pranced up out of it a foot high, white-gold with a clean cerulean core.

"Roxanna," Dad said, "it's a miraculous place." He was sitting beside her. The firelight had restored his face to healthy color, and she—all Frenchbraided, scarf unslung—resembled an opportunity missed by Rembrandt. I looked at Swede and saw hope showing in her face and felt it in my own.

"Come on, Reuben," Swede said, "let's explore!" So off we went with not so much as a caution from Dad, for he was looking at Roxanna through what I fancied were new eyes, she having worked a fairy tale in bringing us to such a place. It was indeed miraculous. How else to describe a valley where spreading fire wakes frozen salamanders with which to scare your sister? We ran all over. We forgot the picnic. We jumped over narrow places in the crack, then dumped in armloads of snow for the thrill of the hiss.

Returning, we saw a covered pan jetting steam beside the fire, also a small Dutch oven, hearty smells emanating from the delicacies we later spooned up—beef stew with pearl onions, golden gingerbread sweetened with fruit. But time was short. Dad was gazing downvalley with a flummoxed expression.

"Is that Martin Andreeson?" he inquired, pointing at a man in a coat picking his way toward us through the rocks.

Roxanna said, "Who?"

"Martin Andreeson," Dad replied. "He works for the FBI."

The fellow was wearing a knee-length coat belted at the waist, and he was stepping carefully alongside the fire vein. He waved at us like some old friend. "It's him," I said.

"What's he want? Who is he?" Roxanna wondered.

Dad didn't answer. Where was he supposed to start?

"Jeremiah?"

Dad sighed. "Well—you'll see."

"Hello," said Martin Andreeson, walking up. "Hello, Jeremiah, Reuben. Say, where's your girl?"

Dad looked round. Swede had disappeared. "Exploring, I guess. You're in time for supper, Mr. Andreeson."

"Thank you. I ate." The putrid fed picked a boulder and sat himself down. He popped loose a cigarette and lit it from the ground fire, then took a big puff and winked at me through the smoke.

"Roxanna, this is Martin Andreeson," Dad said.

"My pleasure, Mrs. Cawley."

It was quiet a moment while Andreeson smoked and looked around. You couldn't help but notice that he was kind of a handsome jerk, sitting there in the glow. He seemed extremely tickled. "Do you know," he said, "I had some car trouble back in Linton."

"Looks like you're fixed up now."

"I'll be honest, Mr. Land. We're getting close to Davy. And the closer we get, the more dangerous for him. I'm not threatening anyone. I'm asking for your help."

"If you're close, you already know more than I do," Dad replied, adding, "Just for the sake of discussion, how close do you suppose you are?"

"He's in the Badlands," Andreeson said.

"You appreciate the Badlands are fair-sized."

Andreeson smoked a little, appeared to decide on forthrightness. "A rancher not far from here keeps losing pigs from his barn."

Dad said, "Wait a minute. You think Davy's here?"

"Not far from here." Andreeson dropped his cigarette into the fire, then peered down after it. "What we'd like, Mr. Land, is for you to come with us for a day or two. Drive around a little."

Through all this Roxanna had held silent. Of course I didn't know how much Dad had told her regarding Davy—nothing in our hearing. Yet watching her, you'd have guessed she not only knew my brother but had raised him herself and tutored him in evading the law. Her face was shut and latched against Andreeson.

"Drive around?" Dad stood up. "Thank you for keeping us informed. Should anything develop, we've taken rooms with Mrs. Cawley. You may reach us there."

Andreeson stood up also, handing Dad a card with a phone number, stressing his hope Dad would reconsider. We watched him walk back down the valley, vanishing amid firelit boulders.

From no hint of Davy to a possible sighting! It went to show that anyone could deliver good news.

I WAS CARRYING A HATFUL OF eggs in from the barn and saw a man sitting a horse on the hillside back of Roxanna's. This was next morning before full light, and he was perhaps a half mile from the house, so what I saw was the black shape of him up there.

The rider was Davy. I knew it without question.

He sat the horse and watched me. The horse was still but for its flapping tail, and as the light improved, we looked at each other across the half mile of clean blue snow. I waved.

The horseman didn't wave back. He turned and started working round the side of the hill. I could see the plunge and heave of the horse through the deep snow. Alarmed lest he leave my sight, I peeled for the house, herded the eggs across the countertop where Swede was waiting to candle them, and churned back outside.

Horse and rider were gone.

"What's going on?" Swede yelled. She was on the back step in an apron. Roxanna had promised to teach us how to make her great-uncle's cinnamon rolls, those he had served to young Butch Cassidy.

"There was a guy on a horse up the hill there." I pointed. I'd certainly have claimed it was Davy, except Roxanna appeared in the door to say her neighbor Lonnie Ford pastured cattle on that hill and that he kept a trail open during the winter.

Swede said, "We're going to make the rolls. You coming in?"

"I'll be just a minute."

The door shut. I jogged to the barn, as though perhaps I'd forgot something out there, slipped in nonchalantly, then sped through to the back door, dislodging hens. From here I could trot off toward the hillside in question without being observed from the house.

It wasn't that I wholly believed anymore the horseman I'd seen was Davy. You can imagine how my hopes slumped when Roxanna mentioned the rancher Lonnie Ford. But it sure had looked like Davy, even if the distance was great and the light poor and the thinking wishful. If nothing else I meant to get up to where that horse trail was and follow it a little ways.

What a hike, though. In the lee of some snowdrifts lay soft pockets that could drop you waist-deep, and then it was a tough slog.

And the horse trail, once reached, was not the clean footpath I'd imagined. I slumped to my haunches. Trail, my eye—it was thigh-deep in snow, the crust broken. The truth is, I nearly cried at this point, for I'd worked so hard to get here. Then I looked back at the house and barn. A very decent stretch, considering I was a pauper in the lung department. It stirred me up. In fact I now saw that the snow up here looked generally hard-swept. Keeping the trail on my right, I trotted ahead. Practically before realizing it, I'd come round and was looking down at a valley beyond which rose steeper hills with barren stratified cliffsides and twisted scrub pine.

Twenty yards down the trail sat Davy on a stamping bay horse.

He had on a green army parka so large the sleeves were rolled back. Over his jaw lay a whiskery scrub that erased the boy I might've expected. When I looked at his face, I felt dizzy and fearful, for it was Davy's face and yet another's also.

But my faintness disappeared when he grinned, saying, "Pretty long climb, wasn't it, Natty Bumppo?"

It was hard to talk at first. He walked the horse up and offered me his hand. I took it, and he lifted me up behind him. I sat back of the saddle on the horse's wide hind end—a slippery arrangement. I kept tilting one way or the other while we worked down the backside of the hill. The horse, name of Fry, kept skidding sideways and catching himself. I grabbed Davy around the ribs.

"It's all right, Rube. He's good at this."

But I hung on tight. It was such a relief to hold on to my brother again, but it was strange, also. Davy's coat smelled smoky. Sulfurish. He was thinner and harder than I remembered. He seemed compressed. We bumped and slid down to a stand of juniper, where the hill leveled out, and there Fry stopped.

"You all right?" Davy asked.

"Sure thing," I said.

"Jump off, why don't you."

"Okay." But when I lay bellywise across the horse with both legs hanging down, I couldn't see my feet. I slipped down, missed the earth, and lit on my back. Davy swung down and grabbed hold of me like I was his little brother for real. The best thing was to hear him laugh, and his laugh was as I remembered, only deeper.

"Tell the truth now," he said. "How'd you know it was me?"

"Well, I could just tell! I knew right away!"

"You didn't tell anybody, did you?"

"Why, no!"

"Good for you, Rube. Man, I'm glad to see you."

The great question suddenly occurred. "But how'd you know where we were?"

"I heard you last night—you and Swede fooling around by that coal vein." He perched back on a deadfall pine. "Swede doesn't sound like anyone else, you know. I tied Fry and prowled up."

"You were watching us?"

He smiled big.

"But you didn't come out! You should've—"

"Good thing I didn't, wouldn't you say?" Davy asked, striking me silent a moment till I recalled how Martin Andreeson had shown up. He said, "Rube, who was that guy?"

So I described the putrid fed. Davy wanted a complete portrayal of Andreeson—how he spoke, what sort of things he said. He got a kick out of him spying on the Airstream, how he saluted driving away. When I told about Swede emptying the Aunt Jemima down Andreeson's tank, Davy laughed so hard he tipped over in the snow.

"Where are you living?" I asked abruptly.

He quit laughing and looked me over. "Not far away. I'd like to show you where, but I better not. Hey—it's all right."

I wasn't getting teary, but it surely wasn't all right.

He said, "It's better if you don't know, Rube."

We sat on the dead pine while Fry pawed the snow for browse. Always one to withhold the personal, Davy seemed more than usually constrained. We talked small awhile—satisfactory in its way, since we were at least sitting together as in more thoughtless times.

"Say," he wondered, "what is it with Dad and that lady?"

So I told how we'd met Roxanna—a little about her goats and her great-uncle who had consorted with famous robbers.

"Is she liking Dad a lot?" Davy asked.

"You saw them," I said cautiously. "What did you think?"

"She likes him. Boy, he looks skinny, though."

"He had pneumonia. He's okay."

"How about you? How're the lungs?"

When I thought about it, they were on the poor side. "Why don't you come down to Roxanna's? I'll go down first and make sure Andreeson's not there or anything. Swede'll go crazy!"

Davy smiled at his feet. "Listen, I really want to. You don't know how much. But it sounds like this putrid fed isn't such a dope."

"He's *kind* of a dope," I said loyally.

"Well, he thinks I'm here, and sure enough I am." Like a gentleman, he didn't suggest that had we not set out from Roofing, Andreeson would have had no call to suspect the Badlands.

We sat a minute, and he said, "I can't come down, that's all. The truth is, Rube, I'm trying real hard to miss the penitentiary."

"What am I supposed to say, then—when I get back?"

"Nothing." He looked at me so alarmed I recognized my idiocy. "Don't tell Dad—and especially don't tell Swede."

"Okay." But I couldn't imagine going back and not telling Swede at least. I wasn't even sure it was possible.

"You know what?" Davy said. "Fry belongs to a friend of mine. A fellow who's helped me out."

"A rancher? Is it Lonnie Ford?"

"Nope, no rancher. This man's in some trouble. Real trouble, Reuben. He's been all right to me, though." At this, my brother seemed to go up on edge. He quit talking to peek here and there. To listen as for a distant summons—as we'd listened sometimes, roaming in the timber, expecting to be whistled down for supper.

Davy said, "It's a long walk back. Here, I'll take you partway." He was in the saddle before I could reply, seizing my hand, hoisting me up. Fry moved out of the trees and headed back up the hill.

I said, "What's your friend's name?"

Nothing right away; then, "Waltzer. Jape Waltzer."

"Jape? Funny name."

He didn't reply. The horse angled up the hill, his front heaving and rearing so I had to grip Davy even tighter than previously. It shot through me that I would not see him again—that the horse with every upward plunge bore us nearer a ruthless parting I was bound to keep secret. My breathing turned thick. Dad came to mind, and I shut my eyes and prayed that when we came round the hillside, he would by divine leading be standing there, his face primed with wisdom and responsibility.

Roxanna's place came into view. Davy said, "Whoa, Fry. Rube, you better walk the rest."

But I didn't let loose of him. How could I, burdened as I was?

"I have to tell *somebody* about you," I said.

He pried my arms away and turned in the saddle. "You can't do it, Reuben. Not yet. You understand?"

But I wouldn't look him in the eyes. "Then show me where you live," I said. "Show me, or I'll tell Dad."

I hung to the cantle and watched Davy consider what I'd said, all the while with the miserable sensation of having wrecked something, but then he nodded. "All right, Rube. But I have to tell Jape you're coming. Can you get out of the house tonight without rousting everybody?"

Well, of course I could. I'd read as much Twain as the next boy.

Davy studied Roxanna's place. "Come out back of the barn this way a couple hundred yards. I'll be close. Come when you can," he said. "I'll be there. I got no other plans."

As I entered Roxanna's kitchen, the cinnamon rolls had just come out, with their beguiling aroma, and Swede was whisking up frosting. "Well, where'd *you* go?" she asked.

"Just a walk. Sorry I missed breakfast."

"You could of told somebody."

"Boy, Swede!"

"I looked in the barn and all over."

"I just hiked around a little."

"Were you looking for Dad? He went out with Mr. Andreeson."

The last thing you expected, right? Me too.

"How come he went?"

Swede punished the frosting. No doubt she'd have been happier had an answer been available. "He left before daylight."

I sat down. The truth is, my lungs felt congealed. I was so tired. I said, "How come he wants to help that guy? He *wants* them to catch Davy now?"

Swede didn't reply. Out front we heard Roxanna enter with a customer. We heard the slide of the cash drawer, the bell ding above the door; then Roxanna swept in. "Reuben!" she exclaimed. "Where'd you go?" She kissed my cheek, first time she ever did so.

"Exploring."

"That's good. Find anything?" She was off hanging up her coat.

I yelled, "Roxanna, how come Dad went?"

She came out of the mudroom and took the chair next to me. I remember how she put her elbows on her knees to look into my eyes. "He felt he had to go, Reuben." She measured me for a beat or two. "He was led to go."

"Led? Led by who? That barf Mr. Andreeson?"

Roxanna turned briskly aside, as if deflecting my vulgarity. For a moment she seemed unable to look at me. When she did, her eyes were so merry I was stumped indeed. She said, "I don't think Mr. Andreeson could influence your father to clear his throat."

"But he went with him!"

"Reuben, he stayed up all night. I woke and heard him. Do you know what he was doing?"

"I suppose praying," I answered miserably.

"Yes—not like I ever heard anybody pray." Roxanna stopped there, still not knowing what to say about it. "I got up," she added, "and we talked awhile. Swede, isn't that frosting a little thick?"

Roxanna showed Swede how to thin it with coffee and warm butter. How we hate waiting for things to make sense! For I can tell you now what Roxanna held back at the time: how she woke to the sound of Dad's voice raised to the pitch of argument. How she thought at first that Andreeson himself had come in the night.

Creeping from her room, she heard Dad articulating grievance against the putrid fed, yet there was no reply. She listened to him savagely racing through King James as if to back up some contention. "He doesn't know You and doesn't want to," Dad said. "Make me willing if You can," he cried, a challenge it still shakes me to think of. Roxanna's muscles went weak. She sat down in the hall and remembers yet the strange warmth that comforted her there. In fact she fell asleep. Waking sometime later, she found Dad at the kitchen table. He was at peace, his Bible closed. He smiled at her; he asked for coffee. When he stood, he held to the back of a chair.

But Roxanna didn't tell us all this at the time. All she said was she got up to keep Dad company and their talk ranged far and wide.

"He told me how you took down that corncrib," she said, "and then bought groceries with the money."

"I wanted a canoe."

"He really did," Swede affirmed.

"Buying those groceries instead of the canoe? It broke your heart, I bet," Roxanna said.

"At first," I admitted.

"Would you say," she wondered, "that you were led to do that?"

"Well, sure," I groused. "Led by Swede."

Which drew Roxanna's low, beautiful laugh. "Come on, Reuben," she said. "Come tell me if these rolls are as good as Mr. Cassidy thought they were."

the little man's country

JUST past midnight that hunched bundle behind the barn was me, Reuben Land, in deep regret. Skittish, that's what I was, and unnerved about walking out into the dark. Here all day I'd imagined the glory of this act, yet I crouched against the barn.

It was a moonless night, and you get little light from stars. In fact—say—no doubt it was too dark for Davy too! How would he find his way on horseback among the hills? I cupped an ear—no stamp or whicker. Relieved, I took a few steps. Even were he not waiting, I had to go some token distance. At fifty steps I stopped. The barn was a starless hump in the night. I said, "Davy, you here?"

Nostrils jetted at a distance, loosening my guts. Fry walked up through the snow. I smelled the steam from his skin, the sulfur of Davy's clothes. Then Davy laid hold and yanked me up behind him.

As earlier, we didn't talk right away. It was too dark and the going too lumpy. It seemed at first we were following the path I'd broke earlier; then it seemed otherwise. We kept rising.

Cresting a long hill, we stopped a moment while Fry blew and stooped and clipped at the snow. I let go of Davy to sit straight. I can't describe what we saw. Here was the whole dizzying sky bowled up over us. We were inside the sky. It didn't make the stars any closer, only clearer. They burned yellow and white, and some of them changed to blue or a cold green or orange. Swede should've been there—she'd have had words.

"Up, Fry," Davy said. "Let's go. Rube, it's pretty, isn't it?"

I was pleased. It was okay to talk. "Do you picture God tossing them out there like that or setting them up one by one?"

We were heading downslope, a more comfortable job.

"Are you waxing poetic on me now?" Davy said.

"No, I don't think so."

"Well, you're waxing something."

Fry was rustling downhill just as though he could see. The sound changed under his hooves, and the air turned cushiony. It took me a few minutes to realize we were among trees.

Davy said, "Was it hard not telling?"

"Nope."

"Dad didn't ask where you'd gone?"

"Nope." Davy hadn't any idea, of course, where Dad had gone. I wondered whether to tell him and decided to wait. The snow seemed less, and Fry eased into a smoother walk. "Do you and Jape live in a tepee?" I asked.

At that he pulled Fry to a stop. He turned in the saddle. "Rube, there's one thing. Listen to me now. Call him Mr. Waltzer. It's a weighty thing to him, how he's addressed."

"Well, sure." I was taken aback. "I'll say mister. What do *you* call him?"

Davy turned forward. "Jape."

Fry resumed trudging under the stars.

"And the girl is Sara," he added.

The rest was a silent ride. Weary travel induces a kind of vacuum. We came up finally into a saddle between two hills, looking down at the same sort of fiery valley where Roxanna had taken us to picnic—a great deal less impressive, however. There was one main fissure, wide as an automobile but glowing only in patches with the cool radiance of a candlelit pumpkin.

Davy said, "Here we are."

I saw the shape of a lighted window set well back from the glowing vein. "You built a cabin?"

He clicked at Fry, who trotted down whickering and was answered by at least one horse below. Beside the window a door opened, and a man stood straight and formally in the thrown box of light. We rode to him, and he clasped his hands behind his back and looked at me as though I were money.

"Little brother Reuben," he said. "It is my honor."

"Hi, Mr. Waltzer," I said.

He took hold of my arm above the elbow and guided me off the horse. Despite all I was to learn about this man, he knew how to make a boy welcome—that is, he took entire control in a way to make you feel older and soldierly. Hands on my shoulders, he amended my posture, tugged at my coat. I looked round for Davy, but he was gone with Fry. Waltzer said, "Look at me, Reuben."

He was of unimposing height, under six feet. A practical build. His hair was dark and tied back in a short bob, and he had two rapscallion eyebrows—upswept, pointed, and mobile.

"Mm," he muttered. Those brows of his scared me—they were like flipped goatees. "Tired from the ride?"

"No sir."

"You mean to do right by your brother, I expect."

"Yes sir."

He leaned down to me. "If I were to tell you that those hills you rode over will be shaken to dust and that waters will rise up in their place and that creatures like none you can think of will swim in that sea—what would you say to that, Reuben?"

He posited this as though it were imminent and as though I were alone with him in the knowledge, and so far was it from anything I'd expected, I didn't even know to be careful.

"I guess I'd want to know what day, Mr. Waltzer."

He searched my eyes, straightened, and blew out hard through his nostrils, like a horse. "Come in and eat."

The cabin was a clean ruin. I have since seen photos of its ancestors: the slave and sharecropper shacks strung beside dirt fields in southern states. It was built up of chinked vertical boards held by stringers top and bottom—four warped walls laced together to approximate a box. It had a sooty tin roof and a floor, except where some boards had been removed for a barrel stove. Yet for all its poverty, the place was livable. The stove flung heat nobly and was topped by a coffeepot and a Dutch oven that smelled of brown sugar. One corner of the room had been enclosed by ropes from which sheets hung like laundry to the floor.

Waltzer took a stool at the table under the window. "Sit down."

I didn't want to—not without Davy there. I angled against the wall and worked at my overshoes.

"He'll be in forthwith. A horse isn't a car. Come sit."

I hung my coat on a peg and sat. He leaned forward on an elbow. "Davy doesn't tell me about his family. You're a surprise."

"I'm sorry."

His eyes were bright as a badger's. "Sorry doesn't matter. We should be honest with each other. I have some questions for you, and you've a few for me. Go ahead."

He was so direct I could only doubt his meaning. He wanted me to grill him? Right now? And then he was going to grill me?

He looked at me with pity and impatience. "Sara," he called, "come meet Reuben, pour him some coffee." Before the sentence ended, a sheet was pulled back and she moved across to the stove, a redhead girl about fourteen, in pants and a man's flannel shirt. Green plaid flannel. When she brought the coffeepot, I saw she had green eyes too, though she didn't aim them at me particularly.

"Davy's brother, Reuben," Waltzer said as she set down three enameled cups and poured. "This is Sara. Thank you, daughter."

She nodded to him and retired behind the sheets. I asked the only thing I could think of—how he knew Davy.

"Here is what happened. I went into Amidon for breakfast. It isn't far, and there's a not bad café there. I sat at a front table and ordered the steak and eggs and sat looking out the window. The telephone rang. The owner, Williams, answered. I heard the word Studebaker. Williams approached my table. There was a car out front, and he asked was that my car. No sir, it is not. Then he went back, and I heard him on the phone again. Not long after, my breakfast arrived. It's hard to do better than steak and eggs. When I looked out again, a county deputy was parked down the block." Waltzer said confidentially, "I was pleased because someone was in trouble and it was not me. Do you understand that, Reuben?"

"No sir."

"He should've been after the fellow he could see through the window eating steak and eggs," he said gleefully, "but he looked straight past me. In sight of wolf he was hunting squirrel!"

At this, praise be, the door whuffed open and Davy stepped in.

Waltzer beamed. "Davy, my squirrel! Your brother's curious how we met. I'm just to the moment you rose from your table at Williams's. Come finish the story!"

Davy sat, sipped the coffee Sara had poured earlier. "I'll just listen. You tell it, Jape."

So he finished it out: how Davy'd gone up and paid his bill, how he'd stopped beside Waltzer's table to observe the street, then returned to the counter and inquired of the whereabouts of the rest room, Williams pointing to the rear of the café. Seeing this, Waltzer

laid money beside his plate and left by the front door. He nodded
to the deputy, rounded the corner, and entered the alley, where
behind the café Davy stood hunched in calculations. Talk ensued,
during which Waltzer was stirred by the boy's assurance under
stress. A quarter hour later the pair were riding an overladen Fry
into the hills above Amidon.

During this summation Sara had emerged from her little room to
lay a feast of medieval plenty. She carried the Dutch oven to the
table and unlidded it before us, stepping back from the steam to
show a knoll of sweet potatoes glazed with brown sugar, encircled
by sausages. She produced half a round of black-crust bread, baked
no doubt in that same oven, which she laid on a checked cloth.
She arranged our plates and tinware, receiving a thankful glance
from Davy. Through all this, Waltzer talked right along. I wondered
what she could think of such a father. Though he wasn't without
appeal—I looked at him, eyebrows rocketing now at the part where
grumpy Fry carried both men into the hills—it was clear he was a
difficult fellow to please.

"Now, Reuben," said Waltzer, reaching for the yams, "your story.
Was Davy dropping breadcrumbs behind him, that you followed so
efficiently?"

I lowered my head in panic. Not for a moment had I believed my
narrative would be required. I guess I shut my eyes a moment.

"Reuben, what are you doing?"

I looked at him through twisting steam from the Dutch oven.
He'd frozen as if detecting betrayal. "Nothing," I said.

"Are you praying over this meal I've provided?"

"No, Mr. Waltzer."

"You are thanking God for the food," he said, "when He did not
give it to you. I gave it to you and did so freely. Thank *me*."

I nodded.

"Thank me, then!"

I looked at Davy, who was watching his plate. I said, "Thank you,
Mr. Waltzer. It looks like a good meal."

"Absolutely it does," Waltzer agreed. He leaned toward me, congenial again. Two fingers, I noted, were missing from his left hand. "No need to wet your pants, Reuben. Tell us how you came here."

"We just came. We got a new Airstream trailer," I said, thinking he might find that interesting.

"Been traveling awhile, then. Looking for Davy all over the place."

"No, we pretty much came straight here."

He looked at Davy, who shrugged. "Straight to us, Reuben? Tell me how you happened to do that."

"Our car broke down, and we got snowed in."

"So no one led you here," he said.

Well, the question was dismaying. Of course we'd been led. Why did everyone keep bringing this up? We'd had leading by the bushel! Even the putrid fed had been part of the old rod and staff employed by the Lord to goose us along.

Waltzer looked at me with eyes from a dead photograph.

"I guess we had great luck," I said, and immediately there came a loathsome squeal from behind the bedsheets and a weighty tumbling, the sheets themselves jerking horribly about. Then out sped some wild leathery being, screeching in torment! It zipped under the table and leapt up into the lap of Jape Waltzer, where it became a small dark pig atremble with terror.

"Ha." Waltzer held the pig firmly. "Ha. Take a breath, little one. Ha-ha—sweet pig. Good Emil. A little bad dream?" he said pleasantly. Without changing his tone, he added, "Daughter?"

Out came Sara. Why in the world had she stayed in there—with a pig!—instead of joining us for supper?

"Please explain this disruption," Waltzer said. His voice was patient in a way that made me afraid.

"He was sleeping out of his box, sir," Sara replied. "I must've stepped on his tail. I'm very sorry." Anyone could hear her voice was worn to the contours of apology.

"It wasn't my tail you damaged," Waltzer said conversationally.

"You're right, sir," Sara replied. "I'm very sorry, Emil." She stepped back and shut the curtains. Dreading to do so, I looked at Waltzer, but his eyes were alive and forgiving.

"Reuben, what are your plans?" he asked.

"My plans? For tonight, Mr. Waltzer?"

He smiled, scratching Emil gently. "In your life," he said.

I tried to think of a reply large enough for Jape Waltzer. Nothing came. My lungs had gotten shallower all through the night.

"I guess breathe," I said.

Waltzer spoke to the pig. "His aspiration is respiration, Emil. He might do well to strive harder—what, are you hungry? Here is a sausage—mm, yes. Good pig, my little cannibal."

Davy spoke up at last. "Jape, Reuben has some lung trouble—just once in a while." He looked at me kindly.

Waltzer let the pig down off his lap. "Is that right. I've heard of this condition. Tell me, is it hard right now? To breathe?"

It sure was.

"Do this." He sat up straight and drew in the deepest breath he could, opening his eyes wide to encourage me likewise.

I straightened and inhaled. It sounded like a dozen slow leaks from an inner tube.

Waltzer leaned in. "No, no. Make the attempt. Make up your mind and *breathe*." And he gave me another example of a man's functioning lungs, a suck of immense force and duration.

I made another attempt. You have to understand this was old ground to me. More than one teacher back in Roofing had been convinced I simply hadn't learned to breathe properly.

Waltzer shook his head. "How do you even live, boy?"

"It's usually better," I said. In fact all this attention to my respiratory apparatus had made it self-conscious. It was shutting down valves all over the place. "May I please be excused?"

He said in evident disbelief, "Are you strangling on me now, Reuben? Has the monster got you by the throat?"

I'll say this: I kept quiet at first. But these attacks have an exponential nature, doubling and quadrupling their hold. They are fearsome enough without some skeptic calling you a fake.

"Rube," Davy said, seeing my look, "you better lie down—"

"Here, Reuben, this is nonsense," Waltzer said, about to try to help me again. "Stop embarrassing yourself. Now when I count three—"

"Shut up!" I gasped. "Shut up and let me be!" It was all the air I had. I paid for some more and added, "Mr. Waltzer." I can't forget how the air in the cabin turned all spotty then, nor the scramble I heard, nor the broken-bat sound that was my head striking the floor.

OF ALL the dreams you ever had, which do you least hope to have again? For me it was the man with the skin bag—the little devilish fellow who slugged my gut and harvested my breath. The moment of highest peril in that dream came when he crouched down, peering at my face. His eyes were windows through which I glimpsed an awful country. I don't like telling about it. The point here is that for a long while I walked in a gray place. A sunless place where the cold boulders were the same color as the dead grass and as the sky. I smelled decay on the wind. I had the sense of walking through an old battlefield upon which the wrong side had prevailed. It was the little man's country. He soon found me. It was colder every second, and the smell of decay mixed with sulfur as I heard his nimble steps. Even shut-eyed I knew what he would do. Now he'd crouch and—

"Reuben," he whispered, "look at me."

What choice did I have? I opened my eyes. Jape Waltzer's face searched mine as I hope never to be searched again.

I couldn't say a thing. I was confused—wondering about the skin bag. It seemed to me Waltzer must have it and that he wanted something more besides. I saw we were outside the cabin, that I lay against it in my coat, and that Waltzer was crouched in the snow against a night of misty stars.

"Ah, you're breathing now," he said. He smiled to reassure me, but in his eyes I saw the same dead country through which I'd just come. "Davy's getting Fry. He'll take you back."

I nodded, dreading to speak aloud lest Waltzer change his mind.

He pressed close to me. "You know not to tell of this place."

I said, "Yes, Mr. Waltzer." Fry cantered up out of the night.

"Come back and see us, Reuben. I'll teach you how to breathe."

Davy lifted a leg over Fry's withers and slipped off frontwise. He gathered me up and carried me to the horse and heaved me aboard, then rocked himself up behind. I honestly had no breath. Fearing another faint, I leaned back into my brother as though his were the mighty Everlasting Arms sung about, and we trotted up out of Waltzer's valley.

AT MY age Teddy Roosevelt's lungs would lock down so tight his father would gallop his fastest horse down gaslit New York boulevards with the boy before him, gaping at the wind. Mr. Roosevelt's idea was to impel air down Teddy's throat by their very speed.

Did this method work for me? Maybe so. I do recall getting my breath as Fry plunged on with confident speed. When we rose over the last hill and trotted down toward Roxanna's, I asked Davy when I could see him next. He wouldn't say. He let me off Fry a few hundred yards back of the barn. The slopes to the west were just showing blue. In less than two hours I'd have to get up and candle eggs.

As it turned out, though, Swede did the candling.

I woke with a rotten fever and Roxanna's cool hand against my forehead. I squinted while she pulled the shades.

"It's still awfully bright," I told her.

She opened a wardrobe, took down a quilt, stepped up on a chair, and tacked it over the window. "Better, darling?"

"Uh-huh," I said.

"Could you drink a little cocoa?"

I shook my head. "No, thank you—"

She came and bent over me, put her hand on my forehead again. She listened to my breathing. I squeezed my eyes shut.

"I'll get a cool cloth," she whispered. "We'll whip that fever."

To my great relief she went from the room, and I wiped my eyes and settled down. The easy way she'd said that—"Better, darling?"—I don't know why, but I could hardly answer her.

Sleep that day was a warm pool into which I dove and stayed, sporadically lifting my head to sense the world. Swede stood by the bed a few times, waiting for me to open my eyes, which I didn't.

Once, I surfaced to the rattle of papers and found her on a chair, pretending to rub out some words on a page. Her regret at my awakening was also counterfeit. She happened to be waist-deep in a new Sundown episode.

Barely conscious, I listened like some drunken editor. You'll recall how Sunny started as ramrod lawman, then found himself compelled to questionable action, and had lately grown into the best of misunderstood outlaws. This new chapter placed him in an undiscovered valley high in the mountains, a snakeless Eden and matchless hideout, its meadows fed by springs and a vigorous brook. Moreover, this valley had but one entrance, a steep slot through canyon walls, which one tucked stick of dynamite could obliterate forever. Yes, Sunny owned a stick. In fact he had tucked it already, back in a crevice away from rain. He hadn't set it off, because first he wanted his wife up there with him.

At roughly this point I drifted off again, and when finally I woke, the blanket over the window was shot with orange pinpricks. The day was over, the fever whipped. I washed up and went downstairs, sticking out my chest like Horatius.

How quickly I'd come to expect Roxanna to make a big deal of me! And how kind she was not to disappoint. At my appearance she smiled, pressed her palm against my forehead—a sensation I enjoyed—remarked on my sturdy constitution to recover so fast, and introduced me to a bowl of vegetable soup. Swede ate too, while Roxanna worked in the kitchen beside us, thumping up crust for a pie. Things were close to perfect.

"When's Dad coming home?" I asked.

"This evening," Roxanna said. "He called earlier."

"How'd it go with Mr. Andreeson?"

"He didn't say much. They didn't find Davy." She rolled out that crust in about six strokes, laid it across a metal pan, and turned to me with an encouraging smile. I saw that she was scared for Davy, though she'd never met him, and I felt underhanded.

"We have to be steadfast," she said. "We have to have faith, you two, that's all." She'd begun to use Dad's language. You notice something like that. I noticed too that she was wearing earrings.

Swede had been eating in unusual quiet. Out of nowhere she said, "If Dad says we have to go home, I'm not gonna let him."

Roxanna scrubbed the counter, all business. "Neither am I."

WE DIDN'T even see who dropped him off. It could've been Andreeson or some underling. Who cared? What we saw was Dad standing in his overcoat between the two gas pumps. At his feet was a small cardboard suitcase. Swede and I were bouncing and waving at the window like a pair of gibbons, but Dad somehow didn't see us. He stood looking up at the front gable like the most hopeful yet constrained boy you ever saw—a boy on his birthday morning, scared to get out of bed for fear everybody forgot.

"Why isn't he coming in?" I asked Swede.

"Ssshhh." She kept her eyes on Dad.

"Good grief," I muttered. Dad was smoothing his hair back with his left hand. Now he looked critically at his shoes. Straightened his overcoat. I started for the door, but Swede had my shirt.

"Come on," I told Swede, but still she held me back.

"Let Roxanna," she said.

"But it's Dad."

"Let *Roxanna*—" hissing it at me, for now we heard Roxanna descending the stairs in a tremendous rustle. I stopped, flat-footed. She was in a deep blue dress, her hair softly curled in front. When Dad stepped inside wearing a weightless expression, Roxanna reached and took his hand. I didn't hear what she said, but I can still see their hands touching—not a passionate clasp, but an easy, timeless transaction as old as Scripture. Then Dad's hand let go and for a moment encircled Roxanna's waist—he was laughing—and when he turned to us, he'd never appeared stronger or more like himself or more capable of stepping up to what might be required.

That very night Dad packed up his clothes and moved out to the Airstream. I didn't fret, for it was plain now that something was forged between them and that no abrupt partings were likely, but it confused me. Following his lead, I started stacking shirts in my own suitcase, but Swede came in and crouched beside me.

"We're not moving out there—only Dad," she said.

"How come he is?"

"He told me he wants to make sure the heater's working in the trailer, but it's really just for honor," she said.

There seemed to be something going unsaid here, though I didn't know how to reach it. I'd have asked my father, but embroiled in deception as I was, I feared a protracted discussion of honor. Honest, I came about this close to telling Dad the works. What kept me from it wasn't my promise to Davy either—it was my intact bewilderment over Dad's having gone off with Andreeson. Three days he'd been gone, and what had come of it?

"I just liked it better when Mr. Andreeson was the enemy," I complained to him finally.

We were in the barn, jacking up the Airstream to lie level so Dad needn't sleep at a tilt. He was kneeling at the ratchet.

"I don't see what's changed," I said. "You even told him we were enemies, right to his face. Remember that?"

"All right," Dad said. "Let's take stock. Why exactly is Mr. Andreeson our enemy? Because he's a bad fellow?"

"He wants to stick Davy in prison."

"And how come? No. Quit that squirming. How come?"

"For what he did," I replied eventually.

"Davy's in the wrong, then?"

"He might be."

"You aren't sure, though." Dad let me stew while he reversed the ratchet and let the trailer sink an inch. He returned to the jack and brought it up a millimeter or two, and while he messed thus, Tommy Basca's last moments reappeared to me.

"Okay," I said. "Davy did a wrong thing."

"Yet you want him to escape consequences."

"Yes sir."

"Consequences represented by Mr. Andreeson—our enemy."

This of course was the indefensible truth.

"Look, Reuben, I want the same thing as you. Davy free and

clear. If you like Mr. Andreeson better as an enemy, keep him one. Maybe that's your job as a brother. My job is different. I'm the dad. I have to heed the Lord's instructions. You remember what the Lord said about enemies?"

In fact I did remember some passages. Once, sick of whiners, the Lord caused the earth to crack open like an old bun and a crowd of them fell right in. And how about the prophet Elijah, slaughtering the priests of Baal? The Old Testament—boy, it suited me.

"Love your enemies," Dad said. "Pray for those who persecute you."

He would pick those verses.

"Rats, huh?" he said.

DAVY came back that afternoon. On some errand, I looked up to the hills. He was exactly where he'd been the first time, riding a different horse now—a paint.

That night he was waiting for me behind the barn.

"Hey, Natty—" he started, but I shushed him. Dad was sleeping in the trailer now; we couldn't afford a whole lot of Nattying.

Davy gave me a hand, and I slipped up behind him.

"Jape's gone tonight," he whispered when we'd gained some distance. "He had to go pay a man some debt he owed. He won't be back for a couple days."

"Can you come home with us, then—since he's gone?"

This brought a silence during which I remembered a salient fact: Davy wasn't scared of Waltzer the way I was. Davy wasn't his hostage but remained by choice.

"Nope," said my brother at last. "Besides, what about Sara? You think I should leave her alone?"

"Bring her along," I suggested hopelessly.

"That," said Davy, grinning so I could hear it, "might be the worst idea you had in a while, Rube."

So we rode on. The paint horse took us up at a walk, round the first hill, then on as before, through treed valleys, choked washes, and across flanneled hillsides, none of which a person could honestly see on account of the clouds that had got between us and moonlight.

In the coming weeks I was to make that ride with Davy three more times. One night, skirting the barn, I heard Dad praying aloud in the Airstream, and I had to fight an ache to go straight to him and admit the weaselly nature I was fast developing. Yet even then Davy was waiting in the dark not a hundred yards away. How could I not go? I told myself we might yet reach a place where Davy would agree to come home. That the things I was learning at Waltzer's table might be of value in my brother's redemption.

And indeed I did learn some things, many of which I've had to grow into.

"We saw Israel Finch's father," I told Davy as we rode. "It was the day we left. He was out in the wind, and he could just barely stand up."

"Well, that old souse," Davy cheerfully replied.

But after talking with Dad, it had come to mean something whether Davy felt anything like repentence. I pressed awkwardly in. "Couldn't help but feel sorry for him—with Israel gone."

The paint horse stepped along at a bright pace. Davy said, "Don't you recommend regret to me, Rube. It's no help."

"I wasn't saying anything."

"Say I did regret it," Davy posited. "What good does it do? I have to go on from here."

Another ride, we got talking about Sara.

"She's not really Jape's daughter. He got her from a fellow in Utah," Davy said. "When she's old enough, she's supposed to marry him. That's what he told me: 'I'm raising myself a wife.' "

Raising a wife? "That's the pukiest idea in the world," I declared. "Why doesn't he go out and get one like everybody else?"

Davy said, "Why don't you ask him that yourself?"

"Did you ask him?"

"Nope."

We walked a heavy fifty paces before I said, "Is Sara afraid?"

"Hard to say," Davy mused, "but Sara's real smart. She should be. I'd say she probably is."

Afraid, he meant. But Davy was right, it was hard to say. Sara had been raised five years by Jape Waltzer. She wasn't accustomed to conversation as you and I think of it.

"Did Mr. Waltzer show you his fingers?" she inquired during my second visit.

He hadn't made a point of it, but I remembered—the index and middle fingers of his left hand gone from the roots up.

"He amputated those fingers himself," Sara declared, her eyes unreadable. Suspecting I was being made foolish, I looked at Davy, who was tilting his chair back, holding coffee in an enameled cup.

"He did, honestly," Sara said. "He made me watch. So I'd learn."

"To cut off *fingers?*" My voice may've been a little high.

"No. It was my fault," she said, apparently in explanation.

"But how come he did it?"

"We were towing a car, and the chain came loose. My foot slipped off the clutch while he was hooking it back up."

Talk about abstaining from detail.

Urged, Sara revealed these particulars: Jape laid the hatchet blade first in a saucepan into which he'd uncorked whiskey. He took the fingers separately with two clean strokes. Sara had to pick them up and drop them into a paper sack. She didn't want to, but Jape told her to get it done or there would be punishment. He was busy at that moment with needle and suture. She picked up the digits and threw them, sack and all, into the crackling stove.

I WOKE close to noon short of breath and with reinstated fever— woke from a rolling-mutter sleep when Dad came in my room and took my hand. "Let me hear you breathe," he said.

I sucked up what I could.

"Pretty short, my friend. Let me get some water boiling."

"Do I have to?" I was hot. Steam would poach me alive.

"All right, let me see if Roxanna's got an aspirin somewhere." He smiled back, and I saw he was wearing good clothes—his suntan khakis and a blue chambray button-down.

"Dad, is it Sunday? You're all dressed up."

"Oh. Well." He looked at me as though I'd thrown him a hard one. "Reuben, I've decided to court Roxanna. What do you think of my chances?"

That he would put such a question to me so directly—well, it sat me right up. I felt older, packed with consequence, and also cautious lest I say something dumb. "How's it going so far?"

Straight-faced but with a shine back of it, he said, "I believe she regards me respectfully."

"Oh, it's more than respectfully," I said, and started to tell about the exchange we'd had when Roxanna was making the pie, but Dad fended off this encouragement with a question.

"Did you and Swede like being here with her while I was gone?"

I nodded.

"I thought you did. I'm glad." He stood up. He really did look good, a clean-shaven courting man with quick arms and steady eyes. He had to know that Roxanna loved him already, but he wouldn't have me pointing it out. Who could blame him? Why sprint through such sweet country? He stopped entering the house casually. He knocked for admittance, often with a hothouse carnation in hand.

There was a poor nursery west of Grassy Butte: A feeble flower is better than none, and the old man there sold them for next to nothing. And one day he gave Dad an old ruined guitar.

NOT to linger on it, but I was getting worse, a fact that seeped in the night Swede volunteered to wash dishes without me. "Go up to bed," she said, taking my plate and glass out of my hands. "That wheeze is awful."

"Thanks."

"You want me to boil some water?"

"Sure." Dad had disappeared—I was too tired to wonder where.

"Go on up," she said, reaching down the vinegar.

But I didn't want to go upstairs alone. I wanted to sit on the bottom step where I could see Swede. I wanted to listen to her talk. Also, the stairs looked steep.

"Tell me about Sunny"—I took a breath—"up in the secret valley."

But she turned on me, not to be fooled with. I went. I recall the climb as tougher than my ascent to the hills that first time seeking Davy. Tougher by far. I leaned in the dark stairwell to rest. Down in the kitchen, Swede banged and rinsed. I climbed a few stairs. Of course I'd had times like this before. Of course I expected to bounce back. But four days had passed. The stairwell now began to turn slowly, as if dangling. I sat on the steps and dozed.

"Reuben?"

I had just entered a dream about hunting at August Shultz's.

"Can you hear me, Rube?"

Smelling brine, I opened my eyes. "Oh," I said.

"My gosh, Reuben, couldn't you even make it upstairs?"

I got to my feet, embarrassed and scared. "Sure. I just got tired—see?" With Swede behind me I went up briskly enough.

"I brought you some steam; here's a towel," she said, pulling up a chair. "Should I read to you now?"

She stayed a long time, reading psalms against fear and twice rising to reboil the brine. But my lungs wouldn't loosen. I remember the room veering slowly, my eyesight tilting. Swede pounded my back without result. The muscles in my legs and chest needled. Dr. Nokes had described to me how oxygen is shipped round the body, and it seemed to me these vessels were docking empty.

Meantime Dad was gone off courting Roxanna.

At this a dread realization occurred. Since arriving at this house, we'd had no miracles whatever.

You'll rightly point out plenty of subsequent wonders: Davy being encamped practically outside Roxanna's door. The alighting of Roxanna herself inside our motherless lives. But in that dark hour I thought only that it had been a long time since Dad walked by grace above the earth or touched a torn saddle and healed it clean.

I thought, Without a miracle, exactly what chance do I have?

I decided then to tell Swede about Davy. I opened my eyes, and she was still there, reading aloud. "I know where he is," I said.

"*In the mountainous Eden unseen,*" she replied patiently. "I have a little more, if you'd like." I realized she was risking some new Sundown on me and nodded to her to continue.

> *"From a spire of stone Sunny watched for his own,*
> *For his raven-haired intrepid bride.*
> *For she'd sworn to seek his Arcadian peak,*
> *Her life to spend by his side.*
> *Then a rider appeared on a day stale and seared*
> *And approached through the undulate heat,*
> *And her horse had the stride of a wearisome ride—*
> *Of a horse too long on its feet.*
> *But deep in the distance and churning up smoke,*
> *Who are the riders come charging for broke?"*

Well, nuts, *I* knew who those riders were. They were some dirty posse trailing Sunny's bride—his intrepid bride—to his hideout. And she so weary and faint.

"What's the matter?" Swede said, for at this I felt such grief I'd taken the towel and made a tent of it over my head.

"Do you hate it?" she demanded.

I shook my head, but I guess in a way I did hate it. "It's just more trouble," I said, a great knot in my throat. "Nothing ever goes right for Sunny. Can't you make something turn out okay once?"

"But it's going to turn out okay." Swede paused, alarmed enough to bend principle. "I haven't written it yet, but listen, Reuben—I'll tell you!" And she did, and as you'd expect, Sunny rode down out of his mountain and swept his brave wife from her failing mount, and there was a wondrous gunfight among the rocks, and the two of them worked their way under relentless fire back up the mountainside, where, yes, the stick of dynamite came into play.

"And then the whole valley's theirs—and apple trees and fish in the stream and good pasture for their animals. You see?"

You know what, though, it was no relief. In fact it was worse, for as she spoke of this perfect valley, all I could see was Davy and the rotten shack he lived in, with its windy chinks and its dark pig and its frightful nutcase awaiting the world's destruction. Arcadian peak, my eye. Again I was gripped with the need to spill all. I had the conviction my lungs weren't going to improve. The bounce back wasn't coming. Heavy with fever and unconfessed sin, I said, "Swede, will you not get mad if I tell you something?"

But she said, "That's Dad," hearing the door below us. Sure enough there was some bootstamping, and up they came, Dad and a slumping fellow with a brown leather bag. Dr. Nickles.

"What do you do for his lungs?" the doctor inquired. He shook down a thermometer and jabbed it under my tongue.

"Steam and vinegar," Dad replied. "Baking soda sometimes."

"Doesn't do any good." Dr. Nickles worked a stethoscope's icy cup against my chest, listening. "Breathe," he said.

I did my best.

"You got a flock of sparrows in there. Turn around." He rammed the scope between my shoulder blades. "Well, no pneumonia. Not yet. Try not to get it, young man. You're a full-blown asthmatic, has anyone told you that?"

"What would you advise, Doctor?" Dad's delivery was crisp.

"I'd advise the hospital in Fairfax—except the hospital's full of flu." The doctor smiled. "Worst in years. It'd finish your boy here, I think." He plucked the thermometer and read it. "Indeed, yes." Snapping open the bag, he produced a handkerchief, spread it on the bed, then laid forth a brown bottle, capped syringe, alcohol, and cotton. He dipped up a cotton ball and asked for my arm. "I'm going to give you a little Adrenalin boost."

"Okay." I looked the other way, felt the point hit. I remember the solid hot-licorice feel of the Adrenalin coming in.

Dad came back upstairs after Dr. Nickles left. I'd been sitting up in bed waiting to feel something, but except for a certain alertness there was no change.

"I'm sorry, Reuben." Dad sat on the bed looking slack and pale. "I would take your place, son," he said.

I knew he would.

"Reuben, the water and vinegar—does it help?"

"Most times it helps—really."

"How about now? The Adrenalin."

"Yes," I told him. The truth was, I'd developed the sensation of standing up. That's my best shot at describing it.

"You should try and sleep," Dad said.

But there's little sleep for the Adrenalin-charged. You mostly dream of this or that ordeal. For me tin pans rang. Trains hurled by. In the dream I was wrenching every muscle in the effort to breathe, and waking from it, the work was no less hard.

The bounce back, and it was a good one, pulled in just before sunup. I went downstairs in the cool gloom, and Dad was at the kitchen table drinking coffee with Martin Andreeson.

"Morning, Rube," said the putrid fed. He was slouched comfortably in his chair, legs crossed. His fedora lay on the table next to Dad's King James, which was turned, I recall, to Romans.

"Morning."

"You're improved," Dad said, looking me over.

"A lot," I said. I wanted to be suspicious of Andreeson, but he sat there so relaxed. Dad too seemed at ease—warm, in fact.

"I was sorry to hear about your lungs," said Andreeson.

"I'm okay."

He looked at Dad, who gave him a nod. "Listen, Rube, I've been showing your brother's picture around—finally found the right man. Over in Amidon. He said he gave your brother a ride the day before yesterday—dropped him off out of town."

I have to be honest: This was kindly spoken. Andreeson seemed a different fed from the one who'd shouldered into our home that first day with his talk of nabbing. Still, his nearness to Davy raised gooseflesh.

"Go on, Martin," Dad said.

Andreeson opened his mouth, shut it again, shook his head. "I just want you folks to know we're going to be careful. Stay near the phone, Jeremiah." He got to his feet. "Reuben, we won't hurt Davy. That's a promise. From me to you."

But I didn't want anything from him to me. "You can't hurt what you can't find," I replied, not looking at Dad.

But Andreeson smiled as he rose. He went out the door all business, setting the felt fedora on his head. My enemy.

That afternoon I went outside on every excuse. After such a scare they were all against it, but I was an exemplary weasel now and eased out the back in my coat and hood, breathing through a scarf to warm the air. I prayed, but the prayers were tangled and dissenting. I walked up and down, attempting to pray as Dad did, but the walking wore me out. I went inside and was rebuked by Swede for taking chances. We repaired to the living room, where I stretched myself on the couch. The idea was to feign sleep until Swede went upstairs, then pop outside, but I dropped off for real and dreamed a river of horses flowing along between banks, backs streaming sun. I woke inside a strange calm recognizable as defeat. Light entered the house, pink and orange. I straggled outside, leaned against the house, and squinted. I didn't see Davy, but somewhere on the side of the darkening hill a horse lifted its voice to neigh. The sound had the clear distance of history.

I WAS to have one last night in the hills—another starry one, as you will hear, but with a moist hush to the air that was like something at full draw—a breath, an arrow.

Jape Waltzer was busy shoeing Fry at a makeshift forge on the place.

"Reuben, I thank you," he said when Davy had ushered me into the shed and I'd said my piece. That was it. He thanked me for the information and seemed otherwise unconcerned.

"He said they're getting close," I reiterated.

"Fry," he said to the horse, who stood short-roped to a ring in the wall, "let's try this on. Davy, his head."

I said, "It's just—he told Dad to stay by the phone."

Waltzer leaned against the horse's left hip and picked up his foot. "It's always the back left one he throws," he said pleasantly. "I don't know why."

We ate a midnight supper in the shack, and still Waltzer would hear nothing of Andreeson. His disinterest was stunning. He turned the conversation to politics, astronomy, the science of well drilling, the superiority of beaver felt over wool. He claimed to have been born with no sense of smell but with extraordinary and compensatory taste buds; he never salted his food, its natural flavor being satisfactory. "For example, your meat there. I suspect you find it bland."

It was a little lump of gray meat on a tin plate. It and a boiled potato were supper. There they lay, all tired out.

"It's fine," I replied. Of course it wasn't yams and sausages.

Waltzer said, "It's pork. Take a bite, Reuben. Describe the flavor."

I bit. The pork had been boiled a long time. It was like chewing a hank of old rope. Waltzer's eyes were alight and curious.

"It's pretty good," I told him.

"I commend your courtesy, but nonsense. I won't take offense. Nor will Emil. Do it for Emil, hm?"

You remember Emil.

I peered at the pork. Waltzer said, "Go on. Assess the piquancy of Emil. It's all the memorial he's bound to get. Poor little Emil."

"It's—stiff," I said cautiously. "A little dry."

Waltzer liked this. "Yes, yes—go on."

"It's dull. Blunt. Stagnant. It tastes like cartilage."

"Yes. Good. Now me." Waltzer took a small mouthful. "Mm, yes." He closed his eyes. "I taste corn—not so much corn as I'd like. I taste beans. Bread. Pigweed, grass, earth." He looked pained. "Unfortunately, I also taste slops. It's a hard gift."

Did I believe him? It doesn't matter. All this time my lungs had worked tolerably well. I understand now this was a period of grace. Waltzer went on treating me as though my presence honored him. Sara stayed apart from us behind her wall of quilts. Later we stood outside the cabin, Waltzer pointing out constellations while Davy went to saddle Fry.

"There's the Great Ring," Waltzer said. "And there is the Totem. There's Hawk and Mouse, the Whale, Boy Ready."

"I never heard of Boy Ready," I said, as though the others were familiar, so he aimed at its points and related the myth of a child who lived in a city of wood that caught fire and burned to fine ash.

Only the boy escaped. One day a passing pilgrim saw him crouched at the river, pursuing fish with his hands. The pilgrim took the boy to the next city, where he charmed all with his bravery and wit, was adopted by the king, and grew up trained in arms and letters. At last he became king himself and was wise and good. It was a passable story until Waltzer revealed that the boy had set the fire himself.

"He couldn't have!" I said.

"Of course he could. Calm down, Reuben. It's only a legend." He put his altered hand on my head. "Don't let it bother you."

THE next day Martin Andreeson called. The fellow who'd given Davy a lift, name of Robinson, had promised to show Andreeson the place he'd dropped him off. They'd been going to meet at the Amidon café, but Robinson never showed. There were three Robinsons in the phone book. Andreeson reached two. The third's phone had been disconnected. Driving eight miles along the edge of the Badlands, he found the house boarded and cold.

"The situation, Martin," Dad said, "requires prayer."

I'd have given quite a bit to hear the fed's response. Whatever it was, Dad said good-bye, then hung up and called me over.

"Chest tight?" he asked—a rhetorical question, for he could hear what had become the usual wheeze.

"Yes sir."

"What can I do?" He'd began approaching it this way ever since Dr. Nickles threw cold water on the vinegar treatment.

"Just pound a little."

He turned me by the shoulders, and I braced against the doorjamb while he worked my back. "Reuben," he said out of nowhere, "is there something you ought to be telling me?"

My insides jelled. "I don't think so."

"You're looking peaked. It wears, this whole thing, doesn't it?"

So it was only my health he was worried about.

"I'm going to the trailer and pray for your brother," he said, such sadness in his face it was as though he knew something I didn't, instead of the reverse.

No word arrived from Andreeson that day. Or the next. What did arrive was a northwest wind. In the Dakotas it needn't snow to blizzard. The wind came low and fast, peeling the drifts. From her window upstairs Swede and I watched wide chunks of snow tear off and fling forward. It was a ground blizzard. Picture a storm to match any in wildness but only eight feet high.

Thinking of the cabin in the hills, with its shrunk chinking and corroded stove, I worried for Davy. Also for Sara. How much firewood did they have—how much food? I worried that I should've told Dad where Davy was, then worried what might've happened had I done so. I worried about my failing lungs, which at rest were breathing six times as fast as Swede's. What I wanted was a great big inhale or, failing that, a little peace. I ventured out to the barn.

Dad was in the Airstream playing the antique guitar. He'd repaired it with a tube of airplane glue and worked out many of the songs we loved in those days—"Amazing Grace," "It Is Well with My Soul," "Happy Trails," and "The Cowboy's Lament." Sometimes Dad sang; sometimes he hummed. Sometimes there was a long search for this or that desired chord. I eased from the barn and shut the door.

Inside the house, Roxanna was stirring up bread, soup asteam in a pan, just as though we were a family not perched at the edge of great loss. Even Swede seemed to have reached some sort of harbor. She sat in her room above the blizzard, fomenting joy for Sunny and his wife now that they'd obliterated the entrance to their secret valley, as well as about half that rotten posse.

The wind blew through a second night, stratifying snowbanks and encumbering roads. Then it wore out. After breakfast the others went out to shovel. I was no good for it, but Dad said someone had to stay by the phone. Andreeson did not call.

This time the county plows reached us by late afternoon. Dad called Andreeson's motel in Rathton. The owner took a message, his annoyance audible in Roxanna's kitchen. He had to go down five doors to Mr. Andreeson's room; the messages were piling up; it was too cold for this.

"When did he leave?" Dad asked.

The owner thought this over. Early the previous day he'd taken a call from one Mr. Robinson. He was in Amidon, at the café. Andreeson was glad for the message—had, in fact, tipped a two-dollar bill for its delivery. Not long afterward, the motel lot already turning humpy with drifts, the owner had watched Andreeson's tan Mercury creeping away through the wind.

Dad hung up the phone. He stood at the window and looked to the broken hills. "Rube," he said, "that Andreeson's a smart fellow, but he doesn't know one thing about winter in North Dakota."

A thought dropped from nowhere like a big snake.

Dad plucked his coat off the hook, heading to the trailer. I plucked mine to follow, then nearly sat down. My legs trembled, hips and kneecaps loose as dominoes.

"Something the matter?" Dad inquired.

"Yes sir." I didn't want to say it—the thought. Yet it coiled around me, irresistible. It squeezed, and I yielded. "Mr. Andreeson's in bad trouble."

He looked at me, and I at his shoes. "What is it, Reuben?"

But the snake had me so hard I could barely speak. I sagged to the floor to shiver. What I saw was Andreeson, encouraged—only days ago—having shown Davy's picture to the right man at last. Then Waltzer, comfortable, talking easily, refusing all concern at my insistence that Andreeson was drawing near.

"Reuben," Dad said.

It was too much to manage all at once. "His name isn't Robinson," I said. "It's Jape Waltzer—and he's with Davy—and he's going to kill Mr. Andreeson."

SO I turned at last. So I betrayed my brother. Before daylight next morning we assembled horseback at Lonnie Ford's ranch. I say we. The party included Mr. Ford; a federal investigator, Harper Juval, who'd driven in from Bismarck; the sheriff; and three skittish ad hoc deputies. Two hours earlier a rancher had found Andreeson's Mercury parked empty on a county road, snow to its fenders. It was briefly argued whether I had any business going.

"What are you, boy? About nine?" This was Mr. Juval.

"Eleven, sir."

"He's the only one of us who's made the trip, Harper," said Lonnie Ford. "At least he can tell us if we're going right."

I'd never made the trip in daylight, so my usefulness was suspect in any case. Juval examined me with distaste. "Mr. Land," he said to Dad, "it's your call. You comfortable with your boy going?" Dad had wanted to go himself, but Juval had nixed that the night before.

"He's up to it," Dad said. "I'm taking you at your word, now," for Juval had promised Davy would be taken without violence.

Juval nodded. Dad looked at me. I saw he was counting on me to see them quickly to the cabin. He wanted it over with—Davy safe, Andreeson alive. Perhaps he also believed that with Davy's little brother close by, the lawmen would be less apt to shoot.

"Let's go, then," Juval said while Lonnie Ford boosted me onto a shaggy bay mare.

We rode single file into the hills, heading for what Mr. Ford supposed from my description to be an old line cabin that had belonged to his ranch long before. It lay an indeterminate distance west in a valley remote enough that no cattle had grazed there in a generation. Also the pasture had cracked open to lignite in the late '30s and caught fire, which had a bewildering effect on livestock. For all Mr. Ford knew, it was burning to this day.

Probably it won't surprise you that Swede took all this badly. That I'd kept Davy a secret from her, she judged the deepest kind of lie; that I'd revealed him compounded the sin. I was both liar *and* traitor. I was an apostate. She went upstairs to fling a tantrum unequaled in her history. I heard papers flying, weeping mixed with wordless growls, and the sound of a pillow being kicked with tremendous gusto. That last, I knew, was me.

IT WAS a longer ride than I remembered. We rode up into timbered breaks that felt familiar and along ridges where it seemed I'd never been. In order of riding I came second, after Mr. Ford and before Mr. Juval. After a time we rode through a fairly open valley I might have recognized, but the wind had erased any tracks. Mr. Juval came abreast. "We going the right way, then?" he asked.

Miserably, I admitted to having no idea.

He rode at my side awhile without comment. He was older than Dad, wore a short-brim cowboy hat, and had a clipped white beard and a web of wrinkles under his eyes. "I consider Martin Andreeson a friend," he said after a time. "You don't, I guess."

"Davy's not the problem for your friend Andreeson," I told him. "It's Jape Waltzer."

Mr. Juval gave me a look I've never forgotten—the look perhaps of years spent in disappointment. He said, "Son, your brother killed two boys, then broke jail. This Robinson, Waltzer, whatever his name is—I don't know him from Adam."

We were getting close, riding now through country I knew for certain, yet we'd slowed. Lonnie Ford, leading, stopped to squint from time to time. Under this faltering progress I had time to think it all over. The nearer we came to the cabin, the more likely it seemed that the enigmatic Robinson really wasn't Jape Waltzer, that he was simply what Mr. Andreeson had supposed, a fellow who'd given Davy a ride, then acquired cold feet about talking to a federal man. So what that Andreeson hadn't found him in the phone book—lots of people didn't have telephones. So what that Waltzer was unconcerned about the putrid fed. The man steered by stars of his own invention. The idea emerged that I'd betrayed my brother needlessly. That Andreeson, while he'd gone out foolishly in a dangerous storm, was in no danger from any Robinson.

Up ahead, Lonnie Ford consulted with Mr. Juval, then turned his horse and loped back to me through the snow. "I lease the ranch," he said. "I never saw this cabin before. I told Mr. Juval that. Does any of this look right to you?"

My first thought was that God in my disconsolate hour had slid open a hatch. Lonnie Ford didn't know where we were! I took stock. We were on a gently beveled hill ringed with cedars and scrub juniper. Ahead to the left rose exhilarating cutrock cliffs.

I knew where we were, all right.

Knew, moreover, if we bore to the left—behind the cliffs—we'd be steering away from Davy.

"We have to bear left," I told Lonnie Ford.

It was a slick climb in places, a steep one in others, and no one really wished to make it. We climbed strung out, so a skidding horse wouldn't panic the others. Only gradually did the incline become less manageable, narrowing then lifting before us until we leaned close over the horses' necks. Briefly I feared for my deception—that Mr. Juval would throw off the climb as impossible. Perhaps he would've, had the way been wide enough for a horse to turn.

Yet we gained the top, coming out on level earth. There was the big cold sky moving over us. I confess to a certain exultation. My artifice had worked. The cabin lay somewhere to the right, in a valley; our way now lay clearly to the left. We were on a mesa of sorts. I slipped off the mare and stood beside her like the other men, the animals blowing and shaking their heads. There on the mesa we enjoyed a prevalent good humor, even if my reasons were unique. The sheriff poured coffee in a thermos lid and passed it around. A deputy came over and told me he was sorry to be hunting my brother. Lonnie Ford—and this ached—shook my hand.

Only Juval remained detached. He swung back on his horse and trotted to a small rise atop the cliffs. He had his binoculars out and peered through them a long time. "Ford," he called.

The rancher heaved aboard and came alongside Juval, who passed him the glasses. Adjusting them to his eyes, he looked over the valley. Next thing the two of them were trotting back to us.

Juval coughed and spat. "It's back down, then, gentlemen," said he, and with barely a pause he rode to the rim and dropped over. In a few words Mr. Ford told the men we'd come the wrong way. Mr. Juval had discerned the cabin down the valley. To say I felt like a caught sneak doesn't touch it. I was a boy caught deceiving honest men.

I went over next to last. If you've never essayed a decline like that on the back of a horse, I don't know what to tell you. There's a separation from ground and a hopeless union with the animal—can't hear a thing but gravel, absolutely can't steer. The mare laid her ears back, splayed her front feet, set haunches to earth, and slid. Lonnie Ford was in front of me by some yards. His horse, a big-barreled quarter, began to skid sideways. I saw it happen—hindquarters bearing right, hooves scrabbling for balance. Then wayward legs struck a boulder, and the horse went down. Mr. Ford was a man of size, but he just disappeared. The horse flipped once, then hit a steep drop and flipped again. All this time I was skidding behind on the mare. At last the gradient eased and the downed horse stopped, lying in the path at an alien angle. My mare clattered to a halt beside it, the last deputy arriving behind me in a spray of broken stone.

THAT Lonnie Ford lived at all commends the resilient design of humans, the rib cage in particular. Ford's rib cage was rolled over not once but twice by an entire American quarter horse, yet his organs remained whole. The rest of Ford was worse off. His arm lay twisted behind in such a way that the sheriff diagnosed a broken collarbone. Over one shoulder a hole had been rubbed through jacket, shirt, and skin. He was down to muscle. His face on the same side was swelling purple as we watched. He was unconscious, which relieved us all.

The sheriff had a kit in his saddlebag. He worked on Ford where he lay, pasting up the shoulder, easing the arm out to the side. He directed a jury-rigged stretcher of poles and tied coats.

While they moved Ford to even ground, Juval steered me away from the others. He asked, "Did you misdirect me on purpose?"

When I didn't answer immediately, he said, "Son?" His tone implied, if not gentleness, at least understanding.

"Yes—I did, sir."

Juval cuffed the right side of my head so hard I spun to my knees; then he told me earnestly five or six specific things he found discouraging about my character. If you don't mind, I'd rather not restate them, but they were by and large true.

They made Lonnie Ford as snug as possible, laying him on a bed of gathered juniper. Though unconscious, the rancher had begun to twist and mutter. When Juval was satisfied Ford wouldn't freeze solid, he gathered the others, who checked cinches and climbed aboard. They were leaving me with Ford and going on to hunt Davy without me. Lucky I was muzzy from being hit. More lucid, I might've wept for grief and outrage.

Every time despair came courting, though, Mr. Ford would moan and thrash. I held his limbs when he dreamed, and I rebunched his juniper pillow. After a bit he started to shiver. We needed a fire.

Which sent me back to the horse. I'd forgotten about him—the poor downed animal lying a few yards away. He was alive, though resigned, the side of his belly rising and falling, nothing else moving but his eyes. I opened the accessible saddlebag and found a can of all-purpose oil and a heavy black pouch containing tools.

The horse sighed heavily. An animal that size gives off so much heat I snuggled against his belly. I knew he should've been shot after the fall. The only reason he wasn't was our nearness to Davy's cabin. Juval wanted to preserve surprise. I tried to brace up. To think of anything besides gunshots from the hills.

It seemed necessary just then to touch base with the Lord. Shutting my eyes, I leaned into the horse. I prayed in words for a little while—for Davy, of course, and for Mr. Ford, whom I could hear making chewing sounds in his sleep, and for my own future, which seemed a boarded-up window—and then language went away, and I prayed in a soft, high-pitched lament any human listener would've termed a whine. We serve a patient God. Andreeson, whom I'd despised, now appeared to mind as he might've to a worried brother. There in the cold, curled against Mr. Ford's sighing horse, I repented of hatred in general and especially that cultivated against the putrid fed. A pain started up, as of live coals inside, and like that, I knew where he was.

Lonnie Ford cried out in an arid voice. I scrambled to him.

"I'm busted up," he observed.

"Yes sir."

"Where'd they all go?"

"After my brother," I replied.

He shut his eyes. "Where's Billy?" he asked. His horse.

"A little ways—that way. He can't lift up his head, Mr. Ford."

"They didn't shoot him."

"No sir."

He lay thinking about this. "Those buggers."

We sat in silence. He'd gone sullen, and it was hard to blame him. Soon Juval and the rest came trotting back in the blackest of moods. They'd come to the cabin, which lay open and empty; they'd found no sign of any person save Andreeson, whose felt fedora sat in rumpled condition on the cold stove. In silence Juval presided over the construction of a travois by which Ford could be carried home. Then we all mounted. Juval shot the horse Billy through the head, and we got away from there.

the red farm

DAD married Roxanna on a wind-blasted Saturday in March. We were back in Roofing, Pastor Reach officiating. I wish I remembered more about it. There was a photographer setting us here and there. I have one of the photos: Roxanna in lace, looking as lustrous as a bride ever did; Dad standing calm, his eyes enjoying the commotion; Swede laughing. At Roxanna's elbow stands her father, Mr. Cawley, the theater operator. I remember thinking he seemed terribly cautious for someone in such a happy line of work. Perhaps he owned misgivings about his new son-in-law, an unemployed janitor nearly his own age. I'm in the photo also, looking like old man.

We had come back to Roofing at the end of February, the ride into the Badlands with Juval having tipped my lungs into steep descent. I won't describe the buried and airless place I seemed to visit. Truth is, it's mostly gone from memory, and with my blessing. I can tell you the doctor returned—Nickles—and insisted on hospitalization, never mind the chance of flu. For a few days, perhaps a week, they braced me up with pillows and Adrenalin; then Nickles released me to Dad, saying, "You take this boy home."

By now there was no question of Roxanna's not coming. By my release her animals were at a neighboring ranch, a classified ad was in the nearest weekly, and a sign saying CLOSED stood out by the gas pumps. We left before daylight next morning. I recall she betrayed no sadness in parting from the place. She got in the Plymouth, leaned back to plump blankets around Swede and me, then flounced up beside Dad in a most girlish motion. It occurred to me that this leaving—which to me ached with failure and despair—was for her a gallant endeavor. Adhering to us must've seemed a risk demanding the deepest reserves of joy and strength. She settled into the freezing Plymouth, humming a dance tune. She opened a thermos of coffee, which steamed in the glow from the dash. She was all but our mother now. I shut my eyes and slept.

We came into Roofing midafternoon as school was letting out. We drove past in silence. Swede and I knew every one of those kids walking home or bunching up in front yards, yet we slouched in the car, unwilling to be seen. They all seemed so little changed.

The house was warm and clean, thanks to Dr. and Mrs. Nokes, whom Dad had telephoned long-distance. The Nokeses boarded Roxanna. Then Swede and I put in a few days at the Nokeses' after the ceremony—Swede writing some verse it embarrassed me to listen to, all about doves in the nest and moonbeams falling, as though something had happened to her mind.

Abruptly we crated our possessions and pulled them seven miles north to a red farm on a hilltop. It had belonged to Pastor Reach's great-aunt Myrtle, who had died in deepest January at the age of a hundred and two. The farm went to Pastor, who'd offered it to us at preposterous rent, at least until Dad found work.

It was a lovely place, the red farm. So called because house, barn, roost, and granary have been painted brick red to the furthest reaches of local memory, it seemed a place of order and rest. In coming years it would prove a paradise of work and exploration, but when we moved in, it was a place to rest and to wait.

Because we were waiting—all of us, I believe, though my sense of it may have been strongest. The beast in my lungs kept me tied close. I remembered Dr. Nickles's inflection when he told Dad to take me home; also the look they exchanged. Swede returned alone to school. Days passed during which I didn't leave the window seat overlooking the meadow. The infirm wait always, and know it.

We waited foremost for word of Davy. With the disappearance of Mr. Andreeson the hunt gained untold federal impetus. For months an irregular stream of investigators came knocking, asking mostly the same questions and once in a while a new one: Was Davy especially strong in mathematics? Had he frequented the movies? Had we acquaintances in South America?

Andreeson, by the way, stayed missing. What happened to him is no secret, for I revealed my conviction repeatedly: Waltzer put him in the vein of burning lignite that ran past the cabin. It used to wake me, sweating—the truth of it glowing inside my bones. Yet the investigators who listened to the idea seemed to give it little credit, which frustrated me until I complained about it to Swede.

"There's no proving it. There's nothing in it for them," she said, disappearing before I could grouse further.

Because this, you understand, was something else I was waiting for—Swede's forgiveness.

She wasn't nasty; that wasn't it. Plainly the fact had dawned: As compadres go, I wasn't trustworthy. Of course I tried to win her back—wondering aloud whether we might get a horse now that we lived on a farm, or asking about some adventure of Sunny's. To none of it would she rise.

One night in deep contrition I went to her room. "Swede," said I when she opened the door, "can't you ever forgive me?"

"Sure," she replied.

"Well, I wish you would. You act like I'm some old leper."

"All right—you tell me how to act, and I'll act that way."

Can a person be both penitent and furious? "Swede, please!"

"You're forgiven," she said, but in a voice still miles removed and with eyes still regarding me as an abstract thing.

ONE THING I WASN'T WAITING for was a miracle. The well appeared dry. Though begrudging Roxanna nothing, neither could I recall a single wonder arriving through Dad's hands since we banged on her door that first Sunday. Blanketed in my window seat, I puzzled it through, concluding that God, feeling overworked on our behalf, had given us Roxanna as a parting gift—just what we'd always wanted, but accompanied by the end of the miraculous. Was it unjust? I'd have thought so not long before, but these activities— whining about what's fair, begging forgiveness, hoping for a miracle—these demand energy, and that was gone from me. Contentment on the other hand demands little, and I drew more and more into its circle. It seemed good to sleep. My clothes got slack and hangy. Mornings I watched the deer that came up through the hardwoods to paw the snow by the corncrib. Evenings Dad played the guitar, and the hymns and ballads and antique waltzes seemed all the marvels I required.

In May the Orchard family came with a blueberry pie. Bethany carried it in, the first I'd seen her since she fed me an orange with her fingers. She wore a dusk-blue dress and had ripened to a supremacy that scotched conversation. It wasn't her fault. She asked how Davy was doing and what it was like riding a horse in the Badlands. I gave it an abbreviated try, but I saw that her interest was nominal and engendered by my lousy health, and anyway my voice had become a spare, unpleasant sound.

Now, it may be Swede spied on this most humble talk. Maybe she even had some notion where Bethany had stood inside my untaught thinking. I only know that when evening came, she slipped under my blanket on the couch, listening to Dad working up some thankful psalm. She sat beside me cross-legged, like a Sioux, and held my hand again, as though we would wait together for whatever was moving toward us. At that moment there was nothing half worth my sister's pardon. Listening to Dad's guitar, halting yet lovely in the search for phrasing, I thought, Fair is whatever God wants to do.

On a wide purple evening in June, a '41 Ford drove up to the red farm. We were all on the porch and so share this memory among us.

The car was covered with pale dust and jounced slowly right to the house and stopped. Then Swede squealed and flew off those steps, for Davy was standing from the Ford, laughing and genuine before our eyes, scooping Swede up, and as we knotted round, he said, "Wait, wait," and the other door opened, and Sara also stood out, one hand atop the car as though she might duck back in. How could she foresee the warmth awaiting? How predict the radiant comfort that was Roxanna's gift? What I remember is clutching my brother's side as we walked up the porch and Swede's feet scissoring in the air, and I remember a strange melodic sound that was Sara's laugh as she entered the house, and I hoped to hear it more.

And did—much more, as you will see. Though neither of them said Waltzer's name, what had transpired was clear enough to me: The man decided Sara had been his daughter long enough. I could shut my eyes and see him. He wanted a wife.

You think my brother Davy would've let that happen?

So they bolted one morning—just five days previous—in a car Jape had bought in Wyoming, where they landed after fleeing the Badlands. Having no better opportunity than Jape stretching his legs, they "motored on out of *that* frying pan," Davy said, the wicked old maxim evidently not worrying him at the time.

"I thought," he added, "maybe Sara could stay with you."

"Of course, and welcome," said Roxanna.

"What about you? Are *you* staying?" Swede asked. Having weaseled onto his lap, she wasn't about to throw him easy ones.

"I can't," he replied. "You know that, Swede." He looked, right then, for the first time in years, his age, which was seventeen.

Back home, he was our leader again, however briefly. He told us details on demand—of meanders alone or with troubled companions, meals rendered almost mannalike in hard circumstances, narrow spots departed in the nick of time. He was expansive and good at the telling. Despite the hour, Roxanna served juice, brewed coffee. Yet he mostly kept quiet about Waltzer, out of consideration, it seemed, for Sara. She'd lived with the man for years, after all. She owed him little, but not nothing.

Davy did allow they'd had a hard scrape getting out of the Badlands cabin. He and Sara had scratched a checkerboard on the dirt floor and were outwaiting the blizzard when Waltzer rode up, his nostrils iced, his eyes prophetic. A vision had come to him out of the snow—a glimpse of horse soldiers. He feared staying put. Following the vein of smoking lignite, he'd arrived at a capacious hole in the native sandstone. He brooked no complaint but packed the horses and drove Davy and Sara toward it. Here they all spent a whole day and more, sitting in the cold. The wind died; the sky cleared. Once, they heard a rifle shot far off. Dusk of the second day, Waltzer sent Davy to scout. The cabin was full of boot marks, the snow around it sacked with hoof tracks and horse manure.

Not one of us asked about Andreeson, though he lit on my heart, staying there like a guest on the porch you hope will give up and leave.

Sara was asleep in her straight-backed chair. It was past eleven. When Dad went upstairs to see about her room, I tagged along.

"It's great, isn't it, Dad?" I asked. The truth is, I could've wept, such sadness hung about us. I fought it back.

"Why, of course it is, Rube. Here, grab the corner." He spread a spare blanket on Sara's bed and shook up the pillow. He wound an old clock on the bedside stand, remarking on the hour.

"Do we have to go to bed, Dad? Can't we stay up?"

He held out his arm toward me, and I went and put my head against his chest. He felt strong and thin—I could feel his pulse in my ear. He said, "Well, of course, stay up—unless Davy wants to sleep. Then we'll let him be, right?"

I nodded. It should have been the best of nights.

Downstairs, we found the others subdued as well. Roxanna sleepwalked Sara to bed and turned in also. Dad asked Davy would he rest, and Davy replied no, he'd be going shortly. Repairing to the front room, we doused lights and sat while the moon rode up over the farm. Strangely, we talked little of present quandaries. There was no speculation on Davy's plans. Andreeson hovered but was not mentioned. Davy said he sure liked Roxanna; he was happy for us all. They talked about Sara, where she'd come from. Then conversation dove and resurfaced in history, picking up happenings from the great long ago like curiosities from a ruin. Davy remembered the time a red fox came toward us as we lay in a fencerow awaiting geese. As Davy recalled, I stood and would've tottered out to meet this doglike and sorrowful spook, but Dad put me behind his back and shot it.

It was deepest night. I remember Davy's shape in the stuffed chair next to the window: clean map of chin and cheekbone. After some silence he rose and stood close to the glass. A herd of deer were crossing the meadow. "Well," Davy said.

Then Swede, desperate to keep him and honor him, begged that he wait. Off she ran, returning with her tousled binder. She turned on a lamp and read aloud all there was of Sundown, beginning to end. Davy loved it all, Sunny's doleful intervals as well as his triumphs. He was particularly attentive to her treatment of Valdez, whom he said was exactly right: savage, random, wolflike—and also probably uncatchable, right down through time. Though, he amended quickly, if anyone living were up to the job, Sundown was that man.

We had him till dawn. By then Roxanna had got up and baked her great-uncle's rolls, which Davy ate with energy to be envied, given no sleep. Finishing up, we cleared our throats and armored our hearts and stepped out into the sunrise.

JAPE Waltzer was sitting beside the granary with a rifle. He'd simply picked a spot—in view of the house and shaded from morning sun—and sat still. He'd even entered the barn and retrieved an old chair to ease the wait.

I am haunted yet by his patience in this business.

Davy was standing by the car fishing for keys when Dad fell across the hood, his forehead smacking like an echo of the shot. From the porch I spotted Waltzer sighting through smoke. He fired, and the Ford's backdoor windows sprayed across the gravel. As Dad skidded off the hood to flop by the front wheel, Roxanna tugged me backward to the door. I heard Dad murmuring, broke Roxanna's hold, and flung down off the porch.

I suppose Jape led me, like a flaring goose.

What I recall isn't pain but a sense of jarring reversal, as of all motion, sound, and light encountering their massive opposites. I felt dirt against my cheek, and sorrow that Dad was shot, and confusion that I couldn't reach him.

Here my terrestrial witness fails.

I shut my eyes, the old *morte* settled its grip, and the next country gathered itself under my feet.

I WADED ashore with measureless relief. Stay with me now. The bank was a slope of waving knee-high grasses, and I came up into them and turned to look back. It was a wide river, mistakable for a lake unless you'd been wading and knew its current. Somehow I'd crossed it and somehow was unsurprised.

At that moment I had no notion of identity. Nor of burden. The meadow hummed as though thick with nests, and the grasses were canyon-colored, lifting their heads as I passed. Up scattered finches, and cheeky longspurs, and every sort of bunting and bobolink and piebald tanager. Butterflies—monarchs, tailed lunas, and others of such spread and hue as to have long disappeared from the gardens of the world. The meadow was layered with flight. In fact it seemed there was nothing that couldn't take wing. Seized with conviction, I spread my arms and ran for it. At times my feet were only brushing the ground.

But I was drawn on. Conscious now that something needed doing, I moved ever higher on the land, here entering an orchard of immense and archaic beauty. All the trees were heavy-trunked and capaciously limbed. Apples, gold-skinned apricots, immaculate pears. The leaves were thick and cool. Touched with a finger, they imparted a palpable rhythm.

It took a long while to traverse the orchard. I began to feel hungry but didn't pause. I felt prodded to appear before the master. The place had a master! I knew he was already aware of me—

comforting and fearful knowledge. I pressed ahead as if obeying a beloved command. I weaved amid curly-horn antelope and bison browsing fruit from the lower branches, through an enormous unwary herd of horses pulling up clover and bluegrass.

Far across a valley I saw a man afoot. His skin was dark, and he wore the buckler and helm of a Spanish knight, and over his shoulder he carried a flag of arcane device. Though battered in appearance, the man moved with spirit. He was like one going to his king, having served to his deepest ability. He was almost running.

And now, from beneath the audible, came a low reverberation. It came up through the soles of my feet. The pulse of the country worked through my body until I recognized it as music. As language. And the language ran everywhere inside me, like blood, and a verse blazed to mind: *O be quick, my soul, to answer Him; be jubilant, my feet!* And sure enough my soul leapt dancing inside my chest, and my feet sprang up and sped me forward, and the pulse of the country came around me, as of voices lifted at great distance, and moved through me as I ran, until the words came clear and I sang with them a beautiful and curious chant.

And now the orchard ended, and a plain reached far ahead to a range of blanched mountains. A stream coursed through this plain. A narrow, raucous stream, it flowed upward against the gradient, and mighty fish arced and swam in it, flinging manes of spray.

Another figure appeared, running upslope beside the water. A man in pants. Flapping colorless pants and a shirt, dismal things most strange in this place. Despite the clothes, his face was incandescent, and when he saw me, he wheeled his arms and came on ever faster. Then history entered me—my own and all the rest of it, more than I could hold, history like a heavy rain—so that I knew the man coming along was my father, Jeremiah Land.

He was beside me in moments, stretching out his hands. What cabled strength! I remember wondering what those arms were made for. No mere reward, they had design in them. They had some work to set about. Meantime Dad was laughing—at my arms, which were similarly strong! He sang out, *You're as big as me!* How had I not noticed? We were like two friends, and I saw he was proud of me, that he knew me better than he'd ever thought to and was not dismayed by the knowledge; and even as I wondered at his ageless face, so clear and at home, his eyes owned up to some small regret, for he knew a thing I didn't.

Let's run, he said. It's true both of us were wild to go on. I tell you, there is no one who compels as does the master of that country. Dad shot ahead like a man who sees all that pleases him most stacked beside the finish, then held back so that we traveled together, he sometimes reaching for my hand as he'd done a thousand times in the past, and the music and living language swept us forth until the mountains lay ahead and up we climbed.

We attained a pass where the stream sang louder than ever, for it swelled with depth and energy the farther it rose. Dad reached it first. I saw him mount a shelf of spray-soaked stone and stand waiting for me, backlighted, silver-lined as though by the sun.

But it wasn't the sun. It was a city.

Joining Dad on the rock, I saw it, at a farther distance than any yet conceived. Still it threw light our sun could only covet. And the longer you looked, the more you saw. Dad pointed below, at movement I took to be rivers—winding, flowing, light coming off them. They came from all directions, streaming toward the city, and dust rose along their banks.

They're people, Dad said. And looking again, I could see them on the march, pouring forth from vast distances—whole tributaries of people, some with untamed faces you would fear in neighbors, and even these were singing a hymn that rose up to us on the mountain, and it was as though they marched in preparation for some imminent and joyous and sanctified war.

We listened a long time. Dad held my hand, and I felt the music growing in his fingers.

Take care of Swede, he said.

From this pass the stream threw itself over a sheer face, where mist drifted up and was struck gold by the light of the city.

Work for Roxanna, Dad told me.

Now I saw the stream regrouped below, flowing alongside the rivers of people, a silver wire winding toward the city.

I thought, Lord, can't I be among them? Can't I come in too?

Tell Davy, Dad said. He sat down on the rock and swung his feet into the stream. It was deep and swift; it would take him in a moment. I seized his arm.

Please, I said.

Soon, he replied, which makes better sense under the rules of that country than ours. *Very soon!* he added, clasping my hands. Then, unable to keep from laughing, he pushed off from the rock like a boy going for the first cold swim of spring, and the current got him. The stream was singing aloud, and I heard him singing with it until he dropped away over the edge.

THE excitement didn't quit while I was away: Jape Waltzer fired three more unhurried rounds at the Ford, where Davy was burrowed in the back seat. He also plugged the house a few times. Windows blew all over the main floor, and one load came straight through the wall into the living room. Amid this ruin Roxanna called the sheriff, Dr. Nokes, and the Lord, doubtless in the opposite order, and shouted at the girls to stay down. But Swede was busy ripping Dad's closet half to shreds, hunting his shotgun. She found it, but no shells. By then the Ford was gone and Davy with it. Waltzer's chair lay tipped in the shade beside the barn.

Dad was propped on an elbow on the gravel, bleeding from a hole in his right side. I was on my face in the lee of the porch.

Here's what I've been told of the next few minutes. Roxanna attended to Dad while Swede pushed me over and explored for heartbeats. Nine years old. Kneeling in blood and foam, she grabbed my wrist, my neck; she felt the big dripping cave of my chest. Dad, tired but lucid, told Roxanna to quit stanching the hole in his side. When she pressed too hard, he couldn't breathe. Let it flow, he told her. Let the blood wash it clean. It put Roxanna in an awful bind. She prayed aloud, wrapping her fist in her dress and jamming it into that wound, Dad coming in and out the while. Then the sound of Swede crying registered on Dad, and she went to him covered in pink froth, so that he started up, thinking she was dying. But she told him it was me. I wasn't breathing. And right about here Dr. Nokes drove up.

His best turned out to be no better than Roxanna's. Ascertaining that I was gone—for my lungshot chest no longer bled, no rhythm moved anywhere, and I lay cooling under his hands—Dr. Nokes turned to Dad, who looked him over without evident recognition and rolled up his eyes. By the time a county car rolled in, there was an atmosphere of crystalline despair in which the doctor broke and sobbed. Through this scene stepped the sheriff and a deputy, yet before an official word was spoken, the deputy yipped, "Look there!" For I had bucked suddenly, as though kicked in the back. And then, reports Swede, I was seized with coughing, and blood and water spouted from my mouth, and Dr. Nokes bolted to my side in a sort of delirium. It was hardly the first time I'd come awake to someone whacking my back, but it seemed a wholly new experience, one I'd come a great distance to try.

"I DON'T know what you were using to breathe," Dr. Nokes told me. It was some weeks later, and he was beside my bed at the red farm. "Not your lungs," he declared.

At first I didn't know what he meant. My lungs felt as large and light as a May afternoon. They felt like they had in the next country, as I ran up through the orchard—except over there I hadn't given them a thought. Back here I woke each morning to the shock of perfect breathing. Had I opened my mouth and spoken Portuguese, the surprise couldn't have been more complete.

For weeks there wasn't a day Dr. Nokes didn't come by. Though professing worry over the chance of infection or of some undissolved clot cruising my arteries, he came for other reasons also. He came so we could miss Dad together, all of us.

One day he said, "Your father should not have died, Reuben. Not just because it's terrible to be without him—" And here Dr. Nokes seemed to slip somewhere in his mind, then catch himself. "I mean, injured where he was. No organs were damaged. He actually shouldn't have died."

And I, conversely, shouldn't have lived. Though I sensed this was the case, it was only years later that Dr. Nokes would explain why. What eleven-year-old should be told that his lungs only recently lay in literal shreds inside his central cavity? Dr. Nokes saw this with his two eyes. Yet mere hours later it was revealed at the hospital in Montrose that my lungs had not only endured an explosive chest wound but in fact seemed as though they hadn't been touched.

Of course they had been touched; that was the very point.

Goodness, I miss Dad.

But here, let me finish quickly. You should know that Roxanna, married to Jeremiah Land three months, became as much our rock as though God himself had placed her beneath our lives. Certainly her sacrifice was no less than Dad's. Who could've poured more courage into us? We were a demanding crew. Sara herself could've emptied the stores of a dozen wise parents. Oh yes—Sara stayed with us, though at a distance she'd acquired living with Waltzer. For many months none but Roxanna closed the distance, and she on tiptoe.

Swede, whom you know reasonably well by now, quit school in frustration at seventeen to write a novel. It didn't publish but won her a sort of watchful uncle at a venerable New York publishing house. Now—after four novels, a history of the Dakota Territories, and a collection of poetry—she gets adoring letters from strangers. Her poetry all rhymes! Reviewers could only gape. One wrote that she was "setting verse back a century" and impelled Swede's poetry onto several bestseller lists.

You should know that Jape Waltzer proved as uncatchable as Valdez. Maybe Waltzer's dead, prancing across some pockmarked landscape trying to keep the flames off, or maybe he's just old, and a more sulfurous poison than before. Maybe he's even old and repentant. I only know he is apart from us, and that, as Mr. Stevenson wrote of Long John, we're pleased to be quit of him.

You should know that Andreeson did indeed perish in the Badlands, and that it was Waltzer who bludgeoned him and rolled his poor corpse into the lignite to hiss. Having this information from Davy, I could hardly volunteer it officially.

Finally, you should know this: One Thanksgiving we were all of us home, all but Davy. Swede had returned from a writing residency in Wyoming, Sara from nursing in St. Paul. I was working for a carpenter in Roofing, putting up Sheetrock and a little proud of my big shoulders. We held hands round the table for a prayer of gratitude. When Roxanna reached amen, Swede released my left hand, but Sara held on to my right.

Or maybe it was I who didn't let go.

AND Davy? Listen: There's a small town in Canada, a prairie town, a place along the broad North American flyway where in autumn the geese move through by the hundreds of thousands. Since August Shultz died—following Birdie by two hard winters—I've gone north to witness that migration. The glory of a single Canada goose gliding in, trimming its angles this way and that, so close you can feel the pressure of its wingbeats—multiply this by ten or twenty thousand across a morning, and you too might begin creeping into frozen rock piles before dawn. In any case, once, I rose in the small hours and walked down from my rented bed to a pine-bench café full of hunters sociably forking down eggs by five in the morning. What I wanted was pancakes and sausage, so I ordered and took a clean cup and helped myself to coffee.

Davy came in before my short stack arrived. He wore a down jacket and lace-up boots. He sat down. "You hunting alone, Rube?"

It's not the easiest way to keep up with your brother. Some years he coasts into that town in my shadow. He's the next man in the café, the voice behind me at the gas station. Some years he doesn't show at all. Exile has its hollow hours. Some years I've noticed odd tilts in his speech. No doubt he has lived among accents, I hope in pleasant places, but he tells me painfully little. He asks and asks.

So I give him the news. He reads all of Swede's work. He sends regards and comments. It drives her wild. Twice Swede has accompanied me, hoping to see him, neither time with success.

Possibly he dreads what she might ask of him.

"You got awfully big," he told me that first morning in the café.

So I told him what happened—about my foray into the next country. Belief is a hard thing to gauge where Davy is concerned.

"And Dad sent you back?"

I told him he didn't exactly send me, but that I could go no farther. That it seemed a transaction had taken place on my behalf.

"Breathe," Davy said. "Let's see you breathe."

Well, that was the easy part. Harder was describing that land itself—its upward-running river, its people on the move and ground astir with song. For just as that music stays outside the pattern I would give it, so does my telling fall pitifully short of what the place is. And so I sound like a man describing a dream.

"Don't you ever doubt it?" Davy asked.

And in fact I have. And perhaps will again. But here is what happens. I look out the window at the red farm—for here we live, Sara and I, in a new house across the meadow, a house built by capable arms and open lungs and joyous sweat. Maybe I see our daughter, home from school, picking plums or apples for Roxanna; maybe one of our sons, reading on the grass or painting an upended canoe. Or maybe Sara comes into the room—my darling Sara—with Mr. Cassidy's beloved rolls on a steaming plate. Then I breathe deeply, and certainty enters into me like light, like a piece of science, and curious music seems to hum inside my fingers.

Is there a single person on whom I can press belief?

No sir. All I can do is say, Here's how it went. Here's what I saw. I've been there and am going back.

Make of it what you will.

LEIF ENGER

Leif Enger wrote Peace Like a River *to read to his sons.*

Leif Enger fondly recalls the evenings of his youth in rural Minnesota when his father read to him from the heroic stories and poems of Robert Louis Stevenson. Now a father of two sons, Ty and John, Enger set out to write a book that he could read to them. Out of that sentiment comes the rhapsodic novel *Peace Like a River,* with its echoes of Stevenson and the outlaw sagas of western folklore.

A reporter/producer for Minnesota Public Radio since 1984, Enger has covered a wide variety of subjects, ranging from Bulgarian sailors and Indian fishing rights to the endangered mince pie and the restoration of antique prairie windmills. His first venture into fiction led to a series of crime novels co-written with his brother, Lin, in the early 1990s. That experience allowed Enger to later claim the distinction of having five books out of print before he was forty years old. This, his first literary novel, has already attracted considerable attention and acclaim.

Enger and his wife, Robin, live with their sons on a farm in Aitkin, Minnesota.

To read an exclusive interview with Leif Enger,
visit the Select Editions website:

ReadersOnly.com
Password: *today*

SUE GRAFTON

P

Is for Peril

Dark clouds are hanging over
Santa Teresa, California,
and Kinsey Millhone
is about to get caught
in the downpour.

1

THE house on Old Reservoir Road appeared to be in the final phases of construction. I spotted the site as I rounded the curve, recognizing the unfinished structure from Fiona Purcell's description. To my right I could see a portion of the reservoir for which the road was named. Brunswick Lake fills the bottom of a geological bowl, a spring-fed body that supplied the town with drinking water for many years. In 1953 a second, larger catch basin was established, and now Brunswick is little more than an irregular blue splotchlet on maps of the area. Swimming and boating are forbidden, but migrating waterbirds rest on the placid surface while they make their way south. The surrounding hills are austere, gentle swells rising to the mountains that mark the northernmost boundary of the Santa Teresa city limits.

I parked my VW on the gravel berm and crossed the two-lane road. The steeply pitched lot was still bare of landscaping and consisted of raw dirt and boulders. A small grove of signs planted in the yard announced the names of the building contractor, the painting contractor, and the architect, though Mrs. Purcell had been quick to assure me by phone that she'd drawn up the plans herself. The design—if that's what you want to call it—could have been approved by the Department of Defense: an implacable series of concrete boxes stacked up against the hillside under a pale November sun. Somewhere to the rear of the house there must have been a driveway leading to garages and a parking pad, but I opted for the stairs built into the barren hillside. At six a.m. I'd done a three-mile jog, but I'd skipped my Friday morning weight lifting to keep this early appointment. It was just now eight o'clock, and I could feel my butt dragging as I mounted the steps.

Behind me I could hear a dog bark. Its deep-throated yaps echoed throughout the canyon. A woman was calling, "Trudy! Truuddy!" while the dog barked on. She emitted a piercing whistle, and a young German shepherd came bounding over the hill and sprinted off. I continued climbing Fiona's wide concrete steps, tacking twice before I reached the upper terrace with its plain limestone portico that shaded the front entrance. By then I was huffing and puffing. I turned, pretending to admire the view while I recovered my breath. From this aerie I could see the broad gray band of the Pacific Ocean stitched to the shoreline some five miles away.

By the time I rang the bell, my breathing had slowed and I'd done a quick review of the subject I was here to discuss. Fiona Purcell's ex-husband, Dr. Dowan Purcell, had been missing for nine weeks, since Friday, September 12. She'd had a messenger deliver a manila envelope filled with newspaper clippings that recapped events surrounding his disappearance. I'd sat in my office, tilted back in my swivel chair, my Sauconys propped on the edge of my desk, while I studied the articles she'd sent. I'd been following the story in the local papers, but I'd never anticipated my involvement in the case.

Dr. Purcell, sixty-nine years old, had practiced family medicine in Santa Teresa since 1944, specializing in geriatrics for the last fifteen years. He'd retired in 1981. Six months later he'd been licensed as the administrator of a nursing-care facility called Pacific Meadows, which was owned by two businessmen. On the Friday night in question he'd worked late.

According to witnesses, it was close to nine o'clock when he paused at the front desk and said good night to the nurses on duty.

At that hour the occupants had settled down for the night, and the corridors were empty. Dr. Purcell had paused to chat with an elderly woman sitting in the lobby in her wheelchair. After a cursory conversation—less than a minute by her report—the doctor passed through the front door and into the night. He retrieved his car from his reserved space at the north side of the complex, pulled out of the lot, and drove off into the inky void from which he'd never emerged. The Santa Teresa Police Department and the Santa Teresa County Sheriff's Department had devoted endless hours to the case, and I couldn't think what avenues remained that hadn't already been explored by local law enforcement.

I rang the bell again. Fiona Purcell had told me she was on her way out of town, a five-day trip to San Francisco to purchase furniture and antiques for a client of her interior design firm. According to the papers, Fiona and the doctor had been divorced for years. Idly I was wondering why she'd been the one who called me instead of his current wife, Crystal.

When she opened the door, I saw that she was already dressed for travel in a double-breasted pin-striped suit. She held a hand out. "Ms. Millhone? Fiona Purcell. Sorry to make you wait. I was at the back of the house. Please come in."

"Thanks. You can call me Kinsey if you like."

We shook hands, and I moved into the entrance hall. I placed her in her late sixties, close to Dr. Purcell's age. She had thinly arched brows and dark smudged eyes, with pronounced streaks of weariness descending from the inner corners. Her hair was dyed a dark brown, parted on one side, with puffy bangs and clusters of artificially constructed curls pulled away from her face and secured by rhinestone combs—a style affected by glamour-girl movie stars of the 1940s. She was saying, "We can talk in the living room. You'll have to pardon the mess."

Scaffolding had been erected in the foyer, reaching to the lofty ceiling. Drop cloths lined the stairs and the wide corridor leading to the rear of the house.

"Your flight's at ten?" I asked.

"Don't worry about it. I'm eight minutes from the airport. We have at least an hour. May I offer you coffee?"

"No, thanks. I've had two cups this morning, and that's my limit."

Fiona moved to the right, and I followed her, crossing a broad expanse of bare cement. I said, "When do the floors go in?"

"These *are* the floors."

I said, "Ah," and made a mental note to quit asking about matters far beyond my ken.

The interior of the house had the cool, faintly damp smell of plaster and fresh paint. All the walls were dazzling white, the windows tall and stark, unadorned by curtains or drapes.

In the living room, Fiona gestured toward one of two matching armchairs, chunky and oversized, upholstered in a neutral-toned fabric that blended with the gray cement floor. A large area rug showed a densely woven grid of black lines on gray. I sat when she did. The furnishings were striking: light wood, tubular steel, stark geometric shapes. A tall silver-and-ivory coffeepot, with a matching creamer and sugar bowl, sat on a silver tray on the beveled-glass coffee table. She refilled her cup, then paused to light a cigarette.

She said, "I don't think I mentioned this when we chatted the other day, but Dana Jaffe suggested I get in touch with you."

"Really. How do you know her?"

"She's now married to one of Dow's associates, Joel Glazer. Do you know Joel? He's partners in a company called Century Comprehensive that owns a chain of nursing homes."

"I know the name Glazer from the papers. I've never met him," I said. Her call was beginning to make sense, though I still wasn't sure how I could be of service. Dana Jaffe's first husband, Wendell, had disappeared in 1979, though the circumstances—on the surface—were very different from the current case. Wendell Jaffe was a self-made real estate tycoon who'd faked his own death, showing up in Mexico shortly after his "widow" had collected half a million dollars in life insurance benefits. He'd been spotted in Mexico by a former acquaintance, and I'd been dispatched by the insurance company, who wanted their money back. I wondered if Fiona suspected her ex-husband had pulled a fast one as well.

She set her coffee cup aside. "You received the articles?"

"A messenger dropped them off at the office yesterday. I read them last night. The police have been thorough. . . ."

"Or so they'd like us to think."

"You're not happy with their progress?"

"Progress! What progress? Dowan is still missing. I'll tell you what they've accomplished. Zilch."

I objected to her attitude but decided not to protest just yet. I think the cops are terrific, but why argue the point? She wanted to hire me, and I was here to determine what, if anything, I could contribute. "What's the latest?" I asked.

"No one's heard a peep from him, at least as far as I've been told." She lowered her eyes. "You realize we're divorced."

"There was reference to that in one of the articles. What about his current wife?"

"I've only spoken to Crystal once throughout this whole ordeal. She's gone to great lengths to keep me out of the loop. I receive updates through my daughters, who've made it a point to stay in close touch with her."

"You have two girls?"

"Correct. My youngest, Blanche, and her husband are only four blocks away. Melanie, the older one, lives in San Francisco. I'll be staying with her 'til Tuesday afternoon of next week."

"Any grandchildren?"

"Mel's never been married. Blanche is expecting her fifth."

I said, "Wow."

"Motherhood's her way of avoiding a real job."

"A 'real' job sounds easier. I couldn't do what she does."

"She barely manages herself. Fortunately, the children have a nanny who's extremely competent."

"How do your daughters get along with Crystal?"

"Fine, I suppose. Then again, what choice do they have? If they don't dance to her tune, she'll make sure they never see their father or their half brother again. You know Dow and Crystal have a son? His name is Griffith. He just turned two."

"I remember mention of the boy. May I call you Fiona?"

She took another drag of her cigarette. "I'd prefer Mrs. Purcell, if it's all the same to you."

"Very well. I'm wondering if you have a theory about your ex-husband's disappearance?"

"You're one of the few who's even bothered to ask. Apparently, my opinion is of no concern. I suspect he's in Europe or South America, biding his time until he's ready to come home. Crystal thinks he's dead—or so I've heard."

"It's not so far-fetched. According to the papers, there's been no activity on his credit cards. There's been no sign of his car and no sign of him."

"Well, that's not quite true. There've been a number of reports. People claim to have spotted him as far away as New Orleans and Seattle. Someone fitting Dow's description tried to cross into Canada but walked away when the immigration officer asked to see his passport—which is missing, by the way."

"Really. That's interesting. The papers didn't mention it. I take it the police have followed up?"

"One can only hope," she remarked.

"You're convinced he's alive?"

"I can't imagine otherwise. The man has no enemies, and I can't conceive of his being the victim of 'foul play,' " she said, forming the quote marks with her fingers. "The idea's absurd."

"Because?"

"Dow's perfectly capable of taking care of himself—physically, at any rate. What he's not capable of doing is facing the problems in life. He's passive. Instead of 'fight or flight,' he lies down and plays dead . . . in a manner of speaking. He'd rather do anything than deal with conflict, especially involving women. This goes back to his mother, but that's another story altogether."

"Has he done anything like this before?"

"As a matter of fact, he has, twice. The first time, Melanie and

Blanche were—what?—probably only six and three. Dowan disappeared for three weeks. He left without warning and returned much the same way."

"Where'd he go?"

"I have no idea. The second time was similar. This was years later, before we separated for good. One day he was here; the next he was gone. He came back a few weeks later without a murmur of explanation or apology. Naturally, I've assumed this recent disappearance was a repeat performance."

"What prompted his departure on those earlier occasions?"

Her gesture was vague, smoke trailing from her cigarette. "I suppose we were having problems. We usually were. One day he simply didn't come home. He'd canceled his appointments, including social engagements, all without a word to me or to anyone else. The first I became aware was when he failed to arrive for dinner. The second time was the same except I didn't go out of my mind with worry."

"So in both instances he behaved much as he did this time?"

"Exactly. The first time it took *hours* before I realized he was gone. The man's a doctor, and naturally, he was often delayed. By midnight I was wild, close to hysterical."

"You called the police?"

"I called everyone I could think of. Then first thing the next morning a note arrived in the mail. He said he'd come home eventually, which is exactly what he did. Fool that I am, I forgave him, and we went on as before. The marriage was good, or good enough from my perspective. I thought he was happy—until this business with Crystal. For all I know, he'd been fooling around with her for years."

"What made you stay?"

"I thought he was a good husband. He tended to be distant, but I didn't fault him. I might have harbored resentments, but I wasn't aware of them until he asked for the divorce. Looking back, I realize there are many ways a man can disappear."

"Such as?"

She shrugged, stubbing out her cigarette. "Television, sleep, alcohol, books, uppers, downers."

"And in his case?"

"Dow buried himself in his work. Went in early, stayed at the office until all hours of the night."

"How long were you married?"

"Close to forty years. We met at Syracuse. I majored in art history, and he was premed. We married shortly after graduation. I stayed home with the girls until they were both in school, and then I went back and got my master's in interior design. I designed the house we built soon afterward in Horton Ravine."

"He still owns that house?"

"Yes, though I've heard Crystal doesn't care for it."

"You didn't ask for the house in the settlement?"

"I couldn't afford the mortgage and upkeep. To hear him tell it, he was fleeced. Believe me, he got the better deal."

She was busy shading my perception, scoring points for her team. It seemed odd when the reason for my visit was to see if I could help search for him. Was she still in love with the man? "It must have been difficult when the marriage broke up," I murmured.

"Humiliating. Devastating. It was such a cliché. Doctor goes through a midlife crisis, leaves his middle-aged wife to take up with some whore."

The papers had had a field day with the fact that Crystal had been a stripper. Still, I questioned Fiona's use of the word "whore." Stripping, as a way of earning money, doesn't necessarily translate into hookerdom. "How did he meet her?"

"You'd have to ask her. The truth is, Dow developed an appetite for, mmm, unusual sexual practices. His hormones were off, or his anxiety levels began to climb as he aged. Whatever, once Dowan turned sixty, he began to falter. He couldn't—let's say—'perform' without stimulus. Pornography, marital aids . . . unspeakable acts that I refused even to *discuss* with him. He finally stopped pressing."

"Because he'd taken up with her?"

"Evidently. He's never admitted it, but I'm sure he went looking. It did cross my mind he'd go out and find someone willing to submit to his perverse requests."

I was secretly panting for an example, but I thought it was wiser (for once) to keep my big mouth shut. Sometimes you don't want to know what people do—or refuse to do—in private. "Did you ask for the divorce or did he?"

"He did. I was completely taken off guard. I presumed he'd get his needs met outside the marriage and keep his family intact. I never thought he'd stoop to divorce at this late stage in his life. I should have known. Dowan's weak. Not that any of us relish owning up to our mistakes, but Dow always abhorred even the *appearance* of failure."

"Meaning what?"

"Well," she said, "I suspect his relationship with Crystal is not the union of souls he'd like others to believe. Some months ago he'd heard she was screwing around on him. Better to disappear than admit he'd been cuckolded."

"Did he have any idea who it was?"

"No, but he was looking into it. After he disappeared, Dana finally confided that she'd known the whole time. The fellow is Crystal's personal trainer. His name is Clint Augustine."

I was sure I'd heard the name before, possibly in the gym where I work out.

"You believe he left because of that?"

"Yes. We had a conversation—a long talk—September tenth. This was two days before he vanished. He was dreadfully unhappy."

"He said that?"

"Not in so many words, but you don't go through forty years of marriage without learning to read between the lines."

"What occasioned the conversation?"

"He came over to the house."

"You were seeing him," I stated.

"Well, yes. Lately he'd been stopping by in the evenings to have a drink with me. That night he was exhausted. His face was *gray* with worry. When I asked what was wrong, he said the pressures at the office were driving him insane. And Crystal was no help. She's extremely narcissistic."

"Were you surprised he'd confide in you after everything he'd put you through?"

"Who else does he have? Anyway, he didn't really talk about her, but I could see the tension in his eyes."

"You're saying he had problems at home as well as at work?"

"That's right. He didn't talk specifics, but he mentioned in passing that he'd like to get away. That's the first thing I thought of when I heard he was gone."

"I assume you told the police."

"Not at first. I thought his absence was voluntary and he'd come home when he was ready. I didn't want him to be embarrassed. Leave it to Crystal to turn this into a media circus."

I could feel myself bristle. "Mrs. Purcell, he's a prominent physician, well known and loved in this community. His disappearance is bound to attract media attention. If you thought he'd gone AWOL, why didn't you speak up?"

"I felt he was entitled to his privacy," she said.

"What about all the time and money being spent on the investigation? Weren't you at all concerned about that?"

"Of course. That's why I spoke to the police," she said. "After six weeks I began to worry. I was expecting a call or a note, *some* indication he was all right. Now that nine weeks have passed, I thought it was time to take matters into my own hands."

"And now you're worried something's happened to him."

"I suppose so. That's why I decided to meet with the detective last week. Odessa was polite. He took notes. He said he'd get back to me, but that's the last I've heard. The police must be working *dozens* of other cases, which means they don't have the time or resources to devote to Dow. I said as much to Dana, and she agrees. That's why she recommended you."

"I don't know what to say. Even if we come to some agreement, I can't spend twenty-four hours a day on this any more than the police can. I have other clients, too."

"I didn't say you'd have to be exclusive."

"Even so, I'm just one person. You'd be better off with a big Los

Angeles agency, one with lots of operatives, who can fan out across the country and overseas to do this properly."

"I don't want a big L.A. agency. I want someone local who's willing to report directly to me."

"But all I'd be doing is repeating what the police have already done."

"You might have ideas they haven't thought of yet. After all, you tracked down Wendell Jaffe *years* after everyone assumed he was dead. What if there's an angle the police have overlooked?"

I was silent for a beat, staring at the floor. "I'll do what I can, but I make no promises."

"Good. We'll talk on Tuesday. Just keep track of the time you put in, and you can give me an invoice as soon as I get back." She glanced at her watch and then rose to her feet.

I stood when she did. "I'll need a retainer."

"A retainer?" She made a show of startlement, but surely she didn't do business without a written agreement and earnest money changing hands. "How much did you have in mind?"

"I charge fifty an hour or a flat four hundred a day, plus expenses, so fifteen hundred dollars should cover it for now. If you give me Melanie's address in San Francisco, I'll overnight you a contract for your signature."

She blinked as though baffled. "What if you fail to find him?"

"That's exactly the point. If I come up empty-handed, you might decide I wasn't worth the hourly wage. Once I take a case, I persevere. I'll follow the trail right out to the bitter end."

"I should hope so," she said. She crossed to an ebony-inlaid console. She removed her checkbook, returned to her chair, and sat down. "And I'm to make the check out to . . ."

"Millhone Investigations."

I watched while she dashed off a check and tore it out of the book, scarcely bothering to disguise her irritation as she handed it to me. I noticed we were bank mates, sharing the same branch of the Santa Teresa City Bank. I said, "You're upset."

"I operate on trust. Apparently, you don't."

"I've learned the hard way. It's nothing personal." I held out the check. "I can return this right now if you'd prefer."

"Just find him. I'll expect a full report the minute I get home."

DRIVING back into town, I noticed my stomach had begun to churn with anxiety. I tried to pinpoint my doubts.

1. I didn't particularly like, or trust, Fiona. She hadn't been candid with the cops, and I didn't think she was being entirely candid with me.

2. I wasn't sure I could be effective. Nine weeks had passed since Dr. Purcell was last seen. Whatever the circumstances surrounding a disappearance, the passage of time seldom works in your favor. Entering the game this late, the likelihood of my making any critical discovery was almost out of the question. Fiona did have a point in that sometimes a fresh perspective can shift the focus of an investigation. But intuition was telling me that any break in the case was going to be the result of serendipity, a term synonymous with unadulterated dumb luck.

I stopped off at McDonald's and ordered coffee and a couple of Egg McMuffins. I needed the comfort of junk food in addition to the nourishment. I munched while I drove.

I might as well take a moment here to identify myself. My name is Kinsey Millhone. I'm a licensed private investigator in Santa Teresa, California, which is ninety-five miles north of Los Angeles. I'm female, thirty-six, twice divorced, childless, and otherwise unencumbered. Aside from my car, I don't own much in the way of material possessions. My business, Millhone Investigations, consists entirely of me. I was a cop for two years early in my twenties, and through personal machinations too tedious to explain, I realized law enforcement didn't suit me. I was way too crabby and uncooperative to adjust to department regulations with all the morals clauses thrown in. I have been known to bend the rules. Plus, the uniform and the belt made my ass look wide.

Having left gainful city employment, I apprenticed myself to a two-man office of private investigators, where I put in the hours necessary to apply for my license. I've been on my own now for a good ten years—licensed, bonded, and heavily insured. A good portion of the last decade, I pursued arson and wrongful-death claims for California Fidelity Insurance—first as a bona fide employee, later as an independent contractor. We parted three years ago, in October 1983, for reasons too complicated to delineate in this brief curriculum vitae. Since then I've rented space from the law firm of Kingman and Ives, an arrangement that I now suspect is on the verge of change.

For the past year Lonnie Kingman had been complaining about the shortage of space. He'd already expanded once, taking over the entire third floor of a building he owns free and clear. He'd now purchased a second building, on lower State Street, where he intended to relocate soon. He'd found a tenant for our current digs, and the only question that remained was whether I'd go with him or find a space of my own. My requirements were modest: room for my desk, a swivel chair, my file cabinets, and a few fake plants. The problem was that everything I liked was too large or too expensive, and anything that fit my budget was either too cramped, too shabby, or too far from downtown. I spend a lot of time at the hall of records, and I like to be within walking distance of the courthouse, the police station, and the public library.

As soon as I reached the two-hundred block of East Capillo, where Lonnie's office was located, I began the usual search for a parking place. One drawback to the current building was the tiny lot attached, which held only twelve cars. Lonnie and his partner were each assigned a slot, as were their two secretaries, Ida Ruth Kenner and Jill Stahl. The remaining eight spots went to the building's other tenants, so the rest of us were forced to ferret out parking where we could. Today I nosed my way into a short length of curb between two commercial driveways I could have sworn was almost legal. It was only later I discovered I'd been ticketed.

I walked the five blocks to the office, climbed the requisite two flights of stairs, and let myself into the suite through an unmarked side door. I crossed the interior hallway to my office, unlocked the door, and stepped in, carefully avoiding Ida Ruth and Jill, who were deep in conversation a short distance away. I knew the subject matter would be the same one they'd been debating for the past two months. Lonnie's partner, John Ives, had suggested they hire his niece, Jeniffer, who was eighteen and a recent high school graduate. This was her first paid position, and despite a lengthy written job description, she seemed thoroughly perplexed about what was expected of her. She showed up in T-shirts and miniskirts, her long blond hair hanging down to her waist, legs bare, her feet shoved into wood-soled clogs. Her phone voice was chirpy, her spelling was atrocious, and she couldn't seem to get the hang of coming in on time.

I put a call through to the Santa Teresa Police Department and asked to speak to Detective Odessa. He was in a meeting, but the woman who took my call said he'd be free in a bit. I made an appointment for ten thirty. I filled in a boilerplate contract and slipped it into an Express Mail envelope that I addressed to Fiona in care of Melanie's home in San Francisco.

At 10:25, I locked the office and walked over to the post office, then continued to the police station, which was four blocks away. The morning air was chilly, and the earlier pale sunlight had faded as the sky clouded over with the first hint of rain.

The small lobby at the police station seemed cozy by comparison. I moved to the L-shaped counter, where I told a uniformed officer of my appointment, and he relayed the information to Detective Odessa's desk by phone. "He'll be right out."

Detective Odessa opened the door and stuck his head around the frame. "Ms. Millhone?"

"That's me."

"Vince Odessa," he said, and we shook hands. "Come on back."

I said, "Thanks."

He held the door, allowing me to pass in front of him. He wore a blue dress shirt, a dark tie, chinos, and shiny black shoes. His hair was dark, and the back of his head was flat, as though he'd slept on his back for his entire infancy. He was taller than I, probably five feet nine to my five feet six. He walked ahead of me, and I followed him through a door marked INVESTIGATIONS. Over his shoulder he said, "Shelly mentioned this was in regard to Dr. Purcell."

"That's right. His ex-wife hired me to look into his disappearance."

Odessa kept his tone neutral. "I had a feeling that was coming. She was in here last week."

"What'd you make of her?"

"I'll have to take the Fifth."

His "office" was tucked into a standard cubicle: shoulder-high gray walls carpeted in a tight synthetic loop. He took a seat at his desk, offering me the only other chair in the compact space. Framed photos of his family were arranged in front of him: wife, three daughters, and a son. His dark brows were fierce over dark blue eyes. "So what can I help you with?"

"I'm not sure. I'd love to hear what you have, if you're willing to share."

"I got no problem with that," he said. He leaned forward, checking through a stack of thick files on one side of his desk. He pulled a three-ring binder from the bottom of the pile, then leafed through numerous pages to the initial incident report. "I just got this promotion. I'm junior man on the team, so this is a training exercise as far as they're concerned. Let's see what we got." His gaze zigzagged along the page. "Crystal Purcell filed a missing persons Tuesday, sixteen September, seventy-two hours after the doctor failed to arrive home as scheduled. Records took the information. As far as we could determine, Purcell wasn't 'at risk,' and there was nothing suspicious about the circumstances of his disappearance." He paused to look at me. "Tell you the truth, we figured he'd gone off on his own. You know how it is. Half the time the guy shows up later with his tail between his legs. Turns out he's got a girlfriend, or he's been off on a bender with the boys somewhere."

He leaned back in his chair. "I called the current Mrs. Purcell and made an appointment for Friday afternoon, September nineteen. Frankly, I stalled, assuming she'd hear something."

"Which she didn't."

"Not then and not since. From what she says, he wasn't suffering any physical condition that raised a flag on that score. She said she'd called and talked to him at the office—this was Friday, twelve September, shortly after lunch. Purcell told her he'd be late, but there was no mention of his not coming home at all. By Saturday morning she was frantic, calling everyone she knew—friends, relatives, his colleagues. Hospitals, California Highway Patrol, the morgue—you name it. There was no sign of him.

"I sat with her for an hour. This was at the house in Horton Ravine. She's got another place at the beach, where she stays most weekends. I asked about habits, hobbies, job, country club memberships. Had a look at his bedroom, went through phone bills, credit card receipts. I checked his credit card accounts for any recent activity, address book, calendar. Over the next couple weeks we went through the mail at his home and at the clinic, arranged a mail cover, talked to his associates, entered him in the Department of Justice missing persons system, and put a stop on his license plate. Meantime, you have to understand, we're not talking about a crime here, so this is strictly a public service. We're doing what we can, but there's no evidence to suggest we got a problem on our hands."

"Fiona tells me his passport's missing."

Odessa smiled ruefully. "So's mine, for that matter. Just because his wife can't lay hands on it, doesn't mean it's gone. We did come across the statement for a savings account at Mid-City Bank. And this is what caught our attention. It looks like he made a series of cash withdrawals—thirty thousand dollars' worth—over the past two years. Balance drops from thirteen grand to three in the past ten months alone. The last activity on the account was August twenty-nine. His wife doesn't seem to know anything about it."

"You think he was prepping for departure?"

"Well, it sure looks that way. Granted, thirty thou won't get you far in this day and age, but it's a start. He might've milked other accounts we haven't come up with yet."

"Could we go back to the passport? If Purcell left the country, wouldn't customs have a record of it?"

"You'd think so. Assuming his was the passport he used. He might have traded in his driver's license, birth certificate, and passport for a set of phony papers, which means he could have flown to Europe or South America under someone else's name. Or he might have driven into Canada, booked a flight, and left from there."

"Or he might be lying low," I said.

"Right."

"Wouldn't someone have spotted his car?"

"No guarantee of that. He could've run it off a cliff or driven into Mexico and sold it to a chop shop."

"What kind of car?"

"Mercedes sedan. Silver. Vanity plate reads Doctor P."

I said, "You haven't mentioned foul play."

"No reason to. It's not like we found bloodstains in the parking lot outside the nursing home. No signs of a struggle, no evidence of assault, and no reason to believe he was forcibly removed."

"Fiona thinks he might have left on his own. What's your take on it?"

"Personally, I don't like the feel of it. Nine weeks with zip. You almost have to assume there's something else going on. We're beginning to backtrack, looking for anything we might have missed the first go-round."

"Did you believe the story Fiona told?"

"She says he's gone off before. Maybe so, maybe not. I believe he left *her*. Whether he was having problems with the current Mrs. P. is anybody's guess." He paused. "Have you met Crystal yet?"

I shook my head.

Odessa lifted his brows and shook his hand as though he'd burned it. "Hard to picture anyone walking out on her."

"You have a theory?"

"Not me," he said.

I indicated the file. "Mind if I take a look?"

"Wish I could, but this is Paglia's case, and he's hell on confidentiality. He doesn't mind us passing on the gist of it when it seems

appropriate. The point is to find the guy, which means we cooper-
ate when we can."

"He won't care if I go back and talk to some of these people?"

"You're free to do anything you want."

When he walked me out, he said, "If you find him, let us know.
He can stay gone if he wants, but I'd hate to keep putting in the
hours if he's in Las Vegas with a snootful of coke."

"You don't believe that."

"No, I don't. Nor do you," he said.

On the way back to the office I made a stop at the bank. I filled
out a deposit slip, endorsed Fiona's check, and waited my turn in
line. When I reached the window, I pointed to the account number
printed on the face. "Could you verify the balance in this account?
I want to be sure the check's good before I make the deposit."
Another lesson learned the hard way. I didn't start work until a
check had cleared.

The teller was one I'd been dealing with for years. She typed in
the account number on her computer keyboard, studied the screen,
then hit the ENTER key.

She looked back at my deposit slip and made a face. "This is covered, but it's close. Want the cash instead?"

"The deposit's fine, but let's do it before another check comes in
and leaves her short."

2

I RETURNED to the office and put a call through to Crystal Purcell
at the house in Horton Ravine. The housekeeper informed me she'd
left for the beach house. She gave me the number, which I dialed
as soon as we'd hung up. When Crystal picked up, I identified
myself, hoping she wouldn't be annoyed by the idea of yet another
detective. I told her I'd met with Fiona that morning and that she'd

asked me to look into Dr. Purcell's disappearance. "I know you've gone over the subject repeatedly, but I'd appreciate hearing the story from you, if you can bear telling it again."

There was a momentary pause. "How much are you charging?"

"Fiona? Fifty an hour."

"Come by at five this afternoon. I'm on Paloma Lane." She gave me the number. "Do you know where that is?"

"I can find it. I'll try not to take too much of your time."

"Take all you want. Fiona's the one paying."

I LEFT the office at four o'clock, stopping by my apartment on my way to Crystal's beach house. The smell of gathering rain had infused the air. I'd left windows open, and I wanted to get the place buttoned down properly against the coming storm. I parked the car out in front and pushed through the gate with its reassuring whine and squeak. I followed the narrow concrete walk around the side of the building to the backyard.

My apartment was formerly a single-car garage converted into living quarters. My studio consists of a small living room, with a sofa bed for guests tucked into a bay window, a built-in desk, a kitchenette, a stacking washer-dryer combination, and a bathroom. Above, accessible by a tiny spiral staircase, I have a sleeping loft with a platform bed and a second bathroom. The interior resembles a sturdy little seagoing vessel, complete with a porthole in the front door and teak-paneled walls. The best part of all is the good soul who makes this possible—my landlord, Henry Pitts. He's eighty-six years old, handsome, thrifty, energetic, and competent. He worked as a commercial baker, and even in retirement, he not only produces a steady stream of baked goods, but he caters luncheons and high teas for all the old ladies in the neighborhood. In addition, he trades his fresh breads and dinner rolls for meals at the corner tavern, where he eats three to four nights a week.

As I turned left onto the patio, I spotted Henry on a ladder outside his bedroom, putting up storm windows. The Santa Teresa temperatures never drop much below fifty, but he's originally from

Michigan, and his lingering attachment to the seasons dictates the installation of window screens in late spring and storm windows in the late fall.

Henry waved from his perch and then eased carefully down the ladder. "You're home early," he remarked.

"I thought I better close my windows before the rain."

Henry said, "Why didn't you call? I could have saved you a trip."

"This was right on my way. I have an appointment at five down on Paloma Lane, so I was heading in this direction. I have a new client. At least I'm ninety-nine percent sure."

"Why the hesitation?"

"I am interested in the case, but I'm not convinced I can be effective. This is the doctor who's been missing."

"I remember reading about that. Still no sign of him?"

"Nope. His ex-wife thinks the cops aren't showing the proper initiative. Frankly, she strikes me as the type who likes to make people jump through hoops, which I hate."

"You'll do fine." With that, he returned to the ladder, which he collapsed and carried back across the patio to the garage. I watched him ease around his 1932 Chevy coup and hang the ladder on the wall. "You have time for tea?" he asked, coming back across the yard.

"Better not. I'll see you later up at Rosie's."

Rosie owns the Hungarian tavern where Henry's older brother, William, now functions as the manager. William and Rosie were married Thanksgiving Day the year before, and they live in an apartment above her restaurant, which is half a block away. William is eighty-seven years old, and where Rosie once swore she was in her sixties, she now admits to being in her seventies.

I let myself into my apartment and dropped my shoulder bag on a kitchen stool. I circled the apartment, closing windows and locking them. Upstairs, I pulled on a clean white turtleneck, which I wore with my jeans. I shrugged into my gray tweed blazer, traded my Sauconys for black boots, and studied myself in the bathroom mirror. The effect was just what you'd expect: a tweed blazer with jeans. Works for me, I thought.

PALOMA LANE IS A SHADY two-lane road that runs between Highway 101 and the Pacific Ocean. Many houses along Paloma sell in the millions and vary in style from pseudo–Cape Cod to mock Tudor to faux Mediterranean to contemporary.

Crystal's house filled a narrow lot. The glass-and-cedar structure was probably forty feet wide and three stories high. To the left an open carport sheltered a silver Audi convertible and a new white Volvo, with a vanity license plate that read CRYSTAL. The end slot was free, probably where Dow Purcell had parked his Mercedes. To the right, there was room for an additional three cars on the gravel stretch where I parked my slightly dinged 1974 VW.

The rear façade of the house was austere, a windowless wall of weathering wood. I trudged across the gravel to the entrance and rang the bell. The woman who answered the door carried a wide martini glass by the rim. She said, "You must be Kinsey. I'm Anica Blackburn. Nica's the name most people use. Why don't you come in? Crystal's just finished her run. She'll be down in a bit. I told her I'd let you in before I headed home." Her dark auburn hair was slicked back, strands looking wet, as though she were fresh from the shower. Her body was slim and straight. She wore a black silk shirt, crisply pressed jeans, and no shoes.

I stepped into the foyer. The lower level widened from the entry, expanding into a great room that utilized the entire width of the house. The floors were a pale wood, covered with pale sisal carpeting. Everything else, from the walls to woodwork to the plump upholstered furniture dressed in wrinkled linen slipcovers, was as white as whole milk.

Beyond the deck, there was an apron of scruffy grass about ten yards wide. Beyond the grass, the ocean looked cold and unforgiving.

Inside, somewhere above, I could hear a voice raised in heat. "Shut up! That's bull. You are such a bitch. I hate you!"

A door slammed.

I glanced at Anica, who had her face upturned, regarding the ceiling with an air of bemusement. "Leila's home for the weekend—Crystal's only daughter, age fourteen. That's skirmish number one.

By Sunday it's all-out war, but then it's back to school for her. Next weekend they start in again." She gestured for me to follow and then moved into the great room and took a seat on the couch.

"She's in boarding school?" I asked.

"Fitch Academy. Malibu. I'm the school guidance counselor, and I provide personal transportation to and from. Not part of my duties. As it happens, I rent two doors down." She had strong, arched brows over dark eyes, high cheekbones with a smattering of freckles, and a pale, wide mouth, showing perfect white teeth. "This particular donnybrook is about whether Leila's going to spend the night with her dad. Four months ago she was fanatical about him. If she couldn't spend the weekend with him, she'd regale everyone in ear range with loud, shrieking fits. Now they're on the outs, and she refuses to go. Girls her age are melodramatic by nature, and Leila's high-strung."

"Fitch is all girls?"

"Thank God. I'd hate to imagine having to deal with boys that age, too. Can I fix you a drink?"

"I better not, but thanks."

She finished the last of her martini and then set her empty glass with a click on the pale wood coffee table. "I understand you're here about Dowan."

"Yes, and I'm sorry to intrude. I'm sure she's been through a lot since this ordeal began. How's she doing?"

"I'd say fair. Of course, the strain's been enormous. She keeps waiting for the phone to ring, looking for his car."

"I'm sure it's hard."

"Impossible. It really gets to her. If it weren't for Griff, I don't know how she'd manage to keep sane."

"Where was she that night, this house or the other one?"

Anica pointed at the floor. "They're usually here on weekends. This is more Crystal's style than that pretentious pile of crap Fiona built in town."

"What about you? When did you hear Dow was missing?"

"Well, I knew something was going on that first night. I'd driven Leila up from Malibu, as usual—we arrived about five o'clock—and she went off to her dad's. He's her stepfather, really, but he's helped raise her from infancy. At any rate, Crystal had already talked to Dow when we pulled in from school. He knew he wasn't going to be free in time for supper, so it was just Crystal and Rand and me."

"Rand?"

"Griff's nanny. He's great. He's been with the baby ever since Griff was born. Anyway, on the twelfth we ate out on the deck. It was gorgeous—very balmy for this time of year. At seven forty-five Rand took Griff and went over to the other house."

"Rand and the baby stay at the house in Horton Ravine?"

"Ordinarily, no. I think Crystal and Dow were looking forward to some time alone. I was probably here until ten o'clock."

"What time did she expect Dow?"

"Anytime after nine. That was usually his pattern when he had to work late. Anyway, she called me at three in the morning when she woke and saw he wasn't in bed. She came downstairs and flicked on the outside lights. His car wasn't there. She put a call through to the clinic, and they said he'd been gone for hours. That's when she called me, and I told her to call the cops."

"What was she thinking? Do you remember what she said?"

"The usual. Car accident, heart attack. She thought he might've been picked up by the cops."

"What for?"

"Driving under the influence."

"He drinks?"

"Dow always has a couple glasses of whiskey at the clinic when he works late. She's warned him about driving home afterward, but he always swears he's fine. She worried he might've run off the road."

"Was he on medication?"

"Hey, at his age, who isn't? He's sixty-nine years old."

"What went through your mind?"

A brief smile flickered. "I thought about Fiona."

"What about Fiona?"

"That she'd finally won. That's all she's angled for since the day he left, using any means she could to get him back."

I thought Anica might say more, but she just got up and padded as far as the wide French doors. "Tell Crystal I'll be at my place whenever she's done with this."

I watched her cross the deck and disappear.

I HEARD someone cross the room just above me, then thirty seconds later Crystal Purcell came down the stairs, barefoot, wearing a short-cropped T-shirt and faded jeans cut low. Her hair was an upscale-salon blond, a little longer than shoulder length, framing her face in a tangle of soft curls. Holding out her hand, she said, "Hello, Kinsey. I'm sorry to keep you waiting." Her grip was strong, her voice mild, her manner pleasant. "Where's Anica?"

"She just left. She asked if you'd call her as soon as you're free."

Crystal moved into the kitchen, sailing her comments in my direction while she crossed to the stainless steel refrigerator and removed a bottle of wine. "She's a good friend. One of the few. Dow's Horton Ravine pals view me as beneath contempt."

I couldn't think how to respond, so I kept my mouth shut.

"How long have you known her?"

"Really, not that long. Sometime early last spring. I saw her out on the beach and then later at Fitch."

She took a corkscrew from the kitchen drawer, opening the bottle as she moved to the kitchen cabinet and fetched herself a glass. "Do you want a drink?"

"It doesn't seem professional, given that I'm here on business."

Bemused, she took out a second glass and held it up. "You sure? It won't count against you. We can sit out on the deck and sip wine while we watch the sun go down."

"Oh, all right. Why not? You talked me into it."

"Great. I hate to drink by myself. If you'll take the glasses and the bottle, I'll make us up a plate of nibbles. That way we won't get looped—or any more looped than we choose."

I took the glasses in one hand and tucked the bottle of white wine in the crook of my arm. Once on the deck, I set the items on a weathered wooden table between two wood-and-canvas sling chairs. The wind gusting in from the ocean was damp and smelled pungent, like an oyster liqueur.

I sat down, crossing my arms as I huddled against the chill. I was grateful for the protection afforded by the long-sleeved turtleneck under my blazer.

Two ornamental lamps came on, and Crystal emerged from the house, carrying a tray of cheese and crackers, arranged with grapes and apple wedges. She'd pulled on a heavy navy sweater. She left the door open behind her, glancing over at me. "You look cold. I'm used to the ocean, but you must be freezing. Why don't I fire up the outside heaters? It'll just take a sec. You can pour the wine."

I did as she suggested and then watched as she lit the two heaters, turning them to face us so that warmth poured out across the space between us. "Is that better?"

"Much."

We sipped wine in silence while I tried to decide how to begin. "I appreciate your taking the time to talk to me. I just want to be clear that any comments you care to make will be safe with me. If you have relevant information, I'll report it to Fiona, but nothing else gets passed on."

"Thank you. I was wondering about that."

"I'm assuming there's no love lost."

"Hardly. Fiona's done everything in her power to make my life hell on earth." Her face was angular; her eyes were gray, her brows pale, her lashes thick and black. Aside from mascara, she seemed to wear little or no makeup. I could tell she'd had her eyes done and probably her nose as well. Crystal's smile was brief. "Look, I know she's busy painting a picture of herself as the victim in all of this, betrayed and put-upon. The truth is, she never gave Dow a thing. It was all take, take, take. Dow reached a point where he had nothing left. Fiona was always coming up with some new harebrained scheme, her current business venture being one. Interior design? Who's she trying to kid? She only has one client—some friend of hers named Dana. . . ."

"She's married to one of Dow's business associates?"

"Joel Glazer—that's right. How do you know him?"

"I don't. I knew her when she was married to someone else."

"She couldn't be too bright. Fiona's milking her for everything she's worth."

"What's your relationship to Dow's daughters?"

Crystal shrugged. "They're all right. They probably hate me, but at least they're too polite to say so. I'm sure they're worried their dad will die and leave all his money to Griffith and me."

She cut into a wedge of Brie, spread the cheese on a cracker, and held it out to me. "With Dow gone, it doesn't seem important. Whatever quarrel I have with Fiona is immaterial."

"Do you believe he's alive?"

"No, not really. But I can't be sure."

"The police detective says close to thirty thousand dollars had been pulled from his savings over the past two years."

"So I heard. I didn't know anything about that until they brought it to my attention. I know he kept a large sum of money somewhere, but he never said anything else about it. The statements were being forwarded to a post-office box that I used to keep. Dow asked about it a couple of months ago, and I told him it'd been canceled. Now it looks like he was paying to keep it open all this time."

"Why did he ask you about it when he already had the answer?"

Crystal shrugged. "Maybe he was wondering how much I knew."

"Could it be extortion?"

"I'm sure he'd have told me if someone were extorting money. Dow told me everything."

"It might have involved you. He might have paid the hush money in your behalf, as protection."

"I don't think so." I could have sworn her cheeks tinted, but in the fading light it was difficult to tell.

I changed tactics, not wanting her to disconnect from the conversation. "Was there anything unusual about the day he disappeared? Any behavior that seems different in retrospect?"

Crystal shook her head. "It was like any other Friday. He was looking forward to the weekend. Saturday he was playing in a tennis tournament at the country club, and we were going out to dinner with friends."

"Can you give me those names?"

"Sure. I'll give you a list before you leave."

"Was he having problems at work?"

"There are always problems at work. Dow takes his job very seriously. Recently he's spent a lot of time going over the books. The fiscal year at the clinic ends November thirtieth, and Dow likes to be on top of it."

"Were . . . are his responsibilities medical or administrative?"

"Both. He's very involved with the residents. Not treating them—they have their own personal physicians for their medical needs—but Dow's there every day keeping an eye on things."

"Is it possible he walked off?"

"No. And you want to know why? Because of Griff. That boy is the light of Dowan's eyes. He'd never leave Griffith voluntarily."

"I understand," I said. "What about the two of you? Are you doing okay?"

"We're very close. In fact, we've been talking about another baby now that Griffith is two."

"So you're convinced something's wrong."

"Very wrong. I just can't think what."

"What about his partners? What can you tell me about them?"

"I really don't know much. As I understand it, Joel Glazer and Harvey Broadus made a fortune in construction, developing retirement communities in the Southwest. They also own a chain of board-and-care homes, plus a number of nursing facilities across the state. After Dow retired, they approached him with regard to Pacific Meadows and asked him to take over the administrative work."

"And they all get along?"

"As far as I know. I mean, they hardly ever see each other. Joel and Harvey seem to be happy with Dow, so they tend to go their way and let him go his. An operating company does the billing."

"How long have they owned the place?"

"They bought it in 1980. It's over on Dave Levine Street at the corner of Nedra Lane. You've probably passed it. Looks like Tara without the acreage."

"How did you and Dow meet?"

"Mom . . ."

Crystal glanced into the great room through the open door. "We're out here." She must have caught sight of Leila because she turned back with an expression of annoyance and disbelief.

I followed her gaze.

Leila was clumping down the stairs in a pair of black satin pumps with heels so high she could hardly stand erect. Under her black leather jacket her top was a see-through confection of chiffon and lace worn with a long, narrow wool skirt. At fourteen she was still in that coltish stage of development: no bust to speak of, narrow hips, and long, bony legs. Her hair was cut short, dyed a white blond, sticking out in all directions. Some strands had been dread-locked while the rest remained as wispy as cotton candy. She came to the open door and stood there staring at us.

Crystal snorted. "You look ridiculous. Please go upstairs and find something decent to wear."

"I can dress any way I want."

"Leila, you're not leaving the house dressed like that."

"Great. I won't go, then. I'd rather stay here."

"You didn't see him last time, and I swore you'd be there."

"You promised I could see Paulie."

"I never said any such thing. And don't change the subject. Paulie's got nothing to do with it. He's your father."

"We're not even related. He's one of your ex-husbands."

"One ex-husband. I've only been married once before," she said. "Why are you being so hostile? Lloyd adores you."

"You think Lloyd's so great, why don't you go see him?"

Crystal closed her eyes, trying to control her temper. "We're not going to do this in front of company. He's got joint custody, okay? He's picking you up at seven, which means he's already on his way over. I'll come get you Sunday morning at ten. Now go back up and change, and pack a bag."

"You are so unfair," Leila said, and clomped back upstairs.

Crystal returned to our conversation, making no reference to Leila. "Dow and I met in Vegas at the home of mutual friends. The first time I saw him, I knew I'd marry him one day."

"Wasn't he married?"

"Well, yes. I mean, technically speaking, but not *happily,*" she said. "You've met Fiona. She's only six months younger than him, but she looks like she's a hundred. She drinks. She smokes two packs a day. She's also hooked on Valium. Dow was sixty-nine last spring, but you'd never guess by looking. Have you seen a picture of him?"

"There was one in the paper."

"Oh, that was terrible. I have a better one. Hang on."

She left the deck and moved into the great room, returning moments later with a framed color photo. She passed the photograph to me. I studied Dow Purcell's face. The picture had been taken on the golf course. His hair was white, trimmed close, and his face was lean. He looked tanned and fit. "Where was this taken?"

"Las Vegas, in 1982. We were married a year later."

I handed the photo back. "Do you play?"

"Some, but I'm terrible." She set the picture on the table.

"There's your mommy," a man said. He stood just inside the door, holding Griffith, who was dressed for bed in flannel jammies. His face was a perfect oval, his cheeks fat, his mouth a small pink bud. His fair hair was still damp. Mutely, he held his arms out, and Crystal reached for him. She fit him along her hip, looking at him closely while she spoke in a high-pitched voice, "Griffie, this is Kinsey."

She took one of his hands and waved it in my direction, saying, "I dotta doh beddy-bye now. Nightie-night."

"Night-night, Griffith," I said, voice high, trying to get into the spirit of the thing. I glanced at Rand. "Hi. You're Rand? Kinsey Millhone."

Rand said, "Nice to meet you." He appeared to be in his early forties, dark-haired, very thin, jeans, white T-shirt.

I said, "I better go and let you get the little one to bed."

Rand took Griffith from his mother and retreated. I waited while she jotted down the names and phone numbers of her husband's business associates and his best friend, Jacob Trigg. I left with her assurance I could call if I needed to.

On the way out, I passed Leila's stepfather, Lloyd, who'd just arrived. He drove an old white Chevy convertible with a shredded sun-faded top. His brush cut was boyish, and he wore glasses with tortoiseshell frames. He had the body of a runner or a cyclist, with long lean legs and no visible body fat. I placed him in his late thirties, though it was hard to determine, since I glanced at him only briefly as he passed. He nodded, murmuring a brief hello as he approached the front door. As I started my car, the first fat drops of rain were beginning to fall.

ASIDE from Henry, Rosie's tavern was empty when I arrived shortly after seven o'clock. The happy-hour crowd had been there and gone, and the neighborhood drinkers hadn't yet wandered in. Henry was sitting alone at a chrome-and-Formica table to the left of the door. I pulled up a chair. "Where's Rosie?"

"In the kitchen making a calf's-liver pudding with anchovy sauce."

"Sounds interesting."

The kitchen door swung open, and William emerged, dressed in a natty three-piece pin-striped suit, a copy of the evening paper tucked under his arm. Like Henry, he's tall and long-limbed, with the same blazing blue eyes and a full head of white hair. The two looked enough alike to be identical twins on whom the years had made a few minor modifications. When William reached the table, he asked permission to join us and Henry gestured him into a chair.

"Evening, Kinsey." William opened his paper, selected the second section, and flapped the first page over to the obituaries.

Henry glanced at him. "Anyone we know?"

William shook his head. "Couple of kids in their seventies."

William turned several pages to the classified ads. He glanced up at me. "Well, here's something. Still need office space? You should check this one out. Five hundred square feet, downtown, two fifty a month, available immediately."

I tilted my head in his direction. "You're kidding. Let me see that."
William handed me the section, pointing to the item, which read:

> For lease: 500 sq. feet in newly renovated Victorian, heart of downtown near courthouse; private bath and separate entrance. $250/month. Call Richard after 6:00 p.m.

The phone number was listed.

"I'll bet it's a dump. They always embellish in these ads."

"It won't hurt to call." He reached into his watch pocket and removed a coin. "Go on."

I took the coin and the paper and crossed the room. The pay phone was in the vestibule, the area dimly illuminated by a neon Budweiser sign. I dialed the number, and when the line was picked up on the other end, I asked to speak to Richard.

"This is he."

"I'm calling with regard to the office space listed in tonight's paper. Can I ask what street it's on?"

"Floresta. About six doors down from the police station."

"The price is two hundred and fifty bucks a month?"

"It's only one room, with a closet and bathroom."

"Would it be possible to see it tonight?"

"My brother's there laying carpet, and I'm on my way over. You want to take a look, I can meet you there in fifteen minutes."

My watch said seven thirty. "Great. What's the address?"

He gave me the information. "My brother's name is Tommy. The last name's Hevener."

"I'm Kinsey Millhone. I'll see you in fifteen minutes."

THE building had clearly once been a single-family residence: a one-story white frame cottage with gables and gingerbread trim. At 7:42, I eased my VW down the driveway and peered out the driver's-side window. The location was ideal—one block away from the office I was in—and the price couldn't have been better. I counted ten parking spaces laid out along the narrow backyard. Looking up, I could see Lonnie's office windows. I parked and got out.

A wide redwood deck had been constructed across the back of the building, complete with a ramp installed for easy wheelchair access. I entered a small foyer. A door stood open to my immediate right. I stepped through, absorbing the room at a glance.

The room was twelve by twelve, with new hand-crank windows on two walls. On the far wall, two doors stood open, one leading to a small bathroom, the other into what was clearly a spacious walk-in closet. A redheaded fellow in jeans, an olive-green T-shirt, and heavy work boots was sitting on the floor kicking a carpet stretcher, forcing the carpet taut along the baseboard. A phone line had been installed, and the phone was currently resting on a cardboard box.

I said, "Hi, I'm Kinsey. Your brother said he'd meet me here at seven forty-five. Are you Tommy?"

"That's me. Richard's always late. I'm the good boy, the one who shows up when I'm expected. Hang on. I'm almost done here." He glanced over, flashing me a smile, all green eyes and white teeth. With his red hair and his ruddy complexion, the effect was electric, like a black-and-white film with a wholly unexpected sequence in Technicolor. I felt myself averting my gaze with a little frisson that danced its way along my spine.

He tossed his mallet aside and sprang to his feet. He held a hand out, saying, "What's your name again?"

"It's Kinsey. The last name's Millhone with two *l*'s."

I pegged him in his late twenties, five feet ten, a hundred and sixty pounds. I'd been a cop for two years early in my career, and I still view men as suspects whom I might be called upon later to identify in a lineup. "Mind if I look around?"

He shrugged. "Help yourself. What kind of business you in?"

I walked into the bathroom. "I'm a private detective."

Toilet, pedestal sink with a built-in medicine cabinet above it. The shower stall was fiberglass with an aluminum-framed glass door. The floor was done in a white ceramic tile.

I moved back into the main room. If I placed my desk facing the window, I could look out at the deck. I leaned against the windowsill. "No termites, no leaky roof?"

"No, ma'am. I can guarantee that because I did the work my-self." His accent was faintly southern. "Place was in pretty bad shape when we took possession. We upgraded plumbing and electrical, put on a new roof and aluminum siding."

"It looks nice. How long have you owned it?"

"About a year. We're new out here. We lost our parents a few years ago. Both passed away." He crossed to the cooler and opened the lid, glancing over at me. "Offer you a beer?"

"Oh, no, thanks."

"Don't like to drink and drive," he remarked, smiling.

"That's part of it," I said.

He pulled out a Diet Pepsi and popped the tab. I held up a hand, but not quick enough to stop him. "Seriously, I'm fine."

His frown was softened by a tone of mock disapproval. "Can's open now. Might as well have a sip," he said, waggling the can coaxingly in my direction. I took it to avoid a fuss.

He reached into the cooler, extracted a bottle of Bass Ale, and seated himself on the floor. He leaned against the wall, his legs extended in front of him. His work boots looked enormous. He gestured at the carpet. "Pull up a seat."

"Thanks." I picked a spot across from him and sat down on the floor, taking a polite sip of Pepsi before I set the can aside.

Tommy took a long draw of beer.

"Where you from?"

"I'm local. Went to Santa Teresa High."

"Me and my brother come from Hatchet, Texas. Right outside Houston. Pop was in real estate. Developed shopping malls, office buildings, commercial properties."

He took another pull of beer. "Private detective. That's a new one on me. You carry a gun?"

"Not often." I dislike being 'drawn out,' though he was probably only being polite until his brother appeared.

He smiled as if picking up on my innate crankiness. "So which do you prefer? Guys way too young for you or guys way too old."

"I never thought about it like that."

He wagged a finger. "Guys way too old."

I felt my cheeks grow warm. Dietz—my occasional boyfriend—really wasn't that old.

"I like women your age," he said. "You seeing someone steady?"

"More or less," I said.

"More or less. I like that. So which is it?"

"More, I guess."

"Can't be much of a romance if you have to guess." He lifted his head, checking his watch as he did. "Here he comes. Fifteen minutes late. You can just about bank on it."

A car door slammed, and shortly afterward Richard Hevener walked in, tapping a clipboard restlessly against the side of his leg. He wore jeans and a black T-shirt, over which he wore a supple-looking black leather sport coat. He was taller than Tommy and a lot stockier, his hair dark. He was the somber brother and seemed to take himself very seriously. I rose to my feet.

"Richard Hevener," he said as he offered me his hand. We shook hands, and then he turned to Tommy. "Looks good."

"Thanks. Finish picking up, and I'm out of here." He lifted a wastebasket full of carpet scraps and carried them outside to the trash bin at the rear of the lot.

"So what do you think of the place?" Richard said, turning to me. "You want to fill out an application?" His accent and his manner of speaking were much less "Texas" than Tommy's. Consequently, he seemed older and more businesslike.

"Sure, I could do that," I said, trying not to sound like I was sucking up.

He passed me the clipboard and a pen. "We pay water and trash. You pay your own electric and phone. There's only one other tenant, and he's a C.P.A."

I leaned on a windowsill and began to fill in the information. By the time I finished, Tommy had left. I heard his truck in the driveway, and then it was gone. I handed Richard the clipboard, watching while he scanned the information.

"I'll call your references and run a credit check. We have a couple people coming by on Monday. I'll be in touch once I've processed all the applications."

"That's great. If you like, I can pay six months in advance." I was starting to sound fawning and insecure.

Richard said, "Really." He studied me, his eyes a dark, brooding brown. "Fifteen hundred dollars, plus one seventy-five for the cleaning deposit."

I thought about Fiona's check for fifteen hundred bucks.

"Sure, no problem. I could give you that right now."

"I'll take that into consideration," he said.

3

SATURDAY I opened my eyes automatically at 5:59 a.m. I stared up at the skylight, which was beaded with rain. As dutiful as I am about exercise, there's still nothing more delicious than the opportunity to sleep in. I burrowed under the covers, ignoring the world until eight thirty, when I finally came up for air.

Once I'd showered and dressed, I made myself a pot of coffee and downed a bowl of cereal while I read the morning paper. I changed my sheets, started a load of laundry, and generally picked up around the place. As a child, my aunt Gin insisted I clean my room on Saturdays before I went out to play. Since we lived in a trailer, the task didn't amount to much, but the habit remains.

At eleven o'clock I hauled out the phone book and turned to the yellow pages, checking out the section that listed nursing homes. There were close to twenty by my count. Many boasted large boxed ads detailing the amenities. Pacific Meadows, the nursing home owned by Purcell and his two partners, touted twenty-four-hour R.N. nursing care and on-site chapel and pastoral services, which were bound to come in handy. It was also certified by Medicare and Medicaid, giving it a decided advantage over some of its private-pay competitors. I decided to make a visit to see the place myself.

I tucked a fresh pack of index cards into my handbag, pulled on my boots, and found my yellow slicker and umbrella. I locked the door behind me and scurried through the puddles to my car parked at the curb. I slid in, fired up the engine, and drove in slow motion.

When I pulled into the parking lot at Pacific Meadows, the sky was dark with clouds and the lights in the windows made the place look cozy and warm. I picked my way across the half-flooded tarmac to the sheltered front entrance and stepped through the door. Dripping raincoats were hung on a row of pegs. I added my slicker and propped up my umbrella in the corner.

Along the wide hallway ahead, I could see a row of six elderly people in wheelchairs arranged against the wall like drooping houseplants. Some were sound asleep, and some simply stared at the floor in a sensory-deprivation daze.

To my right, aluminum walkers were bunched together like grocery carts outside a supermarket. The day's menu was posted on the wall, behind glass, like a painting on exhibit. Saturday lunch consisted of a ground chicken patty, creamed corn, lettuce, tomato, fruit cup, and an oatmeal cookie. I thought about fries and a Quarter Pounder with Cheese and nearly fled the premises.

French doors opened into the dining room, where I could see the residents at lunch. Some wore street clothes, but the majority were still dressed in their robes and slippers. Many turned to stare at me with a touching air of expectation. Had I come for a visit? Was I there to take them home? Sheepishly, I raised my hand and waved. A tentative chorus of hands rose in response. Their smiles were so sweet and forgiving I felt pricked with gratitude.

I backed away from the dining room and cruised down the corridor, guided by signs indicating the services of a dietary supervisor, a nursing supervisor, and a clutch of occupational, speech, and physical therapists. All three doors were open, but the offices were empty. Across the hallway I saw a sign for ADMISSIONS and BILLING. Next door was MEDICAL RECORDS. I thought I'd start there.

The overhead lights were on, and I moved through the door.

There was no one in evidence. I waited at the counter, idly dangling my fingers near a basket full of mail. By fanning the corners and tilting my head, I could read most of the return addresses. The usual bills and two manila envelopes from Santa Teresa Hospital, better known as St. Terry's.

"Can I help you?"

Startled, I straightened up and said, "Hi. How're you?"

A young woman in her early twenties had emerged from the door connecting administration to medical records. She wore glasses with red plastic frames. The names Merry and Pacific Meadows were machine-embroidered on the breast pocket of her green smock.

She crossed to the counter, passing through a hinged door, and took her place on the far side.

"Are you here to see someone?"

"I'm here on business," I said. I removed my wallet from my shoulder bag and flipped it open. I pointed at my P.I. license. "I've been hired to look into Dr. Purcell's disappearance."

Merry squinted at my license.

I said, "Are you the office manager?"

She shook her head. "I'm temping here on weekends while the other girl's out on maternity leave. Monday through Friday I'm Mrs. Stegler's assistant."

"Really. That's great. And what does that entail?"

"You know—typing, filing. I answer phones and distribute mail to all the residents, whatever needs doing."

"Is Mrs. Stegler the one I should be talking to?"

"I guess, but she won't be back until Monday."

"What about Mr. Glazer or Mr. Broadus?"

"They have an office downtown. You have a business card? I can have Mrs. Stegler call you as soon as she gets in."

"That'd be great." I took my time fumbling through my handbag to find a business card. "How long have you been here?"

"Three months December first. I'm still on probation."

I put my card on the counter. "You like the work?"

"It's boring but okay. Not that I'll stick around long. I'm two semesters short of my college degree in elementary ed. Besides, Mrs. S. is real moody. One day she's sweet, and then she turns around and acts all crabby. I mean, what is her *problem?*"

"What's your guess?"

"She thinks she should be promoted instead of just being used is how she put it."

"If she did get promoted, who would she replace?"

"Mrs. Delacorte. She's the one who got canned."

Not only was she bored, but she hadn't learned the basic rules, the most compelling of which is never never confide company secrets in the likes of me. I said, "Golly, that's too bad. Why was she fired?" My lies and fake behavior are usually heralded by gollys and gees.

"She wasn't fired exactly. It's more like she was laid off."

"Oh, right. And when was that?"

"The same time as Ms. Bart. She's the bookkeeper since way back when. They were interviewing for her position the same time I applied for this one."

"How come the bookkeeper and the administrator got laid off at the same time? Was that coincidence?"

"Not at all," she said. "Ms. Bart was let go, and Mrs. Delacorte got upset and raised a stink. Mr. Harrington suggested she might be happier finding work somewhere else, so that's what she did. This is all stuff I heard." She stopped what she was saying, and her eyes seemed to widen behind the red plastic frames. "You're not taking notes. I'm not supposed to gossip."

"I'm just making conversation 'til the rain lets up."

She patted her chest. "Whew! For a minute I got nervous. I'd never blab anybody's private business. It's not in my nature."

"You and me both," I said. "So who's Mr. Harrington?"

"He works for the billing company in Santa Maria."

"And he's the one who hired you?"

"Kind of. He interviewed me by phone, but only after Mrs. S. had already approved my application."

"I thought Dr. Purcell did all the hiring and firing."

"I don't know anything about that. I was here less than two

weeks when he, you know, ran off or whatever. I think that's why Mr. Harrington was forced to step in."

"Where's Mrs. Delacorte work now? Has anybody said?"

"She's over at St. Terry's. I know because last week she stopped by to visit with Mrs. S. Turns out she found a great job."

"What about Ms. Bart?"

"I don't know where she went."

"Did you know Dr. Purcell?"

"I knew who he was, but that's about it. That's his office in there. He just like, you know, vanished." She lowered her voice. "Mrs. S. thinks he left the country."

I lowered my voice, too. "Because of . . ."

"Medicare. F-R-A-U-D. Last winter the O.I.G.—"

"O.I.G.?"

"Oh, that's the Office of Inspector General. They're part of the Department of Health and Human Services. Anyway, O.I.G. faxed us this list of charts and billing records they wanted to see. They wanted a bunch of stuff covering the past two years. That's when Dr. P. came in. The way Mrs. S. tells it, if Pacific Meadows loses its funding, the place'll be shut down. Not to mention all the fines and restitution. She says, maybe even jail time, plus the public embarrassment. Dr. P. was the one lined up to take the brunt of it. Like his butt's in a sling. Those are her words, not mine."

"What about his employers?"

"Oh, they don't have anything to do with the hands-on stuff. They're all over the state, taking care of other business."

"When did this first come up?"

"I think last January, way before my time. Then, in March, these two guys from M.F.C.U. swooped in unannounced—that's the Medicaid Fraud Control Unit. They came loaded with questions and all the charts they wanted pulled. Everybody scrambled around. Dr. P. was notified of this big list of violations. We're talking half a million dollars at least, and that's just scratching the surface. He could turn out to be a major big-time crook."

"So she thinks he bolted to avoid punishment?"

"Well, I sure would if I was in his place."

I glanced over my shoulder. A nurse in a white uniform was standing in the doorway. She had fixed us with a look that was both shrewd and intimidating. I cleared my throat and said, "Well, Merry, I better scoot and let you get back to work. I'll stop back on Monday and chat with Mrs. Stegler."

"I'll tell her you were here."

Once in my car, I opened my pack of index cards and started taking notes—one fact per card—until I'd emptied my brain.

AFTER I left Pacific Meadows, I stopped by my office at Kingman and Ives. I hung up my slicker, then pulled out my portable Smith-Corona and placed it on my desk. I sat down in my swivel chair, took out the file I'd opened, and began sorting through the notes I'd assembled, adding the information on the index cards.

Looming large in my mind was Fiona's return on Tuesday. I could already see her, arms crossed, one foot tapping with impatience while I brought her up to date. She'd have dollar signs dancing like sugarplums above her head, thinking, *Fifty bucks an hour for this?* My strategy was to outfox the woman by presenting a beautifully constructed, typewritten report that would make it look as if I'd done a lot more than drive around chatting with folks.

When I was satisfied the document was as polished as I could make it, I took out my calculator and added up my hours. So far, I'd earned only one hundred and seventy-five dollars out of the fifteen hundred she'd paid me up front, which meant I still owed her thirteen hundred and twenty-five dollars' worth of my life. Oh, well. I typed the invoice and attached it to the original of my report, then placed the copies in the folder.

My report seemed okay, but I thought I'd let it sit for a day. I'd be adding interviews, once I figured out who I'd be talking to next. I drew up a list from the possibilities I'd gleaned. Purcell's business associates were among the top five names, along with Dow's best friend. I made sure I had the necessary phone numbers and then decided I'd done enough and it was time to go home.

FOR LUNCH I MADE MYSELF some milk-of-tomato soup and a gooey grilled cheese sandwich, which I dipped in my bowl and lifted dripping to my lips. The liquid red of the soup against the crunchy golden surface of the bread was a culinary portrait of early childhood consolation. Aunt Gin first served me this confection when I was five years old, mourning my parents who'd been killed in a car wreck the previous May. The ooze of melted Velveeta will always prompt the curious sensation of sorrow and satisfaction commingling on the surface of my tongue. This sandwich, I confess, was the highlight of my weekend, which is what life boils down to when you're celibate.

Afterward I settled on the sofa, covered myself in a big puffy comforter, and started reading a book. Within minutes I'd sunk like a stone into a river of dreams.

The phone rang, the sound annoyingly shrill, and I was disoriented by the need to surface. I reached back, fumbling for the phone, which was resting on the end table above my head.

"Ms. Millhone? This is Blanche McKee."

The name meant nothing. I rubbed my face. "Who?"

"Fiona Purcell's daughter. I understand Mother's hired you. I just wanted you to know how relieved we all are. We've been urging her to do this ever since Daddy disappeared."

"Oh, right. Sorry. I couldn't place the name."

"I'm not sure how much Mother's told you, but I'm assuming you'll want my impressions as well. If you have a minute this afternoon, you might want us to get together."

I hesitated. I hadn't forgotten Fiona's barely disguised contempt for her younger daughter, mother of four, soon to be mother of five. On the other hand, maybe Fiona'd told Blanche about me in order to test my perseverance. "Gee, I have an appointment. Tomorrow might be possible. I could be there by ten o'clock."

"That won't work for me. Isn't there *any* way you could stop by? I feel it's terribly important."

What I personally felt was a surge of irritation. I could just see Fiona returning from San Francisco, carping because I hadn't taken time to interview Blanche. I said, "I could be there by five thirty, but only for half an hour. That's the best I can do."

"Perfect. We're up on Edenside at the corner of Monterey Terrace. The number's 1236. It's a two-story Spanish."

THE house at the corner of Edenside Road and Monterey Terrace was indeed a two-story Spanish hacienda. I pulled in at the curb, locked my car, and approached the house, passing through a tile-paved courtyard.

I rang the bell. Within seconds I could hear shrieks, barking dogs, and the clattering of small feet. As the door opened, a girl of perhaps five turned to sock the smaller boy-child behind her. Meanwhile, the toddler bringing up the rear got knocked on his diaper by two Jack Russell terriers and set up a howl. Another girl was walking down the hallway toward the rear of the house, bellowing, "Mom! Mooommy! Heather's socking Josh."

Swaybacked, Blanche lumbered into sight, the sphere of her belly so large it looked like a rogue moon held in orbit by unseen gravitational forces. She swooped down and gathered up the howling baby, whom she settled on her hip. She grabbed Heather by the arm, hauling her away from her brother. "You kids go out in the backyard."

"But we want to watch cartoons!"

"Too bad. You do what I say. And no running," Blanche warned.

I glanced at my watch, a gesture that wasn't lost on her.

"I know you're in a hurry, so I'll get to the point. Has Mother filled you in on Crystal's past?"

"I know she was a stripper before she married your dad."

"I'm not talking about that. Did she mention Crystal's fourteen-year-old daughter was born out of wedlock? I'm not even sure Crystal knows who the father is."

I squinted. "And you think this is somehow connected to your father's disappearance?"

She seemed startled. "Well, no, but I wanted to fill in the picture so you could see what you're up against."

"Meaning what?"

Blanche said, "Doesn't Crystal's behavior strike you as odd? She doesn't seem at all distraught about what's happened. Crystal's never made a public appeal for information about Daddy. She's never offered a reward. She's never sent out any flyers. I think he left the office and drove out to the beach house, as usual. Only something went terribly wrong. Of course, Crystal denies this. She claims he never arrived, but we only have her word for it."

"So you think she knows where he is and she's covering?"

"Well, yes," she said, as though surprised I'd ask. "She could have knocked him out and driven him away somewhere."

"And done what with his car?"

"There could have been two of 'em. She could have hired someone. How do I know? I'm just telling you. Nothing would suit her better than to have him out of the way."

"Why?"

Blanche leaned forward. "Before she married my father, she signed a prenuptial agreement, according to which she gets nothing if they divorce in the first five years."

"Wait a minute. Back up. You still haven't told me how she intends to profit if she had him snatched."

"I didn't say she had him kidnapped. I said she knows where he is."

"What's that have to do with a prenup?"

"She's been having an affair."

"Your mother mentioned that as well. This is Clint Augustine?"

"Exactly. Now she wants her freedom, but she wants the money, too. If she tries to divorce him, she'll end up with nothing. The only way she benefits is if Daddy dies."

"How did you find out?"

"From Mother's friend Dana Glazer. She and her husband have a house in Horton Ravine. The Glazer property backs right up to Daddy's, with just a little fence in between. They have a guest cottage back there, and Crystal asked if they'd consider renting it temporarily to a friend of hers. This was back in January. Anyway, the Glazers don't use the cottage, so they decided, hey, why not? Of course, once Dana realized what was going on, she was horrified. She found it thoroughly repulsive, which is why she's never said a word to my mother. For fear of hurting her."

"Why'd she tell you?"

"She didn't. I heard it from another friend. Dana confirmed the story, but only because I pressed. Poor Mother still thinks Daddy's coming back to her. Bad enough he left her for such a . . . *tart,* but the fact that Crystal's still *doing* it makes Daddy look like an even bigger fool."

"Which leads us to what conclusion?"

"Crystal wants him out of the way. If Daddy dies, she inherits the bulk of his estate. If she divorces him, she gets nothing."

"All right, let me see what I can do to check it out. So far, this is pure theory, but I can appreciate the worry."

THE minute I got home, I went to my desk and began writing down the list of possibilities for Dowan Purcell's fate. I'd dismissed the notion that he'd been kidnapped, but maybe I was wrong. He could have left voluntarily, been on the run or hiding out. He could have met with an accident while driving under the influence. If he were lying at the bottom of a canyon, it would certainly explain the fact that his Mercedes hadn't been spotted either.

Or he could have established a secret life, having slipped now from one persona into the next. What else? Fearing disgrace, he could have killed himself. Or, as Blanche suggested, someone could have killed him for gain or to cover something worse.

My only hope was to plod my way systematically from friend to friend, colleague to associate, current wife to ex, daughter to daughter in hopes of a lead. All I needed was one tiny snag in the fabric of his life that I might use to unravel his current whereabouts.

The next day, Sunday, went by in a blur. I gave myself the day off and spent the time puttering around my apartment, taking care of minor chores.

Monday morning, after a three-mile jog, I picked up my gym bag and headed over to the gym. I signed in, asking Keith, at the desk, if he knew Clint Augustine. Keith's in his twenties, with a gleaming shaved head.

He said, "Sure, I know Clint. You remember him. Big guy, white-blond hair. He used to come in here regular, maybe eight, ten times a week with his clients, mostly married chicks. They're a specialty of his. But it's been months since I've seen him. He might have moved his clients to another gym."

"I heard he'd been working with Crystal Purcell."

"He did for a while. They'd come in late afternoon—Mondays, Wednesdays, and Fridays. Isn't she the wife of the guy who disappeared? Something skanky going on there."

"Could be," I said. "Anyway, I gotta get a move on. Thanks for the info."

AFTER my workout I returned home, showered, pulled on a turtle-neck, jeans, and my boots, grabbed a bite of breakfast, and packed myself a brown-bag lunch. I reached the office at nine o'clock and put a call through to the police department, where Detective Odessa assured me he'd do yet another computer check to see if there was any sign of Dow Purcell.

I briefed him on the people I'd spoken to so far, and I noted, once more, that I was being ever so faintly protective of Crystal. I could have told him the unconfirmed rumor about her affair, but I decided to hold off until I had a chance to check it out. By the end of the conversation it was clear we were both still in the dark.

I put in a call to Jacob Trigg and spoke briefly to him. We set up an appointment for ten o'clock Tuesday morning at his place. I then called Joel Glazer's office number. His secretary told me he was working from home and gave me the phone number there. I called and briefly identified myself. He seemed pleasant and cooperative, and we set up a meeting for one o'clock that afternoon. I then called Santa Teresa Hospital and learned that Penelope Delacorte was now director of nursing services. I decided to try her after my meeting with Glazer. Lastly, on my own behalf, I made a call to Richard Hevener, whose machine picked up. I left a message inquiring about the status of my rental application. I tried to sound winsome on the phone in hopes that might tip the odds in my favor.

At lunchtime I sat at my desk and ate the peanut butter and pickle sandwich I'd brought from home. At twelve thirty I left the building and walked to my car.

Horton Ravine, where I was headed, is a moneyed enclave. I took Highway 101 as far as the La Cuesta off-ramp, turned left, and followed the road around to the right, heading for the main entrance, which consisted of two massive stone pillars, with Horton Ravine spelled out in curlicue wrought iron arching between the two.

The Glazers lived on Vía Bueno. The house was 1960s modern. Three soaring stories were variously angled and cantilevered with a steeply pitched tower driving straight up out of the center of the mass. When I'd first met Dana Jaffe Glazer, she was living in a small housing tract in Perdido, thirty miles to the south. I wondered if she was as conscious as I of how far she'd come.

I parked in a circular driveway and crossed to the wide sweeping stairs that led up to the front door. A few minutes passed, and then she answered the bell. I could have sworn she was wearing the same outfit I'd seen her in the first time we met: tight, faded jeans and a plain white T-shirt. Her hair was still the color of honey, with silver now in the mix. Her eyes were hazel, under softly feathered brows. Her most arresting feature was her mouth. Her teeth were slightly occluded, and the overbite made her lips appear plump and pouty.

She said, "Hello, Kinsey. Joel said you'd be stopping by. Please come in. Let me take that."

"This is beautiful," I said as I stepped inside, slipping off my slicker, which I handed to her. While she hung it in the closet, I had time to gape. The interior was cathedral-like, a vast space crowned by a vaulted ceiling thirty feet above. Bridges and catwalks connected the irregular levels of the house.

Dana joined me, saying, "Fiona probably told you we're redoing the place."

"She mentioned that," I said. "She also said you suggested me for this job, which I appreciate. How well did you know Dow?"

"I ran into him occasionally because of Joel, but we weren't friends. I met Fiona after they divorced, so I tend to side with her. Joel's in his office. I'll walk you to the elevator."

JOEL Glazer's office was located on the third floor—a spacious, airy tower room with windows on all four sides. His views were spectacular: the ocean, the coastline, the mountains, and the western edges of Horton Ravine. The thickened cloud cover spread gloom across the landscape, at the same time making the deep blue of the mountains and the dark green of the vegetation seem more intense.

Joel rose from behind the refectory table he used for a desk, and the two of us shook hands. His looks surprised me. I was so enamored of Dana's beauty that I'd imagined a mate for her equally good-looking. Joel was in his sixties, with a high balding forehead. When he stood up to greet me, I realized he was shorter than I, probably only five feet four. He was portly, and his shoulders were hunched in a way that made me want to monitor my calcium intake. "Nice to meet you, Miss Millhone. Have a seat."

I settled into a brown leather wing chair.

He sat back in his chair. "Fiona tells us she's hired you to track Dow down. I'll tell you what I can, but I'm not sure that's going to be much help."

"I understand," I said. "Could we start with Pacific Meadows? I gather there's been a problem with the Medicare billing."

"My fault entirely. I blame myself for that. I should have kept an unofficial eye on the day-to-day operations. Harvey Broadus and I—don't know if you've met him, my partner . . ."

I shook my head in the negative, allowing him to continue.

"We've had a host of projects in the works this past six months. We've been in business for years. My background's business and finance, where his is real estate and construction—a match made in heaven. We met on the golf course fifteen years ago and decided to go into partnership building retirement communities and board-and-care homes. Both of us had parents who were deceased by then, but the need for attractive housing and skilled nursing care for the

elderly was something we'd both struggled to find and not always
with success. Anyway, long story short, we've now put together an
impressive chain of residential health-care and intermediate-care
facilities. Pacific Meadows we acquired in 1980. At the time, it was
shabby and poorly run. We poured close to a million dollars into
the renovation and improvements. Shortly after that we made the
lease arrangement with Genesis Financial Management Services.
Somebody—I forget now who—suggested Dow's name to Genesis as
a possible administrator. I'd known him socially and could certainly
vouch for his reputation in the medical community. Seemed like a
worthwhile arrangement for all the parties concerned."

"What happened?"

"I wish I knew. Harvey and I are often out of town, crisscrossing
the state. We've probably taken on more than we should." The
phone on his desk began to ring. He glanced at it briefly.

"You need to get that?"

"Dana will pick up. I should go back and fill you in on how this
business works. What you have essentially are three separate enti-
ties. Harvey and I own the property through Century Comprehensive, which is a company we formed back in 1971. By property I'm
talking now about the land and the building occupied by Pacific
Meadows. The nursing home is actually operated by Genesis. They
lease the physical plant from us. They also handle all the billing:
accounts payable and receivable, Medicare and Medicaid billing,
medical equipment purchases. Genesis falls under the larger umbrella of a company called Millennium Health Care. Millennium is
publicly held, and as such, they're required by law to submit financial information to Social Security, and by that I mean lists of
assets, liabilities, and the return on equity capital. A certified public accountant has to verify those figures."

"Where did Dr. Purcell fit in?"

"Dow's the medical administrator of the facility, responsible for
the day-in, day-out nuts-and-bolts decisions, which is where he may
have gotten into trouble."

"The three of you are partners?"

"Not really. We couldn't be in partnership with Dow or the management company that runs the business. The government gets very testy about any agreement that isn't the result of an arm's-length negotiation. Dow could hardly make unbiased decisions about billing practices if he stood to profit. Harvey and I both thought Pacific Meadows would be the perfect venue for a man with Dow's experience and reputation. I see now he may not have had quite the head for business I'd been led to believe. We first heard about this Medicare business last May. I thought then, and I'm still convinced, any discrepancies will turn out to be clerical mistakes. The notion of Dowan actively debunking the government is incomprehensible."

"Suppose he did, though. I don't understand how he benefits. If Medicare or Medicaid is overbilled, aren't those monies paid to the operating company? Seems like it's their responsibility."

"Absolutely. But outside providers, such as ambulance companies and medical-supply businesses, can collect thousands of dollars for services never rendered, or goods not delivered, or goods billed out at inflated prices. If someone in Dow's position were in league with them, the contracts could mean thousands of dollars to the companies involved. For this he'd receive remuneration—kickbacks—perhaps under the heading of a referral fee. Now the Health Care Financing Administration, which regulates Medicare and Medicaid, is insisting on documentation for every such transaction, including the lease agreement, which is where we come in."

"But you don't think he's really guilty."

"I don't. At the same time, it isn't looking good for him."

"You think he left to avoid disgrace?"

"Possibly," he said. "He's a man in big trouble."

"When did you see him last?"

"September twelfth, the day he disappeared. I took him to lunch."

"Was this at his request or yours?"

"His. He called and asked to see me. Of course, I said yes. By then I knew about his difficulties. We met at a little place in walking distance of Pacific Meadows, a mock English pub called Dickens. It's quiet and affords a measure of privacy."

"Did he talk about the problems with Medicare?"

"He seemed to want reassurances that Harvey and I would come to his defense. I did what I could to put his mind at rest, but I told him I couldn't condone anything underhanded. If the charges turn out to be provable, then there's no way I'd be willing to cover for him, even if I could."

"But why would he risk it? Especially at his age and station in life. He couldn't need the money."

"I'm not so sure about that. Dow always did well for himself financially, but Crystal is high-maintenance."

The phone rang again. His eyes didn't even flicker, so I went right on. "You think she married him for his money?"

He shook his head. "I wouldn't say that. I think she genuinely loves the guy, but she's been poor all her life. She wants to make sure she's safe, just in case something happens to him."

"Did Dr. Purcell say anything to suggest he might flee?"

Joel shook his head. "I don't remember anything of the kind. But if he ran, he'd have to continue running for the rest of his life."

I saw his gaze shift. "What's going through your mind?"

"It crossed my mind—after seeing him that day—he might have been thinking of doing himself in. He wasn't sure Crystal would stick with him once the scandal came to light. You have to ask yourself just how despondent he was and how far he'd go to get relief."

"Joel?"

We both turned to find Dana standing in the doorway.

"Harvey's on line two. This is the second time he's called."

"Sorry. I better get this."

"Sure, go ahead. I appreciate your time. It's possible I'll want to talk to you again at a later date."

"Anytime," he said. He stood up when I did, and the two of us shook hands across his desk. By the time I reached the door, he'd picked up the phone.

Dana walked me to the elevator. During its slow, whirring descent I said, "What's the story on Clint Augustine?"

"Simple. For the six months he rented from us, Dow would go

off to work, and the next thing you know, Crystal would come sneaking out her back door, through the trees, and into Clint's cottage. She'd be there an hour or so and then slip back home. It got to be the talk of the neighborhood."

"Couldn't there be another explanation?"

Dana's smile was jaded as she handed me my slicker. "Maybe they were having tea."

4

IT WAS not quite two o'clock when I walked into the hospital lobby of Santa Teresa Hospital. I inquired at the information desk and was given directions to the office of the director of nursing services.

I found Penelope Delacorte seated at her desk in a small private office. When I knocked on the doorframe, she peered at me above a pair of half-glasses with tortoiseshell frames. She was in her early fifties, at that stage where she hadn't quite decided whether to dye her graying hair.

"You're Ms. Delacorte?"

"Yes." Her attitude was cautious.

"Kinsey Millhone," I said. "I'm a private investigator here in town, and I've been hired to look into Dr. Purcell's disappearance. May I have a few minutes?"

Without much in the way of encouragement I entered her office and eased myself into the chair near her desk.

Penelope Delacorte got up and closed her office door. "I'm not sure what I can tell you." She sat down and put her hands in her lap. "I was gone by the time he . . . went missing."

"How long did you work for Pacific Meadows?"

"I was the administrator there for the past eight years, until August twenty-third. I worked with Dr. Purcell for the last forty-seven months of that."

"I thought he was the administrator."

"His title was medical director slash administrator. I was the associate administrator, so I suppose you're correct."

"Can you tell me why you left?"

"Genesis, the management company that oversees the operation of Pacific Meadows, received notification that Medicare was conducting a rigorous audit of our records."

I raised my hand. "What prompted them to do that?"

"Probably a complaint."

"From?"

"One of the patients, a guardian, a disgruntled employee. I'm not sure what it was, but they seemed to know what they were doing. Apparently, the clinic was suspected of any number of violations from overpaying our suppliers to submitting false or inflated claims for services. Dr. Purcell was in a panic and blamed the bookkeeper, Tina Bart, which was absurd and unfair. I went to bat for her. She didn't make the decisions. She didn't even pay the bills. Genesis did that."

"Why isn't Genesis considered responsible for the problem if they pay the bills?"

"We supply them the information. As a rule, they don't stop to verify the data, nor did Ms. Bart."

"But she was fired anyway."

"Yes, she was, and I turned in my notice the very same day. I was determined to complain to the Labor Relations Board."

"What was their response?"

"I never got that far. I had second thoughts and decided not to go through with it. Tina Bart didn't want to make a fuss. She was as reluctant as I was to call attention to Dr. Purcell's situation."

"His situation?"

"Well, yes. We're all fond of him. He's a darling human being and a wonderful doctor. He just had no clue when it came to the Medicare rules and regulations—which items were billable and which would automatically be disallowed, co-payments, deductibles, claims for fee-based services. I grant you, it's enormously complicated. Make one mistake—you put a code in the wrong place or leave even one window blank—and the form comes right back at you, usually without a hint about where you've erred."

I said, "Do you think Dr. Purcell was intentionally cheating the government?"

"I doubt it. I can't see how he'd benefit unless he had some covert arrangement with Genesis or the various providers. The point is, Dr. Purcell was on the premises. Genesis wasn't, and neither was Mr. Glazer or Mr. Broadus. It was his responsibility, and ultimately, he's the one who'll be held to answer."

"What do you think happened to him?"

"I can't answer that. I was gone by then."

"Just one more thing. Where did Tina Bart end up?"

"You're the detective. You figure it out."

WHEN I got back to the office, I picked up a message slip on which Jeniffer had written, "Richard Heaven called. Pleas return his call." I could actually feel my heart begin to thump as I moved down the corridor to my office and unlocked the door. I dumped my shoulder bag on the desk and snatched up the telephone. When I reached Richard, he said, "I've been through the rest of these applicants, and none of them panned out. Bunch of bums out there. Anyway, the place is yours if you want it."

"That's great. When can I take possession?"

"I'm heading over there now. If you have a few minutes, maybe you could give me a check. That's sixteen hundred and seventy-five dollars, with the cleaning deposit, made out to Hevener Properties."

"Sure, I could do that. I'm just across the alley."

"I didn't realize that. Why don't you join me in a bit, and as soon as the lease is signed, I'll give you the key." He seemed to be uncomfortable discussing money, and I wondered how much experience he had in landlord-tenant relationships.

"I'll see you shortly, and thanks."

As soon as I hung up, I did a little dance of joy, my attention already darting forward to the practicalities of moving. I tucked my tape measure into my shoulder bag, grabbed a yellow legal pad and pencil, made sure my answering machine was on, then walked to my brand-new digs.

I was already feeling extraordinarily possessive as I trotted along the driveway from the rear of the lot. Once inside the back door, I was careful to wipe my feet on the cotton doormat provided for that purpose. The door to the back office was standing open, and I could smell fresh paint. I peered in and found Tommy on his hands and knees, touching up the baseboards with a brush and a can of white latex paint. He flashed me a quick smile and continued with his work.

I said, "Hi. How are you?"

"Doing good. I hear you're the new tenant."

"Well, it looks that way. Richard said he'd meet me over here to do the paperwork." There was something nice about the fact that his attention was fixed on the job in front of him. It allowed me to study his shoulders and the soft reddish hair on his forearms where his sleeves were rolled up.

He glanced over his shoulder at me. "How's the boyfriend?"

"He's fine." I wondered if Tommy had a girlfriend.

"Hope he's treating you good."

"Actually, he's out of town." I winced when I said it because it sounded like a come-on.

"What's he do for a living? He some fancy-pants attorney?"

"He's a P.I. like me. Semiretired. He was laid up for a while with a knee replacement." Mentally, I crossed my eyes. The way I was describing Dietz made him sound like some old geezer who could barely walk. In truth, Dietz had been gone so long that my claiming him as a boyfriend was patently ridiculous.

"Sounds old."

"He's not. He's only fifty-three."

Tommy smiled to himself. "Now see? I knew you'd be the type to go for somebody old. What are you, thirty-five?"

"Thirty-six."

"I'm twenty-eight myself, which I figure is prime for a guy." He lifted his head slightly. "Here comes Richard."

"How do you do that? I didn't hear him pull in."

"Radar," he said. He sealed the can of paint.

Richard appeared in the doorway wearing a black raincoat. He wasn't nearly as appealing as his brother and certainly not as friendly, meeting my gaze with only a flicker of his eyes. "I thought you had something else to do today," he said to Tommy.

"Yeah, well, I wanted to finish this."

There was something edgy going on between them, but I couldn't figure out what. Tommy went into the bathroom to clean his paintbrush, then came out and began to gather up his tools.

"Let me write that check," I said, trying to inject a warmer note. I reached for my bag and took out my checkbook and a pen, leaning against the wall while I filled in the date. "Hevener Properties?"

"That's right." Richard watched me idly as I wrote in the amount. As Tommy headed for the door, I saw the two exchange a glance. His gaze moved to mine, and he smiled at me before he disappeared through the door.

I ripped the check from the book and handed it to Richard, who removed the lease from the inner pocket of his raincoat. I began to read through the lines of minuscule print. Seemed like standard fare—no tricks, no hidden clauses, no unusual restrictions.

Richard watched me read. "What kind of cases do you handle?"

"Just about anything. Right now I'm looking into the disappearance of a doctor who's been gone for nearly ten weeks."

"Mostly local?"

"For the most part, yes. Occasionally I go out of state, but it's usually cheaper for a client to hire a P.I. in their own geographic area. That way they don't have to pay travel." I scribbled my name at the bottom of the lease. "I'm always saying this, but the job's a lot duller than it sounds. Background checks and paper searches at the hall of records."

He said, "Well, I better give you a key." From his raincoat pocket he pulled out a key and dropped it into the palm of my hand.

"Thanks." I took out my key ring and added it to my collection.

After he departed, I pulled out my tape measure and began to lay out the dimensions of the room. I made a crude drawing on my legal pad, and then I sat in the middle of the carpet, studying the room. Outside the window the day was dreary, but inside, where I was, there was a sense of new beginnings.

I was just about to pack up when the phone rang. I must have jumped a foot, and then I stared at the instrument sitting on a cardboard box. Someone looking for Richard or Tommy. Couldn't be for me. I picked up, feeling hesitant. "Hello?"

The drawl again. "Hey, it's me. My brother still there?"

"He just left."

"I thought maybe the two of us might go out for a drink." His voice on the phone was low and flirtatious.

"Why?"

"Why?" His laugh bubbled up. "Why do you think?"

"It's only four o'clock. I have work to do yet."

"When will you finish?"

"Probably closer to six."

"Good. We'll make it dinner instead."

"Not dinner. A drink. And only one," I said.

"You're callin' the shots. Name the place, and I'll be there."

I thought for a moment, tempted by the idea of Rosie's, which was off the beaten path. This all felt sneaky, like it wouldn't be good for Richard to see us together. Still, I couldn't see the harm in having one drink. "There's a place near the beach," I said, and gave him Rosie's address. "You know where that is?"

"I'll find it."

After I hung up, I wondered if I'd made a mistake. It's not a smart move to mix the professional with the personal. On the other hand, it did cheer me up, the notion of seeing him again. With luck he'd turn out to be a jerk, and I'd politely decline any further contact.

In the meantime, I knew I had to get down to the business of Dow Purcell. I'd go back to square one, starting at Pacific Meadows and the night he vanished from the face of the earth.

THE parking lot at Pacific Meadows was full. I tucked my VW into the very last slot on the left, locked my car, and slopped through shallow puddles to the front door. I leaned my umbrella against the wall and hung up my slicker on a peg. As this was a weekday, there seemed to be more residents moving about in the hall.

I proceeded to the administration office, where I found Merry laying out a hand of solitaire. She looked up and said, "Hi. How are you?" I could tell she'd recognized my face but was drawing a blank on the name.

"Kinsey Millhone," I said. "I thought I'd stop by and see if Mrs. Stegler was here. I hope she hasn't left for the day."

Merry pointed to her right just as a woman emerged from the inner office. Her hair was cut quite short. She wore a brown blazer, a shirt, a tie, and a pair of mannish pants.

"Mrs. Stegler? My name's Kinsey Millhone. I'm hoping you can give me some information about Dr. Purcell. His first wife, Fiona, hired me in hopes I could get a line on him. She felt a conversation with you was the logical place to begin."

Mrs. Stegler shook her head. "I'm sorry, but I was gone by the time the doctor left the building that night," she said.

"Did you talk to him that day?"

Mrs. Stegler signaled with her eyes that Merry was listening to every word we said. "Perhaps you'd like to step into his office. We can talk in there."

We entered Dr. Purcell's office, which was small and neat. Desk, swivel chair, two upholstered guest chairs, and a bookcase filled with medical textbooks. I'd have given a lot for the chance to go through his desk drawers, but the chances of that looked dim.

It was clear Mrs. Stegler thought it inappropriate to sit at his desk. She perched on one of his guest chairs, and I took the other, which put us nearly knee to knee.

"I'd appreciate your telling me about his last day at work," I said. "Detective Odessa told me you were very helpful."

"And you won't quote me out of context?"

"I won't quote you at all."

"I've been divorced for years." Her voice was so tight and so raspy I could hardly understand what she said. "Dr. Purcell . . .

was the closest . . . thing to a . . . friend I had. I can't believe he's gone." She took a deep breath, humming with the kind of sorrow that didn't lend itself to words.

I realized she was the first person who'd shown any real emotional reaction to his vanishing. I leaned forward and clutched her cold hands. "I know this is hard. Take your time. My only purpose here is to help. Trust me on that."

"What do you want?"

"Just tell me what you know."

She must have decided to trust me because she took a deep breath and opened up. "That last day, he seemed preoccupied. I think he was worried. I mean, why wouldn't he be? Mrs. Purcell— the first one, Fiona—stopped by to see him, but he'd gone out to lunch. She waited for a while, thinking he might return, and then she left him a note. When he came back, he worked in his office for the rest of the day. He had a glass of whiskey sitting at his desk. This was late in the day."

"Did he go out for dinner?"

"I don't believe so. When I tapped on his door to say good night, he was just sitting there."

"Any phone calls or visitors that you know of?"

Mrs. S. shook her head. "Not that I remember."

"Didn't I read in the paper he had a brief chat that night with an elderly woman sitting in the lobby?"

"That would be Mrs. Curtsinger. Ruby. She's been a resident here since 1975. I'll have Merry take you over to her room."

MERRY walked me down the hall. We took a left, passing a series of residential rooms. Many doors were closed, but through the doors that remained open, I caught glimpses of twin-size beds with floral spreads, photographs of family members lined up on the chests of drawers. Each room looked out onto an outside courtyard.

Ruby Curtsinger was sitting in an upholstered chair beside a set of sliding glass doors, one of which was pushed back to admit a breath of damp, fresh air. Ruby was a tiny, shrunken woman with a small bony face and arms as thin as sticks. She turned a pair of bright blue eyes toward us and smiled, showing the many gaps in her lower teeth. Merry introduced us and explained what I wanted before she withdrew.

Ruby said, "You should talk to Charles. He saw Dr. Purcell after I said good night to him."

"I don't think I've heard of Charles."

"He's an orderly on the night staff. When I have trouble sleeping, I ring for him and he'll put me in my chair and push me up and down the halls. The night you're asking about—when I last saw the doctor—I took my usual pills, but nothing helped. I rang for Charles, and he said he'd take me on the Toad's Wild Ride. That's what he calls it. In truth, he wanted to smoke, so he parked me in the lobby and went outside. Dr. Purcell doesn't allow anyone to smoke in here. He says too many people have problems breathing as it is."

"What time was this?"

"Five minutes to nine or so. We didn't chat long. We talked about the weather. Felt just like spring, and I believe the moon was almost full. He went through the door, and that's the last I saw of him."

A Hispanic woman in scrubs appeared at the door. "I have your dinner tray, Mrs. Curtsinger." She crossed to Ruby's chair and set the dinner tray on a small rolling table that she pulled in close.

"Thank you," Ruby said, and then she smiled at me. "Will you come back and see me, dear? I like talking to you."

"I'll do what I can."

I walked down the hall as far as the staff lounge, where I stuck my head in and said, "I'm looking for Charles."

The man I saw sitting at the table with the evening paper was nut-brown, scrawny, in his fifties, and dressed in scrubs. He set his paper aside and got to his feet. "Charles Biedler," he said. "How may I help you, miss?"

I explained who I was and what I wanted, repeating what Ruby Curtsinger had told me. "It would really be a help if you'd tell me what you remember."

"I could show you where he was parked that night."

"I'd love that," I said. I retrieved my umbrella and my slicker. Charles used his newspaper as a rain hat, and we hurried outside. The walkway continued along the side of the building, and Charles paused at the end, pointing toward the cars. "See where that little blue VW's parked? Doctor was right there. I saw him crossing the lot, and then he got in his car and pulled out right around to here."

"You didn't see anyone else?"

"No, but that corner of the parking lot was darker at nine o'clock than it is right now."

"So he unlocked the car door. Did the interior light go on?"

"Might have. After he got in, he sat awhile, and then he started up the engine and swung this way so he could drive out the front."

"Was that his pattern?"

Charles blinked, shaking his head. "Most times."

"Let's get out of this rain," I said.

We headed back to the entrance, pausing outside the front door. I said, "You didn't see anyone in the car with him?"

Charles shook his head.

"Well, I appreciate your time. If you think of anything else, would you give me a call? I can be reached at this number." I handed him a business card and started out across the parking lot.

Once I got into my car, I sat thinking about the fact that I was parked right where Dow Purcell had been on the night of September 12. What had happened to him? He hadn't been assaulted. He'd gotten in his car; he'd sat there awhile. . . . Doing what? I started the car and headed, as Purcell had, toward Dave Levine Street.

I turned right, scanning the street. The area was residential. No bars or restaurants where he might have stopped for a drink. Once I reached the next intersection, it was impossible to guess which way he might have gone.

I PARKED my car in front of my apartment and dogtrotted the half block to Rosie's. I pushed open the door, dumped my umbrella, and left my slicker on a peg. The place was jammed. Both the juke-box and the television set were going full blast. I searched the crowd, wondering if I'd managed to arrive before Tommy Hevener. I felt a plucking at my sleeve and looked down to find him looking up at me from the first booth on the right.

Oh, my. He was freshly shaved, and he'd changed into a white dress shirt with a sky-blue wool crewneck pulled over it. He said something I missed. I leaned closer to him. When he repeated himself, his voice in my ear set up a tickling chill that went down to my feet. "Let's get out of here," he said. He got up and grabbed his raincoat from the seat across from him.

I nodded and began to inch my way toward the door again. I could feel him following, one hand against my back. I collected my slicker and my umbrella, and he shrugged into his raincoat. "Where to?" he asked.

"Emile's-at-the-Beach, one block over. We can walk."

His umbrella was the larger, so he raised it and held it over my head as we emerged into the pelting rain. The rain was coming down so hard, the water was propelled through the umbrella fabric like a mist.

Tommy stopped. "This is nuts. I've got a car right here." He took his keys out and unlocked the passenger-side door on a new Porsche painted candy-apple red. I stepped from the curb to the interior. He closed me in on my side and then circled in front of the car to his.

"Where's your pickup?" I said.

"That's business. This is play. You look great."

We chatted about nothing in particular on the short drive over to Emile's, where we were seated at a table for two. The atmosphere was intimate, with only half the tables occupied because of the rain. The waiter brought us two menus, and after a quick consultation Tommy ordered a bottle of California chardonnay.

"I went back and read your rental application. You're divorced," he said.

I held up two fingers.

"I've never been married. Too much of a rolling stone."

"I tend to appeal to guys on the move," I said.

"Maybe I'll surprise you. Where's your family?"

"My parents died in a car accident when I was five. I was raised by my mother's sister, my aunt Gin. She's dead now, too."

"No siblings?"

I shook my head.

"What about the husbands? Who were they?"

"The first was a cop. I met him as a rookie. . . ."

"You were a cop?"

"For two years. Then some other stuff went down, and I left the department. The second ex was a musician. Very talented. Not so good at being faithful, but he was nice in other ways. He cooked and played piano."

"Skills I admire. And where is he now?"

"I haven't any idea. You said your parents were gone?"

"It's weird being an adult orphan, though not as bad as you'd think. What'd your father do for a living?"

"Mail carrier. My folks were married fifteen years before I came along."

"So you only had five years together as a family."

"I guess that's right. I hadn't thought of it that way."

The waiter returned with our chardonnay and poured two glasses while we looked at the menus. I ended up ordering the roast chicken, and Tommy ordered the pasta puttanesca. Once the entrées arrived, Tommy said, "Tell me about the boyfriend."

I lowered my fork, feeling defensive on Dietz's behalf. "Why should I talk to you about him?"

"I'd like to know what's going on here. Between us."

"Nothing's going on. We're having dinner."

"I think there's more to it than that."

"What are we doing here, defining our relationship? I haven't known you long enough. Besides, you're too young."

He lifted his brows, and I found myself blushing.

I said, "How'd you decide to move to Santa Teresa?"

"You're changing the subject."

"I don't like to be pushed," I said.

"You cook?"

"No, but I'm a tidy little thing."

"Me, too. My brother's a pig. You'd never guess it by looking. He dresses okay, but his car's a mess."

We chattered on in this fashion, and I found myself liking his face. Also, I was not exactly unaware of his body, lean and muscular. Few men appeal to me, not so much because I'm picky about *them*. I'm protective of myself, which means I disqualify all but the most— What? I couldn't think what it was that allowed some men to get through my defenses. Chemistry, I guess. I focused on cutting my chicken, trying a sample of mashed potatoes, which rank right up there with peanut butter, in my opinion.

Tommy touched my hand. "Where'd you disappear to?"

I looked up to find him staring at me. "Is this a date?"

"Yes."

"I don't date. I'm not good at this boy-girl stuff."

"You do fine. Lighten up."

Humbled, I said, "Okay."

When we left the restaurant at nine o'clock, the streets were still glistening with the rain, which had passed. I waited while he unlocked his Porsche and let me in. Once he fired up the engine, he said, "Something I want to show you. Okay?"

He drove west, passing the yacht harbor. Without being told, I knew we were on our way to Horton Ravine. He smiled over at me. "I want to show you the house."

"What about Richard? Won't he object?"

"He drove down to Bell Garden to play poker tonight. He won't come back until morning, whatever happens."

We drove through the stone pillars that marked the rear entrance to Horton Ravine. At length, he turned up a short driveway to a half-moon motor court. I caught a sweeping glimpse of the house: stucco walls, massive lines, red tile roof. He reached for the remote garage-door opener, pressed a button, and then swung into the open bay of a four-car garage. I opened the car door on my side and got out while Tommy let us into the utility area off the kitchen. The indicator on the alarm panel by the door was dark. There were stacks of junk mail on the kitchen counters—catalogues and flyers. In a separate pile there were instruction manuals for the answering machine, the microwave oven, and the Cuisinart, which had clearly never been used. Tommy tossed his keys onto the white tile kitchen counter. "So what do you think?"

"No alarm system? That seems odd in a house this size."

"Spoken like a cop. There was actually one installed, but it isn't hooked up. When we first moved in, Richard set it off so often, the company started charging us fifty bucks a pop and the cops refused to show. We figured, what's the point?"

"Let's hope the burglars haven't heard."

"We're insured. Come on, and I'll give you the ten-cent tour."

He walked me through the house. On the first level, wide-plank oak floors stretched through the living room, dining room, family room, paneled den, and two guest rooms. The upstairs was fully carpeted in cream-colored wool—two master suites, a workout room, and enough closet space for ten. Many rooms were empty. I didn't see any art or books. In the bedrooms it was clear they'd purchased entire suites of furniture off the showroom floor.

We made the complete circuit and ended up back in the kitchen. Both of us were conscious of the passage of time. Despite his nonchalance, he seemed aware that Richard might roll in at any moment. In a show of bravado he said, "Would you like a drink?"

"I think not, but thanks. I have work to do. I appreciate the tour. This is really great."

"You'll have to see it by day. The landscaping's beautiful." He checked his watch. "I better get you home."

In the confines of the Porsche I was conscious of the charge in the air between us. We chatted on the drive, but it was make-work in the face of my attraction to him. He found a parking space near Rosie's, half a block from my place. He parked and came around the car to let me out.

We stood together for a moment, neither of us sure how to say good night. He reached over idly and adjusted the metal clasp on the front of my slicker. "Don't want you wet. Can I walk you home?"

"I'm just down there. You can almost see it from here."

He smiled. "I know. I got the address from your application and checked it out earlier. Looks nice."

"You're nosy."

"Where you're concerned," he said, smiling again.

We both said "Well" at the same time and laughed. I walked backward a few steps, watching while he opened the door and folded himself under the steering wheel. Moments later he took off with a roar.

5

TUESDAY morning dawned in a haze of damp fog. After a jog and breakfast I spent some time working at home, finishing revisions on my report for Fiona.

I left my apartment at 9:35. My appointment with Dow Purcell's best friend, Jacob Trigg, was scheduled for ten o'clock at his home in the heart of Horton Ravine. I drove east along Cabana Boulevard and ascended the hill as it swept up from the beach. I turned left on Promontory Drive and followed the road along the bluffs that paralleled the beach. I turned left and drove through the back entrance to Horton Ravine. Tommy crossed my mind, and I smiled in a goofy glow I found embarrassing.

A mile down the road I saw the house number I was looking for. I parked and got out. All the ground-floor windows were disconcertingly dark. There was no doorbell, and no one answered my repeated knocks. Had Trigg stood me up?

I started down the sloping lawn, hoping to come across someone who'd tell me if Trigg was home. At the end of a row of ornamental pears I spotted a greenhouse with a small potting shed attached. An electric golf cart was parked nearby.

I could see a man working at a high bench just inside the shed.

Despite the cold, he wore khaki shorts. There were braces on both legs. Propped up against the counter beside him was a pair of forearm crutches. The cap he wore covered a thatch of gray hair. On the redwood surface in front of him there were five or six potted plants.

I paused in the doorway, waiting for acknowledgment before I went in. "Hi. Sorry to interrupt, but are you Mr. Trigg?"

He scarcely looked up. "That's me. What can I do for you?"

"I'm Kinsey Millhone."

He turned and looked at me blankly. I guessed he was in his early sixties—red-nosed, jowly, and heavy through his chest.

"I was hoping you could answer some questions about Dr. Purcell," I prompted.

His confusion seemed to clear. "Oh, sorry. I forgot you were coming, or I'd have waited at the house."

"I should have called to remind you. I appreciate your taking the time to talk to me."

"Hope I can be of help," he said.

I said, "I take it you're an old friend of Dr. Purcell?"

"A good twenty years. I was a patient of his. He testified in my behalf in the lawsuit following my auto accident."

I smiled. "What kind of work did you do?"

"I was a detail man—drug sales, calling on doctors. I met Dow when he had his office over near St. Terry's."

"You must have done well. This property's impressive."

"So was the settlement. Not that it's any compensation. I used to jog and play tennis. Take your body for granted until it goes out on you, but I'm luckier than some." He peered over at me. "How's it going so far?"

"It's frustrating. I've met with a lot of people, but all I've picked up are theories when what I need are facts."

His eyebrows met in the middle. "I suspect I'm only going to add to the confusion. I'm as baffled as anyone."

"How often did you see him?"

"Once or twice a week. He'd stop by for coffee in the mornings on his way to Pacific Meadows. I felt comfortable telling him just about anything. He confided in me as well. Crystal tells me Fiona hired you."

"That's right. She's in San Francisco, but she's coming back this afternoon. I'm scrambling around, talking to as many people as I can, hoping to persuade her the money's well spent."

"Who's on your list, aside from me?"

"Well, I've talked to one of his two business associates—Joel Glazer. I haven't talked to Harvey Broadus. I talked to people at the clinic and his daughter Blanche."

"What about Crystal's ex-husband? Have you spoken to him?"

"I hadn't thought to, but I could. How does he fit in?"

"He might or might not. About four months back, Dow went to see Lloyd. I assumed it had something to do with Leila, but maybe not. You know, Leila lived with Lloyd briefly. Crystal got tired of fighting her, so Leila went to Lloyd's. She started eighth grade in the public schools up here. Wasn't there two months, and she was out of control. Grades fell; she was truant, into alcohol and drugs. Dow put his foot down and enrolled her in Fitch. Now she's strictly regulated, and she blames Dow for that."

"I gather Lloyd and Crystal get along okay."

"More or less. She still tends to lick his boots. Crystal was always under Lloyd's thumb."

"How so?"

"He lived off her earnings when she worked as a stripper in Las Vegas. They had one of those hotheaded relationships full of drinking and fights. After she met Dow, she moved to Santa Teresa with the girl. I guess she saw Dow as her ticket out, which he was. Problem was, Lloyd followed her, and he was furious."

"How do you know all this?"

"I heard it from Dow," he said. "I think he was worried Lloyd would find a way to reassert his dominance. He was also upset about Fiona pressing him for money. She was convinced he was coming back to her, and that distressed him no end. That's why he was on his way up there."

"What do you mean, up there?"

"He was going to see Fiona to clarify the situation."

"The night he disappeared?"

"That's what he told me. We had breakfast together that Friday morning, and he said she'd insisted on a meeting. She was always insisting on something. She couldn't stop his leaving her, but she could surely make him pay."

"Fiona tells me Dow disappeared on two previous occasions. Any idea where?"

"Rehab. He told me he went to a 'dry out' farm."

"Alcohol?"

"That's right. He didn't want it known, felt his patients would lose confidence if they knew his drinking was out of control."

"I've heard he was drinking again."

"Probably Fiona's influence. She'd drive any man to drink."

"Could he have checked into another rehab facility?"

"I hope so, but you'd think he'd have let someone know."

"Fiona says he didn't say a word to anyone before."

"That's not quite true. He told me."

"What do you know about the business at Pacific Meadows?"

Trigg shook his head. "Not much. I know it wasn't looking good. I told him to hire an attorney, but he said he didn't want to do that yet. He had his suspicions about what was going on, but he wanted to check it out himself before he did anything else."

"Someone told me he was worried Crystal would jump ship if the uproar became public."

"Maybe that's what Fiona was counting on," he said.

I WALKED into the office at 11:25 to find Jeniffer bending over a file drawer in a skirt so short two crescent-shaped bulges of her heinie were hanging out the back. I said, "Jeniffer, you're really going to have to wear longer skirts."

She jerked upright and tugged at the hem of her skirt.

"Any messages?" I asked.

"Just one. Mrs. Purcell said she's back and she's expecting you at two o'clock."

"When? Today or tomorrow?"

"Oh."

"Don't worry about it. I can figure it out. Anything else?"

"Someone's here to see you. Mariah *something*. I showed her into your office."

"You left her in my office by herself?"

"I have work to do. I couldn't stay."

I could feel my heat gauge rising into the red zone. "How long's she been there?"

"Twenty minutes. Maybe a little more."

"Jeniffer, in that length of time she could have ripped me off for everything I own."

"I'm sorry."

"Forget about sorry. Don't do it again." I headed down the inner corridor. I looked back at her. "And get some panty hose," I snapped.

My office door was closed. I barged in to find a woman sitting in the guest chair. Scanning the surface of the desk, I could've sworn my files were slightly disarranged. I looked at her quizzically, and she returned my gaze with eyes as blank and blue as a Siamese cat's.

She couldn't have been more than twenty-six, but her hair was a startling silver-gray. The skirt of her gray wool business suit was cut short, and sheer black hose emphasized her shapely knees. There was a black briefcase resting near the left side of her chair. She looked like an expensive lawyer. Maybe I was being sued.

Warily I moved around my desk and sat down.

"I'm Mariah Talbot," she said as she reached across the desk to shake hands. She had long oval nails painted a neutral shade.

"Do we have an appointment?" I asked, unable to keep the testiness out of my voice.

"We don't, but I'm here on a matter I think will interest you," she said, unruffled. She leaned forward, placing her business card on the desk in front of me. The face of it read MARIAH TALBOT, SPECIAL INVESTIGATIONS UNIT, GUARDIAN CASUALTY INSURANCE, with an address and phone number I scarcely stopped to read. "We need to have a chat about your landlord."

"Henry?"

"Richard Hevener."

I don't know what I expected, but not that. "What about him?"

"You may not be aware of this, but Richard and Tommy are fraternal twins. They murdered their parents back in Texas in 1983."

She went on, her manner completely matter-of-fact. "They hired someone to break into the house. As nearly as we can tell, the plan was for the burglar to drill the safe and walk off with a substantial amount of cash, plus jewelry valued at close to a million dollars. The boys' mother, Brenda, inherited a stunning family jewelry collection that she left, by will, to her only sister, Karen."

Mariah reached into her briefcase, removed a manila folder, and passed it over to me. "These are the newspaper clippings. Plus one copy each of the two wills."

I opened the file and glanced at the first few newspaper clippings, dated January 15, 22, and 29 of 1983. In all three articles Richard and Tommy were pictured, looking solemn and withdrawn. Headlines indicated the two were being questioned in the ongoing investigation of the homicides of Jared and Brenda Hevener.

Mariah Talbot went on. "The burglar was a punk named Casey Stonehart, who'd already been jailed six times for a variety of crimes ranging from petty theft to arson. We believe he opened the safe using the combination they'd given him. Then he dismantled the smoke detectors and set a blaze meant to cover up the crime. Apparently—and this is only a guess—the deal was, he'd take the bulk of the jewelry, which he was in a position to fence. The boys would take the cash and maybe a few choice pieces, then submit a claim to the insurance company for the house, its contents, the jewelry, and anything else they could get away with. Mr. and Mrs. Hevener were found bound and gagged in the master-bedroom closet. They died of smoke inhalation. Both boys were out of town and had ironclad alibis," she said. "Stonehart disappeared soon afterward—probably dead and buried somewhere. He's been missing ever since, so it's a safe bet they got rid of him."

"Couldn't he be in hiding?"

"If he were, he'd have been in touch with his family. The sheriff's department put a mail check in place, and there's a trace on the phone. This is a kid with big dependency issues. If he were alive, he couldn't tolerate the separation."

"When was this again?"

"In 1983. Hatchet, Texas. It didn't take long for suspicion to fall on the two boys, but they'd been extremely clever."

Anything I'd felt for Tommy had evaporated. "What made the cops fix on them?"

"For one thing, neither of them can act. They put on a good show, but the feelings were all phony, strictly crocodile tears. At the time, both were still living at home. Tommy was a perpetual college student. Richard fancied himself an 'entrepreneur,' which meant he borrowed and squandered money as fast as it came into his hands. Jared was thoroughly disgusted with them. Brenda, too. This we heard about later from close friends of theirs."

"I'm assuming the brothers were charged?"

Mariah shook her head. "Police investigators couldn't cobble together sufficient evidence to satisfy the D.A. Of course, the insurance company balked at paying, but the boys filed suit. Since they hadn't been arrested, charged with, or convicted of any crime, Guardian Casualty had no choice but to pay up."

"How much?"

"Two hundred and fifty thousand each in life insurance. The homeowner's and auto claims came to a little over three quarters of a million dollars. Along with the insurance, you add the cash in the safe—probably another hundred grand—and the jewelry on top of that, and you can see they did well. Guardian Casualty and Karen Atcheson, the boys' aunt, are preparing to file a civil suit to recover their losses. We're convinced the boys still have the jewelry."

"Why now, when the murders were three years ago?"

"An informant's come forward—very hush-hush. This is the arsonist, a professional. Casey was relying on his expertise because the job was much bigger than anything he'd done in his piddling career."

"What was the arsonist getting in return?"

"A piece of Casey's action. Once the arsonist found out about the killings, he wasn't willing to fess up to any part in it. Now he's decided to do what's right."

"Why doesn't he go to the cops and let them handle it?"

"He will if Guardian Casualty comes up with the evidence."

I pushed the file aside. "And you're here to do what?"

Mariah smiled to herself as though privately amused. "I've been nosing around. It looks like funds are low and the boys are getting on each other's nerves. We're counting on the fact they're having cash-flow problems. That's why Richard agreed to lease the place to you, if you haven't figured that out. You offered him six months' rent in advance, and he needed the bucks."

"How'd you find out about that?"

"We gimmicked up another applicant. The cash is the explanation Richard gave when he turned him down. At any rate, the friction between the brothers could really work for us. I'm always hoping one will break down and rat the other one out."

"What's that got to do with me?"

"We'd like for you to pass along the name of a fence in Los Angeles. He's a jeweler by trade. With money getting scarce, the boys might be tempted to dip into the stash."

"So I pass along the information about the jeweler, and then what?"

"We wait to see if they take the bait. Once we know the jewelry's on the premises, we'll ask for a warrant and go in."

"Based on what?"

"We'll have the fence, and the fence will have a portion of the jewelry. The boys are going to have a hell of a time explaining that."

"What if they don't make contact with him?"

"We have another scheme in mind that I'd rather not go into."

"What makes you so sure they still have the jewelry?"

"We know they bought a safe from a local locksmith. The problem is, we have no legitimate means of getting in."

"Funny you should say that. I was there last night. Richard was gone. Tommy took me over and showed me around."

"I don't suppose you spotted the safe."

"I'm afraid not. There's barely any furniture and no wall art.

"When will you see him again?"

"I'm not going to see him again! After what you've told me?"

"Too bad. We could really use your help."

"I'd have no reason to tour the house again. Besides, even if I found the safe, I wouldn't have the faintest idea how to open it."

"We wouldn't want you to do that. All we need is the location, which couldn't be that hard. Once we have the warrant, we don't want the boys disposing of the evidence."

I thought about it briefly. "I won't do anything illegal."

Mariah smiled. "Oh, come now. From what we've heard, you're willing to cut corners when it suits you."

I stared at her. "You ran a background on me?"

"We had to know who we were dealing with. All we're asking you to do is pass along the information about the fence." She placed a slip of paper on the desk with a name and address written across the face of it. "This is the name of the jeweler. I'll leave it up to you how you play out the information."

I took the paper and looked at the name. "You have a number where I can reach you?"

"I've been moving around. In an emergency you can use the number on my card, but it'd be better if I called you. I'll touch base in a day or so. Meanwhile, I don't want the boys to know I'm here. If they find out we've spoken, you're in the soup, so take care."

BY 1:45, HAVING confirmed my appointment with Fiona, I found myself driving once more along Old Reservoir Road. I wasn't looking forward to the meeting, but it was better than having to think about Richard and Tommy Hevener. That problem was stuck in my throat like a bone. My first impulse was to bail on the new office space, thus severing all ties, but how could I get out of my deal with them? And by breaking off all contact, I was, in effect, refusing to help Mariah Talbot. I seldom shied away from risk.

Fiona must have been waiting because I'd barely touched the bell before she opened the door. Her outfit that day consisted of a long-sleeved crepe blouse modeled on a postwar Eisenhower jacket that tied at the waist. Her black wool skirt was tubular.

As she stepped away from the door, I held out the brown manila envelope.

"What's this?" she asked suspiciously.

"You said you wanted a report."

She opened the envelope and peered at the pages. "Thank you," she said, dismissing my labors with a glance. "I hope you won't object to talking in the bedroom. I'd like to unpack."

"Fine with me." In truth I was curious to see the rest of the place.

She picked up a makeup case she'd stashed in the hall. She barely glanced at the larger suitcase. "Grab that for me."

I picked up the hard-sided suitcase, feeling like a pack mule as I followed her up the stairs. We turned right at the landing and went into the white-on-white master suite. I set her suitcase on the floor.

Fiona moved to the four-poster bed, where a second hard-sided suitcase was already laid open on the pristine spread. She began to remove articles of clothing. "Why don't you start from the beginning and fill me in."

I opened my verbal recital with an improvisational medley of interviews, going back over my report in a series of beautifully articulated summations of events. I began with Detective Odessa, segued into my visit with Crystal Purcell, and then moved on to Pacific Meadows, at which point I delineated the nature of the difficulties Dow Purcell was facing, then related my visit to Blanche.

Fiona turned to me. "You went over to see Blanche? Why in the world did you do that?"

"She called me at home. I got the impression you'd already spoken to her."

"I did no such thing, and I can't believe you'd take such a step without consulting me. If I'd wanted you to see Blanche, I'd have given you her number. How much did you tell her?"

"I really don't remember. I'm sorry, but she acted as if she knew all about me, so I assumed she'd talked to you or to Melanie."

"I'll pass on information to the girls if it seems relevant, but I think it's inappropriate coming from you. Is that clear?"

"Of course," I said, stung.

"How do you intend to go about finding him?"

"Ah," said I. "Well, I have some other people I want to talk to first, and then we'll see where we stand." In truth, I was at a loss.

Her eyes glittered briefly, and I thought she might challenge me, but she seemed to think better of it.

"A question," I said. "Why didn't you tell me he was on his way over here that night?"

"He never arrived. I thought it was a miscommunication. I tried calling his office the next day, but he was already gone by then."

"Why was he coming?"

"I don't see why it matters, since he never showed."

"Was anyone else in the house with you that night?" I asked.

"To support my story?"

"That'd be nice, don't you think?"

"I'm afraid I can't help. This is a small town. Tongues wag. I wouldn't even let him leave his car on the parking pad. I had him pull into the empty garage. No one knew about his visits."

"At least no one you told."

"He swore he wouldn't tell Crystal."

"I didn't say he told Crystal. This was someone else."

"Trigg."

I said, "Yes." After all, it was her money. "What about Lloyd Muscoe? Did Dow ever talk to you about him?"

"A bit. They disliked each other and avoided contact whenever possible. At first it was territorial. Later the friction between them was more about Leila's relationship with Lloyd. I'm sure Lloyd resented Dow's interference. Instead of taking time with Blanche, you should have been talking to him."

I left Fiona in the bedroom and went outside to the car to consider my options. The simplest course of action would be to ask Crystal where Lloyd lived. Since the two shared custody, I assumed she'd know. I turned the key in the ignition and headed for Horton Ravine.

DR. PURCELL'S HOUSE WAS built on a lush, wooded knoll with a narrow view of the ocean. The residence itself wasn't impressive, despite Fiona's boasting about her talent for design. In typical fashion she'd piled box on box in tiers to a flat concrete roof. It was clearly not Crystal's taste, and I could see where she'd chafe at having to live there. The white Volvo and the Audi convertible were parked in the drive, along with a snappy little black Jaguar I hadn't seen before.

I rang the bell, and within a minute Crystal appeared at the door. She was wearing boots, black wool slacks, and a heavy black wool sweater. "Good. Maybe you can help. Nica, it's Kinsey! Come on in," she said to me, harried.

I stepped through the door. "What's going on?"

"Anica's just driven up from Fitch," she said. "Leila left campus without permission, and we're trying to track her down before she blows it. She'll be kicked out of school if they realize she's gone."

Anica appeared from the kitchen, wearing navy-blue slacks and a red blazer with a gold-stitched FITCH ACADEMY patch on the breast. She managed a wide smile despite Crystal's distress. "Hello, Kinsey. How are you?"

"Fine. You think Leila's heading this way?"

"Let's hope," Crystal said on her way into the kitchen. "I'm making coffee while we try to decide what to do. She knows she's not allowed to hitchhike. I'd be sick with worry if I wasn't so mad at her. How do you take yours, Kinsey?"

"Black's fine with me."

Anica and I followed her into the kitchen. Anica perched on one of the stools lined up along the length of a speckled-gray granite island while Crystal took cups and saucers from the nearest cabinet, saying, "She'll be grounded for months. What time did she take off?"

Anica said, "She had an appointment with me at ten. When she didn't show for that, I tracked down her roommate, Amy, who told me she'd seen Leila leaving campus with her backpack."

"Mind if I look in her room?" I asked.

Crystal said, "Go right ahead. It's the second door to the right, at the head of the stairs."

The room was done in frilly pastels. Talk about wishful thinking. She was at that stage where the half-nudie rock posters ran neck and neck with the stuffed animals of her youth. The floor was carpeted in discarded clothes, which were also draped over two chairs and a window seat.

I did a quick but thorough search of the room. The only discovery of interest was the narrow metal lockbox hidden between the mattress and box spring. I shook it but heard only the softest of sounds in response. Probably her dope stash. I didn't have time enough to pick the lock and returned the box to its hiding place.

Going back to the kitchen, I studied the family calendar for November that sat open on the desk. I could see that three different people had added notes about social events and other activities. Judging from handwriting and the nature of the events posted, I was guessing that Leila's was the oversized printing—angled *t*'s, puffy *i*'s. Crystal's was the elegant cursive in red ink, and Rand's was the scrawl. Notes on alternate weekends indicated Leila's return from school. I leafed back three months to July and August, noting a fourth handwriting: bold block letters in black. This (I surmised) was Dr. Purcell, whose presence was visible up until Monday, September 8, four days before he vanished. He'd jotted in notes about two board meetings, a medical symposium at U.C.L.A., and a golf date at the country club.

"I've had it with her," Crystal was saying.

Anica said, "She's probably on her way to Lloyd's."

"Great. Let him deal with her. I'm sick of it. This is about Paulie. I'll bet you dollars to doughnuts."

"Is Paulie her boyfriend?" I asked.

"Girlfriend," Anica said. "Name's Pauline."

I picked up the calendar and moved over to the island, where I claimed my coffee cup. "Mind if I ask about this?"

Crystal glanced over at me, distracted. "What do you need?"

I placed the calendar on the counter and tapped at the page. "I gather Leila doesn't come home every weekend."

"For the most part, she does. Lloyd and I usually alternate visits, but things do come up."

"Like what?"

Crystal glanced at the page, pointing to the second weekend in July. "This was the weekend she had an invitation to go home with her friend Sherry, in Malibu Colony. Her father's in the movie business, and he takes the girls to all the big premières."

I pointed to the weekend of September 12, when Dow Purcell disappeared. "And this?"

"Same thing, different friend. Emily's family owns horses. Actually, I think Emily got sick, and Leila ended up over at Lloyd's. Why do you ask?"

I shrugged, checking back through the months. It looked as if Leila went off with her school friends on an average of once a month. "I'm thinking she might have left campus with one of her classmates from Fitch."

Crystal turned to Anica. "What do you think?"

"It wouldn't hurt to check."

Then Crystal said, "Hold on a second, and let me try Lloyd again." She picked up the phone and punched in seven numbers, listened for a moment, and then replaced the handset. "He's still not answering. He's there, if I know him. He's always got collection agencies on his case, so he refuses to pick up."

I said, "Look, I need an excuse to talk to him anyway. Why don't you let me go over to his place and see if Leila's there?"

"That's not a bad idea. Nica and I can stay here in case she decides to make an appearance." Crystal reached for a pen and scribbled down some numbers on a scratch pad, tearing off the sheet. "My number and Lloyd's address and phone. If you find Lloyd, tell him it's time he took his fair share of the load."

Walking out to my car, I had to wonder how kids of divorced parents survive all the bickering.

LLOYD lived on a street called Gramercy Lane, which looped along the foothills. I sailed through the stone pillars that marked the front entrance to Horton Ravine and followed the road as it curved around to the right. At the first red light I glanced at my map.

Gramercy Lane was within a two-mile radius of the Purcell house in the ravine. If Leila had thumbed a ride from Malibu, traveling north on the 101, she'd probably ask to be let off at Little Pony Road, which was one off-ramp south.

I took the Little Pony off-ramp. At the top, I turned left and headed toward the mountains, scanning both sides of the four-lane road. I passed a couple huddled under an umbrella. They were walking on my side of the road with their backs to me. It wasn't until I passed them, catching a second glimpse in my side-view mirror, that I identified Leila's cottony white-blond hair and her long coltish legs. Her companion was tall and lean, toting a backpack. I slowed and pulled in at the curb just ahead of them. As they walked by my car, I leaned over and rolled down the window on the passenger side. "Can I give you a ride?"

Leila leaned forward. She knew she knew me, but she didn't remember how. The kid with her leveled a gaze at me filled with hostility and disdain. This had to be Paulie.

I focused on Leila. "Hi. I'm Kinsey Millhone. We met last Friday at the beach house. I just came from your mom's. She's worried about you. You should have let her know you were leaving school."

"I'm fine, but tell her thanks for her concern."

"I think you should tell her yourself."

Paulie said something to Leila under her breath. She eased the backpack from her shoulders, passed it to Leila after a few murmured words, and took off toward the highway.

Leila leaned closer to the half-opened window. "You can't make me go home."

"I'm not here to *make* you do anything," I said. "Come on. Get in. I'll drop you off at your dad's."

She opened the door and slid into the passenger seat, shoving her backpack into the cramped space at her feet. I pulled onto the road.

"How'd you know where I was going?" she asked.

"Your mother figured it out. When we get to a phone, I want you to call and tell her where you are. She's been worried sick."

"Why don't you do it? You'll talk to her anyway."

"Of course I will." We drove for a block in silence. Then I said, "I don't get what's bugging you."

"I hate Fitch. The girls are such snobs."

"I thought you had friends."

"Well, I don't."

"What about Sherry?"

Leila stole a look at me. "What about her?"

"I'm just wondering how you enjoyed yourself in Malibu."

"Fine. It was fun."

"What about Emily? Your mom said you liked riding horses at her place."

"Why are you asking me all these questions?"

"Here's my best guess. I'll bet you skipped both those visits and spent the weekend with Paulie."

"So what if I saw Paulie? What's the big deal about that?"

"How'd you two meet?"

"In Juvie."

"You were in Juvenile Hall? When was this?"

"A year ago July. Bunch of us got picked up."

"Doing what?"

"The cops said loitering and trespass, which is crap. We were just hanging around some boarded-up old house."

"What time of day?"

"What are you, a district attorney? It was late, like two in the morning. Half the kids ran. Cops took the rest of us in."

I turned left on Gramercy, and Leila pointed at a weathered A-frame sitting on a dirt rise. I pulled into the driveway and killed the engine. "You want to see if he's there? I'd like to talk to him."

"What about?"

"Dr. Purcell, if it's all the same to you," I said.

Leila snatched open the door and reached for her backpack, which I snagged with one hand. "Leave that with me. I'll bring it in if he's home. I don't want you taking off on me."

She sighed, exasperated, but did as she was told. She knocked on the door and then huddled with folded arms. The place looked dark to me. She knocked again, then splashed her way back to the car and let herself in. "He's probably coming right back. I know where he keeps the key, so I can wait for him here."

"Good. I'll wait with you."

We got out of the car, and I followed her along the path with her backpack. Once we reached the house, Leila shifted a pot of dead geraniums and removed the house key from its terribly original hiding place. I waited while she unlocked the door and let us in.

"Does he rent this?"

"Nuhn-uhn. He's house-sitting for a friend."

The interior was basically one big room. The ceiling soared to a peak. To the right, a narrow staircase led to a sleeping loft. In the living area below, the wood furniture was clumsily constructed, covered with imitation Indian rugs. I spotted the phone sitting on a small side table. "You want to call your mom or should I?"

"You do it. I'm going to the bathroom."

While she availed herself of the facilities, I called Crystal. "I'm going to stay here until Lloyd gets home. If it gets too late, I'll try to talk Leila into coming back to your place."

"Honestly, I'm so mad at her I don't want to see her. Anica's calling the school. I have no idea what she'll tell them."

"I'll keep you posted on our progress," I said.

Leila emerged from the bathroom and moved over to the sofa. "What'd she say?"

"Nothing much. She's not real happy with you, Leila."

Ignoring me, she opened her backpack and took out a compact so she could study her face. She cleaned up the smeared mascara and then peered closer at herself.

"Tell me about Dow," I said. "And don't get all huffy. I'm bored with that."

"Like what do you want to know?"

"When did you see him last?"

"I don't remember stuff like that."

"Here, I'll help. September twelfth was a Friday. Emily was sick and she canceled, so were you at the beach house?"

"Nuhn-uhn. I was here."

"Where do you think Dow is?"

"In Canada."

"Interesting. What makes you say that?"

"I heard him talking to some woman on the phone. Six months ago these people came into the clinic and picked up financial records and a lot of patient files. Whatever it was, I guess he could have gone to jail for it, so I think he skipped."

"Who was he talking to?"

"I don't know. He never said her name, and I didn't recognize her voice. Just about then, he figured out I was on the line, so he waited 'til I got off before he said anything else."

"You were listening in?"

"I was up in my room. I wanted to make a phone call. How was I supposed to know he was on the line?"

"When was this?"

"Couple weeks before he went."

"Did you tell the police?"

"Nobody asked. Can I watch TV now?"

"Sure."

She picked up the remote control, MTV came blasting on, and Leila sunk into that hypnotic state television generates. The A-frame was getting dark. I flipped on some lights. Since she was paying absolutely no attention, I took advantage of the moment to search the desk drawers. Most seemed to be filled with the other fellow's junk. I sifted through a handful of Lloyd's bills, all overdue.

I moved across the great room and climbed the stairs to the loft. A check of the dresser drawers revealed nothing except a wide array of flashy-looking boxer shorts. I turned and surveyed the area. There was a telescope on a tripod standing by the window, and that interested me. I crossed and studied the view with my naked eye at first, orienting myself to my surroundings. Startled, I realized Lloyd's current digs were located just across the reservoir from Fiona Purcell. I could see the barren outline of her house. I bent to the eyepiece on the telescope, squinted through the lens, and adjusted the knob. Abruptly the far shore came into sharp relief. I could see the scarring on a boulder standing out in such sharp contrast; it looked as if it rested just a foot away from me. The water in the reservoir was ragged where the raindrops hit. I caught movement to the right and shifted my view a hair.

There was Trudy, the German shepherd I'd seen at Fiona's, barking at a stick—one of those brainless behaviors dogs seem to thrive on. Behind her, a wide path through the undergrowth had been flattened, and I could see white where a line of saplings had been snapped off at ground level. Maybe a boat trailer had been backed down close to the water's edge to launch an outboard.

I let my gaze come to rest on the narrow end of the reservoir where the vegetation grew densely all the way to the point where the water met the hill. A sign was posted on a fence post, and I could read the larger of the lines. Swimming and boating were forbidden. The light was fading rapidly. I lifted my eyes and stared at the gathering dark. What had I seen?

I turned and trotted down the stairs. Leila emerged from her trance long enough to look up at me.

I said, "I have to go out for a few minutes. Will you be all right by yourself?"

"Yeah." She turned her attention to the set again.

I closed the front door behind me and picked my way down the muddy path to my car. The rain wasn't falling hard, but it was annoying nonetheless. I slid under the wheel and popped open the glove compartment. I took out my flashlight and laid it on the passenger seat while I started the car and backed out of Lloyd's short drive. I swung around and headed back to the main road. At the intersection I turned right, drove half a mile, turned right again onto Old Reservoir Road, and began the winding ascent.

Ahead, Fiona's house came into view, and I pulled over on the berm. I grabbed my flashlight from the glove compartment, got out, and set off on foot. Out here, there was still enough ambient light that I could see my way. I climbed the wet grassy hill, my feet slipping out from under me when I least expected it.

Traversing the downside of the hill was even trickier. At the bottom I turned on my flashlight. The water was black near the shoreline and showed no evidence of a current. I shone the beam of my flashlight along the hill behind me, locating the boulder I'd seen and the path of broken saplings. I turned my beam on the silty water, tracing the shallows. The lake bottom apparently dropped off abruptly, but I could see the curve of a chrome bumper glowing dully, like buried treasure. I couldn't read the name on the vanity plate, but I knew I was looking at the trunk of Dow Purcell's silver Mercedes submerged in the depths.

6

AN ACCIDENT scene at night is as bleak and gaudy as a carnival. It was now fully dark, close to eight p.m. The coroner's car, the mobile crime lab, and a Ford sedan were parked on the berm, along with two patrol cars with red-and-blue bar lights flashing, radios squawking insistently between spurts of static.

Five minutes after I'd spotted the submerged Mercedes, I'd scrambled up the hill and down the other side to the road. I'd crossed and climbed Fiona's stairs two at a time, not pausing for breath until I reached the top. I pounded on her front door and rang the bell simultaneously, willing her to respond. It didn't take much to persuade me she was still out somewhere.

Fiona's nearest neighbor was just across the road. I rang the bell, talking to myself the whole time: *Come on, be here. Help me out here.* I peered through the glass side panels, which afforded me an abbreviated view of the foyer. Someone appeared in the hall and approached the front door. She was middle-aged, in a sweater and slacks. She turned on the porch light and studied me with caution.

I spoke loudly. "I'm a friend of Fiona's. She's out, and I need to use your phone." I saw her eyes stray toward Fiona's house while she assimilated the request; then she let me in and showed me to the phone.

Seven minutes later the first black-and-white patrol car had come careering up the road.

Nearly two hours had passed, and neighbors from many of the surrounding houses had straggled out to the road. They stood in clusters under their umbrellas, conversing in subdued and fragmentary bursts while the rain pattered on. Word had apparently spread that the doctor's car had been found.

I sat in my car feeling tense with the cold. At intervals I fired up the engine so I could keep the heater running and the windshield wipers on. From the water's edge the floodlights glowed eerily, silhouetting the few scrub trees stretched out along the crest. Occassionally the light was broken by shadows as the police went about their business. I'd spoken briefly with Odessa when he'd first reached the scene. He'd asked me to stay and said they'd put a diver in the water to check the car's interior before they hauled it out of the lake.

At some point Leila had appeared, accompanied by her stepfather, Lloyd, who'd come home while I was in the process of discovering Dow's car. I was guessing the two had been attracted by the lights and had hopped into Lloyd's car. Down the road I spotted two Minicam crews—one from KWST-TV, the other from KEST-TV. The blond reporter from KEST was already picking up film clips and interviews for the eleven-o'clock news. She stood under a big black umbrella, talking to one of the neighbors.

I adjusted my rearview mirror, watching as a pair of headlights swept into view around the curve in the road, then parked on the berm just ahead of me. I was hoping to see Fiona, but the vehicle turned out to be Crystal's white Volvo.

I grabbed my slicker from the back seat and held it over my head as I left the comfort of my VW and moved gingerly along the road to her car. She turned and caught sight of me and rolled down her window. Her face was drawn, her hair pulled back in an untidy knot at the nape of her neck.

She looked as if she'd dressed in haste, pulling on jeans and a gray sweatshirt. She said, "I was already in my robe and slippers when the officer came to the door. He wanted to bring me over in his patrol car, but I wanted my own wheels. What's happening?"

"Nothing much. Where's Anica?"

"She had to get back to school. Hop in."

I said, "Thanks." I opened the door and slid into the front seat. "How are you?"

"Numb."

I said, "The car might have been abandoned."

"Let's hope that's all it is. When did you get here?" she asked, as though talking in her sleep.

"Hours ago. At six."

"They said not to hurry. I was watching TV when the officer arrived at the door."

"You're lucky. I'm starving. I'm about to eat my arm."

Crystal reached over to the glove compartment and flipped the door down. "Try this." She removed a battered Hershey's bar and passed it over to me. "How'd they find the car?"

"I was the one who spotted it and called nine one one." I broke the candy bar into perfect squares and placed one section on my tongue. I could almost read the softly engraved letter H as I pressed the softening chocolate against the roof of my mouth.

We were silent. Then Crystal said, "I take it they haven't pulled the car out of the water yet."

"They're waiting for the tow truck." I ate an E and stuck the rest of the Hershey's in my shoulder bag.

Crystal made a sound that was half sigh and half weariness. "I knew he was dead. That's the only explanation that made any sense. I told you he wouldn't walk off and leave Griff."

"Crystal, they haven't even brought the car up. We don't know he's in there."

"He's there. Leila's going to freak."

"How so? She doesn't like him."

"Of course not. She treated him like dirt. How's she going to make her peace with that? I'm not sure how I'm going to tell her about all this."

"She's here. Didn't you see her back there with Lloyd?"

Crystal sat up abruptly. "I had no idea. Where?"

"Far side of the road, about three cars back."

"I better see how she's doing." Crystal reached around the seat for an umbrella and opened the car door.

"Thanks for the Hershey's. You saved my life."

"You're welcome."

The tow truck appeared, its headlights illuminating the roadway as far as the next curve. I retreated to my car and watched the tow truck lumber backward up the hill to the top. I couldn't imagine how they'd manage to haul the Mercedes out of the water and up the sodden hillside.

I turned sideways, looking over the back seat to check Crystal's progress. She'd reached Leila, who was standing by the side of the road with Lloyd. Lloyd had his arm around her, but the minute Leila saw Crystal, she fled to her mother's embrace.

Detective Odessa, in a hooded water-repellent jacket, appeared at the crest of the hill and began his descent. He spotted my VW and began to tack in my direction. I leaned over and cranked down the window. He reached the car and peered in. "I want you to meet Detective Paglia. He'll be the case manager on this."

I said, "Sure." I rolled up the window and got out, shrugging into my slicker and following him up the hill.

I said, "Anybody heard from Fiona?"

"Nope. We notified the daughter. She says she'll put in a few calls and see if she can track her down. Otherwise we wait and hope she comes home."

We scrambled the last few yards to the top of the hill and stood there together staring down at the lake. The light from the flood lamps had washed the color from the scene. With the angle of the light the butt end of the Mercedes glimmered incongruously in the murky water. "Is he in there?"

"Don't know yet. We've got a diver in the water. The shelf drops off sharply to a depth of twenty feet. Car got hung up against a boulder, or it'd be down on the bottom and we'd be out of luck."

The diver surfaced, removed his mouthpiece, and lifted off his face mask. Once onshore the coroner and another man intercepted him and listened while he reported.

Odessa nodded. "That's Paglia with the coroner."

"I gathered as much."

As if on cue, the other detective turned and caught sight of us. He excused himself and headed toward us across soft ground already trampled with footprints. When he reached us, Detective Paglia held out his hand. "Ms. Millhone. Jim Paglia." His voice was deep and uninflected. I placed him in his fifties. His head was shaved, his freckled forehead etched with a trellis of vertical and horizontal lines. He wore small oval glasses with thin metal frames.

We shook hands and said hi-how-are-you-type things. "We owe you a big one. How'd you happen to come down?"

Odessa touched my sleeve. "You two go ahead. I'll be right back."

I watched him cross to the diver, whom he engaged in conversation. I turned my attention to Detective Paglia, whose gaze had settled unrelentingly on mine. "I'm not sure how to describe the process. I was up at Lloyd's. He's Crystal's ex-husband."

"Leila's stepdad."

"Right. This morning she left boarding school without permission, and Crystal figured she was headed for his place. I told Crystal I'd see if I could track her down, so I began cruising the area there at Little Pony Road and the 101. She must have hitchhiked because I spotted her walking on the berm. I talked her into letting me drive her up to Lloyd's. He was gone when we got there, so she let us into the house. His is that A-frame," I said, and pointed to the far side of the lake. Leila was watching TV, and I went up to the loft. I saw the telescope and thought it'd be interesting to take a peek. I was surprised to see where I was. I hadn't realized that section of Gramercy put him directly across the reservoir from Fiona.

"Anyway, when I looked through the telescope, I saw the dog—a German shepherd named Trudy. I'd seen her up here on a visit to Fiona's house, and she was in this area, barking her head off. I could see she was excited, but I had no idea why. Aside from Trudy, I could see some scarring on that boulder halfway up the slope. There was also damage to the vegetation, saplings snapped off. At first I figured somebody must have backed a trailer down to launch a boat, but then I caught sight of the posted warning and I remembered that swimming and boating were forbidden."

Paglia seemed to study me, his expression one of calculated kindness. "I still don't understand how you made the connection."

"The idea suddenly made sense. Dr. Purcell was last seen at the clinic. I'd heard he was on his way up here to see Fiona, so I—"

"Who told you that?"

"A friend of Purcell's, a fellow named Jacob Trigg. Dow told him he had a meeting scheduled with her that night."

"You talk to her about this?"

"Well, I *asked* her. Why not? I work for her. She should have given me the information the moment I hired on."

"What'd she say?"

"She claims he didn't show, called it a miscommunication. I assumed he stood her up and she was too embarrassed to admit it."

"Too bad she didn't mention it to us. We could have canvassed up here. Somebody might've heard the car."

Behind him, I heard the high whine of the gear as a cable was wound around the drum, dragging the Mercedes from the lake. The car was now suspended in a forward tilt, front end down, three of the four windows opened. Lake water poured from every crack and crevice. The window on the driver's side had been shattered, the bottom half still a maze of crazed glass, the upper portion gone. In the front seat I caught a glimpse of a vaguely human shape—amorphous, all bloat and slime, face turned toward the window gap as if peeking at the view. After weeks in the water the once living flesh was bloodless, bleached a pearly white. I turned my head abruptly and made an involuntary sound. His mouth was open, his jaw relaxed. His lips had widened in a final O of joy or surprise—a howl of rage, perhaps.

"I'll be in the car," I said.

Paglia didn't hear me. He was heading for the Mercedes. The

morgue crew stood back. Peripherally I saw flashes as the police photographer documented her work. I couldn't watch anymore. Ordinarily at such a scene, after the first jolt of revulsion, I can become detached. Here I couldn't manage it, couldn't shake off the feeling that I was in the presence of evil. Purcell—assuming the body was his—had either killed himself or been killed. There was no way he could have driven up that hill and down into the lake by accident.

BY THE time I returned to my apartment, it was after ten o'clock. The crime-scene technicians were still busy at the reservoir, though I couldn't imagine what remained to be done. I'd hung around for a while and then headed home. I'd never eaten dinner. In fact, as nearly as I remembered, I hadn't eaten lunch. Hunger had asserted itself and then faded at least twice during the evening and now had dissipated altogether, leaving a nagging headache in its wake.

Mercifully, the rain had moved on, and the temperature had warmed. The streets seemed to smoke, vapor rising in drifts. The sidewalks were still wet, water dripping from the tree limbs as silently as snow. The gutters gurgled merrily, miniature rivers diverted by debris as the runoff traveled downstream into sewers to the sea. A dense fog began to accumulate, making the world seem hushed and dense. My neighborhood looked unfamiliar, a landscape made alien by mist. Depths were flattened to two dimensions, bare branches no more than ink lines bleeding onto a page. I paused in the process of unlocking my door. Henry's kitchen window was aglow, a small square of yellow in the hovering mist. I tucked the keys into my pocket and crossed the flagstone patio.

I peered into the upper portion of his back door. He was seated at the table, reaching for his glass of Jack Daniel's. I called, "Henry," and then tapped on the glass. He let me in. While I doffed my slicker and hung it over the back of the chair, he opened the freezer door and removed a handful of ice cubes, which he plunked in his glass, pouring a fresh round of whiskey over them.

"So what's up? You look beat." He took a seat at the table.

"I am." He handed me his drink.

I said, "Thanks," and took a swallow of Jack Daniel's. I could feel my tension ease and realized, belatedly, how tired I was. I passed the glass back to him and sank into a chair.

"What's going on?" he asked.

"We found Dr. Purcell's car and his body—assuming it's him." I gave Henry a summary of events leading up to my discovery.

"I understand," he said. "So what now?"

"Dr. Yee will do the autopsy in the morning. Don't know how much they'll learn, given the shape the body's in."

Henry picked up the glass and took it to the sink. He rinsed it and set it in the rack. "By the way, I saw a friend of yours tonight."

"Really. Who?"

He took a seat. "Tommy Hevener came into Rosie's. He was looking for you, of course, but we ended up having quite a chat. He seems like a nice fellow, and he's clearly smitten. He asked a lot of questions about you."

"I have a lot of questions about him, too. Turns out Tommy and his brother hired a punk down in Texas to break into the family home and steal the valuables, including close to a million in jewels. The burglar did as instructed and then set fire to the house to cover his tracks. What the boys failed to mention to him was that Mom and Dad were bound and gagged in the closet. They died of smoke inhalation while the place burned down around them."

Henry blinked. "No. That can't be true."

"It is," I said. "The insurance investigator—a woman named Mariah Talbot—came to the office this morning and showed me the clippings from the Hatchet *Daily News Gazette.*"

"But if that's the case, why aren't they in jail?"

"There was never enough evidence, and since the 'boys' were never charged, they managed to collect on the fire loss, life insurance, and the inheritance. All told, they walked off with a couple million bucks. Their aunt and the insurance company are preparing a civil suit, hoping to recover whatever assets remain."

"But how do they know the burglar didn't surprise the parents? Maybe he was the one who tied them up and gagged them."

"Unfortunately, the burglar hasn't been heard from since. Speculation has it, they killed him, too."

"How can you do business with them?"

"That's what I'm getting to. I signed a year's lease and paid six months in advance. Now I can't figure how to get out of it."

"Let Lonnie handle it. He'll know what to do."

"Good thought," I said. "Not that it ends there."

"Why not?"

"Mariah thinks the jewelry's still somewhere in that big fancy house of theirs. She's hoping I can locate the safe so the cops can get a search warrant. She says the Heveners' funds are just about depleted. She's hoping they'll try to sell at least a portion of the jewelry. Since they filed a claim for the loss, it's not going to look good. If she can get them to tip their hand, the cops will step in with a warrant for their arrest."

"How's she going to persuade them?"

"Ah. She's not. She wants me to do it." I fished the piece of paper from my jeans. "She gave me the name of a fence in Los Angeles and asked me to pass the information on to them."

Henry took the scrap of paper on which she'd written the jeweler's name. "Cyril Lambrou's a pawnbroker?"

"A jeweler. She says he runs a legitimate business. He also deals in stolen property when the goods warrant it."

"Why can't *she* give them the information?"

"Because they know who she is, and they'd never fall for it."

"But why you?"

Henry's tone was becoming belligerent, and I could feel my face heat. "Because Tommy's interested in me."

"But they're going to smell a rat. You mention a jeweler. They pawn the stuff, and shortly afterward they're arrested and thrown in jail? You can't be serious."

"By then it's too late. They're already behind bars."

Exasperated, Henry leaned back in his chair and stared at me. "Don't do this. Don't get involved. It's none of your business."

"I didn't say I would."

"How're you going to find the safe? You'll have to get into the house."

"Tommy's taken me up there once. All I have to do is talk him into taking me again."

"But why take the risk? I don't think you should be alone with either one of them."

"Henry, I promise you I won't act in haste. I haven't even figured out what I'll say. . . . You know, assuming I decide to take the job."

"Why do this to yourself? You don't need the money."

"Money isn't the issue. Let's quit arguing. You worry too much."

"And you don't worry enough!"

MUCH of Wednesday I was occupied tidying up odds and ends. At six that morning I'd managed to squeeze in a three-mile jog between cloudbursts, after which I'd gone to the gym. I'd come home, cleaned up, eaten breakfast, and arrived at the office at nine fifteen. I spent the bulk of the day catching up on paperwork, including my personal bills, which I paid with the usual sense of triumph. I love keeping the wolves at bay.

I left the office just before three o'clock and walked over to the bank. The check I'd written to Hevener Properties hadn't yet cleared. I put a stop-payment on the check, returned to the office, and wrote Richard a brief apologetic note, indicating that circumstances had changed and I wouldn't be renting space from him after all. He might well take me to small-claims court, but I didn't think so. Surely, in his position, he'd prefer to avoid legal wrangles. At five thirty I locked up. On my way home I drove by the main post office and dropped the letter into the outside box. I reached my apartment twelve minutes later, feeling lighter than I had all day.

Before I unlocked my front door, I tapped on Henry's kitchen window, but there was no sign of him. I picked up the tantalizing scent of one of his oven-baked stews, so I didn't think he'd gone far.

I returned to my apartment and let myself in. The message light on the answering machine was blinking merrily. I pushed PLAY.

Tommy Hevener.

"Hey, it's me. I've been thinking about you. Maybe I'll catch you later. Give me a call when you get in."

I pressed ERASE, wishing I could do the same with him.

I went into the kitchen. Saturday's can of tomato soup was the last I had, so I already knew there was nothing in the house to eat. I picked up my bag and headed out the door. Dinner at Rosie's— what a pleasant change of pace.

The night air was misty and smelled of basements. It had been raining off and on now for six full days. The ground was saturated, and the creek beds ran high, a noisy rush of water pushing debris in its path. Unless we had a few dry days, the torrents would jump the banks and flood the low-lying areas.

At Rosie's, the bar area was teeming. The noise level had risen to a harsh, edgy pitch that seemed to reflect the mounting irritability levels. People were tired of raincoats, wet shoes, and mold spores that made their allergies flare up in a rush of sneezes and clogged sinuses.

I left my umbrella propped up against the wall by Rosie's front door, shed my slicker, and hung it up. As I stepped through the inner door, I spotted Tommy Hevener at a table near the front. I felt a flash of irritation, feeling cornered. How was I going to get him out of my life? He was drinking a martini when he caught sight of me. I halted in my tracks—a split second of indecision—because the second person I saw was Mariah Talbot sitting in a booth at the rear. Her telltale silver hair had been concealed beneath a dark, shag-cut wig, her blue eyes masked by glasses with plastic-and-rhinestone frames. The raincoat she wore made her body appear bulky. The minute Mariah and I made eye contact, she rose from the booth and slipped into the seat on the opposite side of the table with her back to us. Abruptly I crossed and sat down at Tommy's table.

He took my hand and placed a kiss in my right palm. I wanted to shiver—not from arousal, but from dread. What had once seemed seductive was only cheap display.

Peripherally I saw Mariah leave the booth and head for the ladies' rest room. I rested my chin on my hand. "Are you free for dinner? We could go back to Emile's or try somewhere else."

"Buy me a drink first, and we can talk about that," he said.

I pointed to his glass. "What are you having?"

"Vodka martini."

I took his empty glass and got up. I crossed to the bar where Henry's brother, William, was at work, pulling beers and mixing drinks. I ordered two vodka martinis and said, "Could you do me a favor? When you're done, will you take those over to that guy in the gray sweater? Tell him I'm in the loo and I'll be back in a second."

"Happy to be of help," William said.

I proceeded to the ladies' room and pushed through the door. Mariah was standing at the basin mirror adjusting her wig.

She said, "What do you think?"

"That disguise is lame. I spotted you the minute I walked in. What are you *doing* here? Do you know how close you've come to blowing it?"

"I tried to call, but all I got was your answering machine. I didn't want to leave a message. You never know who's going to be there when those things are played back. I figured it'd be easier to find you here. I walk in, thinking I'm safe, and there he sits. What are the chances you can get him out of here?"

"I'm doing what I can, but I don't like it. I'm trying to turn him off, and now I have to suck up to him to cover for you."

"Life's tough." She smiled to herself. "Here's a piece of good news. All their credit cards are maxed out. They're making minimum payments, just trying to keep afloat."

"They're completely broke?"

"They will be if they don't act fast." Her eyes met mine in the mirror. "I don't suppose you've had time to tell Tommy about the fence."

"I'm not going to. I can't help you there. I'm sorry."

"Don't sweat it. I'll get them with or without your help."

"How'd this become so personal?"

"Murder's personal. I take offense when I see guys like them getting off scot-free." Behind the glasses her eyes were a clear blue and very cold. "You better get out there. Prince Charming awaits."

I left the rest room, pushed my way through the crowd, and returned to the table where Tommy waited. Henry had joined him, and he was sipping his usual glass of Black Jack over ice.

I sat down. "Hi, Henry. I knocked on your door earlier, but I couldn't seem to rouse you."

"I popped over to the market. I needed some fresh parsley to finish off my stew."

"Henry's stews are legendary," I said in Tommy's direction, though I couldn't meet his eyes. I lifted the martini glass and took a sip, then steadied the wobbling glass as I set it down.

Henry glanced over at me, and we exchanged a brief look. I knew what he was up to. He had no intention of letting me consort with the enemy unchaperoned. He said, "By the way, I looked into that business you were asking me about."

I said, "Ah." Thinking, business? What business?

"The guy you want to try is Cyril Lambrou in downtown Los Angeles. The woman I talked to sold an assortment of her mother's jewelry. This was stuff she hardly ever wore, and she was tired of paying the exorbitant insurance premiums."

I felt myself separating from my body. I'd backed away from Mariah's scheme, and here Henry was laying out the bait. I knew why he was doing it. If the jeweler's name came from him, how could I be blamed for it later when the deal went sour? Henry and Tommy had spent the previous evening together. Tommy trusted him.

I said, "I don't blame her. I pay a fortune for insurance, and I could use the cash." My voice sounded hollow.

Meanwhile, Henry went on as smoothly as a con artist with an easy mark. "I called the fellow myself, and we had a nice chat. I described the diamond, and he was definitely interested. I know you don't want to *give* the ring away, but you have to be realistic."

My mouth was dry. "How much? Did he give you any idea?"

"Between eight and ten thousand. He says it depends on the stone and whether there's any secondary market, but he swore he'd be fair."

"The ring's worth five times that," I said indignantly.

Henry shrugged. "Check around if you want. There are other jewelers, but as he says, better the devil you know."

"Maybe. We'll see about that."

Tommy's expression hadn't changed. He listened politely, no more and no less interested than any ordinary guy would be.

Henry said, "Well, I better get back to my stew before it starts sticking to the pan." I knew he didn't want to leave me, but he didn't dare persist. Henry and Tommy exchanged chitchat, and next thing I knew, he was gone. I had to get out of there.

"You know what? I've got work to do. I'll have to take a rain check on dinner."

The notion of an evening alone with him was intolerable. Mariah had to be gone by now, and if not, that was her problem.

"Why the sudden change of heart?" He was staring at me. "Has someone told you something about me?"

I could feel my jaw set. "What's there to tell, Tommy? You have something to hide?"

"No. Of course not, but people make things up."

"Well, I don't. If I say I've got work, you can take my word for it."

He gave my fingers a squeeze. "I better let you go, then. Why don't I call you tomorrow? Or better yet, you call me."

"Right."

We stood at the same time. Tommy shrugged into his raincoat and picked up his umbrella. When we reached the entrance, I retrieved my slicker and umbrella. Tommy held the door. I made short work of the fare-thee-wells. I turned toward my apartment while he walked off in the opposite direction. I forced myself to stroll, though my impulse was to scurry, putting as much distance as possible between him and me.

I WENT back to my apartment and locked myself in. I sat down at my desk and found Mariah Talbot's business card. I was nervous about my association with her. Tommy'd been uncanny in his suspicions about me. In the eerie way of all psychopaths he'd picked up on my newly minted fear of him. He must be wondering who or what had caused my attitude to shift.

I sat down at my desk and dialed Mariah's Texas area code and the number on the card. I knew I wouldn't reach her, but at least I could leave her a message to get in touch with me. I thought about how deftly Henry had stepped in with the name of the fence. He'd lied as well as I did and with the same finesse. The question now was whether Tommy would act on the information.

AT NINE a.m. the next morning, I called Fiona. Naturally, I didn't reach her. In the message I left, I told her I was hoping to track down the thirty thousand dollars missing from Purcell's account, and I implied that someone in Crystal's household might be responsible for the theft. I proposed putting in a couple more hours' work if she'd approve the expense. I was hoping she'd take advantage of the possibility of incriminating Crystal or someone dear to her. If not, I'd probably pursue it anyway, just to satisfy myself. Not everything in this business is about the bucks.

It was not quite noon by the time I cleared my office calendar and dealt with phone messages from the day before. I walked to the police station hoping to catch Detective Odessa before he went to lunch. Apparently, he and another detective had left five minutes before I'd arrived. I asked the desk officer if he had any idea where they'd gone. "Probably the Del Mar. If not, try the Arcade."

I put a business card on the desk. "Thanks. If I miss him, would you have him call me?"

"Sure thing."

There was no sign of Odessa in the Del Mar, so I hoofed it the half block to the Arcade—a sandwich shop with a pint-size interior, consisting of a counter, three tables, and assorted bent-wire chairs. Detective Odessa was hunched over a red plastic basket that contained a massive paper-wrapped burger and a load of fries. The detective sitting across the table from him was Jonah Robb.

I'd met Jonah about four years before, when he was working missing persons and I was looking for one. He'd since been transferred to homicide, promoted to lieutenant, and made unit supervisor— Paglia's boss, in effect. At the time we became acquainted, Jonah's on-again, off-again marriage was in one of its off-again phases, and we'd dallied for a season on my Wonder Woman sheets. Subsequently, his wife, Camilla, returned with their two girls in tow.

Vince Odessa spotted me and waved.

I said, "Hi, guys."

Odessa gestured. "Sit down. Are you having lunch?"

Jonah promptly held out his plastic basket. "Here. You can have half of mine. Camilla's bugging me to diet."

I sat down beside him and checked his sandwich: bacon, lettuce, and tomato, with a gruel of guacamole in between the layers of mayonnaise. I added a snow flurry of salt to the mix. I hate to pass up a chance to give my kidneys a thrill.

"We were just talking about Purcell," Odessa said. "Jonah attended the post."

"Such as it was. Condition of the body, Dr. Yee says he can't run biochemical or biophysical tests. From the gross, it looks like he died from a single contact shot to the head. We found the gun on the front seat. A Charter Arms Bulldog .357 Mag with one shot fired. The cartridge casing was still in the cylinder. Yee says he was probably dead when he went into the water."

"The gun was his?" I asked.

Jonah wiped his mouth. "He bought it before he and Fiona split. Crystal wouldn't let him keep it in the house on account of the kid. She thinks he either kept it in his desk drawer at work or in the glove compartment of his car."

Odessa said, "We're trying to figure out how he got up to the reservoir in the first place."

I raised my hand. "He was supposed to go see Fiona. She says he never showed, but she could be lying."

Odessa nodded. "Don't think it's escaped our attention that the guy turns up dead practically in her front yard."

"And she's the sole beneficiary on a life insurance policy. Part of the divorce settlement," Jonah said.

"How much?"

"A million."

"Risky to kill the guy so close to home," I remarked.

"Maybe that's the beauty of it," Jonah said. "Could have been someone else. Lure him up there and put a bullet in his head."

Odessa made a face. "How're you going to get him up there?"

Jonah said, "Ride in the same car. You arrange a meeting, say you want to go someplace quiet and talk, but you need a lift."

"How do you get back down the road in the dark?"

Jonah said, "You hike. It's not that far."

I said, "What if you're seen?"

Odessa said, "Could have been two of them. One meets him up there and does the job while the other one waits in a car parked somewhere down the road."

"But doesn't adding a co-conspirator increase the risk?"

"Depends on who it is." Jonah sipped his Coke.

I said, "On the other hand, Purcell was in trouble with the feds and facing social disgrace. He must have considered suicide. Wouldn't you in his shoes?"

Jonah said, "I guess." He sounded glum at the prospect. "The guys are still working on the Mercedes. He had this mohair blanket over his lap, empty whiskey bottle on the floor of the passenger side. Headlights off. Key in the ignition, which was turned to the 'on' position. ID, his wallet was on the body."

Odessa said, "What else?"

"Not much. The tempered glass in the driver's-side window was crazed—some glass missing, but most of it intact—where the bullet exited. I sent two guys back over there with a metal detector, hoping they can pick it up. The passenger-side window and the two in the back seat were rolled down, ostensibly to speed the water pouring in."

Odessa wadded up his paper napkin. "I'm not sold on suicide."

Jonah said, "Let's assume he shot himself. How did he manage to sink the car? And why even bother?"

"Maybe he was embarrassed," Odessa said. "Ashamed to kill himself, so he hopes the whole business will disappear."

"What about the window on the driver's side? Why leave that up when all the others are rolled down?"

"To muffle the sound of the shot," I said.

"Yeah, but what's it to him if someone hears the gun go off?"

"Wouldn't muffle much anyway if the other three windows were wide-open," Odessa pointed out.

Jonah said, "Exactly. I don't like the redundancy. Shoot yourself before you drown? Why double up the effort?"

Odessa said, "People do it all the time. Take an overdose of pills and put your head in a plastic bag. Mix vodka and Valium before you slit your wrists. One doesn't work, you have the other to fall back on."

"Another thing. I don't like the whiskey bottle. Guy wants to off himself, why's he need to take a drink?"

"To calm his nerves?" I suggested. "He did drink. A friend of his told me when he disappeared before, he was off at rehab getting dried out. I guess he fell off the wagon the last six months or so."

Jonah was still feeling argumentative. "It bugs me there's no note. The guy might've been desperate, but he's not mean-spirited. Suppose the car is never found. Why leave everyone hanging? And why put the car at the bottom of the lake?"

"Right," Jonah said. "So let's say somebody did it for him. You shoot the guy, get out, give the car a quick shove, and send it on its merry way."

Odessa said, "Look at it as murder; then the sinking of the car makes a lot more sense."

"The killer assumes the car's gone for good," I said.

"Exactly. Now the scenario heats up. You find the car, and now he's forced to cope with something he never counted on."

I said, "If you're looking for a motive, I heard a rumor that Crystal was having an affair."

"Who with?"

"A personal trainer of hers. Someone she worked with eight or ten months ago."

Odessa glanced at his watch. "Hey, I gotta run an errand." He stood up. "I'll see you back at the place, Jonah."

"I better be going myself. You walking in that direction?"

"Sure, if you don't mind."

I picked up my shoulder bag, and we walked for a beat in silence. I said, "You really believe he was murdered?"

"I think we'll operate on that assumption until we hear otherwise."

I WENT back to the office. Fiona had left me a message, authorizing two hours but no more. I sat in my swivel chair and stared at the phone. I was reluctant to call Crystal in the midst of the current crisis, but I tried the number at the beach house. Anica answered after two rings.

"Anica, it's Kinsey. How's she doing?"

"She's a mess. I think it's the finality that's getting to her. She swore something happened to him, but the whole time she must have been praying she was wrong."

"What about Leila? How's she taking it?"

"Oh, you know her. She was up in her room listening to music at top volume, driving everyone nuts. I finally called Lloyd and asked him to pick her up and take her for the day."

"What about the funeral?"

"Crystal's talking about Saturday, if she can pull it together. She'll have to get the notice in the paper and an officiant lined up. I just called the mortuary, and they said they'd pick him up. She's having him cremated—not that she has a lot of choice in the matter."

"I guess not."

"What happened? Detective Paglia never said, but I'm assuming he drowned."

I could feel my heart lurch. "Ah, I don't know. They're still working to determine that. In the meantime, is there anything I can do to help?" The question seemed false even to my lie-corrupted ear, but I had to get her off the subject.

"Not at the moment, but thanks anyway. I should probably get back, but I'll tell Crystal you called."

"While I have you on the line, I wondered if I could get some information. Crystal mentioned a post-office box she used to keep here in town. I need the number and location."

"Hang on for a second." Anica placed a palm across the mouthpiece, and I heard her muffled conversation with someone.

Anica removed her hand. "P.O. box 505. She says it's the Mail & More over in Laguna Plaza. Let her know what you find."

"I'll do that."

I'd no more put the phone down than it rang.

Mariah Talbot said, "Hi. What's up?"

"Well, here's the situation." I went on to describe the conversation at Rosie's the previous night when Henry had laid out the bait about the jeweler in L.A.

"You think Tommy bought it?"

"I have no idea. I thought I'd report it because the last time we spoke, I told you I wasn't going to help. Now the deed's been done, but only because Henry stepped in and did it."

"What a cool move on his part. If it's coming from him, it'll never occur to Tommy he's being conned," she said. "Where did you and Prince Charming end up? Not in the bedroom, I hope."

"Absolutely not," I said. "I canceled our dinner plans, which he didn't like. He pretended it was okay, but he was pissed. I wish I knew how to dump the guy without setting him off."

"Good luck. He's never going to let you get away with that. Tommy's an egomaniac. He dumps you. You don't dump him."

"He's like a spider. Every time I go somewhere, he crawls out."

"Well, what do you expect? These boys are both wacko. The thing about them is, both would rather forfeit everything than see the other enjoy his half. Happened with a girl once, and she ended up dead."

"You're really cheering me up, but happily I'm hanging up my spurs. I called to fill you in, in case one of 'em makes a move."

"Come on. You can't leave me now with the job half done. What about the safe? You have to hang in until you locate that."

"No, thanks. Nice doing business with you. It was fun," I said, and hung up. I looked up to find Richard Hevener standing at my door. I had no idea how long he'd been there, and I couldn't remember if I'd mentioned his name or Tommy's in the final moments of my conversation. I didn't think I'd used hers.

I said, "Hello," trying to sound unconcerned.

"What's this?" He tossed my letter on the desk.

My heart began to thump. "I feel bad about that. I don't want the space. I thought I did, but now I don't."

"You signed a lease."

"I know, and I apologize for the inconvenience—"

"It's not a matter of inconvenience. We have an agreement."

"What do you want from me?"

"I want you to honor the terms of the lease you signed."

"You know what? Why don't you talk to my attorney about that. His name is Lonnie Kingman. He's right down the hall."

Ida Ruth appeared in the hall behind him. "Everything okay?"

Richard said, "Everything's fine. I'm sure we'll find the perfect solution to the little problem we have."

He backed out of the room, careful not to touch Ida Ruth as he passed.

"What's with him?" she asked. "Is he nuts or what?"

"You don't know the half of it. If he shows up again, call the cops."

LAGUNA Plaza is an aging L-shaped strip mall. I pulled my VW into a slot directly in front of Mail & More, a franchise that boasted private mailbox rentals, mail receiving and forwarding, copy machines, a notary public, custom business cards, rubber stamps, and twenty-four-hour access, seven days a week.

The interior was divided into two large areas, separated from each other by a glass wall and lockable glass door. The space on the right contained a counter and a clerk to assist with the packaging and mailing services. The clerk was gone. Not a soul in sight.

I crossed to the glass wall and peered into the adjoining space—a veritable cellblock of mailboxes, numbered and glass-fronted, with a slot on the far wall for the mailing of letters and small packages. I followed the numbers in sequence and found box 505. I leaned over and looked into the tiny beveled-glass window. No mail in evidence, but I was treated to a truncated view of the room beyond, where I could see a guy moving down the line distributing letters from a stack in his hand. When he reached my row, I knocked on the window of 505.

The fellow leaned down, so his face was even with mine.

I said, "Can I talk to you? I need some help out here."

He pointed to my right. "Go down to the slot."

We both moved in that direction. The slot was at chest height. The guy said, "What's the problem?"

I stuck a business card through the slot so he could see who I was. "I need information about the party renting box 505."

He took my card and studied it. "What for?"

"It's a murder investigation. I need a peek at the rental form to see who's renting it."

"Why?"

"All I want to know is who filled out the form."

"I'm not supposed to do that."

"Couldn't you make an exception? It could make a really big difference."

I could see him staring at the floor. He appeared to be forty, way too old for this line of work. I could well imagine his debate. On one hand, the rules were the rules, though I personally doubted there was any kind of policy to cover my request. He wasn't a federal employee, and his job didn't require a security clearance. He'd be lucky to earn fifty cents an hour over the minimum wage.

I said, "I just talked to the police and told them I'd be doing this, and they said it was fine."

No response.

I said, "I'll give you twenty bucks."

"Wait right there."

He disappeared for what felt like an interminable length of time. I pulled the twenty from my wallet, folded it lengthwise, bent it, and balanced it on the lip of the slot. While I waited, I kept my back to the wall, my attention fixed on the entrance. I entertained a brief fantasy of Richard Hevener crashing his sports car through the plateglass window, squashing me up against the wall like a dead person.

"Lady?"

The guy had reappeared, and the twenty I'd left in the slot was gone. He had the rental form with him, but he held it behind his back. I tried asking him some easy questions, just to get him in the mood. This is called private-eye foreplay. "How's this done? Someone comes in and pays the fee for the coming year?"

"Something like that. It can also be done by mail. We put a notice in the box when the annual fee comes up."

"They pay in cash?"

"Or personal check. Either way."

"So you might never actually see the person renting the box?"

"Most of them we don't see. We don't care who they are as long as they pay the money when it's due."

"Can you push the form through the slot so I can see it better?"

"Nope. I don't want you touching it. You can look for thirty seconds, but that's the best I can do."

He held the card up on his side, angled so I could see it. The rental form was a no-brainer. The signature on the bottom line appeared to be Dow's, but he hadn't written in the data on the lines above. The printing was Leila's, complete with the angled *t*'s and puffy *i*'s. Well, well, well.

I said, "One more tiny thing. Would you spit on your finger and run it across the signature?"

"Why?"

This guy was worse than a four-year-old. "Because I'm wondering if it was done with a pen or a copier."

Frowning, he licked his index finger and rubbed the signature. No ink smear. He said, "Hnh."

"I appreciate your help. Thanks so much."

I returned to my car and sat, considering the implications. I had to conclude that Leila'd intercepted the rental renewal notice when it arrived with its request for the annual fee. Crystal had told me the Mid-City Bank statements were being routed to the P.O. box. Very likely Leila had notified the bank, perhaps typing the request on a sheet of Pacific Meadows letterhead, forging Purcell's signature or affixing a photocopy, and asking that the statements for that account be mailed to 505. She could have stopped by the Mail & More when she was up from school.

I started my car and headed for the exit. When I reached the street, I realized the Laguna Plaza branch of the Mid-City Bank was located on the opposite corner. Even from this distance I could see the ATM she'd used to drain the account. All she really needed was the bank card and pin number for the account, which Dow probably left in his desk at home.

When I got back to the office, I called Jonah. "This is Kinsey. If you don't scrutinize my methods, I'll tell you what I found out."

I explained my trip to the Mail & More, leaning heavily on Leila's behavior while glossing over mine.

Jonah didn't say much, but I could tell he was taking notes. "You better give me the location of the P.O. box."

"The Mail & More at Laguna Plaza. The number's 505."

"I'll check it out," he said. "Any idea where she is now?"

"I heard she was up at Lloyd's, but maybe I should check it out. Leila's got a friend named Paulie, some gal she met in Juvie. The two of them might be planning to take off. It might be interesting to track Paulie's history and see what she's done."

He told me he'd check into it, and I hung up. I was already feeling guilty. The last thing Crystal needed was to have her only daughter brought up on charges of grand theft.

APPROACHING Lloyd's A-frame, I could see that lights were on. I pulled up to the driveway, parked the car, and got out. Lloyd was working in the small unattached garage. He'd raised the hood on his convertible, and his hands were dark with grease. He looked over at me without reaction, as though my arrival at his doorstep was an everyday occurrence.

"You're Millhone," he remarked as much to himself as to me.

"And you're Lloyd Muscoe. Is Leila here?"

He smiled slightly to himself. "Depends on what you want."

I studied the exposed engine. "What's wrong with the car?"

"Nothing. I'm changing the oil, putting in new spark plugs."

"A tune-up."

"Of sorts. I'm taking off in a couple days."

"Where to?"

"Vegas. I thought I'd ask Crystal if I could take Leila with me. What d'you think?"

"I can't believe she'd say yes."

"Never know with her. She's tired of Leila's problems."

"That doesn't mean she'd kick her out," I said. "You think it'd be good for Leila, moving her again?"

"At least over in Vegas she behaved herself. She hates that school she's in. Bunch of spoiled, rich debutantes."

"She seems to hate everything."

"She needs handling, that's all." His tone of voice turned wry. "You ever going to get around to telling me why you came?"

"Sure," I said. "I understand Purcell came up here to talk to you about four months ago. I was wondering why."

"He heard a rumor Crystal was having an affair. He assumed it was me. Too bad I couldn't up and confess. I'd have taken a certain satisfaction shoving that in his face."

"It wasn't you."

"I'm afraid not."

"How'd you get along with Dow?"

"Considering he walked off with my wife, we did fine."

"You remember where you were?"

He smiled, shaking his head. "The night he took a dive? I was working. I had a gig driving cabs—it's on the company books. Leila was here with her friend Paulie, watching videos."

"Why are you going back to Vegas?"

"Here's my theory. Things get bad? Think about the last place you were happy and go there."

IN A FIT OF GUILT I DEVOTED all of Friday to other clients. Nothing exciting went down, but at least it paid the bills. On Saturday afternoon Tommy Hevener called.

He said, "Hey, babe. It's me." His tone was both intimate and assured, as if I'd been waiting all day in hopes of hearing from him. The sound of his voice gave me a jolt. I had to remind myself that while I didn't want to see him, I might need his help in getting Richard calmed down.

I ignored his seductive manner and said, "Hi. How are you?"

"What'd you do to Richard? What happened?"

"Ah. What happened. Well . . . " Think, think, think. The lie lurched from my lips. "Lonnie wanted me to stay in the office, so he offered me a fifty percent discount on the rent."

"Why didn't you say so? Richard would've understood."

"He was in such a rage, I never had a chance."

"Why didn't you tell me? We could have worked something out. And then on top of that, he found out you went and put a stop on the check. He was screaming at the top of his lungs. You don't know what he's capable of once he gets like this."

"Can't you talk to him for me?"

"That's what I've been trying to do. I thought if I heard your version of the story, I could reason with him. You blew this one bad."

"What do you think will happen next?"

"Hard to say with him. Maybe the whole thing will blow over," he said. "Anyway, enough about him. When can we get together? I've missed you."

I tried to keep my tone mild, but I knew my message wasn't one he'd accept. "Look, I don't think this relationship is going to work for me. It's time to let go."

There was dead silence. I could hear him breathing on his end. Finally he said, "This is your pattern, isn't it? Distancing yourself. You can't let anyone get close."

"Maybe so. Fair enough. I can see how you'd think that."

"I know you've been hurt, and I'm sorry about that, but give me a chance. Don't shut me out. I deserve better than that."

"I agree. You do deserve better. Truly, I wish you well, and I'm sorry if I gave you the wrong impression—"

"Who the hell are you, thinking you can talk to me like this? You were the one came on to me."

"I'm hanging up now. Good-bye." I set the phone down in the cradle. My heart began to bang like someone dribbling a basketball.

I sat at my desk and took a few deep breaths. I was not going to let the guy get to me. I took out my index cards and turned to the card for Tina Bart, the bookkeeper at Pacific Meadows who'd been fired. Where had she gone? No doubt Penelope Delacorte knew, but she wasn't about to tell me. On impulse I hauled out the phone book and turned to the B's. Five Barts were listed, none of them Tina or T. There was a C. Bart, no address, conceivably short for Christine or Christina. I tried the number for C. Bart. After two rings a machine cut in. The voice on the other end was one of those computer-generated robots who talked as if he were living in a tin can. "Please leave a message." Use of this proto-male was a device used by single women who like to create the illusion of a guy on the scene. I reached for the city directory and looked for the phone number listed for C. Bart. The address was on Dave Levine Street, not far from Pacific Meadows. Time to find out how much she knew.

Before I left the apartment, I searched for my old Davis .32 semi-automatic and tucked it into my shoulder bag. I didn't believe Richard or Tommy would actually come after me, but I couldn't be sure. And that, of course, was the nature of the game they played.

IT WAS close to five o'clock as I traveled down Dave Levine Street scrutinizing house numbers. The building I was looking for was only a block away from Pacific Meadows. I found parking on the street and approached on foot, hunched against the misting rain.

The structure was a plain stucco box, four units in all, two up and two down, with an open stairwell up the middle. The name Bart had been written in black marker pen and attached to the mailbox for apartment 3. Lights were on in several rooms on the front right-hand side. I climbed the stairs, knocked on the door, and waited.

"Who is it?"

"Ms. Bart?"

I heard her secure the chain, and then she opened the door a crack. "Yes?"

"I'm Kinsey Millhone. I'm a private investigator working for Dr. Purcell's ex-wife. Could I talk to you?"

"I don't know anything. I haven't seen him in months."

"I'm assuming you heard his body was found?"

"I read that. What happened? The paper didn't really say."

"Would it make a difference to you?"

"Well, I don't believe he killed himself, if that's what they're trying to prove."

"I tend to agree, but we may never know. Meanwhile, I'm trying to reconstruct events that led up to his death."

"How do I know you're who you say you are?"

I reached into my handbag and took out my wallet. I pulled my license from the windowed slot and pushed it through the crack to her. She studied it briefly and then handed it back. She closed the door, undid the chain, and opened the door again.

I stepped inside, removed my slicker, and hung it on a hat rack near the door. Tina indicated that I could take a seat in a gray upholstered chair while she returned to her place on the couch. She was younger than I expected. Penelope Delacorte was in her early fifties, and I'd pictured Tina to be the same age. She was in her mid-thirties and so lacking in animation I thought she might be tranquilized. Her hair was the color of oak in old hardwood floors. She wore a gray sweat suit. "Why come to me?"

"Last Monday I went over to St. Terry's and talked with Penelope Delacorte. Your name came up, so I thought maybe you could fill in some blanks. May I call you Tina?" I asked.

She lifted one shoulder in a careless shrug, which I took as assent. "How long did you work for Pacific Meadows?"

"Fifteen years. I was hired as a file clerk and worked my way up."

"Who owned the building before Glazer and Broadus?"

"A company called Silver Age Enterprises. I never knew the

owner's name. There might have been more than one. Before that, there was another company, called the Endeavor Group."

I reached into my handbag, took out a little spiral-bound notebook, and made a note of the two names.

"I saw Pacific Meadows change hands three times, and the price came close to doubling with each transaction," she added.

"At what point did you start keeping the books?"

"After the Endeavor Group. Actually, I think Silver Age was a subsidiary of Endeavor. The head of Endeavor was a woman named Peabody. She used to run all her personal expenses through our accounts payable. She'd renovate her house and write it off to Pacific Meadows as 'maintenance and repairs.' Groceries, utility bills, travel and entertainment—she never missed a trick."

"Isn't that illegal?"

"Mostly. I called a few items to the administrator's attention, but he told me, in effect, I'd better mind my own business."

"Did anything change when Dr. Purcell arrived on the scene?"

"Not the first couple of months. Then I noticed an increase in the number of charge slips for things like ambulance service and physical therapy, portable X-ray equipment, wheelchairs. I started keeping notes, and then I wrote a memo to Mr. Harrington, the head of the billing department at Genesis. That was a mistake, as it turned out. He never said as much, but I'm sure he didn't appreciate the effort, because it put him on the spot."

"So even before the audit, they were unhappy with you."

She nodded and said, "Very. They let some time pass, and then they fired me. Dr. Purcell tried to intervene, but he was overruled. Penelope got upset, and she quit in a huff, which really worked in their favor. It made it look like we were guilty of wrongdoing and Genesis was cleaning house. That still gave them Dr. Purcell as a fire wall if the investigation proceeded—which it did."

"As I remember it, Joel told me Genesis was part of a group called Millennium Health Care."

"It is, but my guess is that some, if not all, of those companies are shell corporations set up to conceal real ownership."

I held a hand up. "Hang on a minute." I'd been wondering about something since I'd arrived at her door. "The night he disappeared, Dr. Purcell left Pacific Meadows at nine o'clock. Did he, by any chance, stop by to talk to you?"

She paused so long I didn't think she'd answer me. "Yes."

"About what?"

"He told me he had a meeting scheduled with the FBI. He'd done some digging of his own. He thought he knew what was going on and who was behind it, namely Harvey and Joel."

"But those two wouldn't have been in any jeopardy, would they? I mean, from what I was told, they had nothing to do with the day-to-day running of Pacific Meadows. The real fiddle must have come from Genesis, since the Medicare checks were sent to them."

"There may be more of a connection than you think. Dr. Purcell must have gotten greedy, because he began to sign off on charges he knew were fraudulent: X-ray and ambulance services among them. He probably took kickbacks for those. The FBI put the squeeze on him, and that's why he agreed to help."

"But what would be the point of silencing him? There must be plenty of other people who know about the scam. You, for one."

"I never had any real authority. Now that he's gone, they can blame it all on him."

"Do you think he told Joel and Harvey what he was up to?"

"Not if he was smart. I know he had lunch with Joel, but he didn't say anything else about it."

"I don't get it. With all these agencies at work, how come they haven't been caught?"

She shrugged. "Most of what they submit is legitimate, and where the figures are false, everything else looks good. They use standard diagnoses and standard treatments. They're careful not to cross the line in any obvious way. They know how far they can push the system before the flags go up."

"Did you tell the fraud investigator about all this?"

"I talked to him last week, but most of what I told him he already had in his files."

8

SUNDAY was full of hard rain and gloom. I spent the day in my sweats, stretched out on the couch under a quilt. I went through one paperback novel and picked up the next. At five o'clock the phone rang. Fiona. She said, "Blanche had her baby yesterday afternoon."

"She did? Congratulations. What'd she have?"

"A little girl named Chloe. Seven pounds eight ounces. We'll bring them home this afternoon. Actually, I'm calling about something else. Last night when I went to the hospital to visit Blanche, I saw Crystal's white Volvo parked in the driveway of a house on Bay. I was curious, so I went over again this morning and there it was. I'm assuming there's a way you can find out whose house it is."

"I can. Why don't you give me the address?" I made a note as she recited it and then said, "What's your concern?"

"I think she's finally showing her true colors. You know the rumor about Crystal's affair with that trainer of hers, Clint Augustine. I put it out of my mind until I spotted her car, and then I began to wonder. Whatever she's up to, I think it's worth pursuing."

"Assuming it was her."

"The license plate said Crystal, big as life. I put a call through to Detective Paglia and told him you'd be looking into it."

After we hung up, I pulled the city directory from my bookcase and leafed through the pages until I found Bay Street. I ran a finger down the house numbers until I came to the relevant address. I'd hoped against hope that Fiona was wrong, but the listed occupant was J. Augustine. I couldn't believe Crystal had gone looking for Clint the very day of Dow's memorial service. I picked up the phone and dialed the house on Bay.

The man who answered had a phone manner that bordered on the rude. "Yes?" His voice was harsh and full of impatience.

"May I speak to Clint?"

"He can't come to the phone. Who's this?"

"Never mind. I'll try later."

THE house on Bay Street was an old two-story white frame Victorian with a wide porch that stretched across the front. A white picket fence surrounded the yard. There was no sign of Crystal's Volvo in the drive.

I cruised past the house, did a turnaround at the corner, and came back. I parked across the street and settled in to wait. Even protected by a gauzy curtain of rain, I felt conspicuous sitting in the car by myself. I adjusted my rearview mirror, ever mindful of Tommy Hevener. Just because I didn't see him didn't mean he wasn't there.

By 6:25, I decided Crystal wasn't going to show. I'd already started my car when a white Volvo headed in my direction. She was at the wheel.

I KILLED the engine and sat watching as Crystal pulled into the drive. I grabbed my umbrella and got out of my car as she was getting out of hers. This was one of those occasions where asking a direct question seemed the obvious route. I wasn't going to peep over windowsills in search of the truth. "Crystal?"

She'd already let herself through the gate when I called her, and she turned to look at me. She wore a rain-repellent parka with the hood pulled up, cowboy boots, and tight jeans. She clutched a neat stack of shirts against her body to protect them from the damp. Her blond hair was pulled into a knot. She stood with one hand on the latch, and I could see her puzzlement.

"Can I talk to you for a minute?"

Her response time was ever so faintly slow. "About what?"

"Clint. We happen to be members of the same gym."

"What do you want?"

I shook my head. "Someone saw your car here and thought you might show up again."

She closed her eyes and then opened them again. "Fiona."

I didn't see much reason to deny it. She knew I'd been working for Fiona, and who else, really, would be dogging her steps? "You should probably be aware she talked to Detective Paglia."

"What's she going to do, monitor my actions the rest of my life?"

"Hey, babe. It wasn't my idea. Take it up with her."

"Oh, right." She paused while she struggled to get a grip on herself. When she spoke again, her tone was more resigned than angry. "Let's get out of the rain."

We went up the front steps and took shelter on the porch.

"You know the entire time I was married to Dow, she did everything she could to make life miserable for me."

"She's not the only one who heard the rumor about Clint."

"Oh, for pity's sake. There's no law that says I can't visit a friend. Clint was my trainer. There was never anything sexual between us. Ask him if you doubt me. I'll be happy to wait out here."

"What would that prove? I'm sure he's too much of a gentleman to kiss and tell."

"Don't you have any male friends? Does everything between a man and a woman have to be sexual?"

"I didn't say you were guilty of anything. I'm telling you how it looks. Tongues have been wagging. Fiona saw your car here yesterday, and here you are again today."

She stared at me briefly and then seemed to make a decision. "Why don't you come in, and I'll introduce you properly."

"Why would I do that?"

"Why not? By the way, I found Dow's passport when I was going through his clothes. It was in the breast pocket of the overcoat he wore when we went to Europe last fall."

"Well, that's one question down. Are those his?" I said, pointing to the shirts.

"Someone might as well get some use out of them."

She unlocked the front door, using a key, I noticed, from her own key chain. She pushed open the door and stepped aside, allowing me to pass in front of her and into the house.

The front room was done up as an old-fashioned parlor with a camelback sofa, occasional tables, and assorted Queen Anne chairs. Every item of furniture sported a hand-crocheted doily. Crystal proceeded down the hallway and through the kitchen to a glassed-in porch. Clint was seated in a La-Z-Boy looking out toward the yard. She put the stack of shirts on a small wooden table next to him. Crystal gave him a brief kiss on the top of his head. "I brought you some shirts, and I also brought a friend, Kinsey. She's a member of your gym."

At first I thought, Not Clint. Mistake. Has to be someone else. But it was Clint. He was suffering contractures of his hands and a muscle weakness so pronounced he could hardly move his head. He'd lost an enormous amount of weight. I could see skin lesions on his forehead and his arms. I tuned the rest of it out. Through the window I could see a burly old guy working in the yard—probably Clint's father, the man who answered the phone.

Crystal was saying, "We just ran into each other, and she was asking about you."

"How're you doing?" I said, feeling like a fool.

"Clint has a systemic connective tissue disease called dermatomyositis. Severe in his case. It may be an autoimmune reaction, though nobody really knows. This has been going on since the end of January. The doctors were hoping he'd go into remission, so it seemed advisable for him to lay low."

"Is that why he rented the Glazers' cottage?"

"That's right. I wanted him close so I could keep an eye on him. After the lease ran out, it seemed best to have him move in with his parents for a while."

"Why didn't you let people know what was going on?"

"Clint asked me not to, and I honored his request."

"I'll have to tell Fiona."

"Of course," she said. "That's what she pays you for."

Crystal smiled at Clint, who was watching her with a doglike devotion. "Cat's out of the bag," she said. "Remember Dow's ex-wife? She finally figured out we were having a torrid love affair. Kinsey's caught us in the act."

I could feel myself flush. Clint seemed to enjoy the joke, and I could hardly protest. I said, "I probably ought to go."

"I'll walk you to the door."

I could feel a brittle rage radiating from her as she accompanied me. "Look, I'm sorry. Did Dow know?"

"Someone might have told him. I certainly didn't."

THE freeway traffic was crawling, cars end to end. I drove home on surface streets to avoid the mess. All the street lamps were on, and the roads gleamed like patent leather in the falling rain. In my neighborhood the houses glowed with light. I found parking right in front of Henry's. I went through the squeaking gate and around the corner of my apartment to the rear. Henry's kitchen lights were out. He was probably over at Rosie's.

I unlocked my door and let myself in. As I closed the door behind me, someone slammed against it from the outside and sent me hurtling. My shoulder bag struck the floor with a thunk, and I saw my key ring sail off and land on the rug. I hit the floor and rolled as Tommy Hevener grabbed me by the hair, pulled me upright, and dragged me backward. I stumbled into him, and he sat down abruptly, pinning me across his knees.

He choked me with one hand and stuck his face against mine. "Henry gave you the name of a jeweler in L.A. Turns out there isn't any such guy, so what was that about?"

The door swung back and banged against the wall. I shrieked, rolling my eyes in that direction. Richard was standing in the doorway in a black raincoat. He closed the door, looking on with indifference as Tommy tightened his grip.

"Answer me."

"I don't know. I never dealt with him. Someone told Henry. He was just passing it on. You were there."

"No." He shook my head, using my hair for leverage.

I clawed at his hand. The pain was excruciating. "Let go, let go. That's it. That's all. I never called the guy. I swear."

"Tell me you didn't find the safe and help yourself."

"What safe?"

"The safe in the office. Don't play dumb. You broke in. You ripped us off, and we want the stuff back."

"What stuff? I don't even know what you're talking about."

Richard said, "Get her up."

Tommy didn't move. His grip on my hair was so tight I thought he'd tear out a hunk of my scalp. I was nearly sick with fear. What had Mariah done? Had she set me up?

Richard said, "Tommy."

Grudgingly Tommy loosened his grip. I turned on my side and rolled away from him. I lifted myself as far as my hands and knees, shaking my head while I gasped for breath. "I don't know anything about a safe. I never saw it. I'd have to be an idiot to break in. I still have a key. It's on my key ring."

I fumbled across the rug for my keys and held them up. Richard took the ring of keys and sorted through them until he found the office key, which he worked out of the bunch. He tossed the remaining keys to Tommy.

Tommy was sitting with his knees drawn up, shaking his head. "You don't know how much trouble we're in. Everything is gone. Every damn—"

"Shut up, Tommy. She doesn't need to know. Let's get her out of here before someone shows up."

"I'm sorry your valuables were stolen, but it wasn't me."

"Yeah, well, we're sunk anyway. Wiped out. It's over."

"Knock it off," Richard said, and lifted me to my feet, half dragging, half carrying me to the door.

I stiffened my knees, forcing him to halt. "Let me get my bag," I said, gesturing. Tommy leaned down and picked up my shoulder bag. He did a quick search. He found the Davis, checked the load, and tucked it into his pocket, tossing the bag aside. There went that hope. I glanced back, watching him turn the lights out and pull the door shut before he joined us on the patio.

The two of them crowded against me, walking in a lockstep that forced me to trot along. We reached Tommy's pickup truck.

Richard opened the door on the passenger side. He flipped the seat forward and shoved me into the narrow space behind the seats, knocking my head against the frame in the process.

I said, "Hey!" This was pissing me off. Tommy got in on the driver's side. The two doors slammed in quick succession, like rifle shots. Tommy jammed the key in the ignition and pulled out with a chirp as I clung to the seat back, trying to assess the situation.

For the moment Tommy was too busy driving to pay attention to me, and Richard didn't have a sufficient angle to turn around and level more abuse. Rain was stinging against the windshield.

I said, "Where'd you have the safe?"

"Don't play dumb." Richard was bored.

Tommy said, "In the closet floor, under the carpeting."

"How many people knew besides the two of you?"

Tommy said, "No one."

Richard snorted. "What's this, twenty questions?"

"Who opened it last?"

"Tommy, this is bull. Are you buying this act?"

"Richard did. We had something we wanted to sell. He goes all the way down to Los Angeles on Friday, and there isn't any such dude."

"When did he get back? Was it late?"

"No, it wasn't late," Richard said, exasperated. "It's five o'clock. I go over to the office and put the piece back in the safe."

"Everything else was still there?"

"Of course it was. Now would you shut up?"

"Maybe someone saw you with the stuff and followed you back. If they saw where the safe was hidden, they could have waited until you left and ripped you off."

"I said, Shut your mouth!" He raised his left arm, torqued around in the seat, and bashed me in the face with a backhanded swing. The blow didn't have much force, but it hurt. I put my hands across my nose, hoping he hadn't broken it.

Tommy said, "Hey! Cut it out."

"Who put you in charge?"

"Just leave her alone."

There was a moment of silence. Then I said, "Anyway, how'd they get the safe open? Was it drilled?"

"You are just not going to shut up, are you?"

I thought the question was a good one, but I shut my mouth and leaned away from the front seat. The space where I was sitting was cramped. I groped around, hoping for a weapon—a wrench or a screwdriver—but found only a ballpoint. I clutched the pen in my fist, wondering what would happen if I jammed it in Richard's ear.

The drive to the house took seven minutes at top speed on the wet-slick roads that wound through Horton Ravine. As Tommy wheeled up the driveway, he picked up the remote control for the two garage doors and hit one of the buttons. The double door on the left rolled open. A light came on, and he pulled in. Tommy's red Porsche sat in the next bay over and, on the other side of that, was a second Porsche, a shiny black one, presumably Richard's.

Richard got out, left the truck door ajar, and peered into the truck bed. He opened the toolbox and fumbled among the contents. I knew I didn't have time to pull the door shut and lock it, so I turned to Tommy. "Who knew the combination? Just the two of you, right?"

Richard came back with a coil of rope. "Nobody asked you. Now get out."

"Tommy, think about it. Please."

Tommy got out of the truck and moved around the front to the passenger side. "Richard, what the hell is that for?"

"I'm going to tie her up and beat the hell out of her until she tells us where she hid the stuff," Richard said. "I told you not to mess with her. This is all your fault."

"Oh, really. Now it's my fault," Tommy said. His annoyance had passed, and there was something new in his face. He put his hands in his coat pocket, where I knew he'd put the gun. "You know, she's got a point. How do I know you didn't clean out the safe yourself?"

Richard snorted. "Why would I do that? I don't have anyone to lay it off on, if you'll remember."

"You say that now. You could have taken everything to L.A. when you went on Friday. You could have sold it all and kept the money. There's only your word you put it back where it was. I never saw the jewelry after you came back."

"That's bull."

"The safe wasn't drilled. There are only two of us who knew the combination. I know it wasn't me, so that leaves you."

"Stick it up your ass," Richard said. He put his hand on the seat back so he could reach for me. I swung the pen in an arc and brought it down hard on the back of his hand. He tried to grab me, but I scooted toward the driver's side of the truck. Enraged, he flipped the seat forward, prepared to haul me out. I leaned back, braced myself, and kicked twice at his hand. I caught him smartly with the heel of my Saucony, jamming three of his fingers.

He pulled his hand back and flashed an angry look at Tommy. "Help me out here."

"Answer my question first."

"Don't be an idiot. I didn't take anything. Now let's get her out of here."

"You and I were the only ones who knew. There wasn't any burglar."

Richard slammed the passenger-side door. "I'm telling you the truth. I didn't do it. You get that? I wouldn't do that to you, but you'd do that to me because you've done it before. So how do I know it wasn't you?"

"I didn't open the safe. You did. You made a point of going down to L.A. alone. The jewelry's gone now, you—"

Richard flew forward and grabbed Tommy by the front of his coat and then shoved. Tommy stumbled but regained his footing and came back at him. I saw Richard's fist fly out, catching Tommy in the mouth. He went down, tumbling backward. I leaned down and reached around the side of the seat, fumbling for the lever that would release the seat back. I opened the door on the driver's side, slithered through the gap, crouched, and came up along the fender. I could hear the chilling sound of flesh on flesh, a grunt as someone took the brunt of a blow. I lifted my head. Tommy was dragging himself to his feet, trying to free the Davis from his coat pocket. His legs weakened, and he went down. There was blood streaming from his nose. He moaned, looking up at his brother in a daze. Richard kicked him, then bent down and took the gun from Tommy's rubbery grip. He stepped back and leveled the Davis at his brother. Almost lazily Tommy put a hand up and said, "Oh, Richie, don't."

Richard fired. The bullet tore into Tommy's chest, though the blood was slow to come.

Richard looked blankly at his brother's body and nudged him with his foot. "Serves you right. Don't accuse me."

He tossed the gun aside. I heard it clatter across the garage floor and skitter under the truck. He hit the button that activated the other garage door. His manner was matter-of-fact as he moved around the red Porsche to the black one and got in. He started the car, backed out of the garage and down the drive.

I crawled over to Tommy to check his pulse, but he was dead. I spotted the gun. I was just about to pick it up when I caught myself. No way would I mar the fingerprints that Richard had left on the gun. I got up and went through the back door, turning the dead bolt behind me as I headed for the phone. I was feeling cold with dread, worried Richard would turn around and come back for me.

I dialed 911 and told the dispatcher about the shooting. I gave her the shooter's name, a description of his Porsche, and Richard's license number, then recited the address. She told me to remain at the scene until the officers arrived. I said, "Sure," hung up, and dialed Lonnie.

I FINALLY crawled into bed at midnight. Detectives Paglia and Odessa arrived at the Heveners' shortly after Lonnie showed up. They viewed me as a witness, not a suspect, which greatly affected their handling of me. Lonnie rode herd on them, nonetheless, protecting my rights anytime he thought they were crossing the line in the course of the interview. They bagged and tagged the Davis as evidence. It would probably be a year before I saw that gun again. Richard Hevener was picked up within the hour on his way to Los Angeles. I figured it was still remotely possible he'd taken the jewelry, but I was not convinced. Lonnie drove me home.

Monday morning I skipped the run and drove to the office. When I walked into the firm, I found Ida Ruth and Jill chatting in the corridor. At the sight of me they fell silent and fixed me with compassionate looks.

I went into my office and dialed Fiona's number. When she answered the phone, we exchanged the obligatory chitchat. I was guessing she hadn't heard about the shooting, because she never mentioned it. Or maybe she didn't care.

I said, "I have the answer to your question about the person living in that house on Bay. Turns out it's Clint Augustine's father, and Clint's living with him."

"I told you they were having an affair."

"Well, not quite."

I went on to describe Clint's medical condition. "I'm guessing that in the last year he's been in no shape to engage in a sexual liaison—or any other kind for that matter."

Fiona's response was grudging. "Perhaps I've misjudged her."

"Hard to know," I said, not wanting to rub it in.

"What about the missing money?"

"The cops are looking into it, so I'll leave that to them."

She seemed to shake off her disappointment. "Well, I suppose that takes care of business. If you like, you can calculate what I owe you and deduct it from the balance of the retainer."

"Sure, I'll put a check in the mail to you this afternoon."

There was a moment's hesitation. "I wonder if I could ask you to bring me that in cash?"

"No problem. I can have it this afternoon."

For an hour I sat at my desk, organizing my files. I really didn't want to work, but the mindless activity eased my anxiety somewhat. I finally lifted the receiver and dialed 713—the Houston, Texas, area code—and then 555-1212, for Directory Assistance. When the operator came on, I asked her for the sheriff's department in the county where Hatchet, Texas, was located. She gave me the number, and I made a note of it. I took out the file Mariah Talbot had given me. I glanced through the news clippings until I spotted the name of the sheriff who'd handled the Hevener murder case. I tried Mariah's number first and got the same recorded message I'd heard before. "Hello, this is Mariah Talbot. You've reached the offices of Guardian Casualty Insurance in Houston, Texas. . . ." I depressed the plunger. Anyone can leave a recorded announcement on an answering machine. Anyone can have business cards printed.

I dialed the Texas number and asked for Sheriff Hollis Cayo. I identified myself. "I'm wondering about two murders you investigated in 1983. This was Jared and Brenda Hevener."

"I remember them," he said. "They were both fine people and deserved better than they got. How can I help?"

"I thought I should pass along some information. Tommy Hevener died last night. His brother shot him in the heat of an argument."

There was a moment of quiet while he took that in. "I can't say I'm surprised. I hope Richard's not headed this way."

"No, no. The cops picked him up and put him in the county jail out here," I said. "One thing I was wondering. Was Casey Stonehart ever caught?"

"No, ma'am. He's gone. He disappeared right after the murders, probably the work of them two boys as well. Our best guess is, he's dead, but we may never know."

"I understand Brenda Hevener's sister and Guardian Casualty Insurance intend to file suit. Have you heard about that?"

"Yes, ma'am. I believe they're in the process of gathering information even as we speak. What's your interest in that?"

"I had an insurance investigator come into my office a week ago, and I wondered if you knew her. Mariah Talbot."

I could hear the smile in his voice. "Yeah, we know her. Mariah the Pariah. You're talking five feet nine, a hundred and forty pounds, twenty-six years old. Her hair's prematurely gray."

"Glad to hear you say that. I was beginning to think she'd misrepresented herself. How long has she worked for Guardian Casualty?"

"I never said she did. Talbot's the name of Casey's older brother. Got another one named Flynn. The whole family's bad. In jail and out, a bunch of sociopaths."

I could feel myself squint. "And what's her connection?"

"She's Casey's sister, Mariah Stonehart."

I said, "Ah." There was no doubt about it: She was slick.

At ten thirty I went over to the courthouse to do a records check. I figured it would be a comfort to bury myself in endless mundane paperwork, and I was genuinely curious about Joel Glazer's business dealings, specifically his connection to Genesis Financial Management Services.

I started with the assessor's office in the county administration building, where I looked up the property tax records for Pacific Meadows. As expected, Glazer and Broadus were listed as the owners. Then I left the assessor's office and walked over to the county recorder's office. I spent an hour working my way through real property sales, grant deeds, trust deeds, tax liens, and reconveyances. The Pacific Meadows building and lot had changed hands three times in the past ten years, and each sale had represented a substantial jump in price. The property was sold to Maureen Peabody in 1970 for $485,000. She'd sold it, in turn, to the Endeavor Group in 1974 for a tidy $775,000. The property sold again in 1976 to Silver Age for $1,500,000 and was finally purchased by Glazer and Broadus's company, Century Comprehensive, in 1980 for a whopping $3 million.

I crossed the street to the public library, where I discovered that Maureen Peabody was the widow of Sanford Peabody, who'd been an officer at the Santa Teresa City Bank from 1952 until his death in the spring of 1976. Maureen had probably used the money she inherited from his estate to buy the nursing home.

On a hunch I returned to the courthouse and checked the marriage records for 1976 and 1977. In February of 1977, I found a record of the marriage license issued to Maureen Peabody and Fredrick Glazer—a second marriage for both. She was fifty-seven at the time, and he was sixty-two. It didn't take much to figure out that Maureen was Joel Glazer's stepmother. I was betting Maureen's name would appear again among the corporate officers of both Endeavor and Silver Age. The only question remaining was who owned Genesis, the operating company for Pacific Meadows. The owner of record was Dana Jaffe, doing business as Genesis Financial Management Services. Joel Glazer had probably talked her into signing an application for registration before they married. She may or may not have understood the significance. On the surface Genesis appeared to be separate and unrelated to Pacific Meadows. In truth, Glazer controlled both, which put him in the perfect position to reap the benefits of all the bogus Medicare claims.

I left the courthouse close to noon, and I was curious as to what was going on with the police investigation. I went by the bank and withdrew the money I owed Fiona, then walked to the Arcade sandwich shop. As I passed the plate-glass window, I caught sight of Odessa sitting by himself. I waved and went in. I sat down across the table from him. He was working on another paper-wrapped burger in a red plastic basket surrounded by fries.

"I've just been nosing around in the public records. It looks like one of Dr. Purcell's business associates is working a Medicare scam and trying to push the blame off on him."

"You're talking about Glazer?"

"And Harvey Broadus. Purcell had figured it out and had a meeting scheduled with the FBI. Who knows how far the two of them were willing to go to keep him quiet. What's the coroner say?"

"He found powder tattooing on Purcell's right temple. He says it looks more like near-contact than a contact wound. Means the gun was held a short distance away instead of pressed right up against the skin. Purcell could have done it himself if his shooting arm was another eight inches long. They went back to scour the area near the reservoir, but so far no bullet. Could be he was shot somewhere else, and then the car was moved."

"That'd be tricky. With him sitting at the wheel?"

"That bugged Jonah, too. He got to thinking about that mohair blanket Purcell had over him. He asked Crystal, and she says a year ago she put together this emergency road kit in case he ever got stuck: snacks, flashlight, bottled water, first-aid supplies—all of which he kept in the trunk of his car. Blanket was part of that. Jonah thinks the killer could have spread it over the body and then sat on his lap to drive him up to where we found the car. The blanket was used to keep the blood off his clothes."

"Wouldn't the mohair leave fibers on his pants?"

"Sure. Blood traces, too, but there's been plenty of time to dispose of the evidence."

I picked up a french fry, doused it in ketchup, and put it down again. "I talked to Crystal last night. She came across his passport in an overcoat pocket from the last trip they took. What about Paulie? What's the story on her?"

"Jonah had me check on that after you talked to him. She got picked up the first time when she was thirteen. Grandmother thought somebody stole her car, so she called the police. Turned out Paulie took it. She also got picked up once for loitering and once for malicious mischief. She's a kid with too much time on her hands and not enough supervision."

"She and Leila are sure trouble."

"We're still working on that. We sent someone down to the school to see if we can get a match on the dates when she was off-campus and the money was being pulled from the ATM. We've subpoenaed the bank records and the records from the mailing service where Purcell kept his post-office box. The D.A. and probation are talking to the judge. We're hoping to wrap that up this afternoon."

"Here's something else. The other day I stopped over at the Horton Ravine house. Leila had left school without permission. Crystal was having fits and gave me permission to search her room. She's got a locked metal box hidden under the mattress. It's probably dope, but it might be the missing money. She and Paulie may be planning to take off. You might keep an eye on them."

"We can do that," he said.

I GOT back to the office at 1:15. The rain was picking up again, and I was tired of it. A curious depression had descended in the wake of the shooting with the adrenaline rush that accompanied it.

I typed up the information I'd unearthed about Genesis and pondered Fiona's request for cash. I didn't think she was seriously concerned my check would bounce, so it had to be something else. The picture that kept coming to mind was of her house with its decor of drop cloths and permanent scaffolding.

I was also brooding about that mohair blanket, about someone sitting on Dow's lap after he'd been shot to death. You wouldn't want to drive far. Certainly not out on public roads, where a driver in the next lane might look over and spot you in the dead man's embrace. If you were the killer, you'd think about the reservoir—how nice if both the dead man and the car disappeared from view. Jonah had been assuming the killer made an unfortunate mistake, miscalculating the position of the boulder, which prevented the car from being fully submerged. Maybe the killer *intended* to have the car found. If Dow's death was meant to look like suicide, then maybe the causal error went the other way. The killer knew the boulder was there and thought the car would still be visible when daylight came. Instead the vehicle veered slightly and sank too far to be seen easily.

It wasn't until late afternoon that I hauled out the phone book, turning to the yellow pages under the section that listed painting contractors. I started with the A's and ran my finger down the names until I found the one I remembered from Fiona's sign out front. One line of print: "Ralph Triplet, Colgate." No street address.

I dialed Ralph Triplet's number. The phone was picked up on the first ring. "Ralph Triplet Painting."

I said, "Hi, Mr. Triplet. My name is Kinsey Millhone. I just finished some work for Fiona Purcell up on Old Reservoir—"

"I hope you got your money up front."

"That's why I'm calling. Is she a slow-pay by any chance?"

"No-pay is more like it. I haven't been paid in weeks. The architect filed a lien against the property, and I'm threatening to do likewise. Meantime, I finally got around to checking her credit. Should have done that in the first place, but how was I to know? She puts on a good show, but she's busy using one credit card to pay off another. What'd you say your name was?"

"Doesn't matter," I said, then hung up.

I pulled out my packet of index cards. I shuffled through them, checking the information I'd picked up in the past week, particularly the details about Dow's last day. In passing, Mrs. Stegler had confided an item that caught my attention in light of everything I'd learned. She said that while he was out at lunch, Fiona had stopped by. She'd waited in his office and had finally departed, leaving him a note. I'd sat in that office myself and know how easily she could have opened his desk drawer and taken his gun.

I DROVE up Old Reservoir Road in the gathering dark. I had an idea, an intuition to verify before I called Jonah Robb. I turned left on the road that angled up beside Fiona's property and pulled into the parking area behind the house.

I went around to the front door and rang the bell. She came to the door decked out in a black wool suit with big shoulder pads and a pinched-in waist. She had her hair concealed in a leopard-print turban. Gloria Swanson had nothing on her. I held out the envelope. "I included an invoice for your records. I hope you don't mind signing for the cash."

"Of course not. Won't you come in?"

I stepped into the foyer.

Fiona scribbled her signature on the receipt. I tore off the top copy and handed it back to her.

"Mind if I use the bathroom?"

"There's one off the kitchen. You can help yourself."

"Be right back," I said.

I walked through the kitchen and unlocked the door leading from the kitchen into the three-car garage. There was a BMW parked in the nearest space, but the other two spaces were empty. She'd told me that when Dow came to visit, she made him pull into the garage each time so the local tongues wouldn't wag. I flipped on the overhead light, which didn't help that much.

I took the flashlight from my shoulder bag and crossed to the far wall. I imagined myself sitting in Dow's Mercedes. I looked to my left and calculated the trajectory of a bullet fired from the front seat through the driver's head, through the car window, and into the wall.

Right about there, I thought. I'd have bet money she never bothered to pry the bullet out of the drywall. Who'd even think to look here?

I ran a hand lightly over the wall, expecting to feel the faintly irregular patch of plaster fill. The wall was unblemished. Not a mark anywhere. I made a circuit of the space, but there was no indication whatever that Dow had been shot to death here before the car was moved. No fragments of glass, no oil patches on the floor where his car had sat. I wanted to wail with disappointment. This had to be right. I had been so sure.

The door to the kitchen opened, and Fiona appeared. She stared at me. "Detective Paglia was here earlier, doing exactly the same thing. He checked the walls for a buried bullet and found none."

I looked at her, my mouth suddenly dry. "Fiona, I'm sorry."

"I'm sure you are." She paused a moment. "One question, please. If I'd actually killed Dow, why in the world would I hire you?"

My cheeks grew warm, but I knew I owed her the truth. "I thought you needed to have the body found to collect on the insurance. If you hired me, you'd appear to be above reproach."

Her gaze bit into me, but she never raised her voice. "You're a very arrogant young woman. Now get out of my house."

She withdrew, closing the door behind her with a sharp report.

I let myself out. I got back in my car and started down the hill, reeling with shame and embarrassment. I'd been wrong about her. I'd been wrong about Crystal and Clint Augustine. I'd been wrong about Mariah, who'd made a fool of me. I turned left at the intersection. I'd driven a block when I caught sight of a familiar figure walking backward along the side of the road: Paulie, with her thumb stuck out.

I slowed and pulled over on the berm while she hurried to catch up. By the time she reached the car, I'd opened the passenger door for her. "Hop in. Are you on your way to see Leila?"

"Yeah. She's staying down at the beach." She got in and slammed the door, smelling of dope and cigarettes. "You can drop me off in town. It's no problem finding a ride from there."

"I don't mind driving you. I could use the air," I said. I pulled onto the road. "Were you up at Lloyd's?"

"Yeah, but he was out, and I couldn't find the key. I didn't want to wait for him in the cold."

"The two of you are friends?"

"Kind of, because of Leila."

"How's she going to feel about it when he moves to Las Vegas? Think she'll miss him?"

"Big time. She was really bummed when she heard."

"Well, maybe she'll get to visit Lloyd once he's settled," I said. "When's he taking off? He said a couple of days."

"Something like that. I'm trying to talk him into taking me."

"Don't you have family here?"

"Just Gram is all, and she wouldn't care."

When we reached Crystal's beach house, I pulled into the gravel parking area and Paulie got out. I didn't think Crystal would be glad to see her, but she'd probably be polite. I figured Leila and Paulie would end up in jail together within the next few hours.

I left the engine running, waiting while Paulie rang the bell and Crystal came to the door. Crystal caught sight of my car and waved. I returned the wave and backed out of the drive, my headlights washing across the open carport, where I could see the Volvo and the convertible. The slot on the extreme left was empty, and I was guessing that was the space where Dow had kept his car. I felt a tiny jolt of electricity. I made the turn onto Paloma Lane, drove half a block, and then pulled the VW over to the side of the road. I got out and walked back to the house.

Crystal had closed the door, and the area was dark.

As I had at Fiona's house, I placed myself in a spot that approximated the location of the Mercedes's front seat, picturing the car parked as it would have been had Dow pulled in that night. Maybe Crystal had promised him such exotic sexual treats that he'd bypassed his scheduled visit with Fiona and come home to his wife. She could have retrieved the .357 Magnum earlier. All she had to do was come out to meet him, open the car door, lean across the seat, and kill him as sweetly as a kiss. Driving the body up to the reservoir was a nice piece of misdirection that put Fiona in the soup.

Given the amount of money Fiona stood to gain, the police would naturally pursue the notion that she'd killed him herself.

I looked left and calculated the trajectory of a bullet speeding in that direction. After all, if a shot had been fired from a Charter Arms .357 Magnum across the space of the front seat and through the doctor's head, one could only imagine the bullet traveling right on, smashing the car window, crossing fifteen feet of open space, and plowing through the shingle siding of the structure next door.

I crossed the patchy stretch of grass that lay between the carport and the structure. It might have once been a detached garage. I took out my flashlight and turned it on. I moved the bushes aside and swept the beam across the rough-hewn shingles. The bullet hole was big and black, like a spider sitting on the side of the house.

I retraced my steps across the gravel parking pad to Crystal's front door. I rang the bell. She opened it with an expression on her face like I might be selling door to door. She said, "Oh, I didn't expect to see you. What's going on?"

"I'd like to use your phone."

She seemed puzzled but stepped back and let me pass in front of her. She peered out. "Where's your car?"

"It's parked on the road. The engine cut out, and I need a way to get home."

"I can do that," she said. "I'll grab my keys."

"No, no. I wouldn't want to trouble you. I have a friend nearby, and he's an experienced mechanic. I'll just ask him to take a look. Maybe he can fix it right here and send me on my way."

"Well, if that doesn't work out, I can always run you home."

From upstairs I could hear music being played at top volume. I pictured Paulie and Leila planning their escape. I really hoped the cops would show up before they made good on their "getaway."

She showed me into the den and then stood in the doorway while I took a seat at the desk. I picked up the receiver and dialed Jonah's home number. When he picked up, I said, "Oh, hi. It's me."

"Kinsey?" He sounded puzzled. "What's up?"

"I'm at Crystal's beach house. I've got a little problem, and I'd love to have you take a look."

"All right," he said cautiously. "Is this important?"

"Completely. You have the address?"

"I know the place. Are you in trouble?"

"Not yet, but I could be. I'll see you shortly, and thanks."

I replaced the receiver, and when I looked up again, Anica had joined Crystal in the doorway. The two stood close together—Crystal in front, Anica slightly behind. Anica's hand was on Crystal's arm, and I suddenly understood what I'd been looking at all along. Anica said, "Is there a problem?"

"Not really. I'm waiting for a friend of mine to come give me some help. I had some trouble with my car."

"Oh. Well, why don't you join us for a glass of chardonnay while you wait."

"I guess I could do that."

I followed them out onto the deck. We sat in the dark, just the three of us, sipping wine and chatting, listening to the surf rumble on the beach until Jonah arrived.

Two days later I received the following note in the mail.

Kinsey,

Sorry I had to do that to you, but I didn't have a choice. Here's the difference between us: Basically, you're decent and have a conscience. I don't.

                                        Mariah Stonehart

SUE GRAFTON

Sue Grafton thinks of her detective Kinsey Millhone as her alter ego.

Sue Grafton began her groundbreaking alphabet mystery series in the early 1980s, a rocky time in her life. In the midst of a bitter divorce and a child custody suit with her ex-husband, she lay awake nights dreaming of ways to do him in. Alas, she knew she could not actually act it out. "I thought, Why don't I put this plot between the covers of a book and get paid for it?" The result was *"A" Is for Alibi,* the bestseller that introduced P.I. Kinsey Millhone to the world.

Now, with the publication of her sixteenth blockbuster, the sixty-one-year-old author still enjoys writing whodunits featuring her irrepressible detective. While Grafton thinks of Kinsey as her alter ego, the two women are more different than alike. Unlike her perpetually single heroine, Grafton is married to a philosophy professor and has three children and two grandchildren. Whereas Kinsey is a nature-hating, junk-food devotee, Grafton loves gardening and good cuisine. "She'll always be thinner, younger, and braver," she says. "Her biography is different, but our sensibilities are identical. Because of Kinsey, I get to lead two lives—hers and mine. Sometimes I'm not sure which I prefer."

To learn more about Sue Grafton and the story behind *"P" Is for Peril,* visit the Select Editions website:

ReadersOnly.com
Password: *today*

KRISTIN HANNAH
Summer Island

*Sometimes
the only way to remember
what you've lost
is to go home again.*

Chapter One

AN EARLY evening rain had fallen. In the encroaching darkness the streets of Seattle lay like mirrored strips between the glittering gray high-rises.

The dot-com revolution had changed this once quiet city, and even after the sun had set, the clattering, hammering sounds of construction beat a constant rhythm. Buildings sprouted overnight, it seemed, reaching higher and higher into the soggy sky. Purple-haired kids with nose rings and ragged clothes zipped through downtown in brand-new, bright red Ferraris.

On a corner lot in the newly fashionable neighborhood of Belltown, there was a squat wooden structure that had been built almost one hundred years earlier, when few people had wanted to live so far from the heart of the city. The owners of radio station KJZZ didn't care that they no longer fit in this trendy area. For fifty years they had broadcast from this lot. They had grown from a scrappy local station to Washington's largest. Part of the reason for their current success was Nora Bridge, the newest sensation in talk radio.

Although her show, *Spiritual Healing with Nora,* had been in syndication for less than a year, it was already a bona fide hit. And her weekly newspaper advice column, Nora Knows Best, appeared in more than 2600 papers nationwide.

Nora had started her career as a household hints adviser for a small-town newspaper, but hard work and a strong vision had moved her up the food chain. The women of Seattle had been the first to discover her unique blend of passion and morality; the rest of the country had soon followed. Reviewers claimed that she could see a way through any emotional conflict; more often than not, they mentioned the purity of her heart.

But they were wrong. It was the *impurity* in her heart that made her successful. She was an ordinary woman who'd made extraordinary mistakes. She understood every nuance of need and loss. Each night, she brought her own regrets to the microphone, and from that wellspring of sorrow she found compassion.

She had managed her career with laserlike focus, carefully feeding the press a palatable past. Her fans knew she'd been divorced and that she had grown daughters. The hows and whys of her family's destruction remained—thankfully—private.

Tonight Nora was on the air. She scooted her wheeled chair closer to the microphone and adjusted her headphones. A computer screen showed her the list of callers on hold. She pushed line two, which read MARGE/MOTHER-DAUGHTER PROBS.

"Hello, Marge. You're on the air with Nora Bridge."

"Hello . . . Nora?" The caller sounded hesitant.

Nora smiled. Her fans, she'd learned, were often anxious. "How can I help you, my friend?" she asked gently.

"I'm having a little trouble with my daughter, Suki."

"How old is Suki, Marge?"

"Sixty-seven this November."

Nora laughed quietly. "I guess some things never change. So, Marge, what's the problem with Suki?"

"Well"—Marge made a snorting sound—"last week she went on a singles cruise, and today she told me she's getting married again, to a man she met on the boat. At *her* age." She snorted again. "I know she wanted me to be happy for her, but how could I?"

Nora asked, "Do you love your daughter?"

"I've always loved her." Marge's voice caught on a little sob. "You can't know what it's like, Nora, to love your daughter so much and watch her stop needing you. What if she marries this man and forgets all about me?"

Nora closed her eyes and cleared her mind. She'd learned long ago that callers were constantly saying things that struck at the heart of her own pain. "Every mother is afraid of that, Marge. The only way to really hold on to our children is to let them go. If Suki has your love for strength, she'll never be too far away."

Marge wept softly. "Maybe I could call her, ask her to bring her boyfriend around for supper."

"That would be a wonderful start. Good luck to you, Marge." Nora cleared her throat and disconnected the call. "Come on, everybody," she said into the microphone. "I know there are plenty of you who have mended families. Call in. Marge and I want to be reminded that love isn't as fragile as it sometimes feels."

For the next two hours Nora gave her heart and soul to her listeners. She never pretended to have all the answers or to be a substitute for doctors or family therapy. Instead she tried to give her friendship to these troubled, ordinary people she'd never met.

When the show was finally over, she returned to her office. There she took the time to write personal thank-you notes to those callers who'd been willing to leave an address with the show's producer. Anyone who'd been courageous enough to publicly ask for advice from Nora deserved a private thank-you.

After she finished, she hurried to her car. Fortunately, it was only a few miles to the hospital. She parked in the underground lot and emerged into the lobby's artificial brightness.

Nora had become a regular visitor—every Saturday and Tuesday for the past month—and she smiled and waved to the nurses' familiar faces as she walked down the corridor toward Eric's room.

Although she saw him often, it was never easy. Eric Sloan was as close to a son as she would have, and watching him battle cancer was unbearable. But she was all he had. His mother and father had written Eric off long ago, unable to accept his life's choices, and his younger brother, Dean, rarely made time to visit.

Nora pushed open the door to his room and saw that he lay in bed sleeping. With his hair almost gone, his cheeks hollow, and his mouth open, he looked as old and beaten as a man could be. And he hadn't yet celebrated his thirty-first birthday.

She went to him, gently caressed the bare top of his head.

He blinked up at her sleepily, trying for a boyish grin and almost succeeding. "I have good news and bad news," he said.

She touched his shoulder and felt how fragile he was. There was a tiny catch in her voice as she said, "What's the good news?"

"No more treatments."

She clutched his shoulder too hard. "And the bad news?"

"No more treatments." He paused. "It was Dr. Calomel's idea."

She nodded dully. In the eleven months since his diagnosis, they'd spent dozens of nights talking about this moment. She'd even thought she was ready for it, but now she saw her naïveté.

Eric closed his eyes, and she wondered if he was remembering the time, a few years before, when his partner, Charlie, had been in a hospital bed like this one, fighting a losing battle with AIDS.

Finally Eric looked up at her. His attempt at a smile brought tears to her eyes. In that second she saw pieces from the whole of his life. She pictured him at eight, sitting at her kitchen table, eating Lucky Charms—a shaggy-haired, freckle-faced boy with banged-up knees and soup-ladle ears.

"I'm going home," he said quietly.

"That's great," she said, smiling too brightly. "I'll visit you during the day. I'll still have to work the show at night, but—"

"I mean the island. I'm going *home.*"

"Are you finally going to call your family?" She hated his decision to handle his cancer privately, but he'd been adamant.

"Oh, yeah. They've been so supportive in the past."

"This is different than coming out of the closet, and you know it. It's time to call Dean. And your parents."

The look he gave her was so hopeless that she wanted to turn away. "What if I told my mother I was dying and she still wouldn't come to see me?"

Nora understood. "At least call your brother." She forced a smile. "If you can wait until Tuesday, I'll drive you—"

"I haven't got much time. I've arranged to be flown up. Lottie's already at the house, getting it ready."

She swallowed hard. "I don't think you should be alone."

"Enough." His voice was soft, but she heard the barest echo of his former strength. He was reminding her that he was an adult, a grown man. "Now," he said, clapping his hands together, "let's talk about something else. I listened to your show tonight. Mothers and daughters. That's always tough on you."

"I never really know what to say. How would Marge feel if she knew I hadn't spoken to my own daughter in eleven years?" It helped Nora that Eric recognized how painful it was to think about her younger daughter. "I wonder what she's doing now."

Eric managed a laugh. "With Ruby it could be anything, from having lunch with Steven Spielberg to piercing her tongue."

Nora laughed, then fell abruptly silent.

Eric leaned forward. There was a sudden earnestness in his eyes. "She's not dead, Nora."

"I know. I try to squeeze hope from that thought all the time."

He grinned. "Now get out the backgammon board. I feel like whooping you."

IT WAS only the second week of June, and already the temperature hovered at one hundred degrees. A freak heat wave they called it on the local news, the kind of weather that usually came to southern California later in the year.

No one could sleep in this heat, and Ruby Bridge was no exception. She lay sprawled in her bed, the sheets shoved down to the floor, a cold pack pressed across her forehead.

The minutes ticked by. She felt lonely. Only a few days earlier her boyfriend, Max, had left her. After five years of living together, he'd simply walked out of her life. All he'd left behind were a few pieces of furniture and a note.

The funny thing was, she didn't miss him. She missed the idea of him. She missed a second plate at the dinner table, another body in bed. Mostly she missed the pretense that she was in love.

At seven a.m. the alarm clock sounded. Ruby slid out of bed on a sluglike trail of perspiration and went to the bathroom, where she took a lukewarm shower. She was sweating again before she was finished drying off. Grabbing the grease-stained black polyester pants and white cotton blouse that lay tangled on the floor, she got dressed and went out into the stifling heat.

She walked downstairs to her battered 1970 Volkswagen Bug. After a few tries the engine turned over, and Ruby drove toward Irma's Hash House, the trendy Venice Beach diner where she'd worked for almost three years.

She'd never meant to stay a waitress. The job was supposed to be temporary, something to pay the bills until she got on her feet, caused a sensation at one of the local comedy clubs, did a guest spot on *Leno,* and—finally—was offered her own sitcom. But at twenty-seven, after almost a decade spent trying to break into comedy, Ruby was brushing up against "too old." Everyone knew that if you didn't make it by thirty, you were toast.

She parked in the crowded parking lot and headed for the diner. When she opened the front door, the bell tinkled overhead.

Irma, her three-story beehive hairdo leading the way, bustled toward Ruby, then came to an abrupt halt in front of her. Irma's heavily mascaraed eyes narrowed. "You were scheduled for last night."

Ruby winced. "Oh, no."

"I'm letting you go," Irma said. "We can't count on you. Debbie had to work a double shift last night. Your final paycheck is at the register. I'll expect the uniform back tomorrow. Cleaned."

Ruby's lips trembled. "Come on, Irma. I *need* this job."

"I'm sorry. Really." She turned and walked away.

Ruby stood there a minute, breathing in the familiar mixture of maple syrup and grease. Then she snagged her paycheck from the counter and walked out of the restaurant.

She got into her car and drove away aimlessly, up one street and down the another. Finally, when it felt as if her face were melting off her skull, she parked in front of a high-rise building on Wilshire Boulevard. Before she had time to talk herself out of it, she went to the elevator and rode it up to the top floor. The doors opened, and she walked briskly down the hallway toward her agent's office.

The receptionist, Maudeen Wachsmith, had her nose buried in a romance novel. Barely looking up, she said, "Hi, Ruby. He's busy today. You'll have to make an appointment."

Ruby rushed past Maudeen and yanked the door open.

Her agent, Valentine Lightner, was seated behind the glassy expanse of his desk. When he saw Ruby, his smile faded into a frown. "Ruby, I wasn't expecting you . . . was I?"

Maudeen rushed in behind Ruby. "I'm sorry, Mr. Lightner."

He raised a slim hand. "Don't worry about it, Maudeen." He leaned back in his chair. "So, Ruby, what's going on?"

She waited for Maudeen to leave. "Is that cruise-ship job still available?" She'd laughed about it three months before—cruise ships were floating morgues for talent—but now it didn't seem beneath her. It seemed above her.

"I've *tried* for you, Ruby. You write funny stuff, but that's no ordinary chip on your shoulder. It's a section of the Hoover Dam. You've burned too many bridges in this business. Remember the job I got you on that sitcom? You slowed down the first week's production and made everyone insane with rewrites."

"My character was an idiot. She didn't have one funny line."

Val looked at her, his eyes narrowing. "Shall I remind you that another—less talented—comedian is now making thirty thousand dollars an episode saying what she's told to say?"

Ruby collapsed into the plush leather chair in front of his desk. "I'm broke. Irma fired me from the diner."

"Why don't you call your mother?"

"Don't go there, Val," she said quietly.

He sighed. "I'll try Asia. They love U.S. comedians overseas. Maybe you can do the nightclub circuit."

She winced, imagining herself in one of those men's bars with naked women writhing up and down silver poles behind her.

Val had always been her champion, her biggest fan. She'd been
~~with him a long time—since her first days~~ at the Comedy Store. But
in the past few years she'd disappointed him. She didn't know what
was wrong with her, except that she seemed to be angry all the time.
"I appreciate everything you've done for me, Val. I know it's hard
to get work for a prima donna with no talent."

He said, "You have as much raw talent as anyone. You light up a
room with your smile, and your wit is as sharp as a blade. Let me
ask you a question. When did you stop smiling, Ruby?"

She knew the answer, of course. It had happened in her junior
year of high school, but she wouldn't think about that.

"I don't know." She wished she could let Val see how frightened
she was, how alone she felt. But she couldn't do it. No matter how
hard she tried, Ruby couldn't let down her guard. Her emotions
were packed tightly inside her, hermetically sealed so that every
wound and memory stayed fresh.

She got to her feet. "Well," she said at last, straightening her
shoulders. She had the fleeting sense that she looked absurd—a
wounded sparrow trying to impress a peregrine falcon. "I guess I'd
better go home and learn to speak Japanese."

"That's my girl." Val smiled wanly. "I'll make the calls about Asia."

"I'm grateful. Sayonara." She wiggled her fingers in an oh-so-
California-darling wave and did her best to sashay out of the office.
It was tough to pull off in a sweat-stained waitress uniform, and
the minute she was out of his office, she let go of her fake smile.

Outside, she headed for her car. There was a parking ticket on
her windshield. She yanked the paper from beneath the rusted
windshield wiper and wadded it into a ball. To her mind, ticketing
this rattrap and expecting to get paid was like leaving a bill on the
pillow at a homeless shelter. She felt the hot sting of tears.

Absurdly, she thought, If only it would rain.

JUNE was a hard month in Seattle. It was in this season, when the
peonies and delphiniums bloomed, that the locals began to complain that they'd been cheated. The rains had started in October. By

the last week in May, even the meteorologically challenged denizens of Seattle had had enough. They'd put up with nearly nine months of dismal weather, and it was past time for the sun to deliver.

So it was hardly surprising that it rained on the day Nora Bridge celebrated her fiftieth birthday. She didn't take the weather as an omen or a portent of bad luck. In retrospect she should have.

She stood at the window in her office sipping her favorite drink—Mumm Champagne with a slice of fresh peach. On her windowsill were dozens of birthday cards. The most treasured card had come from her elder daughter, Caroline. Of course, the joy of that card was tempered by the fact that, again this year, there had been no card from Ruby.

Nora gave herself a little time to wallow in regret, and then she rallied. Fifteen years of therapy had granted her this skill; she could compartmentalize. She turned away from the window and glanced at the crystal clock on her desk. It was four thirty-eight.

They were down in the conference room now, setting out food, bottles of Champagne, plates filled with peach slices. Assistants, publicists, staff writers, producers—they were all putting together a "surprise" party for the newest star of talk radio.

Nora set her champagne flute down, then headed out of the office. She walked into the conference room.

It was empty. The long table was bare; no food was spread out. A HAPPY BIRTHDAY banner hung from the overhead lights. It looked as if someone had started to decorate for a party and then suddenly stopped.

It was a moment before Nora noticed the two men standing to her left: Bob Wharton, the station's owner and manager, and Jason Close, the lead in-house attorney.

Nora smiled warmly. "Hello, Bob. Jason. It's good to see you."

The men exchanged a quick glance.

"We have some bad news," Bob said.

Jason eased past Bob and came up to Nora. "Earlier today Bob took a call from a man named Vince Corell."

Nora felt as if she'd been smacked in the face.

"He claimed he'd had an affair with you while you were married. He wanted us to pay him to keep quiet."

"An *affair,* Nora," Bob sputtered angrily. "While your kids were at home. You should have told us."

"I could say he was lying," she said, wincing when she heard the breathy, desperate tone of her voice.

Jason opened his briefcase, took out a manila envelope, and handed it to her. Her hands were shaking as she opened it.

There were black-and-white photographs inside. She pulled the top one halfway out. "Oh, God," she whispered. She crammed it back into the envelope. "There must be a way to stop this. An injunction. Those are private photographs."

"Yes, they are," Jason said. "His. It's obvious that you . . . knew the camera was there. You're posing."

She looked at them. "How much does he want?"

There was a pregnant pause. "A half-million dollars," Jason said.

"I can get that amount—"

"Money never kills this kind of thing, Nora. You know that."

She understood immediately. "You told him no," she said woodenly. "And now he's going to go to the tabloids."

Jason nodded. "I'm sorry, Nora."

"I can explain this to my fans," she said. "They'll underst—"

"You give *moral* advice, Nora." Bob shook his head. "This is going to be a hell of a scandal. When these photos hit the air, we'll lose advertisers instantly. We've been promoting you as a modern version of Mother Teresa. Now it turns out you're Debbie Does Dallas."

Nora tried to appear calm. "What do we do?"

"We want you to take some time off." Jason touched her shoulder gently. "You've spent the better part of the past decade telling people to honor their commitments and put their families first. How long do you think it will take the press to uncover that you haven't spoken to your own daughter since the divorce?"

And just like that, Nora's life slipped beyond her grasp. "It'll blow over," she whispered, knowing in her heart that it wasn't true. "I'll take a few weeks off. See what happens."

"For the record," Jason said, "this is a scheduled vacation. We won't admit that it has anything to do with the scandal."

"Thank you."

"I hope you make it through this," Jason said. "We all do."

There was an awkward silence. Then Jason and Bob walked past Nora. The door clicked shut behind them.

She stood there, alone now, her gaze blurred by tears. After eleven years of working seventy-hour weeks, it was over, blown apart by a few naked photographs taken a lifetime ago. The world would see her hypocrisy, and so too—oh, God—would her daughters.

They would know at last that their mother had had an affair and that she'd lied to them when she walked out of her marriage.

RUBY had a pounding headache. She'd slept on and off all day. Finally she stumbled into the living room, leaned against the wall, and slid down to a sit, her legs stretched out. She should walk down to Chang's Mini-Mart and pick up a newspaper, but the thought of turning to the want ads was more than she could bear.

The phone rang. Ruby didn't want to answer. It could hardly be good news. At best it would be Caroline, her *über*-yuppie Junior League sister, who had two perfect kids and a hunk of a husband.

It was *possible* that Dad had finally remembered her, but Ruby doubted it. Since he'd remarried and started a second family, her father was more interested in midnight baby feedings than in the goings-on of his adult daughter's life. The ringing went on and on.

Finally she crawled across the shag carpet and answered on the fourth ring. "Hello?" She heard the snarl in her voice.

"It's me, darlin', your favorite agent."

She frowned. "Val? You sound pretty happy, considering that my career is circling the hole in the toilet bowl."

Val laughed. It was a great, booming sound. "I *am* happy. You won't believe who called me today." There was a palpable pause. "Joe Cochran. He had a cancellation and wants to book you for tomorrow's show."

How could a world spin around so quickly? Yesterday Ruby had been pond scum; today the host of *Uproar,* the hottest, hippest talk show in the country, wanted her. The show had been patterned after *Politically Correct,* but because *Uproar* was broadcast on cable, it explored racier issues. It was a young comedian's dream gig.

"He's giving you two minutes to do stand-up. So, kiddo, this is it. I'll send a car around to pick you up at eleven tomorrow morning."

"Thanks, Val." Before she hung up, Ruby remembered to ask, "Hey, what's the topic of the show?"

"It's called 'Crime and Punishment: Are Mommy and Daddy to Blame for Everything?' "

"They want me because I'm *her* daughter."

"Do you care why?"

"No." It was true. This was her shot. Finally, after years of play dates in smoke-infested barrooms in towns whose names she couldn't remember, she was getting national exposure.

She thanked Val again, then hung up the phone. Her heart was racing so hard, she felt dizzy. She ran to her bedroom and flung open the doors of her closet. She couldn't afford anything new.

Then she remembered the black cashmere sweater. It had come from her mother two Christmases earlier, disguised in a box from Caroline. Although Ruby routinely sent back her mother's guilty gifts unopened, this one had seduced her. Once she'd touched that beautiful fabric, she couldn't mail it back.

She grabbed the black V-neck sweater off its hanger and tossed it on the bed. Tomorrow she'd jazz it up with necklaces and wear it over a black leather miniskirt with black tights.

When Ruby had picked out her clothes, she kicked the bedroom door shut. A mirror on the back of the door caught her image. Her short black hair had been molded by last night's sweatfest into a perfect imitation of Johnny Rotten. "I'm Ruby Bridge," she said, grabbing a hairbrush off the dresser to use as a mike. "And yes, you're right if you recognize the last name. I'm her daughter, Nora Bridge's, spiritual guru to Middle America." She flung her hip out, picturing herself as she would look tomorrow. "Look at me. Should that woman be telling you how to raise kids? It's like—"

The phone rang.

"Damn." Ruby raced into the living room and yanked the cord out of the wall. She couldn't be bothered for the next twenty-four hours. Nothing mattered except getting ready for the show.

LIKE all big cities, San Francisco looked beautiful at night. Multicolored lights glittered throughout downtown, creating a neon sculpture garden tucked along the black bay.

Dean Sloan glanced longingly at the wall of windows that framed the panoramic view. Unfortunately, he couldn't leave his seat. He was, as always, trapped by the flypaper of good manners.

Scattered through the ornately gilded ballroom of this Russian Hill mansion were a dozen or so tables, each of which seated four or five couples. The women were expensively, beautifully gowned, and the men wore tuxedos. The party's hostess, a local socialite, had hand-chosen the guest list from among the wealthiest of San Francisco's families. Tonight's charity was the opera.

Dean's date was a pale, exquisite woman named Sarah. "That was a lovely sentiment, don't you think?" she said softly.

Dean had no idea what she was talking about, but a quick look around the room enlightened him. An elderly, well-preserved woman was standing alongside the ebony Steinway. No doubt she'd been waxing poetic about the opera and thanking her guests in advance for their unselfish contributions. There was a smattering of quiet applause, then the sound of chairs being scooted back.

Dean took hold of Sarah's hand, and they slipped into the whispering crowd. The band was playing something soft and romantic. On the dance floor he pulled Sarah close, slid his hand down the bare expanse of her back, felt her shiver at his touch. If he cared to, he could lead her out of this crush and take her to his bed. After that he would call her, and they would probably sleep together a few times. Then, somehow, he would forget her. Last year a local magazine had named him San Francisco's most *in*eligible bachelor because of his reputation for nanosecond affairs.

But what the reporter hadn't known, hadn't even imagined, was how tired Dean was of it all. He wasn't even twenty-nine years old, and already he felt aged. For more than a year now, he had felt that something was wrong with his life. Missing. At first he'd assumed it was a business problem, and he'd rededicated himself to work, logging upward of eighty hours a week at Harcourt and Sons. But all he'd managed to do was make more money, and the ache in his gut had steadily sharpened.

He'd spoken to his parents about it, but that had proved pointless. Edward Sloan was now—and always had been—a charming playboy who jumped at his wife's every command. It was Mother who held the ambition, and she'd never been one to care about things like fulfillment or satisfaction. Her comment had been as he'd expected: "I ran this company for thirty years; now it's your turn. No whining allowed." He supposed she'd earned that right. Under his mother's iron fist the family business had become a hundred-million-dollar enterprise. That had always been enough for her, but that same success felt hollow to Dean.

He'd tried to talk to his friends about it, and though they'd wanted to help, none of them understood his feelings. It wasn't so surprising. Dean had grown up in a slightly different world than they.

Lopez Island. Summer Island.

He'd spent ten perfect years in the San Juan Islands. There he and his brother, Eric, had been—for a short time—ordinary boys. Those remote islands had formed and defined Dean, provided a place he felt whole. Of course, Ruby had been there. And before she went crazy and ruined everything, she'd taught him how love felt.

Then she'd shown him how easily it was broken.

Dean sighed, wishing he hadn't thought about Ruby now, when he had a beautiful, willing woman in his arms. Suddenly he was tired. He simply didn't have the energy to spend tonight with another woman he didn't care about.

"I'm not feeling well, and I've got a crack-of-dawn conference call from Tokyo," he said. "I think I'll take you home, if you don't mind."

She pouted prettily, and he wondered if that was one of the things they taught wealthy young girls at schools like Miss Porter's.

Once he'd made his decision, Dean couldn't get out of the room fast enough. He maneuvered through the crowd like a Tour de France cyclist, saying good night to the few people who really mattered, then hurried out with Sarah to his car. They made idle chitchat on the way to her father's hilltop mansion.

Less than fifteen minutes after Dean had dropped Sarah off, he was standing in his living room, staring out at the night-clad city. On the walls all around him were framed photographs—his hobby. Once, the sight of them had pleased him. Now all he saw when he looked at his photographs was how wrong his life had gone.

Behind him the phone rang. He strode to the suede sofa, collapsed onto the down-filled cushion, and answered it.

"Dino? Is that you?"

"Uh . . . Eric? How in the world are you?" Dean was stunned. He hadn't heard from his brother in what? Eighteen months?

"Are you sitting down?"

"That doesn't sound good."

"It isn't. I'm dying."

Dean felt as if he'd been punched in the gut. "AIDS?"

Eric laughed. "We *do* get other diseases, you know. My personal favorite is cancer." He took a deep breath. "I don't have much time left."

Dean couldn't seem to draw a decent breath. "You're thirty years old," he said helplessly, as if age were relevant.

"I should've told you when I was first diagnosed, but I kept thinking I'd tell you when it was over, and we'd laugh about it."

"Is there *any* chance we'll someday laugh about it?"

It took Eric a moment to answer. "No."

"What can I do?"

"I'm going back to the island. Lottie's already there."

"The island," Dean repeated slowly. A strange sense of inevitability drifted into the room. It was as if Dean had always known that someday they'd end up back there, where everything had begun. Where everything had gone so wrong.

"Will you come up?"

"Of course."

"I want us to be brothers again."

"We've always been brothers," Dean answered uncomfortably.

"No," Eric said softly. "We've been members of the same family. We haven't been brothers in years."

Chapter Two

𝒯HE scandal broke with gale force. Those humiliating photographs were everywhere, and the newspapers and television stations that didn't own them described them in excruciating detail.

Nora sat huddled in her living room, refusing to go anywhere. The thought of being seen terrified her.

Her assistant, Dee Langhor, had shown up bright and early in the morning. Now Dee was in Nora's home office, fielding calls.

With everything on Nora's mind, one thing kept rising to the surface—she should have called Caroline the day before to warn her. But in the end, Nora had chosen to handle the impending disaster as she handled all difficult things: She'd taken two sleeping pills and turned off her phone. Now, with the story on every morning show, she had no choice. She had to call. She reached for the phone, accessed the second line, and pushed number one on the speed-dial list.

"Hello?"

It took Nora a moment to respond. "Caro? It's me—Mom."

There was a pause that seemed to strip away a layer of Nora's tender flesh. "Well, I found out this morning when I dropped Jenny off at preschool." Caroline laughed sharply. "Mona Carlson asked me how it felt to see pictures of my mother like that. How it *felt.*"

Nora didn't know how to respond. Defending herself was pointless. "I'm sorry. I couldn't . . . call."

"Of course you couldn't." Caroline was quiet for a moment. "I can't believe I let it hurt my feelings. It's just that I thought—"

"I know. We've been getting closer."

"No. Apparently *I've* been getting closer. You've been like some Stepford mom, pretending, saying the right things but never really feeling connected to me at all. I don't know when I got stupid enough to expect honesty from you."

"I know I screwed up. Don't shut me out of your life again."

"You really don't get it, do you? I'm not the one who shuts people out. Maybe Ruby was the smart one—she hasn't let you hurt her in years. Now, I've got to go."

"I love you, Caroline," Nora said in a rush, desperate to say the words before it was too late.

"You know what's sad about that?" Caroline's voice broke. A little sob sounded in her throat. "I believe you." She hung up.

The dial tone buzzed in Nora's ears.

Dee rushed into the living room, her eyes wide. "Mr. Adams is on the phone. I told him you weren't here, but he said to tell you to pick up the phone, or he was going to call his lawyers."

Nora sighed. Of course. Tom Adams hadn't become a newspaper mogul by playing nice. "Put him through."

"Thanks," Dee said, hurrying back into Nora's office.

Nora answered the phone. "Hello, Tom."

"Nora, what in the Sam Hill were you thinking? I heard about this godawful mess when I was eating breakfast. If I hadn't had the television on, I don't know when I'da found out."

"Sorry, Tom. I was caught off guard by the whole thing myself."

"Well, you're on guard now, little lady. You haven't gotten any letters yet, but you will."

"You've got two months' worth of columns from me on file. That'll give me some time to figure out how I want to handle this."

He made a barking sound. "I pay you a wagonload of money to answer readers' letters, and now that they finally got something interesting to ask about, you aren't going to play possum. Scandals sell newspapers, and I mean to cash in on your heartache. Sorry, Nora. I've always liked you, but business is business."

Nora felt sick. "The radio station is giving me some time off—"

"Don't you confuse me with those tie-wearin' pantywaists. I haven't backed down from a fight in my life."

"Okay, Tom," Nora said softly. "Give me a few days. Use what you have for now, and then I'll start to answer the hate mail."

He chuckled. "I knew you'd see the light, Nora. Bye now."

She hung up. Tom actually expected her to read angry, disappointed letters from the very people who used to love her.

Impossible.

RUBY stood in her steam-clouded bathroom staring through the mist at her watery reflection. The lines beneath her puffy eyes looked like they'd been stitched in place by a sewing machine. It wouldn't do to look this old, not in Hollywood. She'd use makeup to take off the years. Enough "heroin-chic" black eyeliner, and people would assume she was young and stupid.

Ruby dressed carefully—cashmere sweater, black leather miniskirt, and black tights. A lot of gel made her hair poke out everywhere. Then she grabbed her handbag and headed outside.

The sleek black limousine was already parked at the curb. A uniformed driver stood beside the car. "Miss Bridge?"

She grinned. No one ever called her that. "That's me."

The driver opened the door for her. Ruby peered into the interior and saw a dozen white roses lying on the back seat. She slid into the seat, heard the satisfying thud of the closing door, and plucked the card from the flowers: "People as talented as you don't need luck. They need a chance, and this is yours. Love, Val."

It felt good, as if those tarnished dreams of hers were finally coming true. She had never meant to need it all so much. But after her mother abandoned them, everything had changed. Ruby had changed. From that moment on, nothing and no one had been quite enough for her. She'd come to need the unconditional acceptance that only fame could provide.

She scooted closer to the window, grinning as the limo pulled up to the security booth at the entrance to Paramount. The twin white arches announced to the world that through these gates was a special world, open only to a lucky few. The guard waved them through.

The driver proceeded to soundstage nine, a hulking flesh-colored building. He stopped the car, then came around, opening Ruby's door.

She took a deep breath and headed toward the entrance. A neon sign read UPROAR! A NEW KIND OF TALK SHOW WITH JOE COCHRAN. Inside was a kaleidoscope of lights, darkened seating, and people scurrying around like ants with clipboards, checking and rechecking.

"You're Ruby Bridge?"

Ruby jumped. She hadn't noticed the small platinum blonde who now stood beside her. "I'm Ruby."

"Good." The woman led her into a small waiting room. On the table beside a brown sofa were a bowl of fruit and a bottle of Perrier on ice. "Sit here. I'll come and get you when it's time to go on." The woman consulted her papers. "You get two minutes up front. Be fast and be funny." She was gone.

Ruby collapsed on the couch. Suddenly she was more than nervous. She was terrified. *Be funny.*

What had she been thinking? She wasn't funny. Her material might be funny, but *she* wasn't. "Calm down, Ruby," she said. She focused on her breathing: in and out, in and out.

There was a knock at the door. The same lady with platinum blond hair stood there. "They're ready for you, Miss Bridge."

"Oh, my God." Ruby shot to her feet. She'd been hyperventilating for thirty minutes, and now she couldn't remember one line of material. She exhaled slowly. "I'm ready," she said.

She followed the woman toward the stage. Ruby was sweating like a geyser. Mascara was probably running down her cheeks. She'd look like something out of *Alien* by the time—

"Ruby Bridge!" Her name roared through the sound system.

Ruby pushed through the curtains. She forced herself not to squint, although the lights were so bright, she couldn't see anything. She just hoped she didn't walk off the end of the stage.

She went to the microphone. "Well," she said, "it's nice to know I'm not the only person who can come to a talk show in the middle of the day. Of course, it's easy for me. I was fired yesterday from a trendy restaurant I won't name, but it sounds like Irma's Hash House. I won't even tell you what I thought we'd be selling—"

A smattering of laughter. It gave her confidence. She grinned, then launched into the rest of her routine, saving the best jokes—about her mother—for last.

At the end of her routine Ruby stepped back from the mike. Amid the sound of applause Joe Cochran crossed the stage toward her. He was smiling. He placed a hand warmly on her shoulder and turned to face the crowd. "You've all met the very funny Ruby Bridge. Now let's meet our other guest—family therapist Elsa Pine, author of the best-selling book *Poisonous Parents.*"

Elsa walked onstage. She and Ruby followed Joe to the artfully arranged leather chairs. Joe sat down and looked up at the audience. "I don't know about you, but I'm sick of the way our judicial system handles criminals. Every time I open the paper, I read about some jerk who killed a little girl and got off because the jury felt sorry for him. I mean, who's looking out for the victims here?"

"Now, Joe," Elsa said, "criminals aren't born. They're made. Some people have been so abused by their parents that they no longer know right from wrong."

Joe looked at Ruby. "You know something about toxic parents, Ruby. Is everything wrong in your life your mother's fault?"

Elsa nodded. "Yes, Ruby. You of all people should understand how deeply a parent can wound a child. I mean, your mother is a huge proponent of marriage. She positively waxes poetic about the sanctity of the vows. You were probably the only person in America who wasn't surprised by the *Tattler* today."

"I don't read the tabloids," Ruby answered.

A whisper moved through the audience. Joe's enthusiastic smile dimmed. "You haven't read today's *Tattler?*"

Ruby's frown deepened. "Is that a crime now?"

Joe reached down, and for the first time, Ruby noticed the newspaper folded beneath his chair. He picked it up, handed it to her. "I'm sorry. You were supposed to have known."

Ruby felt a sudden tension in the room. She took the newspaper from him. At first all she noticed was the headline: RAISING MORE THAN SPIRITS. Then she saw the photo. It was a blurry, grainy shot of two naked people entwined. The editors had carefully placed black privacy strips across the pertinent body parts, but there was no denying what was going on. Or who the woman was.

Ruby looked helplessly at the faces around her, then tossed the newspaper down in disgust. "There's a lesson to women everywhere in this. When your lover says, 'One little photo, honey, just for us,' you better cover yourself and run."

Elsa leaned forward. "How does it make you feel to see—"

Joe raised his hands. "We're getting off the topic here. The question is, how much of our screwups are our fault? Does a bad parent give someone a free ride to commit crime?"

Ruby sat perfectly still. There was no reason for her to speak. She knew she'd given *Uproar* what it had wanted—a reaction. By tomorrow her blank-eyed, dim-witted response to the scandal would lead every report. She should have known it would be like this—her big break. What a joke. How could she have been so naïve?

Finally she heard Joe wrapping up. The APPLAUSE sign lit up, and the audience responded immediately, clapping thunderously.

Ruby rose from her chair and moved blindly across the stage.

"Ruby?" Joe was standing beside her, his handsome face drawn into a frown. "I'm sorry about ambushing you. The story broke yesterday. It never occurred to us that you'd miss it. And since so much of your material is about your relationship with your mother . . ."

"I turned off my phone and television," she answered, then added, "I was getting ready for the show."

"You thought this was your big break. And it turned out—"

"Not to be." She cut him off. The pity in his eyes was more than she could bear. "I have to go now." Without glancing at anyone, she raced out of the studio.

IN HER apartment, Ruby closed all the blinds and turned off the lights. She slumped onto her worn sofa.

Mommy Dearest had an affair after all.

It didn't surprise her. Any woman who would leave her children to go in search of fame and fortune wouldn't think twice about having an affair. What surprised Ruby was how much it still hurt.

Her fingers shook as she reached for the phone and dialed her sister's number. Caroline answered on the second ring. "Hello?"

"Hey, sis," Ruby said, feeling a sudden tide of loneliness.

"So you finally plugged your phone in. I've been going crazy trying to reach you."

"Sorry," Ruby said softly. Her throat felt embarrassingly tight. "I saw the pictures. Did you know about the affair?"

"I suspected."

"Why didn't you ever tell me?"

"Come on, Rube. You've never mentioned her name to me all these years. You didn't want to know anything about her."

"I suppose you've already forgiven her, Caroline the Saint."

"No," Caro said softly. "I'm having a hard time with this one. Yesterday I said some really nasty things to her. I couldn't seem to help myself. I'm going to call her back when I calm down. Maybe we can finally talk about some of the stuff that matters."

"Nothing she has to say matters, Caro."

"You're wrong about that, Rube. Someday you'll see that."

Before Ruby could respond, the doorbell rang. "I gotta run, Caroline. There's someone here to see me."

She hung up, then padded across the shag carpeting and peered through the peephole. It was Val, standing beside a woman so thin she looked like a windshield wiper.

Ruby wrenched the door open. Val grinned at her. He leaned forward and kissed her cheek. "How's my newest star?"

"Up yours," she whispered. "I never saw it coming."

Val drew back, frowning. "I tried to call you."

Ruby would have said more, but the way the lady was watching them made her uncomfortable. She turned to her, noticing the woman's severe haircut and expensive black dress. "I'm Ruby Bridge," she said, extending her hand.

The woman shook it. Firm grip. Clammy skin. "Joan Pinon."

"Come on in." Ruby backed away from the door. She tried not to see the apartment through their eyes, but it was impossible—tacky furniture, dusty shag carpeting, garage-sale decor.

Val sat down on the old velour Barcalounger. Joan perched on the end of the sofa. Ruby flopped down on the sofa's other cushion.

Val leaned forward. "Joan is an editor for *Caché* magazine in New York. She's here because of your mother."

Ruby turned to Joan. "What do you want?"

"We'd like you to write an exposé on your mother." Joan smiled. "Val tells me you're a first-rate writer."

A compliment. That felt good. Ruby settled back in her seat, eyeing Joan. "You want a daughter's betrayal."

"Who betrayed whom?" Joan said. "Your mother has been telling America to honor commitments and put their children first. These photographs prove that she's a liar and a hypocrite."

"It's just an article, Ruby," Val said. "No more than fifteen thousand words. And it could make you famous."

"*Rich* and famous," Joan added.

Ruby looked at Joan. "How rich?"

"Fifty thousand dollars. I'm prepared to pay you half right now and the other half when you deliver the article."

"Fifty thousand *dollars?*" For a few measly words. And all she had to do was serve up her mother's life for public consumption. "I don't know my mother that well," Ruby said slowly, trying to think through it. "The last time I saw her was at my sister's wedding nine years ago. We didn't speak."

"We don't want cold facts. We want your opinions and thoughts on what kind of a person she is, what kind of a mother she was."

"That's easy. She'd step on your grandmother's throat to get ahead. Nothing—and no one—matters to her except herself."

"You see?" Joan said, eyes shining. "That's exactly the perspective we want. I brought the contract with me and a check for twenty-five thousand dollars." She reached into her black briefcase and pulled out a stack of papers with the check on top.

Ruby stared at all those zeros and swallowed hard. She'd never had that much money at one time.

"This is your chance, Ruby," Val said. "Think of the exposure. The networks will be fighting over you."

She felt flushed. She heard herself say, "I'm a good writer."

Joan was smiling. "We've tentatively booked you on *The Sarah Purcell Show* for a week from now to promote the article."

Ruby wanted it so much. She'd clawed through life for so long, been a nobody. She thought of all the reasons she should say no— the moral, ethical reasons—but none of them found a place to stick. Slowly she reached for the check. "Okay," she said. "I'll do it."

RUBY cranked the Volkswagen's radio to full blast. A raucous Metallica song blared through the small black speakers.

Fifty thousand dollars. She wanted so badly to share this day with someone. If only she had Max's new number—she'd call him and tell him what he'd missed out on.

She drove into Beverly Hills. Usually she didn't even drive past this area, but today she was flying high. She felt invincible.

When she saw an open spot on Rodeo Drive, she pulled over and parked. Grabbing her purse—with the deposit slip for twenty-five thousand dollars inside—she got out of the car.

She strolled around for a while, then looked into a store window and saw a sheer, beaded, silvery blue dress with a plunging V neckline and a split in the side that came up to mid-thigh. It was the most perfect dress she'd ever seen, the kind of thing she'd never imagined she could own. She pushed through the doors.

A saleswoman came over. "May I help you?"

"I saw a blue dress in the window," Ruby said.

"You have excellent taste." The woman led Ruby to a dressing room that was bigger than the average bedroom. "Would you like a glass of Champagne?"

Ruby laughed. Now, *this* was shopping. "I'd love some."

Within a minute a man in a black tuxedo was handing Ruby a sparkling glass of Champagne.

"Thanks," she said, collapsing onto the cushy seat in the dressing room. For the first time in years, she felt like somebody.

The saleslady peeked in. "Here you go. Holler if you need me."

Ruby trailed her fingers down the beaded, sheer-as-tissue fabric, then quickly undressed and slipped into the dress. Self-consciously she stepped out of the dressing room and walked over to the wall-size mirrors in the corner. Her breath caught. Even with her hair too short and her makeup too heavy, she looked beautiful. The plunging neckline accentuated her small breasts. Her waist appeared tiny, and the slit slimmed her fleshy thighs.

"Oh, my," the saleswoman said wistfully. "It's perfect."

"I'll take it," Ruby said in a thick voice.

She wrote a check—almost thirty-five hundred dollars—and hung the dress carefully in the back seat of the Volkswagen.

Then, cranking the music up again, she sped toward the freeway. She was almost home when she passed the Porsche dealer. Ruby laughed and slammed on the brakes.

NORA lay curled on the elegant sofa in her darkened living room. Hours ago she'd sent Dee home and disconnected the phone. Then she'd watched the news.

Every station had the story. They showed the lurid blacked-out photographs again and again, usually followed with sound bites of Nora expounding on the sanctity of the marriage vows. What hurt the most were the man-in-the-street interviews. Her fans had turned on her; some women even cried at the betrayal they felt.

She knew what was happening in the lobby downstairs. The press was outside, cameras at the ready. One sighting of Nora Bridge, and they would spring on her like wild dogs. Her doorman claimed that the garage was safe, but she was afraid to chance it.

She sat up, then walked to the makeshift bar in the kitchen that she kept for guests. Nora hadn't taken a drink in years. But now she needed *something* to help her out of this hole. She poured herself a tumbler full of gin. It tasted awful at first, but after a few gulps the booze slid down easily.

On her way back into the living room, she paused at the grand piano, her attention arrested by the framed photographs on the gleaming ebony surface. She almost never looked at them, not closely. It was like closing her hand around a shard of broken glass.

Still, one caught her eye. It was a picture of her and her ex-husband, Rand, and their two daughters. They'd been standing in front of the family beach house, their smiles honest and bright.

Nora finished the drink, then went back for another. By the time she finished that one, she could barely walk straight. She swayed drunkenly and plugged the phone into the wall. Bleary-eyed, she dialed her psychiatrist.

A moment later a woman answered. "Dr. Allbright's office."

"Hi, Midge. It's Nora Bridge." She hoped she wasn't slurring her words. "Is the doctor in?"

A sniff. "He's not in, Ms. Bridge. Shall I take a message?"

Ms. Bridge. Only days ago it had been Nora.

"I can put you through to his service. Or he left Dr. Hornby's number for emergencies."

"Thanks, Midge. There's no need for that." Nora hung up. Then she ripped the cord out of the wall again.

Eric. He would be on the island by now. If she hurried, maybe she could still make the last ferry.

She grabbed her car keys and staggered into her bedroom. On the bedside table she found her sleeping pills. Of course it would be bad—wrong—to take one now in her drunken state. But she wanted to. She tossed the brown plastic bottle into her purse and left the apartment, tottering toward the elevator.

Once inside, she prayed there wouldn't be a stop in the lobby. She got lucky; the elevator went all the way down to the parking garage, where it stopped with a clang and the doors opened.

She peered out; the garage was empty. She careened unsteadily toward her car, collapsing against the jet-black side of her Mercedes. It took her several tries to get the key into the lock, but she finally managed. She slid awkwardly into the soft leather seat. The engine started easily—a roar of sound in the darkness.

"Please," she whispered, "let Eric still be there."

She slammed the car into reverse and backed out of the spot. Then she headed forward and hit the gas. She didn't even glance left for traffic as she sped out onto Second Avenue.

DEAN stood on the slatted wooden dock. The seaplane taxied across the choppy blue waves and lifted skyward, its engine chattering as it banked left and headed back to Seattle.

He'd forgotten how beautiful this place was, how peaceful.

The tide was out now, and the beach smelled of sand that had baked in the hot sun, of kelp that was slowly curling into leathery strips. It was a smell that pulled him back in time. Here he and Eric had built their forts and had buried treasures made of foil-wrapped poker chips; they'd gone from rock to rock, searching for the tiny crabs that lived beneath the stones. They had been the best of friends.

Of the two of them, Eric had been the strong one, the golden boy who did everything well and fought for his heart's desires. At seven Eric had demanded to be taken to Granddad's island house on Lopez, and it was Eric who'd first convinced Mother to let them stay and go to the island school.

Dean hated what had brought him home, hated how he felt about Eric now. They'd grown so far apart. It was all Dean's fault.

It had happened on a seemingly ordinary Sunday. Dean had moved off the island by then, gone to prep school; Eric had been at Princeton. They were still brothers then, and they'd spoken on the phone every Sunday. One phone call had changed everything.

I've fallen in love, little bro. Get ready for a shock. His name is Charlie, and he's . . .

Dean had never been able to remember more than that. Somehow, in that weird, disorienting moment, he'd felt suddenly betrayed, as if the brother he'd known and loved was a stranger.

After that they had drifted apart. By the time Dean graduated from Stanford and went to work for the family business, too much time had passed. Eric had moved to Seattle and begun teaching high school English. Dean had meant to pick up the phone, but every time he reached for it, he wondered what in the world he could say.

He turned away now from the water and walked down the dock, then climbed the split-log stairs to the top of the bluff.

The Victorian house was exactly as he remembered it—salmony pink siding, steeply pitched roof, elegant white trim. The lawn was still as flat and green as a patch of Christmas felt.

As Dean headed toward the house, a glint of silver caught his eye. He turned and saw the swing set, rusted now and forgotten. The sight of it dragged out an unwelcome memory.

Ruby. She'd been right there, leaning against the slanted metal support pole, with her arms crossed.

It was the moment—the exact second—he'd realized that his best friend was a *girl* and that he loved her. He'd wanted to say the words to her, but he'd been afraid, and so he'd kissed her instead. It had been the first kiss for both of them, and to this day, when Dean kissed a woman, he longed for the smell of the sea.

He spun away from the swing set and strode purposefully toward the house. At the front door he paused, gathering courage, then knocked.

The door burst open, and Lottie was there. His old nanny flung open her pudgy arms. "Dean!"

He walked into the arms that had held him in his youth, then drew back, smiling. "It's good to see you, Lottie."

She gave him the look—one thick gray eyebrow arched upward. "I'm surprised you could still find your way here."

Though he hadn't seen her in more than a decade, she had barely aged. Her ruddy skin was still wrinkle free, and her bright green eyes were those of a woman who'd enjoyed her life. He realized suddenly how much he'd missed her. Lottie had never had any children, and Eric and Dean had become her surrogate sons. She'd raised them for the ten years they'd lived on Lopez.

"I wish I were here for an ordinary visit," Dean said.

She blinked up at him. "It seems like only yesterday I was wiping chocolate off his little-boy face. I can't believe it."

He followed her into the living room. Cream-colored sofas on carved wooden legs faced each other. A large, oval rosewood coffee table stood between them.

Dean glanced toward the stairway. "How is he?"

Lottie's green eyes filled with sadness. "Not so good, I'm sorry to say. The trip up here was hard on him."

"Did Eric call our parents, tell them about the cancer?"

"He did. They're in Greece—Athens."

"I know. Did he speak to Mother?"

Lottie glanced down at her hands. "Your mother's assistant spoke to him. It seems your mother was shopping when he called."

Dean's voice was purposely soft. He was afraid that if he raised it, he'd be yelling. "And has she returned his call?"

"No."

Dean released his breath in a tired sigh.

"Go on up." Lottie smiled gently. "He's a bit the worse for wear, but he's still our boy."

Dean nodded stiffly, resettled the garment bag over his shoulder, and headed upstairs. He passed his old bedroom and came to Eric's door. He paused, then walked into his brother's room. The first thing he noticed was the hospital bed—big, metal-railed, and tilted up like a lounging chair. Lottie had positioned it to look out the window.

Eric was asleep. Dean seemed to see everything at once—the way Eric's black hair had thinned to show patches of skin, the yellowed pallor of his sunken cheeks, the smudged black circles beneath his eyes. Only the palest shadow of his brother lay here.

Dean grabbed the bedrail for support; the metal rattled beneath his grasp. Eric's eyes slowly opened.

And there he was—the boy Dean had known and loved. "Eric," he said, wishing his voice weren't so thick.

Eric looked up at Dean, his rheumy eyes filled with a terrible, harrowing honesty. "I didn't think you'd come."

"Of course I came. You should have told me . . . before."

"Like when I told you I was gay? Believe me, I learned a long time ago that my family didn't handle bad news well."

Dean fought to hold back tears and then gave up. They were the

kind of tears that hurt deep in your heart. He felt a stinging sense
of shame that he'd been a bad person, that he'd hurt his brother
deeply and known it and never bothered to make it right.

Eric smiled weakly. "You're here now. That's enough."

Dean wanted to smooth the thin strands of hair from Eric's damp
forehead, but his hands were trembling, and he drew back. He
would give anything to erase the past, to be able to go back to that
Sunday afternoon, listen to that same confession of love from his
brother, and simply be happy. But how did you do that? How did
two people move backward through time?

"Just talk to me," Eric said sleepily, smiling again. "Just talk, little brother. Like we used to."

Chapter Three

𝒯HE phone rang in the middle of the night. Ruby groaned and
glanced bleary-eyed at the bedside clock: one fifteen. It had to be
one of those idiot reporters. She reached across the bed, yanked the
phone off the hook, and brought it to her ear. "Bite me."

"I gave that up in kindergarten."

Ruby laughed sleepily. "Caro? Oh, sorry. I thought you were one
of those bottom-feeders from the *Tattler*." Through the phone lines
Ruby could hear a baby crying—a high-pitched wailing only dogs
should be able to hear. "Does the baby always wail like that?"

"Mom's been in a car accident."

Ruby gasped. "What happened?"

"I don't know. All I know is that she's at Bayview. Apparently
she'd been drinking."

"She never drinks. I mean, she never used to. How bad is it?"

"I don't know. I'm going to go to the hospital first thing in the
morning. But I don't want to do this alone. Will you come?"

"I don't know, Car—"

"She could be dying," Caroline said sharply.

Ruby sighed heavily. "Okay. I'll be there by noon." She hung up.

She had been angry at her mother forever. She couldn't really remember *not* hating her. But now . . . an accident. Horrible images slammed through her mind: paralysis, brain damage, death.

Ruby closed her eyes. It took her a moment to realize she was praying. "Take care of her," she whispered. "Please?"

WHEN Nora woke up the next morning, she had a moment of pure, heart-pumping fear. She was in a strange bed. Then she remembered she'd been in a car accident. She recalled the ambulance ride, the flashing red lights, and the doctors. The orthopedist who'd spoken to her just before and after the X rays: *a severe break above the ankle, another small fracture below the knee, a sprained wrist.*

Now her leg was in a cast. The flesh itched, and her bone ached. She sighed, feeling sorry for herself and deeply ashamed. Drinking and driving. As if the *Tattler*'s photographs weren't enough to ruin her career, she'd added a crime to the list.

There was a knock at the door, short and sharp, and then Caroline swept into the room. Her back was ramrod straight. She wore a pair of camel-colored pants and a matching sweater set. Her silvery blond hair was cut in a perfect bob. "Hello, Mother."

"Hi, honey. It's nice of you to come." Nora recognized instantly how distant she sounded, and it shamed her.

Caroline glanced at Nora. She looked vulnerable suddenly.

Nora couldn't stand the awkward silence that fell between them. She said the first thing that popped into her mind. "The doctors say I'll need to be in a wheelchair for a few days, just until my wrist gets strong enough to make crutches possible."

"Who is going to take care of you?"

"I guess I'll hire someone. The big question is, where will I go? I can't go back to my condo. The press has it staked out."

Caroline took a step toward the bed. "You could use the summerhouse. Jere and I never find time to make it up there, and Ruby won't step foot on the island. The house is just sitting there."

The house on Summer Island. A stone's throw from Eric. It would be perfect. "You'd do that for me?" Nora asked.

Caroline gave her a look of infinite sadness. "I wish you knew me."

Nora had said the wrong thing again. "I'm sorry."

"God, I've heard that from you so often. Quit saying you're sorry and start acting like it." Caroline reached into her purse and fished out a set of keys. Pulling a single key from the ring, she set it down on the bedside table, then stepped back, putting distance between them. "I have to go now."

Nora nodded stiffly. "Of course. Thanks for coming." She wanted to reach out for Caroline, hold her daughter's hand and never let go.

"Good-bye, Mom." And she was gone.

RUBY stepped out of the main terminal at SeaTac International Airport. Rain thumped on the skybridge and studded the street. The early morning air smelled of evergreen trees and fertile black earth. Like a dash of spice in a complex recipe, there was the barest tang of the sea, a scent only a local would recognize.

Ruby hailed a cab and climbed in, tossing her carry-on bag beside her. "Bayview," she said, thumping back into the seat.

When they arrived, she handed the driver the fare and tip. Then she grabbed her bag and headed toward the hospital's double glass doors, where a few people stood milling about.

Ruby was almost in their midst when she realized they were reporters. They turned to her, yelling and elbowing for position.

"Was your mother drunk at the time of—"

"What did you think of the photographs—"

Ruby heard every shutter click, every picture frame advance. She pushed through the crowd, holding her head up, looking straight ahead. Their questions followed her as she strode through the pneumatic doors. They whooshed shut behind her.

Inside, the lobby was quiet. The air smelled of disinfectant.

"Ruby!" Caroline rushed forward. Her hug almost knocked Ruby off her feet. As she held her sister, Ruby could feel the tremble in Caroline's body. At last they drew back.

"So how is Nora?" Ruby asked.

Caroline gave her a sharp look. "She still hates it when we call her that."

"Really? I'd forgotten."

"I'll bet you did. Anyway, her leg is broken, her wrist sprained. She'll be in a wheelchair for a few days. That makes it pretty tough to do the ordinary bits and pieces of life. She'll need help."

"I pity the poor nurse who takes *that* job."

"Would *you* want to be cared for by a stranger?"

It took Ruby a minute to get her sister's drift. When she did, she burst out laughing. "You're delusional."

"Ruby," Caroline said, "a stranger could sell her out to the tabloids. She needs someone she can trust."

"She can't trust me."

Caroline looked disgusted. "You're going to be thirty in a few years. Mom's fifty. When are you going to get to know her?"

"Who says I'm *ever* going to?"

Caro moved closer. "Tell me you didn't think about it last night."

Ruby couldn't swallow. "About what?"

"Losing her."

The words hit dangerously near their mark. There was no doubt in Ruby's mind what she should do—go out those front doors and fly home. But it wasn't quite so easy this time, especially with the *Caché* article out there to write. A little time with Nora Bridge would certainly make the piece better. A lot better.

Ruby took a deep breath. "One week," she said evenly. "I'll stay with her for one week."

Caroline pulled Ruby into a fierce hug. "I knew you'd do the right thing. Go tell her. She's in 612 west. I'll wait for you here."

"Coward." Ruby flashed her a nervous smile, then headed for her mother's room.

The door was ajar, and Ruby stepped inside.

Nora was asleep. Ruby stared down at her and felt an unexpected tug of longing. She had to remind herself that this lovely red-haired woman who looked like Susan Sarandon wasn't really her mother.

Ruby's mother—the woman who'd played Scrabble and made chocolate chip pancakes every Sunday morning—had died eleven years ago. This was the woman who'd killed her.

Nora opened her eyes, gasped, and scooted up to a sit. "You came," she said softly, a note of wonder in her voice.

"How are you?" Ruby felt off-balance.

"I'm fine." Nora smiled, but it was an odd, uncertain smile.

"So I guess you've lost your good-driver discount."

"That's my Ruby—quick with a joke."

"I wouldn't say *your* Ruby."

"I'm sure you wouldn't." Nora exhaled softly. "I see you still think you know everything and you still don't take any prisoners."

"I don't know everything," Ruby said evenly. "I don't think I ever knew my mother."

Nora laughed—a tired sound. "That makes two of us."

Already Ruby knew she couldn't spend a week with this woman and feel nothing. The anger was so sharp, it overwhelmed her. But she had no choice. "I thought I'd stay with you, help you get settled."

Nora's surprise was almost comical. "Why?"

Ruby shrugged. "You could have died. Maybe I thought of what it would be like to lose you. Or maybe this is your darkest hour, the loss of everything you left your family for, and I don't want to miss a minute of your misery. Or maybe I got a contract to write a magazine article about you, and I need to get the inside scoop. Or maybe I—"

"I get it. You obviously have nothing better to do."

"How do you do it—slam me in the middle of a thank-you?"

"Let's not start, okay?" Nora's fingers slid close to touch Ruby. She looked up. "You know I'm going to the summerhouse, right?"

Ruby couldn't have heard correctly. *"What?"*

"Reporters are camped outside my condo. I can't face them." Nora's gaze lowered. "Your sister offered me use of the summerhouse. If you want to change your mind, I'll understand."

It had seemed doable a few moments ago—go to this woman's glass-walled high-rise that success had purchased, make a few meals, look through a few old photo albums, ask a few questions.

But at the summerhouse—it was where so many of the memories were buried, both good and bad.

Fifty thousand dollars. That's what she had to think about. "I guess it doesn't matter where we are."

"You mean it?" There was a disturbing wistfulness in her mother's voice. "You'll need to rent me a wheelchair, and I'll need a few things from my apartment."

"I can do that."

"I'll talk to my doctor and get checked out of here. We'll have to leave quietly, through the back way maybe."

"I'll rent a car and pick you up in—what? Three hours."

"Okay. My purse is in the closet. Use the platinum Visa for anything you need. And Ruby, get a nice car, okay?"

Ruby tried to smile. This was going to be bad. Her mother was already making demands—and judgments. "Only the best for you, Nora." She went to the closet, saw the expensive black handbag, and grabbed it. Without a backward glance she headed out.

Her mother's voice stopped her. "Ruby? Thank you."

Ruby shut the door behind her.

RUBY walked into her mother's penthouse condominium and closed the door behind her. She dropped her jacket onto the gleaming marble floor, then turned the corner and literally had to catch her breath. It was the most incredible room she'd ever seen.

A wall of floor-to-ceiling windows wrapped around the whole living room, showcasing a panoramic view of Elliott Bay. Brocade-covered furniture sat in a cluster around a beautiful gold-and-glass coffee table. In one corner stood an ebony Steinway, its lacquered top cluttered with framed photographs.

A dimly lit hallway led to the master bedroom. Here the windows were dressed in steel-gray silk curtains that matched the woven cashmere bedspread. There were two huge walk-in closets. Ruby opened the first one. There were two rows of clothes—designer silks, cashmeres, expensive woolens—organized by color. The thought *This is what she left us for* winged through Ruby's mind.

She backed out, closing the closet door. At the rosewood gilt-trimmed bombé chest she opened the top drawer. Little piles of perfectly folded lingerie lay there. She picked out a few pieces, then gathered up some shorts and cap-sleeved tops from the second drawer. She moved to the other closet.

The clothes here looked as if they belonged to another woman—worn gray sweatpants; baggy, stained sweatshirts; old jeans; a few brightly colored sundresses.

As she reached for a sundress, Ruby saw that the hem was caught on the upraised flap of a cardboard box. On the side of the box, written in red ink, was the word Ruby. Her heart skipped a beat. She fell to her knees, dragging the box toward her. Her fingers were trembling as she opened it.

Inside, there were dozens of wrapped packages, some in the reds and greens of Christmas, some in bright silvery paper with balloons and candles. Birthdays and Christmases.

She counted the packages: twenty-one—two each year for the eleven Nora had been gone from them, less the black cashmere sweater that Caroline had sneaked past Ruby's guard. These were the gifts that Nora had bought every year and sent to Ruby, the same ones Ruby had ruthlessly returned unopened.

"Oh, man." She let out her breath in a sigh and reached for a small box wrapped in birthday paper. Carefully she peeled the paper away and lifted the lid. Inside, on a bed of opalescent tissue, lay a silver charm. It was a birthday cake, complete with candles. Inscribed on the back was "Happy 21st. Love, Mom."

The silver charm blurred.

Ruby could imagine her mother, dressed perfectly, going from store to store for the ideal gift, saying to the salespeople, *My daughter is twenty-one today. I need something extra special.* Pretending that everything was normal, that she hadn't abandoned her children when they needed her most.

At that, Ruby felt a rush of cold anger. What mattered was not what Nora had tried to give Ruby, but rather what she'd taken away. A few nicely wrapped gifts couldn't change that.

RUBY SHOULD HAVE RENTED a Winnebago. This minivan was too small for her and Nora. With the windows rolled up, there seemed to be no air left to breathe and nothing to do but talk. Ruby cranked up the radio. Celine Dion's voice filled the car.

"Could you turn it down?" Nora said. "I'm getting a headache."

Ruby's gaze flicked sideways. Nora looked tired. Her skin, normally pale, now appeared to have the translucence of bone china. Tiny blue veins webbed the sunken flesh at her temples. She turned to Ruby and attempted a smile, but in truth, her mouth barely trembled before she closed her eyes. She looked fragile. Ruby couldn't wrap her arms around that thought. Her mother had always been made of steel.

"Ruby? The music?"

Ruby snapped the radio off. The metronomic whoosh-thump, whoosh-thump of the windshield wipers filled the sudden silence.

A few miles from downtown Seattle, the city gave way to a sprawling collection of strip malls. A few miles more, and they were in farming land. Rolling tree-shrouded hills and green pastures fanned out on either side of the freeway.

At Anacortes, the tiny seaside town perched at the water's edge, Ruby bought a one-way ferry ticket and pulled into line. An orange-vested attendant directed her car to the bow of the ferry, where she parked and set the emergency brake.

The Sound was rainy-day flat. Watery gray skies melted into the sea. Puppy-faced seals crawled over one another to find a comfortable perch on the swaying red harbor buoy.

Ruby glanced sideways and saw that Nora was asleep. She got out of the car and went upstairs onto the deck. The rain had diminished to little more than a heavy mist. Lush green islands dotted the tinfoil sea, their carved granite coastlines a stark contrast to the flat silver water. Houses were scattered here and there, but for the most part the islands looked empty.

Ruby closed her eyes, breathing in the salty, familiar sea air. In eighth grade she had started taking the ferry to school at Friday Harbor on San Juan Island. She and Dean had always stood together at just this spot, right at the bow, even when it was raining.

Dean. It had been more than a decade since she'd seen him, and still it hurt to remember him. Sometimes when she woke in the middle of a hot, lonely night and found that her cheeks were slicked and wet, she knew she'd been dreaming of him. She knew from Caroline (who knew from Nora) that he'd followed in his mother's footsteps, that he was running the empire now. Ruby had always known that he would.

At last the ferry turned toward Summer Island. The captain came on the loudspeaker, urging passengers to return to their vehicles.

Ruby raced downstairs and jumped into the minivan. The captain cut the engine, and after the boat docked, Ruby drove off the ferry, past the post office and general store. What struck her first was the total lack of meaningful change. Here, on Summer Island, with only one hundred year-round residents, it was still 1985.

To her left the land was a Monet painting, all golden grass and green trees and washed-out silvery skies. To her right lay Bottleneck Bay, and beyond that was the forested green hump of Shaw Island. Weathered gray fishing boats sat keeled on the pebbly beach.

As Nora blinked awake, Ruby approached the beach road and turned. The narrow one-lane road wound snakelike through the towering trees. At last they came to the driveway. The knee-high grass that grew in a wild strip down the center of the road thumped and scraped the undercarriage. At the end of the treelined road Ruby hit the brakes.

And stared through the windshield at her childhood.

The farmhouse was layered in thick white clapboards, with red trim around the casement windows. A porch wrapped around three sides of the house. It sat in the midst of a pie-shaped clearing that jutted toward the sea. A white picket fence created a nicely squared yard. Inside it, the garden was in full bloom.

With a tired sigh Ruby got out of the car.

The tide made a low, snoring sound. Birds chattered overhead.

Ruby went around to the back of the van and pulled out the wheelchair, then helped Nora into the seat. Ruby pushed her mother down the path. At the gate she stopped and unlatched it.

Ruby cautiously guided the wheelchair in front of her. They had just reached the edge of the porch when her mother suddenly said, "Let me sit here for a minute, will you? Go on in." Nora handed the key to Ruby. "You can come back and tell me how it looks."

"You'd rather sit in the rain than go into the house?"

"That pretty much sums up my feelings right now."

Ruby walked onto the porch. The wide-planked floor wobbled beneath her feet like piano keys, releasing a melody of creaks and groans. At the front door she slipped the key into the lock.

"Wait!" her mother cried out.

Ruby turned. Nora was smiling, but it was grim, that smile. "I . . . think we should go in together."

"Let's not make an opera out of it. We're going into an old house. That's all." Ruby shoved the door open, then went back for Nora. She maneuvered the wheelchair up onto the porch, bumped it over the threshold, and wheeled her mother inside.

The furniture, draped in old sheets, huddled ghostlike in the middle of the room. Ruby could remember spreading those sheets every autumn, snapping them in the air above the furniture.

"Caroline took good care of the place. I'm surprised she left everything exactly as it was." There was wonder in Nora's voice.

"You know Caro," Ruby said. "She likes to keep everything pretty on the surface."

"That's not fair. Caro—"

Ruby spun around. "*Tell* me you aren't going to explain my sister to me."

Nora's mouth snapped shut. Then she sneezed. And again. Her eyes were watering as she said, "I'm allergic to dust. I know there's not much, but I'm really sensitive. You'll need to dust right away."

Ruby looked at her. "Your leg's broken, not your hand."

"I can't handle it. Allergies."

"Fine. I'll dust," Ruby said.

"I guess I'll have to sleep in your old room. There's no way we can get me upstairs."

Ruby dutifully wheeled Nora into the downstairs bedroom, where two twin beds lay beneath a layer of sheeting. Between them was a gingham-curtained window.

"I think I'll lie down," Nora said. "I'm still fighting a headache."

Ruby nodded. "Can you get out of the chair by yourself?"

"I guess I'd better learn."

"I guess so." Ruby turned for the door.

She was almost there when her mother's voice hooked her back. "Thanks. I really appreciate this."

Ruby knew she should say something nice, but she couldn't think of anything. The memories in this room were like gnats, buzzing around her head. She slammed the door shut behind her.

Chapter Four

DEAN tossed his garment bag on the floor of his old bedroom and sat down on the end of the bed. Everything was exactly as he'd left it. Dusty baseball and soccer trophies cluttered the bureau's top. Posters covered the cream-colored walls, their edges yellow and curled. An autographed GO SEAHAWKS pennant hung above the desk.

Dean hadn't taken anything with him when he left here, not even a photograph of Ruby. *Especially* not a picture of her. He got to his feet and crossed the room. At the bureau he bent down and pulled at the bottom drawer; it screeched and slid open.

And there they were, reminders of Ruby. There were pictures, shells they'd collected together on the beach, and a couple of dried boutonnieres. He reached randomly inside, drawing out a small strip of black-and-white pictures—a series that had been taken in one of those booths at the Island County Fair. In them she was sitting on Dean's lap, smiling, then frowning, then sticking her tongue out at the unseen camera. In the last frame they were kissing.

Someone knocked at the door, and Dean opened it.

Lottie stood clutching a purse. "I'm off to the store." She thrust a champagne glass at him. Inside was a thick pink liquid. "This is your brother's medicine. He needs it now. Bye."

Dean walked slowly to Eric's bedroom and went in. The room felt stuffy, and the curtains were drawn. Eric was asleep. Dean moved quietly toward the bedside table and set down the glass.

"I *hope* that's my Viagra," Eric said sleepily.

"Actually, it's a double shot of Cuervo Gold. I added the Pepto-Bismol to save you time."

Eric laughed, and Dean opened the windows and flung back the curtains. The windows boxed a gray and rainy day and let a little watery light into the room.

"Thanks. Bless Lottie, but she thinks I need peace and quiet. I haven't the nerve to tell her I'm getting a little scared of the dark. Too coffinlike for me." He grinned. "I'll be there soon enough."

Dean turned to him. "Don't talk about that."

Eric gave Dean a gentle look. "What am I supposed to talk about? The Mariners' next season? The long-term effects of global warming?" He sighed. "We used to be so close," he said quietly.

"I know." Dean saw Eric move, the sudden pain sucking the color from his cheeks. "Here," Dean said quickly.

Eric's hands were shaking as he brought the glass to his colorless lips. Wincing, he swallowed the whole amount.

"Will that medication help?" Dean asked.

"Sure. In ten minutes I'll be able to leap tall buildings in a single bound." Eric laughed.

Dean relaxed a little. "It's good to hear you laugh. It's been a long time." He moved idly to a chest of drawers where a collection of pictures sat clustered together. Most of them were photographs of Dean and Eric as boys. There was one shot of the brothers and another boy standing with their arms around each other, grinning. It looked ordinary enough, but when Dean turned back to Eric, he couldn't help wondering, Had it been there all along, the difference between them? Had Dean simply missed the obvious?

"I wish I'd never told you I was gay," Eric said. It was as if he had read Dean's mind. "I knew our folks wouldn't accept it. But you . . . You I didn't expect. You broke my heart."

"I never meant to."

"You stopped calling me."

Dean sighed. "You were away at college, so you didn't know what it was like back here. The technicolor meltdown of the Bridge family. And then Ruby and I broke up."

"I always wondered what happened between you two. I—"

"It was awful," Dean said quickly, unwilling to delve into that heartache. "I called Mother and demanded to be transferred to Choate. I hated it there. I couldn't seem to make friends. But every Sunday night my brother called, and that one hour made the rest of the week bearable. Then one Sunday you forgot to call. When you finally did, you told me about Charlie. I was seventeen and nursing a broken heart. I didn't want to hear about your love life. And yeah, the fact that it was with another man was hard for me to handle."

Eric leaned deeper into the pillows. "When you stopped returning my calls, I assumed it was because you hated me. I never thought about what it was like for you. I'm sorry."

"Yeah. I'm sorry, too."

"Where do these apologies take us?"

"Who the hell knows? I'm here. Isn't that enough?"

"No."

Suddenly Dean understood what Eric wanted. "You want me to remember who we used to be, to remember you, and then . . . watch you die."

"I want *someone* in my family to love me while I'm alive." Eric closed his eyes, as if the conversation had exhausted him. "Just stay here until I fall asleep. Can you do that for me?"

Dean's throat felt tight. "Sure."

He stayed at his brother's bedside until long after Eric's breathing had become regular and his mouth had slipped open.

He would have given his fortune—hell, he'd have given everything he had or owned or could borrow—in exchange for the one thing he'd always taken for granted, the one thing Eric needed: Time.

NORA SHIFTED AGAINST THE bed and leaned back against the wobbly wooden headboard. She knew she needed to handle Ruby with kid gloves, to let her make all the first moves toward a reconciliation. No matter how much it hurt, how deeply the ache went, Nora didn't want to bulldoze the situation.

If they'd gone somewhere else, maybe this would have been easier, but nothing new could grow here, not in this soil contaminated by the past. It was in this house that Nora had made her biggest mistake. This was where she'd come when she had left Rand. She had meant for it to be temporary. At the time she'd simply thought, If I don't get some space, I'll start screaming and never stop. She remembered that summer and the bad years that had preceded it, how it had felt—that slowly descending depression, like a thick glass jar that closed around you, sucking away the air you needed to breathe.

She picked up the bedside phone and dialed her psychiatrist's number. Dr. Allbright answered on the second ring. "Hello?"

"Hi, Leo. It's me—Nora."

"How are you?"

"I'm fine," she said.

"You don't sound fine."

"Well, Ruby and I are crowded in with a lot of old ghosts."

"I don't think you should be there. With all that's happening, you should be in the city."

"And let the vultures pick at me?" She smiled ruefully. "It appears to be open season on Nora Bridge wherever I go."

"If Ruby hates you, it's because she doesn't understand."

"I don't understand it all either."

"You owe it to yourself and to Ruby to tell her the truth."

She sighed wearily. "You ask too much of me, Leo."

"And you ask too little, Nora. You're so afraid of your past. Talk to her. Try this: Tell her one personal thing about you every day, and try to find out one thing about her. That would be a start."

Nora considered it. Yes, she could do that. It wasn't much, and it wouldn't change everything, but it felt possible.

RUBY STRODE THROUGH THE house, yanking the gingham cotton curtains open, letting what little light was possible into every room. By now it was nearly three o'clock; soon there would be no daylight through the clouds at all. She wanted to catch what she could. At last she found herself in the kitchen/dining room.

A round maple table sat beneath the window, its four ladder-back chairs pulled in close. A centerpiece of dirty pink plastic dahlias was flanked by a set of porcelain salt and pepper shakers shaped like tiny lighthouses. A cookbook was in its rack on the kitchen counter.

Ruby passed into the living room, where an overstuffed sofa and two leather chairs faced a rock fireplace. On the back wall were bookcases. There was an RCA stereo, and a red plastic milk box held all of the family's favorite albums. The photos on the mantel caught her eye. They were in different frames from the ones she remembered. Frowning, she walked toward the fireplace.

All the pictures were of Caroline's children. There was not a single shot of Ruby. Not even one of Ruby and Caroline.

"Nice, Caro," she said, turning away and heading up the creaking narrow steps to the second floor. She felt forgotten.

She pushed the door open to her parents' old bedroom. A big brass bed filled the room, flanked by two French provincial end tables. The bedside lamps were yellow.

Ruby remembered her grandmother, sitting in that corner rocker, her veiny hands making knitting needles work like pistons. *You can never have too many afghans,* she'd said every time she started a new one. It had been a long time since Ruby had had so clear a memory of her nana. Maybe all she'd needed to remember the good times was to see this place again. It was exactly as Nana had made it. Nora had never bothered to redecorate. When Nana and Pop had died, they had willed the house to Ruby and Caroline. Dad had then moved their family into the bigger house on Lopez Island, and left this house for summer use.

Ruby crossed the room and went to the French doors, opening them wide. Sweet, rain-scented air made the lacy curtains tremble and dance. She stepped out onto the tiny second-floor balcony. A pair of white deck chairs sat on either side of her, their slatted backs beaded with rain. For a split second she couldn't imagine that she'd ever lived in a valley so hot and airless that boiling water sometimes squirted out of ordinary green garden hoses.

Ruby backed off the balcony and turned into the room. Out of the corner of her eye she noticed the new photographs on the bedside table. They were all pictures of Caroline's new life.

Frowning, Ruby marched back downstairs and went outside. She grabbed the suitcases from the car and carried them inside, dropping her mother's in front of the closed bedroom door.

Upstairs, she opened the closet's louvered doors, then yanked down on the light chain. A lightbulb came on in the empty closet and shone on a cardboard box with "Before" written across the top in black marker pen. Inside the box Ruby found the photographs that used to sit on every flat surface in this house—pictures of two little girls in matching pink dresses, of Dean and Eric in Little League uniforms, of Dad waving from the *Captain Hook.* And one of Nora.

Now Ruby understood what Caroline had done. Caro, who couldn't stand conflict, who just wanted everything to be *normal.* It had hurt her sister to look back on these years. Better to start over, pretend there had never been happy summers spent in these rooms.

Ruby released her breath in a heavy sigh and boxed the photographs up. She'd already lost her equilibrium in this house, and it had only been a day. She had to get back on track.

The magazine article—*that* would keep her focused.

She unzipped her suitcase and withdrew a yellow legal pad and a blue pen. Then she crawled up onto the bed, drew her knees in, and wrote the first thing that came to mind.

In the interest of full disclosure I must tell you that I was paid to write this article. Paid handsomely, as they say in the kind of restaurants where a person like me can't afford to order a dinner salad. Enough so that I could trade in my beat-up Volkswagen Bug for a slightly less beat-up Porsche.

I should also tell you that I dislike my mother. No, that's not true. I dislike the snotty salesclerk who works the night shift at my local video store. I hate my mother.

The story of us starts eleven years ago in the San Juan Islands up in Washington State. My dad was—is—a commercial fisherman who repairs boat engines in the winter months to make ends meet. He was born and raised on Lopez Island. Although my mother was born off-island, she was a local by the time I came along. She volunteered for every town charity event and was a fixture around school. In other words, we were a perfect family in a quiet little town where nothing ever happened. In all my growing-up years I never heard my parents argue.

Then, in the summer before my seventeenth birthday, everything changed. My mother left us. Walked out the door, got into her car, and drove away.

I can't remember now how long I waited for her to return, but I know that somewhere along the way she became my mother and then, finally, Nora. My mom was gone. I accepted the fact that whatever she wanted out of life, it wasn't me.

The worst of it was my father. For my last two years of high school I watched him disintegrate. He drank; he sat in his darkened bedroom; he wept.

And so when *Caché* came to me, asking for my story, I said yes. I figured it was time that America knew who they were listening to, who was giving them moral advice—a woman who walked out on her marriage and abandoned her children and—

"Ruby! Can you breathe okay with all this dust?"

Ruby rolled her eyes. As always, her mother was as subtle as an exclamation mark. "I see you found enough air in your lungs to scream at me," she muttered, hurrying downstairs.

In the kitchen, she knelt in front of the cabinet beneath the sink and opened the doors. Everything she needed stood in four straight rows. When she realized that the supplies were organized in alphabetical order, she burst out laughing. "Poor Caro," she whispered. "You were *definitely* born into the wrong family."

NORA TRIED NOT TO WATCH her daughter clean the house. It was simply too irritating. Ruby dusted without moving anything, and she clearly thought a dry rag would do the job. When she started mopping the floor with soapless water, Nora couldn't help herself. "Aren't you going to sweep first?" she asked from her wheelchair.

Ruby slowly turned around. "Excuse me?"

Nora wished she'd kept silent, but now there was nowhere to go except forward. "You need to sweep the floor before you mop, and soap in the water is a big help."

Ruby let go of the mop. The wooden handle clattered to the floor. "You're criticizing my cleaning technique?"

"I wouldn't call it a technique. It's just common sense to—"

"So I have no common sense either." Ruby stomped into the kitchen, grabbed some liquid soap, and squirted a stream into the bucket. Then she began mopping again; her strokes were vicious.

Nora tried a different approach. "Maybe I could help?"

Ruby didn't look at her. "I stripped the bed upstairs. You could take care of your bed and start a load of laundry."

Nora nodded. It took her almost an hour to strip the sheets off her bed, maneuver her wheelchair into the cubicle-size laundry room, and start the first load. By the time she rolled back into the kitchen, she found the room sparkling clean. Ruby had even replaced the horrid plastic flowers on the table with a fragrant bouquet of roses.

"Oh," Nora said, taking her first decent breath since coming into the house. "It looks beautiful." She looked at her daughter. "I thought I'd help you make dinner."

Ruby turned to her. "I don't know how to cook."

"I could teach you." Nora scavenged through the cupboards, finding several cans of tomatoes, a bag of angel-hair pasta, a bottle of olive oil, jars of marinated artichoke hearts and capers, and a container of dried Parmesan cheese. She said, "See that big frying pan hanging on the rack? Put it on the front burner. Put about a tablespoon of olive oil in it, and turn on the gas."

The pan hit with a clang. Ruby then opened the oil and poured in at least a half cup.

Nora bit back a comment as she opened the canned tomatoes. "Here, add these and turn the flame to low."

When Ruby had done that, Nora went on. "Cut up the artichoke hearts and add them."

Ruby went to the counter and began chopping. "Ow!"

Nora spun toward her daughter. "Are you okay?"

Blood was dripping in a steady stream from Ruby's index finger. Nora yanked a clean towel off the oven door. "Come here, honey." She gently took hold of her daughter's hand. Seeing that blood—her child's—made Nora's own hand throb. She coiled the towel around the wound and, without thinking, wrapped her own hands around Ruby's. When she looked up, Nora saw the emotion in Ruby's eyes and knew that her daughter remembered this simple routine. The only thing missing was a kiss to make it all better.

Ruby yanked her hand back. "It's just a cut, for God's sake."

That gap yawned between them again, and Nora wondered if she'd imagined the longing in her daughter's eyes. Her voice was shaking when she said, "Put a big pot of water on to boil, won't you?"

For the next thirty minutes Ruby did as she was told. Finally the meal was ready, and they were seated across from each other at the round wooden kitchen table. Ruby picked up her fork and rammed it into the pasta, twirling it. Nora tried to eat, but the silence tore at her nerves. Leo's advice came back to her: *one personal thing.*

She was still trolling for an icebreaker when Ruby got up from the table and started filling the sink with water.

Nora hadn't realized that eating was a timed event. She cleared the table, stacked the dishes on the counter at Ruby's elbow. In an unnerving silence Ruby washed and Nora dried. When they were finished, Nora wheeled herself into the living room. Ruby swept past her, practically running, and headed for the stairs.

Nora had to think fast. "Why don't you make us a fire? June nights are always chilly."

Without answering, Ruby went to the hearth, knelt down, and built a fire exactly as she'd been taught by Grandpa Bridge.

"I guess some things you never forget," Nora said.

Ruby sat back on her heels and held her hands out toward the fire. "Except how it feels to have a mother."

"That's not fair. You and Caroline were my whole world."

Ruby laughed dryly. "We weren't your whole world the summer I was sixteen. That was the year you walked into the living room, dropped your suitcase on the floor, and announced that you were leaving, wasn't it? And what was it you said to us? 'Who wants to come with me?' As if Caroline and I would move away from our dad just because you decided you didn't want to be here."

"I didn't decide. I left because—"

"I don't care *why* you left. That's what you care about."

Nora longed to make Ruby understand. "You don't know everything about me." She thought she saw a war going on inside her daughter, as if Ruby wanted both to keep fighting and to stop.

"Tell me something about you, then," Ruby said at last.

This was Nora's chance. "Okay. Let's go sit on the porch, like we used to. We'll each share one piece of information about ourselves."

Ruby laughed. "I asked you to tell me about *you*. I didn't offer to reciprocate."

Nora stood her ground. "I need to know about you, too."

Ruby studied her. "This should be interesting. I'm twenty-seven. You were fifty . . . When? The day before yesterday? I guess it's time we talked. Come on."

Nora finally allowed herself to smile—Ruby had remembered her birthday. She followed Ruby onto the porch, thankful to see that the rain had finally stopped. The cool night air breezed across her cheeks. Sunset tinted the sky purple and pink.

Ruby looked young and vulnerable, with her black hair so poorly cut and her clothes all tattered and torn. The urge to reach out, to brush the hair off Ruby's face and say softly—

"Don't say it, Nora."

Nora frowned. "Say what?"

" 'Ah, Ruby, you could be so beautiful if you'd just try a little.' "

It startled Nora—that bit of mind reading. Sure, she'd said that often to Ruby, had thought in fact to say it a second ago, but it meant nothing. To Nora the comment had simply been grains of sand in the desert of a mother's advice. Obviously, Ruby had felt otherwise, and she'd carried the words into womanhood with her.

Nora was ashamed. "I'm sorry, Ruby. What I should have said is, 'You're beautiful just the way you are.'"

Silence settled between them, broken only by the sounds of the sea and the occasional caw of a lone crow hidden in the trees.

"Okay, Nora," Ruby said, leaning with feigned nonchalance against the porch rail. "Tell me something I don't know."

"You think I don't understand you," Nora began softly, "but I know how it feels to turn your back on a parent. On the day I graduated from high school, I left home and never went back again."

"Did you run away?"

"From my father, yes. I loved my mother."

"And you never saw him again?"

"Never again." Nora wished those two words didn't hurt so much. "I didn't even attend his funeral, and all my life I've had to live with that decision. It's not regret I feel so much, but I wish he had been a different man. Most of all, I wish I could have loved him."

"Did you ever try to forgive him?"

Nora wanted to lie. It was easy to see that Ruby was asking as much about *their* relationship as she was about Nora and her father's. But there was little enough chance for Nora and Ruby; with deception there would be none at all. "After I'd had my own children—and lost their love—I regretted how I'd treated him. As a young woman, I didn't understand how hard life can be. Of course, that understanding came too late. He was already gone."

"So I should forgive you now, while I still have the time?"

Nora looked at Ruby sharply. "Not everything is about you. I told you something painful about me tonight. I expect you to handle my life with respect if you can't manage care."

Ruby looked abashed. "I'm sorry."

"Apology accepted. Now tell me something about you."

Ruby stared at Nora. "One night, the summer after you left, I just . . . snapped. I drove to Seattle and went to a dance club. I picked up some kid. I went back to his apartment and let him have sex with me." She paused for effect. "It was my first time. I did it to hurt you. I thought you'd come home eventually, and then I'd tell you. I used to imagine the look on your face when I described it."

"You wanted to see me cry."

"At the very least."

"I would have, if that makes you feel better."

"It's too late for any of us to be feeling better." Ruby sighed. "Dean didn't take it very well either."

That was all it took—the simple mentioning of Dean's name— and Nora was lost. That's how the grief hit her lately. Sometimes she went whole hours without thinking about Eric, and then she would suddenly be reminded. She knew she should say something—the pain in Ruby's eyes when she said Dean's name was unmistakable— but Nora's throat was blocked too tightly to speak.

"That's enough quid pro quo for one night," Ruby said sharply. "I'm going to go upstairs and take a bath."

Nora watched her daughter leave. Then quietly she said, "Good night, Ruby."

RUBY went upstairs, where she grabbed her yellow legal pad and crawled up onto the bed.

My mother and I have battles to fight. But I'm afraid to ask the questions, and she, I can tell, is afraid to answer them.

My secret for one of yours—this is the game we have begun to play. I will learn things about my mother that I don't want to know. I know, for instance, that she ran away from home after high school and never spoke to her father again.

Even yesterday I wouldn't have been surprised by that. I would have said, "Of course. Running away is what Nora Bridge does best." But I watched her eyes as she spoke of her father. I saw the pain. Part of me wishes I hadn't seen that, be- cause as I stood there, listening to my mother's heartache, I wondered for the first time if it hurt her to leave her children.

Chapter Five

$\mathscr{D}$EAN sat cross-legged on the end of the dock watching the sun rise. The Sound was rough now at the changing of the tides. He heard the sound of motors in the distance, and he smiled.

The fishing boats were going out. How many times had he and Ruby stood on the dock watching Rand's boat chug out to sea? She'd always squeezed Dean's hand when the *Captain Hook* rounded the point and disappeared. He had known, without her telling him, that she lived with the fear that one day her father wouldn't return.

Tiredly he got to his feet and turned around. To his right the old family sailboat bobbed wearily in the tide. The mast—once a bright white—had been discolored by the endless rain and pitted by the wind. The deck around the steering wheel was hidden beneath a layer of slimy leaves and green-gray mold.

He heard her voice. *Let's take out the* Wind Lass, *Dino. Come on!*

He closed his eyes, remembering Ruby. In the beginning he'd flinched at every memory and waited for the images to pass, but then he'd gone in search of them, reaching out like a blind man.

He grabbed the line, pulled the boat closer to the dock, and stepped aboard. He had always felt free on this boat. The flapping sound of sails catching the wind had buoyed his spirits like nothing else, and yet he'd walked away from it, let sailing be part of the life he'd left behind. Suddenly he knew what he needed to do: He would restore the *Wind Lass*—scrape the old paint away, strip the wood and reoil it. If he could get Eric out here for just a single afternoon, maybe the wind and the sea could take them back in time.

RUBY woke to the smell of frying bacon and brewing coffee. Snagging yesterday's leggings off the floor, she pulled them on underneath her long nightshirt and padded downstairs.

Nora was in the kitchen, maneuvering the wheelchair like General Patton along the front. There were two cast-iron skillets on the stove, one with steam climbing out. Nora smiled up at Ruby. "Good morning. Did you sleep well?"

"Fine." Ruby poured herself a cup of coffee. After a sip she felt more human. She saw that her mother had made bacon and pancakes. "I haven't eaten breakfast like this since you left us."

It was an effort for her mother to keep smiling. "Do you want me to put an M&M face on your pancakes like I used to?"

"No, thanks. I avoid carbohydrates layered with chocolate."

Ruby set the table, then dished up two plates and sat down.

Nora sat across from her. "Did you sleep well?" she asked.

"You already asked me that."

Nora's fork clanged on the plate edge. "Tomorrow I'll remember to wear a Kevlar vest under my nightgown."

"What am I supposed to do? Be like Caroline—pretend everything is fine between us?"

"My relationship with Caroline is not for you to judge," Nora said sharply. "You've always thought you knew everything, but there's a dark side to all that certainty, Ruby. You . . . hurt people." Ruby saw her mother swell up with anger and then as quickly fade. "But I suppose it's not entirely your fault."

"Not *entirely?* How about not at all my fault?"

"I left Caroline, too. It didn't make her cold and hard and unable to love people."

"Who said I can't love people? I lived with Max for five years."

"And where is he now?"

Ruby pushed back from the table and stood.

Nora looked up. There was a gentle understanding in her gaze. "Sit down. We won't talk about anything that matters."

Her mother spoke in one of those voices that immediately turned a grown woman into a child. Ruby did as she was told.

Nora took a bite of bacon. "We need to go grocery shopping."

"Fine. We'll leave in about thirty minutes?"

"Make it an hour. I have to figure out how to bathe."

"I could lasso your leg and lower you into the tub."

Nora laughed. "No, thanks. I don't want to drown naked with my leg stuck up in the air."

The remark took a moment to sink in. When it did, Ruby said, "I wouldn't let you drown."

"I know. But would you rescue me?" Without waiting for an answer, Nora spun around and rolled into her bedroom.

LATER that afternoon Ruby sat on the bed in her parents' old bedroom with her yellow pad in her lap. She had surreptitiously bought a copy of *USA Today* when they were grocery shopping and hidden it until she got up to her room. The headline in the upper right-hand corner read WHERE IS NORA BRIDGE HIDING? A grainy photograph of her mother stared up at her from the page.

> My mother is being destroyed in the press. It's only fitting, I suppose. She ruined her family in pursuit of a career, and now that career is detonating.
>
> It's what I wanted to happen, if not for vengeance, then for fairness. And yet something about it doesn't sit well with me.

"Ruby! Come help me make dinner."

Ruby yanked open the top drawer in her mother's nightstand. Pens and junk clattered forward. As she started to put her pad away, she saw a brown prescription bottle: VALIUM. NORA BRIDGE. 1985. The doctor listed was Allbright.

Ruby frowned. Her mother was on Valium in 1985? In 1985 everything had been fine. Or so Ruby had thought.

She went downstairs and found Nora already in the kitchen.

"We're going to make chicken divan. How does that sound?"

Ruby groaned. "Cooking together."

For the next half hour they worked side by side. Ruby chopped broccoli and cut up the chicken, while Nora did everything else. Finally the casserole was in the oven.

"I have a surprise for you," Nora said. "There's a big cardboard box in my closet. Will you get it?"

Ruby went into the bedroom and found the box. She took it into the living room and set it down on the coffee table.

Nora had followed her into the living room. "Open it."

Ruby pulled the flaps apart and peered inside the box. It was their sixteen-millimeter movie projector and a reel of film.

"Home movies," Nora said with a forced smile.

Ruby was trapped. She reached deeper into the box and found a folded white sheet and a set of thumbtacks—their old "screen." She set up the projector on a table in the living room, tacked the sheet onto the wall, and turned off the lights. With a dull, clacking sound the film started. Ruby lowered herself to the sofa. There was a buzz of people talking, then her mother's voice: "Rand, she's coming."

Ruby couldn't have been more than five years old—a scrawny, puffy-cheeked kindergartner dressed in a ragged pink tutu. She twirled and swirled drunkenly across the stage.

"Oh, Rand, she's perfect."

"Hush. I'm trying to concentrate."

The picture went dark, then stuttered back to life. This time they were down at the beach. Caroline, in a skirted one-piece bathing suit, was splashing in the ankle-deep water, laughing. Ruby was wearing a bikini. Her mother was looking through a plastic bucket full of shells and rocks. Ruby ran over to her. Mom leaned over and fixed a strap on her sandal, then pulled a wiggly, laughing Ruby into her arms for a kiss. Mom . . .

How was it Ruby had forgotten how much they'd laughed or how regularly her mother had hugged and kissed her?

There was Dad, twirling Ruby around and around in a circle; Mom, teaching Ruby how to tie her shoe; a rainy Halloween with two princesses skipping hand in hand, carrying pumpkin-headed flashlights; Mom and Dad, dancing in the living room.

By the time the final bit of film flapped out of the reel and the screen went black, Ruby felt as if she'd run a ten-mile race. She was unsteady as she turned off the camera and hit the lights.

Her mother (*Nora,* she reminded herself) sat hunched in her wheelchair. Tears glistened on her cheeks and lashes.

At the sight of her mother's tears Ruby felt something inside of her break away. "You and Dad looked so happy together."

Nora smiled unevenly. "We were happy for a lot of years. And then . . . we weren't."

"You mean *you* weren't. I saw what it did to him when you walked out. Believe me, he loved you."

"Ah, Ruby, there's so much you don't know. No child can judge her parents' marriage."

Ruby wanted to be angry, but in truth, she was too battered. The movies had hurt so much, she couldn't think straight. "I had forgotten you," Ruby said softly. "I've never dreamed of you or had a single childhood memory with you in it. But tonight I remembered the locket you gave me on my eleventh birthday."

Nora wiped her eyes and nodded. "Do you still have it?"

Ruby got up. She'd been sixteen the last day she'd worn it.

That summer, the Bridge family had stayed huddled in their too quiet house. Dad had started drinking and smoking when Nora left in June. By August he never came out of his room. The *Captain Hook* sat idle, and by the fall Dad had had to sell off another chunk of land to pay their bills. Finally, on the first day of school, Ruby had taken the locket off and thrown it to the ground.

She turned and looked at her mother. "I threw it away."

"I see."

"No, you don't. I didn't throw it away because I hated you. I threw it out because it hurt too much to remember you."

"Oh, Ruby . . ."

In the kitchen the oven's timer went off.

Ruby lurched to her feet. "Thank God. Let's eat."

NORA wrestled through a long and sleepless night. Around dawn she gave up and went out onto the porch to watch the sunrise. *I had forgotten you.* Nora had known that Ruby blamed her, hated her. But to have *forgotten* her? Nora didn't know how to combat that. She needed to attack the problem with Ruby aggressively. But how?

"Okay," she sighed. "Pretend this is a reader letter."

Dear Nora:

Years ago I walked out on my marriage and left my children. My daughter has never forgiven me. Now she tells me that she's forgotten all memories of me. How do I make amends?

She took a deep breath, thinking it through. If Nora had received a letter like this, she would have taken the woman to task for her unpardonable behavior. Then, after moralizing for a few sentences, she would have said, *Force her to remember you.*

The answer came easily when offered to a stranger.

Behind her the screen door squeaked open. "Nora?"

Nora wheeled around, smiling brightly. "Hi, honey."

Ruby frowned. "You're awfully chipper for eight in the morning. Do you want a cup of coffee?"

"I've got some. Why don't you get a cup and join me?"

Wordlessly Ruby went back inside, then came out a few minutes later and sat down in the rocker.

Nora took a sip of her coffee. "Remember the Fourth of July barbecues we used to have out here? Your dad was always gone fishing, and the three of us girls would load up on firecrackers."

Ruby smiled. "Sparklers were my favorite. I couldn't wait for it to get dark."

"We wrote things in the light, remember? I always wrote, 'I love my girls.' You only wrote Dean's name. Year after year."

"Yeah. He and Eric always showed up right when you put the salmon on the barbecue." Ruby sighed. "Caroline tells me you've stayed in touch with Eric. How is he?"

Nora had known this moment was coming. She'd thought she was prepared for it, but she wasn't. How did you tell your daughter that one of her best childhood friends was dying? Nora wiped her eyes and met her daughter's expectant gaze. "Eric has cancer."

Ruby paled. "Oh, my God. Is he going to die?"

It hurt to answer. "Yes, honey, he is."

Ruby buried her head in her hands. "I should have stayed in contact with him." She fell silent, shaking her head, and Nora knew her daughter was crying. "It seems like yesterday we were all together. I can't imagine him sick. Can we visit him?"

"Of course. He's staying at the house on Lopez. I know he'd love to see you." Nora leaned back and stared out at the Sound.

Inside the house, the phone rang. Ruby got slowly to her feet and went inside. "Nora!" she yelled. "It's your assistant—Dee."

Nora wheeled into the kitchen and took the phone. "Dee?"

"Oh, Nora, a box of letters just landed on your desk. There was nothing I could do about it. Tom Adams called. He threatened to get me fired if I didn't forward them to you."

"Did you read the letters? How bad are they?"

"It's ugly, Nora. A lady in Iowa went on TV last night and said she was going to file a lawsuit against you. Fraudulent advice."

"Okay, Dee. Send me the letters."

"I thought I'd send your 'Best Of' file, too. In case you wanted to sneak some old letters in. Tom wouldn't know."

"Good thinking. Thanks for everything, Dee. Really. Good-bye." Nora leaned forward and hung up the phone.

Ruby stood by the refrigerator. "What was that all about?"

"My boss at the newspaper expects me to answer some rather unflattering letters from my readers."

"Well, it *is* your job."

Nora didn't bother answering. Ruby didn't know how it felt to *need* acceptance and how, without it, you felt invisible.

Nora heard Ruby run upstairs. In a minute she was back, holding a section of newspaper. "I bought this yesterday at the store. Maybe you should read what they're writing about you."

Nora took the paper and glanced through the article. "It's over," she said dully, letting the newspaper fall to the floor.

Ruby frowned. "You'll get through this. Look at Monica Lewinsky. She's selling expensive handbags now."

"Thank you for that comforting comparison, Ruby. My career is over. I have no intention of answering a single letter. I'm going to hide out until this is over. Another story will come along, and they'll forget about me. Then I'll just fade away."

"But with the right spin, you can—"

"You don't understand my career, Ruby. Everything I think and feel and believe is found in my words to strangers. That's why they believed in me—they sensed my honesty."

"According to the press, your columns said you believed in marriage. Is that the kind of honesty they got from you?"

"I *do* believe in marriage. And love and family and commitments. I just . . . failed at it."

Ruby looked surprised by that answer. "I would have thought you'd see leaving us as a success. You did it so well. Like leaving a job you hate. You might miss the income, but you're proud of yourself for finding the guts to quit."

"I wasn't proud of myself."

"Why?" Ruby asked the question in a whispered voice. "Why did you do it? Couldn't you have a career *and* raise children?"

Nora sighed. "What happened to us isn't some event, like the sinking of the *Titanic*. It's little things, strung together over decades. To really understand it all, you'd have to see the way things really were in our family, but you don't want to do that. You want to forget I ever existed, forget *we* ever existed."

"It's easier that way," Ruby said quietly.

"Yes. And it's easier for me to walk away from my career. I can't fight these charges, not with the choices I've made in my life."

"I never saw you as a quitter."

Nora gave her a sad, knowing smile. "Ah, Ruby, of all people, you should have."

THE package arrived in the late afternoon while her mother was taking a nap. Ruby knew what it was. She debated with herself for a few moments—after all, she'd never chosen to read her mother's newspaper columns—but the *Caché* article changed things. Now Ruby needed to know what Nora Knows Best had been about.

She opened the box and pulled out a manila envelope marked BEST OF. She withdrew a pile of clippings. The one on top was dated December 1989.

Dear Nora:

Do you have any tips for getting red wine out of white silk? At my sister's wedding I got a little drunk and spilled a glassful on her gown. Now she's not talking to me, and I feel awful.

Wedding Dress Blues

Nora's answer was short and sweet.

Dear Wedding Dress Blues:

Only your dry cleaner can get the stain out. If it can't be done, you must offer to replace the gown. This is more than an ordinary accident, and your sister deserves a perfect reminder of her special day. It may take you a while to save the money, but in the end, you'll feel better. It's so easy to do the wrong thing in life, don't you think? When we see a clear road to being a better person, we ought to take it.

Reading the columns, Ruby noticed that her mother's mail changed gradually from household-hint questions to earnest, heartfelt questions about life. Ruby had to admit that her mother was good at this. Her answers were concise, wise, and compassionate.

As she read a column from a sixteen-year-old who was having a problem with drugs, Ruby remembered the time in her own life when she'd been fourteen, and Lopez Island—and her own family—had seemed hopelessly small and uncool. For a time, skipping school and smoking pot had offered Ruby a better way.

Dad had gone ballistic when Ruby got suspended, but not Nora. Her mother had picked Ruby up from the principal's office and driven her to the tip of the island. She'd dragged Ruby down to the secluded patch of beach that overlooked the distant glitter of downtown Victoria and plopped down cross-legged on the sand. Then she had reached into her pocket and pulled out the joint that had been found in Ruby's locker. Amazingly, she had put it in her mouth and lit up. Then she had held it out to Ruby.

Stunned, Ruby had sat down by her mother. They'd smoked the whole thing together, and all the while, neither of them had spoken.

Gradually night had fallen, and Nora said, "Do you notice anything different about Victoria?"

Ruby had found it difficult to focus. "It looks farther away."

"It *is* farther away. That's the thing about drugs. When you use them, everything you want in life is farther away." Nora had turned to her. "How cool is it to do something that anyone with a match can do? Cool is becoming an astronaut or a comedian or a scientist who cures cancer. Don't throw your chances away. We don't get as many of them as we need." She stood up. "It's your choice. Your life."

Ruby remembered that she'd been shaking as she'd stood up. That's how deeply her mother's words had reached. Very softly she'd said, "I love you, Mom." That was Ruby's last specific memory of saying those words to her mother.

She turned her attention back to the columns now. The item on top was a handwritten letter.

Dear Nora:

My daughter—my precious baby girl—was killed by a drunk driver this year. I find that I can't talk to people anymore, not even my wife. I see her sitting on the end of the bed, her hair unwashed, her eyes rimmed in red, and I can't reach out to her, can't offer comfort.

I want to gather my belongings, put them in a shopping cart, and disappear into the faceless crowd of vagrants in Pioneer Square. But I haven't the strength even for that. So I sit in my house, seeing the endless reminders of what I once had, and I ask myself why I bother to breathe at all.

Lost and Lonely

Across the top of that letter someone had written, "FedEx the attached letter to this man's return address immediately." Paperclipped to the letter was a photocopy of a handwritten note.

Dear Lost and Lonely:

I will not waste time with the pretty words we wrap around grief. You are in danger; you are not so far gone that you don't know this. I am going to do what I have never done before. You will come and talk to me. I will not take no for an answer.

My secretary will be expecting your call tomorrow, and she will set up an appointment. Please, please, do not disappoint me. I know how much life can wound even the strongest heart, and sometimes all it takes to save us is the touch of a single stranger's hand. Reach out for me. I'll be there.

Nora

Ruby's hands were trembling. No wonder these readers loved her mother. She carefully put the columns and letters back in the manila envelope and left the package on the kitchen table for her mother to find. Then she went upstairs.

She hadn't realized that she was going to call Caroline until she'd picked up the phone. But it made sense. Ruby felt unsteady, and Caroline had always been her solid ground.

Caro answered on the third ring. "Hello?"

Ruby couldn't help noticing how tired her sister sounded when she answered. "Hey, sis. You sound like you need a nap."

Caroline laughed. "I always need a nap. So what's going on up there? How are you and Mom doing?"

"She's not who I thought she was," Ruby admitted softly. "Like, did you know she was seeing a shrink when she was married to Dad or that she took Valium in 1985?"

"Wow. I wonder if her doctor told her to leave Dad."

"Why would he do that?"

Caroline laughed softly. "That's what they do, Ruby. They tell unhappy women to find happiness. I wish I had a buck for every time my therapist told me to leave Jere."

"You see a shrink, too? But I thought you and Mr. Quarterback had a perfect life."

"We have our problems, just like anyone else, but I'd rather talk about— Aah! Darn it, Jenny! I gotta run, Ruby. Your niece just poured a cup of grape juice on her brother's head."

Before Ruby could answer, Caroline hung up.

EVERYTHING WAS READY. Dean knocked on Eric's door and went inside.

Eric was sitting up in bed, reading. When he saw Dean, he smiled. "Hey, bro. It's almost dinnertime. Where have you been?"

"I've been working on something," Dean said. Slowly he lowered the metal bedrail. "Are you up to a little trip?"

"Are you kidding? I'm so sick of this bed, I could cry."

Dean leaned forward and lifted his brother up from the bed. *God, he weighed nothing at all.* It was like holding a fragile child. Dean carried him downstairs, through the house, across the lawn, and down the bank to the beach. On the slanted wooden dock, he'd already set up an oversized Adirondack chair and piled pillows onto it.

"The *Wind Lass,*" Eric said softly.

Dean carefully placed his brother in the chair, then tucked a cashmere blanket tightly around his thin body.

It was nearing sunset. The sky was low enough to touch. The last rays of the setting sun turned everything pink—the waves, the clouds, the pebbled beach. The sailboat was still in bad shape, but at least she was clean.

Dean sat down beside Eric. "I still have some work to do on her. The sail should be done tomorrow. The cushions are being cleaned. I thought maybe if we could take her out—"

"We could remember how it used to be," Eric said. "How *we* used to be."

Of course Eric had understood. "Yeah."

Eric drew the blanket tighter against his chin. "So what's it like being the favored son?"

"Lonely."

Eric sighed. "Remember when she loved me? When I was a star athlete with awesome grades and a promising future."

Dean remembered. Their mother had adored Eric. The only time Mom and Dad came on the island was football season. Every homecoming game, Mom had dressed in her best "casual" clothes and gone to the game, where she cheered on her quarterback son. When the season ended, they were gone again.

"I heard the phone ring last night about eleven o'clock," Eric said. "It was her, wasn't it?"

Dean looked away. Eye contact was impossible. "Yeah."

"Are they coming to see me?"

There was no point in lying. "No."

Eric released a thready sigh. "What good is an agonizing death by cancer if your own family won't weep by your bedside?"

"I'm here," Dean said softly. "You're not alone."

Tears came to Eric's eyes. "I know, baby brother. I know."

Dean swallowed hard. "You can't let her get to you."

Eric closed his eyes. "Someday she'll be sorry. It'll be too late, though." His eyes blinked open again, and he smiled sleepily. "Tell me about your life."

"There's not much to tell. I work."

"Very funny. I get the San Francisco newspapers just to read about you and the folks. You seem to be quite the bachelor-about-town. If I didn't know better, I'd say you had everything."

Dean wanted to laugh and say, *I do. I do have everything a man could want,* but it was a lie. "There's something . . . missing in my life. I don't know what it is."

"Do you like your job?"

Dean was surprised by the question. "No."

"Are you in love with anyone?"

"No. It's been a long time since I was in love."

"And you can't figure out what's *missing* in your life? Come on, Dino. The question isn't what's missing. The question is, what *is* your life?" Eric yawned. "Remember Camp Orkila?" he said suddenly.

"When we met Ruby," Dean said softly. "She climbed up into that big tree by the beach, remember? She said arts and crafts were for babies and she was a big girl."

"She wouldn't come down until you asked her to."

"Yeah. That was the beginning. We'd never seen a real family before. . . ." Dean let the words string out, find each other, and connect. Like threads, he wove them together, sewed a quilt from the strands of their life, and tucked it around his brother's body.

$\mathcal{N}$ORA woke up groggy from her nap. She lay in bed for a minute, listening to the gentle whooshing sound of the sea through her open window. It was almost nighttime. *Eric.*

She pulled the phone onto her lap and dialed the number.

Eric came on the line. "Nora? Well, it's about time."

She laughed. "I've had an . . . interesting last few days. I'm on Summer Island. Caroline is letting me relax here for a while."

"Ah, the lifestyles of the rich and famous. I suppose it's tough to make time for a friend who is facing the grim reaper." Eric laughed at his own joke, but the laughter dwindled into a cough.

Nora made an instant decision: She wouldn't tell him about the scandal. He didn't need to worry about her. But she had to tell him *something*—she couldn't just show up at his house in a wheelchair. "I had an accident and wound up in Bayview."

"Are you okay?"

"For a fifty-year-old woman who drove into a tree, I'm great. I came out of it with a broken leg and a sprained wrist. Nothing to worry about. But that's why I haven't been to see you."

"There's something you're not telling me."

She forced a laugh. "No, really, I—" She started to cry.

"Nora, you know you can talk to me about anything."

"You don't need to hear about my troubles."

"Who sat by me in the hospital while Charlie was dying? Who held my hand at the grave? Who was there when I began chemotherapy?"

Nora swallowed hard. "Me."

"So talk."

She didn't cry. She was almost preternaturally calm, in fact. "The *Tattler* just published naked pictures of me in bed with a man."

"Oh, God." His voice was a whisper.

"That's not even the worst of it. The photos were dated, proving that I was married to Rand at the time they were taken. The press is crucifying me. My career is over."

"This is *America*. Celebrities screw up all the time. Hold your head up, cry when you admit your mistake, and beg for a second chance. Your fans will love you more for being like them—human."

"That's why I love you, Eric. The glass is always half full." Nora sighed. "How about if I come to see you tomorrow? Between the wheelchair and the hospital bed, we'll look like a scene from *Cuckoo's Nest*."

"That'd be great. And you won't believe who's here."

Nora laughed. "Believe me, you won't believe who is *here* either."

"Dean—"

"Ruby—"

They spoke at the same time.

Nora was the first to recover. "Dean is on the island? How is it between you two?"

"Awkward. A little unsure. And Ruby?"

"Angry. Truthfully, she hates me."

"But she's there. That means something. Hey, do you know what happened between Dean and Ruby? He won't talk about it."

"She won't either."

"It must've been bad. Dean went all the way to boarding school to get away from her. But it's interesting neither ever married."

"Are you thinking what I'm thinking?"

"How do we get them together?"

Nora grinned. It felt great to talk about something besides Eric's illness or her own scandal. And this made her feel like a mother for the first time in years. "Carefully, my boy. Very carefully."

AFTER Nora hung up, she wheeled herself out of the room and was halfway into the kitchen when she saw the package on the table. She stopped dead. Slowly she wheeled closer. It had been opened.

She pulled the slim box onto her lap and went into the living room. Her fingers were shaking as she pulled out the stack of mail marked NEW LETTERS. On top was an envelope postmarked GREAT FALLS, MONTANA. She opened it and began to read.

Nora:

I've written to you a dozen times over the last few years. Twice you have published my letters, and once you wrote me a private letter, saying that you hoped things were getting better.

Can you imagine how it now feels to know the kind of person I've been taking advice from?

Don't bother answering this letter. I don't care about your opinion, and I certainly won't be reading your columns anymore. If I want to read fiction, I'll go to the library.

May God forgive you, Nora Bridge. Your fans will not.

Nora folded the letter and slid it back into the envelope.

After reading a few more, she couldn't seem to move. A tremor was spreading through her, chilling her from the inside out.

"Nora?" Ruby came into the room and sat down on the leather chair across from Nora. "Did you sleep well?"

Nora stared down at her own hands and thought, Oh, please, just go away, don't talk to me now. "Yes," she managed.

"I take it you read a few of your new letters," Ruby said.

Nora wanted to say something casual and flip, but she couldn't. "They hate me now."

"They're strangers. They don't even know you." Ruby flashed a smile. "Leave the big, ugly emotions to your family."

That only made it worse. "What family?" Nora moaned quietly. "Really, Ruby, what family have I left myself?"

Ruby looked at her for a long minute, then said, "Do you remember when I was twelve and my class elected me to run the dance where the girls asked the boys?"

Nora sniffled. "Yeah, I remember that."

"I wanted the local newspaper to cover the event. You were the only one who didn't laugh at me." Ruby smiled. "I watched you charm that fat old editor from the *Island Times*."

Nora remembered that day. "The minute I walked into that

office, I loved it. For the first time in my life I felt as if I *belonged* somewhere. I'd always known I had words banging around in my chest, but I'd never known what to do with them."

"I realized later that I'd shown you the way out of our lives."

"I didn't leave my family for a career, Ruby. That had nothing to do with it. For me, leaving your dad started before I met him."

"I don't understand."

Nora stared out the window. "My dad was an alcoholic. When he was sober, he was almost human, but when he was drunk—which was most of the time—he was pit-bull mean. It was a secret I learned to keep from everyone. Hell, it took me fifteen years of therapy to even say the word alcoholic."

Ruby's mouth fell open. "You never told us that."

"On our farm the neighbors couldn't hear a woman's scream. Or a girl's. And you learn fast that it doesn't help to cry out. Instead you try to get smaller and smaller, hoping that if you can become tiny enough and still enough, he'll pass you by."

"He abused you?"

"He didn't do the worst thing a father can do to his daughter, but he . . . molded me. I grew up trying to be invisible, flinching all the time." Nora made direct eye contact with her daughter. "For years I thought that if I didn't talk about my dad, I could forget him."

Ruby drew in a sharp breath. "Did it work?"

Nora knew her daughter was making the connection. "No. All it did was give him more power and turn me into a woman who couldn't imagine being loved. Not unlike how a girl would feel if her own mother abandoned her." Nora wouldn't let herself look away. "Did you ever fall in love after Dean?"

"I lived with Max for almost five years. Then I came home from work one day and he'd moved out."

"Did you ever tell him you loved him?"

"Almost. Practically."

"Did he say he loved you?"

"Yeah, but Max was like that. He told the checker at Safeway he loved her."

Nora could see she'd have to be more direct. "My point is this: You lived with a man for almost five years and never told him you loved him, even after he'd said those precious words to you. The question isn't why he left. It's why he stayed so long."

Ruby looked helplessly at Nora. "I never thought of it like that."

"I told your father I loved him the first time we made love. I'd never said the words before to anyone. It wasn't the sort of thing my family did. And do you know when Rand told me he loved me?"

"When?"

"Never. I waited for it like a child waits for Christmas."

Ruby shook her head. "No more. Please."

"I wanted to raise you to be strong and sure of yourself, and instead I turned you into me. I made you afraid to love. I was a bad mother. I'm so, so sorry for that."

"You weren't a bad mother," Ruby said, "until you left."

Nora was pathetically grateful for that. "Thank you." She knew she was following a dangerous path, falling in love with her daughter all over again, but she couldn't help herself. "I still remember the little girl who cried every time a baby bird fell out of its nest."

Ruby got to her feet. "That girl is long gone."

"You'll find her again," Nora said softly. "Probably about the same time you fall in love. And when it's real, Ruby, you'll know it, and you'll stop being afraid."

DEAN carried the breakfast tray up to his brother's bedroom. He found him already awake, sitting up in bed.

"Heya, Dino," Eric said.

Dean carefully placed the tray across Eric's lap. He noticed how wan his brother looked this morning. "Bad night?"

Eric nodded. "I can't seem to sleep anymore, which is pretty ironic, since it's all I do. The pain cocktail knocks me out, but it's not the same as a good night's sleep." He smiled tiredly.

Dean pulled a chair up, sat down, and held his brother's hand.

Eric turned to him. "I always thought we'd come back to this house as old men. I pictured us watching your kids run up and down the dock, looking for shrimp." Eric's eyes fluttered shut. "You and Ruby used to play down on that dock for hours."

Dean swallowed hard. He thought about changing the subject, but suddenly he wanted to remember her.

"I thought I'd be the best man at your wedding. You and Ruby were sixteen years old, but I thought it was true love."

"I thought so, too."

Eric looked at him. "And now?"

"Now I know it was."

"She's on Summer Island."

Dean frowned. It took a moment for the full impact of those words to hit him. "Ruby's at the summerhouse?"

Eric grinned. "Yep."

Dean leaned back. "What . . . With her husband and kids?"

"She's never been married. I wonder why that is?"

Dean's heart was beating so fast, he felt faint. *Ruby is here.*

"Go see her," Eric said softly.

DEAN grabbed his ten-speed from its resting place beneath the eaves. The sun was shining brightly as he pedaled down the winding hill to the Lopez Island dock. A ferry was loading. He got right on and stood with his bike at the bow of the boat, barely noticing the cars streaming into lines behind him.

On Summer Island, he bicycled off the boat onto the dock. By the time he swooped onto the Bridges' driveway, he was sweating and out of breath. He jumped off the bike and let it clatter to the ground.

Then Dean stopped. For the first time he wondered what he was doing, running toward his first love as if eleven years hadn't passed. Their last day together came at him in a rush of images.

The sky had been robin's-egg blue. Strangely, he remembered looking up, seeing the white trail from a passing jet. When he'd turned to point it out to Ruby, he saw what he should have seen before: She'd been crying.

I had sex with a boy last night. She'd said it without preamble, as if she'd wanted to wound him with her confession.

He had pulled the whole sordid story out of her, one painful syllable at a time, and when she was finished, he knew all the facts, but they hadn't added up to a whole truth he could understand. If he'd been older, more sexually experienced, he would have known the question to ask: Why? But he'd been seventeen and a virgin himself. All he'd cared about was the promise he and Ruby had made—to wait for each other until marriage.

Anger and hurt had overwhelmed him. He'd felt foolish and used. He waited for her to beg for forgiveness, but she just stood there, close enough to touch and yet so far away, he couldn't see her clearly. Or maybe it was his tears that were blurring the world, turning her into a girl he'd never seen before.

Go ahead, she'd said, staring dully up at him. *Go. It's over.*

He'd had to leave fast, before she could see that he was crying. He'd turned away from her and run back to his bike. He'd pedaled hard, trying to outdistance the pain, but it had raged inside of him.

Now Dean released his breath in a steady, even stream. There was no turning back. He walked down the path, stepped up onto the porch, and knocked.

And she answered.

"Ruby," he whispered. It actually hurt to say her name. She was so beautiful that for a second he couldn't breathe.

"Dean," she said, her eyes widening.

The moment felt spun from sugar, so fragile that a soft breeze could shatter it. "I . . . uh . . . I came home to see Eric."

"How is he?" Her voice was barely audible.

"Not good."

"I'm here with my mother. She had a car accident, and I'm taking care of her."

"You?" It slipped out, an intimate observation from a man who'd once known the girl. He was instantly afraid he'd offended her. "So you've forgiven her, then."

Sadness darkened her eyes. "Forgiveness doesn't matter, does it? When a thing is done, it's done. You can't unring a bell." She smiled, but it wasn't the smile he remembered, the one that crinkled her whole face and sparkled in her eyes. She seemed to be waiting for him to say something, but he couldn't think fast enough, and she didn't wait long. "Well, it was good seeing you again. Say hello to Nora before you leave. She'd hate to miss you."

And with that, she walked past him, heading for the beach.

RUBY thought she was going to be sick. That was why she'd left Dean so quickly. She couldn't stand there, making polite conversation, not when it felt as if carbonated water had replaced her blood. She ran down the path toward the beach and sat down on her favorite moss-covered rock.

"Ruby?"

She heard her name, spoken softly, and she froze. Her heart picked up a wild beat. She hadn't heard his footsteps.

"Can I sit with you?"

Ruby sidled to the right, and Dean sat down beside her. She felt his thigh along hers, and she ached to lay her hand on his the way she'd done so many times before. But she'd lost that right. In her angry, confused youth she'd thrown it away.

"This brings back memories," he said softly.

She didn't mean to turn to him, but she couldn't help herself. When she gazed into his blue eyes, she was sixteen again. Except he had become a man. If it were possible, he was even more handsome now. She felt a rush of shame. If only she'd worn better clothes today than torn shorts and a ragged T-shirt. He was probably disgusted that she'd let herself get so ugly. She reached deep inside for a casual voice. "I hear from Caro that you're a corporate bigwig now."

"It doesn't mean much."

"Spoken like a rich man." She tried to smile.

"I saw your act once. At the Comedy Store. I thought you were really funny."

Her smile softened into the real thing. "Really?"

"I wanted to talk to you after the show, but there was a man—"

"Max." She felt the sting of that missed opportunity. "We broke up a while ago. And what about you? Are you married?"

"No. Never."

She felt euphoria. Then it fell away, left her even more confused. She'd loved him so much, and yet she'd broken his heart. "That summer . . . I found out from Lottie that you'd moved away."

"I couldn't face you," he answered, looking at her. "You didn't just hurt me, Ruby. You ruined me."

"I know." She lurched to her feet, terrified that she would burst into tears. "I have to get back to Nora."

Slowly he got to his feet and reached for her. She stumbled back so fast, she almost fell. His hand dropped back to his side, and she could see the disappointment in his eyes. "Time is precious," he said. "If I didn't know that before this week, I know it now. So I'm just going to say it: I missed you."

She couldn't imagine what to say next. She had missed him, too. A more trusting person could have changed the future in this very moment, but Ruby couldn't imagine that kind of strength.

He waited, and the silence stretched out between them. Then slowly he turned and walked away.

NORA sat on the porch. She could see Dean and Ruby sitting on that old rock of theirs. Ruby was the first to stand. Dean followed. They stood frozen, close enough to kiss. Then Dean turned and headed back toward the house, leaving Ruby behind.

He saw Nora on the porch and came up to her. "Hey, Miz Bridge."

She smiled. "Call me Nora. It's good to see you again, Dean."

"It's good to see you, too." In his eyes she saw pain. "Thank you, Nora," he said softly. "You're everything to him."

She nodded, knowing she didn't need to say anything.

Dean turned back, stared down at the beach. Finally he pulled away. "Will you guys come over on Saturday? I've got the *Wind Lass* working. I'm going to take Eric sailing."

"That would be great."

Dean shot a last, lingering look at Ruby, then walked away.

A few minutes later Ruby headed up the path. When she saw Nora on the porch, she paused.

Nora noticed that her daughter's eyes were red. Her heart went out to her. "Come," she said, "sit with me."

Ruby walked onto the porch and sat on the railing.

Nora longed to touch her daughter. But such intimacy was still impossible between them. "You know what I was remembering just now? The winter I was pregnant with you. The snow came earlier that year than anyone could remember. Just after Thanksgiving. For almost a month after that, things on the island went a little crazy. Roses bloomed on prickly bushes that had been dead for weeks. Rain fell from cloudless skies. We believed it was magic. But what I remember most of all were the sunsets. From then until the new year came, the night sky was always red. We called it the ruby season."

Ruby said softly, "Is that where my name came from?"

"We never talked about naming you after it, but when you came, we knew. You'd be our Ruby. Our own bit of magic." Nora paused and looked at her. "Dean invited us to go sailing on Saturday."

"What will I say to Eric?"

"Oh, Ruby," Nora said gently, "you start with hello."

RUBY barely slept that night. She knew that she had hurt people, and she didn't want to hurt Dean again. He deserved a woman who could return his love as fully and freely as he gave it.

Finally, at about three thirty, she went out onto the balcony and sat. *Write. That'll get your mind off everything.* Then for the first time she considered the impact of her article. She'd agreed to write it because she'd *wanted* to hurt her mother, to strike back for all the pain she'd suffered as a young girl. But she wasn't a child anymore. And Ruby had glimpsed images in the past days that didn't fit with the picture she'd drawn of her mother.

She closed her eyes and remembered a cold, crisp October day a few months after her mother had left home.

Dad had been in the living room, sitting in that leather chair of his, drinking and smoking cigarettes. Caroline had been gone on a field trip to Seattle. Ruby had been in the bedroom, reading *Misery* by Stephen King. There was a knock at the front door. Ruby heard her dad's footsteps, then heard him say "Nora" in a voice that was too loud, belligerent.

Ruby froze. Then she crept to the door of her room.

Dad was in his chair. Mom was kneeling in front of him.

"Rand," Mom said quietly, "we need to talk."

He stared down at her; his hair was too long, and dirty. "It's too late for talking."

Ruby couldn't stand it another minute, seeing her father's pain in such sharp relief. "Get out," she yelled.

Mom got to her feet, turned around. "Oh, Ruby," she said, holding her arms out.

As Mom came toward her, Ruby saw the changes in her mother— the gray pallor in her cheeks, the weight she'd lost, the way her hands, always so strong and sure, were blue-veined and trembling.

Ruby sprang back. "G-go away. We don't want you anymore."

Mom stopped, her hands falling to her sides. "Don't say that, honey. There are things you don't understand. You're so young."

"I understand how it feels to be left behind, as if you were . . . nothing." Ruby's traitorous voice broke, and the sudden rawness of her pain made it difficult to breathe. "Go away, Mother. No one here loves you anymore."

Mom glanced back at Dad, who'd slumped into his chair again. He was holding his head in his hands.

Ruby wanted to put her arms around him and tell him she loved him, but it was all she could do to keep from wailing. She stepped back into her bedroom and slammed the door shut.

She didn't know how long she stood there. After a while she heard footsteps crossing the living room, then the quiet opening and closing of the front door. Outside, a car engine started; tires crunched through gravel. And quiet fell once again, broken only by the sound of a grown man crying.

Even then her mother had had a story to tell, but no one had wanted to hear it. Now Ruby was ready. She wanted to learn what had happened more than a decade earlier within her own family.

She would ask her father.

Chapter Seven

*I*T HAD been easy to get out of the house. Ruby had simply left a note—"Gone to Dad's"—on the kitchen table. Now she was in the minivan, driving up the treelined road that led away from the Lopez Island ferry dock.

Ruby was a fourth-generation islander, and at this moment, seeing all the new houses and bed-and-breakfasts that had sprouted on Lopez, the full impact of that heritage hit her. She had roots here, a past that grew deep into the rich black island soil.

Her great-great-grandfather had come here from a dreary, industrialized section of England. He'd homesteaded two hundred acres on Lopez. His brother had staked his own claim on Summer Island. Both had become successful apple and sheep farmers. Now, more than one hundred years later, there were only ten acres on Lopez that belonged to her father.

Randall Bridge was an island man through and through. He'd grown up on this tiny, floating world, and he'd raised his children here. He lived on a financial shoestring, from one fishing season to the next, making it through the lean months doing boat repairs.

Ruby turned off the main road. A gravel road wound through acres of apple trees. At last she was home. She parked alongside her dad's battered Ford truck and got out of the car. The yellow clapboard house sat wedged between two huge willow trees.

It was exactly as she remembered. She walked toward the back porch. The yard was still a riot of weeds and untended flowers. A tattered screen door hung slanted, a set of screws missing.

She paused on the porch, steeling herself for the sight of her dad's new family. She knew she'd be entering another woman's house—a woman she barely knew—seeing a baby brother for the first time. Taking a deep breath, she knocked on the door and waited. When there was no answer, she eased the screen door open and stepped into the kitchen. "Dad?" Her voice was weak. She stepped past the table into the living room.

He was there, kneeling in front of the small black woodstove, loading logs into the fire. When he looked up and saw her, his eyes widened in surprise; then a great smile swept across his lined face. "I don't believe it. You're here." He clanged the stove's door shut, got to his feet, and pulled her into an awkward hug. "Caroline told me you were home. I wondered if you'd come see me."

She clung to him, fighting an urge to cry. "Of course I'd come," she said shakily, drawing back, although both of them knew it was a half-truth, a wished-for belief. She hadn't even called him, and the realization of her own selfishness tasted black and bitter.

He touched her cheek. "I missed you," he said.

"I missed you, too." It was true. She had missed him every day and all the time. She glanced uneasily up the stairs, wondering where Marilyn was. "I don't want to intrude—"

"Mari took Ethan off-island for a doctor's appointment." He grinned. "And don't even pretend you aren't happy about that."

Ruby smiled sheepishly. "Well, I wanted to see the kid. My brother," she added when she saw the way he was looking at her. She winced, wishing she'd said it right the first time.

"Don't worry about it." But she knew she'd hurt his feelings. He sat down on the threadbare floral sofa, cocked one leg over his knee. "How's it going between you and your mom?"

She flopped down onto the big overstuffed chair near the fire. "Picture Laverne and Shirley on crack."

"I don't see any visible bruising. I have to admit, I was shocked when Caro told me you'd volunteered to take care of Nora. Shocked and proud."

"She isn't quite what I expected." Ruby experienced a momentary lapse in courage. She drew a deep breath. "What happened between you two?"

He got to his feet and walked past her to the window. "Are you in for the long haul this time, Ruby?"

"What do you mean?"

"Ah, Rube." He sighed. "You have a way of moving on. You went off to California and started a new life without us. But after a while it was *our* fault—Caroline's and mine. We didn't call enough or not on the right days, or we didn't say the right things when we did call. You didn't come to my wedding or call when your brother was born or come to see Caroline when she suffered through that terrible labor. Now you want to stir up an old pot. Will you be here tomorrow or next month to see what comes of it?"

Ruby wanted to say he was *wrong*. But she couldn't. "I don't know, Dad." It was all she could manage now.

He stared down at her for a long time, then headed into the kitchen. Ruby followed him through the doorway. Her father was standing at the table with a bottle of tequila. He thumped it down hard, then yanked out a chair and sat down.

The sight of her father holding a bottle of booze shook Ruby to the core. "I thought you'd quit drinking."

"I did."

"You're scaring me."

"Honey, I haven't begun to scare you. Sit down."

Ruby pulled a chair out and perched nervously on its edge.

Her dad seemed different. This man, hunched over, staring at a full bottle of Cuervo Gold, looked as if he hadn't smiled in years. He looked up suddenly. "I love you. I want you to remember that."

She saw the emotion in his eyes. "I could never forget that."

"I don't know. You're good at forgetting the people who love you. The story starts in 1967, just a few years before the whole damn world exploded. I was at the University of Washington, finishing my senior year, and I was certain I'd get drafted into the NFL. So certain, I never bothered to get a degree.

"And then I met Nora. She was scrawny and scared. Still, she was the most beautiful girl I'd ever seen. She believed absolutely that I'd play pro football." Her dad slumped forward a little. "But it didn't happen. No one called. Then my draft number came up. I could have gotten out of it, but I hated this island, and I wanted someone to wait for me, to write me letters. So I asked Nora to marry me."

Ruby frowned. She'd heard this story a thousand times in her childhood, and this was not the way it went. "You didn't love her?"

"Not when I married her. No, that's not true. I'd just loved other women more. Anyway, we got married, spent a wonderful honeymoon at Lake Quinalt Lodge, and I shipped out.

"Your mom's letters kept me alive over there. It's funny. I fell in love with your mother when she wasn't even on the same continent. I meant to *stay* in love with her, but I didn't come home the same cocky, confident kid who'd left. Vietnam, war—it did something to us." He smiled sadly. "Anyway, I turned cynical and hard. Your mom tried to put me back together, and for a few years we were happy. Caroline was born, then you.

"When I came home, your mom and I moved into the house on Summer. I went to work at the feedstore. Everyone thought I was a failure. I hated my life. I didn't mean for it to happen."

Ruby swallowed convulsively. "Don't say—"

"I slept with other women."

"No."

"Your mom didn't know at first. I was drinking a lot by then—God knows *that* didn't help—and I knew when she started to suspect. But she always gave me the benefit of the doubt. Finally that summer someone told her the truth. She confronted me. Unfortunately, I was drunk at the time. I said . . . things. It was ugly. The next day she left."

Ruby felt as if she were drowning or falling.

"We've all been carrying this baggage for too long. Some of us have tried to go on." He looked at her. "And some of us have refused to. But all of us are hurting. She's your mother. Whatever she's done or hasn't done, or said or hasn't said, she's a part of you and you're a part of her. Don't you see that you can't be whole without her?"

Ruby's past seemed to be crumbling around her. There was nothing solid to hold on to. "I'm leaving."

He smiled sadly. "Of course you are."

"Call Nora. Tell her I'm going to Caroline's."

"I love you, Ruby," he said. "Please don't forget that."

She knew he was waiting for her to say the words back to him, but she couldn't do it.

RUBY had never been to her sister's house, but the address was imprinted on her brain. Caroline was the only person on earth who regularly received a Christmas card from Ruby.

The traffic was stop-and-go as she crept toward the sprawling suburb of Redmond. Not so many years earlier this had been the sticks. Now it was Microsoftland. Ruby checked the handy rental-car map and turned down Emerald Lane. One big brick-faced house followed another, each built to the edge of its lot. At last she found it: 12712 Emerald Lane.

She drove up the stamped blue concrete driveway and parked next to a silver Mercedes station wagon, then headed up the path to a pair of oak doors trimmed in beaded brass.

She knocked. From inside came a muffled "Just a minute."

Suddenly the door sprang open, and Caroline stood there smiling, looking flawless at one o'clock in the afternoon. "Ruby!" She took Ruby into her arms, holding her tightly. Finally Caro drew back. "I'm so glad you came." She pulled Ruby into the house.

Of course, it was perfect—uncluttered and flawlessly decorated. Not a thing was out of place. Caro led her through the pristine kitchen, then through the formal dining room and into the living room, where two wing chairs, upholstered in a brandy-colored silk, flanked a gold-and-bronze tapestried sofa.

"Where are the kids?"

Caroline brought a finger to her lips and said, "Shh. We don't want to wake them up. Trust me."

Ruby got a glimpse of something behind Caro's perfect face, but it was gone so fast, it left no imprint. She felt a prickle of unease. "Something's going on with you," Ruby said. "What is it?"

Caro sat on the edge of the chair. Her perfectly manicured hands were clasped so tightly together, the skin had gone pale. A smile flashed across her face. "It's nothing, really. Just a bad week."

Ruby couldn't put her finger on it exactly, but *something* was wrong here. Suddenly she knew. "You're having an affair!"

There was no mistaking the genuineness of Caro's smile. It showed how false the others had been. "Since Fred was born, I'd rather hit myself in the head with a jackhammer than have sex."

"Maybe that's your problem. I try to have sex at least twice a week, sometimes even with someone else."

Caro laughed. "Oh, Ruby, I missed you." She sounded normal now. "So what brought you racing to my door? You left Mom strapped to the wheelchair and ran screaming out of the house?" Caro grinned at her own black humor.

Ruby couldn't even smile. "I went to Dad's house today." She didn't know how to put a pretty spin on such ugliness, so she just said it. "When Nora left, Dad was having an affair."

Caroline sat back. "Oh, *that.*"

"You *knew?*"

"Everyone on the island knew."

"Not me. She's not who I thought she was, Caro. We're trapped in that house together, and I'm getting to know her. We talk."

"*You're* getting to know her?" Something passed through Caroline's eyes. If Ruby hadn't known better, she'd have called it envy. Suddenly Caro walked out of the room. A few minutes later she returned with a pack of cigarettes.

Ruby laughed. "Smoking? You're kidding, right?"

"No jokes, Ruby. Please." She opened the French doors and led Ruby to a seat at an umbrellaed table. A golf course stretched alongside the flowered yard.

Caroline pulled a cigarette from the pack and lit up. "I've been talking to Mom for years, meeting her now and then for lunch, calling her on Sunday mornings, being the daughter she expects, and we're polite strangers. And *you*"—she shot Ruby a narrowed gaze—"you, who treats her like Typhoid Mary, she talks to."

"Have you forgiven her?" Ruby asked. "I mean *really?*"

"I tried to forget it, you know? Most of the time I do, too. It's like it happened to another family, not mine."

A scream blared through the open window behind them.

Ruby jumped. "Good God. Has someone been shot?"

Caroline deflated. Her shoulders caved downward, and the color seemed to seep out of her cheeks. "The princess is up."

Ruby moved closer to her sister. "Are you okay?"

The smile was too fleeting to be real. "I'll be fine," Caro said. She got up and walked woodenly back into the house.

Ruby followed her. This time there were two screams.

"Go," Caro said with a tired smile. "Save yourself."

The screams were getting louder. Ruby fought the urge to cover her ears. "Let's go upstairs. I want to see my niece and nephew."

"Not when Jenny's in this mood." Caroline turned to her. "You'd better get going. The ferry lines are hell this time of day."

Ruby checked her watch. "You're right."

Caroline looped an arm around Ruby and guided her toward the door. "I'm sorry you had to find out about Dad, but maybe it'll help. We're human, Ruby. All of us. Just human."

Ruby hugged her sister. She had the strange thought that if she said anything except good-bye, Caro would simply shatter.

So good-bye was all she said.

NORA sat at the kitchen table staring down at the package of letters. Idly she rubbed her throbbing wrist. She'd spent an hour in the morning practicing with her crutches. By the end of the week she hoped to be out of the damned chair completely.

She'd tried giving herself a little pep talk. The letters were just words from strangers, she told herself. Certainly she could find the strength to pick up a pen and fashion some kind of response. Not true. Every response she'd attempted began, "I'm more sorry than you can know" or "How can I begin to say what's in my heart?"

But there was never a second sentence. And if all that wasn't bad enough, she was worried about Ruby. Her gaze landed on the note she'd found on the kitchen table: "Gone to Dad's."

It looked innocuous enough, but appearances were often deceiving. Ruby wasn't coming back. It was Nora's own fault. She'd pushed her younger daughter too hard in the past few days, and her daughter had had enough.

Nora heard a car drive up, footsteps on the porch. The door opened, and Rand stepped into the kitchen.

Nora understood instantly: Ruby had sent her father to deliver the bad news. "Hey, Randall," she said. "Have a seat."

He glanced around. "I've got a better idea." He crossed the room, scooped her into his arms, and carried her outside. He walked across the shaggy lawn to the edge of the bank and gingerly set her down beneath a huge madrona tree, then sat down beside her.

"Still can't stand to be inside on a sunny day?" she said.

"Some things never change." His face was solemn. "I'm sorry, Nora."

"About what?"

He stared at a point just beyond her left shoulder. "I should have said it a long time ago."

She drew in a breath. Time seemed to hang suspended between them. She smelled the familiar fragrance of the sea at low tide.

He looked at her finally, and in his dark eyes she saw the sad reflection of their life together. "I'm sorry," he said again, knowing that this time she understood. He touched her face. "It was *my* fault. All mine. I was young and stupid and cocky. I didn't know how special we were."

Nora was surprised by how easy it was to smile. Maybe that was all she'd needed all these years. Just those few, simple words. She finally felt at peace. "We were both at fault, Rand."

He leaned closer. She thought for a breathless moment that he was going to kiss her. But at the last second he drew back, gave her a smile so tender that it was better than a kiss. "That day you came back, I should have dropped to my knees and begged you to stay. In my heart I knew it was what I wanted, but I'd heard about you and that guy, and all I could think of was *me*. How would it look if I took you back after that?" He laughed—a bitter, harsh sound. "*Me*, worrying about that after the way I'd treated you. It makes me sick."

Nora reached out, brushed the hair from his eyes. "You've gone on now. Married. I'm happy for that." She realized how true it was. "And are you being a good boy, Randall?"

He laughed. "Even a stupid dog doesn't get hit by the same bus twice." He gazed at her. "I told Ruby the truth about us."

Nora felt sick. "That was a foolish thing to do."

"It's something I should have done a long time ago."

"Perhaps, but when you didn't—when I didn't—we buried that little piece of family history. You shouldn't have dug it up. It won't make a difference now."

"After all these years you deserved it, Nora," he said.

"Oh, Rand, she believed in you. This will break her heart."

"You know what I learned from us, Nora?" He touched her face. "Love doesn't die. And that's what Ruby's going to discover. She's always loved you. I just gave her a reason to admit it."

AFTER two hours of waiting for the ferry, Ruby remembered why she'd been so eager to move off-island. Timing your life around a state-operated transportation system was miserable.

Finally she drove aboard, and as the ferry left the dock, she adjusted her seat to a more comfortable position and closed her eyes. She still felt shaky, as if the foundation of her life had turned to warm Jell-O and was letting her sink.

I slept with other women.

One thing she knew: Her novelization of the past, with Dad cast as hero and her mother as villain, wouldn't work anymore.

She reached under the seat and pulled out the pen and legal pad she'd packed in the morning. She started to write.

> I was sixteen years old when my mother left us. It was an ordinary June day; the sun rode high in a robin's-egg blue sky. It's funny the things you remember.
>
> We were an average family. My father, Rand, was an islander through and through, a commercial fisherman who repaired boats in the off-season. It never occurred to any of us, or to me anyway, that he was anything less than the perfect father.

There was no yelling in our family, no raging arguments. I often look back on those quiet years, searching for an inciting incident, a moment where I could say, "Aha! There it is, the beginning of the end." But I never found one. Until now.

Today my parents pulled back the curtain, and my dad was revealed to be an ordinary man.

I didn't know that then, of course. All I knew was that on a beautiful day my mother dragged a suitcase into the living room. "I'm leaving. Is anyone coming with me?"

That's what she said to my sister and me.

That was the day I learned the concept of before and after. Her leaving sliced through our family with the precision of a scalpel. I saw what her absence did to my father. He drank; he smoked; he spent the day in his pajamas. He ate only when Caroline or I cooked for him. He let his business go to hell.

I formed an image of my mother that summer. From the hard stone of everything that happened, I carved the image of a woman and called it Mother. The statue was a collection of hard edges—selfishness, lies, and abandonment.

But now I know the truth: My father was unfaithful to my mother. He wore a wedding ring and had sex with women other than the one he'd sworn to love, honor, and protect.

My mother didn't leave him—and us—for fame and fortune, but simply because the man she loved had broken her heart.

Before she could finish, the ferry honked its horn. They were docking on Lopez. As soon as the ferry had unloaded a few cars, the boat would turn to Orcas Island. Summer Island was the last stop before the boat turned back to the mainland.

Ruby made a snap decision. She started the car, pulled out of line, bumped over the ramp, and drove off.

The Sloan house was only a few blocks from the ferry terminal. She pulled the minivan into the driveway. It was twilight now; a purple haze fell across the garden. Ruby walked up the pathway to the front door. She gathered her courage and knocked.

Lottie opened the door. She looked just as Ruby remembered her. "Ruby Elizabeth!" Lottie said, pulling her into a hug.

Ruby drew back, trying to maintain a smile. "I came to see Eric."

"He's upstairs. Dean had to fly to Seattle on business."

Ruby was relieved. "Can I go up?"

"Why, I'd beat you with a stick if you didn't."

Ruby took a deep breath and released it, then slowly mounted the stairs. She turned toward Eric's room. The door was closed. She gave it the tiniest push to open it. "Eric?"

"Ruby? Is that you?"

"It's me, buddy." She walked into his room.

Only sheer willpower kept her from gasping. His beautiful black hair was practically gone. Bruise-dark shadows circled his eyes. His cheekbones stood out above the pale, sunken flesh.

He gave her a smile that broke her heart. "I must be dead if Ruby Bridge is back on the island."

"I'm home," she said, looking away quickly.

"It's okay, Ruby," he said softly. "I know how I look."

Suddenly she couldn't pretend, couldn't make small talk. "I should have stayed in better touch with you. What happened between Dean and me—I shouldn't have let that extend to you."

"You broke his heart," Eric said softly.

"All of our hearts got broken that year, I guess, and the king's horsemen couldn't put us back together."

"What your mother did—it was really bad. But you're not sixteen anymore. You ought to be able to see things more clearly."

"Like what?"

"Come on, Ruby. The whole island knew your dad was screwing other women. Don't you think that makes a difference?"

So it was true: Everyone did know. "Caroline and I didn't do anything, and she left us, too."

There it was, the thing she still couldn't get past.

"You know who got me through those tough times when I first realized I was gay and my parents disowned me?"

"Dean?"

"Your mother. I wrote to her column, anonymously at first. She wrote back praising my bravery, telling me to keep my chin up, that my mom was sure to come around. It gave me hope. But after a few more years I knew she was wrong." He grabbed his wallet from the bedside table. Opening it, he withdrew a piece of paper and carefully unfolded it. "Here. Read this."

Ruby took the piece of paper from him. It was yellowed from age and veined with tiny fold lines.

Dear Eric:

    I can't express the depth of my sympathy for your pain. That you would choose to share it with me is an honor I do not take lightly.

    For me you will always be Eric, the rope-swing king. When I close my eyes, I see you hanging monkeylike from that old rope at Anderson Lake, yelling "Banzai!" as you let go. I remember a sixth-grade boy, his face reddened by new pimples, his voice sliding down the scale, who was never afraid to hold Mrs. Bridge's hand as they walked down the school corridor.

    This is who you are, Eric. Whom you choose to love is a part of you, but not the biggest part. I hope and pray that someday your mother will wake up and remember the very special boy she gave birth to, and smile at the man he has become. But if she does not, please don't let it tear your heart apart. You must go on. Life is full of people who are different, broken, hurting, who simply put one foot in front of the other and keep moving.

    It is your mother I fear for. If she continues on this path, it will eat her up from the inside. She will find that certain pains are endless. So forgive her. It is the only way to lighten this ache in your heart. Forgive her and go on.

    I love you, Eric Sloan. You and your brother are the sons I never had, and I am proud of who you've become.

                                 Nora

Ruby folded the letter back into a small triangle that fit in his wallet. "That's a beautiful letter."

"It saved me. Literally. It took lots of work, but I forgave my mom, and when I did that, my chest stopped hurting all the time." He smiled. "Forgive your mother, Ruby."

She looked down at him. "How do you forgive someone?"

"You just . . . let go. Unclench." He kissed the tips of his own fingers, then pressed the kiss to her cheek. "I love you, Ruby. Don't forget that."

"Never," she whispered. "Never."

THE next morning Ruby woke late. A shower made her feel almost human, and she stayed in it until the water turned lukewarm. Then she stepped out and through the mist saw herself in the mirror.

She experienced one of those rare moments when, for a split second, you see yourself through a stranger's eyes. Her hair was too short and raggedly cut. And what had made her choose to dye it Elvira Mistress of the Dark black? Ruby realized she'd been *trying* to make herself unattractive. All that mascara, the black eyeliner, the haircut and color—all of it was a camouflage.

She dropped her makeup bag in the metal trash can. It hit with a satisfying clang. No more heroin-chic makeup or refugee clothing. She'd even quit dyeing her hair and find out what color it really was. Her last memory was of a nice, ordinary chestnut brown.

The decision made her feel better. She dressed in jeans and a jade-green V-neck T-shirt, then hurried downstairs.

Nora was standing by the counter, leaning on her crutches. The plop-drip-plop of the coffeemaker filled the kitchen with steady sound. She looked up as Ruby entered the room. An almost comical look of surprise crossed her face. "You look . . . beautiful." She flushed. "I'm sorry. I shouldn't have sounded surprised."

"It's okay." Ruby laughed, and it felt good. "I guess I didn't look so great with all that makeup on. I need a haircut badly. Is there still a beauty salon in Friday Harbor?"

"I used to cut your hair."

Ruby hadn't remembered until that moment, but suddenly it came rushing back: Sunday evenings in the kitchen, a dishrag pinned around her neck with a clothespin, the soothing clip-clip-clip of the scissors. "Could you cut it again?"

"Of course. Get the stool from the laundry room and take it outside. It's such a pretty morning."

Ruby gathered up the necessary supplies and carried everything outside. She set the stool on a nice flat patch of grass overlooking the bay and sat down on it. She heard Nora coming toward her: Thump, step. Thump, step. Her mother moved around behind Ruby, wrapped a towel around Ruby's neck, and pinned it in place. "I'm just going to give it some shape."

The steady snip-snip-snip of the scissors seemed to hypnotize Ruby—that and the comforting familiarity of her mother's touch.

A few minutes later Nora said, "Ah, there we are." She stepped aside and handed Ruby a mirror.

Ruby looked at her reflection. She looked young again—a woman with most of her life ahead of her, instead of a bitter, struggling comic who'd left her youth sitting on a barstool. "It looks great," she said, turning to her mother.

Their eyes met, locked. Understanding passed between them.

"I went to see Dad yesterday."

"I know. He came to see me."

Ruby should have guessed. "We have to talk about it."

Nora sighed. "Yes." She bent down and retrieved her crutches. "I don't know about you, but I'll *definitely* need to sit down." Without waiting, she hobbled toward the porch.

Ruby followed. Nora sat on the love seat; Ruby chose the rocker.

"Dad told me he'd been unfaithful to you," Ruby said in a rush. "What else?"

"Well, he sort of blamed it on Vietnam, but I got the feeling he thought he would have fooled around anyway."

"Don't judge him too harshly, Ruby. His infidelity was only part of what broke us up. I needed so much reassurance and love, I sucked him dry. No man can fill up all the dark places in a woman's soul. I knew he'd be unfaithful sooner or later."

Ruby didn't understand. "You *knew* he'd be unfaithful?"

"You lived with a man. Did you expect him to be faithful?"

"Of course." Ruby said it quickly. Too quickly. Then she sighed and sat back. "No. I didn't expect him to want only me."

"Of course not. If a girl's mother doesn't love her enough to stick around, why should a man?" The smile Nora gave Ruby was sad. "That's the gift my father gave me, the one I passed on to you."

Ruby walked toward the railing and stared out at the Sound. "I remember the day you came back." She heard her mother's sharp intake of breath and turned around.

Nora was sitting there, hunched over, as if waiting for a blow. "I don't like thinking about that day."

"I'm sorry . . . Mom," Ruby said quietly. "I said some horrible things to you."

Tears filled her mother's eyes. "You called me *Mom*." She stood up, hobbled toward Ruby. "Don't feel guilty over what you said to me that day. You were a child, and I'd broken your heart."

"Why did you come home that day?"

"I missed you girls so much."

"I know why you left Dad, but why did you stay away?"

Nora gazed at her steadily. "The leaving, the staying away—to you these were the beginning of the story. To me it was deep into the middle." She took a deep breath and dove in. "Everyone thought Rand and I were the perfect couple. I was young then, and I cared about appearances more than substance. Living with an alcoholic will do that to you.

"It hurt me to suspect your dad of having affairs, but that wasn't the worst of it. The worst was his drinking. He started drinking after dinner, and by ten o'clock he was wobbly, and by eleven he was stumbling drunk. And he got mean. Every time he yelled at me, I heard my dad's voice, and though Rand never hit me, I started expecting it, flinching away from him, and that only made him madder." She went on, "So, you see, I was half of the problem. I couldn't separate my past from my present. But I was handling everything okay until Emmaline Fergusson told me about Shirley Comstock."

Ruby gasped. "My soccer coach?"

"It's a small island," Nora said ruefully. "There weren't a lot of women to choose from. He started drinking more and coming home less, and I fell apart. It started with insomnia. I simply stopped sleeping. Then the panic attacks hit. I got a prescription for Valium, but it didn't help. I would lie awake at night with my heart pounding and sweat pouring off me. Every time I picked you up from soccer, I went home and threw up. Finally I started to black out. I'd wake up lying on the kitchen floor, and I couldn't remember huge chunks of my day."

Nora wondered if it was possible to make a single twenty-seven-year-old woman understand how stifling marriage and motherhood could sometimes be. Then the early summer day she'd worked so hard to keep at bay welled up inside her. She'd gone to the soccer field early to drop off cookies, and she'd seen them—Rand and Shirley kissing right out in the open, as if they had every right. "I took too many sleeping pills. I don't remember if I meant to or if it was an accident, but when I woke up in the hospital, I knew that if I didn't do something quickly, I was going to die. So I packed my bag and ran. I only meant to stay away for a few days. I thought I'd come here, get some rest, and be healthy."

"And?"

Nora stared down at her hands. "And I met Vince Corell."

"The guy who sold the pictures to the *Tattler.*"

"He was a photographer, taking pictures of the islands for a calendar. He told me I was the most beautiful woman in the world. By then your father and I hadn't been intimate in a long time, and I *wasn't* beautiful. I was rail-thin, and I trembled all the time. When Vince touched me, I let him. We had a wonderful week together. For the first time I found someone I could talk to about my dreams, and once I'd said them aloud, I couldn't go back to the way I'd been living. And then he was gone.

"I was devastated. I knew your father would have heard about Vince. When the affair was over and I realized I'd thrown my marriage away and lost my girls, I took too many sleeping pills again. This time I ended up in a mental institution in Everett."

"How long were you there?" Ruby's voice was whisper-soft.

"Three months. It was Dr. Allbright who saved me. He came every day and talked to me. I worked so hard to get better so I could come home. But when I did—"

"Oh, God," Ruby said softly. "That was the day."

Nora felt tears sting her eyes. "It's not your fault," she said.

"But Dad should have let you come home."

"I didn't want my marriage back. I wanted . . . me. It's a horrible thing to say. But it's the only truth I can give you. The world is full of regrets and times where you think 'If only . . .' We have to move past that. Your dad was angry and arrogant. I was frightened and fragile. You were heartbroken. And on that one day we came together, and we hurt each other." She longed to take her daughter into her arms. "But I want you to know this, Ruby. I never stopped loving you or thinking about you. I never stopped missing you."

Ruby stared at her. Then softly she said, "I believe you."

And Nora knew the healing had finally begun.

Chapter Eight

RUBY retreated to her bedroom, opened the nightstand drawer, and pulled out her legal pad. She'd learned that it calmed her to write down her thoughts. She sat on the bed and drew her knees up, angling the pad against her thighs.

I'd always believed that the truth was easily spotted, a dark line on white paper. Now I wonder.

My mother was in a mental institution. This is her newest revelation. Tonight Mom painted a portrait of our family I'd never imagined—a drunken, unfaithful husband and a depressed, overwhelmingly unhappy wife. She was right to hide this truth from me. Even now I wish I didn't know it.

The phone rang. Ruby was startled by the sound. Tossing the pad aside, she leaned over and answered, "Hello?"

"Ruby?"

It was Caroline's voice, soft and thready. Ruby immediately felt the hairs on the back of her neck stand up. "What's wrong?"

"Wrong? Nothing. Can't a girl just call her little sister?"

"Of course. You just sounded . . . tired."

Caro laughed. "I have two small children. I'm *always* tired."

"Is motherhood really like that, Caro?"

Caroline was quiet for a minute. "I used to dream of going to Paris. Now I just want privacy when I use the toilet."

"How come we never talk about things like that?"

"There's nothing to say."

"Are you happy, Caro?"

"Happy? Of course I'm—" Caro started to cry.

The soft, heartbreaking sound tore at Ruby's heart. "Caro?"

"Sorry. Bad day in suburbia."

"Ruby!" It was Mom's voice. She must be at the bottom of the stairs.

Ruby held the phone to her chest. "I'll be right down. Hey, Caro," she said, coming back on the line. "Why don't you come up here? Spend the night."

"Oh, I can't. The kids—"

"Leave them with the stud muffin. It's not like you're stapled to the house."

Caroline's laughter was sharp. "That's exactly what it's like."

"Ruby! Can you hear me?" It was Mom's voice again.

Ruby accepted defeat. "I gotta go. I love you, big sis."

She hung up, then hurried downstairs. "Good God, is there a fire in the—" She skidded to a stop in the kitchen.

Dean was there, holding a bouquet of Shasta daisies.

"Oh," Ruby said, feeling heat climb into her face.

Mom stood beside the table grinning. "You have a visitor."

Dean handed Ruby the flowers. "We need to talk." His voice matched the soft pleading in his eyes. "Please."

The way he said it made her shiver. "Okay."

They stood there, staring at each other. Finally Mom thumped toward them and gently tugged the flowers out of Ruby's hand. "I'll put them in water," she said.

"Thanks, Mom."

Ruby turned to Dean. He gave her a quick smile; then they headed out the door.

Outside, there were two bicycles. Ruby stopped. "You've obviously confused me with a woman who likes to sweat."

He smiled. "Too old to ride a bike, Rube? Or too out of shape?"

He *knew* she couldn't refuse a challenge. She grabbed the handlebars and yanked the bike around. "Lead on."

Dean jumped on his bike and pedaled on ahead of her out of the driveway. Ruby sped up to him. Soon they were flying, racing side by side down the long, two-lane road. Golden pastures studded with apple trees rushed past them. The road wound into a long, even S curve and into the entrance of Trout Lake State Park.

Ruby should have known he'd bring her here. "No fair, Dino," she said softly, wondering if he even heard her.

He did. "What's that they say about love and war?"

"Which one is this?"

"That's up to you."

Ruby jumped off her bike and set it against a wooden bike rack, then walked toward the lake. She had forgotten how beautiful it was here. The heart-shaped sapphire-blue lake was surrounded by lush green trees and rimmed in granite. A ribbon of water cascaded over the "giant's lip"—a flat, jutting rock at the top of the cliffs— and splashed onto the placid surface of the lake.

Dean came up beside her. "Are you up for a climb?"

"Lead on."

Side by side, they walked around to the western side of the lake, through the hoard of picnickers, Frisbee-catching dogs, and screaming children. When they reached the heavy fringe of trees, they left the people behind. The gurgling, splashing sound of falling water grew louder and louder.

The trail was rocky and narrow, corkscrewing straight up through the trees. Finally they reached the top—the giant's lip. It was a slab of gray granite as big as a swimming pool and as flat as a quarter. Thick green moss furred the stone.

Ruby stepped onto the rock and saw the picnic basket. It was sitting on a familiar plaid blanket, which Dean had carefully spread out on a spot where the moss was several inches thick.

They sat down, and Ruby leaned back on her elbows. "We used to come up here all the time."

"This is where you first told me you were going to be a comedian. You said you wanted to be famous."

"I still do. And you wanted to be a prizewinning photographer." She didn't look at him. It was better to stay separate, as if they were just two old high school friends.

"I still wish for it. If I could, I'd throw everything away and start over. Money sure doesn't make you happy."

A quiet settled between them, and she was vaguely afraid of what he would say, so she said, "I saw Eric yesterday."

"He told me. It really meant a lot to him."

"I wish I'd stayed in better touch with him."

"*You?* I'm his brother, and I hadn't seen him in years."

That surprised Ruby. She rolled onto her side. "You guys were always so close."

He stared up at the sky. "I seem to have a problem with really knowing the people I love. I get blindsided."

"You're talking about his being gay?"

He looked at her. "That's part of what I'm talking about."

She understood and knew it was time. For more than ten years she'd sworn to herself that if she ever got the chance with Dean, she would say the thing that mattered. "I'm sorry, Dean," she said. "I didn't want to hurt you."

He rolled onto his side, facing her. "You didn't want to hurt me? Ruby, you were my whole world. I tried to take care of you after your mom left, but it was hard. You were constantly picking a fight with me. But I kept loving you."

Ruby didn't know how to explain it to him. "You believed in something I didn't. Every time I closed my eyes at night, I dreamed about you leaving me."

"What made you so sure I would leave you?"

"Come on, Dean, we were kids. I knew you'd go off to some college I couldn't afford and forget about me."

Their faces were close, and if she'd let herself, she could have lost her way in the blue sea of his eyes.

"So you dumped me before I had a chance to dump you."

She smiled sadly. "Pretty much. Now let's change the subject. Tell me about your life. How is it to be a jet-setting bachelor?"

"What if I said I still love you?"

Ruby gasped. "Don't say that . . . please."

He took her face in his hands, gently forced her to look up at him. "Did you stop loving me, Ruby?"

She wanted to say *Of course; we were just kids,* but when she opened her mouth, the sound she made was a quiet sigh of surrender. His lips brushed against hers, and she melted against him, moaning his name as his hand curled around the back of her neck. It was the kind of kiss they'd never shared before, the kind of achingly lonely kiss a pair of teenagers couldn't imagine.

When he drew back, he said, "I've waited a long time for a second chance with you, Ruby."

She battled a wave of helplessness. She wished desperately to have grown up, to have been profoundly changed by all that she'd seen and learned in the past days. But it wasn't that easy. Her fear of abandonment was so deep, she couldn't get past it. She'd discovered a long time ago why the poets called it falling in love. It was a plunging, eye-watering descent, and she'd lost her ability to believe that anyone would catch her. She pushed him away. "I can't do this. It's too much too fast. You've always wanted too much from me."

"Damn it, Ruby," he said. "Have you grown up at all?"

"I won't hurt you again," she said.

He touched her face. "Ah, Rube, just looking at you hurts me."

DEAN FOLLOWED RUBY BACK down the trail. Though they didn't talk, the forest was alive with sounds. Birds squawked and chirped in the trees overhead, squirrels chattered, water splashed.

At the park, he tossed the picnic basket—still filled with a lunch unpacked and uneaten—in the trash can. Curling the heavy blanket around his shoulders, he climbed tiredly onto his bike.

When they reached the summerhouse, he pulled off to the side of the road and got off his bike.

Ruby stopped and turned to him. "I guess this is good-bye."

The crack in her voice gave him hope. "For now," he said.

"It was just a kiss. Don't turn it into *Gone With the Wind*."

He took a step toward her. "You must have confused me with one of your Hollywood idiot boys."

She wanted to move backward. "Wh-what do you mean?"

Now he was close enough to touch her, but he stood still. "I know you, Ruby. You can pretend all you want, but that kiss meant something. Tonight we'll both lie in bed and think about it."

Ruby flushed. "You knew a teenager a decade ago. That doesn't mean you know *me*."

He smiled. "You might have built a wall around your heart, but somewhere, deep inside, you're still the girl I fell in love with." At last he touched her cheek—a fleeting caress.

Her mouth trembled. "I'm afraid."

"The girl I knew wasn't afraid of anything."

"That girl's been gone for years."

"Isn't there some part of her left?"

She stood there a long time, staring up at him.

He knew she wasn't going to answer. "Okay," he said, "I'll concede this round." He climbed onto his bike and started to go.

"Wait."

He stumbled off his bike so fast, he almost fell. It clattered to the ground as he spun back to face her.

She took a step closer. "You sound so sure."

He smiled. "You taught me love, Ruby. Every time you held my hand, I learned a little more about it. Maybe when we were kids, I took that for granted, but I've spent a lot of years alone, and every date I went on only proved again how special we were."

"My parents were special," she said slowly.

It saddened him, knowing how her heart, once so open and pure, had been trampled by the people who should have protected it. "Okay, love hurts. But what about loneliness?"

"I'm not lonely." She stepped away from him. Without a backward look she jumped on her bike and rode away.

"Go ahead," he called. "Run away. You can only go so far."

RUBY walked into the kitchen and found her mother at the stove stirring something in an old iron pot.

"Ruby," Nora said, looking up in surprise, "I didn't expect you back so soon." She glanced at the door. "Where's Dino?"

The kitchen smelled of pot roast, slow-cooking all day with carrots and oven-browned potatoes. Homemade biscuits were rising on the counter. And unless Ruby missed her guess, that was vanilla custard Mom was stirring. She'd made Ruby's all-time favorite dinner.

Ruby didn't know which hurt more—the effort her mother had made to please her or the fact that Dean wasn't here to share it.

"Dean went home," she said.

A frown darted across her mother's face. She turned off the burner. "What happened?"

"I don't know. I guess we started something we couldn't finish. Or maybe we finished something we'd started a long time ago."

"This won't be like Max," her mother said.

"I love Dean," Ruby admitted. "But that's not enough. It wouldn't last anyway."

"Love is nothing without faith."

"I lost that faith a long time ago."

"Can you let yourself jump without a net? Because that's what love is, what faith is. You're looking for a guarantee, and those come with auto parts. Not love."

It felt good to talk to her mother this way—as friends. It was something Ruby had never imagined. She'd *missed* her mother so much that the only way she'd been able to go on in the world was to pretend she was alone.

I'm not alone anymore. That one sentence, once thought, formed a road that led Ruby to herself. *I can't write the article.*

"I've got to go upstairs," she said suddenly, seeing the surprise on her mother's face. Ruby didn't care. She ran upstairs, went to the phone, and dialed Val's number.

Maudeen answered on the second ring.

"Hi, Maudeen. It's Ruby Bridge. Is the Great Oz in?"

Maudeen laughed. "No. He's in New York, but he's calling in."

"Okay. Tell him I won't be delivering my article."

"Oh, my. You'd better give me your address and phone number again. He'll want to talk to you."

Ruby gave out the information, then hung up. She reached for her writing pad and slowly began to write.

> I have just called my agent. When he calls back, I will tell him that I can't turn in this article. I never thought about what it meant to write an exposé on my own mother.
>
> I dreamed. I imagined. I saw myself on *Leno*—a witty, charming guest plugging her own skyrocketing career. I never noticed that I'd be standing on my mother's broken back to reach the microphone. But my dreams were all about me, and now I know what the price of my selfish actions will be.
>
> As I write, I am reminded of that passage from the Bible— the one that is read at every wedding: *When I was a child, I spake as a child, I understood as a child, I thought as a child.*
>
> Now I understand as an adult. Maybe for the first time in my life. This article would break my mother's heart. That didn't matter to me a week ago; in fact, I wanted to hurt her then.
>
> I can't do it anymore—not to her and not to me. For the first time I have drawn back the dark curtain of anger and seen the bright day beyond. I can be my mother's daughter again. She is the keeper of my past. She knows the secret moments that have formed me, and even with all that I have done to her, she still loves me. Will anyone else ever love me so unconditionally?

IN FRIDAY HARBOR ON SAN Juan Island, the marina was a hive of activity—boats coming in and going out, kids racing along the docks. The downtown area was an eclectic mix of art galleries, souvenir shops, gift emporiums, and restaurants.

Dean walked aimlessly up and down the streets. Today had depressed him, and it shouldn't have. Nothing had ever been easy with Ruby. Love would be the most difficult of all.

He heard the ferry's horn and knew it was time to get down to the dock. He jumped on his bike, raced downhill, and followed the last car onto the boat.

On Lopez, he stopped by the grocery store and bought a few things. Then he pedaled home as fast as he could. When he reached the house, he hurried up the stairs to Eric's room.

"Hey, bro," Eric said. "How was your bike ride?"

Dean went to him. "Guess what I bought?" He opened a small blue insulated bag and withdrew a melting Popsicle.

Eric's eyes widened. "A Rainbow Rocket. I didn't think they still made them."

Dean unwrapped the soggy white wrapper and handed his brother the dripping multicolored Popsicle. Eric made groaning sounds of pleasure as he licked it. When he finished, he set the gooey stick on the bedside tray. "That was great," he said. "I'd forgotten how much I loved those things."

"I remembered. I've been remembering a lot of things lately." Dean leaned over the bedrail. "I went to see Ruby today."

"And?"

"Let's just say the door hit me in the ass on the way out."

Eric laughed. "That's our Ruby. Never gives an inch. So when is round two?"

Dean sighed. "I don't know. Maybe something will happen tomorrow when we all go sailing."

"Well, I hope it works out fast. I wanted to be the best man at your wedding."

"You will be." Dean struggled to keep his voice even. Their eyes met, and in his brother's gaze he saw the sad truth. They both knew

Eric would not be putting on a tuxedo and standing in shiny shoes beside Dean at the altar.

"I'm glad you came home, Dino. I couldn't have done this without you." Eric reached out. His pale, blue-veined hand covered Dean's. He smiled tiredly and closed his eyes, and Dean could see that he was losing his brother to sleep once again. "Since you're back, I dream again. It's nice." Eric's voice was barely a whisper.

"Dream," Dean said softly, placing his brother's hand on top of the blanket. "Dream of who you would have been and who you were—the bravest, smartest, best brother a kid ever had."

AFTER dinner Nora went out to the porch and sat in her favorite rocking chair. In this magical hour, poised between day and night, the sky was the soft hue of a girl's ballet slipper.

The screen door squeaked open and banged shut. "I brought you some tea," Ruby said, stepping into the porch light's glow.

"Thanks," Nora said. "Join me."

Before Ruby could sit down, she heard the sound of a car driving up. It parked, and a door slammed shut. Ruby glanced toward the garden. "Are we expecting someone?"

"No."

Footsteps rattled on gravel. A rusty gate creaked open. Someone thumped up the porch steps and walked into the light.

Nora stared up at her elder daughter in shock, wondering what had brought her here. It was unlike her daughter to do anything spontaneously. "Caroline?" she whispered.

"I don't *believe* it!" Ruby pulled her sister into a fierce hug.

Nora got awkwardly to her feet and limped forward. "Hey, Caro. It's good to see you."

Caroline drew back from Ruby's embrace. "Hello, Mother." Her smile seemed forced. It wasn't surprising—even as a child, she'd been able to smile when her heart was breaking.

Nora studied Caroline. She was flawlessly dressed in a pair of white linen pants and a rose-colored silk blouse. Not a strand of silvery blond hair was out of place. And yet in all that perfection there was a strange undercurrent of fragility. As if she were hiding some tiny, hairline crack.

Ruby peered around her sister's shoulder. "Where are the kids?"

"I left them with Jere's mom for the night." She glanced nervously at Nora. "It's just me. I hope that's okay."

"Are you *kidding?* I begged you to come," Ruby said.

She looped an arm around her sister's narrow shoulders. The two women moved into the house, their heads tilted together. Nora limped along behind them.

In the living room, Caro turned toward Nora. She offered a smile that didn't reach her eyes. "Would you like to see the newest photos of your grandchildren?"

"We could start there," Nora said. "But if we really want to get to know each other, it will take more than pictures."

Caroline paled, then went on seamlessly. "Good." She unzipped her overnight bag and took out a flat photo album. She went to the sofa and sat down. Ruby rushed over and sat beside her, and Nora sat down on the other side of Caroline.

Slowly Caroline opened the book. The first photograph was an eight-by-ten color shot of her wedding. In it Caroline stood tall, sheathed in an elegant beaded-silk off-the-shoulder gown. Jere was beside her, breathtakingly handsome in a black Prada tuxedo.

"Sorry," Caro said quickly. "The new photos are in the back." She started to turn the page.

Nora boldly laid her hand on top of Caroline's. "Wait."

Who gives this woman to be married to this man? When the priest had asked that question, it had been Rand alone who'd answered, *I do.* Nora had been in the back of the church, doing her best not to weep. It should have been *We do—her mother and I.*

Nora had been there for Caroline's wedding, but she hadn't *been* there. Caroline had invited her, placed her at a table reserved for special guests, but not family. Nora had known that she was a detail to her daughter on that day, no more or less important than the floral arrangements. And Nora, lost in her own guilt, had thanked God for even that.

Who had acted as Caroline's mother on that day? Who had sewn the last-minute beads on Caro's dress or taken her shopping for ridiculously expensive lingerie? Who had held her one last time as an unmarried young woman and whispered, "I love you"?

Nora drew her hand back, and Caroline quickly turned another page. "This is our honeymoon. We went to Kauai."

Nora noticed that Caroline's fingers were trembling. "You look so happy," she said gently.

"We were."

Nora saw the sadness stamped on her daughter's face. And she knew. "Oh, Caro . . ."

"Enough honeymoon shots," Ruby said. "Where are the kids?"

Caroline turned to a photograph of a hospital room. She was in bed, and for once, her hair was a mess. She held a tiny baby in her arms. Here at last was a genuine smile.

Nora should have seen that smile in person, but she hadn't. Oh, she'd visited Caroline in the hospital, of course. She had come bearing an armload of expensive gifts. She'd commented to her daughter on how pretty the baby was . . . and then she'd left.

Nora hadn't been there when Caroline realized how terrifying motherhood was. Who had said to her, *It's okay, Caro—God made you for this.* No one.

Nora clamped a hand over her mouth, but it was too late. A small noise escaped. She felt the tears streak down her cheeks. She tried to hold her breath, but it broke into little gasps.

"Mom?" Caroline said, looking at her.

Nora couldn't meet her daughter's gaze. "I'm sorry."

Caroline was quiet. Nora didn't realize that her daughter was crying until a tear splashed onto the album.

"That was the day I missed you most," Caroline said. Another tear fell. "I remember the first night. Jenny was in a bed beside me. I kept reaching out for her, touching her little fingers. I dreamed you were standing beside my bed, telling me it would be okay, not to be afraid. But I always woke up alone."

Nora swallowed hard. "Oh, Caro, there aren't enough words in this galaxy to say how sorry I am for what I did to you and Ruby."

Caroline let Nora take her in her arms.

Nora's heart cracked open like an egg. She was crying so hard, she started to hiccup. When Nora drew back, she saw Ruby, her face pale. Only her eyes revealed emotion; they were shimmering with unshed tears.

Ruby stood up. "We need to drink."

Caroline wiped her eyes self-consciously. "I don't drink."

"Since when? At the junior prom you—"

"It's a dozen lovely memories like that one that keep me sober. In college Jere used to call me E.D., for easy drunk."

"E.D.? *E.D.?* Oh, this is too good. I'm twenty-seven years old, and I haven't gotten drunk with my sister since before it was legal. Tonight we're changing all that."

Nora laughed. "The last time I drank, I drove into a tree."

"Don't worry. I won't let you drive," Ruby promised.

Caroline laughed. "Okay. One drink. *One.*"

Ruby did a cha-cha-cha toward the kitchen, threw back her head, and said, "Margaritas!" Before Nora had figured out how to start another conversation with Caroline, Ruby was back, in the living room with glasses that could have doubled as Easter baskets.

Nora took her drink, then laughed out loud when Ruby went to the record player, picked an album, and put it on.

"*We will, we will, rock you . . .*" blared through the old speakers. Ruby had the volume so high, the windows rattled.

She took a laughing gulp of her drink, slammed it down on the coffee table, then snapped a hand toward Caroline. "Come on, dance with Hollywood's worst comic."

Caroline grabbed Ruby's hand and let herself be pulled into a twirl. Nora cautiously sipped her cocktail. Her daughters looked so happy and carefree, it actually hurt Nora's heart.

The girls danced and drank and laughed together until Caroline held up her hands. "No more, Ruby. I'm getting dizzy."

"Ha! You're not dizzy enough. That's your problem." She handed her sister her margarita. "Bottoms up."

Caroline wiped the damp hair off her face. "Oh, what the hell." She drank the rest of her margarita without stopping, then held out the empty glass. "Another one, please."

"Yee ha!" Ruby danced into the kitchen.

On the stereo the next album dropped down—an old album by the Eurythmics. "*Sweet dreams are made of this . . .*" pulsed through the speakers.

Caroline stumbled unsteadily to one side and held her hand out. "Dance with me, Mom."

"If I step on your foot, I'll break every bone."

Caroline laughed. "Don't worry. I'm anesthetized." The last word came out hopelessly mangled, and Caroline laughed again. "Drunk," she said sternly. *"Drunk."*

Nora grabbed a crutch and limped over to Caroline. She slipped one arm around her daughter's tiny waist and used the crutch for support. Slowly they began to sway from side to side.

"This is the song I had them play at my wedding, remember?"

Nora nodded. She was going to say something impersonal, but then she noticed the way Caroline was looking at her. "Do you want to talk about it?" Nora asked gently.

"Talk about what?"

Nora stopped dancing. "Your marriage."

Caroline's beautiful face crumpled. Her mouth quavered. "Oh, Mom, I wouldn't know where to start."

Ruby spun into the room, singing, "Margaritas for the senoras." She saw Nora and Caro standing there and stopped in her tracks. "I leave you two for five minutes, and the waterworks start again."

Caroline took an unsteady step backward. She looked from Nora to Ruby and back to Nora. She was weeping silently, and it was a heart-wrenching sight. It was the way a woman wept in the middle of a dark night with her husband beside her in bed.

"I wasn't going to tell you," Caro said in a broken voice.

Ruby stepped toward her, hand outstretched.

"Don't touch me!" Caro said. "I'll fall apart if you touch me, and I'm so damn sick of falling apart, I could scream."

Caroline sank slowly to her knees on the floor. Ruby sat down beside her, and Nora followed awkwardly.

"Have you and Jere talked about this?" Nora asked.

Caroline shook her head. "I can't tell him. We're always going in different directions. I feel like a single parent most of the time. And I'm lonely. I'm so lonely sometimes, I can't stand it."

"I know what you're going through, believe me," Nora said. "You're at that place where your own life overwhelms you and you can't see a way to break free. And you're suffocating."

Caroline drew in a gulping, hiccuping breath. Her eyes rounded. "How did you know that?"

Nora touched her cheek. "I know," was all she said for now. "Is Jere seeing another woman?"

"Everyone always said he was just like Daddy." Caroline wiped her eyes. "I'm going to leave him."

"Do you love him?" Nora asked gently.

Caroline went pale. Her lower lip trembled. "So much . . ."

Nora's heart felt as if it were breaking. Here was another legacy of her motherhood: She'd taught her children that marriages were disposable. "Let me tell you what it's like, this decision you think you've made," she said to Caroline. "When you leave a man you love, you feel like your heart is splitting in half. You lie in your lonely bed, and you miss him. You drink your coffee in the morning, and you miss him. You get a haircut, and all you can think is that no one will notice but you. But that's not the worst of it. The worst is what you do to your children. You tell yourself it's okay—divorces happen all the time, and your children will get over it. Maybe that's true if the love is really gone from your marriage. But if you still love him and you leave him without trying to save your family, you will . . . break. You don't just cry in the middle of the night. You cry forever, all the time, until your insides are so dry, there are no tears left, and then you learn what real pain is."

Nora knew that what she was saying wasn't true for all marriages. But she was certain that Caroline hadn't tried hard enough, not yet, not if she loved Jere. "Maybe you even find a career that makes you rich and famous. But you find out it doesn't matter. You know that somewhere your daughters are out there, holding someone else's hand, crying on someone else's shoulder. And every single day, you live with what you did to them. Don't make my mistake," Nora said fiercely. "*Fight.* Fight for your love and your family. In the end, it's all there is, Caroline. All there is."

Caroline whispered, "What if I lose him anyway?"

"Ah, Caro," Nora said, "what if you find him again?"

Chapter Nine

*T*HE next morning, Nora woke feeling refreshed and rejuvenated. Almost young again. She thanked God that she'd sipped a single margarita all night.

In the living room, she saw the relics of last night's blowout: three glasses—each with at least an inch of slime-green liquid in the bottom—an ashtray filled with the cigarettes Caroline had furtively smoked, a pile of discarded record albums. For the first time this summer, the house looked lived in.

Nora limped upstairs. The bedroom door was closed, and she pushed it open. Caroline and Ruby were still sleeping. They looked young and vulnerable. Caroline slept curled in a ball, her body pressed to the mattress's edge. Ruby, on the other hand, lay spread-eagle, her arms and legs flung out above the bedding.

Nora walked to the bed. Slowly she reached down and caressed Ruby's pink, sleep-lined cheek. "Wake up, sleepyheads."

Ruby blinked awake, smacking her lips together as if she could still taste the last margarita. "Hi, Mom."

Caro awakened beside her, stretching her arms. She saw Nora and tried to sit up. Halfway there, she groaned and flopped backward. "Oh, my God, my head is swollen."

Nora clapped her hands. "Get a move on, girls. We're going sailing today with Dean and Eric. Remember, Ruby? Lottie has dinner planned for us around seven."

Caroline turned green. "Sailing?" She rolled out of bed and dropped onto the floor, landing on all fours. Then she crawled toward the bathroom. At the door she hauled herself upright and gave Ruby a pained smile. "First in the shower!"

Ruby sagged forward. "Don't use all the hot water."

Nora smiled. "It's like old times around here. I'm going to start breakfast and pack us a light lunch. Dean's supposed to bring the boat around eleven."

She turned and headed downstairs, thumping down each step. She was halfway down when she heard a car drive up. She made it into the kitchen just as a rattling knock struck the door. She opened it.

Standing on her porch was one of the best-looking young men she'd ever seen. Though she hadn't seen him since the wedding, she'd recognize her son-in-law anywhere. "Hi, Jeremy," she said, smiling.

He looked surprised. "Nora?"

"I guess it's a shock to realize you have a mother-in-law." She took a step backward, motioning for him to come inside.

He smiled tiredly. "Given my other shocks in the past twenty-four hours, that's nothing."

Nora nodded. "Caro is upstairs. I'll get her. You wait here."

"I'm here."

Nora and Jere both spun around. Caroline stood there, wearing the same silk and linen clothes from last night, only now they were wrinkled beyond recognition. Flecks of caked mascara turned her eyes into twin bruises. "Hi, Jere," she said softly. "I heard your voice."

Ruby came stumbling down the stairs and rammed into her sister. "Sorry, Caro, I—" She saw Jeremy and stopped.

Jere walked over to Caroline. "Care?"

The tenderness in his voice told Nora all she needed to know. There might be trouble between Caro and Jere, but underneath all that there was love, and with love they had a chance.

"You shouldn't have come," Caro said, crossing her arms.

"No," he said softly. "You shouldn't have left. Not without talking to me first. Can you imagine how I felt when I got your letter that says you'll be back when you feel like it?" His voice cracked.

Caro looked up at him. "I thought you'd be glad I left, and I couldn't stand to see that."

"Come home," he whispered. "Mom's watching the kids for the rest of the weekend."

Caroline smiled. "She'll be bleeding from her ears before tomorrow morning."

"That's *her* problem. We need some time alone."

"Okay." Caroline went upstairs. She came down a minute later with her overnight bag. She enfolded Ruby in a fierce hug, then walked across the kitchen to Nora. "Thanks," she said quietly. "I won't miss you anymore."

"No way. You can't get rid of me now. I love you, Caro."

"And I love you, Mom." Nora pulled her daughter into her arms and held her tightly, then slowly released her.

Jeremy took the overnight bag from his wife, then held on to her hand. Together they left the house.

Ruby and Nora watched as the gray Mercedes followed the white Range Rover out of the driveway.

Ruby sidled up to Nora. "I'm sorry, Mom."

Nora turned to face her daughter. "For what?"

"For all the presents I sent back and all the years I stayed away. But mostly I'm sorry for being so unforgiving."

Nora wasn't sure how it happened, but suddenly they were clinging to each other, laughing and crying at the same time.

AT EXACTLY eleven a boat horn blared—a loud a*h-oo-gah, ah-oo-gah*. The *Wind Lass* pulled up to the dock.

Ruby glanced toward the water, watching Dean tie the boat down. "They're here." There was a strand of worry in her voice. She hoped that she could find the courage today to tell Dean that she wanted to love and be loved.

Nora understood. "Are you afraid to see Dean?"

Ruby nodded.

"You could travel the world, and you wouldn't find a better man than Dean Sloan. Just let go. Have fun. Let yourself remember the good times, not only the bad."

Ruby looked at her. "I want that so much."

The sailboat honked its horn again.

"Grab the picnic basket," Nora said.

Within minutes they were headed down the path to the beach. Dean was on the bow of the boat. "Welcome aboard."

Nora stepped carefully onto the boat. She took her crutches and tossed them belowdecks. Then, limping awkwardly, she sidled around the giant silver wheel and sat down beside Eric. A pillow rested behind his head, and a blanket covered his body. Although he was smiling, he looked terribly pale and weak. Nora curled an arm around him gently and drew him close.

Dean started the engine. Ruby untied the boat and jumped aboard. They motored out of the bay, and when they passed the tip of the island, Dean rigged up the mainsail. The boat immediately heeled starboard, caught a gust of wind, and sliced through the water.

Eric pressed his face into the wind, smiling brightly. Nora tilted her head against his and stared out at the lush green islands. Ruby was standing on the bow. Nora didn't have to see her daughter's face to know that she was grinning.

Eric looked at Ruby, then at Dean. They were the full boat length apart, each trying not to get caught staring at the other. He said to Nora, "You think they'll figure it out?"

"I hope so. They need each other."

A swift breeze rose suddenly, filling the canvas sail with a tharumping noise.

Dean looked at Eric. "Do you want to take the wheel?"

Eric's face lit up. "Oh, yeah."

Dean slipped an arm around his brother's frail body and helped him hobble toward the wheel. Eric took hold. Dean stood behind and beside him, keeping him steady.

Wind tears streaked across Eric's temples, and his thinning hair flapped against the sides of his face. "I'm the queen of the world!" he yelled, flinging his arms out. He laughed, and for the first time in weeks it was *his* laughter, not the weak, watered-down version that cancer had left him with.

Nora knew that when she looked back on Eric's life, she would picture him now—standing tall, squinting into the sun, laughing.

WHEN they got back to the house, Lottie served them a delicious dinner of Dungeness crabs, Caesar salad, and French bread. They'd descended on dinner like *Survivor* contestants. Eric had even managed to eat a few tender, buttery bites.

While "the girls" washed and dried the dishes, Dean carried Eric up to bed. Finally Nora and Ruby went upstairs, and they all stood around Eric's bed talking softly until he fell asleep.

Now the three of them were back on the *Wind Lass,* headed for Summer Island. The trip, being undertaken at night, took twice the usual amount of time. And still Ruby hadn't found the courage to hand Dean her heart. All day she'd waited for the Moment, when she could turn to him and say she wasn't afraid anymore. She was still waiting when the *Wind Lass* glided up to the Bridges' dock.

"Get the lines, Ruby," Dean yelled.

She grabbed the lines and jumped onto the dock. She was tying the boat down when her mother stepped onto the dock. "Thanks, Dean," she heard her mother say. "Ruby? Honey, I'll need some help up to the house. The bank is slippery."

Ruby shot a glance at the boat; it was all shadows. She couldn't see Dean. What if he left before she could get back?

"Ruby?"

She dropped the excess line and headed toward her mother. And there he was, beside the wheel. She could make out his golden hair and yellow sweater. "Bye," he said in a subdued voice.

"Uh, if you need help leaving—you know, untying or something—I could come right back down," Ruby said.

There was a pause before he answered, "I can always use help."

Ruby felt a rush of relief. She took hold of her mother's shoulders, and together they walked up the bank and across the lawn.

At the front door, Mom smiled. "Go ahead. And Ruby?"

Ruby reached down for the afghan on the rocker and slung it around her shoulders. It was getting chilly out here. "Yeah?"

"He loves you. Try not to be your usual obnoxious self."

Ruby couldn't help laughing. "Thanks, Mom."

She hurried across the yard. At the edge of the bank she paused. Dean was standing at the end of the dock with his back to her. She moved soundlessly down the bank and stepped onto the dock. Her footsteps were indistinguishable from the creaks and moans of old wood. "I remember when we used to jump off of this dock at high tide," she said softly.

He spun around.

She was afraid to speak. She wanted to simply put her arms around him and kiss him. But she couldn't do it. For once, she had to do the right thing. She owed Dean a few words—small, simple words—and she couldn't be too cowardly to speak. "I remember the first time you kissed me. I got so dizzy, I couldn't breathe. I was glad we were sitting down, because I would have fallen. But I fell anyway, didn't I? I fell in love with my best friend. When we were seven, you promised that someday we'd own a boat as big as a ferry, with a bathtub in the master stateroom, and that Elvis would sing at our wedding." She gave him a smile. "We should have known we were in trouble when Elvis died."

Dean closed his eyes, and she wondered if it hurt Dean to hear the old dreams. "Yeah," he said woodenly. "We were young."

"I tried to forget how it felt when you kissed me," she said. "I kept telling myself it was a crush, that I'd grow up and go on and feel that way again. But I didn't." She was exposed now, vulnerable.

"You never fell in love again?"

"How could I . . . when I never fell out of love the first time?"

"Say it."

She tilted her face up to his. "I love you, Dean Sloan."

He didn't respond for a heartbeat, just stared down at her. Then he pulled her into his arms and kissed her the way she'd always dreamed of being kissed. And suddenly she wanted more. More . . .

She fumbled with his T-shirt, shoved it over his head, and let her fingers explore the hair on his chest. She moved her hands across the hardness of his shoulders, down the small of his back.

He yanked the afghan down, letting it puddle on the dock around their feet. With a groan he slipped his hands beneath her shirt, scooped it off her, and tossed it away.

Kissing and groping, they knelt on the blanket, then collapsed on top of it, laughing at their awkward movements. And then he was kissing her again, and she couldn't think. Her body was on fire. His hands were everywhere, and Ruby gave in to sex in a way she never had before.

She threw her head back and closed her eyes. . . .

AFTERWARD she buried her face in his chest.

He held on to her tightly. "We should have done that a long time ago."

"Believe me, it wouldn't have been as good." She rolled onto her side and stared at him. "Let's live together."

He gave her a strange look. "In Hollyweird?"

"No way." She didn't want to live there anymore. "I could live in San Francisco."

He laughed. "No, thanks." He reached up, touched her hair. "We've had those lives, Ruby. I don't know about you, but I don't want to go back to anything that came before. I want to start over. And I'm *not* going to live with you."

She felt as if he'd stomped on her heart. "Oh."

"We're getting married, Ruby Elizabeth. No more excuses or running away. My vote is that we move back here and try to find out what we want to do with the rest of our lives. I'm going to give photography a try. It's what I've always wanted to do. Most importantly, we're going to grow old together."

"We'll have children," she said, dreaming of it for the first time.

"At least two, so they'll each have a best friend."

"And our son—we'll name him Eric."

RUBY WOULD HAVE SLEPT ON the dock all night, wrapped in Dean's arms and that old blanket, but he wanted to get back to Eric, and so they kissed—and kissed and kissed—good-bye. Then she helped him untie the boat and walked to the top of the bank to watch him leave.

After Dean's boat disappeared into the choppy silver-tipped sea, Ruby turned and went to the house. The kitchen light was on, and Mom's bedroom door was closed. She was just about to knock when the phone rang. She ran for the kitchen and answered the phone. "Hello?"

"Ruby, where have you been? I've been calling all night."

"Val?" She glanced at the clock. It was one in the morning.

"What is this about you not turning in the article?"

"Oh, that. I'm not going to deliver, that's all."

"That's *all?* Look, comedy princess, *Caché* magazine has reserved the space in the issue. They've printed the cover—with *your* picture on it, I might add—and leaked the story." He paused. "And I've gotten some interest in you from the networks—NBC wants to talk to you about writing a pilot."

"A . . . pilot? My own sitcom?" Ruby felt sick.

"Yeah, your own sitcom. So no dicking around. You're supposed to deliver the article tomorrow. I FedExed your plane tickets yesterday. They're probably at your front door now. You're scheduled for *Sarah Purcell* on Monday morning."

"I can't do it, Val." Panic rushed through her.

Val drew in a deep breath, then exhaled. "I gave them my word, Ruby. You can't just break your contract. Is the piece written?"

She hated the weakness that made her answer. "Yes."

"And the problem is . . ."

"I like her." Ruby felt like crying. "No. I love her."

Val was quiet for a moment. Then he said, "I'm sorry, Ruby."

"I am, too," she answered dully.

"You'll be on the plane, right? I'll have Bertram pick you up."

Ruby hung up the phone in a daze. She wandered out onto the porch, found the FedEx envelope. Inside, there was a first-class ticket and a short itinerary. They were taking her to Spago to celebrate after the taping of *Sarah Purcell*.

With a sigh she turned and went upstairs. She flopped onto the bed and reached for her pad of paper.

> I just got off the phone with my agent. The joke is on me, it seems. I can't get out of this deal. I have to deliver the article as promised. Monday I will appear on *The Sarah Purcell Show*.
>
> And I will lose my mother—this woman whom I've waited and longed for all of my life. Whatever we could have become will be gone. And this time it will be all my fault.
>
> But I want to say this for the record, although I'm aware it comes too late and at too great a price: I love my mother.

NORA sat at the kitchen table sipping a cup of coffee. She was waiting for Ruby to come downstairs. Nora had tried to wait up for her daughter the previous night, but at about twelve thirty she'd given up. It had to be a good sign that Ruby hadn't come home early. At least that's what Nora told herself.

The phone rang. Ignoring the crutches leaning against the wall, she hobbled to the counter and answered, "Hello?"

"It's me—Dee."

"Hi, Dee. What excellent news do you have today?"

"You're not going to like it. I just got off the phone with Tom Adams. He called me to tell me to tell you that if you didn't get those blankety-blank columns on his desk by Wednesday morning, he was going to slap a ten-million-dollar lawsuit on you."

"He can't do that," Nora said, though, of course, she had no idea whether or not he could. "What else is going on there?"

"The *Tattler* reported that the guy in the pictures wasn't your first . . . affair. They're saying that you and your husband had an 'open' marriage and you both slept with other people. And sometimes"—Dee's voice dropped to a conspiratorial whisper—"you did it in groups. Like in that movie *Eyes Wide Shut*."

Nora's head was spinning. For the first time since this whole mess began, she started to get mad. *Group sex?* She'd made mistakes—big ones, bad ones—but this she didn't deserve. They were trying to make her out to be some kind of whore. "Is that it? Or am I carrying some space alien's mutant child, too?"

Dee laughed nervously. "That's mostly it. Except there was a thing in Liz Smith's column that made it sound as if someone close to you was writing an ugly tell-all story about you."

"I see." Nora had expected this, and yet still it hurt. "Good-bye, Dee." She hung up and wrenched the cupboard doors open.

There they were—the cheap yellow crockery plates she'd bought at a garage sale a lifetime ago. She picked one up, felt the heft of it in her hand. And hesitated. There was no point in making a mess.

Like Eyes Wide Shut . . . *group sex.*

She wound her arm back and threw the plate. It went flying through the air and smacked the wall by the arch, shattering.

Open marriage.

She threw another. It hit with a satisfying smack. She should have tried this years ago. It actually helped. She reached for another plate.

Just then, Ruby came running downstairs. "What in the—" She ducked. The plate brushed past her head and hit the wall. "Jeez, Mom, if you don't like the plates, buy a new set."

Nora sank to her knees on the hard, cold floor. She laughed until tears leaked out of her eyes, and then she was crying.

"Mom?" Ruby knelt in front of her. "What happened?"

"Someone close to me—apparently a friend—is writing an ugly tell-all about my life. Oh, and don't be surprised when you hear that your dad and I engaged in group sex." She tried to smile. "But don't you worry. I can get through this. I've been through worse. The only thing that matters is how much I love you."

Ruby jerked back. "Oh, man," she whispered.

Nora got awkwardly to her feet, hobbled to the kitchen table, and slumped onto a chair. It occurred to her then, as she watched her daughter, who still knelt on the floor with her head bowed, that there was no silence more cruel and empty than the one that followed "I love you." She'd spent a childhood waiting to hear those words from her father, then an eternity waiting to hear them from her husband. Now, it seemed, she was destined to wait again.

"Would you like some coffee?" she asked.

Ruby looked up at her. "Don't pretend you didn't say it. Please." She got up, turned, and went upstairs.

Nora heard each footfall on the steps. She couldn't seem to draw a steady breath. *What in the world just happened?*

Then she heard the steps again—Ruby was coming back downstairs. She walked into the kitchen carrying a suitcase in one hand and a tablet of yellow paper in the other.

Nora's hand flew to her mouth. "I'm sorry. I thought we'd gotten to the point where I could say that to you."

Ruby dropped the suitcase. It landed with a thunk. Tears welled in her dark eyes, bled down her cheeks. "I love you."

Ruby's voice was so soft, Nora thought at first she'd imagined the words. "You love me?" she dared to whisper.

Ruby stood there, a little unsteady. "Just try to remember that, okay?" She slapped the yellow pad of paper on the table. "I spent all of last night making you a copy of this. Read it."

Nora peered down at the paper, squinting.

> In the interest of full disclosure I must tell you that I was paid to write this article. Paid handsomely, as they say in the kind of restaurants where a person like me can't afford to order a dinner salad. Enough so that I could trade in my beat-up Volkswagen Bug for a slightly less beat-up Porsche.
>
> I should also tell you that I dislike my mother. No, that's not true. I dislike the snotty salesclerk who works the night shift at my local video store. I hate my mother.

Nora looked up sharply.

Ruby was crying now, so hard her shoulders were trembling. "It's an article for *C-Caché* magazine."

Nora knew it was all in her eyes—the stinging betrayal, the aching sadness . . . and yes, the anger. "How could you?"

Ruby grabbed the suitcase and ran out of the house. Nora heard the car start up and speed away. She tried not to look at the yellow pages, but she couldn't help herself: *I hate my mother.*

Her hands were shaking as she lifted the pad and began to read. It was only a few sentences later that Nora began to cry.

RUBY made it all the way to the end of the driveway. Then she slammed on the brakes. She was running away again, but there was nowhere to hide on this one. She'd done a terrible, selfish thing, and she owed more to her mother than an empty house.

She put the minivan in reverse and backed down the driveway. She parked, then walked out to the edge of the bank, sat down on the grass, and closed her eyes. When Mom finished the article, she would undoubtedly head for the porch—it was her favorite place. Then she would see her daughter sitting out on the edge of the property.

Ruby knew she would remember this day for the rest of her life and at the oddest times—when she was elbow-deep in sudsy water, washing the dinner dishes; in the shower, with the sweet, citrusy scent of shampoo all around her; or holding the babies she prayed someday to have. In a very real way this would be the beginning of her adult life. Everything that grew afterward would be planted in the soil of what she and her mother said to each other right here.

"Hey, Rube."

Ruby opened her eyes and saw her mother standing beside her. She was leaning awkwardly forward on her crutches.

Ruby jackknifed up. "Mom," she whispered.

"I'm glad you came back. You can't get away from me so easily on an island, I guess." Nora tossed her crutches aside and sat on the grass. "I read every word you wrote, and I have to admit, it broke my heart."

"I knew those words would hurt you. In the beginning that's what I wanted to do, and now I'd give anything to take them back."

Nora smiled sadly. "The truth always hurts, Ruby." She glanced out at the Sound. "When I read your article, I saw myself. That doesn't seem like much, but I've spent a lifetime running away from who I am and where I came from. When I started my advice column, I knew people wouldn't like me, so I made up Nora Bridge, a woman they could trust and admire, and then I tried to live up to that creation. But how could I? The mistakes I'd made kept me on the outside all the time, looking in at my own life." She looked at Ruby. "But I trusted you."

Ruby squeezed her eyes shut. "I know."

"I was right to trust you, Ruby. I knew it when I finished reading. You listened, and you wrote, and you revealed *me*. From the girl who hid under the stairs to the woman who hid behind the metal bars of a mental institution to the woman who hid behind a microphone to this woman, who isn't hiding now."

"I'm not going to publish the article. I won't do that to you."

"Oh, yes, you are." Nora took Ruby's hands. "I *want* you to publish this article. It's a beautiful, powerful portrait of who we are, and it shows who we can be. It shows how love can go wrong and how it can find its way back if you believe in it."

Ruby swallowed hard. "I do love you, Mom. And I'm sor—"

"Shh. No more of that. We're family. We're going to trample all over each other's feelings now and again." Her eyes were bright with unshed tears. "And now we're going to go call your agent. I'm appearing on *Sarah Purcell* with you."

"No way. They'll eat you alive."

"Let 'em. I'll be holding my daughter's hand for strength."

Ruby stared at her mother in awe. "You're amazing."

Nora laughed. "It took you long enough to notice."

I HAD my fifteen minutes of fame, and amazingly, when the clock struck the quarter hour, I was still famous. My mother and I had become, it seems, symbols that the world wasn't on such a fast and ugly track after all.

What Mom and I discovered was that people want good news as well as bad, and they loved the story of my redemption. They loved it. They loved me. But most of all, they loved my mother. They heard the story of her whole life laid out before them like a novel, and they cheered at what she had overcome.

I listen to her on the radio now. Every now and then she gets an angry caller who labels her a hypocrite and a loser. The old Nora Bridge, I think, would have fallen apart at such a personal attack. Now she listens and agrees and then goes on, talking about the gift of mistakes and the miracle of family. By the end of the show her listeners are reaching for tissues and thinking about how to find their way back to their own families. The smart ones are reaching for the telephone.

There's no substitute for talking to the people you love. But someone has to make the first move. I guess that's one of the things I learned this summer. As mothers and daughters, we are connected with one another. My mother is in the bones of my spine, keeping me straight and true. She is in my blood, making sure it runs rich and strong. I cannot now imagine a life without her. A daughter without her mother is a woman broken.

I left Los Angeles a bitter, cynical woman. On Summer Island I became complete. And it was all so easy. I see that now.

I went in search of my mother's life and found my own.

"Do you think they'll be coming home soon?"

Dean didn't need to ask who Eric was talking about. In the three days since Nora and Ruby had left, he and Eric had speculated endlessly about their return. Dean knew that Eric often forgot their conversations on the subject. Sometimes they would end one discussion, and moments later Eric would ask the question again: "Do you think they'll be coming home soon?"

"They'll be here any day," Dean answered. Although he always answered similarly, he wasn't so sure, and the uncertainty was killing him. It was Nora who called every night to talk to Eric. Ruby was always off somewhere, doing publicity or "taking a meeting." She'd talked to them only once, and although she'd said all the right words to Dean, he'd felt a distance between them.

"Can we go outside?" Eric asked. "I can see what a beautiful day it is."

"Sure." Dean ran outside and set up a wooden lounge chair so that his brother could see all the way to the beach. Then he bundled

Eric in heavy blankets, carried him outside, placing him in the chair.

Eric settled back into the mound of pillows. "Man, that sun feels good on my face."

Dean looked at his brother. What he saw wasn't a thin, balding young man huddled in a multicolored blanket. What he saw was courage, distilled to its purest essence. He lay down in the grass beside Eric.

"Do you think they'll be home soon?"

"Any day now." Dean rolled onto his side. "Ruby's famous. Remember we saw her on *Entertainment Tonight* yesterday?"

"You think *fame* is what she wanted?"

"It can be a pretty wild thing, everybody loving you."

"That's not love. She'll come back to you, and if she doesn't, she's too stupid to live." Eric closed his eyes. Then suddenly he woke up. "Where did I leave my eraser?"

Dean touched his brother's forearm. "It's on the kitchen table."

He stroked Eric's forehead. When he heard his brother's breathing even out into sleep, he lay back in the grass and closed his own eyes.

He woke when a car drove up. "Hey, Lottie," he called out, waving sleepily.

"Is that any way to greet your newly famous fiancée?"

Dean's eyes snapped open. Ruby was standing beside him. He scrambled to his feet and swept her into his arms, giving her the kisses he'd been counting since she left.

She drew back, laughing. "I'm going to make a point to leave *lots* in our marriage. Coming home is great." She bent down to Eric, who was still sleeping. "Hey, Eric," she said softly.

Eric blinked up at her. "Hi, Sally."

She frowned at Dean.

"He's getting pretty bad," he whispered. "Keeps forgetting where he is."

Ruby sagged against him. Dean anchored her in place with an arm around her waist. "We watched you and Nora on *The Sarah Purcell Show.* You were great."

Ruby grinned. "It was fun. In a 'reporters following you into the bathroom stall' sort of way. Being famous is harsh. I turned down the sitcom offers and took a book deal. A novel this time. I figured it was something I could do up here."

"Hey, guys!" Nora shouted, waving. She limped up beside them.

Eric's eyes opened again, focused. "Nora? Is that you?"

She bent down to him. "I'm here, Eric."

"I knew you'd be here any minute. Have you seen my eraser?"

"No, honey, I haven't seen it." Her voice was throaty. "But do you know what day it is? It's the Fourth of July."

"Are we gonna have our party?"

"Of course."

"With sparklers?" He smiled sleepily.

"You go ahead and sleep for a minute. I'll get your brother to start the barbecue."

Nora leaned forward and kissed Eric's cheek. When she turned around, Dean saw the moisture in her eyes. He reached for her hand, held it. The three of them stood there, holding hands in the middle of the yard for a long, long time. No one spoke.

Finally Ruby said, "Let's get this party rolling." June hadn't yet turned into July, but this party was exactly what Eric needed.

While Nora and Ruby set the groceries and supplies out on the picnic table, Dean went upstairs and turned on the stereo. He stuck the old-fashioned black speakers in the open window, pointing them toward the yard. By the time he got back outside, Nora and Ruby had everything ready. The corn on the cob had been shucked and wrapped in tinfoil, and the salmon was seasoned and layered in slices of Walla Walla sweet onions and lemons.

They spent the rest of the day laughing, it seemed. They reminisced about the old days. They ate dinner off paper plates balanced on their laps. Eric even managed a few bites of salmon. And when darkness finally came, they lit up the sparklers.

Ruby stood at the bank with her back to the Sound and wrote RUBY LOVES DEAN in glittering white bursts of light. Beside her, Nora wrote I LOVE MY GIRLS and SUMMER ISLAND FOREVER. They were both grinning as they waved at Dean and Eric.

Eric turned his head. When their gazes met, Dean felt fear. His brother looked hopelessly old and tired. "I love you, baby brother."

"I love you, too, Eric."

"No funeral. I want you guys to have a party, something like this. Then throw my ashes off the *Wind Lass.*"

Dean couldn't imagine that—standing on the boat, watching gray ashes float on the surface of the choppy green sea.

Eric's breathing grew labored. He closed his eyes. "Get Mom, would you? I need to talk to her. She's here, isn't she?"

Dean nodded quickly, wiping the tears from his eyes. "Of course she's here. I'll go get her." It seemed to take him an hour to cross the small patch of lawn.

"Come on, Dino," Ruby laughed, reaching for him. "You haven't written my name yet."

Dean couldn't hold out his hand. He felt as if he were unraveling and the slightest movement could ruin him. "He's asking for Mom."

Nora covered her mouth with her hand. A small gasp escaped anyway. Ruby dropped her sparkler. It shot sparks up from the grass, and she carefully stomped it out with her foot.

In utter silence the three of them walked toward Eric. Ruby was the first to kneel beside him. Dean could see the tears in her eyes.

Eric smiled up at her. "You're unclenched . . ."

Dean frowned at the garbled words. Amazingly, Ruby seemed to understand. "I am," she said softly, then kissed his cheek.

"You take care of my brother."

"I will."

Eric fell asleep for a few minutes, then opened his eyes. "Mom?" There was an edge of panic to his voice. "Mom?"

Dean clung to Ruby's hand. The feel of her was a lifeline, the only thing that kept him steady.

Nora lowered herself to the chair, sitting on the edge beside Eric. "I'm here, honey. I'm right here."

Eric stared up at her, his eyes glassy. "Dino came home to me. I knew you would, too. I knew you wouldn't stay away."

Nora stroked his forehead. "Of course I came home."

Eric smiled, and for a split second his eyes were clear. "Take care of Dino for me. He's going to need you now."

Nora swallowed hard. "Your dad and I will watch over him."

"Thanks . . . Nora. You were always my mom." Eric smiled and closed his eyes. A moment later he whispered, "Charlie, is that you?" And he was gone.

Epilogue

𝒯HE chapel on Summer Island was a narrow, pitch-roofed clapboard building set on the crest of a small rise. Even now, in December, the building was cloaked in glossy green ivy.

"I can't believe you wouldn't let me fill the church with flowers."

Ruby laughed at her mother. They were standing in the tiny parking lot adjacent to the church, waiting for the ferry to dock.

"This is exactly how we wanted it. There's only one decoration that matters to me."

"It's the dead of winter. You know there's no heat in the chapel." Nora crossed her arms. Her elegant green St. John knit suit set off the flawless ivory of her skin. Unfortunately, it was about thirty degrees—unusually cold for Christmas week. She tried to smile. "I wanted to plan this day for you. Make it perfect in every way."

Ruby's smile was soft and understanding. "No, Mom. You wanted to plan it for you."

"And that's my right, damn it." Nora moved closer. "I love you, Ruby. Oh, I'm crying already."

Ruby started to say something, but the ferry honked its horn. Within minutes three cars drove up, parked side by side. The doors opened, and the rest of the gang appeared.

Caroline, looking as cool and elegant as a water flower, was in pale ice-blue silk. Beside her, Jere brought up the kids.

Caroline's eyes were full of tears as she smiled. "My baby sister in—" She frowned. "What are you wearing?"

Ruby posed. What had once been her dress of shame had become her wedding gown. "Isn't it great? It's Versace."

Caroline grinned, noticing the plunging neckline and the slit up the side. "It certainly is. You look gorgeous."

Then Rand was there, wearing an elegant black tuxedo. Marilyn was beside him, holding their son. Lottie was there, too.

Rand kissed Ruby, whispering, "Heya, Hollywood, you look like a princess," before he drew back.

"Hey, Dad." Ruby looked at Marilyn, who stood back from the crowd. Ruby gave her a bright smile. "Hi, Marilyn. It's good to have you here. How's my beautiful baby brother?"

Marilyn broke into a smile. "He's great. You look fabulous."

After that they all started talking at once. Then another car roared into the parking lot, and Dean stepped out. In his Armani tux he was so handsome that for a moment Ruby couldn't breathe. He gave her a slow, seductive smile. Gently he took her hands. "Are we ready to do this thing?"

Her heart was so full, she could only nod.

Together they went into the church. Inside, an aisle separated two short rows of benches. The altar was a plain wooden trestle table that held two thick white candles. In the corner stood a small fir that sparkled with white Christmas lights.

The family found their seats and crowded in. Dean walked down the aisle alone and took his place at the altar.

"Are you ready?"

Ruby heard her father's voice and turned slightly. She slipped her arm through his and let him guide her down the aisle.

At the altar he leaned down and kissed her cheek. "I love you, Hollywood," he whispered, leaving her standing beside Dean.

In front of them, on the altar, was a big photograph framed in ornate gilded wood. The only decoration that mattered: Eric.

In it he was fifteen years old, standing on the bow of the *Wind Lass,* half turned to face the camera. His smile was pure Eric.

Dean stared at the picture, and she knew he was remembering. She slipped her hand in his and whispered, "He's here."

"I know," he answered, holding her hand tightly. "I know."

"Dearly beloved, we are gathered here to celebrate the union of this man and this woman in holy matrimony." The priest's rich, melodious voice filled the small chapel.

Finally he came to, "Who gives this woman to be wed?"

It was the only thing Ruby had requested of this service—that question—and when she turned around and saw her mom and dad standing together, she knew she'd done the right thing.

Rand looked at Nora, who was weeping openly. He slipped his arm around her. "We do," he said proudly. "Her mother and I."

Caroline was crying now, too, and Ruby saw the way Jere moved closer to her, sliding his arm around her waist. Then Ruby gazed up at Dean and forgot everyone else. The service kept going, words thrown into a silence broken only by the soft organ music.

"You may kiss the bride."

Dean stared down at her, his eyes moist. "I've waited a lifetime for this," he said softly. "I'll always love you, Ruby."

"That's good," she said, grinning up at him, tasting the salty moisture of her own tears. She knew she was ruining the makeover her mother had paid for, but she didn't care.

He leaned down and kissed her.

Behind them the family clapped and cheered and laughed.

Suddenly Elvis—in a full beaded white jumpsuit—pushed through the doors. The King ran a hand through his pompadour, gave a sneering little half smile, and burst into song.

He was all shook up.

KRISTIN HANNAH

Kristin Hannah finds inspiration in the magical San Juan Islands.

Like her heroine Ruby Bridge, Kristin Hannah knows how difficult it is to break into the entertainment field—her husband is in the movie business, and they count several actors and celebrities among their friends. But the competitive world of Hollywood is about as far as you can get from the remote tranquillity of the San Juan Islands off Washington State, the setting for *Summer Island*. It turns out that Hannah knows these islands well. Her great-grandfather homesteaded five hundred acres there, and for Hannah—whose family still keeps a house on one of the islands—this magical setting seems slightly "out of step with the rest of the world." Time moves more slowly there, and readers who didn't grow up on the islands might wish that they had.

Kristin Hannah practiced law before she became a novelist. When she was in her last year of law school, her mother died. *Summer Island* took shape as Hannah wondered "what it would be like to be with my mother now that we are adults." Hannah is now a mother herself to a thirteen-year-old son. She and her family live in a small town in the Pacific Northwest.

To learn more about Kristin Hannah and the story behind *Summer Island,* visit the Select Editions website:

📖 ReadersOnly.com
Password: *today*

Who: The President of the United States.

What: An assassination attempt.

When: Twelve days before the next election.

Where: An exclusive Maryland golf course.

Why: That's what newshound Jack Flynn is determined to find out.

# Chapter One

ONE hour and counting until dusk, the time of the day Curtis Black liked best. The time when the distant sky left the illusion of light but the enveloping haze provided the cover of dark. A time when if you knew what you were doing, if you knew how and you knew why, the uncertainty of the moment served as your most reliable ally. For Curtis Black it was a time of day to make his mark.

Black shook his Johnnie Walker along the top of the rickety Formica table, the cubes of ice smashing softly against the side of the glass. His eyes drifted across the diagrams spread out before him, then out the window at the waning afternoon light.

Good help is hard to find. That's what he kept thinking over and over again. Good help is hard to find and harder still to keep. Kind of ironic, but the better you do, the quicker guys are to move on. To succeed, you have to keep taking on new people, and every new person represents a new risk. But what else are you going to do? Go it alone? Go straight? Black took a small sip of Scotch and bore in on the closest diagram.

The two-man armored truck would come down Prince Street and take a right on Hanover, then drive two blocks through heavy early rush-hour traffic. There would be a dark blue delivery van idling in the spot where the armored truck usually double-parked, but given the time of day, that shouldn't seem unusual. As a matter of fact, the last two Tuesdays, Black had sat in that idling delivery van himself, positioned in that precise spot, to watch how the armored car driver would react, and both times the driver had pulled up in front, parked, and made his pickup from the Shawmut Bank.

The entire operation from start to a successful getaway should be over in ten minutes—unless someone screwed up. Which got back to this thought that good help is hard to find. One mistake by any one of Black's five guys, and the whole thing could turn to bedlam in a fraction of a second, and that fraction of one second could haunt the rest of a lifetime. Maybe even dictate a lifetime. So it comes down to the execution more than the plans, and the execution was in the hands of five guys he barely knew. He took another pull of whisky.

Black was fretting about one of his men, Rocco Manupelli, who went by the worrisome nickname of Rocky. "Call me Rocky," he had said, jovially, that first time they had met. Black had just rolled his eyes. There are no résumés in this business and no reliable lists of references. So much is done on feel, and suddenly, in the lengthening shadows of that crucial afternoon, Black didn't feel so good about this one.

He took a final sip of whisky, draining the glass. He wanted more but wouldn't allow himself any. He had to be aware, be on top of his game, even if everyone knew that the best part of Curtis Black's game was in the planning, not the execution. Indeed, his planning was so good that Black never saw fit to carry a gun. All that would do was add ten years to the jail term on the off chance he was ever caught, and the guys who worked for him were carrying anyways.

He focused on the top diagram, envisioning the Wells Fargo security guard pushing a dolly carrying a duffel bag filled with cash. Everything goes right, and three men in ski masks jump out of the back of the blue van and surround him. A fourth man comes up from behind and disarms the second guard, who is standing beside the truck. Black would be directing the operation from the driver's seat of the van, barking orders into a tiny microphone that the others could hear through their own earpieces. In three minutes the men should be off the street and in a getaway car, no shots, no worries. They'd leave the stolen van behind.

The knock on the door downstairs startled Black, even though he had been waiting for it. He looked at his watch and saw it was four twenty-five p.m. Right on time. He picked up a photograph resting on the windowsill and smiled wistfully at the three people who were smiling back at him—a woman sitting on a sofa, holding a toddler, and a man, a younger version of himself, kneeling nearby.

He pulled himself up from the metal chair and ambled down the crooked stairs to open the door. One hour to showtime.

Present Day
Thursday, October 26

IT'S always odd meeting someone famous. On television they never look at you unless they're giving a speech, and in that case, they are perfectly made up, every hair in place. In newspaper pictures they are staring straight ahead, dead still, like a corpse. But in person their eyes move as if some mannequin had sprung eerily to life. They have blemishes, their hair is out of place, and your blood races the first few times they use your name.

It was like that on a perfect autumn dawn amid the rolling hills of Congressional Country Club, the type of day when the air is as crisp as an apple and the bright red and orange leaves look as if they were painted by God himself. It was just after six a.m. when I wheeled my Honda Accord into a space between a Jaguar and a Lexus. Before I could pop the key into my trunk, a woman flashed a Secret Service badge at me, spoke my name, and asked if I would raise my arms while she scanned my body with a metal detector. A couple of members happened by, glanced at my car and at the agent frisking me, and shot me a look as if I must be some criminal—or worse, a trespasser.

But their expressions changed abruptly when a man in golf cleats came clicking across the parking lot. "Jack," he called out to me from ten feet away in a voice as familiar as Sinatra's. "Jack, Clay Hutchins. It's a pleasure to meet you."

The introduction was hardly necessary, but I wondered what else you do if you're him: Clayton Hutchins is the President of the United States. He was taking a break from a heated election campaign to play an early morning round of golf. Me? I'm a Washington-based reporter for the Boston *Record.* And what was I doing playing golf with the President at his private club in Maryland? Good question. One day I called his press secretary on a story about presidential pardons; a few days later I'm summoned onto a golf course with the President himself. I suspected I'd find out the reason soon enough.

"Mr. President, the pleasure is certainly mine," I said.

"What do you say we hit a few putts before we head out, Jack," the President said.

A valet came running up and grabbed my golf bag. An advance man spoke into a walkie-talkie, and in the distance a caravan of golf carts moved around the practice green. As I walked toward the putting green with the President, past the clubhouse, a man in knickers, a bright argyle sweater, and a golf beret happened out the front door. The President leaned toward me and whispered, "What a horse's ass, but he's the best the pro tour could do for me this week." Louder, in that booming voice of his: "Jack, I want you to meet Skeeter Davis. Skeeter, this is Jack Flynn. Skeeter's going to give us a few tips today, turn us into pros. Right, Skeeter?"

We all made proper introductions and swapped small talk. On the practice green, I took measure of the situation. Here was the President of the United States treating me like his new best friend. And Skeeter Davis, one of the country's foremost golf champions, ready to give me lessons. There were a dozen golf carts lining the green, some with burly Secret Service agents talking into their wrists and listening through plastic earpieces. Two other carts carried four agents dressed in black ninja jumpsuits, armed with laser-trained automatic rifles. Over in the distance were a few members of the White House press corps, mostly photographers with zoom lenses.

There was a lot to think about here, but most of all, what I was think-ing was this: Please don't duck hook my first drive into the woods.

"You boys ready?" the President boomed. His voice was like steel, meant to last, maybe even at times make history. "It's going to be a memorable day."

ON THE tenth hole Hutchins cut to the point. By then he had already sliced seven balls deep into the woods, in places where no federal employee had ever gone before. And after each ball floated aimlessly over the tree line and into the woods, Skeeter Davis was right there saying, "Excellent swing, Mr. President. Let me just make one small suggestion."

Well, for what it was worth, my game was on, not that anyone really noticed. The Secret Service was looking for trouble. Davis was looking at Hutchins. Hutchins was looking at God knows what, but it wasn't me. Not until the tenth tee, when Davis stepped away to grab some lemonade from a nearby cart and Hutchins turned to me with a businesslike look on his face and asked, "How would you feel about coming over to the White House after the election, tak-ing over as my press secretary?"

I was about to open my mouth, but to say what, I didn't know. Luckily, Hutchins cut me off just as I began to stammer.

"Look, you know my situation. I have no doubt I'm going to win this election. I'm two points up in our internal polls right now. That's off the record, I hope. I have a staff I inherited, and they have no loyalty. Not my type, anyways. Pointy-heads. Intellectuals. Wing-nut conservatives. I've got to get my own people around me." He paused to see if his sales pitch was having any impact. "We'll finish this conversation later," he said as Skeeter came back.

Hutchins then pushed a tee into the moist turf and stroked his best drive of the day, the ball soaring a good two hundred and twenty yards straight down the fairway before gently bouncing along the grass like a little lamb trotting across a dewy meadow. Davis seemed about to have an orgasm, shouting, "Perfect, Mr. President. Perfect."

I got up and duck hooked my drive hard against a tree ninety yards out, and from the sounds of it, the ball hit about four more pines as it zigzagged into the woods.

"Would have made that offer earlier if I had known it would help me this much," Hutchins said, a twinkle in his eye. And as I made my way down the fairway, bewildered over where this day was taking me, I couldn't help but begin to like the guy.

"YOU'RE starting to suck, Jack."

That was the President on the fourteenth tee after I hit my fifth consecutive drive into the woods. He nurtured a reputation as a guy who liked to speak his mind, a no-nonsense businessman who had flourished in the house of mirrors known as national politics, all the while remaining as blunt as he had been when he started out a political neophyte in the state of Iowa a mere six years ago. He wasn't much different out here, and these words were spoken with a lopsided grin and a dose of self-satisfaction.

How could I predict on this day that the floor would fall out of my game because of an offer to be the presidential press secretary, one of the most visible jobs in America and a position that would eventually lead to great fortune for anyone who did it? There would be book contracts and grossly overpaid appearances performing punditry on network television. Not to mention that you might be able to work for what you believe in, perhaps even do some good for the country, if only for a short time.

Hutchins seemed to understand the reason for my golfing collapse, and he was reveling in it as I made my way into the woods in search of my errant drive. He began clicking his five iron off the fairway as pure as silk, his ball attracted to the green like a magnet.

On the sixteenth hole I skimmed four balls along the fairway and ended up inside a sand trap in front of the green, my ball pancaked hard into the grain. Hutchins hit two beautiful shots but caught a bad break and wound up in the same trap.

"Here we are, Jack, together at last," he said, stepping onto the sand, so happy he hardly seemed able to contain himself.

Skeeter stepped into the trap as well and began giving us a few tips, looking far more at the President than at me. He demonstrated one shot and hit it within a few feet of the pin.

Hutchins addressed his ball, and I stood about six feet behind him. As he finished his last practice swing, there was a dull crack. Water began shooting every which way.

"Damn," Hutchins yelled. Two aides raced toward him with golf umbrellas and dry towels. I saw the Secret Service SWAT team leap from their carts on the other side of the fairway and take aim with their automatic rifles at sites unknown. The four agents around us pulled their guns and surrounded the President.

"The sprinkler system was mistakenly activated," one agent called out loudly. "It should be off in a minute."

Within a few seconds the spouting water retreated into nothing. Several aides helped dry Hutchins off. The Secret Service agents walked away, the sense of impending doom having been replaced by a rainbow that hung in the air over the green.

And then, much louder this time, *crack.* And then again, *crack.* I saw Hutchins fall hard into the sand. I saw the quick spray of blood. I heard Davis scream. I felt a strange sensation in my lower chest, as if someone had pressed a hot iron against me, then tried to dig the sharp end of that iron into my flesh. I remember falling down hard into the sand myself.

Then there was bedlam. Three more shots, to the best of my count. Huge men rocketed into the sand trap, diving over the President, then squatting low and carrying him to an ambulance that had suddenly appeared beside the green.

Finally three rescue workers slammed a stretcher down beside me, picked me up, and raced me to the ambulance. When I got there, they were loading Hutchins inside.

It's odd to say this, but the next thing I recall is my father standing over me—odd because my father is dead. He was with Gus Fitzpatrick, his fellow worker in the pressroom, who pulled a sheet across my chest, smoothed it out, and told me I was going to be fine. Then I heard a phone ringing—a loud, cutting ring that must have jarred me out of a deep sleep. Barely awake, I remember reaching for it, and as I lifted my arm, I saw, with horror, that needles, tubes, and wires extended up my forearm to my biceps. As I got my hand to the phone, a nurse appeared, muttering, "Who could be calling this line?"

When I had the receiver in my hand, I couldn't speak, my throat thick with sleep. On the other end there was the proper, crystal-clear voice of what sounded like an elderly gentleman.

"Mr. Flynn, listen carefully to me," he said. "Nothing is as it seems. Do not believe anything that they tell you. There are strange, complex motives involved in this shooting. I will call you again soon."

He hung up. The nurse, oddly exasperated with me, snatched the phone from my hand and slammed it down, then yanked the cord out of the wall. More gently she pushed my head back against the pillows and stuck a thermometer into my mouth. I remember floating on a raft in a bobbing sea, finally asleep.

SOMEBODY was poking me in the shoulder. As I opened my eyes, I saw Peter Martin, Washington bureau chief of the Boston *Record,* at my bedside. I'm a reporter, so I figured I'd ask the questions, beginning with the obvious. "Where am I?"

"Oh, boy," Martin said, shaking his head, then looking toward the door nervously, like maybe he should summon help. "You're at Bethesda Naval Hospital. You know what you're doing here?"

I said, "Just help me out for a minute. I've been shot, right? Tell me what happened. Is Hutchins dead?"

Martin's never really been one to trot around the issues. "Jack, I hate to do this, but it's deadline. It's Thursday night, eight o'clock. The national desk up in Boston is screaming. You were a witness to an assassination attempt on the President of the United States in the middle of a cutthroat campaign, and we all thought it might be kind of nice to put this into a story."

Attempt. He said "attempt," so Hutchins wasn't dead, which was good. Neither was I, which, for me, was even better.

"Look, Peter, I'll do what I can. But first fill me in. What the hell happened? Is Hutchins all right? Am I all right?"

"Here's what I know, which isn't much," Martin said. "I'm counting on you to tell me more. You were out playing golf with the President this morning. By the way, Bob Appleton"—the editor in chief of the paper—"is curious as to exactly why you were doing that. So am I. Anyway, you're on the sixteenth hole. The two of you were in a sand trap with some pro golfer. All of a sudden you're shot.

"The FBI is saying that it was a militia member, disguised as a maintenance worker at the course, who shot you from the other side of the fairway. The first bullet hit your club, ricocheted off, then grazed Hutchins's shoulder. A second shot struck you in the ribs. I think it broke your rib bone or severely bruised it. The diagnosis is good, and you're expected to be out of here soon."

"How is Hutchins?" I asked.

"He's fine. A slight shoulder injury, and now the guy's a national hero. A local paramedic told a network television crew that as they were loading him into the ambulance, he looked at them with a wide grin and said, 'What kind of jerk would shoot me right in the middle of the best round of golf of my life?' He's been slipping in the public polls for days, but now analysts are saying this shooting could win him the election."

"How's Skeeter Davis, the golfer?" I asked. "He dead?"

"He wasn't even hit."

"What happened to the shooter?" I asked.

"Dead. Secret Service says he pointed a gun at one of their agents, and they mowed him down. Six bullets in the head."

Martin was getting increasingly nervous—looking at the door, at his watch, and at me—like some caged animal. He's anxious by nature and slightly bookish. But he knows Capitol Hill front and back. He knows things about the budget process that Cabinet secretaries don't know. He knows the years when all nine Supreme Court Justices were appointed. In a city where most bureau chiefs survive on television appearances, Martin survives on his brains and willingness to work.

"If you're well enough," he said, "we'd like a first-person account of what happened out there. It's a blockbuster. Biggest event in the world, and no one else will have what we have."

As Martin talked, a young man in a navy suit strode through the door and abruptly asked, "Is your telephone not hooked up?" He came around the bed to the phone, where he held up the disconnected telephone cord in the air and plugged it back into the wall. Almost immediately it rang. "For you," he said.

Through the earpiece a voice boomed out. "Jack, Jack, that you? I'm five pars into the best nine holes of my life, and some horse's ass feels the need to take a potshot at us. What's that all about?" Then came the sound of loud wheezing laughter.

It was Hutchins. I motioned to Martin for a pen, and he searched furiously through a shoulder bag for a pad and a writing instrument, placing them carefully in my lap.

"I think that was my club pro, Mr. President, ticked off that you were taking me to the cleaners." I heard him laugh into the phone.

As I was shaking off the grogginess and moving around my bed, it struck me just how much pain I was in. My ribs felt like they were about to snap, and even normal breathing began to hurt. My arms throbbed from all the needles sticking in them.

But journalism is a funny business. There is no sympathy, only opportunity, and the fact that I was laid out in a hospital bed in Bethesda, Maryland, with a bullet hole in my chest was seen by my superiors as a major boon for the paper and probably for me. And lying there, I began to see it that way myself.

"Mr. President, you mind if I throw a few questions at you for tomorrow's story?"

"You're in a hospital bed, and you're writing a story for tomorrow morning's paper?" Hutchins asked, incredulous. "You guys just don't give it a rest, do you? But what the hell, fire away."

With that pun he burst out laughing, then quickly calmed himself down. I proceeded to ask him a series of questions, and he easily answered each one as I scribbled notes.

I asked him about the likely impact on the election, which was only twelve days away. "Look," he said, "my doctors, my security team, they're telling me I'm going to be confined to the White House. Hear me clear right now. That's not going to happen. I'll be back on the stump, if not tomorrow, then Saturday. The American people have a right to see and judge the candidates for President."

All the while, Martin was circling my bed at an excitable pace. I was off the phone maybe two seconds when he placed an open laptop computer in my lap and told me to tap away. "We'll go with two stories: your interview with Hutchins, and then your own first-person account. This stuff should write itself. Just hit the keys as fast as you can."

And I did. When I was done, Martin took the computer and sat in one of those standard-issue hospital chairs and read, shaking his head all the while, rarely typing in any edits. "I hate to tell you this, but you're good," he said finally.

Then he plugged the computer into the phone jack and transmitted the two stories up to Boston. When he finished, he turned to me and said, "Okay, so tell me. Why were you playing golf with the President of the United States?"

I said, "I'm doing that story on presidential pardons that you and I discussed, trying to figure out if there's any rhyme or reason to the pardons that the White House gave out last summer and then last month. It's unusual for them to pardon convicts in the middle of a campaign, and there are a couple of names I'm curious about, so I call the White House press office. The next thing I know, the President's press secretary, Royal Dalton, calls and wants to know if I play golf. If I play, he says, I might be able to lob Hutchins a question or two on the pardon issue."

Martin nodded, then asked the obvious question. "Did you?"

"Never got the chance," I replied.

I was so tired I could barely speak. Mid-conversation I faded in and out of consciousness. I vaguely recall a doctor coming in, checking my pulse, talking softly with Martin. Two other visitors stepped into the room and showed the doctor badges. "FBI," I heard one of them say, a guy with a trench coat. The other was a younger woman with luxuriant black hair. The doctor chatted with them a while, and then they left. Half asleep, I remembered my earlier mysterious telephone call: a man's voice, a stern warning. Lies, everyone's telling lies. And I faded out again, this time to a place so blissful I would never find it again.

Friday, October 27

THERE is that final scene in *The Wizard of Oz,* when Dorothy regains consciousness, surrounded by her farmhands and neighbors— all of whom resemble the characters in her visit to the Emerald City. That's what I felt like, only it was the Bethesda Naval Hospital, not Kansas, and gathered around me were a pair of FBI agents, Peter Martin, my pal Gus Fitzpatrick, a man in a white laboratory coat who my deductive skills led me to believe was my doctor, and a few other people. Everyone, it seemed, but the Joint Chiefs of Staff.

Martin tossed the morning *Record* into my lap. PRESIDENT SURVIVES ASSASSINATION ATTEMPT, the headline screamed. SECRET SERVICE KILLS GUNMAN; BELIEVED TO BE MILITIA MEMBER. 11TH-HOUR ELECTION TURMOIL EXPECTED. And under that, over two separate stories, *RECORD* REPORTER, INJURED BY GUNFIRE, WITNESSES EVENT and HUTCHINS: "I WILL NOT BOW TO THREATS."

"We're the best paper on the biggest story in the country today," Martin said, absolutely exhilarated. "You're a celebrity. The publisher and editor both wanted me to thank you and ask if there's anything the paper can do for you during your recovery."

Martin paused, and a man spoke from the back of the room. "Mr. Flynn," he said, "Keith Madigan, the hospital's public relations director. I have a room of sixty reporters downstairs, and every one of them keeps asking when you're coming down to talk."

He had barely finished his sentence when the female FBI agent spoke out. "Samantha Stevens, special agent with the Federal Bureau of Investigation. This is Kent Drinker, assistant director. Before you go anywhere, we need to speak with you."

From the back of the room the doctor was next. "Look, before anyone does anything, I have to talk some things over with Mr. Flynn and do some tests. I'm going—"

He wasn't quite finished, but I had already had enough. "First could I just get a moment alone with"—I looked around the room real fast for someone who could just give me a breather and explain how upside-down my world had become—"Gus."

I noticed that all of the needles and tubes had been pulled out of my arms and replaced by small bandages covering gauze pads. I was glad I hadn't been awake for that. I felt better physically. My chest still had the sensation that someone quite heavy was nonchalantly standing on top of it. But the pain wasn't all that bad, and I felt quite rested.

As everyone but Gus slowly shuffled out of the room, the telephone rang. I grabbed it before anyone else could, having a nagging sense of who might be on the other end. The female FBI agent, Stevens, must have sensed a change in my voice, because she shot me a quizzical look as I spoke my greetings.

"Mr. Flynn," the voice said, dignified, "this is not a joke. This is not a game. There are things happening that you must learn. I will help you, but I can only do so much. You will be leaving the hospital tomorrow morning. I will telephone you tomorrow afternoon at your house, when you will have more privacy."

How did he know when I was leaving the hospital? I looked over in the direction of the door and saw Stevens staring at me.

"I'll look forward to that," I said in a booming voice. "I can't believe you were this nice to call. Take care."

I hung up, and everyone left except for Gus, who I think was both confused and delighted by my request that he stay.

"Gus, what is going on here?" I asked. "Am I all right?"

"All right? You're a star, kid. Your performance in today's paper is the talk of the country."

Gus works in the pressroom of the *Record.* He was my father's best friend at work—back when they worked the overnight shift at the *Record,* keeping watch over the mammoth printing presses, recasting inks, and refilling the massive rolls of newsprint that turned into the next day's newspaper. It was, I used to think and probably still do, the most important job in the world, the manifestation of which used to be on our kitchen table every morning when my father arrived home from work and I awoke to go to school.

As a kid of twelve, I told my father I wanted to work at the *Record,* and he assumed I wanted to do what he did. It wasn't until I was maybe seventeen that I explained to him I wanted to be a reporter. He didn't say much. No one in his family had ever been to college, and I'm not sure he knew how to react. When I was a senior in college, he died of a stroke. He never saw me walk into the newsroom of the paper he had worked at for more than thirty-five years.

Gus did, though. That first day in the newsroom was the culmination of my dreams. There I was, among all the people I had read for so long—Pulitzer prizewinners, editors who jetted across the country on presidential campaigns. Dressed in a crisp Brooks Brothers pinpoint shirt, striped tie, and woolen trousers to a smart gray suit, I stood arranging a few books at my desk. Gus came walking up to me. I suspect he had never been in the newsroom during business hours. He was short and balding, and he stopped in front of me, staring with a proud gaze.

He extended his hand, and I knew what my father would have felt. I moved past his hand into a soft embrace. Gus wrapped his right arm tightly around me, speaking into my ear, "You're going to be the best reporter this place has ever had." He stepped back and said, "Your father helped me get this job at a tough time in my life. If I can do anything to help you, I will." Then he walked away, leaving a black ink smudge on my new shirt.

"Well," I now said to Gus, who had settled into the chair beside my hospital bed, "tell me, what on earth is going on here?"

"What's going on here is that you're the witness to an assassination attempt on the President of the United States."

"Doesn't get much bigger, does it?" I said.

Gus said, "I want you to be careful. Everyone's going to want a piece of you—the FBI, the TV cameras, even the President. Just do your job, and everything else will take care of itself."

These were the reassuring words I wanted to hear, and lying in bed, I said quietly, "Thanks."

We made small talk, and after a while Gus stood up to leave. "You going to be all right at home?" he asked.

Suddenly I thought of my dog, alone there over the past twenty-four hours. "Do you know if Baker is all right?" I said.

"The dog is fine. Your dog sitter came over and picked him up yesterday afternoon when she saw your picture on television. She said she'll bring him back when you get home."

I paused, basking in the relief. "I'll be fine," I said.

"I'll get the doctor. And I have to get back to Boston. I have to work tonight." And with that, a proud smile came over Gus's face. He gave my hand a long squeeze, whispered, "Jack, do your job," then walked out of the room.

COPS and reporters share a like goal: to gather information for presentation in the public domain. Police prepare for court cases. Reporters compile information for their newspapers. But how they go about it is vastly different. Police detectives can take the most theatrical, most sensational case and break it down into the dull sum of its scientific parts—semen and blood samples, fingerprints and fibers. They move with a painstaking methodology.

Reporters, meanwhile, like to interview people in action. A good reporter can take the most mundane murder, inject it with human emotion, and end up with what the average reader might be convinced is the crime of the century. Reporters are constantly looking at the whole at the expense of some of its parts. Best to have an incomplete story first than the entire tale last. And virtually everything, they believe, is appropriate in the public realm, allowing readers to decide what is right or wrong.

So it is all the more fruitful when a reporter is able to strike up a relationship with a police detective, and I take no small amount of pride in saying that much of the success I've had in my career has been due to my ability to get along with cops.

None of this, though, seemed to have any bearing on my new

relationship with Samantha Stevens. She didn't spend a lot of time on niceties when she and Drinker strode into my hospital room just a moment after the doctor had left. "Why don't we start with the basics," she said. "What were you doing playing golf with the President?"

Her partner stood impassively against the wall.

"He invited me," I said, taken aback.

"Why's that?" she asked, aloof, almost clinical.

"Why don't you ask him?" I said, and I watched as her very becoming face flushed red.

"We are conducting the most important investigation in the Bureau right now, Mr. Flynn," she said. "Forgive my manner if you are offended by it, but I have to dedicate myself to getting to the bottom of this case as quickly as possible. And such a mission doesn't accord me much time for excessive civility."

"Apparently not," I said. "If it would help, I could call my lawyer and have him come down and sit in."

That seemed to take Stevens by surprise. "That would be a mistake for all of us," she said. "Look, I just want you to understand the gravity of this investigation. I didn't appreciate reading your eyewitness account in the newspaper before we had a chance to talk. This is first and foremost an FBI investigation of an assassination attempt on the President, not some sensational story to help you sell more papers. Why don't we revisit this tomorrow, and I'm sure we'll make some more progress."

"That would be fine," I said.

She turned around to leave, and Drinker followed without even so much as looking my way. At the door he turned back around. "By the way, who was that who called you earlier, when everyone was in the room?" His tone was soft, even pleasant.

"Oh, just an old friend of mine," I said, fumbling for an answer.

"What's the friend's name?" he asked.

I'm sure he saw the uncertainty on my face or sensed the flustered tone of my voice. "That's personal," I said eventually, and Drinker simply nodded as the two of them headed out the door.

Chapter Two

WHEN the doctor told me I could head home the following morning, I prevailed on him to endorse my departure for that very night. The press corps treated me as well as I could have hoped, given that a few of the network stars were miffed about being on the sidelines while an ink-stained wretch from an out-of-town paper basked in the limelight. I spent half an hour before the cameras, then headed home in a taxi.

We soon pulled up in front of my brick town house, in the heart of Georgetown. Katherine and I had bought it two years earlier. I was enchanted by the enormous bowfront window, and even though we first saw it in August, I pictured how it would look with a towering Christmas tree. She was smitten with the condition of the place, which was atrocious, so we could gut it and start anew.

I paid the driver and ambled up the stairs. This should have been a pleasant homecoming. I was a celebrity, the President wanted me to be his next press secretary, and I had the terrific story of an assassination attempt a dozen days before a presidential election. But as I stepped inside my dark, empty house, I felt a sense of melancholy. More than anything, I missed Katherine. It was just over one year that she had been gone. We had been married three years and were far from a perfect couple, but for my money we were more perfect than most.

We bought the house and renovated it top to bottom. We bought a golden retriever and named him Baker. We had sex in spurts. There were weeks when we couldn't keep our hands off each other; we would steal away from work in the late afternoon and have sex in the waning sunlight of our second-floor bedroom. Afterward we would lie in bed, telling each other of our day. Of course, other times we were more physically aloof. One or the other of us was tired or preoccupied, and then we would enjoy our friendship. More than anything else, Katherine was my friend, and trite as it is to say, she could make me laugh.

Her pregnancy brought on a real potpourri of emotions. She was constantly sick at first. I, meanwhile, was coming to terms with the thought of fatherhood. Initially the responsibility petrified me. But by the sixth month or so, I had arrived at an inner peace, and I couldn't wait to greet my newborn into our house.

Katherine was due in mid-October. By the second, I was a basket case, nervous to the point of being unable to work. So I stayed home that day and played with the dog and puttered around the house. Katherine, meanwhile, continued to make calls to her public relations clients from our upstairs office. She did this right up to the time when she came walking out the French doors onto our back patio and announced to me that the time had come to head to Georgetown Hospital.

In the delivery room her pain seemed almost unbearable. She pushed and counted, counted and pushed, when suddenly a nurse monitoring her vital signs snapped up a telephone and had the receptionist page our obstetrician. The doctor came rushing in, took measure of the situation, and told me to leave the room. In the waiting area I sat staring at my feet for the next two hours.

Dr. Joyce was one of Washington's top ob/gyns. As I sat, lost in my fears, she came up so quietly I never saw her, took me by the hand, and began walking back toward the delivery room. For a moment all my dreadful thoughts gave way to the sparkling optimism that we were heading to see my wife and newborn baby. But before we arrived at the maternity ward, Dr. Joyce pulled me into a conference room, directed me into a seat, and spoke.

"There's no good way to say this, Jack. Katherine died during delivery. She had a placental tear, and she died from internal bleeding. We did everything we could, but the bleeding was too much." I had never felt so alone, so detached from everything and everyone I had ever known. My head bowed in a storm of salty, silent tears. The doctor continued to speak. "Jack, I can't imagine how tough this is, but I also have to explain to you, your daughter was still-born. She never really had a chance."

I don't know if we were in that conference room for five minutes or five hours. At some point the doctor led me back into the delivery room, now empty but for a lifeless form on a gurney, and pulled back the sheet from Katherine's face, still wet from the sweat of her pain. I kissed her forehead and then let my lips linger on hers until a tear rolled off my nose and onto her face. And I walked out of the room, forever changed, always something less than I should have been.

THESE were the thoughts that filled my mind as I slumped down in my moss-green couch and punched a code into the telephone to access my voice-mail messages. Agent Samantha Stevens of the FBI had called. "We'd like to talk with you again as soon as you feel able," she said. "I'll call you in the morning."

Without Baker trotting around, the house seemed vacant. As I climbed the stairs to bed, there was an uncomfortable silence. Arriving upstairs, I looked at the closed door of the nursery. When I came home from the hospital after my wife's death, I pulled the door shut and hadn't been in there since. Friends, family have all offered to pack up the crib, the changing table, and stuffed animals. I've always said no.

I pulled the door open, flicked on the light, and walked inside. The little blankets were still spread in the crib, waiting for our baby to come home. Though shuttered for many months, the room had the aroma of newness—new woods of the crib and changing table, new stuffed animals on the bureau. I walked around the room, peering into the crib, running my hand across the top of an elephant-shaped toy chest that was a gift from Katherine's mother. I thought about what should have been: fatherhood, an ever changing relationship with my wife, the laughs and the responsibilities. The meaningfulness of it all.

Then I flicked the light out and sat down on the floor, on a Winnie-the-Pooh rug. After a minute I lay down on my back. And I slept, fitfully, until the birds chirped outside and the sun hit me in the eyes. When I awoke, I felt as if my melancholy had lifted. I pulled myself to my feet and lurched out the door toward the shower. A small part of me felt as if I had just conquered something, but most of me just felt an unfamiliar sense of peace.

Saturday, October 28

I PICKED up the telephone on the first ring.

"Have you seen *The New York Times* yet?" It was Peter Martin.

I replied, "I'm feeling much better, thanks. And how are you?"

"Look, this story is out of control. You ready to come to work?"

Someone banged on the front door, and I hurried downstairs with the portable phone still at my ear. When I opened the door, Baker, in all his glory, came charging inside. He circled me twice, his tail wagging, then lunged for his stuffed hedgehog, which was lying on the rug, and paced about the room with the toy lodged deep in his mouth. The hedgehog was squealing; the dog was snorting. I was down on one knee, smacking him lovingly on his side. "Hold on, Peter," I said into the phone, putting it down.

"Kristen, this was really great of you," I said to the dog sitter, an adorable graduate student who lives down the street. "Let me grab you some money." Kristen had fallen in love with Baker in the local park two years earlier and told Katherine and me that if we ever needed a sitter, she would appreciate the chance.

"That's all right, Jack. I'll get it some other time. By the way, you looked great on TV."

Before I could say anything, she was gone, Baker was sprawled on the floor, and I was back on the phone with Peter.

"What's the *Times* have?" I asked.

"It's kind of strange," he said. "They have a front-page story, quoting anonymous sources, saying that the FBI can't pin the gunman in the assassination attempt, identified as Tony Clawson from California, with a specific militia group. They ran a head shot of Clawson from some ID badge he wore at his job at Home Depot. Scary-looking guy. These same sources said that no militia group has yet to claim any knowledge of the assassination attempt, which probably isn't surprising. But here's what I think is interesting: About halfway through the story the FBI spokesman says they *believe* that the gunman was a militia member. To me that seems like the feds are backing away from how definitive they were right after the incident."

I was with him ninety percent. "So what are you saying?" I asked.

"We need to be on this right away." His tone changed, becoming softer. "I know you're not going to like this, but Havlicek is on his way out to California from Boston. I didn't know how you were feeling physically and guessed you wouldn't want to make that flight. He'll be good to do the initial sweep on Clawson."

I was fine about it. Steve Havlicek was in his late fifties, a Pulitzer prizewinning investigative reporter with a near manic drive to land stories that he knew no one else could get. He was the chief investigative reporter in Washington before I was, and Martin was nervous that I would feel threatened by him poaching on my turf. In fact, Havlicek was an old friend, a quasi-mentor, and I welcomed the help. "We'll work well together," I said.

"You have a line in with the FBI?" Martin asked. "The President? Can you flip any of these guys, put them on your side?"

My call-waiting tone sounded, and I took a pass on it.

"The FBI agent, Stevens, seems pretty standoffish. She's going to be tough work, but I'll stay on her. I'll spread some other calls out from home this morning and give you a ring if I get anything back. Have Havlicek give me a call when he gets to California."

It suddenly struck me: the anonymous caller. Maybe I had just lost his call by not picking up the other line.

"One more thing, Peter," I said, and then caught myself, quickly deciding not to tip my hand yet, not even to Martin. I had no real reason to keep it secret, but my instincts told me to maintain my own counsel on this right now, until I knew more.

"What?" he said urgently.

My mind raced to fill in the blank. "You remember the militia series I did last year? I made some good friends on that one, including one guy in Idaho, a militia leader, who is well plugged in nationally. I might be able to squeeze him."

It worked, strangely enough.

"That's right. Maybe you ought to just get out there and see whether this guy has anything. I'm going to check the flight schedules, and I'll call you later."

I hung up the phone, wondering what I had just done to myself. I checked to see if my caller had left a message on my voice mail. I was in luck. It was Samantha Stevens requesting an audience at three o'clock that afternoon at my house.

Immediately I tapped out the number for the *Record*'s library up in Boston, and my favorite researcher answered the phone.

"Dorothy," I said, "Jack Flynn here. Howaya?"

"Jack, you're all over CNN. A reporter was in here last night interviewing people about you. I told them I thought you were a gifted writer and was thrilled that you finally decided to confront your impotency problem."

Ah, that Dorothy, such a card. "You're a laugh a minute. Listen, can you pull me some background on one Samantha Stevens, an agent of the Federal Bureau of Investigation, the pride of this great land? And while you're in the system, could you see if there's anything on another agent, by the name of Kent Drinker?"

"Coming your way. I'll ship it through the computer."

IN THE journalism business we look at shards of people's lives and pretend we see the whole. We spend maybe an hour with someone, talk to neighbors, get some quotes about the time the suspect returned a borrowed rake with a sack of nuts from a gourmet food store, then write as if we understood the very fiber of his soul. I'm as guilty as anyone else, but I've been around long enough to know that what I'm doing might not be entirely right.

Which is exactly how I felt as I sat in my study and scrolled through the computer file that Dorothy had sent me. There was nothing on Stevens. But on Drinker the stories were voluminous. According to the accounts, Drinker worked as an FBI liaison to the U.S. marshals' witness protection program at the start of his career, rising steadily through the hierarchy. In an enormous promotion for largely thankless work, he was moved to Los Angeles to take the number two slot in the FBI's regional office.

He wasn't there but a year when a story broke in the Los Angeles *Times* that the special agent in charge of the region, an FBI man by the name of Skip Weaver, had been blocking the promotions of Hispanic agents in favor of less qualified white agents. The paper quoted from highly sensitive personnel documents that it said it had obtained from sources familiar with the office. Shortly after that the paper conducted a review and found that the Bureau arrested Hispanics in greater proportion than any other racial or ethnic group. This was enough to unleash a racial backlash the likes of which had not been seen there since the Rodney King riots. The city's race relations commission launched its own investigation. So did the FBI, but rather than investigate its arrest policies, it probed into who had leaked the documents to the newspaper. Unbelievably, the *Times* reporter informed investigators that Kent Drinker was his source. Drinker was immediately called back to Washington. In law enforcement there is the code of silence, and he had just violated it. He was assigned a menial desk job. That was all nearly a decade ago.

For several years he committed himself to the pick-and-shovel work of rejuvenation, keeping a low profile, doing whatever he was asked. His fortunes took a sharp turn for the better almost four years ago when Hutchins came to the White House as Vice President. From the depths of penance Drinker was pulled to nearly the pinnacle of the agency—named assistant director—a move interpreted by the national press as a message that the new administration wanted an honest, open government.

So what did this tell me? Perhaps it explained why he had been so quiet with me in the hospital room. Because he had been burned by reporters before, perhaps he simply didn't like us.

The telephone rang, and I picked it up.

"Hey, old boy. I have to get on an airplane and fly all the way to California just to bail out your fat ass." It was Havlicek.

"Not what I heard," I said. "I heard there's an issue over your output up in Boston, and they decided to put you on this story to work with the master for a while. They want you to kneel at my knee. Watch and learn. Watch and learn." Now that this macho turf ritual was over, I cut to the point. "What do you have?"

"Nothing yet," Havlicek said. "I'm on an airplane. I'll be on the ground soon. We're just trying to play catch-up with the *Times* for tomorrow. When are you on board?"

"Well, I have a couple of FBI agents coming over this afternoon, and I'm going to see if I can trade information with them. I'll be working the phone all day, trying to find out anything I can on Clawson and the militia angle from here. If I get anything, I'll write it up, obviously, and we'll probably feed it into whatever you get. Otherwise I'll be in the bureau tomorrow."

"All right. Call me if you hear something worthwhile."

THEY arrived fashionably late for the interview, Stevens and Drinker. After a day spent accomplishing frustratingly little from my dozens of phone calls spread around official Washington, they were an oddly welcome sight. Poor Baker was nearly beside himself at the concept of female companionship at home.

"Hopefully," Drinker said as we had taken our seats in the living room, "all of us are in a better frame of mind today."

That, I think, was the closest I would get to an apology from this duo, so I accepted it gracefully and said, "I'm sure we all are."

The brief informalities behind us, Stevens briskly took up where she left off the day before. "I'm hoping you can run through with me just what it is you saw at Congressional."

I regarded her for a moment. Her jet-black hair had little wisps flowing in various directions, sexy, yet with a sense of innocence. It highlighted her alabaster skin. She was tall and slender, and her tan suit clung in some places. I began talking, and she scribbled furiously in her tiny notebook as fast as she could write.

"Very helpful," she said finally, when I had run out of things to describe. As witnesses go, I'm probably a pretty good one, considering that's what I do for a living. We met eyes a couple of times, and she never looked away. The frost of the previous day seemed to be melting away. "Your house is beautiful," she said, looking around, in a signal that the interrogation had ended.

"Thanks," I said. "My wife and I bought and renovated it a couple of years back."

"I know," she said. I shot her a quizzical look, and she smiled and shrugged. "Homework."

"Do you mind if I ask something?" I said, adopting my reporter voice. "There seems to be some discrepancy in public accounts on whether the shooting was militia-sponsored."

Stevens began to pronounce the first syllable of what I expect was going to be an answer when Drinker firmly cut her off.

"We're not getting into these games," he said, looking at her, then at me. "Call our spokesman. You know who he is."

As they were leaving, Drinker said, "I don't mean to belabor the point, but that telephone call yesterday in the hospital: You said it was a friend. But it came in on a direct-dial line. That friend couldn't have been transferred from the hospital switchboard. For someone to have called you, you would have had to have given your number out. The telephone records show that you hadn't made any calls. And the nurses said you hadn't had any visitors the night before, except for Peter Martin. And Martin was in the room, so it wasn't him."

This all sounded confusing, but I think I knew what he was getting at. Basically I was cornered and screwed. I had nothing to lose, so I gave it my best shot at staving him off. "Last I checked, I'm a witness, not a suspect," I said. "It was just a call from an old friend. I guess Martin must have given out my number."

Drinker didn't push the issue. He bade me farewell, and behind him, Stevens threw me what I took to be a cool parting look. I wondered what it meant: the questions, the persistence, and more than any of that, this intriguing agent with the beautiful hair.

NIGHTFALL brought Baker's evening walk. I grabbed a tennis ball, which he quickly scooped up in his mouth, and some money, which I hoped to spend on dinner. We stopped at our usual park, down on K Street, to toss and fetch. For dinner I took a place at a patio table at a French restaurant on Thirty-first Street, Café la Ruche. I leaned down to tie Baker's leash to my chair, then looked up into the eyes of a stunning waitress, who presented me a menu and cooed at Baker. She took my order and brought me back a Miller. When she brought my food about fifteen minutes later, she reached into her apron and pulled out an envelope.

"A gentleman asked me to pass this along to you," she said.

I looked around curiously, first at the other diners, to see if there was anyone I knew. Nothing. I looked out along the sidewalk and down the street—again, nothing. Before I put my fork into my swordfish, I carefully tore the envelope open to see what was inside. It was a short computer-generated note: "Meet me alone, at the Newseum, Sunday, five thirty p.m."

Well, it provided the where, what, and when you hear so much about in journalism school, but it lacked the all-important who and why. I waved to my waitress, and she came bouncing right over.

"I'm trying to figure out who this envelope came from," I said. "Is he still here?"

She looked around thoughtfully. "I don't see him," she said. "Tell you the truth, I didn't even get a good look at him."

"Older, younger? Do you recall what he was wearing?"

"I really don't," she said, walking away. "I'm sorry."

I sat there on the restaurant patio—Baker blithely sleeping at my feet—spooning rice and swordfish into my face, wondering if my anonymous caller was watching me now, wondering why.

The walk home, to say the least, was an anxious one, every crunch of the leaves sending my head turning in search of any mysterious presence. A man in a sweatshirt, carrying a briefcase, walked about ten yards behind me. A van approached and seemed to slow down as I walked up Twenty-eighth Street, the man with the briefcase still behind me. Suddenly I didn't hear his footsteps anymore. I turned around, and he was gone, and so was the van.

As I arrived at my front door, that same van rounded the corner and slowly passed my house. I hurriedly jammed the key into the lock and stepped inside.

# Chapter Three

IN A world where precise planning and endless advance work serve as the foundation for success, every morning a motley group of highly educated reporters start the day from scratch, floating into America's newsrooms and bureaus, thinking big thoughts, working the telephones, pecking away at keyboards, making and breaking careers in the communities they cover.

Reporters can pick up the telephone and reach governors, Senators, captains of commerce. A few reporters, and I immodestly put myself in this category now, can reach the President of the United States. A reporter's story can cause the indictment of a mayor or the release of a prisoner wrongly convicted on false testimony. All this, and no license required, nothing but the ability to ferret out the truth and to present it in a readable and stylish way. At the end of the day, when it all comes together, the publication of a newspaper is nothing short of a daily miracle, an act of democracy and freedom celebrated with a simple read.

I was thinking about all this as I walked into the bureau Sunday morning for the first time since I was shot.

Peter Martin hustled up to my desk moments after I arrived. It was not quite nine a.m. "You see the *Times* this morning?" he asked breathlessly. "They're way out front again."

I had read the *Times* already, after my morning walk with Baker. FBI sources, quoted anonymously, said they had serious questions over the motive of the assassination attempt, mostly because they had no clear idea of who the would-be killer was. No family members of the attempted assassin, Clawson, could be found, no history, no criminal record based on his fingerprints.

"A good story," I said. Before I could go on, Martin cut me off.

"Look, we need a larger piece of this. This is our story. You were there. You were almost killed. Somebody's got to want to help us."

As he spoke, the telephone rang, and a pleasant woman's voice asked if I could hold the line for the President of the United States.

"I'd be honored to talk to the President," I said.

Martin, pacing, looked at me skeptically. "Quit screwing around," he said after a moment. "We have a lot of work to get done."

I ignored him as the booming voice of President Hutchins filled my ear. "The hell are you doing back at work? You nuts?"

"Mr. President, democracy needs to be protected every day of the week, injury or no injury. You know my devotion." He laughed at that. He didn't seem like such a bad guy. Martin's eyes were glued to mine.

"You have a few minutes to come over to the house and chat?" Hutchins asked. By house, I assumed he meant the White House.

I knew full well what he wanted to chat about, but I also knew I could trade on that for another story or at least the pieces of another story. And if I had this anonymous source filling my ear, it was good to get as much exposure to Hutchins as I could.

"Of course I could come to the White House, sir," I said, speaking more formally than before. Martin pumped his fist into the air.

"Good. How about noon? Just show up at the gate, and someone will guide you in."

Hanging up, I said to Martin as casually as I could, "Going in to see the President at noon."

Looking exuberant, he appeared ready to sit in my lap. One thought did strike him, and he expressed it. "Why?" he asked.

"Don't know. Maybe he likes my company. Maybe it's good PR for him, visiting with the injured reporter."

Martin left my desk in a half trot, half skip.

By now a few more colleagues were filtering into the room. As one or two gave me a hard time about my newfound fame, Havlicek walked into the bureau and stood over a desk on the other side of the room, having just arrived on a red-eye from the West Coast. "About time you ended that vacation," he bellowed across the way. I gave him the finger as I calmly looked the other way. A few minutes later I pulled myself to my feet, grimacing at my sore ribs, and walked across the room. We met halfway, and he gave me a half hug, saying quietly, "Welcome back."

Newsrooms are inherently cluttered places. In a world of Internet searches and CD-ROMs, they are inexplicably filled with piles of newspapers, manila folders, and opened books strewn on chaotic desktops. The floors are lined with cardboard boxes holding files and documents. Phones are ringing every minute. A bank of facsimile machines gives off an uninterrupted beep, and there is the omnipresent click of computer keyboards. And more than any of that, there is the mystique.

This place was all that and more. Located smack in the middle of downtown Washington, just blocks from the White House, the bureau was one large open room, with a dozen desks spread like quiltwork. Off to one side was a large, plush conference room, and beside that was Martin's office. Both had walls of glass.

Havlicek and I agreed to make a round of calls and talk over our angles in the afternoon. First thing I did was punch out a number on my phone that got me into the J. Edgar Hoover Building, headquarters of the FBI. A familiar voice answered on the first ring.

"Ron, Flynn here," I said in my typically warm way. "Still stuck with the weekend shift, huh?"

"As I live and breathe, if it isn't the star of the city," said Ron Hancock, a veteran special agent of the FBI.

I interjected, "Tell you what. First thing tomorrow I'm going to sign a few glossies for the wife and kids and send them on over."

"I'll lay them down, and the dog will piss all over them."

Now that we had the niceties out of the way, I said, "Listen, a question's been bothering me since I woke up in the hospital staring into her pretty face: What's the line on Samantha Stevens? Good woman? Bad woman? Respected agent?"

Despite the threat to allow his dog to urinate on the likeness of my face, Hancock was a solid man and an even better agent. He worked in the intelligence division of the FBI, mostly tracking terrorist activity, and was always willing to lend a hand.

He just kind of snickered. "I don't know a lot about her, aside from the fact that she's divorced and the male agents seem to like her. The boss must too, if they put her on a case like this."

I added, "And Kent Drinker?"

"Well, that one's a little trickier. You know his checkered background, yet his renaissance here has been something to behold."

I said, "Yeah, his history, to say the least, is complex."

I intentionally left a void of silence open, hoping he would fill it with some information he might not otherwise have felt inclined to offer. An old reporter's trick. But Hancock's too good for that. So instead we just had an awkward pause. Finally I asked innocently, "You don't even want to know how I am?"

He laughed. "Next time. I've got to run."

After he hung up, I typed what I knew into my computer. First, there was a gunman whom the FBI, seemingly without any foundation, had reported was a militia member. Second, there was this anonymous source, telling me this shooting was not what it seemed. Third, the outcome of a presidential election hung in the balance, affected by this gunman's errant shot.

"What do you think of Idaho?"

That was Martin, bursting my concentration. I sprinted around the hallways of my mind, wondering what he meant by Idaho. The militia leader, I realized.

"I don't know," I said. "I've just been trying to piece together the holes we have right now. There are a lot of them."

"We need a break on this, and we need it fast. You think you should just get on a plane, try to break some news on the militia front? If it ends up that these groups are disavowing any knowledge of this gunman, it raises a whole lot of questions."

I weighed my options. I didn't want to jump on a plane for the backwoods of America—not now, not with what I had going on. I was due in the Oval Office at noon and at the Newseum at five thirty, for a meeting with my anonymous source that could change the direction of this entire story. On the other hand, suppose my source had nothing new? Suppose he was just another crazy?

"Why don't we hold off on a definitive plan until we see what happens with Hutchins," I said, finding neutral ground.

"That's good, very good," Martin said. "Of course, that leaves us with nothing definitive in the works."

My meeting at the Newseum could fix that, but I wasn't ready to share that with him yet.

I picked up the phone and punched out a number in Sand Falls, Idaho, specifically a ranch called Freedom Lake, headquarters for one of the most far-reaching militia groups in America. A young man picked up on the second ring.

"Minutemen," he said.

I put on my sternest voice. "Daniel there?" I said.

"Who wants to know?" the kid said.

"Jack Flynn from the Boston *Record*," I said sharply. I had met with Daniel Nathaniel—yes, it's his real name—a year ago, and we had hit it off in an odd kind of way.

The kid put me on hold without saying anything, and next thing I heard was the voice of Nathaniel. "Do you know how hard it is to keep good soldiers inspired in a revolution, Jack? And you trying to scare my best receptionist away?"

"Sorry about that, old man," I said. "Here's the thing. I need some help, and I think you're in a position to give it. I need to know what you're picking up on this Hutchins assassination attempt. Where'd this Harvey Oswald wannabe come from?"

"What I have would surprise you," Nathaniel said. "But you know I'm not going to talk about it over the phone like this."

Of course not. Daniel Nathaniel, like every red-blooded militia revolutionary, believed that the federal government, in its role of Big Brother, was listening to every conversation of every citizen every day. I would have to hotfoot it to Idaho after all.

"You going to be around for the next few days?" I asked.

"Where would I go?" he said. "I'm in God's country out here."

AT THE entrance to the West Wing of the White House, a marine in full-dress uniform stands so straight that visitors think he might be a toy soldier, until he snaps open the substantial door with a flip of his brawny wrist. Inside, in the lush reception area, an inevitably becoming woman escorts callers to their destination.

I don't know why I bring this up, because as a reporter, I am required to enter through the press briefing room. It looks nice on television, when presidential spokesman Royal Dalton stands before a deep blue curtain with a White House emblem at his afternoon briefings. The podium gleams, the room looks spacious and official. In point of fact, though, it is an absolute pit. The threadbare rug is stained by the slush of too many winters, and the chairbacks are soiled by pencil gouges and graffiti marks.

Sunday noon brought me through this very room. I climbed the few steps into the West Wing from the press area and announced myself to a uniformed Secret Service agent.

"I have an appointment with the President," I said.

He picked up the telephone, had a brief conversation, then led me past the Cabinet Room into an anteroom with two secretaries, one of whom greeted me with an enormous smile.

"Sylvia Weinrich," she said, holding out a perfectly manicured hand. "It's delightful to see you. Why don't we head right in. The President will want to get started."

Sylvia brought me through a pair of wide doors into one of the most incredible places I have ever been: the Oval Office. The rug was such a colorful blue you could almost get lost in it. In the middle was an eagle within the presidential seal. Sunlight streamed in through French doors. Magnificent portraits decorated the walls, including an unfinished one of George Washington hanging over the fireplace. Hutchins was at his enormous oak desk at the far end of the room. It was a desk where Presidents have signed declarations of war and treaties of peace, addressed the nation in times of crisis, and taped conversations that would haunt them to their graves. He stood up and boomed, "Jack Flynn, damned nice of you to come over."

"A pleasure, sir," I said as Sylvia backed quietly out of the room.

"Let's sit," Hutchins said, lowering his hand toward a blue-and-white-striped couch that I'd seen on television many times. Hutchins settled in a pale yellow upholstered chair.

"How are your ribs?" he asked as I lowered myself gingerly onto the couch. Then he answered his own question. "Doctors tell me you're doing pretty well. Helps to be young and virile, huh?"

The door to the office swung open, and the tall White House chief of staff, Lincoln Powers, came striding into the room.

"Sorry to interrupt, Mr. President," Powers said. He handed Hutchins an official-looking memorandum, then turned to me. "Well, you look even more handsome in person than on TV. I'm Lincoln Powers, Mr. Flynn. Nice to meet you."

The story of Clayton Hutchins and Lincoln Powers was an unusual one—how the lives of two men had intersected at a time of national crisis, and how they had bonded together ever since.

Hutchins's, mostly, was the amazing story. He had made his mark as a successful businessman in Des Moines, Iowa, taking a start-up technology company that produced personal finance software, called Cookie Jar, into the big leagues, eventually earning its inventor hundreds of millions of dollars. Across Iowa, Hutchins became a folk hero, lauded for his ambitions and his brains and loved for his massive acts of philanthropy. His was a uniquely American story— born and raised on a farm, schooled at home, college-educated later in life, entirely self-made in the worlds of both commerce and government.

His entrance to politics was unconventional. A few months before the Iowa governor's race six years ago, a group of business leaders, dissatisfied with the candidates for the two major parties, launched a massive draft-Hutchins movement. Hutchins reluctantly accepted. He won with forty-five percent of the vote.

Hutchins came in with a refreshing ability to speak the truth and the simple promise that he would run the government like a business. He balanced the state's budget. He fired a string of high-level managers who had long been suspected of corruption. He spoke his mind, spoke it often, and spoke it well.

Two years later the Republican front-runner for the presidency,

Senator Wordsworth Cole, found himself getting battered in Iowa public opinion polls a week before the caucus. So Hutchins unleashed his power to help Cole win, and win he did. From there, Cole steamrolled into New Hampshire and then across the country and all the way to the Republican nomination.

Flash ahead to three weeks before the November election. *The New York Times* published a report that Cole's vice presidential running mate, Senator Steven Sugara of Wyoming, had been addicted to Prozac two years earlier but had never disclosed the fact. The Cole campaign went into a tailspin. Hutchins met up with Cole on the campaign trail and told him to stand behind his nominee. He did and staggered to a slim victory. A week later Sugara resigned. Hutchins was picked as Vice President, and he continued like that for three and a half years.

At first my brethren in the news media thought his personality might not fit the role. Hutchins was blunt. His voice was hard, as if it had been pounded by rocks. He was built like a fireplug, at five feet ten inches. His face was rough, his hair thinning, and he was anything but handsome, yet when he met with contributors or businessmen, he spawned many imitators. He was someone who seemed to expect wild success, but when he achieved it, he gave the impression it would never change him.

As Vice President, he was strong, but he knew his place. He was fully aware he had not been elected. Then this past August, one week before the Republican Convention, President Cole dropped dead of a massive heart attack. By nightfall Hutchins had taken the oath of office. Like Jerry Ford, he became President without ever winning a single vote on a national ticket.

Hutchins accepted his party's nomination at a subdued convention in Chicago. Throughout the campaign he remained silent as his Democratic opponent, the respected Senator from Colorado, Stanny Nichols, got pelted by accusations over some decade-old income tax issue back home. It was still a tight race, but Hutchins was watching his poll numbers climb in the wake of the attempt on his life. As I sat in the Oval Office on this day, two months into

Hutchins's presidency, victory had become more realistic than at any other point in the campaign.

Back in August one of the first things he did after taking the oath was call Lincoln Powers's sprawling cattle ranch to plead with the elegant Texan to return to the White House for one last tour of duty. Powers was the most experienced, most respected political adviser in America, a confidant to Republican Presidents for three decades. He knew Washington and he knew power, and I suspect he had been an invaluable part of Hutchins's transition.

"Sorry to cut in on you here," Powers said to me as the President penned a note in the margin of the memorandum. As Powers took the papers back and walked from the room, a telephone rang. I looked down and saw a red light blink along a column that had various agencies listed: CIA, State, Chief of Staff, Treasury. The light illuminated beside the FBI.

"Yes," Hutchins said, sounding annoyed as he answered the phone. There was a pause as he listened; then he hung up without saying good-bye and turned to me. "So where are you in terms of our discussion Thursday?"

My eyes drifted around the room. I looked out the French doors, into the Rose Garden, where the last of the season's hardiest flowers fluttered in the autumn breeze. I looked down to the South Lawn and imagined walking across the grass to Marine One and lifting off for Camp David. Finally, I looked at Hutchins, and not a moment too soon, because he seemed to be getting aggravated with me. "You have to understand, I've had a lot going on these past couple of days, and my first obligation is to the newspaper."

"I understand that," he fired back. "I also have an election to win, then a country to run. And I need people like you with me, at least for the latter. And not just people *like* you, but specifically you. I know the timing could be better on all of this, but you owe it to your country to make a decision."

"I just want to be sure. Tell me again what you have in mind."

"You come aboard here as the White House press secretary. My plan is to ship Dalton off to an agency, maybe Interior."

"Why me?" I asked.

"You come highly recommended. I used to read you when I was campaigning in New Hampshire and grew to be a fan. You also have a way with people. I also don't have a clue what your politics are, which I like. In short, I think we'd work well together. Here's the bottom line. I'm going to need a decision on Friday. That gives you five days. If not you, I have to move on and look for someone else." He began to stand up.

"Sir," I said in as calm and confident a voice as I could, "any idea who this dead would-be assassin is?"

Hutchins sat back down in his chair. "FBI still tells me they think he's a militia member, despite what you guys are saying about the government's inability to link him with a group. Hell, the Secret Service has a security alert going. Their vast preference is for me not to even leave the White House. They want to make me a prisoner of this place, only I have a campaign to run and win. I can't afford to play anything safe right now."

And that, ladies and gentlemen, is what you call news. I jotted down what he said on a yellow legal pad.

"We on the record?" Hutchins asked.

I nodded. "As far as I'm concerned, sir. Is that a problem?"

The President chuckled. "You're some piece of work," he said. "I like that, though. I like that a lot."

I pressed on with more bravado. "And you're satisfied with the FBI investigation so far?" I asked, then quickly added, "And what is it that leads them to believe that this was a militiaman?"

"Two different questions," Hutchins said. "To the first, hell, they're the greatest law-enforcement agency on the earth. If they tell me they believe it was a militiaman who tried to kill me, then I believe it was a militiaman who tried to kill me. On the evidence they're basing that on, you know I can't get into that."

Hutchins stood up. He walked over to his desk, pulled a sheet of paper out of a drawer, and walked back over toward me. "You didn't get this from me," he said, placing it in my hands.

I quickly scanned the document. It was on Treasury Department letterhead, Secret Service Division, dated October 18. It began, "Dear Mr. President, It has come to our attention through the Federal Bureau of Investigation that there has been a secondhand threat on your life. This memo is an advisory of several security measures being taken for your protection."

I soaked in every word, then scribbled furiously into my notebook as Hutchins sat back in his chair, waiting patiently. When I looked up, he told me, "You'll identify me as one of those *senior* White House officials you bastards are always quoting without names. Now I want you to think about our other issue. Come over here and work in the White House. It will be the best experience you've ever had."

I stood up, and we shook hands. On the way out, the carpet was so thick it was like walking on air, or maybe it was the euphoria that comes with a nice news hit.

MARTIN was sitting at my desk when I glided into the newsroom. I put my notebook down and slowly peeled off my jacket.

"C'mon. What do you have?" he asked.

"Nothing. A big zero."

"What are you talking about? You sit with the President of the United States three days after he has been shot and nine days before the election, and you walked out of there with nothing?" His face had flushed to an extraordinary shade of crimson.

"Get a grip," I said. "And get out of my chair. I have a lot of work to do. Would you call a high-level security alert a good story? What if the President said the FBI is still telling him that this assassination attempt was the result of the militia movement?"

"So you're saying this is what you have?" Martin asked, afraid to get excited in case I was pulling another prank on him.

"This is what I have," I said.

Martin looked stunned, but in a good way. "I'll call Boston," he said, moving away from the chair.

I settled in at my desk, got comfortable, and took my readers on a brisk walk through a flowering garden, as an old editor of mine used to say. The prose flowed nicely, and after I shipped the story to

Martin, I wondered if it would trigger another call from my anonymous voice, and if it did, what he might say.

"Idaho?" That was Martin, who had appeared at my desk, his euphoria ebbing toward the needs of the next news cycle.

"Hutchins's story does give Idaho more weight, doesn't it?"

"More than ever. I'll assume you're in the air tomorrow."

THERE is an exhibit at the Newseum—a museum dedicated to the journalism industry, of all things—that allows tourists to stand before a camera, with the White House as a backdrop, and broadcast their own news story on a nearby television screen.

I took comfort in this knowledge, figuring that my meeting with this anonymous source might actually give these network wannabes something to report on. At about five twenty p.m. I paid my admission to the museum, which sits in Rosslyn, Virginia, just across the Potomac River, and began walking around the exhibits.

The Newseum closes at six. Soon I heard footsteps coming from across the hard tile floor; then a man called to me, "Excuse me, sir, but we're closing down for the evening." I turned to see a gentleman in a security uniform. He looked startled when he saw my face and added, "Oh, Mr. Flynn, I had no idea it was you. We'll be doing some cleaning for a while. Feel free to enjoy the museum in the meantime."

"Thank you," I said. So celebrity has its advantages.

I poked around for about thirty minutes, until it was quite obvious I was the only one in the place. Suddenly, to my left, a wall of television screens, twenty feet high and maybe twice that in length, popped to life—hundreds of screens, each filled with the image of Peter Jennings broadcasting ABC's *World News Tonight*. I'll admit I like Peter Jennings, but enough is enough.

"Tonight, growing questions on Thursday's assassination attempt against President Clayton Hutchins," Jennings said.

I looked around to see if anyone was watching me watch Peter, but the rest of the museum was empty.

"At FBI headquarters the official line remains that investigators continue to probe whether the shooting is tied to the nation's militia movement," Jennings said. "But within the FBI, sources tell ABC News there is a paucity of evidence pointing in that direction. Meanwhile, those who knew the dead would-be assassin, Tony Clawson, express surprise. We go now to Jackie Judd in Fresno, California, for a report on the life and death of Tony Clawson."

The image of a Home Depot store flashed on all those screens as the reporter's voice filled the Newseum. Around a nearby bend I heard what sounded like shoes on tile. I stared in that direction.

"Mr. Flynn?"

It was an urgent voice, emanating from the balcony above me. My eyes bolted upward, but I could see nothing but darkness.

"Who is it?" I yelled back.

"Stay right there, Mr. Flynn." The voice was younger than I had expected, given that the phone calls sounded like they came from a reasonably old man.

I stayed silent, waiting, but nothing happened. "Where are you?" I yelled, but got no response. It was beginning to dawn on me that this wasn't just some innocent meeting between a reporter and a confidential source. Problem is, that thought struck me just as I heard a loud crack—a sound that was becoming all too familiar these past few days.

I'm not sure whether I ducked or just flinched. Nor was I sure where the bullet came from. Because of that, I didn't know which way to run and feared that if I peeled off in any given direction, I might find myself face to face with my stalking gunman. Times like these, I wish I had just become a copy editor.

I looked behind me to see Peter Jennings's face blown out on one of the television screens, and that image sent a convulsion through my body. It also prompted me to get flat to the floor and begin crawling toward the door, figuring that was probably the best direction to head. I strained to hear any other sounds, but all I could really hear, Jennings aside, was the sound of my own heavy breathing. So I kept crawling to the entrance, about forty feet away, across the center of the museum floor. Every inch I covered, I wondered whether I was an inch closer to safety or death.

About halfway there I veered toward a heavy door marked with an illuminated sign that read EMERGENCY EXIT. ALARM WILL SOUND. Maybe sounding alarms wasn't such a bad idea. I braced myself on all fours and hurled myself against the door. It flew open, and a shrieking alarm filled the air. I found myself on some nondescript street in Rosslyn. I ran the one block to the Metro station. A train was sliding toward the platform as I bounded down the escalator. The doors rolled open, and I grabbed a pole to hold and stared out the rear window as we pulled away.

I'M IRISH. I have the ability to brood for hours at a time. If I ever needed bypass surgery, I'm convinced my doctors would open up my chest and find that my heart is an alarming shade of black. I love to drink, to tell stories, to laugh hard. But if you really want to see ethnic, take a look at Steve Havlicek.

He stands about five feet six inches, though he doesn't seem short. His face is like a Rand McNally map of wrinkles. His hair, graying, is often matted against his big scalp or sticking up in various directions in wisps. He talks loud. He laughs even louder. His wife, Margaret, his high school sweetheart, is gorgeous. They have two grown children. They seem to have an ideal relationship, the type of love that tears barriers down. Ah, but there I go getting deep.

"What a place." That was Havlicek, walking into the paneled Grille Room at the University Club, an establishment where I have remained a member in good standing for many years. The University Club is my one true indulgence. Years ago it was my refuge, a place to steal away for a few hours from the grind of work. Now, with Katherine gone, the club had become something of a second home for me.

Havlicek looked around the lounge and said, "High-roller city, huh? I bet lots of big guns come in here."

I don't think he quite understood the general code of conduct at all private clubs—one of understated appreciation. Members neither gawk at nor mock each other, at least in a forum as public as the club bar. So I ignored that.

I had arrived comfortably ahead of him, giving myself enough time to clean myself up in the marble men's room, knock down a Miller High Life, and try to calm my nerves.

Lyle, the bartender, caught Havlicek's eye. "Can I get you something, sir?" he asked.

"You bet. I'll have a Heineken."

Havlicek wrapped his hairy hand around the ice-cold bottle and took a long gulp before Lyle could even hurry down the bar with a frosted pilsner glass. "That overnight flight wiped me out, so I didn't get much today," he said to me, his eyes meeting mine for the first time since he walked in. Then, urgently, "What happened to you? I thought I was a mess, but look at you, you're a wreck."

"A tough day. Let me regroup first, and I'll tell you about it."

I had already decided to tell him about the anonymous calls and note, for a couple of reasons. First, he would probably be of help on it. He had one of the best investigative minds in the country. Second, it would be vastly unfair to withhold information from him on this story. If anyone did it to me, I would be furious. And given what had just happened to me, I really had no choice anymore, for my own safety and perhaps his as well.

"So we've got a dead assassin wannabe who no one knows who the hell he is," I said as we leaned on the bar. "We've got the FBI pointing the finger at the militias, and no one knows why. Basically we've got nothing."

"Martin says you might fly out and talk to a militia pal of yours in Idaho? That might be a good idea, just to be able to print that the militias definitively say they don't know who this guy is."

I tugged Havlicek toward an empty table. "Look," I said after we sat down, "I think someone just took a shot at me." I saw the look of confusion on his face. "Let me start from the beginning. An anonymous caller rang me up in the hospital Thursday afternoon, then again on Friday morning. Then someone followed me to a restaurant last night and gave the waitress a note telling me to meet him at the Newseum tonight at five thirty."

"What happened?" Havlicek said.

I told him the details. When I was through, Havlicek said, "That's some story. You never saw the guy?"

"Not even a glimpse."

Havlicek said, "What's the caller sound like?"

"He's older and very eloquent. He's polite but forceful."

"Was that the voice that called out to you at the Newseum?"

"That's the thing," I replied. "I don't think it was. The voice there sounded much younger, much livelier, less formal."

"Probably two different people," Havlicek said. "One person wants to help you get information. The other person wants to make sure you never get it. The good guy, assuming there is one—how did he leave it with you?"

"Says he'll help me more once he's convinced I'm serious."

"Well, the answer is to keep getting hits on this story."

A waiter came over with some menus.

Havlicek said, "Something's been bothering me. Why were you playing golf with Hutchins in the first place?"

"Presidential pardons," I said. "Every year the President pardons any given number of convicts. Most have easy explanations, like a convict in a questionable murder conviction becomes a model inmate and is freed to spend his dying days with his family. I came across one in Massachusetts—a Paul Stemple, involved in an armored car heist back in the late 1970s—that lacked an easy answer. So I asked Royal Dalton about it, but he never properly explained the genesis of the pardon. Then, out of nowhere, he says the President would like to know if I might be available for a game of golf."

Havlicek cut in and said, "So you asked Hutchins about it?"

"Well, I planned to, yes. But before I could, we got shot."

"Let me ask you something far-fetched," Havlicek said. "You don't think there's any way Hutchins or his people might have staged this assassination attempt as some sort of preelection ploy?"

I nodded my head slowly. "I'll admit I've thought about that. But come on. How dangerous is that?"

"Yeah, too stupid. So somebody wants to help you. Somebody else wants to kill you. You have to watch your back."

I nodded, and we both turned to the menu. We ordered some smoked salmon, a couple of hamburgers. At ten o'clock Havlicek announced he had to head back to his hotel and call his wife.

Watch your back. I started to walk outside, then thought better of it. The dog was with Kristen, so I ambled up to the front desk, got a guest key, and slept in one of the overnight rooms upstairs.

Chapter Four

Boston, Massachusetts
February 13, 1979

FINALLY Curtis Black decided it was time to break the heavy silence. For ten minutes, as he drove the blue van out of Chelsea, then into Boston, no one had uttered a word, not Black himself, not his three men sitting on the floor in the back. All of the men wore gloves; all of them were dressed in gray; all of them were packing a 9-mm semiautomatic weapon that Black hoped they would never have to use. The fourth man would be meeting them on Hanover Street in the getaway car—a 1978 Lincoln Continental, stolen the week before. A fifth man would be meeting them on the Boston Fish Pier in a second getaway car, a Mercury station wagon.

They had gone over their plan one final time, sitting around the little kitchen table of Black's Chelsea apartment. They had run through a checklist of actions. Everyone knew his role.

Black was heading for the North End. The sun had given way to afternoon clouds and the threat of rain, which might be good. Clear the streets of passersby—each one a potential witness.

"About three minutes, and we're there," Black called out to the men in back. "Coming down Prince Street."

Black checked his watch. It was four forty-four p.m., about twelve minutes until action. So many things to go wrong. But he reminded himself: He was the most meticulous criminal strategist in Boston, a mastermind of bank heists and store holdups whose reputation was held in awe. This job, though, represented his most daring venture—a daylight armored car strike involving a take of anywhere from $600,000 to $1 million. This was a sleeper of a bank branch, a repository for Mafia money that was usually deposited every Tuesday afternoon after the weekend receipts.

"On Hanover Street. One minute to arrival."

He scanned the street, looking for anything unusual, but saw nothing. He double-parked the van in the precise spot where he had for the past couple of scouting missions.

A minute later, in his rearview mirror, Black saw the Lincoln pull up about two car lengths behind him and double-park, filling him with relief. "Getaway car has arrived," he called out.

Four minutes later Black said, "Put your earpieces in place," and the three men in back inserted small wires into their ears. "Test them," Black said. He spoke quietly into the microphone pinned to the wrist of his shirt. "Testing, one, two, three. Testing. Please acknowledge."

"Gotcha," Rocco responded.

"Fine," Cox said.

Stemple, the third man in the van, added, "With you."

Black said, "Car two, hold up your hand if you can hear." He looked in his rearview mirror and received the signal he wanted.

Suddenly, a problem. In the mirror Black's eye caught something he didn't expect. A meter maid—a man, actually—walking purposefully down the street with his ticket book in hand.

Black cracked his window and watched in his side mirror as the man approached the getaway car behind him. He saw the meter man and his driver exchange words, then saw the meter man write out a ticket and insert it under the windshield wiper. Now the meter man was coming toward the van. He said loudly, "Move it along. Move along."

Black ignored him, hiding his face with his arm in as casual a way as he could. Even as he did this, the ramifications flashed through his mind. This meter man would place the robbers at the scene. He would be asked to help with composite drawings. Those drawings would eventually be broadcast on television.

The meter man stood at the cracked window. "Move your van."

Black still ignored him. So the meter man wrote out a ticket with a flourish, stuck it under the windshield wiper, and proclaimed, "That's fifty bucks, jerk." With that, he walked on.

At that exact moment Black saw the armored car slowly fill his side mirror, then lumber in front of him. His mind raced. He had two choices: Pull the plug on the operation, at least for now, or he could go on as planned and hope that the composite sketches looked nothing like anything that would matter.

In front of him the armored car was backing up toward the van. Urgently Black kept asking himself, Stay or go? Stay or go?

The driver's-side door opened slowly on the armored car. Black said softly into his microphone, "Truck has arrived. Driver getting out. Ski masks on. Four minutes to action."

Present Day
Monday, October 30

EVERYONE is waiting for something—waiting for a better job, waiting for true love. Me, I was waiting too, though I wasn't exactly sure what for. After Katherine died, I looked neither at my past nor toward my future. I lost myself in work, hoping the pain would eventually pass—and waiting was the only way I knew how.

Which is why I like flying. There is no shame in sitting back and doing nothing but waiting. I like to doze in and out while reading a trashy novel. I like to stare out the window. I especially like sitting in first class on long flights, when leggy stewardesses—I'm sorry, flight attendants—supply me with hot towels, newspapers, a choice between salmon and filet mignon for dinner.

Monday morning found me in this precise situation, in the first-class cabin of a US Airways Boeing 757 destined for Seattle, where I would connect to Spokane. It struck me, somewhere between the Mississippi and the Dakotas, that I had a particularly significant amount of waiting going on. I was waiting for a break in the biggest story of my life. And I was waiting to arrive at a decision on the White House press secretary's position.

At the Spokane airport, I rented a Grand Am and headed west, through Coeur d'Alene, then north up to Sand Falls. All the way, I traveled a two-lane highway rimmed by towering pines and verdant hills—beauty that hides a land of inner desperation and racism. The boys up here, they'll rail against anything from the federal government to the blacks who steal the rightful jobs of white men.

Daniel Nathaniel was exactly this kind of guy. He was a former undertaker who had lost his family funeral home to the IRS for reasons that were suspect at best. After a brief prison stint for tax evasion, he had hooked up with a group of militant farmers and formed the Idaho Minutemen. Within months he ascended to the position of commander, inherited a farmhouse from one of the members, and surrounded himself with a team of bodyguards.

I arrived at the farmhouse on Freedom Lake at one p.m. and was stopped at a gatehouse by a skinny kid with droopy eyes.

"Stop right there," he shouted, stepping out in front of my car.

With this postadolescent playing the role of Patton, I couldn't control my disdain. Rolling down my window, I said dismissively, "Let Daniel Nathaniel know that Jack Flynn is here."

"Is the commander expecting you?" the kid asked, equally dismissive. I didn't like that.

"I don't know what the commander is expecting. You'll have to ask him that when you call to tell him I'm here."

The kid looked at me. I wasn't sure whether he was unclear on what to do next or unwilling to honor my request, so I asked him, "That a new squirt gun in your Batman belt? It looks really neat."

"Screw you," he said, putting his hand on some sort of weapon. He walked away to get his two-way radio in the guard shack.

After a couple of minutes he approached my car window. "You want to go straight along this dirt road—"

"Yeah, I've been here before," I said. I drove off along a dirt road about two miles. At the dilapidated farmhouse two men came running down off the porch to meet my car. These guys were Nathaniel's bodyguards, and one of them frisked me.

They led me into the main room of the farmhouse. Nathaniel was sitting behind a metal desk at the far end of the room. He stood up when I walked in and stretched his hand toward me.

"Welcome back," he said in a serious tone. "You here to enlist?"

I gave him a polite laugh. "You'd never take me," I said. "Flat feet. My father's black. Oh, and I'm gay."

He didn't laugh at my humor. Never has, come to think of it. And I saw his young bodyguards flash each other a look before scurrying from the room like a pair of rodents.

"How's the fight going?" I asked as I settled into a chair.

"We're going to win," he said. "The government is weak—weaker than you think. And one day we will rise to conquer."

I said, smiling, "Hopefully that day won't be today, because I was hoping you had a little time for me."

"All the time you need," he said.

I asked, "So, what do you know?"

"About what?" he replied.

I rolled my eyes, but only to myself. He wanted to make a game over this, and I had no choice but to play along. "You mind tape?" I asked, pulling a microcassette out of my jacket.

He said, "My words are meant to last forever."

"Good. The President tells me that the FBI has evidence that the militia movement is behind the recent assassination attempt against him. I'm wondering whether you believe this to be true."

"Maybe," he said.

"What do you mean, maybe?" I said, trying to maintain patience.

"Maybe. Maybe means maybe. Possibly. Perhaps."

This was getting sophomoric, but I had to play along. "Help me out. I'm not precisely sure what you mean by maybe."

He cast his eyes on my microcassette.

I said, "You want me to turn that off?"

He nodded. So much for his everlasting words.

"What do you know about this?" I asked.

He paused. "I have reliable information that this assassination attempt was sponsored by a group of freedom fighters based in Wyoming. They're a relatively new unit with a commander who's hell-bent on making a national mark. This was intended to be it."

I sat for a moment in stunned silence. Nathaniel was essentially confirming the initial FBI line on the shooting, cutting against the grain of most other stories since. This was a significant development. A story indicating that a high-placed source within the militia movement was suggesting that the assassination attempt was militia-related would put me and the *Record* way ahead of the game.

"Okay," I said, adrenaline flowing, "what's the guy's name in Wyoming?"

"Billy Walbin. Billy Joe Walbin to his friends."

I asked, "He accessible?"

"I don't know. Maybe not if one of his guys just took a potshot at the President and bought the farm."

I said, "I need to get this into print. Back in Washington the FBI brass is saying one thing. The rank and file is leaking something decidedly different to *The New York Times* and the rest of the press. I need your information to get something together on this. I need to know how you know."

He said, "Take the information to the bank."

I replied, "The only place I can take it is to my editor, who's going to demand to know how you know. And unless you tell me, it will never see the light of day."

After a pause Nathaniel looked me in the eye and said, "I have a pipeline into his group, but if that gets into print, my source is dead and maybe so am I. The information is good."

That takes care of that. I felt my hand balling up into a fist. All that adrenaline. "What conditions are we talking under?" I asked.

"A source familiar with the nation's militia movement," he said.

That was too vague, leaving open the possibility that it was a law-enforcement official. "How about a well-placed militia leader?"

"And the day you print that, you can come out and cover the assassination of Daniel Nathaniel for your paper."

"An authority who monitors developments within the militia movement?" I suspected he'd like being called an authority.

He thought for a moment and said, "Good."

I checked my watch for the time: two thirty p.m. Pacific, meaning five thirty in Boston. West Coast stories are a killer, given the deadline issues. Much to my joy, I had achieved more than I thought I would on this trip. The problem now was getting it into print.

"You learned about this but didn't go to the feds with it?" I said.

"I don't like the feds."

Good point. I pressed him but didn't get any more. Finally I said, "I have to run. I appreciate your help."

He hit a button on his desk, and his two security goons came in. The interview was over. I bade a quick farewell to Nathaniel.

Outside, I drove down the dusty road as fast as the Grand Am would take me, slowing down at the guard shack on the way out only so the kid there could see me flipping him the middle finger.

Decision time. No matter how I argued it in my own mind, I knew this story would benefit from another day of reporting. I was caught in what is known as a cycle, when newspapers breathlessly publish scraps of information, half-truths, even nontruths. This was about competition, not about reader enlightenment.

I replayed the day. A prominent militia leader was saying, for the first time, that the assassination attempt was likely part of a militia-related conspiracy born in the hills of rural Wyoming. Whether this was enough of a story to get the anonymous old man to call me again, I couldn't be sure.

Still, there were many unanswered questions here, chief among them, Who was Billy Walbin, and what might he have to say about this? Could Stevens or Drinker add anything? Would they? Was the FBI already onto the Wyoming angle, or would this be news to them? Right now the story had more holes in it than Tony Clawson. Near deadline on a Monday evening, I doubted whether I would be able to fill them. I decided that Drinker would be my best shot, so I placed a call on my cell phone to FBI headquarters in Washington.

"Kent Drinker's office, please," I told the receptionist.

The phone rang six times before it kicked over to his voice mail. I left my cell phone number and hung up. I then called my travel agent to see what time the last flight of the day left Spokane.

As I cruised down the highway toward Coeur d'Alene, I wondered what Katherine and I might have been doing on this Monday night. Maybe we would be spooning little bits of mashed vegetables to our baby. Maybe we'd be strolling the neighborhood, pushing the carriage, with the dog padding along beside us.

As I stared blankly out the window, the cellular telephone rang.

"Jack Flynn here," I said, my throat surprisingly thick.

"Kent Drinker here. What can I do for you?"

I replied, "I'm running with a story tomorrow saying that an authority familiar with the inner workings of the militia movement believes the assassination attempt was orchestrated by a newly formed militia unit in Wyoming. I'm trying to see if the FBI has been pursuing that lead."

There was nothing but dead air on the other end of the line. "Hello?" I finally asked.

"Hold on," Drinker said. "I'm just trying to figure out what I can safely tell you." Another stretch of silence; then he added, "You would not be inaccurate in reporting that FBI investigators have been probing the relationship of a Wyoming militia group to this assassination attempt. I would be willing to say that, on the condition of anonymity, as a senior law-enforcement official."

I asked, "How did you get turned on to the Wyoming group?"

"No way am I going that far with you," he said. "You have enough for a significant story. You sure have more than your competition." And then the click of his telephone.

It was abrupt, but it didn't really matter. I had hit pay dirt. I dialed directory assistance in Cody, Wyoming, the hometown of the Wyoming Freedomfighters. They weren't listed, but a B. J. Walbin was, so I called. On the other end I got a snotty kid who referred me to their spokesman, who declined to comment.

Finally, I called Peter Martin at the office. I walked him briskly through what I had and told him where I wanted to go.

"How long before you can file?" he asked.

I said, "I'll have to write it from the road and hunt down someplace to transmit. Can you buy me a couple of hours?"

"No sweat. File to me. I'll buy you time in Boston."

I was urgently scanning the darkening road for a place to pull over, when I spotted a red neon sign that announced THE DEW DROP INN. Outside were about a dozen pickup trucks.

Inside, everything was made of particleboard. Smoke filled the air, along with the smell of beer. I stepped toward the bartender and said, "White wine spritzer please, with a wedge of lemon."

Just kidding. Mrs. Flynn didn't raise any fools. I ordered a Budweiser, specifically saying, "Longneck."

The bartender popped it down on the bar. "Buck and a quarter."

My, my, I thought. Maybe this place wasn't so bad after all. "You mind if I plug a laptop in over at that booth?" I asked.

"All yours," he said.

I laid a pair of twenties between us. "Hit the bar all around."

That gesture of goodwill bought me exactly what I had hoped: some privacy to type out a story as fast as I could, without interruption. When I was done, the bartender, Gerry, allowed me the use of his telephone to send my story east. Once it was gone, I had some time before my flight, so I ordered another Bud and took a seat at the bar.

A few minutes later my pager sounded, and I took a quick look at it. "Great show. Peter," it said, his signal that he was done editing. Another trip, another success.

But life tends to throw you little curveballs, and one came at me at that moment in the form of the skinny guard from Nathaniel's compound, walking through the door of the Dew Drop Inn. He took the barstool next to mine and ordered a rum and Coke. I was packing my computer away in its case when he said, "The little faggot's going to run right on out of here, huh? Scared?"

"Faggot's not exactly scared," I explained to him as I zipped up the case and put my arms through my coat. "Got a plane to catch."

As my arms were just going into the sleeves of my coat, his left hand shot out, grabbed the back of my head, and slammed my face down into the bar. When I pulled my head up in something of a daze, he kneed me in the crotch, causing me to double over in pain.

As I gasped for air, all the other nice patrons pushed their barstools out and surrounded us. He was one of them, a homeboy. I was the guy who an hour ago had bought everyone a round of beer. One guy called out, "Don't go too hard on him, Bo."

Bo didn't adhere to what I thought was reasoned and reasonable counsel. As I remained crunched down, he took a roundhouse swing at the side of my face. His fist grazed my cheek and kept going. That's when he glared at me and said, "I should have kicked the crap out of the last fed who came here too."

Kicked the crap out of the last fed. I didn't know what he meant, but I had a nagging suspicion. I rose up out of my pain-induced crouch and faked a punch to Bo's face. He overreacted, bringing his arms toward his head, exposing his midsection. I zeroed in and punched his stomach so hard he landed on his ass. I grabbed him by his hair, asking, "What fed, Bo? What fed?"

He was actually crying now. Crying. I forced his head around in the grit, and he barely resisted. "What fed?"

He continued to whimper and took a flailing shot at my face with his right fist. He missed.

I pushed his face around on the dirty floor again. "Tell me about the fed before I break your neck."

"He was here two weeks ago," Bo said, collecting himself. "Someone said he was an FBI guy named Kent. Met with the commander at headquarters for two hours. First him, now's you. I'd like to know what's going on."

"I'll tell you over tea sometime," I said to him. I got up, pulled a twenty and a ten out of my pocket, put them on the bar in front of Gerry, and said, "Set Bo up with his next couple of drinks, and buy the rest of the boys a round."

I gathered up my stuff and was off into the night. Hurtling down that two-lane road, I called Peter Martin's condominium in Arlington, Virginia. He answered on the first ring.

"Flynn here," I said. "Kill that story in the second edition."

"What?"

"I think maybe we've been had. I just found out that Drinker might have been out here a couple of weeks ago, before the assassination attempt. I don't know why, but I don't like it."

"We kill that story," Martin said, "and we look ridiculous."

"We leave it in for the full run, and we look negligent."

There was a silence before Martin said, "I'll do what I can."

It was a long ride to the airport and an even longer walk down to my room in the miserable airport hotel where I was forced to spend the night because I had missed the last flight. It gave me time to convince myself that by screwing up, perhaps I learned something far more valuable than anything I previously had.

Tuesday, October 31

WHEN I awoke the next morning, Tuesday morning, I couldn't help but wonder if my anonymous source had read the version of the Boston *Record* with my story or without it.

The flight back to Washington seemed arduously long, even with another soft leather seat up in first class. From the airport, as they announced the final boarding, I called my message services at home and work for the third time of the morning. Nothing. My pager sounded, and I fairly jumped through the ceiling of the US Airways Club. "Jack," the message scrolled, "have new information. Need to discuss. University Club at eight? Steve."

I picked up a telephone and belted out Havlicek's number at the bureau, but got no answer, so I left a message saying eight was fine.

On the plane, I ordered the Sonoma chicken and opted for water instead of wine. Ends up, the chicken was a smart move. Everyone who ordered the fish seemed to be sick as a dog.

The guy in front of me was groaning in his seat. I had to just get out of there. Mother Teresa I am not. So I headed for the back of the plane. I dawdled. I chatted with the stewardesses in the galley.

When I settled back into my seat and leaned toward the seat pocket for a book, I felt something crinkle beneath me. I reached behind my back and pulled out a folded sheet of white paper with my name written across it. I gingerly opened the sheet up and saw a few lines of perfect penmanship. "Dear Mr. Flynn," it began.

"You are on the right track. I am here to help you. I will be in touch in the next couple of days to guide you. Do not believe what they tell you. The would-be assassin is not Tony Clawson."

My informant was right here on the plane! Quickly I flagged a flight attendant. "Ma'am, did you happen to see the person who dropped this paper on my seat?" I asked as I held up the note.

She said, "No, I'm sorry. We've been really busy," as she pushed past me. I scanned everyone's face around me, looking for some reaction. I got none. Obviously, this guy meant business. Either he was on the plane or an emissary was. He had followed me across the country. He watched me diligently, waiting for me to get up so he could drop this. What was the point of catching me mid-flight? Did he just want to show me how serious he was? And had he read the story I had in the early edition today?

I sat rigid in my seat for the next three hours, assuming I was being watched. When we landed, I self-consciously collected my carry-ons, walked off the plane, and jumped into a cab.

BY THE time I had made my way through the Grille Room, Lyle had already drawn me a Sam Adams Autumn Brew.

I joined Havlicek at a nearby table. He looked at the bruise on my left cheek and said, "Whoa, you look like hell."

"Yeah, violent business we're in. I took a shot from one of Nathaniel's lackeys. The whole trip was something worse than strange. First, though, I want to hear what you have."

Havlicek pulled a manila folder out of his briefcase. "Good stuff," he said. "Not sure what it means yet, but I know it's good stuff." He flipped through a sheaf of papers. "Here's the photograph everyone was running of Clawson after the shooting—from a Home Depot security badge out in Fresno."

A waiter stopped by the table. We ordered hamburgers, onion rings, and smoked salmon. Havlicek continued, "So remember, the Secret Service shoots this guy six times in the head. Every one of them connects. You have any idea what a guy looks like who's been shot six times in the head?"

"I really don't."

"Like this." With that, Havlicek slid a large glossy photograph toward me. It was a picture, I believe, of Tony Clawson. My first instinct was to vomit. Chunks of the man's face had been torn out. What remained was almost beyond recognition as a human head. Oddly enough, one eye remained in place, and that eye was open for the photo shoot. I was stunned into silence. I wondered if I could trade that hamburger in for a little bowl of fruit salad.

Havlicek said, "Take a look at that eye. What color is that?"

I said, "Looks to be brown."

"Bingo," he said. "Now take another look at the Home Depot ID photo. What do you see?"

"Blue eyes," I said. I paused, then added, "Oh, my God."

The waiter returned with the food. Havlicek bit into his burger like a ravenous dog. I opted to let mine sit for a while.

I said, "But we can't jump to conclusions. One, this eye is barely an eye, and the color might be off in the photo, or if it isn't, he might be wearing tinted contacts."

"Right. Which is why I got my hands on this." Havlicek slid me a folder marked CONFIDENTIAL. I opened it up to see an autopsy report. Halfway down, under eye color, there it was: brown.

I smiled up at Havlicek as we locked eyes—his brown, mine an ocean blue. "So you have yourself an issue."

"What we have," he said, "is pretty good proof that the man they shot at Congressional isn't the man they say is Tony Clawson, a California drifter with antigovernment tendencies. It's a different guy. I'd like to put that fact in the newspaper."

I took a bite out of my hamburger, forced it down, then pushed the plate to the side. "What's it all mean?" I asked.

Havlicek said, "I don't have a clue."

"I've got two new developments on my front," I said. "First, I heard from my anonymous source again. He gave me this." I handed him the handwritten note.

Havlicek read through it slowly. He looked up and said, "We're really onto something. How'd you get this?"

I said, "On the damned airplane. He—or I should say, someone—left it on my seat when I went into the bathroom."

Havlicek said, "Let me ask you two quick questions. Who is this guy, and what else does he have?"

"I don't know," I said. "Point two, I think there's something strange going on between the FBI and this militia leader I know."

"Go ahead."

I told him of the interview with Daniel Nathaniel, the visit to the bar, the fight with this kid Bo, and of course, Bo's accusations and rantings about the fed named Drinker.

When I was done, Havlicek asked, "So you pulled the plug on your story?"

"I didn't think I had any choice. You think otherwise?"

"No. You did the right thing. But you should know about this."

He slid a computer printout toward me of an Associated Press story that began, "The Boston *Record* first published, then later deleted, a story from its editions today asserting that a newly formed Wyoming-based militia group had sponsored last Thursday's assassination attempt against President Clayton Hutchins. The story was pulled without explanation in an apparent belief that the paper had published wrong or unsupportable information."

"I had too many doubts," I said. "I admit I rushed something I shouldn't have rushed."

Havlicek said, "Screw 'em all. By tomorrow, this is yesterday's news. We're onto even better things right now."

I allowed my thoughts to broaden. I asked half rhetorically, "What is really going on here? We have some anonymous source who has told us that things aren't as they seem, not to believe what others want us to believe. And now we have a point of fact where he's right. The shooter isn't who the feds say the shooter is. That means the motive may not be what the feds say the motive is. And now we have reason to believe that the feds have some bizarre relationship with the militia movement they are accusing of trying to kill the President. Where does that take us?"

"Look back at the Kennedy assassination," Havlicek said. "It's almost forty years after the fact, and people are still arguing over who pulled the trigger and for what reason. For all we know, there is some mysterious force who tries to knock off our Presidents every three decades. Maybe that's what this is all about."

Nothing much to add, and I was getting tired, so I said, "Pretty strange. I've been out of touch all day. Anything happen in the campaign I should know about?"

"No. The polls show Hutchins inching ahead but probably not by as much as Nichols was expecting. The Washington *Post* had another story this morning on that suspicious real estate deal of Nichols's, though I'm not sure the public cares."

"You still think Hutchins could have cooked this shooting up?"

Havlicek only nodded. He said, "Don't be out of touch tomorrow, not even for a moment. We don't want to blow a call from the anonymous one. I'm going to write up this autopsy stuff and put it in the paper. This note makes me more confident than ever that we're right, that we're onto something big. I actually called my wife before I came over. I told her I wouldn't be home until after the election. My sense is, this thing gets a lot bigger before it goes away, and we're with it all the way through, me and you."

SAMANTHA Stevens's recorded voice was far more inviting than it had been in person. This time there was a tinge of concern in her tone, as if something was wrong. And the very fact that she asked me to call her whenever I got the message, regardless of the hour, was telling. I sat on my couch and wondered what she had.

It was only ten p.m. I dialed up Stevens. Ends up, she had left her pager number, which was interesting. Even worried FBI agents don't give their home phone numbers to key witnesses whom they have an enormous crush on. Okay, so I made up the part about the crush. But it wasn't one minute before the phone rang.

"Jack, Samantha Stevens," she said in a fetching tone.

"What can I do for you?" I asked.

She said, "I'd really like to talk about a few things on this case. Would you be available to get together tomorrow?"

I said, "I've got a ton going on at work, obviously. Not every day Presidents get shot in the middle of a campaign. Not every day reporters get shot either, thank God."

Nothing. Not even so much as a chuckle.

"What about tomorrow evening?" she asked.

"That works. How about a drink at Lespinasse, seven thirty."

"Good," she said. "I'll see you there."

# Chapter Five

Wednesday, November 1

WEDNESDAY morning brought a fresh batch of polls to an election that was just six days away—polls that showed Hutchins holding on to a three-point lead over his Democratic rival, Senator Stanny Nichols. A week and a half ago the presidential race was a statistical dead heat, pardon the pun. But the President had received a critical shot in the arm from that, well, shot in the arm. His approval ratings were rising.

Despite Hutchins's good fortune, there was in the country a sense of unease with him, a lack of familiarity—and voters like to feel as if they know their President. Some of that unease was erased out at Congressional Country Club when that nice paramedic was kind enough to poke Hutchins's words around and make him seem a nonchalant, combat-tested hero, cut right out of the American flag.

Give Nichols credit for hanging tough. He had been plagued by allegations of corruption—specifically, using his standing as a United States Senator to receive a highly favorable purchase price on a Breckenridge chalet from the owner of a major ski resort and then failing to pay taxes on it. When all of the major Democrats took a pass on the race because they assumed they'd be running against Hutchins's popular predecessor, Wordsworth Cole, Nichols was the only one who stepped in to fill the void. After Cole died, Nichols had suddenly become a contender. Smartly, he made the press a major issue in his campaign, saying it was time that the news media stopped hindering the rich dialogue of a great nation with two-bit tattletale stories about old, misreported events. It was a message that seemed to resonate with the voting public.

Meanwhile, Hutchins had performed flawlessly in his brief tenure as President. He paid public respect to Cole every chance he got. At the same time, in policy decisions he made clear what he would always call his "respectful" differences.

Then, in an impromptu press conference, a journalist asked Hutchins about his opinion on abortion. It was the first time he had been asked about the issue as President.

"What the hell business is it of mine what a pregnant woman does to herself?" Hutchins growled at the reporter. "Do I want her to have an abortion? No. That's not good for anyone. Am I willing to tell her you can't do this or that with your own body? No again. That's just not what I'm in public life to do."

His answer sent shock waves across the country. The mainstream Republican Party was uneasy about his stand but quickly realized there was nothing anyone could do about it. Hutchins was President, and like it or not, he was their candidate in the November election. And now he was three points ahead.

"What are you doing?"

Peter Martin, arriving at my desk, jarred me back to reality. It was eight thirty a.m. I was in the bureau, hoping my anonymous source would call soon and etching out some questions on a pad to ask him.

"Nothing," I said, feeling like a kid just caught stealing his sister's crayons. I still hadn't told him about this anonymous voice.

"That's some hit Havlicek has for morning, no?" Martin asked.

I said, "It's a great one. I'm going to work the telephones to see if I can help him out on my end."

"Good. I've got to tell you that Appleton"—the editor in chief of the paper—"is none too happy about putting a story on the front page of the first edition yesterday, then having to pull it off."

I said, "Look, Peter, I screwed up. But I think someone was inten- tionally trying to screw me up, and that someone might be the militia leader and the FBI. This could be a much larger story, an exclusive story, because I made that mistake."

Martin started wringing his hands together. He said, "Go on."

I told him what happened. I told of the talk with Nathaniel, of the phone call with Kent Drinker, of the encounter with the kid at the Dew Drop Inn. "The obvious question is, why is an assistant director of the FBI paying a house call on one of the nation's emerging militia leaders the week before a presidential assassination attempt in which the militia is blamed?"

Martin rolled up a chair and sat down beside my desk. He said, "To concoct a story. That's what you think, right?"

I replied, "Well, maybe. But that presupposes that Drinker would know about an assassination attempt, doesn't it?"

"That it does. So why else?" He paused, looking at me, and added, "Because Drinker had a tip about an assassination attempt? He wanted to check it out with the militia."

"Could be," I said. "But then, why the coordinated story lines now about this guy in Wyoming, Billy Walbin?"

We both sat there, baffled.

I said, "Havlicek and I were bouncing around the idea that this could have been staged, you know, like some election ploy."

Martin shook his head. "I can't imagine that anyone would dare pull such a stunt and that it could be kept secret. Hutchins didn't need anything this dramatic."

Good points, all, but I was still unconvinced. The timing of the assassination attempt bugged me, the shooter's poor aim, the resulting rise in Hutchins's favorability ratings. Still, it was far-fetched, so I felt silly pushing it. I said, "At the least, we need to get someone to Wyoming to pay a call on this militia leader, and I don't know if that's what I ought to be doing right now."

"You're right," Martin said. "I'll send Phil Braxton"—another bureau reporter—"out there." Then he got up and went to his office.

I turned up the volume on the ringer of my telephone and roamed across the room, toward Havlicek.

"Hey there, slugger," he said.

I said, "I'll spread around a few calls on the autopsy report, but only to people who'll keep the information close. I don't want to let word get around on what we have."

"Good show," he said. "Let me know what you turn up. More important, let me know when you hear from your guy."

"Of course. Let's just hope he calls."

"He'll call," Havlicek said. "He's in this thing and wants to get in deeper, and he knows we're a good vehicle. If he doesn't know that now, he'll know it tomorrow when he reads this story."

At that moment I heard my telephone ring across the room and sprinted around desks and over one chair in my attempt to reach it. I caught the phone mid-ring. The caller promptly hung up.

Rather than agonize over what I may have missed, I called the main switchboard at the FBI and asked for Kent Drinker.

When Drinker came on the line, I said, "Sir, I'm going with a story tomorrow detailing the highly unusual fact that you paid a call on one of the nation's leading militia leaders a week before the assassination attempt on President Hutchins. I was hoping that you would provide me with some rationale for your visit."

All I heard on the other end was dead air. Finally he spoke. "You have wrong information."

"Well, if it is, then I'll run a correction. But I don't think that's going to happen. I have it reliably on the record that you were up at Freedom Lake the week before the assassination attempt. If you want to deny it or dispute it, you do so at your own peril."

Drinker said, "Can we talk off the record?"

"No. Not until I get some sort of on-the-record explanation."

That was met with more silence. Eventually Drinker said, "Then maybe I'll just refer you to the Bureau public relations person."

"Fine," I replied. "Either way, there's a story in tomorrow's paper about you flying out to Idaho two weeks ago. You can either enlighten me or ignore me. Your choice."

"If I tell you the truth and it gets published, it puts someone's life in danger. We need to be off the record."

In the news media there are four conditions of discussions between sources of information and reporters. The first is known as "on the record," meaning anything that a person tells you can be used in the newspaper, fully attributable to whoever said it. Unfortunately, people might be fired for talking to reporters—or even endangered—so conversations between sources and reporters often tend to be "on background." That means all the information is fully usable, attributable to some mutually negotiated title such as a "senior administration official." The third condition is "deep background," which means a source will provide information to a reporter provided it is not attributable to anyone. The fourth, and most extreme, is "off the record," which means the source is providing the information only to give the reporter a better understanding of what is happening, but the information cannot be used in a story unless obtained elsewhere.

I said, "All right. Tell me off the record."

"Daniel Nathaniel is a paid federal informant. I received a tip on an assassination conspiracy, and I went to him to measure its validity. On other cases, he's always proven helpful and reliable."

I was stunned. Here was a guy whose entire purpose in life was supposed to be rallying against the federal government, and instead, he was on the FBI payroll. And I thought I knew the guy.

In the verbal gap Drinker said, "You see what I mean. You write this, Nathaniel's underlings kill him by tomorrow night."

That they would, but that wasn't my particular problem. I asked, "So were the two of you on the level about this Wyoming militia leader, or was that a concocted story?"

"We believe it to be true, though obviously I don't have it hard enough to bring charges yet."

"So are you saying that you suspected an assassination attempt was coming before the President ever got shot?"

"Yes."

"And you couldn't do anything about it?"

"Well, we tried."

"I'd like to put that part on background, that an unnamed federal informant confirmed your suspicions of a conspiracy."

He paused for a moment, then said, "Sounds reasonable."

I said, "One more thing. On the record, you're sure that corpse you have is of a guy named Tony Clawson?"

Sounding taken aback, he said, "We have no reason at this moment to think it's anyone different." Interesting.

I said, "I'll be in touch."

He replied, "Do that. This case is breaking fast."

We hung up. I was left to wonder, Breaking as in breaking news, or breaking as in breaking apart?

THERE is something wonderful about the bar at Lespinasse, a French restaurant in the heart of downtown Washington. The polished mahogany walls soar perhaps thirty feet toward a frescoed ceiling. Portraits of Presidents gaze at waiters quietly shuffling across the thick floral carpet. If nothing else, it is a haven from the constant slights and indignities of official Washington.

The bar seemed particularly soothing this evening. At the very least, I was fairly confident no one would take a shot at me. So I ordered a Heineken and slumped deeply into a soft upholstered settee with my eyes closed. When I opened my eyes, I found the alluring figure of Agent Samantha Stevens looming above me.

She looked beautiful, her face void of makeup, her jet-black hair glowing in the soft light, her short skirt revealing toned legs. She settled into a leather chair across from me. I was increasingly smitten by her, though I recognized the need to rein it in.

"I appreciate you meeting me on short notice," she said.

I said, "You've piqued my curiosity. Did I miss something from the shooting scene? Is there something I heard or saw wrong?"

She said, "Actually, it's not that at all." She paused, staring down at the glass of merlot that the waiter had just brought her.

You have a crush, I said to myself. You've developed a crush on me, and you don't know how to tell me.

She said, "I wanted to ask you about that story in yesterday's paper that you ended up killing for the later editions."

Oh, well. I stayed quiet. She continued, "I've read your story, and there are a couple of things I don't understand, as in, A, how you got that information and, B, why it is that you decided it wasn't any good. I thought you might be able to share."

"I love to share," I said. "But when I share, I usually expect something in return."

She took a sip of her wine, looked me in the eye, and said, "Okay, I'm interested in what else you know about Wyoming."

"Big, beautiful state," I said. "And I love the Tetons."

She didn't even pretend to find humor. "The militia," she said.

"No way. Let's start with you and what you have for me."

"Why?" she asked. "I'm the one who called you."

"I don't trust you." There, I said it.

"You don't trust me?" she asked, taken aback.

"I don't trust anyone. Check that. I do trust my dog, but even that took me a couple of years."

"What do you want to know from me?"

"We could start with why you people couldn't prevent a presidential assassination attempt that you knew about in advance. Then we could take up the real identity of this would-be assassin, because we both know it's not this guy you call Tony Clawson."

Now her forehead was scrunched up in confusion. "The shooter's name is Tony Clawson. Case closed," she said snappily.

I shot back, "Read tomorrow's *Record,* then decide if you want to close that case so fast. Because you'll either learn something about your own investigation, or everyone else will learn something that you're trying to hide."

Stevens's cheeks suddenly flared red. "I'm not hiding anything," she said, her voice seething.

"I'm sorry," I said. "I am not implying that you are. What I'm saying is, I have some serious questions. You don't seem inclined to provide answers. But still, you expect me to help your cause."

"My cause is to solve a major crime—the assassination attempt on the President. I thought you might want to help."

I said nothing in return. I wasn't in the mood to deliver a lecture on the role of the press, which in this case seemed to involve making sure the FBI was not pulling one over on the public.

"I'll be straight with you," Stevens said, leaning closer. "I had never heard of Mr. Walbin before your ditched story."

Finally something of significance—an FBI agent admitting to a reporter that she has not been fully apprised of the important details of her own investigation. I struggled to conceal my shock. Then, of course, I began wondering if I was being snookered, by Drinker or by Stevens. "Are you aware of any sort of tip that the Bureau had received prior to the assassination attempt?" I asked.

"No."

There was silence.

She asked, "Why did you pull that story?"

"The honest truth is, I wasn't sure if it was true."

"How sure are you on the Wyoming information?"

I replied, "It's out there. It's in circulation. I keep hearing about it, and because I keep hearing about it, I have to run with something on it, because if I don't, someone else will."

She considered that. "I'll be straight again. I've never been in an investigation where crucial facts were withheld from me."

"Have you approached Drinker or your direct superiors?"

"No. Not until I know more. I'm not playing from a position of ignorance anymore."

I liked this lack of blind loyalty, these street smarts. I said, "You should read tomorrow's *Record* and tell me what you think."

"What do you have?"

I shook my head. "Can't," I said.

Stevens locked her gaze on me and said, "Looks like I've given you more than you've given me."

I caught the waiter's eye as he walked by, thinking it might be time to get a check, get out while I was ahead. When he came to the table, Stevens quickly said, "Another glass of the merlot, please." I added, "And another Heineken for me."

"So you've been a reporter your entire adult life?" she asked, displaying her knowledge of me and offering to change the tone of the conversation. I didn't say anything, so she added, "I'm tired, and you look like hell. Why don't we just have a drink?"

It wasn't a bad idea. We sipped our beverages; we traded small talk about the newspaper business and the FBI and growing up in rural Indiana, as she did, as compared to South Boston, as I did.

Outside, she offered to drop me in Georgetown on the way to her Arlington condominium. At my house she asked, "Could I use your bathroom?"

In the foyer she knelt down on the floor, skirt and all, to give Baker an enormous hug and a kiss on his fluffy ears.

"Don't you need to use the bathroom?" I asked finally as she stroked Baker's head with no apparent inclination to move.

She laughed and said, "No. I was just looking for an excuse to say hello to your dog. I absolutely adore him. Sorry."

We both smiled over that, and the telephone rang.

"I'll just let that kick over to my answering service," I said.

"Why don't you pick up the telephone?" she said with a mischievous grin. "A hot woman? An anonymous source? Maybe the President of the United States leaking to you again?"

She walked toward the telephone as I tried not to panic. She reached over and picked it up, saying in a playful voice, "Flynn residence, may I help you?" Then she slowly put the phone back on the hook. "Hung up," she said. "I must have scared her off."

Thursday, November 2

THE dream was one of those hazy ones. I remember realizing I was supposed to meet Katherine, but couldn't recall where or when or why. She wasn't at home and wasn't at work, so I sat at my desk in the bureau trying to figure out what time we said we would be getting together and where we were supposed to meet.

It was about here that the jagged sound smashed into my subconscious and stirred me. At first I thought it was my alarm clock; then I realized it was the phone, and it occurred to me that Katherine might be calling to say she was dining with her sister and wanted to know if I'd meet them for dessert. To say the least, I was confused. I glanced at the illuminated clock and saw it was four thirty in the morning, which only added to the fog.

When finally I found the phone on the night table, the familiar, haunting voice on the other end brought me back to reality.

"You're a hard man to reach, Mr. Flynn," the anonymous source said in that dignified voice. Before I could say anything, he kept talking. "You must realize you are being fed lies, lies that mask important truths that will someday astound you. You must keep working, keep digging, and get at these truths."

"That wasn't you who wanted to meet me at the Newseum?"

"The Newseum? No. I don't understand."

This verified what Havlicek and I believed all along: that someone was trying to help me, even while someone else was trying to kill me. I asked, "You didn't have a note delivered to me at a restaurant Saturday night asking to meet you at the Newseum?"

"No."

I asked, "Then who would try to kill me?"

"Mr. Flynn, given the sensitivity of the information involved, there are people who would kill rather than see you get to the bottom of this story. I must warn you that if you continue to accept my help and pursue these leads, you are in danger."

I said, "You haven't given me any leads yet, only general guidance. I need specifics. If I'm going to be in danger, you might as well give me more help. I need you to tell me what you know or at least guide me along." I sat up in the dark on one elbow.

"I'm prepared to bring you to the core of this situation," he said. "But it's crucial for you to understand, as we get further along, your life will be threatened anew."

Obviously my Deep Throat had a flair for the dramatic. If he thought he was scaring me, he thought wrong. The two most intriguing things you can say to any reporter worth the ink in his pen are that he may have to go to jail if he doesn't give up his source and that his life is in danger.

"I've already accepted the danger," I said. "What I want is to get to the bottom of this story."

There was a pause. I could hear him breathing. Finally he said, "You've been to Chelsea, Massachusetts."

I said, "Yes, I've been to Chelsea." And indeed, I had. It's a tiny city near Boston, full of decrepit slums and abandoned storefronts.

"You should travel there," he said. "You should find out everything you can about a man named Curtis Black. Learn about him, and you will have dug to the core of this case."

I asked, "Just a casual question: What does a Curtis Black in Chelsea, Massachusetts, have to do with an assassination attempt on the most powerful figure in the world?"

"Everything," he said. "I've given you all I can right now. It's up to you to find out why."

I asked, "Will you ever reveal yourself to me?" He paused again and said, "Perhaps someday if I think it will help."

"Have you seen today's *Record?*"

"No, I haven't."

"We have two stories," I said. "We have a story saying the triggerman cannot be the same man the feds say he is. Their ID, this guy named Tony Clawson, has eyes of a different color from the corpse. The second story says that the FBI had a prior tip, confirmed by a federal informant, that a Wyoming-based militia group was plotting an attack on the President."

"You have it about half right," my source said. "You're going to want to find out about Curtis Black even faster now." He hesitated, then added, "Just be careful," and hung up.

AT SEVEN thirty in the morning at the Washington bureau of a big-city newspaper, I should have been a good two hours from seeing another human. Except, at the far end of the otherwise darkened newsroom, Steve Havlicek sat hunched under a single light at his computer, staring intently at the words on his screen.

I approached quietly. "What are you doing here at this hour?"

"Big story here," he said, jovial as ever. "We've got work to do and no time to waste. Howaya, slugger?"

I shook my head. I was holding a bag with two toasted bagels and offered him one. He didn't hesitate in accepting and was already biting into the second half before I even got mine unwrapped.

"These stories are going to catch fire today," he said, his mouth full. "When the boys over at CNN and Fox get in, they'll be all over us. This is officially hell day at the FBI."

I said, "What do you think the FBI is going to do?"

"They can't very well deny it," Havlicek said. "My bet is that they don't say a thing, or they simply say the investigation is continuing down many avenues."

"And the White House? I mean, Hutchins has got to weigh in with something stronger than he has full faith in the FBI."

"This will be a great day," Havlicek said. "Strap yourself in."

"Well, I've got something that might make it even greater. I got a call this morning at four thirty from the anonymous one."

"What did he say?"

I told him about Chelsea and Curtis Black and the source's kind words about our work so far. I told him of the danger he said we would face, of the shocking truths waiting to be uncovered. Havlicek was sitting in his chair just staring at me, his mouth agape.

"This is either one elaborate hoax or one wonderful newspaper story we're onto," he finally said.

"I think I ought to hold off on going up to Boston, just for the day," I said. "This town is going to flip over these stories, and we both ought to be around to handle the fallout."

At that precise moment, on the small color TV on Havlicek's desk, a photo of the front page of the day's *Record* appeared behind a CNN anchorman. Havlicek turned up the volume.

"The newspaper reports the FBI has misidentified the attempted assassin in the shooting of President Clayton Hutchins—"

Havlicek hit the MUTE button, and I heard the ringing sound of my telephone on the other side of the room. I did my usual sprint and grabbed the phone on the fourth ring, barking, "Flynn."

"Why the hell didn't you tell me you had these stories?" It was the rather angry voice of Samantha Stevens.

"Excuse me?" I said, buying time, unsure of the right answer.

"I spill my guts to you last night, and you can't even tell me what the rest of the world is going to be told in twelve hours?"

"Hey there, easy does it," I said. "Last I checked, you're not my editor. And if you'll think back, I told you that Clawson wasn't who you people say he is. As I recall, you told me, 'Case closed.' "

She said, getting angrier, "Look, I'm in a position to help you, but unless I know it goes two ways, you can go screw yourself."

With that, she hung up. No matter. My phone was ringing off the hook. Next up was my close friend Ron Hancock of the FBI.

"Well, you've stirred up quite a hornet's nest," he said. "The director has his entire top staff in his office now. There's so much chatter between here and the White House this morning that they might as well just hook up two cans to a piece of string."

I said, "What does it all mean? Who is this guy you have over in the morgue, why is the FBI screwing up a presidential assassination attempt, and is the FBI screwing up or covering up?"

"I don't know," he said, and I believed him.

I asked, "Do you think they'll admit they made a mistake?"

"No idea," he said. "Those decisions are made about ten pay grades above mine." He paused, then added, "You have anything else? Anything else I should know about?"

"Shot our load today," I said. "But I'll be in touch."

When I turned around, Peter Martin was standing by my desk, almost levitating. "We have this city by the balls today," he said, making a little vise grip with his chalky palm that made me flinch.

I didn't engage. It was time for me to fill him in. "We have to talk about an anonymous source and a guy named Curtis Black," I said. "Let's go into your office."

And we did. After I was done with all the sordid details, from the first calls in the hospital to the encounter at the Newseum to the note on the airplane to the telephone tip in the dark that morning, Martin looked a shade lighter than Casper the ghost. As I sat in one of his leather club chairs, he paced around the office.

He said, "I understand why you didn't, and I am not going to hold it against you, but I wish you had told me earlier. Tell me your gut feeling. Is this guy on the level?"

"Well, he had the Tony Clawson part right at the same time

Havlicek was getting it. He sounds educated. He's not spinning crazy conspiracy theories. I don't know enough to draw a judgment, but I know enough to know that we have to keep playing his game, or we're going to regret it for the rest of our careers."

"Yeah, you're right," Martin said, collapsing onto his couch. "I want you to hang in here today, mop up with Havlicek, and tomorrow get on up to Chelsea and work like a tyrant on this guy Black. I have a hunch we'll know whether this information is any good in the next day or so."

I said, "Sounds like a plan."

Chapter Six

IT WAS around one p.m. when White House press secretary Royal Dalton slid open the doors that separate the press office from the briefing room and walked awkwardly up to the podium.

Hutchins was laying over in Washington amid a weeklong campaign trip. The room was electric. There is nothing that makes reporters happier than catching the government in a mistake or a lie, and this one about Tony Clawson could cut either way. The room was filled with reporters and cameramen.

Dalton looked uneasy. "I have a few policy announcements," he said, trying to maintain a casual demeanor as he looked around the room in something approaching fear. He went on to talk about a Medicare proposal that Republicans had been trying to sell for years.

After that, he opened the session to questions, and first up was Moose Myers, senior White House correspondent for CNN. Moose asked, "Has President Hutchins talked to the FBI director this morning, and has he lost faith in the FBI's ability to conduct this investigation, given the revelations in today's Boston *Record?*"

Sitting three rows behind him, I made a mental note to thank him for that high-profile mention. It doesn't get much better than that. I actually had the feeling that my colleagues were looking at me—and trust me when I say this is a tough lot to impress.

Dalton had obviously patched together a precisely worded answer. Here it came: "The President has spoken to Director Callinger of the FBI by telephone this morning. He was assured that the investigation is moving ahead with significant progress. The President is obviously in no position to discuss the particulars of the investigation. He was the victim. He is not a detective. But I am told the FBI will have more to say on this shortly."

Immediately a dozen hands and as many voices filled the air. Myers, the CNN reporter, talked down his colleagues. "Royal, you didn't answer me. Has the President lost faith in the FBI, given what the *Record* is saying today about the misidentified shooter and the fact that they had previously identified a specific militia group but were unable to stop the assassination attempt?"

"Look," Dalton said, "the President believes today what he's always believed, that the FBI is the most talented, most exhaustive, most prestigious law-enforcement agency in the world. He hasn't changed his opinion because of a newspaper story in Boston."

Dalton spat out those last words as if they were some distasteful bit of phlegm. But if he thought he could outsmart the gathered press, he was about to learn the folly of his ways. Immediately the Associated Press reporter shouted, "So the President believes the FBI was right, that the dead man is actually Tony Clawson?"

Good one. Dalton hesitated at the podium. You could see him twitching. "As I indicated before," he said, "the President is not a detective. He does not involve himself in the particulars of this investigation. He leaves that up to the trained inspectors with the most successful law-enforcement agency in the world."

The Washington *Post* reporter asked loudly, "Does the President still have faith in that agency and its director?"

Dalton: "He does not see any reason, at this juncture, not to have faith in the FBI. He wants to let them proceed with their investigation, which is certainly difficult to do given the intense publicity and the second-guessing that we're seeing now in the news media."

Basically, from my read, Dalton was shying away from saying that the President had full faith in the FBI. He had purposefully not used those words, probably out of fear that the FBI had screwed up. Dalton was also going to great lengths to distance the President from the investigation, repeatedly calling him a victim. This was odd. White House aides prefer to depict the President as someone all-powerful, in control, not some hapless casualty of unfortunate circumstance. They were being cautious. The question was, why?

As Dalton went around and around with reporters, my pager sounded. This message was better than the norm, which usually consists of "Call Peter Martin immediately." I read my beeper twice to be sure I saw it right. "Jack, you're an ass. Come see me ASAP. C.H."

I couldn't get up in the middle of this briefing, mostly because the only way into the West Wing was directly past the podium. "Royal," I said, and I could feel all eyes riveted on me. "As President, as Commander in Chief, shouldn't President Hutchins be taking a keen interest in the progress of this investigation and the abilities of the investigators, given the potentially serious consequences on the well-being of the administration?"

I liked it. Dalton froze at the podium. Finally he punted. "Look, he is as concerned as anyone else with today's report. But he is also leaving the particulars of the investigation to those who are expert investigators." Finally a usable quote. Hutchins is concerned.

Eventually the briefing tailed off, with reporters talking to each other and cameramen packing up their equipment. I quickly pushed my way through the masses to a wall phone, dialed the White House switchboard, and asked for Sylvia Weinrich, Hutchins's assistant.

"Miss Weinrich speaking," she said in her finishing-school tone.

"Hello, Miss Weinrich. Jack Flynn here."

"Mr. Flynn, the President wanted to see you as soon as possible. He has some office time right now and was wondering how soon you might be able to come in."

I explained that I was in the building. Marvelous, we both agreed, and in a matter of minutes I was inconspicuously walking from the briefing room, through the West Wing, and into the Oval Office for the second time in my life.

HE WAS sitting at that big oak desk, wearing a pair of half-glasses, looking dignified, reading a sheaf of papers.

I sat on one of the two couches at the far end of the room, quietly waiting. My eyes scanned around from the busts of Franklin Delano Roosevelt and John F. Kennedy near his desk to the biographies of Truman and Lincoln on the pale yellow shelves. It was mesmerizing, this room where history wasn't just made but prodded and pulled, nipped and formed. As the moments drifted into minutes, I started wondering if he knew I was here.

"Dammit." That was Hutchins, finally. He stood up from his desk, snapped his glasses off his face, and slowly walked toward me, looking haggard. "You have any idea how much money this country sends to Israel every year in federal dollars?" he asked. "Three billion. You have any idea how much private U.S. money is raised for Israel annually? Try another billion." He took a seat on the opposite couch. "How good are we to them? The second call I made after I was sworn in was to Jerusalem. No changes in policy, I said. And how do they say thanks to all this money, to all this friendship, to the promise of all this history if they can reach a simple accord with people they'll be living beside from now to eternity? They build tunnels and housing on sacred Palestinian land. Then they just shrug and ask me, 'Are you with us or not?' And what can I say? 'Yes, I am, though, gee, I was hoping you might behave differently.' "

This scene was astounding for a few reasons, most notably that this was five days before a presidential election. Hutchins should be basking in the glow of favorable public-opinion polls, looking down the pipe to four years in the White House in his own right. Granted, he was taking only a brief breather here, but the respite should not be spent laboring over the finer points of the Middle East peace process. The *Record* story might be one reason why Hutchins wasn't happier. The reality of his life was another. He was childless, wifeless, and really had no one with whom to share the moment, aside from a group of aides I don't think he particularly liked.

I sat in silence, watching the sad look on Hutchins's face, the toll of this job. His reputation was that of a hard-charging bull—a man who, I once wrote, had a steakhouse charm about him: straightforward, with few garnishments. Today he appeared wilted.

"And you," he said. "Where are you on our proposal? You ready to join the team? I'm about to win four more years. I'll be able to do anything I want, go anywhere I want to go. You could be there every step of the way, for all the applause."

I said, "I'm putting an enormous amount of thought into your offer, sir. But I think it's fair to warn you that I don't think this is an appropriate time for me."

Hutchins just kind of looked at me for a minute, probing.

"Howa your ribs?" he asked, surprising me.

"Much better," I said. "I'm getting a lot more comfortable."

"Hasn't affected your work, for Chrisake," he said, getting that mischievous smile again.

I smiled. "Busy time."

"Oh, it's a busy time all right. It's a damn busy time."

He let that hang there, and the two of us sat facing each other.

I broke the silence. "Sir, do you have any reaction, beyond what Dalton has said, on the performance of the FBI?"

He resumed his serious tone. "I can't help you on this one." Then he did. "Look, they're the FBI. You look at their reputation, and you just have to believe they're going to get things right."

Nice little quote that my paper will have exclusively—certainly a lot better than that patter of Dalton's.

"Here's the point, though," he continued. "You're a smart kid. I want you in my trench, not shooting at me from someone else's. If it takes money, I promise you, we'll max out on your pay. I'll give you hiring power over at the press office. You bring in whoever you want. I'll give you virtually open access to the Oval. You'll be one of my most important advisers."

Good Lord. Essentially, what he was now offering me wasn't just the position of press secretary. He was talking about senior presidential adviser, at the center of his inner circle. Senators would kiss my ass. Network anchors would vie for my time. My financial future would be set. This was interesting, though probably not interesting enough to sway me. The story—this assassination attempt and all the mystery that surrounded it—was too good.

"It's all very flattering," I said. "I really will think about it."

"Take whatever time you need," he said.

I said, "I don't want to leave you hanging. I'll move as quickly as I can. But to be perfectly honest, I'm leaning against it."

There was a moment of silence. I gazed around the room again, thinking this could be in some way mine, this hold on power. I took a chance. "You don't look so good, sir. Given that the polls show you creeping ahead, I would think you'd be in a better frame of mind."

He looked at me, his eyes almost pleading. "Are we talking, me and you, or am I talking to seven hundred thousand *Record* readers?"

"Me and you, sir," I said.

He sighed. "This job, it's not what you might think. There is the swarm of attention and, in the middle of that swarm, the sense of total isolation. There is the dangling prospect of accomplishment matched against the overriding reality of constant failure."

He looked out toward the Rose Garden. "Look, it sounds foolish to complain about all this. There's a lot that's great—this house, the limousines, the helicopter, Air Force One, Camp David. I have a staff of valets who lay out my clothes every day, freshly pressed, always nice and clean. I can play golf at any private club in America without even calling for a tee time. But I can't go for a walk in my own neighborhood. Hell, I don't really even have a neighborhood. I am the neighborhood." He was on a roll. "I'm not a professional politician. I didn't spend my entire life praying and scheming to be President. I didn't ask for this job."

He paused, and I cut in. "Sir, with all due respect, you did ask for this job. You're in the process of asking for it now, in this election."

He seemed not in the least bit offended. "Yeah, you're right, I am asking for it," he said. "Look, I'm unloading too much. I'm tired from the campaign. Maybe I'm intimidated by the work ahead. And when a guy takes a shot at you, you think about the fragile nature of life. Bottom line: I'm going to be fine."

Hutchins slapped his hands against his knees in a sign that the conversation was over. I rose slowly from the couch. "Your wife, she died, right?" he asked.

I said, "She did, about a year ago."

I was standing now. He was sitting, deep in the couch, showing no signs of getting up. He said, "I'm sorry. I hope you find someone else. No matter who you are, life isn't meant to be lived alone."

I nodded at him. "I think you're right," I said. I walked out the door, leaving him slumped into the couch, looking painfully sad.

"HEY there, slugger. You hear about the FBI statement?"

That was Havlicek, looking up from his computer.

I said, "I've been out of touch for an hour. What'd they say?"

Peter Martin approached from his office and leaned on Havlicek's desk without saying anything.

Havlicek began, "They issued a response that the original identification of Clawson was tentative, and it only became public because it was released by a junior agent speaking without authorization. They also said they had realized in the past forty-eight hours that this initial identification was wrong, and they had reopened that facet of their investigation to learn the identity of the attempted assassin."

I asked, "So they still don't know who the guy is?"

"They won't say. They said that because of the initial, false release of the tentative ID, they will make certain that in the future no parts of their investigation are released to the news media until they are ready. They claim that today's story hindered their investigation, so they're going to button down even tighter."

I laughed a sneering laugh. "Those jackasses. They screw up, then blame us for hindering them."

"Bingo. But at least they've essentially confirmed our story. This makes for good print tomorrow."

Martin spoke for the first time. "This also means that every paper in the country has to mention us in tomorrow's stories, giving us full credit. The FBI made sure of that today by admitting this and blaming us at the same time. This couldn't be better."

"Well, yeah," I said, "it could be better if we could prove those bastards are lying—that they really didn't know they had the wrong ID, or that they did know, but they misled us on purpose." For the first time, I brought up Hutchins. "And they'll all have to follow us again tomorrow. I have exclusive quotes from the President."

Martin made a move as if he might hug me. "This keeps getting better," he said. "We're on a colossal roll."

The three of us fell quiet. It was nearing four p.m., so we divvied up the workload. Havlicek is the best, most dogged reporter I know, but he writes as if English were a second language. With that in mind, Martin suggested that he type up what he had and ship it to me, and I would combine it with my White House reaction and meld it into one story. But as I settled in at my desk, the telephone rang.

"You're tough to reach." It was Ron Hancock.

"Been in with the President all afternoon," I said.

"Yeah, right." He just kind of snickered. "They're feeding you a line of crap over here," he said. "It's bull. They were calling this victim Tony Clawson right up until six a.m., when the news broke from your paper that they had the wrong ID."

"Can you prove it?" I asked, starting to get excited.

"Of course I can prove it. Go stand by your fax machine. I'm sending you something. You don't know where you got it from. If they stick bamboo shoots under your fingernails and make you eat boiled horsemeat for dinner, you tell them nothing."

There are weeks, even months, in this strange business of newspaper reporting when absolutely nothing goes right. I mention this because this obviously was not one of these times. In fact, on my way to the fax machine, I kept pumping my fist. By the time I got there, it was spitting out a plain sheet of paper with the words "For Jack Flynn. Personal and Confidential."

What followed was a detailed FBI internal case summary, dated the day before, which discussed the identity of the killer as Tony Clawson. I notified Martin and Havlicek. There was much backslapping and hand-wringing, and in the end, the three of us pored over every word of the story that I began writing.

"Nice clean hit," Martin said when we shipped the story to the national desk. We were in his office. The bureau was mostly empty. "I assume you're on an early flight to Boston tomorrow."

Before I could answer, Havlicek appeared in the doorway, smiling. "Let's head out. Drinks are on me," he said.

"Where to?" I asked as Martin put his coat on.

Havlicek said, "University Club. Love that bar."

"Give me five minutes," I said.

At my desk I clicked through my electronic Rolodex to the telephone number for a dining and drinking establishment in Chelsea, Massachusetts, named the Pigpen.

"Sammy there?" I said in a tone as gruff as I could gather.

The guy who answered the phone said, "Who wants to know?"

"Jack Flynn."

I heard the receiver hit a hard surface, probably the bar. After a minute someone picked up on another line.

"What do you want now? I thought I made you into some bigtime Washington reporter."

A word about Sammy Markowitz: He is about sixty. He has droopy eyes and smokes Camels all day—sitting in a back booth of the Pigpen, which he owns. He is the most powerful force in Chelsea's most important industry: bookmaking.

Many years before, I dedicated weeks of my life to researching his bookie network, for a story I hoped to do about the anatomy of an illegal gaming operation. Truth be known, I was making very little progress when I was told by Markowitz in no uncertain terms that I should walk away from the story. In a matter of days he played a critical role laying out a substitute story for me about a group of a dozen Chelsea police officers who had led a decade-long reign of terror in the community they were paid to protect. The story resulted in the imprisonment of the cops, the resignation of the police chief, and the recall of the mayor. I was named a finalist for the Pulitzer Prize. I hadn't spoken to Markowitz since.

"I'm well, Sammy, and I hope you are too." No reaction, so I continued. "I'm looking for someone, and I've got a hunch you can help me find him. I'm in town tomorrow. What if I stop by?"

"Yeah? Well, maybe I'm here, maybe I'm not."

He's always there, so I took that as an invitation. "Good," I said. "I'll see you tomorrow. Drinks are on you."

Next I called Diego Rodriguez, an assistant U.S. attorney in Boston and a sometime source of information, leaving a message that I needed to speak to him tomorrow in his office.

FRANK Sinatra was singing "The Best Is Yet to Come" as I strode through the wide doors of the University Club and up to the bar, where Peter Martin and Steve Havlicek were talking animatedly.

"Boys, boys," I said, "why don't we sit at a table?"

We sat down, and before long a waiter stopped by the table with hamburgers for each of us and a basket of onion rings. We were just three newspaper guys sitting around a table, with a few beers and some red meat, discussing a good story.

Frank was singing "Hello Dolly" by now. Waiters were carrying plates of prime rib and shrimp. The room was filled with the hum of conversation, staccato bursts of laughter. Out of the corner of my eye I caught an unusual sight—at least, for this club: a beautiful woman coming through the doorway, alone, and taking a place at a corner table. I turned to look, and my heart almost came through my chest. This was no beautiful woman: It was Samantha Stevens, special agent with the FBI, smiling at me from across the room.

After the boys took their leave, I made my way to her table and said, "This is an unexpected surprise."

"Most surprises are unexpected," she replied. Good one. I made a mental note to stop using that cliché after all these years.

She was drinking red wine on a tab I had carefully and quietly established for her with the waiter. "Sorry to intrude on your sanctuary, but I need to talk to you in confidence. May I?"

"Of course you can," I said, taking a seat at the table.

She stared down at the wine. After a moment she looked up at me and said, "I'm being excluded from every major decision on this case. Drinker's barely speaking to me, and he seems to have carte blanche to do whatever he wants. I don't even think my boss is clued in. Drinker speaks only to Callinger. I think they're the only two guys who know what's going on."

I let that sit out there as I processed it. I was still leery of being played for the fool and harbored suspicions that this was a setup, an attempt to get me to divulge that I was working with an anonymous source. "Do you and Drinker talk every day?"

She shrugged. "He might stop by my office and ask me to do something like call this militia outpost or some gun store or something that seems peripherally connected, at best."

"You think about going to Callinger?"

"I did," she said. "I said it was bothering me, the way this investigation was being handled. He told me to stick with it and not to worry about how it's going, that there were already plenty enough people worrying for me." Stevens took a sip of wine. "I'm hopeful that if you have information about FBI wrongdoing on this case, you might pass it on to me to investigate."

"I don't have anything right now except what I've written for tomorrow morning's paper, which is a story quoting from an internal document saying that the FBI was identifying the shooter as Tony Clawson at least as recently as yesterday afternoon."

She just stared at me with that one. "Well, there's no way that I'm going to just sit back and watch while this investigation spirals out of control. Let me ask you something. That story of yours today. Do you know who the federal informant is?"

An interesting question, meaning, apparently, that she didn't.

I replied, "Yes. I agreed not to publish the identity so the informant wouldn't be killed, as could well be the case if word got out."

She nodded and asked, "Is it Daniel Nathaniel?"

I didn't answer. She added, "If it is, don't say anything." I didn't, and she eventually looked away.

She spread a hard gaze over my face and said, "Then I have something else." Her tone had changed.

I coolly met her gaze and said, "Go ahead."

"I got access to some computer files. The files detail all federally paid informants. The point is, Drinker told me about telling you of how Daniel Nathaniel is a federal informant. Anyways, this guy Nathaniel, he's not on the list. There's not even a militia member on our ledgers from Idaho."

I drank that in for a moment, stunned at the baldness of Drinker's lie. What did it mean? If Drinker was fabricating, it meant that he worked with Nathaniel to concoct the story about the Wyoming militia, in all likelihood to hide something else.

Much as I wanted to pursue it right there and then with Stevens, some inner voice told me not to. "That's, well, more than interesting," I said, dropping it at that.

We sat in a long stretch of silence until the waiter, in a display of impeccable timing, said, "Check, Mr. Flynn?" I said, "Yeah, that would be great."

DAYLIGHT had long since drained from the early winter sky as Baker and I arrived at Rose Park in Georgetown for our regular game of fetch. As soon as we stepped on the soft grass, Baker tossed the tennis ball excitedly from his mouth, gawked as it hit my shoes, stepped back four paces, and sat, the look on his face one of unbridled joy at the event that was to come.

On my first throw he scooped the ball up in his mouth and whipped his head around as if he were breaking the ball's neck, if it had one. That feat accomplished, he tossed it back at my shoes and set out across the field again as I led him by ten feet or so with another perfect throw. He caught it on the first bounce.

Standing there, I decided to take an inventory of all that was going wrong. I had an enormous story that seemed to be slipping out of my control. I had an anonymous source who might be sending me on a wild-goose chase. I had someone taking an occasional shot at me. I had a fetching FBI agent showing an inordinate interest in me, though I wasn't sure if this came under what was going wrong or what might be right. And, I should add, at that moment I had an ominous-looking man in a trench coat walking across the otherwise empty field, heading in my direction.

Baker spotted him after I did and, being the faithful protector of all things Jack, bounded angrily across the field and grabbed the man's leg, bringing him down in a heap of blood and pain.

Actually, I lie. Baker joyfully trotted up to the guy, dropped the ball at his feet, and stepped back in anticipation of the throw he assumed was to come. The man kept walking, ignoring him.

"Be careful," I called out. "He's vicious."

"I'll be all right." The man was getting closer.

"I was talking to my dog," I said with a shallow laugh.

And out of the dark and into my life once again stepped Kent Drinker, assistant director of the FBI.

I said, flat, "What can I do for you this fine night?"

"I was hoping I might get some help and give some help."

That sounded interesting, though rehearsed. I picked up the ball and tossed it for Baker, then turned my gaze to Drinker. "Everything I have, I think I've given you already," I said.

There was a long pause between us, broken only by Baker's once again presenting me with the ball and my once again throwing it.

"Look, I've dealt with reporters before," Drinker said finally. "And I was more than helpful in my day. I also got more than burned. My whole career got fried. Now I've been given a rare second chance in the Bureau. I'm trying to solve a presidential assassination attempt after the Secret Service put six bullets into my prime suspect and rendered him useless to me. And I have you and your paper staring over my shoulder, second-guessing me every step of the way, getting in the way of a good investigation." He paused. "I need some room. I need some time. And I need some help."

"I give you time, space, and help, what do I get in return?"

"I can help you on this case, just like I helped that reporter out in L.A., only I'm hoping you're a little more loyal."

I said, "I think Benedict Arnold was slightly more loyal than the last reporter you dealt with."

He almost smiled in spite of himself. I looked him over. Despite my finely honed abilities in the area of character judgment, I couldn't get a full handle on Kent Drinker. I wasn't sure if he was driving events or if the events were driving him, whether he was mishandling the investigation or trying to conceal some larger truth.

The facts were these: He had misidentified the presidential assassin. He had shown great interest in who had called my hospital room. He had apparently consorted with a militia leader to concoct a story about motive and then lied to me about it. He might have lied to me about that militia leader being a paid informant. He had iced out even his top subordinate, Stevens, in trying to solve the case. Or trying not to solve it. I didn't know, and thus, my dilemma. Had he really iced out Stevens, or was I being played for a moron?

He kicked softly at a small stone in the field and said, "You drew too hasty a conclusion on Tony Clawson."

"Yeah?" I replied, my tone incredulous.

"You were right about some parts, wrong about others."

"Let's see," I began. "You publicly named a suspect who didn't even have the same eye color as the guy the Secret Service shot dead at Congressional. Tell me what we might have gotten wrong."

He asked, "Can I talk to you off the record?"

I said, "I'd rather talk on the record."

Drinker stayed silent for a moment. "Once more, I'd like to, but I can't," he said. "I'd be fired in an hour. I want to stress, I have some information that's important for you to know."

Well, I didn't know whether to believe him, believe Stevens, or believe my own instincts, which told me not to believe anyone. "Okay, on background, attributable to a law-enforcement official."

"No way. There are only about three people who know what I know. I'd be fingered immediately."

There was a lengthy silence between us as I mulled my options. The last thing I expected on this night was for Drinker to perhaps give me my biggest break on the case. It wouldn't serve me well to shut him off. "All right, off the record," I said.

Drinker started talking as if I had just turned on a spout. "I'll admit up front, this shooting has nothing to do with the militia. You have us cold on that. And the dead shooter is not the Tony Clawson we offered up in that Home Depot ID. Good work on that, by the way. Sometimes I wish my people were as thorough."

"So you were lying last time when you told me Nathaniel was a paid informant?"

"I was protecting the truth. It's a different Tony Clawson. And it's his background that's so potentially devastating to my agency."

I stayed silent, hoping the dead air would prod him to continue. He stayed silent too. I finally said, "Devastating how?"

He shook his head. "Can't go that far. Find out who Tony Clawson is, or was, and you'll know exactly what I mean."

Everyone had a suggestion. I thought of what the anonymous caller had said about Curtis Black early that morning. *Learn about him, and you will have dug to the core of this case.* So the question now—beyond the obvious questions about Clawson—was what Curtis Black had to do with Tony Clawson.

Drinker said, "I need to ask you one more time. Who was that on the telephone in your hospital room that day?"

I didn't utter a word. In the void Drinker added, "Look, I'll admit we have a full-court press on you in trying to find the identity of your caller. I tried the hard approach. Stevens is trying the soft approach. You've been more than resistant. Here's the truth: I think I know who called you that day. That person's been in touch with you since. That person can screw up this entire investigation and, in effect, screw up the entire story that I'm more than ready to help you with. You help me. I help you."

It was as if I had just been kneed in the gut. So perhaps my first instincts were right: Stevens and Drinker really were in this together, trying to play with my mind. Or perhaps not. My head was starting to hurt. I said, "Truth is, I really don't know who was on the phone, and that's all I'm saying about it right now."

Drinker looked me over carefully. "There's a lot at stake for both of us," he said. With that, he turned around silently and walked back across the field from whence he had come, his tan raincoat fading and then melding into the dark of the night.

# Chapter Seven

CURTIS Black sat in the front of the van as if he were watching a movie. And, just like a movie, everything was proceeding as if it were all part of a tightly written script.

The driver stood casually beside the Wells Fargo truck—oblivious to everything going on around him, including Black's attention. His cohort came from the back of the truck, pulled out a dolly, and walked into the bank, where he would collect the day's receipts. He should be visible in the door in about seven minutes.

"Be alert," Black said into the microphone pinned to his wrist. Inside the van the three men crouched against the back door.

Black continued staring out the window. The hazy dusk had grown thick. A mist gathered on the windshield. All in all, Black thought, ideal conditions for a heist. He glanced at his watch. According to the plan, the guard should be approaching the door in roughly three minutes. "Sanchez, come on up," Black said into the microphone.

The driver of the getaway car opened his door and walked up to the side of the van, his ski mask on top of his head like a wool hat, with the part that covered his face not yet pulled down. He stood looking at the ground, concealing his face from any passersby.

And just as planned, the guard appeared inside the door of the bank, pushing a dolly with a duffel bag on it. He turned around and opened the door with his backside.

"Showtime," Black announced into his wrist. "Go."

The rear door of the van burst open. The three men jumped out into the moist air, their black masks shielding their faces. They fanned out, then sprinted toward the guard at the bank door.

"Freeze," Stemple yelled. The guard was instinctively reaching for the semiautomatic pistol in his side holster when Rocco hit him with a body slam at full running speed. The guard sprawled out on the pavement, dazed. When he rolled over to get up, Cox was already on top of him, stripping his gun away.

Meantime, at the van, Sanchez yanked his mask down over his face and approached the driver of the armored car from behind. His sole job was to immobilize the driver. Black watched as the driver reached for his side arm. Just as the driver pulled his weapon out, Sanchez grabbed his coat, preparing for a headlock.

It was misting out. The drops of moisture had balled up on the driver's water-repellent jacket. Sanchez's hands slipped, and the driver squirmed loose. Sanchez lost his balance—not enough to fall, but enough to leave a gaping canyon of opportunity for any decent shot. Barely stopping to aim, the driver fired his gun in the direction of the bank door, where Stemple and Rocco, grabbing the duffel bag filled with money, fell to their knees at the sound of the shot. Cox took shelter by crouching down behind the incapacitated guard. Never had Curtis Black felt the raw terror he did at this instant, watching his heist spiral out of control.

He watched as Sanchez regained his balance, then shifted his body weight in preparation to lunge at the gun-wielding driver. On the sidewalk he saw Stemple and Rocco reaching inside their jackets, though he couldn't tell who was who, since they both wore ski masks and were dressed identically.

"Hold fire," Black yelled into his wrist microphone.

Crack. Crack. Shots echoed down Hanover Street. Passersby screamed, scattering down the sidewalk like frightened animals. Black watched in horror as the driver dropped his gun, then crumpled to the pavement. Blood flowed from a cavity in his neck. Sanchez stood over him for a moment, then bolted back toward the getaway car.

Stemple and Rocco ran toward the car with the duffel bag. Cox stood up and sprinted after them.

Black flung the driver's-side door open on the van, lowered his head to conceal his features, and raced to the getaway car, where he snapped the rear door open and settled into the back seat. Rocco and Stemple flung the money into the trunk and got into the back beside him. Cox settled into the front. Sanchez drove. The group squealed away, a tiny band of silence amid so much chaos.

In a parking lot at the end of the Boston Fish Pier, where the group switched getaway cars, Black paused in the darkening night. "Who killed him?" he shouted. "Who killed him?"

No answer.

The new driver, who had met them at the pier, took in the scene with panicked eyes. It wasn't supposed to be like this, he knew. "What happened?" the driver asked nervously.

No answer. Rather, the men silently but hurriedly folded themselves into the new vehicle, ignoring the question. Stemple paused at the door and flung his gun far into the harbor. Black could only shake his head. What was the point now? he wondered. Would it do any good to yell at a man who had just committed cold-blooded murder? His life, he knew, would never be the same.

Present Day
Friday, November 3

A THIN, cold mist descended on downtown Chelsea. Grown men, mostly Asians, gathered aimlessly on street corners. In front of the Goodwill store a man with a bullhorn read from the Bible.

With this as my backdrop, I pushed against the heavy wooden door into the dark haze of the Pigpen, which looked and smelled just as I had remembered it, which is to say dirty and of stale beer. A couple of barflies, middle-aged men with stubble on their faces and defeat in their eyes, looked my way. Across the room I saw Sammy Markowitz sitting at his usual booth in the back.

I began walking in his direction, when a sizable gentleman in an ill-fitting black sports jacket blocked my path. I said, "Perhaps you could go tell Mr. Markowitz that his friend Jack Flynn is here."

A minute later I was led to the back of the restaurant, where Markowitz stood to greet me and said, "To think, a few years ago I almost had you killed. You've turned out so handsome."

"My dog thanks you for rethinking your plan. And so do I."

We engaged in small talk about the Celtics and the new Boston mayor. Then he said unceremoniously, "So what do you want?"

"Curtis Black," I said. "I need to find Curtis Black."

He looked at me for a moment, an unlit cigarette dangling on his lower lip. Finally he said to me, "Don't know him."

"Bull," I said. "You know him. I don't ask a whole lot from you. But I need you right now. I'm asking for your help."

Markowitz said, "Why are you asking about him?"

I said, "He's into something. I'm not a hundred percent sure what it is yet, but I know it's something of consequence."

"What do you know about him already?"

"Very little."

And that was the truth. Before I got on the airplane, I had called Dorothy at the *Record* library and asked her to pull up everything she could find on Curtis Black. She left me a voice mail saying she had found only two news briefs. The first one was about the arrest of Curtis Black and several other men for a 1979 armored car heist in Boston's North End in which a guard was shot and killed. The second one was about their arraignment in U.S. district court. She shipped the stories to my computer, but I hadn't logged in yet from my laptop.

I added, "I know he's into armored car robberies, or he was. Beyond that I don't know much of anything."

"You want to know about Curtis Black, you should go ask our federal government. They're the ones who know about him."

"Because of the charges?" I said.

"Because of the charges and everything else," Markowitz said.

I asked, "Is Black in jail?"

Markowitz said, "No, he's not. And that's what you might want to talk to your federal government about."

"Sammy, come on. I need you on this. What do you mean?"

To this, I got nothing. "I've gone as far as I can go," he said.

"When I know more," I said, "you mind if I come back at you?"

He said, "You know where to find me. And you know how I work. I confirm, but I don't provide."

I headed for the door. Markowitz had told me to go check with the federal government, so that's what I decided to do next.

DIEGO RODRIGUEZ LOOKED resplendent in his Louis suit, in his fifth-floor office in the U.S. district court with a view of Logan International Airport. We exchanged the type of needling that only old battlefield friends can indulge.

"I have a hunch and a hope," I said, cutting to the quick. "My hunch is you know a thing or two about a former armored car robber named Curtis Black. My hope is you can share it with me."

Rodriguez was leaning back in his chair, behind his desk. I was sitting across from him in a wing chair.

Diego Rodriguez was a federal prosecutor assigned to many of the most glamorous cases in his office. For me he had provided information on cases from Irish gunrunning to Mob surveillance. He respected and understood the role of the news media, and he respected and liked me. Which is why I was so surprised when he said, "I'm not sure I can help you with this one."

I asked, "Do you know who I'm talking about?"

Rodriguez nodded. He said, "I know him."

I told him, "Look, Diego, I need you. This one is important to me. This could be important to a lot more people than just me. Help me out."

"I wish I could," he said. "You know the case, right? That armored car hit in the North End. That's all public record."

I replied, "I'm vaguely familiar with it. My understanding is that Mr. Black didn't do any time."

"This goes a lot deeper than that," he said.

"How deep?" I asked.

Rodriguez looked like he was about to say something; then he just shook his head. "I can't," he said. "I'm not trying to play games with you. I'm truly sorry. All I can tell you right now is that you really don't want to be mucking around in this."

I asked, "What do you mean by that?"

He shook his head again. "Sometimes people change. Sometimes people change, and it's tough to keep up with them." Then he stood and added, "I've got to run to court. Just take my word on this. You don't want to push this too far."

THE NICE MEMBERS OF THE Copley Plaza hotel's management team saw fit to upgrade me to a suite overlooking Copley Square. Once upstairs, I quickly perused the room service menu and called down for a hamburger. Then I fired up my laptop.

The stories from Dorothy were sitting in my queue, as promised, the first headlined FIVE NORTH SHORE MEN ARRESTED IN FATAL NORTH END WELLS FARGO HEIST. I quickly scanned through, seeing Black's name at the top of the second paragraph, then the name of Rocco Manupelli, who was described as a rising member of the New England Mob. My eyes scanned through the rest of the list of suspects, from Marcio Sanchez to Joe Cox and then to the name that stopped my heart cold: Paul Stemple. Paul Stemple. I know that name. It rang so familiar in my mind, but I couldn't place it.

And then, bang. It was as if someone had flicked a fork against a fine crystal glass. Paul Stemple. He was the man who had received the presidential pardon, the man whom I intended to ask Hutchins about at Congressional Country Club. Paul Stemple connected to Curtis Black. Curtis Black connected to the shooting. I stared at the computer screen until the letters turned fuzzy.

Someone knocked at the door. I jumped in surprise, then remembered my call to room service. I pulled the door open and had begun to say, "Bring it right in here," when I saw that the person on my threshold wasn't the waiter, but was none other than my old friend Gus Fitzpatrick. He had a sheepish look on his face.

"They told me in the D.C. bureau that you were in Boston for the night. I figured you'd be here," he said.

"Gus," I said, "what a welcome sight. Come in."

We shook hands, then settled in, he on the couch, me on a chair.

Gus said, "So you, my friend, are hitting home runs every day of the week. You're knocking this story out of the park. You have any idea how proud I am?"

"Oh, c'mon. Thanks. But the more I find out, the less it is I seem to know. I just can't piece the damned thing together."

"Why are you being so hard on yourself? You're finding out things that other reporters aren't. You're the most important reporter in the country on the most important story of the moment."

I said, "Thanks, Gus. Maybe I'm just too much in the thick of it to step back and appreciate what's going on."

Another knock at the door. I let the room service waiter in, and he left the tray on the coffee table. Gus declined my offer to split the hamburger.

As I ate, he asked, "So why all this frustration on your part?"

"Because," I said, "every time I learn something, there are three other things that don't make sense. Everything seems so within reach but so far out of my reach at the same time."

"You have to take it one step at a time. You can only do what you can do. And you have to be careful."

That sounded strange to me. "What do you mean, be careful?" I asked as I salted my pile of french fries.

"Just what I said," he replied. "This can be a dangerous business. You know that. You're tired, Jack. You've done great work. You're about to do even better work. Get some rest."

He stood up, motioning for me to stay down. I got up anyway. As we walked toward the door, he asked, "You ever wish you could just change your identity and become an entirely different person?"

"Right now I do, yeah," I answered.

"You shouldn't," he said. "You have a great life, young man." With that, he squeezed my arm and walked out the door.

I finished my hamburger in the silence of the suite. Curtis Black and Paul Stemple. What did this bizarre connection mean to the story? They are cohorts in a failed armored car heist two decades ago. They are both charged in the death of a guard. Over twenty years later the President of the United States is shot.

I'm told that Curtis Black is key to the shooting, though I have no idea how. Mobsters won't talk about him. Neither will federal prosecutors. I can't find Black. He's apparently not in prison. And Stemple is for some reason pardoned by this President just before the assassination is attempted. So what is the connection? Could Black have masterminded the assassination attempt? Could he have been angry over the Stemple pardon and sought revenge? Could he be acting on behalf of another one of the armored car robbers still in jail?

All these questions made my head hurt. I leaned my head against the back of the chair. A new identity. It was an interesting concept Gus had raised. Someone else had raised that same point today, or something like it, no? Yes, Diego Rodriguez, at the end of our meeting. "Sometimes people change," he said. And he said something else—that when people change, it's tough to keep up with them.

Then there was Markowitz. I had asked him if Black was in jail, and he said no. I asked him why, and he said I should ask the feds about that. Ask the feds why Black isn't in jail. It was as if all these pieces of a puzzle started zipping into place.

I grabbed my coat, my computer, and my overnight bag, side-stepped the coffee table, and bolted out the door.

WATER dripped from my hair as I stood over the booth of Sammy Markowitz, who looked up at me.

"So soon?" he asked, not really surprised.

"Tell me if I'm right," I said. "Curtis Black turned state's witness, entered the witness protection program, and changed his identity. That's why he's not in jail. That's why the feds would know more about him than you do." Pause, then, "Sammy, you'll confirm, but you won't provide. Those have always been the rules."

He replied, "I don't have to go by rules, kid."

"Yes or no, Sammy. That's all I need. Yes or no."

He stared up at me in silence, taking an occasional puff from his cigarette. He took a final drag, stubbed it out, and said, "Yes."

I asked, "You know who he is now, who he became?"

"No one does. Black disappeared in the program. You probably know as much about where he went as anyone right now."

"Thank you," I said, and made for the door, for my idling taxi that would take me to the airport. I placed a call from my cell phone to Lincoln Powers at the White House and told him I'd neared a decision and would like to meet with the President. He sounded pleased and told me he could give me a few minutes the following morning in Chicago, on a campaign stop there.

My next call was to Havlicek. "Hey, old man," I said.

"Where are you and what'd you learn?"

"I'm in Boston. Going to meet up with Hutchins tomorrow in Chicago. Find out as much as you can about the witness protection program. I'll explain more tomorrow when I get in."

Saturday, November 4

A HIGH school band exploded into "Hail to the Chief" as I walked inside the ballroom of the Chicago Sheraton. A pair of Secret Service agents escorted me to a holding area near the dais.

The crowd of several thousand Republican partisans was up on its feet cheering wildly. Hutchins, who had just walked to the podium, waved his arms above his head, stopping only to point out people in the audience whom he recognized, giving them a thumbs-up sign as he mouthed their names. He actually did this to me, letting his eyes linger a moment on mine. He appeared elated, the antithesis of that last time I called on him in the Oval Office.

And why shouldn't he be? He was barnstorming across the country, unveiling a series of policy initiatives designed to take the public discourse beyond partisanship to a place he called the American Way. Pollsters said his lead had increased to about five points. It was a combination, they said, of the honeymoon that any President gets when he takes over at a trying time, his survival of an assassin's bullet, and his newly floated battery of ideas.

"Not a bad little reception, huh?" That was Royal Dalton, the White House press secretary, who had taken the job in the first days of the Cole administration and was about to lose it, though I'm not entirely sure if he realized that fact yet.

Speaking of which, my intention was to reject the press secretary's job. I'm a newspaper reporter—always have been, always will be. I don't look good on television. I don't particularly like politics. I disdain the idea that, as a press secretary, I'd ever have to suck up to someone like myself, some cynical reporter who virtually explodes at the suspicion of a lie. That said, I'd use the rejection as a chance to ask some much needed and belated questions.

The crowd had broken out into a chant of "Clay's Way, Clay's Way." Hutchins held his hands up in a plea for quiet.

"Ladies and gentlemen," he shouted into the microphone. "I have an election to win, an agenda to put into place. I have to get back to Washington to ensure those career politicians aren't misusing our money and dampening our American dream."

The crowd went crazy, cheers swirling toward the ceiling.

Dalton said, "It's been like this at every stop."

Hutchins appeared to be on a roll. "Look," he said, enjoying himself, "let's make a deal. I like deals. Deals are what helped me get rich before I came to Washington. Here's the deal I want to cut with the American people. I talk about the American dream an awful lot, and I happen to think the American dream is the backbone of this wonderful country. The government's role should be to make sure that every American—and that's every single American, black or white or red or brown, male or female, young or old, gay or straight—has the *opportunity* to pursue his or her dream. So here's what I want to do. I promise you I will work until the day I leave office to make sure that every American gets the education they need to pursue their dream. I also promise you we will not allow discrimination—not here in America.

"Here's what I want in return. I want you to be Americans. That means showing compassion for those less fortunate. That means helping those who can work find a job. Let's end crime. Let's put our time and our money toward making this country a better place to live. That's the deal I'm ready to cut with you, the deal that's going to make an already great country even greater."

The crowd jumped to its feet in a massive roar. Red, white, and blue balloons showered down like a patriotic snowfall.

HUTCHINS sat at the head of an antique dining table, drinking from a can of Diet Coke, in what must have been the largest hotel suite I had ever seen. Two aides stood on either side, pointing out something on a sheaf of documents spread out before them. I had arrived in the company of one of the Secret Service agents.

Hutchins pulled off his half-glasses when he saw me come in and advised me where to sit. He handed the papers to one of his aides, saying in that rock-hard voice, "Tell Benny to hand-deliver these to Senator Mitchellson on Monday morning. Tell Benny to tell Mitchellson I'm ready to meet him halfway. Then tell him if he's not ready to meet me, we'll cut his legs out from under him. Tell him he'll need a wheelchair just to get around the Senate floor."

"Yes, sir," the aide said, then sprinted from the room. Hutchins told the other aides he preferred to conduct the interview in private, and after everyone had left, he said, "What'd you think?"

He had just stood before thousands of cheering supporters screaming his name, three days before the election. Network TV crews were beaming the appearance into living rooms across the nation. And here he was, asking what I thought about it all.

"I thought your tie didn't match your suit."

I was hoping for one of those belly laughs. Instead, he gave me a bemused look and said, "This is one of my favorite ties."

He picked up his half-glasses and twirled them in his hand. "So here's what I have in mind," he said. "You heard me out there. I have lots of thoughts. But they're little more than unformed ideas. I have to figure out how to translate them to the policymaking structures of the West Wing and the rest of that rathole we call Washington. That's where you come in. First, you help me translate my thoughts into policy initiatives. Second, once we figure out a set of proposals, you help create the message around them to sell them to the public. My idea is to announce your arrival on Thursday, two days after the election. We'll keep Dalton around until right after the holidays. Then I have a slot saved for him over in the U.S. trade representative's office."

He wasn't really asking me about this; he was telling me. A weaker man might have said, "Yes, this all sounds good."

Instead, I said, "Sir, I have no government experience whatsoever. I really don't believe I'm the guy you need in there."

"I didn't have any presidential experience when I came to the Oval Office, and look at me. I'm up in virtually every poll. I'd rather have someone from outside government than from within.

I'd rather have someone who's skeptical of what I'm saying than another pansy-assed yes-man. You also understand the news media, and that's exactly what I need."

I started to think that, yes, I could help the President, that I was precisely what he needed. Then this voice popped into my mind— that crystal-clear voice of an aging man who was warning me that this assassination attempt wasn't what it seemed. Well, we were trying to figure out what it was, Havlicek and me. Some of the pieces were starting to come together. I had names to go on now, names like Paul Stemple and Curtis Black.

"Mr. President, before I go on with my decision, I need to ask you something. Why did you pardon Paul Stemple?"

Hutchins's forehead scrunched into an expression that may have been concern but may just as well have been anger.

"Jack," he finally said, betraying neither anger nor surprise, "I don't really know. My best recollection is that Mr. Stemple was going to be pardoned by President Cole. I believe he was on his list after I was sworn in, so I went ahead and issued the pardon. I believe that's the case, though I'd have to double-check."

He had me with that answer. How was I supposed to check with Cole or get one of his aides to dig up such minutiae in the throes of the last weekend of an election campaign?

Hutchins continued, his voice taking on an edge. "But here's what I do know. I'm the best damned President who'll ever seek your help. As far as why I was shot, I'm hoping like hell to find that out as soon as I can. I really don't want to be shot again. I think you'll join me in agreement that it's not a fun thing."

Well, that all seemed like an effective evasion, leaving me little in the way of follow-up questions. I gave it one more try, saying, "There's something terribly odd about that assassination attempt."

Okay, so now he seemed exasperated. "We have an army of FBI agents working on this issue. The only odd thing is that they haven't nailed down an exact motive yet. They will, Jack. Sometimes these investigations aren't easy, and sometimes they don't work out in the neatly set schedules that you press people demand."

I said, "Maybe you're right," though I didn't think he was. Then I breathed a long sigh and said, "Sir, I've thought your offer over hard. I really have. I'm honored by it. But I can't accept it. I'm a newspaper reporter. It's just what I do and what I'll continue to do and what I sometimes fear I'll always do."

He stared at me. He was the President, the leader of the free world. Yet here he was stewing that he couldn't persuade a reporter to come work on his staff. "You're making an enormous mistake, young man," he said sternly. He pushed his chair out and lifted himself up to show me to the door. "We're all done here."

I got up and walked to the door, and when I got within a few feet of him, I stuck my hand out to shake his. He ignored me and said, "This is a decision you'll regret for a long time to come."

Chapter Eight

As I stepped off the flight from Chicago O'Hare to National at eight thirty p.m. Saturday and headed outside for a cab, a familiar female voice said from behind me, "Come here often?"

I turned slowly, not wanting to make a jackass out of myself in case the woman was actually talking to someone else. There, walking two paces in back of me, was Samantha Stevens. "Only when I travel," I said. "You pulling into town or heading out?"

"Neither. I'm buying you dinner."

It seemed like a good idea. My mind was about to explode, there was so much going on in it. I needed to give it a rest before I briefed Havlicek and Martin. On the flight back to D.C., I had made a series of calls to lawyers and police detectives I knew from my days on the Boston crime beat. I learned that Curtis Black was a Tom Sawyer type, a gang leader who could convince the others to whitewash the fence while he sat back and watched. He had a college education and was widely known on the streets for his brains and his gregariousness. He was believed to be without a gun on the occasion of the heist, which would explain why the feds granted him immunity, certain that he couldn't have been the triggerman. His lack of practice might also explain why he was such an awful shot at the golf course that day, assuming that it was him. And yes, he had brown eyes, just like the dead shooter at Congressional Country Club.

What I hadn't learned was where Black had gone and who he had become, and it didn't seem like I was about to. That left me with one option: find Paul Stemple. The problem was, it wasn't clear where or how I was going to find him. All of this is a longer than necessary way of saying that a friendly face and a beer seemed like just the quick fix I needed.

"How did you know I was coming in tonight?" I asked.

"We have our ways," she said, smiling.

"Well, name the place," I said.

"Kinkead's. Do you have your car here? I cabbed over."

"I do."

We made chitchat on the way to the restaurant. Once inside, she settled gracefully into the booth. She wore her black hair tied back in a low ponytail, scrunched at the end by a nondescript band. She looked ravishing. Put those feelings away right now, I told myself.

We ordered some seafood ravioli and a plate of Ipswich fried clams to start, and I suggested that she try the pepita-crusted salmon, the signature dish of owner Bob Kinkead. She did.

More chitchat until she spooned clams and a ravioli off the appetizer plates and onto hers. She took a bite, exclaiming her approval in a sound I hoped to hear someday in a different venue.

Out of nowhere, she said, "The only point I want to make before we get too far into dinner is that we need to have a working relationship. That's all I want right now."

Oh, my. There were about a million ways to read that declaration. My first take was that this was good news. She flatly stated that she wanted a working relationship, meaning she'd continue to bring something valuable to the exchange. This was good. My second take was that she seemed to be saying she wanted no personal relationship. That said, she indicated she wanted a working relationship right now, which could be her way of saying we should get this investigation out of the way before we go off and have sex like two wolves in the Montana wilderness.

"I'm all for working together." I was playing this safe.

"Good," she said. "I hear you have some interesting stuff. Word in our shop is that you and your colleague are on the verge of springing another major story, one that might answer the question of who the Secret Service shot that day at the golf course."

I tried not to bat an eye. I said, "We're working hard, Havlicek and me. We're getting some leads, and we're following them."

We locked eyes for a long moment in an attempt to size each other up. She said, "Well, you boys better put a move on it, or you're going to let a whole bureau of federal agents down." She smiled, and so did I.

I regarded her for another moment. Samantha Stevens seemed poised, confident. I had the inclination to rest my hand on top of hers. Instead, I pulled a piece of crusty bread from the basket, took a bite, and said, "Why don't you tell me what you have?"

She smiled at that too. "By my calculation, it's your turn."

"Sam, we have what we hope are some good leads, but I don't know yet if they're going to pan out. My sense is that you're not in as active a stage as I am, so it might be better if you helped me, rather than vice versa, or at least went first in this exchange."

I have no idea about the logic of this argument. The salient fact to take away is that it marked the first time that I addressed her as Sam, and that to me meant that a significant bridge had been crossed. Score one for Jack, even if no one was keeping score.

She seemed to think all this over, perhaps even the Sam part. As she stared at points unknown, our waiter arrived with our entrées.

After he left, Stevens said, "Here's what I'm learning about Drinker. He answers only to the director. He barely speaks to me." She hesitated for a second. "And here's the interesting part. I know he and the President talk on the phone all the time—almost every day. I saw Drinker's call logs."

"Would that be so unusual, an investigating agent talking regularly to the victim of the crime?"

"Well, this is no normal crime and no normal victim. The President's a busy guy. He's trying to win an election. He doesn't need constant contact with the investigator on the case. If he did want regular updates, he'd more likely get them from the FBI director. We're pretty big on the chain of command over there."

We both fell quiet. By now the entrées were done and our waiter had delivered two orders of chocolate dacquoise with cappuccino sauce, and two glasses of port.

I said to Stevens, "Okay, I concede the point. It is unusual those two would be talking as much as you say they are."

She took a bite of the dacquoise and declared she was on her way to heaven. She looked rail thin yet packed down food like there would be breadlines come morning. She'd make a wonderfully expressive bedmate, I thought.

She said, "Not to force the issue, but let's put work aside for a while and see if we can chat like two regular human beings."

Truth be known, I still wasn't a hundred percent confident that Drinker and my new friend Sam weren't conspiring to set me up, playing off each other to learn the identity of my informant. "That sounds good, but just one more thing," I said. "Does Drinker ask about the phone call in the hospital room anymore?"

"No. Though I have to admit, I'm still curious."

Interesting answer. I decided to take a modest risk. "The name Black mean anything to you in this investigation?"

She looked at me blankly. "Not a thing. Should it?"

My question was designed to accomplish two goals: first, see if, in fact, I did get any response and, second, to gauge in the future whether she passed this information to Drinker.

I said, "Probably not. Just scratching at dirt."

"No, really. What do you have?"

"Really, nothing solid," I said.

We both sat in silence, sipping our port. She began making small talk—about her desire for a Caribbean vacation, her raves about my four-legged friend, Baker. It became all very casual, breezy, just how I usually like it. Still, I was looking for meaning within, and this conversation exposed none of it. We tossed down another glass of port before I paid the bill and we walked outside.

The night was cold, the street crowded with cars, creating a blur, even as my eyes focused on Samantha. I could never precisely explain the hints I got, whether they were from her posture or her proximity, but inexplicably I placed my hand on her forehead, brushed her hair softly, then let my fingers run down her cheek. She glided closer to me, and before I could think about what was happening, she placed her warm lips fully against mine for a kiss that was hard and soft, passionate and affectionate, all at the same time.

Then she pushed me away gently and said, "There's a cab right here. It's better if I just leave." She walked slowly to the curb. As she settled into the taxi, she gave me an odd, even goofy smile. I stood on the sidewalk until all I could see were the taillights of her car driving down Pennsylvania Avenue, and I thought, This finally feels like something called home.

As I pulled out my keys on my darkened front stoop, there was the sound from inside the house of someone talking. I froze. I leaned over the railing to look in the window, but the shutters were drawn closed. I could see a light was on, but that would make sense, given that Kristen had been supposed to drop Baker off earlier in the night. I strained to hear, thinking it might be Kristen inside, but it sounded more like a male voice.

It was coming up toward eleven thirty. There were no passersby, no moon, no lights on in any of the neighbors' houses. Inside mine, the sound droned on. And it struck me in a wave of panic that if Kristen had dropped Baker off as she said she would, then he was inside with God only knows who.

I remembered that I had left a pair of old pruning shears beside the stoop, in my little patch of a garden in front of my house. I silently walked down the two stairs, hunched down in the dark, and found them protruding from a pile of soggy leaves.

With the shears in hand I stepped cautiously back up on the stoop. I pushed the key into my lock. My mind raced through what I might find inside: perhaps Assistant Director Drinker. Maybe my anonymous source. Probably some nameless thug ready to carry out someone else's dirty work.

So without more thought, I snapped the lock, threw the door open, and burst inside, holding the shears ahead of me. "Freeze," I yelled.

The warm air of the house hit me in the face. Sitting on my couch, with his feet on the coffee table and my telephone up to his ear, Steve Havlicek calmly said, "Hold on one second, honey." To me: "Boy, am I glad I'm not some overgrown bush."

At the same time, Baker bolted up from a sound sleep and ran into the kitchen, barking at the back door. Wrong way, pal. I made a mental note to get his ears flushed out.

I let the shears fall to my side, closed the door behind me, and said breathlessly, "What the hell are you doing in here?"

Havlicek said into the phone, "Honey, I've got to run. Jack just got in. Seems a bit out of sorts. Tell Mary I said I'll make it back for her play-off game. . . . Good. . . . Yeah. . . . I love you too."

He hung up the phone, took a sip from a can of Pabst Blue Ribbon beer, and said, "Howaya, slugger?"

"I'm almost dead from a heart attack. How'd you get in here?"

"You don't have a dead bolt on your back door."

By now Baker had trotted back out into the living room with a confused look on his face. I knelt down and rubbed behind his ears, relieved that he was all right.

"You scared the hell out of me," I said to Havlicek.

"Sorry about that. Hey, before you sit, grab yourself a beer. I've got some Pabst in the fridge." As I walked into the kitchen, he called after me, "Grab me another too."

As I slumped down into a chair with a can of beer, Havlicek said, "We've got to talk. I'm dying to know what you learned."

I told him of my discussions with Markowitz and Diego Rodriguez, of my deduction about the witness protection program.

"So we've got an armored car robber named Curtis Black in the witness protection program," I said. "We're told we need to find out his relationship with the President that was just shot. Black's a fellow crook of a guy named Paul Stemple. Stemple's pardoned by the President in the middle of the campaign."

"I know a thing or two about the witness protection program," Havlicek said. "The way it goes is, if you have something worthwhile, you cut a deal with the FBI to enter the program. Before a trial you're given protection. Once you do your thing or the other side pleads guilty because they know you're waiting to testify, you're given your freedom and a different identity."

Havlicek looked at me. "Literally, Jack Flynn would cease to exist. Your house would be sold along with everything in it, and the marshals would cart you off. You get to pick the region of the country where you want to move. They'll help you buy a new house or apartment. They'll get you started on getting new identification, like a Social Security card and a driver's license. You come up with a story of who you are and where you're from. I'm told that only about three people in the entire Marshals Service ever get to learn your new identity—that's how closely held the secret is."

"So the odds of us learning who Black became and where he went are not exceedingly good," I said.

Havlicek said, "Suppose Black is the one sitting in that morgue, the unsuccessful assassin. Suppose it looks like the feds gave a free pass to some armored car robber more than twenty years ago, and he turns into some sort of presidential assassin."

"Why does some robber flunky from Chelsea, Massachusetts, end up shooting at the President, especially after he's taken a ride on the federal gravy train? And what's the role of Paul Stemple?"

Havlicek replied, "Maybe it was a hired hit. Maybe the guy's in the program, working a menial job, not making the money he was used to when he was hitting banks and Brink's trucks. Along comes this offer. Maybe it's so good it makes him rich for life."

"Black's too sharp," I said. "He's a chief, not an Indian. He's not going to get his hands dirty like that for the cash."

Havlicek took a pull of beer and said, "Well, maybe he really wanted this President to be dead for some reason."

"That's what bothers me," I said. "And that's what gets to the point of my anonymous friend, who seems to think that if we find out about the relationship between Black and the President, we'll know why this shooting occurred. And it seems like stating the obvious to say Stemple's pardon must be involved, no?"

Havlicek nodded.

"So our immediate mission now," I concluded, "is to find Stemple and find him fast. There's an election at stake in this, and that gives us two days. We find him, we get some answers."

"On that point," Havlicek said, "we're in luck. I think I have a line on where Stemple is living now, and it's here in D.C. I got ahold of his Social Security number through a contact I have. I used that to nail his bank records. I found out that he made some recent withdrawals in Washington. I canvassed some short-term real estate brokers on Capitol Hill, where one of the withdrawals was made, and one guy told me he rented an apartment to him." He made a motion to stand up. "So next stop: his house."

As he stretched his back, Havlicek added, "We have a member of the witness protection program, Curtis Black, who is in some way involved in an assassination attempt. We have someone taking shots at you. And we have some anonymous source who seems to have all the world's information in the palm of his hand. One quick question: Who plays me in the movie?"

I replied, "I don't know. Ernest Borgnine?"

"Screw you. He's about fifty pounds heavier than me." He ambled off to the kitchen with a few empty cans.

I looked at the clock and saw that it was edging past midnight.

As we gathered our coats, Havlicek asked, "You ever think about what you'd do if you came into a million dollars? Would you work late at night like this, go through all the deadline stress that we have? Or would you kick back and live a life of leisure?"

"What, you just find out you're an heir to the throne of Poland, and they want you to come home and live in the castle?" I asked.

He gave me a look and said, "I get two million bucks, I wouldn't change anything. This thing is too much fun. Let's go."

On the sidewalk, he said, "I bet they get De Niro to play me."

I said, "What, you on heroin? Try Leslie Nielsen."

He smiled, this man unlike any other I had ever known.

MY CAR was parked at the curb out front. When I started it up, the engine turned bravely in the cold. Havlicek closed his coat around him in an exaggerated plea for heat.

"Hey, I talked to your FBI friend Stevens today," he said.

"Oh, yeah? You trying to steal my sources?" I asked jokingly.

He patted the pockets of his coat, looked at me more urgently, and said, "I forgot a tape recorder. You have one?"

"Damn, it's inside." I had started to pull the keys out of the ignition when politeness got the better of me. Knowing I had a spare house key stashed under a loose brick in my garden, I let the engine run so the heat would crank up. "I'll be right back."

I'll never forget his words: "Hurry up. I'm freezing."

Inside, I had hit the third step on my way up to my study when I heard what sounded like a truck backfiring on the street outside. That was followed by what could have been a plane hitting my house or an enormous clap of thunder, so strong that the resulting vibrations flung me to the ground, leaving me tumbling down the stairs.

In a daze, I recall windows smashing in, the spray of glass, the blast of cold air. I recall seeing lamps falling off tables, pictures plummeting from walls, a chandelier crashing down from above.

I picked myself up and raced out the front door. On the sidewalk and street various parts of my car were strewn asunder.

I scanned the area furiously, looking for Havlicek. There was singed, broken glass everywhere. Finally my eyes were drawn to his still, tattered body slumped against my house, his legs splayed open, his head concealed by one of his arms.

I raced over to him and saw that his skull was cracked open. He was no longer wearing any shoes, and soot or burn marks covered most of his clothing. I felt his throat and found a pulse.

"Steve, you're going to be all right," I said softly. I yanked my coat off and laid it over his form. "Stay with me, Steve. Just stay with me. Everything's going to be all right."

I glanced around the neighborhood and saw several people emerge onto their front stoops, a look of panic on their faces. I shattered the silence, yelling, "Is there a doctor around?" I got no response. Someone finally hollered back, "I've called for help."

I turned back to Havlicek. His neck was resting in one of my hands. His blood was dripping onto my wrist and coagulating on the cold ground. "Everything's all right," I said, talking as much to myself as to him. "We're not going to let those bastards beat us." Eventually I heard the vague sound of a siren in the distance, and over my shoulder a voice said to me, "Here, I have some towels." I took the towels and pressed them gently to Havlicek's head, trying to stem the flow of blood. Then he opened one eye and looked at me. Summoning an inordinate amount of energy, he blurted out, "My pocket. Coat."

In the background the siren kept getting closer, weaving through Georgetown. In the foreground people were gawking at us, as if they'd never had a car bomb explode on their block before in the early hours of a Sunday morning.

I reached into the inside pocket of his blazer and found a sheet of white paper. I put it in my pocket without looking at it. He seemed content and closed his eyes. "Don't go anywhere, Steve," I said.

I didn't even realize he had been gripping one of my fingers until I felt his grip loosen. He gave one hard exhale, and his facial expression changed. When I put a finger under his nose, his breathing seemed to have stopped. "Come on, Steve. We've come too far. We don't have that much further to go. Stay with me."

I started to breathe into his mouth; then the ambulance pulled up and the EMTs leaped out. One of the men put an oxygen cup over his mouth. Another thumped at his chest. Two more raced over with a stretcher. I backed away.

At that precise moment it hit me—the dog. I turned and raced toward the house and into the front door. On the floor in the middle of the living room, Baker was sprawled out on the rug, the shattered chandelier pinning him to the floor. When I knelt down in the shards of glass, he whimpered, his eyes pleading.

I kissed his muzzle and told him he was going to be fine. I pulled part of the chandelier off his back end. He seemed unable to move. I scooped him up in my arms and took him outside.

"This dog," I said to a policewoman who seemed to be working crowd control. "He's mine, and he desperately needs help. Could someone rush him to the Friendship Animal Hospital?"

"Follow me," she said. She led me to a station wagon, opened the back, and I gently slid Baker inside. He kept looking at me, frightened and in pain. I borrowed the woman's cellular telephone, called Kristen, and told her of my situation. About two minutes later she was standing in front of me, out of breath. She slid into the back of the car beside Baker, and lights blazing, they were off.

As I turned back toward Havlicek, a pair of EMTs were pushing his stretcher into an ambulance. I raced over, said, "I'm with him," and climbed into the back cabin. The doors shut behind me. Inside, two EMTs worked furiously on Havlicek.

Within about four minutes he was wheeled into the emergency room of Georgetown Hospital. As I tried to follow, a nurse blocked my path and said, "You'll wait out here." I was too dazed to argue. I slumped down in a chair in a hallway.

Soon a doctor appeared in front of me. This time it was a man, not a woman. "Your friend, Mr. Havlicek," the doctor said, aloof. "I'm afraid I must inform you that he's dead."

IT FELT like my entire world had just abandoned me. I was, admittedly, frightened. Someone had just tried to blow me up along with Havlicek, or more likely it was just me they were after.

Havlicek's death had left me without my crucial partner on the biggest story of my life. More important, it left Margaret Havlicek without the husband she adored, something I can relate to. And it left their two children without a father. This was a sadness that transcended every other, which is why I finally lifted myself up off that chair, walked heavily to a pay telephone, and dialed the Havlicek household in Braintree, Massachusetts.

"Hello." It was the unfailingly pleasant, though sleepy, voice of Margaret Havlicek, picking up the phone.

"Margaret," I said, "Jack Flynn here." I spoke in the most soothing tone I could muster. "Margaret, it hurts me terribly to tell you this. Your husband died about twenty minutes ago. We were about to drive to an interview tonight in my car, and he was alone in the front seat while I ran into the house to get a tape recorder, and it exploded. It appears someone planted a bomb."

There was silence on the other end as she processed what I had just told her. Then I heard her soft voice say, "No, I just talked to him a couple of hours ago. I just heard his voice. This can't be right." She had become almost too choked up to talk. "Oh, my God," she said; then came the sounds of sobbing.

"How?" she asked, her voice soaked in a cascade of tears. "Who? Why? Why would someone do this?"

"I don't know yet, but you can be sure we're going to find out. Margaret, I work with words every day, but I could never find the right ones to tell you just how sorry I am. Steve said just two hours ago how much he loved his life, how he wouldn't trade it for all the money in the world. He talked about you and the kids all the time."

"Thank you, Jack," she said through her tears. "Steve really enjoyed working with you." I could still hear her sobbing. She said, "I'm going to go now. I don't know what I'm going to do, but I think I should go." And with that, she hung up the telephone to face a life alone that she never wanted or expected.

After that the call to Peter Martin was relatively easy. He was upset—and not just over having the story delayed yet again. "This means you're in grave danger," he said. "I want you out of your house. Check in at a hotel somewhere; then call me."

I ambled outside into the cold—coatless, dried blood on one of my arms, my hair mussed. I flagged a taxi and settled into the back seat. "Friendship Animal Hospital," I said.

When Kristen saw me, she said, "The doctor wants to put Baker to sleep. I told her she couldn't do anything until you got here."

Some sort of veterinary assistant led me into a visiting room. He opened the door, and I saw Baker sprawled out on top of a stainless steel examination table, tied down. Baker saw me as well. Without lifting his head, he whacked his tail on the table several times. I leaned over and kissed his muzzle, then gently stroked his soft ears. The assistant said, "The doctor will be right with you."

When the door shut behind him, I pulled up a stool and sat. My head was close to Baker's, and I whispered to him, "You are my very best friend." It was the truth, almost from the minute I met him. I got Baker a little under two years ago. Katherine and I had just moved into our new house in Georgetown and decked it out for the holidays. I arrived home from work on Christmas Eve to our plans for a quiet dinner alone. She was sitting in the living room, sipping a glass of red wine, wearing a red satin dress.

"I'm going to give you your gift now," Katherine said. She pulled a large hatbox out from under the coffee table. When I lifted the top, all I saw was a ball of fuzzy blond fur.

"Oh, my God!" I remember exclaiming. I looked at this frightened puppy, scooped him up in one hand, and held him tight to my face. His fur mopped up a tear that Katherine never saw.

Two years later he is the only living, breathing remnant of our marriage, aside from me. If this veterinarian thought she was about to put him to sleep, she had no idea how wrong she was.

"Mr. Flynn, hi, I'm Dr. Gabby Parins." A pretty young woman with blond hair and glasses came through the door.

She told me of the extensive injury to Baker's hips, the fractures in both his hind legs. He might never walk again, she said, and he would certainly never be able to run the same way. She could perform surgery, but it might fail, and he could easily die on the operating table. Her recommendation was to put him to sleep.

"That doesn't seem humane," I said. "Not to him, not to me."

"On the contrary, Mr. Flynn, given the extent of the injuries, I think it's the most humane thing you could do right now."

I looked down at the dog. I thought of the first night I had him, this vanilla fluff ball walking on city sidewalks for the first time, people padding their way in the snowy dusk, squealing as they saw him. I thought of the way he moped around the house when I came home from the hospital that awful day without Katherine, how he sniffed at her side of the bed. I was not about to give him up now, to say good-bye to him and all he represented.

"Doctor," I said, my voice thick, "please, perform the surgery. Perform it well. Let's take it one step at a time."

She nodded. "Okay, I'll do that. We'll keep an open mind."

While I still stood there, she shot him with a sedative. I rubbed his head until he fell sound asleep. I went out and told Kristen that Baker was going to have surgery. She shed some tears of relief and asked if she could wait with the dog.

I dug into my pocket to see if I had enough money for a cab. When I did, my hand came across a crumpled piece of paper. I pulled it out, unfolded it, then read the handwritten line: "Paul Stemple, 898 C Street, SE, Washington, D.C."

Chapter Nine

Sunday, November 5

IT WOULD be impossible to realize how fully my world had just changed. I had to come to terms with the fact that danger now lurked beyond every corner. Marbled into all that danger were answers to the most significant questions that I may ever ask. It seemed evident right then that I had to confront the danger to obtain the information that Havlicek would so badly want me to get. I essentially had two days to the election, two days to answer these questions before Hutchins won his own four-year term.

These thoughts raced through my brain as I stood frozen in that waiting room. I asked the veterinary assistant if there were any other exits. He looked at me strangely, but then led me down a set of basement stairs toward a door that opened into a small backyard.

Outside, I hopped over the fence into another yard, then another fence to another yard. Eventually I emerged onto a side street. It was after three a.m., and through luck, I flagged a cab.

"Capitol Hill, please," I said to the taxi driver.

On the Hill, I asked him to take a drive past 898 C Street, Southeast. It was a two-story brownstone town house in an advanced state of disrepair. All the windows were dark.

"I'll get out at the corner," I told the driver.

I walked down the street toward the house, unsure of exactly what I was about to do but positive that I had to do it. The way I saw it, by morning I would be ordered off the story by the paper's editors for safety reasons, and if I wasn't, then whoever was attempting to abbreviate my life would be trying anew.

I took a deep breath and climbed the stairs to the front door of the house. I knocked on the decrepit door and waited. I stepped back, looking at the upstairs windows to see if any lights clicked on, but none did. I rang the doorbell and heard a loud buzz inside. Still nothing. I fingered the doorknob, and to my amazement it turned, creaking open into an entryway that led into a larger room. I stepped inside, keeping the door open behind me.

"Anyone home?" I yelled. No response, nothing. I groped around for a light switch and flicked it on. A bare bulb illuminated overhead, revealing peeling wallpaper covering ravaged walls that rose from a filthy linoleum floor. The only other item in the tiny space was a toilet plunger. Don't ask me why, but I grabbed it.

I stepped into the main room and flicked on a switch. Spread out before me was the living room, ransacked from one end to the other. Right next to me a desk drawer had been pulled out and thrown to the floor, its contents tossed about on a threadbare rug. The cushions of the old, ragged couch had been pulled off and cut open. A small television was smashed on the floor. My eyes sprinted around the room in search of a person or a body.

"Paul, come on out!" I hollered. Sweat rolled down my face. My voice, bouncing off the bare walls, frightened me even more. Carrying the plunger with both hands, I walked into the kitchen and turned on an overhead fluorescent lamp. Cabinet doors were flung open, drawers thrown onto the floor, a few dishes broken on the scratched Formica countertops. About a dozen roaches sprinted across the floor to escape the light.

I walked back into the living room and went slowly toward the staircase in the corner of the room. I started up the stairs, each creaking louder than the one before. On the top stair something flashed across the wooden floor. I raised the plunger to take a swing at whatever demonic figure was coming my way. I looked down in time to see a rat race by my feet into a darkened room. When I looked closer, I saw bloody animal tracks where the rat had just run. He was either bleeding or had just stepped in blood. I looked warily at the open door from which he had come.

I could see it was the bathroom. I reached hesitantly inside the door, found a light switch, and flipped it on. My eyes raced from the toilet to the sink to a pair of soiled towels flung on the floor. That's when I looked into the tub and saw the lifeless form of a human being, face down in a fetal position, as if in self-defense.

As I got closer, I saw that the body was of a white-haired man, wearing a sweatshirt, khaki pants, and sneakers. It appeared he'd been shot a couple of times in the head. Blood had flowed down the side of his face and formed a puddle in the tub. I put my hand gently on his exposed neck. His skin was warmer than I expected. I'd guess that he had been killed in the last few hours.

His wallet lay opened in the tub beside him, some of the contents spilled around his legs and midsection as if someone had rifled through it before throwing it back at him. I snatched up a few pieces of paper. No names, no identification.

I grabbed another handful of papers and sifted through them. The last slip sent a chill up my spine. It was a torn sheet of paper, and on it were my work and home telephone numbers. I shoved the paper into my pocket and made my way for the door.

I crept down the stairs and toward the front door. I stopped suddenly in the middle of the living room, walked back into the kitchen, and saw what I had thought I remembered: a telephone answering machine on the counter. I pressed a button that said GREETING and recognized immediately a voice that haunted me to my soul. "You've reached 282-4572. Please leave a message." It was the voice of my anonymous source, Paul Stemple. Now he too was dead.

Once outside I bolted toward Massachusetts Avenue. I stopped at a pay telephone, called 911, and informed the dispatcher of a possible homicide at 898 C Street in Southeast. I hung up, found a nearby ATM machine, and withdrew five hundred dollars. As I flagged a cab, two police cruisers raced past, their lights flashing.

REGARDLESS of what I looked like, the front-desk clerk at the Jefferson Hotel would have treated me with suspicion, given the hour, which was four a.m., and the fact that I wasn't carrying any luggage. When he took into account my appearance, he called for security, and a nice guard stood politely nearby as I tried to arrange for a room.

"Name, please?" the clerk asked.

"Bird. Lawrence Bird."

"What sort of credit card will you be using, Mr. Bird?"

"I'm not. I'd like to pay with cash." I pulled the thick wad of bills from my pocket and put them on the counter.

"Certainly. You have some form of identification?"

"I don't. I was just in a car accident, and I lost my wallet."

He typed on his computer keyboard. "Unfortunately Mr., um, Bird, we don't have any availability right now. I'm very sorry."

I pulled two twenty-dollar bills from the pile, pushed them toward him, and said, "I'll take anything."

He typed for another moment. "Oh, it seems there's a king bedroom available on the fourth floor that I didn't see."

He required an up-front payment of three hundred dollars.

Once in the room, I called Martin and told him where I was and my assumed name. Within minutes I was fast asleep.

I AWOKE four hours later thinking thoughts that were way too complex. Foremost among them were images of Samantha Stevens meeting me at the airport, Samantha Stevens alone knowing that my car was at Kinkead's, Samantha Stevens jumping into a cab before I could offer her a ride home. She was the only person in any way connected to the assassination attempt who had monitored my whereabouts in the hours before the explosion.

I thought of my anonymous source, the grotesque way he had died, all because of his mission of truth. Of course I thought of Havlicek, fighting for the story right to the end. I questioned whether it was time to abandon my efforts, then dismissed that thought as unworthy of another second's consideration.

Then I thought of Kent Drinker, so desperate for the last week-plus to learn the identity of the person who had called me in the hospital. And a few hours ago I found that person murdered.

It's a different Tony Clawson. And it's his background that's so potentially devastating to my agency. I played Drinker's strange words out in my mind as I showered. Pink and powdered, I sat down in the fluffy terry cloth robe—I had no fresh clothes—and called downstairs for a laptop computer with Internet access. A few minutes later a bellman delivered it to my door.

I settled in at the computer to conduct a cyberspace manhunt. First I checked Social Security records for all Tony Clawsons in the country in the last twenty years. For each one I found, I checked for current telephone numbers. If they didn't have a phone number, I checked for death records. If they didn't have a phone number or a death record, I checked for a credit report.

On the fifteenth Tony Clawson, this one in the suburbs of Chicago, I could find nothing—no death record, no phone number, no credit activity. I checked for a birth record, and again, nothing.

I went deeper into his Social Security history and saw that he hadn't been assigned a Social Security number until 1979, when he was listed as forty years old. That was unusual. Clawson, my computer told me, had begun paying into the system in 1979 and continued for nine years. In late 1988 he abruptly stopped.

More keystrokes, more information. Social Security never paid a death benefit to any Clawson survivors. In 1988 Tony Clawson of Rosemont, Illinois, ceased to exist.

This was interesting because in 1979 Curtis Black had ceased to exist, the year Tony Clawson took shape. Best as I could tell, Curtis Black became Tony Clawson in the witness protection program in 1979. Interesting, though, that Clawson himself then disappeared from sight in 1988. Drinker had implied in the park that it was this Clawson who had resurfaced at Congressional with a gun and a mission. The cryptic words of Diego Rodriguez popped into my mind. *Sometimes people change, and it's tough to keep up with them.* So this is what he meant. But one question still lingered: Why?

The ringing phone crashed through my thoughts. "I've got two engineers in the lobby," Martin told me. "They're going to set up separate phone and fax lines in your room that match your office phone, so you'll get all incoming calls. The phones will be untraceable, so you can make calls. I've also got a pair of security guards standing on your floor, so no one will have access to your room. I've put down an untraceable credit card to hold your room for as long as you need it. Now what the hell is going on here?"

I walked him through the bombing. I told him about making a tentative match between Clawson and Black. I finished with the part about finding Stemple dead and hearing his voice—the voice of my secret informant—greet callers on his answering tape.

"Damn," he said. "Havlicek's dead. You're in grave danger, and we don't even have a publishable story explaining why."

Someone knocked at my door. The phone engineers. As they set up a telephone and fax, I asked Martin, "Did we get news of the explosion into the final edition?"

"No. It happened too late." He paused. "The FBI called this morning, wanting to question you about last night. They said you left the scene of the bombing and they were unable to find you."

My mind flashed again to Stevens at Kinkead's, to Drinker's inquisition about my source, and to Stemple in the bathtub. "No way."

"I already told them that," Martin replied. "I told them it was our responsibility now to assure your safety."

"I need some new clothes," I said.

"I'll be there in an hour," Martin said. "Stay put until then."

He hung up, and the engineers left.

My first call was to Stevens and was a test. When she picked up the phone, I blurted out, "You'll live with Havlicek's blood on your soul for the rest of your life." I hung up before she could reply.

My next call was to Drinker.

"I'm sorry about your colleague," he said. "That's just awful. We have some agents looking to collect information from you."

"I'll get around to that," I said. "First, though, let me run something past you. Tony Clawson used to go under the name of Curtis Black. Curtis Black used to be an armored car robber in Massachusetts, before he entered the witness protection program in the late 1970s. Is this something you can guide me on?"

There was a lengthy silence between us. In a measured tone he said, "I am unable to dispute what you've found."

I rolled my eyes at his lapse into officialese. "I need more than that. What you're saying doesn't help me get this into print."

Another long silence. Then, carefully, Drinker said, "If this is what you've found, then you understand why the director wanted to offer up a different photo of Clawson. It wouldn't reflect well on the FBI to have a former federal witness, who lived for a while with a government subsidy and government protection, then become an attempted assassin rather than spend a lengthy stretch of time in jail."

I asked, "And the motive for the shooting?"

"That I don't know," he said.

I said, "I need to use you as a source, identified only as an official familiar with the investigation. I need that official to say that Clawson and Black are the same guy."

"Can't," he said. "That'd cost me my job. But give me a while to think of another way. You have a fax number?"

I gave it to him, and we hung up. Five minutes later a document rolled out of my fax machine, stamped TOP SECRET beneath letterhead for the Federal Bureau of Investigation. My eyes raced down the page to see the name Curtis Black, along with his last known address in 1979, in Chelsea, Massachusetts. Beneath Curtis Black was the name Tony Clawson, with an address in Springvale, Illinois, and the year 1979. At the bottom of the page were the words "Identity transition, c/o U.S. Marshals Service."

The telephone rang. "That going to help you?" Drinker asked.

"It will help, but it doesn't give me everything I need."

A tone of frustration, even disdain, filled Drinker's voice. "This lays it right out for you. What the hell else is there?"

"First of all, the last official statement from the FBI was an agreement that Clawson was not, in fact, the shooter. I have no one from your agency saying he was. Second, I have no motive. Third, I have a loose end left to tie up, a guy named Paul Stemple."

There was a long silence again before he spoke. "One, you ask the agency, they will have to tell you Clawson is still a suspect. Two, Black was probably doing this for the money. Third, I don't know who Paul Stemple is, but he doesn't have anything to do with this case."

The Stemple mention, I'll admit, seemed to shake him up. It may not have been the wisest maneuver on my part—a fear that was fulfilled about forty minutes later when my phone rang again. It was Martin telling me to tune the TV to CNN. I did.

On the screen an anchor was saying, "So we'll go live now to Washington and hear this surprising new development on that car bomb explosion this morning straight from the FBI." The picture flipped to a press conference. Drinker was at the podium.

"At approximately one a.m. today," Drinker said, "a car carrying Steven Havlicek, a reporter with the Boston *Record,* exploded in the Georgetown neighborhood of Washington, D.C. Mr. Havlicek was killed in the explosion. The owner of the car, Jack Flynn, also a reporter with the Boston *Record,* was not hurt.

"The FBI, along with the Washington, D.C., police, have determined that an explosive device was hooked up to the engine of Mr. Flynn's automobile and was timed to ignite several minutes after the engine started. In answer to your anticipated questions on whether we have any suspects, we don't. But in light of this being Mr. Flynn's automobile that was specifically targeted in this explosion, we are reviewing our investigation into the shooting on October 26 at Congressional Country Club to determine if Mr. Flynn may have been the intended target and President Hutchins an unintended victim."

I could hear the collective gasp of my reporter brethren in the room, and trust me when I tell you, reporters don't gasp easily.

A reporter asked, "Have you learned anything about Jack Flynn that would make you suspicious of such an attack?"

Drinker: "Not definitively, but we are pursuing leads and several lines of inquiry." Not with me, he wasn't. The jackass hadn't even given me the courtesy of a heads-up when we were on the telephone. I didn't know what to think.

Another reporter asked, "Since Mr. Flynn was one of the most active reporters investigating the unsolved shooting of President Hutchins, might that not make him a target in this explosion for anyone who fears he is getting too close to the truth?"

Drinker replied, "That is one explanation. However, I would caution that the attempted assassin is dead. And though we initially investigated the Congressional shooting as a possible conspiracy, we do not have definitive evidence that is the case. So the question remains, who alive would try to kill Mr. Flynn?"

Sitting there on the edge of my bed in the Jefferson Hotel, I felt as if I was watching my life flash before my eyes.

A few minutes later there was a knock on my door. I opened it, keeping the safety chain still fastened, and saw Peter Martin and Bob Appleton, the editor in chief of the *Record*. From the look on their faces I knew this conversation would not be one that I appreciated.

"Boys," I said, "good to see you."

They came in and settled in my sitting area.

Martin began, "Bob's worried, and I have to agree, that with the FBI's theory that you may be a target of some killer, you should not be putting yourself at risk by staying on this story."

"Well," I said, "suppose I wasn't the target of the killer. Suppose that there was a presidential assassin at work, and since we were the lead newspaper in the nation covering that assassination attempt, someone tried to kill us because they didn't like what we were reporting. If this is the case, by pulling me off the story, you are in effect surrendering to whoever killed Havlicek."

There was silence in the room. The feeling, within me anyway, was one of utter loneliness.

Martin said, "Jack, I can only imagine how you feel. Steve is dead. We're all devastated. You've busted your ass on this story, and you've come a long way. But now you've become part of the story. The FBI's having press conferences about you. You're going to be on the front page of every major paper tomorrow."

"It's Drinker who made us part of the story. You want to give in to him now? The FBI doesn't want me on this story. Havlicek's dead. My anonymous source is dead. We're knocking on the door of some really serious answers, and you want to give in?"

Appleton spoke for the first time. "Jack, we're not giving in, not by any stretch. I'm going to send people down to relieve you. I know it's best, for your own safety and for the reputation of this newspaper, if you bow out for a while and stay in hiding."

"You're making the biggest mistake of your careers," I said.

That remark seemed to get under Appleton's skin. "We all make mistakes," he said. "Though this decision doesn't happen to be one of them. I know you were engaging in discussions with Hutchins about becoming his press secretary at the same time you were covering this story. Based on that alone, the decision to pull you off the story was made. What happened today just makes it an easy one."

I said, "Hutchins pursued me, even when I said no. I just used his offer to get a couple of interviews for this newspaper."

Appleton was on his feet now. Martin, still sitting, said, "Jack, my only worry is for your safety. I ask that you not leave this room until the election is over. The funeral service for Havlicek is in Boston tomorrow. I'm afraid I have to forbid you from attending. We cannot put your safety at further risk."

Appleton was at the door. He said to me, "We have your best interests at heart. I'm not sure you could say the same thing to us."

Martin rose. "Jack, I'll call you later tonight."

And with that, they were gone. It made me think of the line from Pete Hamill, the journalism icon. "Newspapers," he once said, "will always break your heart."

Chapter Ten

THEY led Curtis Black into the small, dingy conference room—a federal agent and a police detective pushing him along from behind like he was a common criminal.

Inside the room, another police detective sat at a table, paging through a file. At first Lieutenant Kevin Morrissey didn't even bother looking up. When he did, he said, "Take his cuffs off."

The detective behind Black freed Black's wrists.

"Sit down, please," Morrissey said, indicating the chair across from him. He nodded at the two standing men, prompting them to retreat. Black heard the door click shut behind them.

Morrissey eyed Black from across the table. "Paul Boyle had two daughters," he said, his voice almost soothing.

Black gulped hard, knowing where Morrissey was leading him.

"Here they are." Morrissey slid a pair of pictures across the table—one of just two girls standing in front of a modest suburban home. The other picture was a formal family portrait—a husband, presumably Paul Boyle, and his wife standing up, their two daughters sitting in chairs in front of them. "Take a look."

For a few seconds Black was riveted by the photographs. Then he felt his head spin. He looked away from the pictures at the empty expanse of the table.

"I'm Kevin Morrissey, Lieutenant Kevin Morrissey. I assume you've been read your rights?"

Black continued to look down.

"Well, it's probably worth repeating the highlights. You have the right to remain silent. You also have the right to a lawyer."

Black nodded and said nothing. A lawyer was never part of his program, never necessary, not until the FBI and Boston police had shown up at his Chelsea apartment that afternoon.

Morrissey said, "So what went wrong? You don't usually kill people, Curtis. That's not your style."

Black sat in silence. The faces on the photos smiled up at him.

Morrissey said, "You ever hear of the charge of felony murder? We have it here in Massachusetts. It's when a victim dies in the commission of a felony—like last week on Hanover Street—everyone involved, whether they pulled the trigger or were driving the car, they all go away for life. That's the sentence: life."

Black gazed down at the table. This was the dreaded climax of what had been a successful career of crime. For the last seven days Black had awaited his destiny. He could have fled, but some part of him told him he had to face the consequences of that deadly dusk on Hanover Street. He had already lost his wife and son in a hit-and-run crash the year before. After that he felt he had nothing left to lose.

"We have a witness," Morrissey said. "An employee of Boston's parking enforcement division saw someone double-parked in a van outside the bank. He tried to get that person to move, then wrote out a ticket. He picked your photo out of a lineup."

Black flinched, a wave of terror working its way up his spine. He lifted his head up. His eyes rested on Morrissey. The men locked stares in silence.

"There is a way out," Morrissey said finally. "Let me tell you how. I don't believe you fired the weapon. Not your style. And I may be able to find a witness who says you never got out of that van, which would make it impossible for you to have fired the gun."

Black stared at him, a hurricane of thoughts churning in his head. Could he avoid doing time? What would that mean to the rest of his life? What would it mean to the others involved?

Morrissey continued. "So we cut a deal, me and you. You give me the names. You tell me who fired the shot that killed Paul Boyle. You tell me who else was involved. I'm especially interested in a convict by the name of Rocco Manupelli, who has connections to La Cosa Nostra. You help us; we protect you. We put you in the federal program. We send you out of state with a new identity and a new and honest way to make a life."

Black wondered if he could do it. Could he be a rat? And what was the alternative? Black needed time to think. He should talk to a lawyer. "We may have a deal. I need to speak to my lawyer first."

Morrissey jumped up out of his seat, the chair almost falling backward because of his sudden force.

"This deal holds right now," Morrissey said, almost seething. "You get a lawyer involved, that creates a whole new level of crap I have to go through. If you hesitate, I hesitate. Let me state it another way. You call a lawyer, I want to be the one who swings that prison door shut on the rest of your life."

Black put his hands up to his head, through his hair, across his forehead and eyes. He said, "I'll give you the guys. All four."

"Who was the shooter?"

"I don't know." He thought of Stemple's pitching his handgun into the harbor. "They wore masks and identical clothes."

"No shooter, no deal," Morrissey said.

Black's mind went into overdrive. Does he tell him Stemple because Stemple ditched his gun? But maybe Stemple fired a shot that missed. Does he tell him Rocco Manupelli because he thinks Rocco was destined to screw this thing up, knows that Morrissey wants to hear that it was Rocco who was the killer? Black said, "Then no deal. I don't know which one fired the deadly shot."

Morrissey walked a slow lap around the table. "You're missing a guy too. Five guys at the scene, including you, and a driver at the fish pier, right? We have witnesses."

Black said, "Three guys were on the guard when he came out of the bank. One guy was on Boyle. I was in the van."

"Yeah, and what about the driver at the pier where you dumped the first getaway car?"

Black hesitated, collected himself, and said, "There was no other driver. We planted a car there. When we got there, I drove."

"Bull. I know how you work. You like having a man on every job, a live person. You don't leave things to chance."

Black thought of his getaway driver on the pier. Older guy, no record, not even any criminal experience. He had needed the money but didn't need it so bad he wanted to be part of the holdup. He took the driver's job for a smaller cut and said it was the only job he'd ever do. Black would spare him. To Morrissey he simply shook his head.

In response the detective strode out of the room, flipping the door shut behind him. Five minutes later the door opened and another man in a blue suit entered the room with Morrissey.

"Curtis," Morrissey said, "this is Special Agent Kent Drinker of the FBI. He, along with the U.S. Attorney here in Boston, has to sign off on anyone entering the witness protection program."

Present Day
Monday, November 6

I HAD been held captive at the Jefferson Hotel all day Sunday, not even allowed to leave to visit my recuperating dog, who, by the way, seemed to be doing better, according to Dr. Parins.

I felt like I didn't have a whole lot left to lose, so come Monday morning I hailed a cab to the airport and grabbed a flight to Logan.

The funeral, held in Havlicek's native Boston neighborhood of Roslindale, was packed. Margaret Havlicek sat in the first row, flanked by her two children. The *Record* publisher was there, as were all the top editors.

Despite the session with Appleton and Martin the day before, I was treated with an utmost sense of respect and dignity. Margaret Havlicek had even called me in Washington and asked me to deliver a short eulogy. I walked to the front of the church and told the gathered mourners of my first days at the *Record,* of this funny man named Havlicek. I talked about his brutal work habits, his commitment to the story, his generosity as a colleague. "Margaret, he loved you more than most people realize is possible, and we need only look around this church today to see the breadth and depth of the love so many people felt for him. Steve," I said, "it's been not just a pleasure, but an honor. You were the best I've ever met."

As I walked past the thirty or so rows of pews to my seat, I passed Samantha Stevens, tears streaming down her cheeks.

After the service, as I stood in the back of the church, Stevens approached and, speaking softly, said, "Drinker doesn't like to lose."

I thought that an odd thing to say. Lose what?

I replied, "Who killed Havlicek? Who planted that bomb?"

She shook her head slowly and sadly. "I don't know."

"How did you know I was arriving at National Saturday night?"

"I called Havlicek, and he told me when you were coming in."

"Why did Curtis Black or Tony Clawson try to kill Hutchins?"

She stared at me. "I don't know."

I was growing angry. "What is it you know?"

"I only know that I was never involved in anything to do with that explosion. And I only know that I don't want to see you hurt in any way." And with that, she turned and walked slowly away.

FUNERALS make me think of everyone else who has died in my life. In the cemetery, as the priest droned on, I thought of my father in the pressroom of the *Record*. I thought of my mother, dying of a broken heart after my father's death, and of course I thought of Katherine, who was supposed to be here with me during difficult times like these. We should be preparing for another holiday season, keeping a camera nearby for our baby's first steps. Instead, I had no one to share with, nothing to look forward to.

What I did have, though, were bodyguards, two of whom had joined me on this Boston excursion. Their presence allowed me some comfort, though I still found myself peering around suspiciously at the gathered crowd.

Which is exactly what I was doing when Gus Fitzpatrick emerged from a cluster of people and walked slowly my way. I held my hand out, and he shook it.

"It's really nice to see you, Gus," I said.

"Thank the Lord you're alive," he said. He looked me up and down and then said something that rocked me to my core. "Nothing is as it seems. Do not believe anything that they tell you."

My jaw dropped. The identical words of my anonymous informant, Paul Stemple, rang through my mind.

"Gus," I replied, "what's going on here?"

I bore in on him. My mind raced through every crucial moment of this case, but I couldn't find Gus's footprints anywhere.

Silence, until Gus said, "Come with me, Jack."

I looked at my bodyguards and gave them a hand signal to follow me. Then I nodded at Gus, and we disappeared over the side of the hill, meandering among the tombstones.

THE two of us stood in a remote loading area at the end of the Boston Fish Pier. On one side of us the magnificent city skyline rose toward the heavens. On the other side the harbor sparkled.

Gus looked at me and spoke for the first time since the graveyard. "Are you familiar with Paul Stemple?" he asked.

"I saw him yesterday morning," I said. "He's dead. Murdered."

Gus grimaced and shook his head slowly. "I had a feeling."

Much as I love Gus, standing there watching him, I couldn't contain my anger. "Havlicek is dead. I couldn't have been warned about this? You couldn't have helped us out?" To my pending question, he stayed silent. "What the hell is going on here?"

"This isn't easy," Gus said. "I know Curtis Black. The guys in that armored car robbery fled in one getaway car with the money and came to this very spot. I met them here in a second car, and we all drove to Providence, where we split up the cash."

I looked at him in shock. Gus, a common criminal, part of a gang of killer armored car robbers. A man died that day—a husband, a father, if I remembered right from the newspaper clips. And Gus was a part of it. My mind became a blur. "I don't get it. If you were involved, why weren't you arrested like the others?"

"Black didn't give me up," Gus said. "When he turned government's witness, he denied there was a second getaway driver—for a simple reason. Had he given me up, I would have made a pretty good government witness. I couldn't have been involved in the shooting. I didn't mastermind the thing. I was just a grunt driving a car.

"Two of the other guys insisted to the feds there was another driver, but they didn't even know my name. It came down to Paul Stemple. He fired a shot that day, but meant to aim high—a warning shot. Manupelli fired a shot too. Stemple was always racked by guilt that he killed the guard. He refused to give me up, because he knew I didn't have anything to do with the death."

I shot a glance toward my bodyguards, standing by their rental car about forty yards down the pier.

Gus continued. "So I went to your old man. We knew each other growing up. I told him that I was in a lot of trouble, that I needed his help. I mean, I didn't get involved in this robbery just for kicks. I needed the money because I got in some gambling trouble, and if I didn't come up with some cash, I was going to be in some serious health trouble, maybe even dead.

"So I owe something to your father. He was a shift supervisor at the *Record,* and he got me a job when I needed it most. And I owe something to Mr. Stemple, and here I am taking care of two debts by trying to help you." A pause. "Does this make sense?"

"It does if I knew what it is you were trying to help me with. I know Curtis Black tried to assassinate the President of the United States. But I don't know why, and I don't have proof. So nothing personal, Gus, but you haven't done a whole lot by me yet."

Gus looked at me in a curious way. "You have it partly right. You know Curtis Black went into the witness protection program, right? So he gets a new identity. I don't know what happened to him in the program. I heard he abandoned his new, government-issued identity and got a third identity on his own."

This coincided with the government records that I had seen the previous morning, which showed that Clawson vanished in 1988.

Gus continued. "So no one knows who he is—not the government who gave him a free ride on a felony murder offense, not the guys he betrayed. No one knows who he is."

I asked, "Then why does Black take a shot at the President?"

"He doesn't," Gus said. He reached into a bag and pulled out a copy of that morning's Boston *Record.* He held out the front page in front of me. I looked at a pair of side-by-side colorful photographs. The first one was of Stanny Nichols at an event in Los Angeles. The second one was of Clayton Hutchins in Milwaukee.

Gus pointed slowly at Hutchins. "That's Curtis Black."

I stared at the photograph, then at Gus.

"He's had cosmetic work done," he said. "He's worked on his Boston accent. But it's him. We knew it was him, but couldn't be sure. So from prison Paul sent a message to him when he was Vice President. The message said simply, 'Paul Stemple knows and needs to be pardoned.' And lo and behold, he was."

My head was swimming, my hands shaking. I asked, "So if Black is the President, not the would-be assassin, and all the other men in the gang are dead or in jail, then who shot at Black and why?"

Gus said, "We can't prove it, but my belief is that it was you they were gunning for, not Hutchins. From what I've heard inside the *Record,* you were nosing around on this pardon early on, and they must have been trying to get you out of the way."

"Why didn't you tell me all this to begin with?" I asked. "We could have avoided a lot of tragedy."

"I've known you a long time, Jack. If I gave you what I had, anonymously, you would have dismissed me as a crackpot. If I had come to you on the record, I would have destroyed my entire life. My wife doesn't know about this armored car heist. My daughters, they don't know about it. You're the best reporter I know. I wanted you to figure this out on your own. It almost worked."

I said, "I need you on the record on this."

Gus shook his head. "I just can't. I've made a life for myself. I'm happy. My wife is happy. I can't destroy all that now."

"Who killed Havlicek and Stemple?" I asked.

"It's either Hutchins or the FBI. I just can't tell you who."

Standing there, I suddenly felt the urge to get somewhere fast. I was sitting on information that no one else in the world had, but I wasn't quite sure how to let anyone else know.

"I've got to get out of here," I said to Gus. I gave my bodyguards a wave to approach. Their car started, and they raced up to where we were standing. Gus reached out to hug me, and I fell into his embrace.

As we stepped back from each other, he said, "I'll never be able to tell you how sorry I am. For everything." He smiled, then added, "You're on your own now, and for you, with your talents, that's not a bad place to be."

SO ON your own means having a newspaper that doesn't want you on the story. It means having a key informant who has nothing else to give. It means the FBI may be trying to kill you. It means returning home to Washington to nothing but danger.

After all that had gone on that day, my hotel room seemed depressing. I flicked the television on and tuned to CNN to see where Hutchins was campaigning. A couple of minutes later the network played footage of him speaking at Rockefeller Center in Manhattan, urging his supporters "to guide our own destiny, to renew that most sacred of institutions, the American dream." The camera showed men and women and children laughing and applauding and shouting. I stared hard at Hutchins, at his smile, his face, his eyes, his graying hair. Frustrated, I flicked the picture off.

So do I call Martin? I decided it wasn't the right time yet. I decided I wanted to be armed with more information. On a legal pad I scribbled down the names of people I needed to call: Kent Drinker and Clayton Hutchins. Hutchins would not be particularly easy to raise, though Drinker might well be all too easy. Chances were, he would find me before I began looking for him.

Which, of course, begged the question: Who was the killer FBI agent—Stevens or Drinker? Or both? Stevens was an obvious suspect, given her presence at the airport. But then I recalled Havlicek telling me in the car before he died that he had talked to her that day. Perhaps he really had given her my arrival time.

I called the White House switchboard and asked to have Royal Dalton paged in New York.

Ten minutes later my telephone rang back. Dalton was on the line, exasperated. "It's the day before the election," he said. "What could you possibly be doing?"

"Trying to hold this democracy together, a task that you people aren't making any easier," I said. "I need to talk to Hutchins."

"Absolutely no way. We just gave you time with him on Saturday, and best I can tell, you haven't done anything with it."

I said, angry, "Well, we've had a few things happen since then, like a car bomb and the death of my colleague. Would you relay a message to Hutchins? Tell him I'm doing a story about Curtis Black, with some new details that could prove, well, explosive."

He replied, "What in the world are you talking about?"

I said, "I'm going with a story tomorrow. It's potentially devastating to Hutchins. If you don't tell him I'm trying to reach him, you're going to be screwed. Take my word for it, Royal."

"You know I can't go to him on the night before the presidential election with no information."

"On this one, you have to. Have him call me. I'll be here."

Now I'd be lying if I said I wasn't getting any satisfaction from this—working the telephone, inching closer to the answers that Havlicek and I had pursued to his death. I was back in my element.

The telephone rang. I picked it up, and it was Lincoln Powers, the chief of staff. "Young man," he said, "I brought your request to the President, and the President said, verbatim, that he doesn't know what you're talking about and has nothing to say."

I replied, "Well, could you tell him that tomorrow's *Record* will carry a story detailing the transformation of Curtis Black, and it will no doubt have a profound impact on the election."

Ten minutes later the telephone rang again, and miraculously, it was the familiar voice of President Hutchins. Without introductions he said, "Curtis Black. What the hell does that mean?"

"I think you know, sir," I said. "I uncovered some crucial new information on Curtis Black and his current identity."

"I don't know what you're talking about."

I replied, "Sir, I've talked to other members of the gang on that Wells Fargo job. They know who you are. They are willing to go public with their information." Well, not exactly.

"Young man, I don't have the slightest idea what you're talking about, but be aware you're talking to the President of the United States of America."

Employing an old reporter's trick, I let that hang out there—my implicit accusation, his pathetic response. This wasn't so much a pause as a protracted silence.

Then, his voice so thick it barely sounded like him, he said, "I'm in New York now, on my way to the airport. Why don't you come over to the White House when I get back, and we'll talk."

"That would be helpful, sir," I said. "What time?"

"Seven." We hung up, leaving just one immediate question, at least for me: Would someone try to kill me before I could get in?

At this point I had no choice but to call Peter Martin, who snapped up the phone on the first ring as if he had been waiting for my call. Just as Havlicek preserved the story in the moments before he died and passed on to me Stemple's address, I needed to make plans in case I came in harm's way.

"Well, we were right about one thing," I said. "Curtis Black was definitely involved in the shooting. Only he was the victim, not the attempted assassin."

Martin said, "What? What are you talking about?"

I said, "Curtis Black is the President of the United States. One of the guys from his criminal gang told me so today." I paused. "Curtis Black became a federal witness. He came out with a new identity, that of Tony Clawson. A few years later he ditched the name Clawson and assumed the name Clayton Hutchins. He went off and made a fortune in computer software. He came into politics almost unwittingly, became governor of Iowa at the last minute, and then he rose up almost in spite of himself. And when it was time to run for President, he had a fabricated background. In a media age when all we do is look for scandal, he didn't have any, because his whole life was made up. And fortunately for him, we all found scandal in his opponent, so we were distracted."

I could hear Martin breathing heavily, playing out every angle of this story. "You have it firm enough to go with?"

"No. But Hutchins has agreed to see me. I'm heading over there in about an hour."

"Is it safe for you to go?" Good question.

"Don't know, but it's even less safe not to go."

"All right. I'll be in the office when you get back. Be careful."

I hung up, then snuck out of the hotel through the kitchen.

It was after dusk, chilly. I scanned the parked cars, checking to see if any of them pulled out and followed me as I walked, but none did. I headed down Sixteenth Street with a baseball cap pulled low over my head. I ducked into the Hay-Adams Hotel, just across Lafayette Park from the White House. I sat at the bar, ordered a Coca-Cola, and wrote out the lead to my story dozens of times on the keyboard of my mind.

About forty minutes later, out the window, I could see Marine One descending from the sky and disappearing from view to land on the South Lawn. I hurried across the park, arrived at the northwest gate, and flashed my badge to a Secret Service agent. I felt safe on the White House grounds, maybe wrongly. He buzzed me in with a bored nod. An interview like never before.

TRUTH be known, I didn't have anything close to what I needed to get this story into print. So what I needed here, like a good cop trying to create an airtight case, was a confession. I needed the President to think that his fate had been decided, at least in terms of the coverage in the Boston *Record.* I needed him to think about the media maelstrom that would follow my story, the classic feeding frenzy from which there would be no escape. I needed him to believe that the best and perhaps only way out was an honest admission of fault.

When I was led into the Oval Office, Hutchins was sitting at his desk alone. In his hand he held a lowball glass filled with what looked to be whisky and ice. As I sat in a chair in front of his desk, he brought the glass up to his face and took a sip.

"You believe in redemption?" he asked me, his voice deep.

"I do, sir. There's something very human about it, something almost moral, and something uniquely American. We have the right to another chance, at least in most cases."

"It's election eve," he said. "My pollsters informed me this afternoon that I'm going to win. You care for a celebratory Scotch?"

Why not? "If it's convenient, sir."

He pressed a button on his desk, and a dark-skinned steward came through a side door. "Raj, get my friend a Johnnie Walker, please," Hutchins said. To me, "Rocks or no rocks?"

"No ice."

"Neat," he said to the steward.

After I got my drink, Hutchins bore into me with his eyes. "I watched you guys go after my opponent early in the campaign. What did he do? Fudge some information on his tax return or something ten years ago, and you guys try ruining his political career. I thought it was sickening then, but it helped me, so I kept my mouth shut." He laughed a bittersweet laugh.

"And now here I am, on the verge of winning the election. I'm going to get my own four-year term. Things are going all right. We're getting a good team in place, even if you're not on it. And you guys, you're bored. You need something to get your teeth into. So you turn on me because that's just what you do."

He stared at me. I stared back. He eventually averted his eyes and said, "All right, tell me what you think you know."

I took a sip of Scotch; then I showed him all my cards. "Sir," I said, "you are living under an alias. You were born Curtis Black. You were a convict in Massachusetts. You turned government's witness. You were relocated under the federal witness protection program under the name of Tony Clawson. After being in the program for nine years, you switched names a second time, to Clayton Hutchins. Through a combination of luck, timing, and skill, you have risen to the top of the world."

He laughed a devilish laugh, then leaned back in his chair. "I'm the President of the United States. President Clayton Hutchins. What you have is some cockamamy story that's been put out by my political opponents in a desperate attempt to defeat me."

"Sir," I said, "I have two men involved in the armored car heist on the record—"

"Bull," he said harshly, leaning forward this time. "Check my biography. I was never involved in any armored car heist."

"Sir," I said, "we have a source who is helping us out. Later tonight this source will agree to go on the record to discuss your case. He is familiar with all the details—the initial criminal charges, the name change, the cosmetic surgery." I eyed him carefully.

Hutchins gazed back at me with a look that was tough to read.

I was physically exhausted and mentally drained, and perhaps because of that, Katherine's image kept rolling through my mind. I thought of that ride to the hospital the year before. I thought of how she put her face against my shoulder and told me that even after we had our baby, I would always be the most important person in her life, the one she cherished the most. Which is why ever since, the emptiness had been so overwhelming.

Then, sitting there in the Oval Office, I had another thought, and it was as if Katherine had all but whispered it to me. "Sir, it's awful to have your wife and child die the way yours did," I said. "Unbearable. I understand that all too well. I understand what it can do to your heart, to your very sense of being."

Hutchins wasn't looking at me, but rather down at his glass.

I said, "I have a hunch you didn't turn to crime until after your wife and son died, when you didn't know what else to do. I have a feeling that you miss them now in a way that only the two of us could ever really understand, that you'd like to be true to them, that you want to stop living this lie."

He still stared down at his desk. I couldn't be positive, but I thought I saw a tear roll off his face and splash into his glass.

I took a deep breath and said, "Sir, tomorrow morning I'm fairly certain I will have a story on the front page of the Boston *Record* explaining that you are a rehabilitated felon." I added in a lame attempt at humor, "At least I think you're rehabilitated."

Hutchins didn't laugh. He still hadn't met my eyes.

"I am Clayton Hutchins," he said finally, his voice softer. "All my records say I'm Clayton Hutchins. I have a birth certificate. I was home-schooled by parents who have since died. I worked on a farm, went to college later in life."

I shook my head slowly in a sign of disappointed disbelief.

He focused on some point beyond me and said, "One thing always drew me to you, Jack. You know what it's like to lose everything, all of your hopes and all of your expectations for the future. You know what it's like to live the rest of your days knowing you can never get it back, no matter who you are, even if you're the President of the United States. You know all that."

I was riveted, fearful that even the slightest movement would stop his inevitable confession.

He continued in a firmer voice. "I paid a steep price. I struck a deal. I traded in my entire life. You know what that's like, to give up your life? And now that I've turned myself around, made it on my own, you're going to hang all that around my neck and choke me to death all over again? I deserve better. You know that. This wasn't part of any deal."

I probably should have felt pity. But all I really felt was relief. Sitting in the Oval Office on deadline on the night before the election with the President of the United States, I had him cold. I had my story. "Sir, you may be right. But you had a deal with the American people to let them know who you are."

His voice grew louder. "I did tell them who I am, dammit. I am Clayton Hutchins. I made my money on my own, with no help from anyone. You think all those people who are planning to vote for me tomorrow believe I'd make a bad President? You think my policies aren't carefully thought out? You think I've been corrupt?"

"Sir," I said, "the voters have a right to know who they voted for. They have a right to know your background, your experiences, the truths in your life and the lies. All of that shapes who you are and dictates how you'll act in the future as the country's leader. The voters have the right to the truth."

I believed this. Light, sunshine, is an amazing thing. It keeps a democracy vibrant by keeping the people informed. Informed people are usually wise people. This wasn't about Hutchins's sex life or some ancient two-bit misdemeanor. This struck at the very foundation of who our President is and, in this case, was.

Hutchins stood up and walked slowly over to the fireplace. He said to me, "How about a deal? How about I resign Wednesday morning, win or lose. I'll tell the public I have some illness or something like that. I'll give you an exclusive interview about it tomorrow night, after the results are in, for Wednesday's paper. And you agree not to write anything about my past."

"I can't, sir," I said. "The public is entitled to the truth."

A flash of anger spread across his face. "The truth is," he said in something just short of a yell, "the truth is that I've been a damned good President. That's the truth. You print that."

"I will, sir. Any story will note your policies, your successes. It will note your popularity. It will also inform voters of your past. They can decide what they want to do with that information."

He collapsed into one of those pale yellow chairs where he was often pictured on television. "I tried to save you," he said.

I asked politely, "Excuse me, sir?"

"I tried to save you and your cohort, Havlicek. When you started asking about Paul Stemple last month, Drinker just wanted to kill you, no questions asked. I wouldn't allow it. I said I could hire you, give you the job as press secretary. You'd be on our side, and the questions about Stemple would never be asked again. I had no idea he was going to try to kill you at Congressional that day."

I gulped hard at this revelation. By now I had moved over to sit on the settee perpendicular to his chair. A single lamp lit this side of the room, leaving both our faces in virtual darkness as we talked. I asked, "Why Drinker? What's his motivation?"

Hutchins said, "He expected to be named the director of the FBI once I became elected, and his expectations were probably going to be fulfilled. He knows my damned secret. He was involved in the case way back when, and when I was about to become Vice President, I had no choice but to call him and make it in his own interest to keep my past the past."

"So it was Drinker who killed Havlicek?"

Hutchins nodded.

"Why?"

"You wouldn't take the press secretary's job. My plan failed. He also believed that Stemple began providing you with information after the Congressional shooting—and he couldn't find Stemple to kill him, so he figured it was easier to kill you. And you guys wouldn't buy into our line that the dead assassin was a federally protected witness named Tony Clawson, which would have been embarrassing for the FBI but would have assured that no one would ever associate me with Clawson. I tried fending Drinker off by pushing you to take the job. You set yourself up by refusing to come aboard."

With that logic I had caused Havlicek's death. But right there and then I refused to dwell.

It was getting late, heading toward the deadline for our first edition. I said, "Sir, I appreciate your help, but I have to leave. Is there anything else you want to make clear to me? More to the point, if we run a story tomorrow, do you plan to resign in the light of these allegations or will you remain in office?"

He sat with his elbows on his knees and his head pointed straight down at the floor, as if in prayer. He looked up at me and said, "I don't know. I just don't know right now."

As I turned to walk out the door, he was still sitting, hunched over, looking nothing like the man I saw on the golf course on that brilliant October morning eleven days earlier.

Chapter Eleven

I GULPED in the fresh night air as I stepped outside the White House. I strode toward the northwest gate, looking out into the patch of black on the other side that was Lafayette Park. As soon as I stepped outside that gate, I was fair game. Drinker could be sitting in that park right now, lurking, waiting, watching me, fingering a gun or a knife shoved into his overcoat pocket.

Staring into the abyss of that park, I quickly turned around and began to trot toward the walkway that led to the adjacent Old Executive Office Building. It was off-limits with my press pass, and the Secret Service uniformed officers could detain me. But detention, I quickly calculated, was preferable to a violent death. At least I could make a phone call to Martin and dictate what I had.

The guard shack between the White House and the ancient and ornate OEOB was usually empty. I scurried down the stairs, across an alleyway, and into the loading entrance. I wended my way through a maze of wide, empty hallways before I finally saw an illuminated EXIT sign. I rounded a corner, saw three officers chatting at a station, and casually walked toward the turnstile. An agent matter-of-factly buzzed me out, and I was on my way.

Out on Seventeenth Street, a taxicab happened by just as I hit the curb. I directed the driver to my office, just a few minutes away.

In front of my building, I slipped him a fin and made a dash for the front door, all within full view of a very friendly security guard named Alan. I ran past him to a waiting elevator and ascended to my office, a place I had feared I would never see again.

The bureau, I was quite sure, was probably as safe a venue as any and more comfortable than most. A writer likes familiarity. A reporter does as well. This was not a story I wanted to type from the small desk of my hotel room, nice as my hotel room might be.

At night my office was a shadowy shade of gray, with the hazy green glare of so many computer screens casting the only light across the vast room. I knew this bureau better than I knew anyplace else, yet it seemed different now, eerie. Speaking aloud, I told myself, "You have to relax." The sound of my own voice made me jumpy but not nearly as much as the sound I heard next.

"Who are you talking to?"

The new voice made me just about leap through the ceiling. My eyes darted about the room until they came to rest on Peter Martin, sitting in the dark at a computer just across from mine. "You're going to scare me to death," I said.

"Actually, it's you who scared me. You should be at your hotel. I've been waiting for you to call." He paused. "Tell me what you have."

I sat down at my computer. He drew his chair up closer, and I walked him through my session in the Oval Office. I read him some of Hutchins's quotes that I had furiously scribbled on a legal pad just after I had left the West Wing.

After my ten-minute monologue Martin looked stricken, as if he might get sick right there on the newsroom rug. In the heavy silence my telephone rang, but when I picked up the receiver, I heard only dead air, followed by the click of someone hanging up on the other end. It made my skin crawl, even if I didn't fully appreciate or understand why.

Martin, on the other hand, seemed not even to notice. Staring not so much at me but through me, he said finally, "You use tape?"

"No."

"You took notes?"

"Right afterward, from memory, on my way out the door."

"Incredible," he said. "The whole thing is incredible." He picked up the telephone. Punching out a number, he added, "Appleton's not going to like the lack of a tape recording, but I have no doubt you did exactly what you should have done."

He talked for a few minutes with Appleton, hung up, and said to me, "Write something out. Appleton wants to see it before he figures out what to do. He says there are no guarantees."

No guarantees. Here we had the President of the United States in an absolute lie that defined his entire life. I had risked my life for this story. Havlicek had lost his. And we had some pencil pusher of an editor in chief sitting in Boston telling us that there were no guarantees he would run the most important story in the country. Screw him, and while we're at it, screw this entire newspaper business as well. But not before I write this story and get it into print.

So I settled in before my computer and began to write. I wrote of the Oval Office interview, of Hutchins's belief that the FBI was behind the shooting, and of how the intended target was me. As promised, I talked of his success as President and the lofty approval ratings that came along with it. I explained the 1979 Wells Fargo heist, the deal that Curtis Black struck with the U.S. Attorney, his disappearance from the program in 1988.

When I was done, Martin sat in front of my computer in absolute silence, his fingers not typing in a single change as he paged through the story. That silence was finally broken by my ringing telephone. Again, dead air on the line, followed by a click. I didn't like that at all.

"Brilliant," Martin said. "If we don't run it, I'll quit."

"Let's just calm down," I said. "It's only the President and the future course of America at stake." Neither of us laughed.

At that moment the sound of shattering glass spilled into the room from the hallway beyond. Martin and I looked at each other in silence, and I started walking across the room toward the door.

As I got halfway toward the hallway, the figure of Kent Drinker appeared in the doorway. The sight of him in my newsroom, daring to invade a place I always considered a sanctuary, made me livid.

"What are you doing here?" I yelled.

He continued walking toward me, holding a gun in front of his chest, the barrel pointed at my forehead. "You don't screw with me, and you don't screw with the FBI," he said.

"I want you out of this building," I replied.

Drinker continued to walk toward me, around a clutter of desks. I stood frozen in the middle of the room. In the heat of the moment I figured it was best to try to engage Drinker. Conversation buys time. So I asked, "What is it you want?" Of course, I knew the answer to that already. Unfortunately for me, his intention was to make sure that I wasn't about to transmit a story to the *Record* that would include details of Hutchins's past life and suspicions that the FBI—specifically he—had killed Havlicek and tried to kill me in an attempt to block the truth from being known. Even less fortunately for me, he also wanted to make sure that I wouldn't live to tell anyone what I knew. The reason he hadn't killed me in the prior twenty seconds was because he didn't know if I had sent the story yet.

He was maybe twenty feet away from me by now.

I was standing by Supreme Court reporter Michael Reston's computer. Drinker was still coming at me. My eyes drifted over Reston's desk to a huge legal volume and then to the telephone. I could throw the book, which weighed more, but the fluttering paper might slow the velocity. The telephone was sleeker and harder.

Drinker was but fifteen feet from me now, a free throw in the NBA. I waited for him to get within range, and in one quick swoop I picked up the phone and fired it at his head. Drinker ducked, and the phone smashed into his wrist, causing the gun to fly out of his hand and slide underneath a nearby desk. He shook his wrist in pain, scanned the floor for the weapon, then looked at me with a hatred I hope never to see again. "You should have been dead at Congressional," he seethed.

Um, Peter, I thought, anytime you want to help out here, please feel free. I shot a glance back and saw him at the computer keyboard, transmitting the story to the *Record*.

When I turned, Drinker saw what I was looking at, and that made him panic. He charged me with the force of a linebacker, throwing his forearms into my sore ribs and causing a measure of pain that I hadn't thought possible. As I saw stars, Drinker raced across the room. From my perch on the floor I could see Martin back away from the computer and could see the story scrolling across the screen, as it does when it is transmitting. When it finally arrives at its destination, the computer beeps twice and the screen says, "File sent without errors."

Drinker arrived at the computer and started pressing keys. Still the story continued to scroll. Frantic, he picked the keyboard up to rip it out of the terminal. Standing now twenty feet or so behind him, I assumed he finally had us, that the force would cause such technological havoc that the computer would shut down and the story of Hutchins's past would end up in some netherworld of information. And we would end up dead.

Martin must have thought the same thing, because at that second he lunged for Drinker and shoved a ballpoint pen deep into the side of his neck. Drinker collapsed, his eyes bugged out. The keyboard tumbled out of his hands and dropped to the floor, and as it did, the monitor beeped twice and the words "File sent without errors" flashed across the screen. Drinker rolled around on the ground, moaning. You'll forgive my lack of restraint in thinking, for a brief moment, as I looked at Drinker's neck, that the pen is indeed mightier than the sword.

Anyway, Martin casually picked up the telephone and called for an ambulance. I picked up Drinker's gun and told him, "You try to stand up, you're dead." As I stood guard, Martin made a second call, this one to Appleton.

"Yeah, you're right," I heard Martin say. "This really is a pain to have this story move so late at night."

Wednesday, November 8

So HOW important is truth, anyway? Do we really need it, or is it just better, easier, to go with what feels good, to tell lies with the understanding that even if lies hurt, the truth too often hurts more? Well, I'm still a fan of the truth. Truth is an immovable foundation. Lies shift and collapse. With truth, even at its most painful, you can build on it and move on. I happen to have a rather high regard for the public. I believe they can take the truth, decide if it's important, and make sound judgments. Which is why journalism, for all its drawbacks, is still a good and decent calling.

Which brings me to the issue of Clayton Hutchins or Tony Clawson or Curtis Black, however you want to refer to him. Do I believe in redemption? Yes. I meant it when I told him there was something uniquely American about it. I also believe the public had a right to know who he really was. There's something American about that as well. The free flow of information, of truths, is arguably the most significant attribute of a democracy.

Hutchins won the election with 50.4 percent of the popular vote and took the electoral college by a nine-vote margin over Senator Stanny Nichols. On Election Day the networks devoted on-air coverage to the *Record* story, quoting liberally from our pages until they were able to confirm key aspects on their own. The all-news cable stations nearly burst at the seams. The Internet all but exploded from overuse. The bottom line: The people knew what they were doing, and enough of them believed in the concept of redemption. Hutchins was the President for the next four years. I think. An independent counsel was named by the Attorney General to investigate the President's possible role in Havlicek's death, though I don't believe he had any.

These were my thoughts as I kicked my feet up on my desk after another difficult deadline on Wednesday, the day after the election. It was the end of a whirlwind day of Washington events, capped by an Oval Office address by Hutchins in which he portrayed his own redemption as being part of the American dream he had long espoused. Now, he said, it was time to heal both himself and the country, and he would like to see the job through.

Ironically, while Hutchins, the admitted criminal, spoke, Drinker, the law-enforcement agent, was being detained under heavy guard at a military hospital outside Washington, facing a battery of charges, among them conspiracy to commit murder. Dozens of FBI agents were working with D.C. police to try to determine who actually fired the shots out at Congressional. They had a body. They just needed an identity to go along with it.

And me? Well, on this Wednesday night, after the bureau cleared out, I wandered over to Steve Havlicek's desk, sat in his chair, and ran my hands over some of his things. I pulled a box out of the supply closet and packed his stuff into it. I wrote out a note saying, "Margaret, we all miss Steve more than we can say. This story is happening because of him. Very best, Jack." I dropped the note in the box, sealed it up, and left it for the mailroom to ship to Boston.

As I walked out, I had the feeling of accomplishment, so much so that after I got home, I walked down to the cellar and pulled out a couple of folded-up moving boxes. I climbed the stairs to the second floor, then pushed open the door to the nursery.

Inside I took several stuffed animals out of the crib, removed the tiny cotton blankets and sheets and folded them up, placed them in a box, then lugged it down to the cellar. Back in the nursery, as Baker sprawled out on the Winnie-the-Pooh rug, I unpacked the toy chest. I took the infant pajamas out of the drawers and put them into one of the boxes. I was picking up a Gund bear on top of the bureau when I heard a knock on the door downstairs.

Baker, of course, was thrilled. He limped down ahead of me. I pulled the door open, and there stood Samantha Stevens. She held a bottle of wine beside her. "I got your message this morning," she said. "Thanks for the apology."

I said, "Don't mention it. I got your message this afternoon saying I'm not such a jackass."

She smiled mischievously and said, "You're not."

"Come in."

She stretched out her arm and handed me the bottle of wine. "Peace offering," she said. As I took the bottle, she pointed to my hand, which still held the blond teddy bear, and said, "New toy?"

I didn't laugh. "Old toy, actually," I replied.

She quickly understood what I meant. We were both quiet. She followed me into the kitchen, and I put the bear down on the counter to open the bottle of wine. When I turned around to face her, she drew close, hardly seeming to move at all. She put her face against mine and kissed me on the lips. Then she pulled away, her eyes closed for a second, then opened, looking into mine. That's when I kissed her. It was a long kiss, not so much passionate, but warm, strangely familiar, so natural.

She said, "I missed you." I glanced at the dog lying on the floor behind her, at the stuffed bear sitting on the countertop. I stared into her eyes for a few silent seconds and said, "I missed you too."

And at that moment a future seemed to emerge from the past, like life from ashes, like wine from old grapes, something with a bit of whimsy and so much more.

"Good," she said. "Don't be a jackass again."

"I'm promising you," I replied. "I won't."

BRIAN McGRORY

Columnist Brian McGrory had a front-row view of the Clinton presidency.

As a roving national reporter for the Boston *Globe*, Brian McGrory has written about everything from a group of persecuted sea lions in Seattle to the standoff between federal agents and the Randy Weaver family in Ruby Ridge, Idaho. When McGrory was named the *Globe*'s White House correspondent, he spent three years reporting on one of America's most controversial Presidents—Bill Clinton. In this role, McGrory accompanied him to such far-flung locales as China, Russia, and Australia. Clinton also allowed McGrory to do research in the seat of power itself—the Oval Office—which the author then re-created in *The Incumbent*.

Though the relationship between a President and the press corps that covers him is at the heart of his new novel, McGrory chose not to explore the scandalous aspects of the Clinton presidency. "Many of the issues were so outrageous that fiction simply couldn't do them justice," he says. As a Metro columnist for the *Globe*, these days McGrory lives in the Back Bay section of Boston. Without being tied to a President's schedule, he now has the freedom to write "pretty much whatever I want."

To read an exclusive interview with Brian McGrory, visit the Select Editions website:

ReadersOnly.com
Password: *today*

The volumes in this series are issued
every two to three months. The typical
volume contains four outstanding books
in condensed form. None of the selections in any
volume has appeared in *Reader's Digest* itself.
Any reader may receive this service by writing
The Reader's Digest Association, Inc.,
Pleasantville, N.Y. 10570
or by calling 1-800-234-9000.

Visit our website at
www.ReadersOnly.com
Password: *today*

Some of the titles in this volume are also
available in a large-print format. For information about
Select Editions Large Type call 1-800-877-5293.

ACKNOWLEDGMENTS

Pages 6–7, 8: illustrations by Phil Boatwright
Page 159: photo by Don Enger
Pages 160–161, 162: illustrations by Brian Sheridan
Page 297: photo © John Earle
Pages 298–299, 300: illustrations by Carolyn Bucha
Page 427: photo by Sigrid Estrada
Pages 428–429, 430: illustrations by John Jinks
Page 575: photo by Mary Beth Montgomery